MAR 1 3 1989

THE FLETCH CHRONICLE: ONE

GREGORY MCDONALD

THE FLETCH CHRONICLE: ONE

FLETCH WON
FLETCH, TOO
FLETCH AND THE WIDOW BRADLEY

Rediscovery Books
HILL & COMPANY, PUBLISHERS • BOSTON

This edition published by Hill & Company,
Publishers, by arrangement with the author.

CIP to come

Designed by Milton Glaser, Inc.
Printed in the United States of America

INTRODUCTION

Rather than ask the question and receive the answer tailored to that question, it is better, if possible, to await the truth.

Thousands of times I have been asked *where Fletch came from.* My answers have been tailored.

My father was a journalist and I served in that capacity myself for seven years. Since throat-high to the breakfast table, later, feet propped on a metal desk in a three A.M. city room, I have heard stories about this guy who always worked for the other newspaper, the other network, who did weird, funny, inventive things, such as call the city desk, report a murder and the murderer, but ask that the photographers hide in the bushes to give the widow time to arrive home and discover the body. As a journalist, as a person, Fletch understands that everyone lies to him, at least that everyone is self-serving; this gives him a certain license to lie back, at least to misrepresent himself. But when it comes time for him to report the story, he tells the absolute truth, as he knows it; sometimes, then, he needs to get out of town as fast as he can. *The blithe spirit of journalism.*

Neither Irwin Maurice Fletcher nor Francis Xavier Flynn could have existed before the end of the twentieth century, prior to thermonuclear power falling into the hands of governments, prior to the universal, cultural, technology-reactive revolution of the late nineteen sixties and early seventies, in their ambivalence regarding authority, their new regard for women, children, blacks, homosexuals, and other minorities. The different does not mean the opposed; we're all in the same car together; empathy sweetens the long ride. Fletch's and Flynn's antecedents were committed to a moral code, seldom more profound than some usually *macho* idea of how a man ought to behave. The tragic, refined to comic, source here may be that now there is no such simple, fixed code of behavior in our increasingly complex and diverse world. One must muddle along eclectically, drawing wisdom from a background however wide. The social contract, which can be unraveled by a single unchallenged lie, is the constitution for Fletch and Flynn, their responsibility as well as their license.

Institutions are tested. Our essential little vanities, clothes and food and even sex, are satirized. Human relations are viewed in the time and space in which they exist, transitory, changing, seldom permanent, never the ultimate. Bombasts are punctured. The inarticulate are heard. Technology is used, sometimes for purposes not intended. Enveloped in steel and concrete, one's physicality is appreciated. The preferred route to truth is intelligence and wit. Violence is a failure of articulation. The truth, not just the factual, scientific, legal truth, but the personal truth, understanding, is the object of diverse and sometimes devious approaches. *The barefoot boy with cheek.*

Am I Fletch? Is Fletch my super ego, my peri-spirit, my other self? No more so than my other friends from the page. Empathy is the instrument which the author plays. Someone once telephoned me after breakfasting in a fancy hotel to ask what Fletch would have had for breakfast, if he had breakfasted in that hotel that morning. I was able to tell him. Not prone to headaches, once my head hurt so much I could not continue work until I realized that Fletch had just gotten hit on the head, and I was suffering. As a journalist, I changed clothes several times a day in a small car to be familiar, legible, to the next person I was to interview. At this writing, I have published eighteen books, seventeen of them fiction, yet I have never told a lie. Some part of each person I try to capture on a page has to be some part of me, at least enough for me to be strongly empathic. I know I have failed utterly to capture some characters, for whom I have had little empathy. I am Fletch's biographer.

Fletcher is an ancient Scottish word for an arrow maker, more specifically, for one who attaches the feathers to an arrow shaft. I'm not sure I knew even that when I began the saga.

Such have been my tailored answers.

The truth? I do not know where Fletch came from. I know he was born and began growing in my mind and heart about three years before I ever took pen to paper and wrote: "What's your name?" I spent the next thirteen years answering that question in nine novels.

We are all mysteries awaiting solution.

I can report three truths without being asked. I'm awfully glad it was to me Fletch occurred. I have enjoyed doing these novels, working with him, immensely. I'm grateful his stories were popular enough to permit me to pursue him to whatever end.

Controversy is noted regarding the best order in which to read the nine Fletch novels.

There is a chronology, with a beginning, a middle, an end, time and place references, recurring characters, a maturing central character, with different, possibly enlarging themes. Some insist this is the best way to read through the novels. This is not a characteristic of other series in the genre, including the Flynn series. The chronology is: *Fletch Won; Fletch, Too; Fletch and the Widow Bradley; Fletch; Carioca Fletch; Confess, Fletch; Fletch's Fortune; Fletch's Moxie; Fletch and the Man Who.*

Others insist the best way to read through the saga is the order in which they were written and published: *Fletch* (1974); *Confess, Fletch* (1976); *Fletch's Fortune* (1978); *Fletch and the Widow Bradley* (1981); *Fletch's Moxie* (1982); *Fletch and the Man Who* (1983); *Carioca Fletch* (1984); *Fletch Won* (1985); *Fletch, Too* (1986).

I suspect most readers to date have read the novels in whatever order they came to hand, and I suppose some think that is the best way to read through them.

Publishing rules required even the three trilogies to appear out of order, the second appearing first. The author has nurtured the hope of being able to make a conclusive presentation of this project some time before the end of the twentieth century.

In this First Trilogy appear: *Fletch Won,* Fletch at his youngest, a neophyte journalist, in which a solid law firm is compared to a house of ill repute; *Fletch, Too,* in which something of Fletch's parentage and moral commitment is revealed; *Fletch and the Widow Bradley,* which mentions sexual identity as a means of noting differences that can exist between the outer and inner person.

If this is your first exposure to these stories I can only wish you enjoy reading them at least a fraction as much as I have enjoyed telling them.

— *Gregory Mcdonald*
Camaldon Farm

FLETCH WON

To Edward (Ned) Leavitt,
scholar, agent and friend.

ONE

"Did I ask to see you?"

"No, Frank, I —"

"I want to see you anyway." Frank Jaffe, The Editor, refolded the competing newspaper, the *Chronicle-Gazette*, and put it under his elbow on the desk. "I have some tough things to say to you."

"Little ol' me?"

"How would you like lifting a shovel eight hours a day, every day, five days a week, maybe half-days Saturdays?"

Fletch looked at his sneakers on the rug of Frank's office. Through the top of his left sneaker he saw the knuckles of three toes. Only the smallest toe showed through the top of his right sneaker. "It's not what I see for myself in the parade of life, Frank."

"That's what I see for you. In the parade of life, what do you see yourself suited for?"

"Journalism."

"And what's journalism, young Fletcher?"

"Developing the skill of ending sentences with prepositions? Especially questions?"

"Did I just do that?" Behind his thick lenses, Frank's watery eyes moved across the top of his messy desk. "I just did that."

"Frank, what I wanted to see you about —"

Frank opened a folder on his desk. "I've dug out your personnel file." The folder was not thick. "You're suited for journalism, or pick-and-shovel work. I wonder which it will be?"

"Why are you looking at my personnel file? You hired me months ago."

"Three months ago. Do you remember why? I don't."

"Because I can be really good, Frank. I —"

"I think I had the idea this newspaper needed a breath of fresh air, young maverick who would shake things up a bit, see things differently, maybe, jerk people out of their ruts."

"How can I do that, Frank, if you won't give me a job?"

"I've given you a job. Lots of jobs."

"Not a real job."

"First, I put you on the copy desk."

"Writing headlines is for poets, Frank."

"And kept you there, over the growing protests of your co-workers, I might add —"

"I spilled orange soda on somebody's terminal keyboard."

"That's not all you did."

"I made it up to him. I bought him a pair of surgical gloves."

"— until you wrote the headline GOVERNOR JOKES ON PURPOSE."

"I thought that was news."

"And somehow the headline appeared in two editions before being killed."

"Sheer poetry, Frank. Not long-lived poetry, I admit, not deathless poetry, but —"

"So then I assigned you to writing obituaries."

"You know I want to write sports, Frank. That's why I came in to see you this morning."

"Not the toughest job in the world, writing obituaries. You answer the phone, listen politely, sometimes you have to check a few facts."

"I'm very good at checking facts."

Frank held up a piece of paper. His hand quivered and his eyes shook as he read the first paragraph from it. " 'Ruth Mulholland died peacefully today, having accomplished nothing in her fifty-six years.' Did you write that?"

"It was a fact, Frank. I checked."

"Fletcher, one of the points in your writing obituaries is in our being able to print them."

"I kept asking her sister, *What did she ever do?* The sister kept talking. But I was listening, you see. This person, Ruth Mulholland, never graduated from anywhere, never got married, never had a baby, never held a job, never even supported herself. I mean, in fifty-six years she never accomplished a damned thing. Finally, I asked the sister, Did she ever make anybody a sweater? Cook a pan of brownies for anybody? Or even for herself? The sister kept saying, No, no, in fact Ruthie never did a damned thing in her life. I said, Well, is that what

I should print? And the sister said, Well, yes, I guess that's the truth about Ruthie. I checked the facts, Frank. Ruthie never applied for Social Security, or a driver's license; she didn't even support her local beauty shop!"

"Fletcher —"

"What, there's not supposed to be any truth in obituaries? When someone has won the Nobel Prize we print that in an obituary. When someone accomplishes exactly nothing in life, why don't we print that? Doing absolutely nothing is a statement, Frank, a response to life. It's news, it's interesting."

"Ruthie didn't get her obituary printed, either." Frank held up another shaking piece of paper. "So you were assigned to writing wedding announcements. That's just a job of taking dictation. You don't even have to be responsible for the main fact, the wedding, because it hasn't taken place yet. Your very first announcement read, 'Sarah and Roland Jameson, first cousins, are to be married Wednesday in a ceremony restricted to family.' "

"Crisp."

"Crisp," Frank agreed.

"Concise."

"Concise."

"To the point."

"Absolutely to the point."

"And," Fletch said, "factual."

"Took talent, to dig that story out."

"Not much. When the mother of the bride called, I simply asked her why both the bride and groom had the same last name."

"And she answered you without hesitation?"

"She hesitated."

"She said they were first cousins?"

"She said their fathers were brothers."

"And neither the bride nor the groom was adopted, right?"

"Frank, I checked. What do you think I am?"

"I think you're an inexperienced journalist."

"If the rules of journalism apply on political and crime and sports pages, why don't they apply on obituaries and wedding-announcement pages? Newspapers are supposed to tell both sides of a story, right? Pah! Sundays we devote pages and pages to wedding announcements. Why don't we give equal space to divorce announcements?"

"Fletcher —"

"News is news, Frank."

"You think that by writing obituaries and wedding announcements in this heavy-handed, factual way is how you're going to get yourself assigned to the sports pages, is that it?"

"Truth is truth, Frank."

"Someday, Fletcher, may you be a victim of someone like yourself." Through his pupils dipped in clam juice, Frank looked at Fletcher. "You're getting married Saturday?"

"Yes. Next Saturday."

"Why?"

"Barbara has the day open."

"Unless the purpose is to have children," Frank said slowly, "marriage is a legal institution guaranteeing only that you get screwed by lawyers."

"You don't believe in true love."

"True Love ran at Saratoga Saturday. Made a strong start, faded fast, and ended at the back of the pack. I suppose you expect time off, for a honeymoon?"

"Barbara's rather counting on it. That's another thing I wanted to see you about."

"You haven't worked here a year yet. In fact, some say you haven't worked here at all yet!"

"Yeah, but, Frank, how many times in life do you have a honeymoon?"

"Don't ask. Why are you so sunburned?"

"I ran in the Sardinal Race yesterday."

"Your hair looks like it hasn't crossed the finish line yet."

Fletch smiled. "There's a story there."

"In your hair? I'd believe anything is in your hair."

"In the race. Do you know about the Ben Franklyn Friend Service?"

"Guess I don't."

"Basically, it's a company specializing in health and prostitution."

"What?"

"You call them and this sultry voice answers, saying, 'Ben Franklyn Friend Service. You want a friend?' Only sometimes she slurs a little, and it sounds more like, 'You want to, friend?' "

"You call them often?"

"The guys on the desk played a joke on me one night. They told me to phone out for pizzas and that was the number they gave me. The girl on the phone was trying to set up an appointment for me, and I kept asking if she had anchovies and pepperoni. I guess she thought I was a pervert. You ought to call them sometime."

"I need a friend."

"So I looked into 'em. Big business. Beautiful girls. All of 'em in great physical condition. They're made to work out, you know?"

"What's the story?"

"They were running yesterday. In the race. All of 'em. A flotilla of call girls. About twelve of them, all together. Running through the city streets. Downtown. Wearing T-shirts that read in front, YOU WANT A FRIEND?, and in back, BEN FRANKLYN. They all made it to the finish, too."

"So what's the story? Don't tell me. I've got it." Frank put his hands to his forehead. "STREETWALKERS JOG —"

"Joggle."

"CALL GIRLS COME RUNNING?"

"Consider their leg muscles, Frank."

"I'm all excited."

"They were advertising their business, Frank."

"So where did you finish in this race?"

"Right behind them. I was following a story, you might say."

"Faithful to the last."

"You're not getting the point."

"I'm not?"

"These call girls were using a city-run health and sports event to advertise their service."

"So a few prostitutes ran in the city footrace yesterday. Why shouldn't they? Not against the law. They wore T-shirts advertising their services. Gave thrills to a few dirty old men leg-watchers standing on the curbs. So where's the story?"

"You ran pictures of them today. On your sports pages. Coming and going. Front and back."

Frank paled. "We did?"

"*You* did."

"Jeez!" Frank grabbed the *News-Tribune* off the floor and turned to the sports pages. "We did."

"There's the story."

"You mean, we're the story."

"Gave a call-girl service a nice big spread. Lots of free publicity. Have you heard from the archbishop yet? How about the district attorney? Any of your advertisers object?"

"Damn. Someone did this on purpose."

"You need me on the sports pages, Frank."

"Look at the caption. Oh, my God. *Physical beauty and stamina ex-*

emplified by employees of the Ben Franklyn Service Company who ran together yesterday in the city's Sardinal Race. Group finished near end of race . . . I can't stand it."

"They weren't in any hurry."

"Neither were you, apparently."

"You were just telling me never to get ahead of my story."

"Get up and come into the office early Monday morning . . ." Frank was tearing through the competing newspaper, the *Chronicle-Gazette*, on his desk, trying to find the sports pages. ". . . Have to waste the damned day firing people . . ."

"The *Gazette* didn't run pictures of the call girls, Frank. Front or back. They just ran pictures of the winners. Jeez, they practice tired old journalism over there."

Frank sat back in his chair. He looked like a boxer between rounds. "Why did I have to start off the week by seeing you?"

"Bring a little freshness to your life. A few laughs. Shake you up a bit. Make you see a few things differently, like a couple of photos on your sports page."

"You own a necktie?"

"Sure."

"I've never seen it."

"It's holding one end of my surfboard off the floor."

"I suppose you're serious. What's holding up the other end?"

Fletch looked down at the top of his jeans. "A belt someone gave me."

"I decided over the weekend to give you one more chance." Frank looked at his watch.

"You're going to try me out as a sportswriter!"

"No. After all, what companies do is expect youth, energy, and experience all from the same person. That's not fair."

"The police beat? Fine!"

"Thought we might try knocking a few of the rough edges off you."

"City Hall? I can do it. Just give me a score card."

"So I figure it's experience, polish, you need. You do own a suit, don't you?"

"The courts! Damn, you want me to cover the courts. I know how the courts work, Frank. Remarkable how little they have to do with the law, you know? I —"

"Society."

"Society?"

"Society. Seeing you're so quick to identify deceased people who never accomplished a damned thing in their lives, and point out to the public first cousins who intend to marry each other, I think you might have a little talent for covering society."

"You mean society, like in high society?"

"High society, low society, you know, lifestyles: all those features that cater to the anxieties of our middle-class readers."

"Frank, I don't believe in society."

"That's okay, Fletch. Society doesn't believe in you, either."

"I'd be no good at it."

"You might be attractive, if you combed your hair."

"Little old ladies slipping vodka into their tea?"

"Habeck. Donald Edwin Habeck."

"Didn't he once try out as goalie for the Red Wings?"

"If you read anything other than the sports pages, Fletcher, you'd know Donald Edwin Habeck is one of this neighborhood's more sensational attorneys."

"Is he on an exciting case?"

"Habeck called me last night and said he and his wife have decided, after much discussion, to give five million dollars to the art museum. You're interested in art, aren't you?"

"Not as poker chips."

"He wants the story treated right, you know? With dignity. No invasion of their privacy, no intrusion into their personal lives."

"Frank, would you mind if I sit down?"

"Help yourself. I forgot you ran slowly in a footrace yesterday."

Fletch sat on the rug.

"Sit anywhere."

"Thanks. La-di-da philanthropy."

"Finish the verse and you may have a hit song."

"Frank, you want me, I.M. Fletcher, to do an arm's length, hands-off, veddy, veddy polite story about some for-God's-sake society couple who are giving five million pieces of tissue paper to the art museum?"

"Polite, yes. Why not polite? Here are a couple of people doing something nice for the world, sharing their wealth. Curb your need to report Mrs. Habeck slips vodka into her tea. Time you learned how to be polite. By the way, I can't see you over the edge of the desk."

"I disappeared."

"Well, you'd better reappear. You're meeting with Habeck in the publisher's office at ten o'clock. Pity your necktie and belt are holding up your surfboard."

"God! Any story which starts with the reporter meeting the subject in the publisher's office isn't worth getting up for."

"See? You're improving as a journalist already. You just ended a sentence with a preposition."

"I won't do it."

"Fletch, I'm pretty sure you'd be just as attractive working a pick and shovel in the city streets. You wouldn't have to wear a necktie, belt, or comb your hair. I can arrange to have you leave here Friday and you and Lucy can take as long a honeymoon as you can afford."

"Might make a nice weekend. And her name's Barbara."

"I thought so. Sunday bliss with Barbara. Tuesday with blisters."

"Frank, why don't you let Habeck write the story himself? He's paying five million dollars for the privilege."

Hamm Starbuck stuck his head around the office door. He looked at Fletch sitting cross-legged on the rug. "It's that kind of morning, is it?"

"So far," Fletch answered. "Floored one. After glancing at certain photos on the sports page, I see I have a few more to floor today."

"Frank, were you expecting Donald Habeck?"

"Not me. John's expecting him. He should be sent to the publisher's office."

"He'll never make it."

"He telephoned?"

"No. He's dead in the parking lot."

Frank asked, "What do you mean?"

"In a dark blue Cadillac Seville. Bullet hole in his temple."

Fletch sprang off the floor without using his hands. "My story!"

"Guess we should call the police."

"Get the photographers down there first," Frank said.

"Already done that."

"Also Biff Wilson. Has he reported in yet?"

"I radioed him. He's on the freeway."

"Biff Wilson!" Fletch said. "Frank, you gave this story to me."

"I haven't given you anything, Fletcher."

"Habeck, Donald Edwin. Was I supposed to interview him at ten o'clock?"

"Fletcher, do me a favor."

"Anything, Frank."

"Get lost. Report to Ann McGarrahan in Society."

"Maybe there's a necktie in my car."

"I just made a career decision," Frank said to his desk.

"What's that, Frank?"
"I'm not coming into the office early Monday mornings anymore."

TWO

"Habeck, Harrison and Haller. Good morning."
"Hello, H cubed?"
"Habeck, Harrison and Haller. May I help you?"
"Mr. Chambers, please."
"I'm sorry, sir. Would you repeat that name?"
"Mr. Chambers." Looking across the city room of the *News-Tribune*, no one could guess that someone had just been shot to death in the parking lot of that building, and that everyone there knew it. Did everyone know it? Absolutely. In a newspaper office, unlike most other companies, the process of rumor becoming gossip becoming fact becoming substantiated, reliable news was professionally accelerated. It happened with the speed of a rocket. Assimilation of news happened just as fast. Journalists are interested in the stories they are working on; some have a mental filing cabinet, some a wastebasket into which they drop all other news. "Alston Chambers, please. He's somewhere down in your stacks, I expect. An intern lawyer, a trainee, whatever you call him. A veteran and a gentleman."
"Oh, yes, sir. A. Chambers."
"Probably drifting around your corridors, without a place to wrinkle his trousers."
"One moment, sir." A line was ringing. The telephone operator had to add, "Excuse me, sir, for not recognizing the name. Mr. Chambers does not have clients."
"Chambers speaking."
"Sounds sepulchral."
"Must be Fletcher."
"Must be."
"Hope you've called me for lunch. I gotta get out of this place."
"In fact, I have. One o'clock at Manolo's?"
"You want to discuss your wedding. You want my advice as to how to get out of it. Does Barbara still have it scheduled for Saturday?"

"No, no, yes. Can't talk right now, Alston. Just want to give you the news."

"Barbara's told you she's pregnant?"

"Habeck, Harrison and Haller. That the law firm you work for?"

"You know it. Bad pay and all the shit I can take."

"Donald Edwin Habeck?"

"One of the senior partners in this den of legal inequity."

"Donald Edwin Habeck won't be in today. Thought I'd call in for him."

"I don't get it. Why not? What's the joke?"

"He's been shot to death."

"This is a joke?"

"Not from his point of view."

"Where, when?"

"At the *News-Tribune*. A few minutes ago. I gotta go."

"I wonder if he left a will."

"Why do you say that?"

"Lawyers are famous for not writing wills for themselves."

"Alston, I'd appreciate it at lunch if you'd talk to me about Habeck. Tell me what you know."

"You on the story?"

"I think so."

"Does anyone else think so?"

"I'm on it until I'm ordered off it."

"Fletch, you're getting married Saturday. This is no time to flirt with unemployment."

"See you at one o'clock at Manolo's."

THREE

"Did he do himself?" Fletch was looking over Biff's shoulder into the front seat of the Cadillac.

A man in his sixties was slumped over the armrest. His left leg hung out of the car. His shoe almost touched the ground.

Biff turned his head slowly to look at Fletch. His look said that plebeians were not supposed to initiate conversations with royalty.

"Or was he shot?"

Not answering, Biff Wilson stood up and turned. He waited for Fletch to move out of the way. Despite the heat, the strong sun in the parking lot, Biff wore a suit jacket and tie, although his shirt collar was loosened. Hair grew out of his ears.

Biff walked the few steps to the three policemen standing by the black-and-white police car. Only two of the police were in uniform.

"Do we know who found him yet?" Biff asked.

"Do *we*?" Fletch said to himself.

The younger uniformed officer was staring at Fletch.

Three cars were parked at odd angles around the blue Cadillac. One was the plainclothesman's unmarked green sedan. The second was the black-and-white sedan, front door open, police radio crackling, red and blue roof lights rotating.

The third said NEWS-TRIBUNE on the sides and back. This was the car Biff Wilson used. Its front door was open, too. Radios crackled from its interior. And a blue light flashed from its roof as well.

The older man in uniform looked at his notebook. "Female employee of the *News-Tribune* named Pilar O'Brien."

Biff let spit drop on the sidewalk between his shoes. "Never heard of her."

"Suppose she's a secretary."

"And she called the cops?"

"She told the security guard at the gate."

"And he called the cops?"

"No," said the plainclothesman. "He called the news desk."

Biff's smile glinted. "Everybody's buckin' for promotion."

"Your photographers have already come and gone," said the older uniform.

"They didn't touch anything," the youngest cop said. "I saw to that. Photographed him from the side and through the windshield. Took a few long shots. Didn't touch the car or the victim."

"Gun been found?" Biff asked.

"Not visible. Might have slipped under the seat," said the plainclothesman. "Where's forensics? I want my coffee."

"Donald E. Habeck," the older uniform read from his notebook. "Anyone know what he was doing here?"

"Yeah," Biff answered. "He was here to see John Winters, the publisher. Ten-o'clock appointment. They were going to set up the announcement that Habeck and his wife are going to, *were* going to, give five million bucks to the art museum."

"How do you know that, Biff?" the plainclothesman asked.

"How do I know everything, Gomez?" Again Biff spat on the sidewalk.

"I know you're the greatest, Biff. I spent all last night tellin' my wife that."

Biff shrugged. "Car telephone, jerk. Hamm Starbuck said Donald Habeck was dead in the parking lot. I asked him, What's he doin' at the *News-Tribune*? Wouldn't you say that's a natural question?"

"That's why I just asked it, Biff." At least Gomez had taken off his coat and rolled up his sleeves.

There was no shade in the parking lot.

The younger uniformed policeman kept giving Fletch long, hard looks.

"Five million dollars. Jeez." The older uniformed policeman rubbed his forehead with his sleeve. "Think of bein' able to give away five million dollars."

"You've never been able to do that?" Biff asked.

"Saturday I gave my niece and her new husband an old couch we had in the den. Slob didn't even come for it. I had to truck it over myself."

"Nice of you," Biff said.

"Didn't get no story about myself in the newspaper for it, though."

"Maybe Biff will write you up a story," Gomez said.

"Sure," Biff said. "Friday night I gave my kid a welt under his left eye. I'm generous, too."

"Here comes your competition, Biff." Gomez nodded toward the security gate.

There were two cars from the *Chronicle-Gazette*.

"Sunday I realized how much I missed that couch. I had to sit up during the ball game. And my back was sore from movin' the damned thing the day before."

The younger uniformed cop touched Biff's sleeve and then pointed to Fletch. He spoke quietly. "He with you?"

Biff considered Fletch from his throne as *News-Tribune* crime writer. "Naw."

"Does he work for the *News-Tribune*?"

"I dunno." Biff was not keeping his voice low. "Maybe I've seen him around. Emptying wastebaskets."

"Didn't know the *News-Tribune* had any wastebaskets," Gomez said. "Just delivery trucks."

At the gate the security guard was delaying the arrival of the

Chronicle-Gazette's reporter and photographer at the scene of the crime.

"Haven't you had any coffee yet this morning?" Biff asked Gomez.

"Only two cups," Gomez said. "Anglo."

"You act like you haven't had any."

"*El mismo*," Gomez said.

"Because I've seen something about that guy," the younger officer said. "Recently. A picture, or something."

Biff fixed Fletch with his distant gaze again. "Maybe on the funnies page."

Finally the two cars from the *Chronicle-Gazette* reached the scene of the crime. Neither had lights flashing nor radios crackling.

"Don't you guys touch anything," the younger uniformed officer shouted at them.

The reporter said, "Shut up." He looked into the car.

The photographer was bending around taking pictures without the reporter in them.

"Who is he?" the reporter asked.

"Not confirmed," Biff answered.

"Employee of the *News-Tribune*?"

"Probably," Biff answered. "Most of us have Caddy Sevilles. I let my kid take mine to school."

"Security guard must know who he is," the reporter said. "He must have given a name when he came in."

"Go ask him," Biff said.

"This is your story, uh, Biff?" the reporter asked.

"It happened in his backyard," Gomez said.

"Yeah," the reporter said. "Expect I can make something of that. Murder in the parking lot of a family newspaper. Tsk, tsk."

"That's Habeck," said the photographer. "Donald Habeck, the attorney. Rich guy. Lives over in The Heights."

"Yeah?" said the reporter. "What's he doin' here?"

"Natural question," said Biff.

"Yet to be determined," said Gomez.

"How long you been workin' for the *News-Tribune*, Gomez?" the reporter asked.

"Nothing's going to be said until the medical examiner and forensics team have come and gone," Gomez answered.

"Not by you." The reporter went to his car and began talking into his telephone.

"Here they come." Gomez nodded at the station wagons coming

through the security gate into the parking lot. "Want to get some coffee inside, Biff?"

Biff looked at the side of the *News-Tribune* building. "Coffee's no good in there, either."

"I'll get Maria to make some special."

"Oh, yeah," Biff said. "I forgot your sister-in-law works in the cafeteria."

"You did like hell. You got her the job."

Fletch began moving out of the area into which the forensics team was moving.

The younger uniformed policeman said to Fletch, "You work here?"

"Naw," said Fletch. "Just makin' a delivery. Just bringin' Mr. Wilson his uppers."

The young cop looked alert. "His uppers?"

"Yeah," said Fletch. "He really messed 'em up last night with taffy apple. Took the dental lab an hour to get 'em clean this morning."

"Oh."

The older uniformed policeman was looking inside the car at Donald Edwin Habeck. "I'll bet my giving away that old couch," he said slowly, "meant more to me than this guy's givin' away five million bucks."

FOUR

"News-Tribune resource desk. Code and name, please."

"Seventeen ninety dash nine," Fletch answered into the car phone. He was driving toward The Heights. "Fletcher."

"I haven't had a call from you before."

"They don't let me out much."

"We have some messages for you."

"I want the address for Mr. and Mrs. Donald Edwin Habeck. I believe that's H-A-B-E-C-K, somewhere in The Heights."

"That's 12339 Palmiera Drive."

"Mapping?"

"It's a little road northwest of Washington Boulevard. There are lots of little roads in there. Winding roads. Your best bet would be to stop at the intersection of Washington and Twenty-third and get exact directions. You'll be turning onto Twenty-third there."

"Okay."

"Messages are, call Barbara Ralton. She wants lunch with you. Says she has things to discuss."

"Like how many babies we're gonna have?"

"My, my. This old mother suggests you have lunch before you pick up on that heavy topic."

"Thank you."

"See how much it costs to feed just two mouths."

"It doesn't cost much to feed a kid. Just squirt orange juice into him a few times a day. Peanut butter."

"Ha."

"Beg pardon?"

"Ha."

"How much does peanut butter cost?"

The bumper sticker on the car in front of Fletch read: NASTINESS WILL GET YOU EVERYWHERE.

"Should have taken my own advice and stayed in bed. One more message for you, Fletcher. From Ann McGarrahan, society-page editor. She said if you phoned in to tell you to report to her immediately. Your assignment has been changed."

"Oh."

"So it looks like you don't need that address in The Heights after all."

"One more question: Who is Pilar O'Brien?"

"Why do you want to know?"

"What kind of answer is that?"

"A personal answer. Why do you want to know?"

"Just heard of her. Does she work for the *News-Tribune*?"

A hesitation slightly longer than normal before the *News-Tribune* resource-desk person said, "You're talking to her."

"Ah! Then you're the lady who found Habeck this morning."

"Who?"

"The guy dead in the parking lot."

"Is that his name? I thought you just asked for the address of —"

"Forget about that, will you?"

"How can I? How can a reporter I never heard of before be asking for the address of —"

"I said, please forget about that. I never asked."

"Mrs. McGarrahan —"

"I'll call her. Tell me about finding Habeck."

"I'm not permitted to talk to any reporters until after the police question me. Then I may only report what I told the police."

"Jeez, you know the rules."

"That's what Mr. Starbuck said."

"When you found him, was the car door opened or closed?"

"I can't answer you."

"It's important."

"Maybe that's why I can't answer you."

"Did you see a gun?"

"What's-your-name . . . Fletcher. Shall I tell Mrs. McGarrahan you're returning to the office?"

"Sure," Fletch said. "Tell her that."

"Would you please give me directions to Palmiera Drive?"

The eyes of the man behind the counter of the liquor store at the intersection of Washington Boulevard and Twenty-third Street shifted from Fletch through the store window to Fletch's Datsun 300 ZX outside the front door, motor running, and back to Fletch. There was a hole in the car's muffler. The engine was noisy.

"I'm looking for the twelve-thousand block of Palmiera Drive, if there is such a thing."

Looking Fletch full in the face, the man behind the counter whistled the first few bars of "Colonel Bogey's March."

"Do I turn right on Twenty-third Street?"

The man raised a .45 automatic pistol from beneath the counter. He pointed it at Fletch's heart.

"Jeez," Fletch said. "I'm being held up by a liquor store!"

Fletch was grabbed from behind. Muscular brown arms, fingers clasped just under Fletch's rib cage, pinned Fletch's own arms to his side.

"Hey!" Fletch yelled. "I asked politely!"

The gun kept Fletch's heart as its target.

The man holding the gun called toward the back of the store, "Rosa! Call the cops!"

"I'll get the muffler fixed!" Fletch said. "I promise!"

"Report a robbery in progress!" the man behind the counter shouted.

"All I did was ask for directions! I didn't even ask for change for a parking meter!"

"He ain't got no gun," the voice behind Fletch's ear rumbled.

The man behind the counter looked at Fletch's hands and then the pockets of his jeans.

"Let me point out to you," Fletch said with great sincerity, "you can't shoot me with that cannon without blowing away the guy behind me."

The gun wavered. The steel bands clamping Fletch's arms to his sides slackened just slightly.

"Workmen's Compensation won't cover!" Fletch yelled as he ran backward, pushing the guy holding him.

Within a meter, they crashed into a tall, wire bottle rack.

Instantly, as bottles smashed, there was the reek of bourbon.

The guy's hands disappeared from in front of Fletch. "I'm gettin' cut," he yelled.

Sitting on the guy's lap, Fletch bounced up and down once or twice, then he leaned back against his chest.

"Ow!" the guy yelled.

Bottles were raining down on them. One landed on Fletch's left knee, causing more pain than Fletch thought possible.

The bottles that hit the floor smashed and splashed bourbon over both of them.

The guy with the gun was moving along the counter trying to get a bead on Fletch, that did not include the guy Fletch was sitting on.

Fletch rolled through broken glass and bourbon puddles to the door. "Last time I'll ask you guys for directions!"

As he stood up he grabbed the door open.

Halfway through the door the gun banged. The breakproof glass in the door shattered.

Opening his car door, Fletch shouted back at the store, "If you don't know where Palmiera Drive is, why don't you just say so?"

At a sedate pace, he turned right off Washington onto Twenty-third.

Sirens filled the air.

FIVE

"Mrs. Habeck?"

The lady with blued hair, flower-patterned dress, and green sneakers sat in a straight chair alone by the swimming pool. There was a red purse near her feet.

"Yes, I'm Mrs. Habeck."

Looking up at Fletch in the sunlight, her nose twitched like a rabbit's.

"I.M. Fletcher. *News-Tribune.* I was to meet your husband at ten o'clock."

"He's not here."

Fletch had spent a moment ringing the front doorbell of 12339 Palmiera Drive. It was a nice property, a brick house floating on rhododendrons, but not, to Fletch's mind, the home of someone who could or would give away five million dollars without taking deep breaths.

And there was no one in the house to open the door to him on a Monday morning.

Fletch had explored through the rhododendrons until he found the blue-haired lady contemplating the clear, unruffled swimming pool.

"One never knows where he is," Mrs. Habeck said. "Donald wanders away. That's the only thing, for certain, that can be said for Donald. He wanders away." She reached out her hand and closed her fingers as if grabbing something that wasn't there. She said, "He wanders."

"Maybe I can talk to you."

Again her nose twitched. "Young man, are you very, very drunk?"

"No, ma'am. Do I seem drunk?"

"You smell drunk."

Fletch held a section of his T-shirt up to his nose and sniffed it. "That's my new deodorant. Do you like it?"

"It's an odorant."

"It's called Bamm-o."

"It's called bourbon." Mrs. Habeck averted her nose. "You reek of bourbon."

Fletch sniffed his T-shirt again. "It is pretty bad, isn't it."

"I know bourbon when I smell it," said Mrs. Habeck. "You're not wearing a very good brand."

"It was on special sale, I think."

"Friday that bourbon did not exist." Mrs. Habeck spoke slowly, and there was sadness in her small, gray eyes. "I've heard of you newspapermen. Donald once told me about a journalist he knew who filled his waterbed with bourbon. He told his friends he had refined the art of being sloshed. Lying there, he could nip from the waterbed's valve. He said he could get the motion of his bourbonbed to match exactly the swing and sway of the world as he got drunk. Well, he sank lower and lower. Within three months he was back sleeping flat on the floor." Mrs. Habeck resettled her hands in her lap. "It was a double bed, too."

Fletch took a deep breath and held it. He sensed that Mrs. Habeck would be offended by laughter.

Tightening his stomach muscles to restrain himself, he looked away across the pool. Down a grassy slope, a gardener wearing a sombrero was weeding a flower bed.

"Oh, my," he finally said, sighing. "Truth is, I had an accident."

"You people always have an excuse for drinking. Good news. Bad news. No news."

"No," Fletch said. "A real accident. I stopped at the liquor store at the intersection of Washington and Twenty-third, and while I was there, a rack of bourbon got tipped over. It splashed all over an employee and me."

Her pale, sad eyes studied Fletch.

"I haven't been drinking. Honest. May I sit down?"

Reluctantly, she said, "All right."

He sat in another wrought-iron straight chair. She was in the shade of the table's umbrella, but he was not.

"About this five million dollars, Mrs. Habeck . . ."

"Five million dollars," she repeated.

". . . you and your husband decided to give to the art museum?"

Slowly, she said, "Yussss," in the hiss of a deflating tire. "Tell me about it."

"What?"

"What about it?" she asked.

Fletch hesitated. "I was hoping you'd tell me about it."

Mrs. Habeck drew herself up slightly in the chair. "Yes, well, my husband and I decided to give five million dollars to the art museum."

"I know that much. Your husband is a lawyer?"

"My husband," said Mrs. Habeck, "wanders off. Away, away. He always has, you know. That's something that can be said about him."

"I see," Fletch said politely. He was beginning to wonder how much vodka Mrs. Habeck had slipped into her morning coffee. "He's senior partner in the firm of Habeck, Harrison and Haller?"

"I told him he shouldn't do that," Mrs. Habeck said, frowning. "Three different *H* sounds. In fact, three different *Ha* sounds." Still frowning, she looked at Fletch. "Don't you agree?"

"Of course," said Fletch. "Disconcerting."

"Gives the impression of inconsistency," she said. "As if, you know, the partners couldn't be counted on to get together on anything. To agree."

"Yes," said Fletch.

"To say nothing of the fact that when people say 'Habeck, Harrison and Haller,' what they actually hear themselves saying, underneath everything, you know? is *Ha Ha Ha.*"

"Ah," said Fletch.

"Except the actual sound *Hay Ha Haw*. Which is worse."

"Much worse," agreed Fletch. His fingers wiped the perspiration off his forehead.

"I wanted him to take on a fourth partner," said Mrs. Habeck. "Named Burke."

"Umm. Didn't Mr. Burke wish to join the firm?"

Mrs. Habeck looked at Fletch resentfully. "Donald said he didn't know anyone named Burke."

"Oh. I see."

"At least not any lawyer named Burke. Not any lawyer named Burke who was free to join the firm."

"Did you know a lawyer named Burke free to join the firm?"

"No."

Sweating in bourbon-soaked clothes in the sunlight, Fletch's head was beginning to reel. He felt like he was on a bourbonbed. "Does your husband do any corporate-law work?"

"No," she said. "He was never a bit cooperative. He was always arguing in court."

There was still no humor in her sad eyes.

"I know his reputation is as a criminal lawyer." Then Fletch cringed, awaiting what Mrs. Habeck would make of *criminal lawyer*.

She said, "Yussss."

Fletch blew air. "Mrs. Habeck, did you or your husband have any income other than that derived from his practice of criminal law, and from his partnership in Habeck, Harrison and Haller?"

"Hay, Ha, Haw," she said.

"I mean, were either of you personally wealthy, had you inherited . . . ?"

Mrs. Habeck said, "My husband is most apt to wear black shoes. You don't see black shoes too often in The Heights. He doesn't like to dress flamboyantly, as many criminal lawyers do."

Fletch waited a moment.

She asked, "You wouldn't think a man who wears black shoes would be so apt to wander away, would you?"

He waited another moment. "It isn't that I'm trying to invade your privacy, Mrs. Habeck."

"I don't have any privacy." She looked at her green sneakers.

"It's just that I'm trying to assess what donating five million dollars to the museum means to you and your husband. I mean, is he almost giving away the proceeds of his life's work?"

"Mister, you're making me sick."

"Beg pardon?"

"The smell of you. You seem sober enough, for a newspaperman, for a young man, but you reek of bourbon. It's beginning to affect my stomach, and my head."

"I'm sorry," Fletch said. "Truth be known, me, too."

"Well? What are we going to do about it?"

Fletch looked at the back of the house. "Maybe I could go take a shower."

"If you said bourbon got splashed all over your clothes, your taking a shower and putting the same clothes back on won't do any good."

"Right," said Fletch. "That's very sensible." He nodded. "Very sensible."

"Why don't you jump in the pool? It's right there."

"I could do that." Fletch began taking things out of his pockets. "With my clothes on."

"Why should you jump into the pool with your clothes on?"

"To get the smell of bourbon off them?"

"But then your clothes would be wet. You want to go around the rest of the day in wet clothes?"

"It's a hot day."

"Hotness has nothing to do with wetness."

"Hotness?"

"My daughter used to say that. When she was a little girl. *Hotness.* No wonder she ended up married to a poet. What's his name?"

"I don't know."

"Tom Farliegh."

"Okay. I was going to ask you about your children."

"They're fine, thank you. Obviously, you take your clothes off before you jump into the pool."

"Then I won't have any clothes on."

"I mind? I'm a mother and a grandmother. I don't mind. This is a private pool." She looked down the slope at the gardener. "That's Pedro. He doesn't mind. If he minds seeing a naked man, he shouldn't be a gardener."

"Clearly."

Mrs. Habeck stood up. "Take off your clothes. I'll avert my eyes so you can tell your girl friend no woman has seen you naked since your mother last changed your diapers. Last week was it?"

Fletch was taking off his sneakers. "Really, I don't mind."

"Leave your clothes on the chair. After you get in the pool, say *Hallooo*, and I'll pick up your clothes, take them inside, and put them in the washer and then the dryer."

"This is very nice of you." Standing, Fletch peeled off his stinking T-shirt.

"Hallooo!" Mrs. Habeck called loudly. She was waving at the gardener.

He raised his head and looked at her from under his sombrero. He did not speak or wave back.

Fletch averted his eyes. He took off his jeans and underpants and dived into the pool.

Enjoying the cool water and getting away from the stink of his clothes, he drifted underwater across the pool, turned, and swam back to the nearer edge.

He stuck his nose above the edge of the pool.

"Hallooo," he said.

Mrs. Habeck was already headed for the house with his clothes and sneakers.

She was also carrying her red pocketbook.

SIX

"Hey!"

It was the third time Fletch had heard someone yell that, but this time, just as he was about to make his turn between laps, the shout was distinct. There could be no doubt it was he who was being hailed. He put his hand on the pool ledge and raised his head.

As water cleared from his opened eyes, he saw Biff Wilson, fully dressed, including suit and tie, standing on the pool edge.

"Hallooo," Fletch said.

"God," Biff said. "It's you."

"No, it's not," said Fletch. "It's Fletcher."

Two meters behind Biff stood Lieutenant Gomez.

"That's your name? Fletcher?"

"Yes, sir."

"You were just in the parking lot of the *News-Tribune*."

"Yes, sir."

"How did you get here so fast?"

"I didn't stop for coffee."

"Are you the reason that young cop asked me if I have false teeth?"

"False what?"

Biff stuck his thumb under his upper front teeth and demonstrated how solid they were. "False feeph!"

"Gee, Biff, that gum cement you use must be pretty good."

Biff gave Gomez a tired look, then turned to Fletch. "Are you or are you not an employee of the *News-Tribune*?"

"I am. Sir."

Biff spoke distinctly. "What is your assignment?"

"I am newly assigned to Society."

"Society." Biff's face expressed the contempt he had for society writers. "What are you doing here?"

"Here?"

"Here. At the home of Donald Edwin Habeck."

"Swimming, sir."

Biff exploded at Gomez. "He's swimming bare-assed!"

Fletch said, "I was assigned to interview Donald Habeck at ten o'clock this morning regarding the five million dollars he and his wife had decided to donate to the art museum."

"But you knew Donald Habeck was dead! I saw you in the parking lot!"

Fletch shrugged. "Obstacles are encountered in doing any story."

As if personally offended, Biff shouted at the sky. "He's swimming bare-assed in the murder victim's pool!"

Lieutenant Gomez stepped closer to the pool edge. "What have you done since you've been here?"

"I interviewed, I tried to interview, Mrs. Habeck."

The eyes of both men widened.

"Did you see Mrs. Habeck?" Gomez asked.

"Yes."

"Tell us about Mrs. Habeck," Biff said. "What does she look like?"

"About sixty. Blue hair. Green sneakers. A sort of weird lady."

Biff and Gomez looked at each other.

"Son," Biff said with heavy patience, "what are you doing swimming bare-assed in Habeck's pool two hours after Habeck was murdered?"

"I didn't smell so good, my clothes —"

"What?" said Gomez.

"Yeah, see, I got held up by this liquor store on my way here, I got bourbon splashed all over me, I was really reeking of the stuff —"

Biff stepped on Fletch's hand on the pool ledge.

"Ow." Fletch went entirely underwater a moment and rubbed his hand.

When he resurfaced, Biff and Gomez were still there, staring down at him.

Fletch placed his left hand in a pool drain.

He asked, "What's the matter with you guys?"

"Oh, nothing," Biff answered. "We should have expected to find a reporter from the *News-Tribune* swimming bare-assed in the murder victim's pool two hours after his death."

Fletch asked, "Isn't that what society writers do?"

"Probably," answered Biff. "I wouldn't know."

"Where are your clothes?" Gomez asked.

"Mrs. Habeck took them."

" 'Mrs. Habeck took them.' " Biff repeated. He sighed.

"Where is she?" Fletch asked. "Didn't she let you in the house?"

"The cook let us into the house," Gomez said. He added, "She had just returned that moment from grocery shopping."

"You haven't talked to Mrs. Habeck?"

"Mrs. Habeck isn't here," Gomez said.

"She isn't? Where are my clothes?"

"I think that's something we'd all like to know," Gomez answered.

"She couldn't have left with my clothes," Fletch said.

"Maybe this Mrs. Habeck wanted to make another donation to a museum." Biff chuckled. "An example of late-twentieth-century bummery costumery."

Gomez laughed.

"I didn't get much out of her anyway," Fletch said.

"Oh, you didn't," said Biff. "She got your clothes off you."

"Frankly, she seemed a little off-the-wall. Weird, you know what I mean?"

"Weird, uh? She got your clothes off you and disappeared with them, and you say *she's* weird?"

"Come on, Biff," Fletch said.

Down the grassy slope Fletch saw the gardener's sombrero rise, move a few meters, and lower from sight again.

Biff said, "You're not supposed to be here, and you know it."

"There's still the story of the donation, Biff. What happens to it now?"

"Your name is Fletcher?" Biff confirmed.

"Spelled with an *F*."

"Get out of my face, Fletcher. Get out of it, and stay out of it."

Dripping and naked, Fletch stood over the gardener.

"Any idea where I can get a towel?"

The gardener looked up at him. His face was younger than Fletch had expected.

Slowly the gardener stood up. He took off his denim shirt and handed it to Fletch.

"Gee, thanks. I really mean it. Those guys just said the cook is in the house." He wrapped the shirt around him. "I'll get it back to you as soon as I find some clothes. Nice guy. Give someone his shirt right off his back."

The gardener knelt down and resumed weeding the flower bed.

"You have any idea where Mrs. Habeck went?"

"La señora no es la señora."

"What?"

"La señora no es la mujer, la esposa."

"What? 'The lady is not the wife.' You speak English better than I do. What are you saying?"

"You mean that broad you were talking to, right?" the gardener asked.

"Right."

"She's not Mrs. Habeck."

"She's not?"

"Mrs. Habeck is young and pretty." The gardener sketched a shapely form in the soil with his finger. "Like that. Blond."

"She said she was Mrs. Habeck."

"She's not."

"She's the cook?"

"The cook is Hispanic. Forty years old. She lives two blocks from me."

"Then who was she?"

"I dunno," the gardener said. "Never saw her before."

As Fletch was going through the Habecks' kitchen, the cook shrieked at the sight of a strange man naked except for a denim shirt hanging from his waist.

As Fletch was going up the stairs, Biff Wilson came out of the living room and said, "I've just talked to Frank Jaffe. He says you're a dumb kid who misunderstood your assignment. You're to get your ass back to the office and report to Ann McGarrahan in Society double quick time."

"Right," said Fletch. "Double quick."

He began taking the stairs two at a time.

"Why are you going upstairs?" Biff yelled.

Fletch yelled back, "I parked my car up here."

As Fletch handed the denim shirt back to the gardener, Fletch said, "Sorry I can't give it back to you washed, dried, and pressed, but that's how I lost my last clothes. They were headed for a wash."

As the gardener stood up and put back on his shirt, his eyes crinkled at the sight of the clothes Fletch was wearing.

Fletch shrugged. "Found this suit in Habeck's closet. He'll never miss it."

"The suit is short and fat."

"I got a belt. Nice tie. The necktie should distract the eye from the rest of the ensemble, right?"

"You're ready to boogie, man."

"Thanks again. The cook yelled at me."

"I heard. I thought it was the noon whistle."

"What would she have done if you hadn't lent me your shirt?"

"Scrambled eggs while they were still in the refrigerator."

"Where did you learn your Spanish?" Fletch asked.

"BHHS."

"BHHS?"

"Yeah," the gardener said, stooping to his work. "Bevery Hills High School."

SEVEN

"Cecilia's Boutique. Cecilia speaking. Have you considered jodhpurs?"

"I'm thinking very seriously about jodhpurs," Fletch said into his car phone.

"They're just coming in, sir. In another month they'll be all the rage. I'm sure your wife would be really impressed if you bought her jodhpurs now. Impressed by your prescience."

"So should the jodhpurs be impressed. I haven't got a wife." Waiting at the red light at the intersection of Washington and Twenty-third, Fletch saw that all was peaceful at the liquor store. Plywood had been nailed over the shattered breakproof glass of the door. They were ready for their next attack. "May I speak with Barbara Ralton, please?"

Cecilia hesitated. "Sales personnel are not to take personal phone calls. May I take a message for her?"

"Sure. This is Fletcher. Tell her I can't see her for lunch today. Please also tell her I look forward to buying her a pair of jodhpurs, at Saks."

"Here I am," Fletch said.

"Here who is?" Ann McGarrahan, society editor of the *News-Tribune*, was a tall broad-shouldered woman in her forties. She sat behind a desk that was too small for her in an office that was distinctly too small for her.

"I thought you people in Society knew everyone."

"Everyone who is anyone," Ann said softly. The corners of her mouth twinged with a smile. "Which obliges me to repeat: Who are you?"

"I.M. Fletcher." Fletch looked at the dead, brown fern on Ann's windowsill. "A nobody. Beneath your attention. May I go now?"

"Where have you been?"

"Oh, I changed clothes." Fletch held out the skirts of Donald Habeck's suit coat. "Frank said something about my needing a suit and tie for this job."

Ann studied him over her half-lenses. "And that's the suit? That's the tie?"

"Good material in it."

"I daresay. Clearly you made your investment in the material, and not the tailoring."

"I've lost weight."

"Gotten taller, too. Your trouser cuffs are a half-foot above your ankles."

"Have you heard that in another month jodhpurs will be all the rage? Lord, what I bring to this department."

"I see. Your sleeves are modified knickers, too, are they? They stop halfway down your forearms."

"I'm ready to cover the social scene."

"The young women around here call you Fletch, don't they?"

"When they call me at all." Fletch sat in a curved-back wooden chair.

"Why don't they use your first name?"

"Irwin?"

"What's wrong with Irwin?"

"Sounds like a hesitant cheer."

"Your middle name then. Don't you have a middle name?"

"Maurice."

"I know lots of nice people called Maury."

"I'm not one of 'em."

"Okay. You're a Fletch. It just sounds so much like a verb."

"To fletch, or not to fletch: that is the copulative."

"Guess I'll have to fletch. Well, Fletch. Not only has Frank Jaffe sent me you, with warnings regarding your appearance which, however dire, were still insufficient, he also sent me a strong suggestion as to what your first assignment might be."

"I know what it is."

"You do?"

"Yeah. Stay on this story concerning the five million dollars Donald Habeck and his wife decided to donate to the art museum. To stay right on it until I get to the bottom of it and everything else concerning the Habecks. Right?"

"Wrong. Of course."

"That was my assignment, for about a minute and a half this morning."

"Wasn't Donald Habeck the man murdered in our parking lot this morning?"

Fletch shrugged. "Just makes the story more interesting."

"Oh, we have an interesting story for you to work on, Fletch. It was Frank's suggestion. In fact, he mentioned the suggestion originally came from you."

"From me? A story for the society pages?"

"We don't really think of this section as being society anymore, Fletch. Although, of course, there's always the social aspect of it. We think of it more as human interest, with the emphasis on women's interests."

"That's why I brought up the latest scoop on jodhpurs."

"It's not just fashion anymore, it's more lifestyle. It's not just beauty, it's health."

"Right: women's healthy lifestyles."

"You'd be surprised at some of the topics some of our younger women writers want to discuss these days." Ann picked up some copy off her desk. "Here's an article comparing the relative merits of manufactured dildos. With pictures, supplied by the manufacturers, I expect. Do you think we should run an article comparing dildos, Fletch?"

"Uh . . ."

"Which do you think is the best dildo in the world today?"

"I can't tell you."

"Why not?"

"I couldn't be disinterested. I'm attached to it. It would be a subjective opinion."

"I see." Again Ann McGarrahan struggled to keep the corners of her mouth straight. She dropped the copy onto her desk. "Ah, the woes of being an editor. Needless to say, I've had that story on my desk for some time."

"Dildo?"

"Yes."

"I'm sure you'll find space for it."

"So, you see, we're into all sorts of areas of interest to you. We are not just concerned with little old ladies who slip vodka into their tea."

"Big-mouth Frank."

"So you haven't yet figured out what your assignment is? I was hoping it would come to you, on your own."

"Something about sexual aids? I know: you want me to do a report on what sexual aids do two out of three gynecologists recommend."

"You ran in the Sardinal Race yesterday."

"Oh, no."

"Didn't you?"

"Yes."

"Frank told me you ran behind a group of about a dozen women you couldn't bring yourself to pass."

"Oh, no."

"These same women received rather wide publicity, it seems, on this morning's sports pages of the *News-Tribune*." As she was saying this, Ann McGarrahan opened the *News-Tribune* to the sports section and looked at the two large photographs, on facing pages, of this group of women, coming, and going. "My, they are attractive, healthy young women, aren't they?"

"Not too shabby."

"For some reason, Frank takes this spread on his sports pages as some sort of personal affront. Also, I suspect he is in his office right now getting considerable flak for it, from the usual groups."

"Oh, boy."

" 'Ben Franklyn Friend Service. A service company,' " Ann appeared to read from the newspaper. "What sort of service do you suppose they provide, Fletch, to have Frank so upset?"

"You're kidding."

Ann jutted her large face across the desk and asked, "Does it have something to do with men?"

"I suspect so."

"Tell me what."

Fletch felt the back of his chair pressing against his shoulder blades. "It's an escort service of the traveling-whorehouse variety, and I suspect you know that."

"Ah! Sounds like there's a story here."

"What? No story . . ."

"As I've outlined to you," Ann said, "on these pages we're concerned with women's interests, their health, how they make their livings —"

"This is a family newspaper!"

"Nice to hear you say so. Your investigation, of course, will be discreetly reported."

"You want me to investigate a whorehouse?"

"Who better?"

"I'm getting married, Saturday!"

"Have you already passed your blood test?"

Fletch took a deep breath.

Ann held up the flat of her hand to him. "This is a new thing, as I understand it: prostitutes who are obliged to stay in prime physical condition. Goes along with several articles we've run on organic gardening, I think. How does this Ben Franklyn Friend Service operate? What is the source of their discipline? How do they entertain men professionally without having to drink a lot themselves? If they are not dependent upon drugs themselves, why are they prostitutes? How much money do they make?" Ann continued to hold up her hand. "Of most importance, who owns Ben Franklyn Friend Service? Who derives the profit?"

Fletch let out his breath, and said nothing.

Ann said, "I think we could have a story here."

"Best way to do it," said Fletch, "might be to send one of your young women writers in to apply for a position with Ben Franklyn Friend Service."

"Ah, but it was your story idea, Fletch. Frank said so himself. It wouldn't be right for us to take it away from you. Of course, we may send a young woman in, too, for a preliminary investigation, that side of the story."

"I said I'm getting married Saturday."

"Doesn't give you much time, does it?"

"Ann —"

"Besides that," Ann said, refolding the newspaper on her desk, "I think Frank feels that such a story — well done, of course — would go a long way toward getting him off the hook for these unfortunate pictures that ran on the sports pages this morning." She folded her hands on the desk. "Not all is tea and biscuits on the lifestyle pages, Fletcher. Definitely, you're the man for the job."

Fletch was looking out the window. "P.S., your fern is dead."

"I happen to like brown fern," Ann said, without looking around. "I feel they make a statement: despair springs eternal."

"Oh, boy."

"Happy to have you in the department, young Mr. Fletcher. At least you won't have your purse snatched."

"It's not my purse I'm worried about." He stood up.

"It will be interesting to see what you turn in."

"You're asking me to 'turn in' under wicked circumstances."

"Oh, and, Fletcher . . . ?"

"Yes, ma'am?"

"Be careful of Biff Wilson. Don't get in his way. You do, and he'll run over you like a fifty-car railroad train. He is a mean, vicious bastard. I ought to know. I was married to him, once."

"Fletch, there's a call waiting for you." The young woman outside Ann McGarrahan's office jangled her bracelets at him. "Line 303. Nice suit. 'Fraid you're goin' to get raped 'round here?"

"Hello," Fletch said into the phone.

"Hello," said Barbara. "I'm furious."

"I'd rather be Fletch."

"What the hell do you mean by chewing out my employer?"

"Did I do that?"

"Cecilia's very serious about jodhpurs just now. She overbought."

"I care. She wouldn't let you come to the phone."

"Company policy. The phone's for the business, not for the employees."

"But I'm the fiancé of her number-one salesperson."

"And what do you mean you can't have lunch with me?"

"Things are a little confused here."

"This is Monday, Fletch. We're getting married Saturday. We have things to discuss, you know?"

"Anyway, I'd already agreed to have lunch with Alston. We want him as my best man, don't I?"

"That's the least of my worries. We don't have much time. You've got to get with it."

"I'm with it."

"I mean, really with it. Look at all you've got to do. Cindy says —"

"Barbara! Cool it! Don't chew me out now!"

"Why not?"

"Because I've just been chewed out by absolutely the best. Next to her, you sound tin-horn."

"Then why don't you marry her, whoever she is?"

"I would," answered Fletch, "except she has other ambitions for my proclivities."

EIGHT

"Good afternoon, Alston." Fletch slid into a chair at the café table.

"Good afternoon," Alston said. "I'm having a beer."

"Enjoy."

"Want a beer?" Fletch nodded. Alston signaled the waiter. "Two beers, please." With the back of his hand, Alston then brushed a speck of lint off the sleeve of his suit jacket. "Fletch, I couldn't help notice, as you scuffed along the sidewalk . . ."

"What?"

"Your suit."

"I've been assigned to the society pages."

Alston grinned. "Well, that's a real to-hell-with-society suit."

"It makes a statement, I think," Fletch said. "Like dead ferns. Despair springs eternal."

"I see you had a super morning, too. Did they finally get you for that headline you wrote?"

"Headline?"

"DOCTOR SAVES LIFE IN ACCIDENT?"

"They never noticed that one." The waiter brought the beers. "Sometimes I think I'm the only one at the *News-Tribune* with any news sense."

"I have that headline hanging on my wall."

"We must look at the bright side, Alston."

"Yeah," Alston said. "Barbara."

"Barbara just chewed me out."

"Oh."

"This morning I was chewed out by the managing editor, Frank Jaffe, the *News-Tribune*'s star crime writer, Biff Wilson, Ann McGarrahan, the society editor, and my fiancée, Barbara Ralton. And it's only Monday."

"In a suit like that — as much as you can be said to be *in* it — I'm surprised anyone takes you seriously."

"Oh, yeah." Fletch removed his coat and put it on the back of his chair. "I was also held up by a liquor store. Shot at."

"Lots of people have been held up in a liquor store. Once, my uncle was in a hurry; you know, before the rabbits started nibbling his toes? And —"

"And I interviewed a nice, kooky lady who said she was someone apparently she isn't."

"You interviewed an impostor?"

"I guess."

"Did you get anything interesting out of her?"

"I did have the feeling I was leading her, Alston."

"I would think you would have to feed answers to an impostor," Alston said. "To get any kind of story."

"What's more, she got my clothes off me. Ran away with them."

"All this happened just this morning?"

"And those sneakers were just getting comfortable."

"Fletcher, are you sure you can make it outside the U.S. Marine Corps?"

"It's hard, Alston, getting a start in life."

Alston held up his beer. "To youth."

"No one takes us young people seriously."

"And we are serious."

"We are indeed. Seriously serious."

The waiter said, "Are you gentlemen ready to order now?"

"Yes," Fletch said. "The usual."

"Sir," the waiter said with poised pen, "it may be usual to you, but whatever it is, is not usual to me."

"You mean I have to tell you my order?"

"You could keep it to yourself, sir. That would cut down on my work."

"I had it here just last week."

"I'm pleased to see it was you who returned, sir, and not whatever it was you had for lunch."

"This is Manolo's, isn't it?"

The waiter glanced at the name on the awning. "That much we've established."

"A peanut-butter-and-sliced-banana sandwich with mayonnaise on pumpernickel," Fletch said.

"Ah," said the waiter. "That is memorable. How could we have forgotten?"

"You make it special for me."

"I would hope so. And you, sir?"

"Liederkranz-and-celery sandwich on light rye," Alston answered. "Just a soupçon of ketchup."

"I beseech Thee, O God, that's another special."

The waiter went away, hurriedly.

"Even the damned waiter doesn't take us seriously," Fletch said.

"No one takes youth seriously. Maturity is too precious to be wasted on the old."

"Aren't we mature? Veterans. You're a lawyer. I'm a journalist."

"People still plunk us in the to-be-seen-and-not-heard category, though."

"Could it be that we're pretty?"

"In that suit, Fletcher, you dim daffodils."

"I should think so."

"This morning I got called into Haller's office. Senior partner. Summoned. You see, I'm supposed to sit in on meetings, keeping my mouth shut, of course, and never, never laugh, let my jaw drop in shock, or stare too much."

"Those the conditions of your employment?"

"You got it. I'm supposed to just listen. Pretend I'm not there. That way, I get to learn how grown-up lawyers work up their fees to the exorbitant, pay the rent for us lesser souls, and maintain their Mercedes."

"Sounds edifyin'."

"Educational. Also, of course, peons such as I are to be present at meetings so we can understand what research, leg work, is to be done on the case underfoot."

"Don't you mean, under consideration, or under advisement, or something?"

"Underfoot. So here's a client, new to Habeck, Harrison and Haller —"

"Ha ha ha."

"Excuse me? I haven't finished yet."

"I should have said, *Hay, Ha, Haw*. Have I got that right?"

"Probably. Whatever it is you're saying."

The waiter put their sandwiches in front of them. He said, "Here's your fodder."

"Yeah," said Fletch. "Thanks, mudder."

"Anyway," continued Alston, while checking his ketchup and apparently finding it satisfactory. "This new client was interrupted Saturday night by the police while removing silver, stereo, and other glittery things from a home up at The Heights. The scandal, and the reason for this gentleman coming to Habeck, Harrison and Haller, is, you see, that the home, silver, stereo, and other glittery objects did not belong to him."

"A burglar."

"Well, someone in the front lines in the theft business."

"Why wasn't he in court this morning?"

"Came directly to us from court, having had the wisdom to ask for and get what will be, I'm sure, the first of many postponements."

"He was out on bail."

"Which modest amount he posted himself. His reason for doing so and rushing off, he told the court, was that he was obliged to take his fifteen-year-old dog to the dentist."

"Had he an appointment?"

"Unbreakable."

"A mission of mercy."

"Doubtlessly the court is now prejudiced in his favor."

"You're not about to tell me he was lying to the court?"

"Well, he told us, or, rather, he told Mr. Haller, that while he was in court, the dog, waiting to be brought to the dentist, was howling so in pain, a neighbor shot him."

Fletch shook his head. "He needn't have rushed." He salted his peanut butter-banana-and-mayonnaise sandwich. "Tell me, did he call up and cancel the dentist's appointment?"

"He didn't say."

"I'm trying to gauge the degree of this man's honesty, you see, his concern for the social contract."

"In meetings, I am not allowed to put forth such questions."

"I forgot. You're a hanging plant."

"That, or whatever is put at the base of plants to aid their growth."

"I'm surprised Mr. Haller, being senior partner in an important law firm, would be interviewing a simple burglar himself. Why would he be taking on a burglar as a client?"

"Ah, Fletch, you are innocent as to how law firms, and thus the law, works."

"I thought I knew a few things."

"I'll bet you thought law firms practice law."

"They don't?"

"That's not their primary function."

"It isn't?"

"No. What they actually practice is something called cooling the client."

"Do they teach that in law school?"

"No. Which is why starters, such as myself, work in law firms a few years at just enough above the minimum wage to keep in clean collars. Because it is not being taught in law schools, we must learn this technique essential to keeping the law firm afloat."

"So what's 'cooling the client'?"

"When a client first knocks on the door of a law firm as ambitious as Habeck, Harrison and Haller, the law firm's first job is to discover how much the client — the client, not the case — is worth. It takes experience and wisdom to make such an assessment."

"I don't see how what the client is worth has to do with what the case is worth."

"Suppose it's a simple, straightforward case. But the senior partner, who conducts the first interview, discovers the client is rich. Under the circumstances, what would you do?"

"Practice law."

"How little you know. You cool the client. The senior partner, having made an assessment of the client's worth, decides how much of his wealth the law firm will take from him in fees, regardless of how simple or complicated the case is. It would amaze you to know how a talented law firm can complicate the most simple case by creating setbacks, other delays, filing wrong or useless motions, petitions, initiating incorrect lines of argument, et cetera. The object, you see, is to keep the case going as long as possible, all the while milking the client for nearly every penny he or she may be worth. If, despite the law firm's best efforts, the case is ever brought to a conclusion, and if the law firm has done a masterful job of cooling the client consistently throughout his ordeal, the client ends up impoverished and very, very grateful."

"Pardon me, Counselor, but isn't that called robbery?"

"In the law, it's called building a solid reputation."

"Supposing, Counselor, in the initial interview, the senior partner discovers this particular client isn't rich enough to be worth robbing?"

"One of three things happens. First, the client could be persuaded that his case could be handled just as well, and more cheaply, by a smaller, less prestigious law firm. Which law firm, incidentally, is expected to kick back to the recommending law firm a percentage of whatever fees the poor client is able to pay."

"The rich get richer."

"And the poor get screwed. Or, second, if the case has any value to the partners socially, or if it might generate beneficial publicity, or whatever, even if the client doesn't have sufficient wherewithal to be worth robbing, the case is taken. It is then handled with such dazzling speed and efficiency the world is breathless as it watches. The old-boy network is used. Private deals are struck. A settlement is arrived at swiftly, and cheaply, not always to the client's complete benefit."

"And the law firm's reputation becomes even more solid."

"I'm giving you the internal workings of your average greedy law firm. At least Habeck, Harrison and Haller. How some lawyers look at the law, you might say."

"You're robbing me of my innocence."

"The third thing that might happen is that which happened this morning, which is what I'm trying to tell you about."

"If a person who engages himself as a lawyer is a fool, what's a person who engages Habeck, Harrison and Haller?"

"You can see why violence is not always an illogical solution."

"A solution discovered by an increasing percentage of our population," Fletch said. "Have you heard the complaint, 'The courts don't work'?"

"Once or twice," Alston admitted. "The third thing that can happen with an impecunious client is what I saw happen this morning. A burglar rushes from the court and finds himself being interviewed by Mr. Haller."

"The presumption can be made that if the burglar had enough money to afford Habeck, Harrison and Haller, he wouldn't be a burglar."

"A lot of burglars do afford Habeck, Harrison and Haller. There's a system to everything, you see."

"The legal system."

"Burglars, obviously, must be represented."

"They have their rights."

"They are in a hazardous profession. No telling when their presence might be requested in a court of law."

"That's the breaks. And entering."

"So Mr. Haller, this morning, after pretending to listen to the bare bones of our new burglar-client's difficulty, explains to the burglar that many of his colleagues in the burglary business retain Habeck, Harrison and Haller on an annual basis. A kind of occupational in-urance, you see. Just in case their earning a living is threatened by an arrest, conviction, and jail sentence. For example, Mr. Haller explains, if our burglar this morning had already paid such a retainer to Habeck, Harrison and Haller, a Habeck, Harrison and Haller lawyer, such as myself, would have been waiting for him at the police station when he was arrested Saturday night, to do the proper and necessary. He wouldn't have even had to set bail for himself."

"How much of a retainer?"

"Ten thousand dollars. Not much, really, when you consider that a burglar in prison is no good to anyone. Not to his family, not to his friends, not to the economy, and not to Habeck, Harrison and Haller. In jail, he can't make a living."

"Alston, if this guy had ten thousand dollars Saturday, who would he go burglarizing Saturday night?"

"That's not the idea. He wouldn't have ten thousand dollars. The law firm would have ten thousand dollars. So the man can go earn his living without fret. Peace of mind, Fletcher, is worth almost any price."

"I've heard."

"So our burglar-client is told this morning by Mr. Haller that if he comes up with ten thousand dollars within ten days — that is, before his next court appearance — he may look forward to the full services, support, and talents of Habeck, Harrison and Haller. If not, Mr. Haller can recommend to the burglar a smaller, cheaper, less prestigious firm which can be counted on to represent the burglar to the best of their limited resources."

"How the hell is a two-bit burglar supposed to come up with ten thousand dollars within ten days?"

"Guess."

"You're kidding."

"I'm not kidding."

"You mean, a senior partner, in a major law firm, is sending a burglar out to burgle?"

"Really, we only want professionals among our clientele."

"Isn't Mr. Haller technically a member of the court?"

"He's a half-decent golfer, and a doting grandparent."

"Did the burglar accept this deal?"

"Of course. Where would his family be if he went to jail? Lock your doors tonight."

"In other words, the burglar is now burglarizing on behalf of Habeck, Harrison and Haller."

"If he's going to be in this profession, obviously his professional fees and expenses have to be guaranteed."

"Supposing he gets arrested again?"

"All the more work, and all the more fees, for Habeck, Harrison and Haller."

"Alston, you're making me sick."

"I'm sure it's not the sandwich you just ate affecting you. What could be more soothing to the stomach than peanut butter, banana, and mayonnaise? I must try it someday."

"Frankly, I'm shocked. In the first place, that your man, Haller, who must have just heard that his partner had been shot dead in a parking lot, would sit down and have a serious discussion with any client, burglar or not."

"It only took fifteen minutes. After the client is hooked by the senior partner, he is spun off to one of the lesser lawyers in the firm. The rent must be paid. The Mercedes must be maintained."

"Alston, do you want a Mercedes?"

"My ambition for one is dimming."

NINE

The waiter stood over them. "Would you gentlemen like some coffee, tea, or would you prefer sludge?"

"What kind of sludge do you have?" Fletch asked.

"Chocolate, vanilla."

"No strawberry?" Alston said. "I wanted strawberry sludge."

"No strawberry," sighed the waiter.

"Guess I'll have coffee," said Fletch.

"I'll have another beer," said Alston. "Put a cherry in it this time, will you?"

"One coffee," said the waiter. "One beer with a cherry."

"Alston," Fletch said, "I'd like to know anything you can find out about Donald Habeck. Anything you can tell me."

"Only actually shook hands with him the day I was hired. A short, pudgy man —"

"I know," Fletch said, adjusting his belt.

"Considered one of the most brilliant criminal trial lawyers in the country."

"That's the point. It can't be too surprising a man with such a wide acquaintance among criminals ends up shot in a parking lot."

"It is surprising," Alston countered. "He's the one person you'd think would be safe from that sort of thing. I should think all the villains around here would consider themselves indebted to him."

"One coffee," said the waiter. "One beer with a cherry in it."

Fletch looked at Alston's beer. "He actually put a cherry in it."

"I wanted a cherry in it."

"Are you going to eat it?"

"You're eyeing my cherry."

"Sorry."

"I mean, just suppose this were a contract murder. A contract were put out to murder Habeck. Who'd accept it? Habeck's defended most of the murderers worthy of the name."

"Hey, a job's a job."

"From what I hear, professional hit men do not like to murder anyone they know, even people toward whom they have nothing but good feelings. Always afraid a connection might be made."

"Someone who isn't grateful to Habeck. Someone Habeck failed, defended improperly, lost the case. For example, I'd look for an ex-client of Habeck who got out of prison lately. Spent time nursing the grudge."

"I doubt there is anyone like that."

"There must be. Habeck can't be successful every time he goes to court."

"Successful in one way or another. Mr. Harrison, the other senior partner, once said to me, 'You can commit mass murder in front of witnesses, including police witnesses, and we can guarantee you'll never go to prison for it. The police or district attorney can always be counted on to make some technical mistake, in the arresting process, indictment, in the gathering and presenting of evidence.' "

"He actually said that?"

"He actually said that."

"That's terrible."

Alston shrugged. "The average policeman in this country has something like six weeks of formal training. The average defense lawyer has more like six years, if you add his internship in a law firm. And district attorneys are hopelessly overworked and understaffed."

"How do people ever succeed in getting to jail?"

"They don't hire Habeck, Harrison and Haller."

"Alston, Habeck could not have won one hundred percent of the cases he brought to trial."

"Pretty near, I'll bet. He gets to choose his own cases. Thanks to plea bargaining, I'll bet even those of his clients who are or have been in jail have been happy to go. On reduced charges, you know?" Alston quaffed his beer. "But, I'll look."

"Was Habeck a rich man?"

"Pretty rich. He knew where his next Bang and Olufsen was coming from."

"Rich enough to give away five million dollars?"

"Is anybody that rich?"

"That's how I heard of him, this morning. He was coming in to see the publisher, John Winters. Habeck wanted to announce that he and his wife were giving five million dollars to the museum but he wanted it announced discreetly, whatever that means, so their privacy wouldn't be invaded."

"He's never been the most flamboyant lawyer, this coast, but he's never shunned publicity before."

"I suspect he's never given away five million dollars before."

"That's an awful lot of money." Alston munched on his beer-soaked cherry.

"What does it mean when someone gives away five million dollars?"

"It means he ought to get lunch. At the minimum."

"No, seriously."

"It means he's a philanthropist. Kindly. Generous. Has the well-being of the world in his heart."

"Is that how you'd describe Donald Habeck?"

"No. As I say, I only met the man once. But that's not now I'd describe him."

"He was a partner in a law firm which keeps murderers out of jail and sends burglars out to burgle."

"In this country, Fletch, everyone has the right to the best defense."

"Come on, Alston. Not all law firms operate the way you describe Habeck, Harrison and Haller."

"Not all. Many do."

"Is it possible for Habeck to have earned so much money simply by being a lawyer?"

"Oh, yes. Over a lifetime. That and more."

"Much more?"

"I'm not sure."

"Why was he giving away five million dollars?"

"Didn't have anything else to do with it, I suppose. A man in his sixties . . ."

Fletch wrinkled his nose in the sunlight. "He had children, I think. Grown, of course. Grandchildren. The impostor I interviewed this morning, the weird lady who said she was Mrs. Habeck and wasn't, mentioned children and grandchildren. The gardener at the Habeck house said the real Mrs. Habeck is young. I don't get it."

"Expiate guilt. Maybe Habeck was trying to rid himself of his own guilt."

"He sounds like a man who spent his life rationalizing away guilt. Professionally. His own and others'."

"Yeah, but he was getting older."

"With a young wife. I don't get it. His home just doesn't look like the home of someone who can give away five million dollars. I mean, if you've got one hundred million dollars, giving away five can be a casual experience. It needn't interrupt the flow of one's life, the rhythm of one's coming and going. But giving away five million when maybe you have six million, a young wife, probably grandchildren . . ."

"Which of you gentlemen would like the bill?" the waiter asked.

"He would," Alston said solemnly.

"No," Fletch said. "Give it to him."

"You invited me to lunch," Alston said.

"You asked me to."

"Shall I pay it?" asked the waiter. "I had the pleasure of serving you."

"He's got a point," Fletch said.

"It would be the ultimate service," agreed Alston. "I mean, it would indicate this waiter did everything possible for us."

"It is the one possibility you haven't considered," concurred the waiter.

"But what about the tip?" Fletch asked. "That presents a moral dilemma. Also practical confusion."

The waiter looked around the outdoor café. "Oh, to work in a grown-up restaurant," he sighed. "One with walls."

"I'll pay the bill," Alston said to Fletch, "if you answer me a question."

"Anything." Fletch watched Alston pay the bill.

"Gee," Alston said after the waiter went away. "Over lunch we talked about philanthropy, murder, and the law, and we didn't get any respect even from the waiter."

"No one respects the young," mourned Fletch. "Not managing editors, crime writers, society editors, liquor-store-counter help —"

"Fiancées."

"Fiancées."

"Waiters."

"Now that you've paid the bill," Fletch said, "I've got a question for you."

"Then why didn't you pay the bill?"

"Will you be my best man?"

"You mean, better man? How many of us do you expect there to be?"

"Saturday morning. Whenever you wake up."

"Did you get that suit for your wedding?"

"Don't you like this suit?"

"Gray doesn't suit you."

"Barbara said something about our getting married naked."

"Stark naked?"

Fletch nodded. "She said it would be honest of us. Fitting. She says a marriage is the coming together of two bodies, male and female . . ."

"You sure you want to marry Barbara?"

"No."

"Wearing anything, or wearing nothing, would be better than wearing that dumb-looking suit."

"So, will you be my best man?"

"My question is: Where did you get that suit? I want to never go there."

"I thought you'd recognize it."

"Why should I recognize it?"

"I thought you might have seen it before."

"Fire hydrants don't usually wear suits."

"Walking along the corridors of Habeck, Harrison and Haller."

Alston's eyes widened. "Habeck? That's Habeck's suit?"

"Now you'll have respect for this suit. Habeck wasn't screwing jurisprudence to get his suits from Goodwill."

"You stole a dead man's suit?"

"I guess you could say that. If you insist."

"I don't know, Fletch. I worry about you."

"So, will you be my best man?"

"Fletch, ol' buddy: you shouldn't go anywhere without a lawyer. Especially to your own wedding."

TEN

"Frank?" Fletch said.

At the urinal, the managing editor jumped. He did not turn around. "Who wants me?"

"That's a different question."

"Different from what?"

In the men's room, empty except for them, Fletch stepped to his own urinal three away from Frank Jaffe's. "Matters in hand," Fletch said.

"Oh, it's you. Nice suit." Frank flushed. "Didn't know the tide came in already this morning."

"Have I invited you to my wedding yet?" Fletch asked.

"God, no."

"It's Saturday, you know."

"Which day is Saturday?" Frank was washing his hands.

"End of the week. Day between Friday and Sunday."

"Yeah: that's the day I try to get away from employees."

Fletch followed Frank to the washbasin. "I'm pleading a case, Mr. Jaffe."

"A case of what? Have you confessed yet to what's-her-name you have a case of something-or-other?"

"That's my point, Frank. Don't want a case. Don't want a dose. Don't want to go near that place."

"What place is that?"

"Frank." Fletch shook his wet hands over the basin and then held them in front of him. "I'm getting married Saturday. And you've got me investigating a whorehouse!"

"Every nook and cranny." Frank dried his hands on a paper towel.

"Is this some kind of an office joke?"

"Not yet," Frank said. "But I'm sure it will be."

"Dump on the kid, is that it?"

"Fletch, you need experience. Don't you?"

"Not that kind, I don't. Not to get married, I don't."

"Come on. You asked for a job, a real job, so I gave you one."

"A whorehouse the week before I'm married?"

"Gives you a chance to show your stuff. Let us see what you can do."

"Very funny."

"We want you to give it your all, kid. Get to the bottom of things. Really get into the crux of the matter. What we want is a penetrating report. We want everybody to get your point."

"You forgot something."

"What did I forget?" Frank looked at his fly.

"My expense account."

"We expect there to be expenses."

"Yeah, but I'm going to write my expense account with accuracy painful to you."

"That will be a novelty."

"In detail. I'm going to write down exactly what money I'm spending on the Ben Franklyn Friend Service, and for what services."

"Expense accounts are never questioned, if the story's worth the expense."

"Frank, I'm gonna file a pornographic expense account."

Frank opened the door to the corridor. "Maybe we'll print that, too."

"What will the publisher say about that?"

Leaving the men's room, Frank said, "Give it your best shot, kid."

ELEVEN

"As I live and breathe," said the Beauty in the Broadbrimmed Hat. "You must be Fletcher."

Standing in the door of her small office, Fletch frowned. "What makes you say that?"

"Your suit, darling. Your suit." Sitting corsetless at her console, Amelia Shurcliffe, society columnist for the *News-Tribune*, perpetually wore the facial expression of someone who had just been invited to a party. Perpetually she had just been invited to a party. Everyone wanted dear Amelia at his or her party. For some, giving parties makes life worthwhile. For everybody, a sentence or two in Amelia's column made giving parties worthwhile. What Amelia did not know about people on the party circuit was not worth knowing. "I've heard so much about you, and your exciting style of dress."

Fletch looked down at Donald Habeck's suit. "Exciting?"

"You don't mean to tell me you don't know what you're doing! At fashion, you're just an unconscious genius!"

"I'm unconscious, all right."

"Look how you're dressed, Fletcher darling." Although Amelia was staring at Fletch, head to toe and back again, she nevertheless kept glancing at her telephone. "That gray businessman's suit is miles too small for you. Surely you know that?"

"One or two have mentioned it."

"Your trousers are up to your shins, your sleeves nearly up to your elbows, and you have yards of extra material around your waist."

"Pretty cool, uh?"

"I'll say. The point of fashion, my dear, if you'll listen to old Amelia, not that you need to, clearly, is to wear clothes which make other people want to get them off you."

"Have I succeeded at that?"

"Brilliantly. You look lost and uncomfortable in that suit."

"I am."

"Anyone, seeing you, would want to tear those clothes off you."

"Would they turn down the air-conditioning first?"

"And you encourage that impulse, you see. The jacket and shirt are much too narrow across your chest and shoulders. Your shirt buttons are straining. Why, you're just ready to burst out of those clothes."

"I'm a fashion plate, am I?"

"So original. What do you call that style?"

Fletch shrugged. "Borrowed."

" 'Borrowed,' " Amelia said with great satisfaction. She typed a few words on her console. "I'll use that."

"Have you heard about jodhpurs?"

"What about jodhpurs?"

"They're going to be all the rage in a month. Cecilia's Boutique is fully stocked with them."

"Jodhpurs, darling, were all the rage months ago."

"Oops."

Amelia glanced at her telephone. "Now, darling, other than your presenting me with a vision of brilliant, new, young fashions, to what do I owe the honor of this visit?"

"Habeck, Donald Edwin. Haven't done any homework on him yet, but I was hoping you'd point me in the right direction."

Amelia's eyelids lowered. "You mean that sleazy criminal lawyer who was shot in our parking lot this morning?"

"The same."

"Not Society, darling. A creature like Donald Edwin Habeck could be shot just anywhere. And was."

"But supposedly he was giving five million dollars to the art museum."

Slowly, Amelia Shurcliffe said, "I should think Biff Wilson would have the exclusive on that story for this newspaper."

"Oh, right," said Fletch. "I'm just tracing down the social aspects of it."

"The social aspects of murder? Are there any other?"

"You know, the five million dollars."

"Did he actually give the five million dollars to the museum?"

"I believe he was just about to announce it."

"Well," Amelia sighed. "People do give money to charities."

"You say Habeck was not socially prominent?"

"People like Habeck exist in a very peculiar way," Amelia said. "One knows of them, of course, but, at best at the other end of a telephone. You know, if one shoots one's husband in the middle of the night, having once mistaken him as one's lover and now wanting to have mistaken him as a burglar, one must have someone to call, mustn't one?"

"I guess."

"One must know people of that sort well enough to be able to call them, but have them to dinner as a regular thing? No. Their presence might give one's husbands ideas."

"I guess you're serious about all this."

"The Habecks of this world are not to be trusted. After all, when we hire someone like Habeck we're hiring someone to lie for us. Isn't that what we're doing? That's what people like Habeck do for a living. They're professional liars. We don't mind hiring them to lie for us. But do we want them to lie to us, at our own dinner tables? Of far more importance, do we want them lying to other people about what happened and what was said at our dinner tables?"

"Generally, aren't lawyers trained to follow rules of evidence?"

Amelia Shurcliffe stared at Fletch a long moment. "Lawyers, my dear, are trained to follow rules of gullibility."

"Okay. How rich was Habeck? Was he rich enough to give away five million dollars?"

"I have no idea. Probably. He's always in the news over some sensational case or other. Although how criminal lawyers get criminals to pay their law bills has always been a puzzle to me. There must be some trick to it."

"I think there is."

"His partner, Harrison, does all the divorces worth doing. These chaps aren't in the law business to serve justice or just make a living, you know."

"What about Mrs. Habeck? I'm a bit puzzled —"

"Have no idea. Don't even know if there is a Mrs. Habeck. I'll have to read Biff Wilson in the morning. As I said, the Habecks of this world do not shine socially."

"Amelia, I was in Habeck's house this morning, very briefly, I admit, but I didn't notice any paintings or other art works that caused me to pause."

"Do you know about paintings?"

"A little bit."

"Of course you do. Foolish of me to ask. Look at the clever way you've dressed yourself."

"Why would a person, especially, as you say, not socially prominent, and who does not have an immediately obvious interest in art, be giving five million dollars to an art museum?"

"I find the generous impulse generally inexplicable."

"What was he buying?"

"Respectability? That's as good an answer as any I can give, in this case. Here's this man, Habeck, whom society has been using like a tissue, employed only when one has sneezed, or, to mix metaphors, like a high-priced prostitute, picked up, used, and dropped off, without ever an invitation to visit hearth and home. He's getting older. Or, he was, when his aging was concluded this morning. Wouldn't such a person, at the age of sixty, have the instinct to do something that says, 'Eh! I'm as good as you are! I can give away five million bucks, too!' "

"Would society then accept him?"

"No. Especially if society knows there isn't another five million bucks to be gotten from him. But it might make him feel better."

"That's very interesting."

"I'm always very interesting. That's my job, you see." Amelia glanced at her phone again. Clearly, Amelia's phone not ringing made her nervous.

"So." Fletch took a step backward toward the door. "Ann McGarrahan and Biff Wilson were married once."

"I forgot that," Amelia answered. "Yes. Years ago. One of the greater mismatches in my experience. They were married for about three weeks perhaps as many as twenty years ago. Why do you ask?"

"What happened?"

"Who ever knows what happens in someone else's marriage, let alone one's own? My opinion would be, if I were rudely asked, that Ann is a strong, intelligent, good, and decent woman who found herself married to a violent, nasty scumbag."

"Phew! I'm glad I didn't ask."

"But you did. You and I are in a rude business, Mr. Fletcher."

"Did Ann ever marry again?"

"To someone who died. She's not now married. If you're interested in Ann McGarrahan, who's old enough to be your mother, dare I cherish hope for me?"

"And Biff Wilson?"

"I shudder to think. Somewhere in Biff's background there lurks a succubus he calls wife. Named Aurora, or some such dim thing. Now, unless you have more social notes regarding sleazy lawyers, or fashion notes regarding jodhpurs —"

"I do, in fact."

"Out with it."

"I'm getting married Saturday."

"To whom?"

"Barbara Ralton."

"I never heard of her."

"She sells jodhpurs. At Cecilia's."

"I should have figured that. Now, darling, the Stanwyks are giving their annual bash for Symphony next week, and I'm absolutely desperate to find out which colors Joan's using for her table settings. You wouldn't happen to know, would you?"

"Me? I don't even know what Stanwyks are."

TWELVE

"Hey, what are you doing at my desk?"

"All right if I use your computer terminal?"

"You're probably screwing it up." Clifton Wolf, religion editor, looked over Fletch's shoulder at the screen. " 'Ha-beck,' " he read. "You doing research for Biff Wilson now?"

"We all work for the same newspaper."

"Like hell we do. I work for my inch of space, you work for your inch. Biff Wilson works for his foot and a half. If you're not on the story, buddy, you'd better get off it."

Fletch turned off the terminal. "Just curious."

"Curious will turn you into dog food. Also, get off my chair."

"I don't have a terminal of my own." Fletch stood up, picking up a sheaf of notes he had made.

"We always wondered why you were hired. Now we know: to cover whorehouses. I don't want anyone who spends his time in whorehouses sitting in my chair."

"Haven't gone to the whorehouse yet. Haven't got my mother's permission."

"No tellin' what you might be givin' out. Al!" Clifton Wolf yelled across the room to the city editor. "Call the disinfectant guys! Fletcher's been using my stuff!"

"I bet you'd like this assignment," Fletch said. "Only place they send you is church."

"Scat!"

"Do you know of a poet named Tom Farliegh?" Fletch asked.

Fletch suspected that, without much deliberation, people who wrote for the various sections of the newspaper dressed like the people about whom they wrote. People in the business section wore business suits; in the society section they always seemed dressed for a lawn party; in the sports section, white socks and checkered jackets seemed to be the style.

Mentally they identified with their subjects, too. Business writers thought in terms of power, profit and loss; society writers cherished an incredible web of lines of the acceptable rudeness of old money versus the crudeness of new money, attractiveness versus beauty, style versus ostentation; sportswriters thought in terms of winners and losers, new talent versus has-beens, and the end-of-life standings.

Standing before him in the dark part of the corridor was Morton Rickmers, the book editor. He wore thick glasses, a challis tie, tweed jacket, baggy trousers, and soft, tire-tread shoes. It was clear from his book reviews that he loved people and their stories honestly told, loved words and putting them together in their most magical, concise form, and considered the good book humans' most notable achievement, perhaps our only raison d'être.

Frequently his reviews were more interesting and better written than the books he was reviewing.

"Why, have you met Tom Farliegh?" Morton asked.

"No."

"I might like to meet him," Morton mused. "I'm not sure."

"Just heard of him."

"First," Morton said, "I might enjoy knowing why you're dressed that way."

His notepapers in hand, Fletch held his arms out to his sides. "I've been assigned to investigate an escort service. Is that an answer?"

"I see. Trying to disguise yourself as an out-of-town businessman? You look more like the victim of a raid, obliged to grab someone else's clothes."

"You're nearly right. I lost my clothes this morning, and had to borrow this rig."

Morton smiled. "I'm sure there's a story behind how you lost your clothes."

"Not much of a one."

"It's been years since I've lost my clothes. In fact, have I ever lost my clothes?"

"I don't know. It's easy to do."

"Make an interesting short story. *How I Lost My Clothes*. Something Ring Lardner might have done."

"Tom Farliegh lives locally, does he?"

"Oh, yes. Teaches something at the university. Being a poet in academia, he's probably wrongly assigned. You know, to teach English or something, instead of music, or math, or equestrian skills."

"Is he the son-in-law of Donald Habeck?"

"How interesting. I have no idea. You mean the man who was shot in the parking lot this morning?"

"Yes."

"That would be fascinating."

"Why?"

"You've never read him?"

"Not that I remember."

"Not many have. But, if you'd read him, you'd remember. He writes what we call a Poetry of Violence. His best-known poem is something called *The Knife, The Blood*. His publisher entitled his book of collected poems after that one poem. I think I have a copy of it in my office. Come with me."

In his bright, book-walled office, Morton took a slim volume from a shelf and handed it to Fletch. "Here's *Knife, Blood*. You can borrow it."

On the cover, bare skin was deeply slashed by a knife. Blood poured from the skin, down the knife onto a satin sheet.

"This is a book of poetry?" Fletch asked. "Looks more like an old-fashioned mystery novel."

"It's unusual poetry. Rather thin on sentiment."

"Thank you."

"I do believe in reading about what you're doing," Morton said, almost apologetically. "Widens the base of your perception."

Skimming through the book, Fletch said, "I don't suppose you know anything personally about Donald Habeck."

"In fact, I do." Morton folded his arms across his chest and turned away from Fletch. "My sister's son, years ago, was accused of stealing a car and then running over someone in it. Intoxication, grand theft, vehicular homicide, at the age of eighteen."

"I'm sorry to hear that."

"It was awful. The boy was your average frustrated, sullen teenager who just went wild one night." With his back still toward Fletch, Morton said, "We hired Donald Habeck. I mean, he's the sort you hire when things look really awful."

"At any price."

"Yes. At any price."

"What happened to the kid?"

"Intoxication charge was dismissed. Habeck proved the police had used the blood-alcohol testing equipment incorrectly. The charge of car theft was reduced to using a car without permission of owner. I suspect Habeck bribed the owner to say he knew the boy and there had been a misunderstanding regarding use of the car. And the vehicular homicide was found to be the fault of the car manufacturer. Apparently that model car had been proven to have something amiss with its steering mechanism." Morton sighed. "My nephew was sentenced to three months probation, no time in prison."

"Wonder they didn't give him the keys to the city."

Morton turned slowly on his heel. "We're still ashamed of the whole thing. My sister and I, well, we ended up feeling like criminals, like we committed a crime."

"In hiring Habeck."

"I think, in miscarrying justice." Morton shrugged. "My nephew, with just enough of a misdemeanor on his record to make him an understanding person, is now a teacher in a San Diego high school, married, three kids of his own. But, you know, I can't think of him without feeling guilty."

"Did Habeck leave your sister with any worldly wealth?"

"Not much. She had to sell their new house, their second car, cash in their savings, and accept a little help from me."

"What did you think this morning when you heard Habeck had been killed?"

"I've been thinking about it all day. When you live by the sword . . ." Behind his thick glasses, Morton's eyes were focused as if reading from a page close to his face. "Ironic, somehow. I see his ghost hurrying up from his corpse to defend the person who murdered him . . . for good long-range results, or bad. . . ."

"But always for money."

"Yes. He used his brilliance to twist the legal system for money. Scoff at him. Hate him for it. But, when it came right down to it, we paid that money, gladly, to save Billy from an utterly ruined life, to give him a second chance, which he, at least, took. I'm not sure how many of Habeck's clients take that second chance, how many of them are just free to maim, kill, destroy again."

"Thanks for the book."

"If you do meet Tom Farliegh, tell me if you think he's worth a feature story."

"What time are you going to be done?"

"Never." Fletch was sitting at another borrowed desk in the city room. Having gone through his notes, he had just picked out items from the voluminous Habeck file he wanted copied.

"What's it today?" Barbara asked over the telephone. "Wedding announcements? Deaths? Or writing headlines for other people's stories?"

"Hey, I'm working hard for you, kid. I'm trying to plant an item in Amelia Shurcliffe's column about jodhpurs. And the place to buy them is Cecilia's Boutique."

"Anything would help. I'm so sick of wearing them."

"You have to wear them in the store?"

"Yeah. A plum pair, would you believe it? Customers are supposed to come in, see me in my jodhpurs, say, 'Oh, darling, they're divine,' and buy themselves, or their daughters, a pair."

"But do they?"

"No. They look me up and down obviously wondering if I'm sufficiently trendy even to wait on them. I'll meet you at the beach house, right?"

"It's an awfully long drive."

"I only have the house another few days. Until the wedding."

"When you gave up your place, why didn't you move into my apartment? It would have been much simpler."

"What's wrong with having a beach house for the week before we get married?"

"Why don't you spend tonight at my apartment? That way I won't have to drive all the way out and back."

"Hey. I'm getting paid for house-sitting. I know it's not much, but we need the money, right?"

"Right. It's just that I'd sort of like to stay in town and keep checking on a few things."

"I hear someone got bumped off in your parking lot this morning."

"True."

"A lawyer of some kind."

"Some kind."

"One of the ones you see in the newspaper all the time. A Perry Mason type. Murder trials, and big drug deals."

"Habeck. Donald Edwin Habeck."

"That's right. Interesting story. I mean, it should be interesting. I look forward to reading Biff Wilson about it."

Fletch said nothing.

"Fletch, you're not doing anything on that Habeck story, are you?"

"Well, there was a coincidence. I was just about to meet him when —"

"You'll get fired."

"Some confidence you've got."

"You haven't written enough wedding announcements yet, to take on a big story like that."

"I haven't taken it on. I just intend to sit and watch it."

"You've never *just sat* in your life."

"Well, maybe not *just sit.*"

"Does anyone know you're sticking your nose into this story?"

"Barbara —"

"We're getting married Saturday, Fletch. First, you don't have time for any such story. Second, it really would be nice, when we come back from our skiing honeymoon, if you had a job. I'm pretty sure Cecilia won't have offloaded all her jodhpurs by then."

"Relax. If I turn up something interesting, something useful, you think the newspaper would turn the information down?"

"Fletch, have nothing more to do with this story. Get away from it. Jealousies on a newspaper can't be any different from anywhere else."

"Anyway, I've been assigned to a different story altogether."
"What is it?"
"I'd rather not tell you, just now."
"Why not?"
"Well, it's not too far removed from wedding announcements, births, deaths. A travel story. You might say it's a travel story. It might even turn into a medical story."
"You're not making much sense."
"That's because I haven't really got ahold of the story yet. I'm writing it for the society pages."
"Fletch, I don't think there have been any society pages in this country for half a century."
"You know what I mean: the life pages, living, style. You know, the anxiety pages."
"You should be all right doing a piece for the anxiety pages."
"Sure. Anxieties, we all have 'em. You see, I was using my new influence to feed Cecilia's jodhpurs into Amelia Shurcliffe's column."
"Nice of you. When will you get to the beach house?"
"Soon as I can."
"What does that mean?"
"It means I have to run off some copies from a file. And then make one phone call."
"Only one?"
"Only one."
"And it has nothing to do with Habeck?"
"No, no," said Fletch. "Nothing to do with Habeck. Has to do with this other story. The one for the anxiety pages."

Fletch hesitated, just slightly, before pushing the button which would make selected copies from Habeck's file.
Sitting at his borrowed desk, he hesitated again, just slightly, before picking up the phone and dialing an in-house number.
"Carradine," the voice answered.
"Jack? This is Fletch."
"Who?"
"Fletcher. I work for the *News-Tribune*."
"Are you sure?" The financial writer's tone was mildly curious. "Oh, yeah. You're the guy who committed that headline a couple of months ago, what was it? Oh, yeah: WESTERN CAN CO. SITS ON ITS ASSETS."
"Yeah, I'm the one."
"That one, eh? Guess we're all young, once."
"Don't know why everybody objected to that."

"Because we'd all heard it before. Did you call for forgiveness, Fletcher, or do you have a hot tip for me on the international debt?"

"You know that guy who was murdered this morning?"

"Habeck? No. I didn't know him. Saw him once at a lunch for the Lakers."

"A couple of guys here are saying he was very rich."

"How rich is very rich?"

"That he was about to give away five million bucks."

"I doubt it. He was a worker. A high-priced worker, but a worker. I doubt he had more than he'd earned. What were his assets? A partnership in an admittedly prosperous law firm. What's that worth, year by year? Also, whatever he had been able to accumulate over a lifetime of work. Maybe he invested in something and struck it rich, but, if he had, I expect I would have heard of it. He was too much of a street person ever to have inherited anything much. And, again, if he had married great wealth, we would have known about it."

"What about the mob?"

"You think he was associated with the mob?"

"A criminal lawyer —"

"Sure, he probably had mob clients. But the mob doesn't make anybody rich but the mob. Despite what you read, the mob's biggest problem is financial constipation. The riskiest thing they do, at least regarding their own safety, is dispersing money. In fact, it's such a problem for them I don't know why they bother making so much."

"What's your guess as to how much money Habeck had when he died this morning?"

"Just a guess?"

"Take your time."

"Working hard all his life, paying his taxes reasonably well, giving little away, not making any big, stupid investments, not running through too many wives, which are a lot of big *ifs*, I'd say he'd be pretty lucky to have five million dollars of his own."

"So," Fletch said. "Sam wins the office pool."

"Who's Sam?"

"Oh," Fletch said. "He drives one of the *News-Tribune* delivery trucks. The downtown run."

Fletch gathered the selected copies from the Habeck file. On top of the stack he put the volume Morton Rickmers had loaned him, *The Knife, The Blood*.

Then he hesitated a long moment before picking up the phone and dialing the number he had once thought belonged to a pizza-delivery establishment.

The voice that answered was young, female, strong, clear, healthy, and friendly. "Ben Franklyn Friend Service. You want a friend?"

Putting thoughts of anchovies and pepperoni out of mind, Fletch said, "I just might."

"Well, we're an escort service. Available twenty-four hours a day. Your place or ours. But first, will you tell me who recommended you to Ben Franklyn?"

Fletch swallowed. "My father."

The girl hesitated. "You have any problems, son?"

"Not that I know of."

"Nice guy, your dad."

"Yeah, he's a good old guy."

"Doesn't want you to be alone in the big city, huh?"

"He doesn't — uh — want me making friends — uh — I can't get rid of. Uh."

Suddenly, he had become very warm in the city room.

"I see. What's your dad's name?"

"Oh, I doubt he ever used your services himself. I mean, personally."

"You'd be surprised. What's his name, anyway?"

"Uh. Jaffe. Archibald Jaffe. Never mind about him. My name is Fletcher Jaffe. I'm the one who's coming. I hope."

"Okay, Fletcher. Why don't you come to the service? We'll check out your health."

"I'm fine, thank you."

"Oh, we're sure you are. By health, we mean just everything. We're friends like you never had before. We take care of all of you. You do exercise, don't you?"

"Oh, yes."

"Well, we want to check out your skin tone, your muscle tone, your diet. Exercise you through to sexual fulfillment. You've never had friends like us before."

"I'm sure."

"We take you all the way, my man, from simple stretches, through deep breathing, to ecstasy."

"Ecstasy! Wow!"

"You don't believe?"

"I've just never heard *ecstasy* used in a sentence before. I don't think. I mean, not conversationally."

"You've never called Ben Franklyn Friend Service before."

"Not for anything without cheese."
"What?"
"Never mind."
"You going to come right over?"
"Not right now. Someone's waiting for me. How about tomorrow?"
"Sure. I guess we can fit you in."
"Ha ha."
"What time?"
"Eleven o'clock."
"In the morning?"
"Right. I want to have my skin toned up."
"Fletcher Jaffe. Eleven o'clock tomorrow morning. We'll see you then. All of you. And you'll see all of us."
The phone clicked.
Fletch hung up.
And then did some deep breathing exercises.

THIRTEEN

"Wow!"

"These bugs are gettin' to me."

"Heck with the bugs. Listen to this."

Sitting on the bench in her swimsuit, Barbara Ralton was scratching her elbow with one hand and her back with the other. "Fletch, the bugs really take over the beach when the sun gets this low."

"Appropriate for what you're about to hear. Listen." His back propped against her beach bag, Fletch read:

Young flesh,
taut skin,
tight over muscle,
smooth over joints,
Revealed
Realized
Explored
Exploited

Felt
Most perfectly
Reviled
Revolted
Explained
Exploded
Sharp
Hard
Shining
Steel
in a blade
draws across the flesh.
Blood bubbles, then
mimics the slit,
becomes a line
of blood;
finding its own way, it
pours down the skin,
thick, red fluid
flowing over the soft
rose pink of skin.

Touch your tongue to the blood.
Bathe your lips in it.
Suck it through your teeth.
Let your eyes see above the slash
the skin draining, turning white,
whiter next the blood, and
watch the palpitations as
skin
reverberates with the ever-quickening
heart rhythm urging
out the blood to air, to
redness, to
flow.

What penetrates more
perfectly the warmth of flesh
than the coolness of steel?
in truth,
were they not just
made for each other?

Barbara, bugs on her, was no longer listening. She said, "That's sick."

"Pretty sharp," Fletch said.

In the red of the setting sun, she shuddered. "Punk."

Fletch ran his fingernail along her calf. "But do you get the point?"

"A little lacking in metaphor," she said.

"But consider the irony."

"Weird!" She moved the book in Fletch's hand to see the cover. "What's that supposed to be?"

"It's a poem by Tom Farliegh called *The Knife, The Blood*."

"That's poetry? Not exactly 'How do I love thee? Let me count the ways . . .' "

"I guess it's called the Poetry of Violence. Tom Farliegh is its inventor, or chief current practitioner, or something."

"Where did you get it, a motorcyclists' convention?"

"Tom Farliegh may or may not be Donald Habeck's son-in-law."

"For a son-in-law I'd rather Attila the Hun."

Fletch rolled onto his stomach. "It is sentimental, of course."

"I prefer Browning."

"At least he gives flesh and a knife their values."

"Oh, yeah. He does that. And why, Irwin, are you carrying around a book of poetry by Habeck's son-in-law the night that Habeck is murdered?"

Even facing away from the sun, Fletch squinted. "Don't you find it fascinating?"

"Fascinating!" she said falsely. "Is the whole book like that?"

"I'll read you another." He reached for it in the sand.

"Not before supper, thank you." She stood up. "Flies and satanic poems. Did you bring anything for supper?"

"Yeah," Fletch answered. "There are some pretzels in the car."

"Great. I could tell you stopped somewhere on your way home. You arrived in nothing but swimming trunks."

"I know how to prepare pretzels."

"Come on. I brought lamb chops. I'll show you how to prepare them."

"I'm going to jump in the ocean." Fletch began to get up slowly. "Wash the sand off."

"You can tell me about your new assignment," Barbara said, beach bag under her arm like a football. "The one that has nothing to do with people getting bullets in the head."

"Yeah, I'll do that," Fletch said absently.

* * *

in truth,
were they not just
made for each other?

FOURTEEN

"So what's your assignment?" At the stove, Barbara wore an apron over her swimsuit.

Fletch munched a pretzel. "Research on Ben Franklyn."

Dark outside, light inside the beach house, the huge plate-glass windows reflected them.

"Somehow Ben Franklin doesn't strike me as news."

Fletch found the brown paper bag in which Barbara had brought the chops, potatoes, peas, and milk. In it, he put Donald Habeck's suit, shirt, tie, drawers, socks, and shoes. "Got some string?"

"Look in that drawer." She pointed with the potato masher. "What's new about Ben Franklin?"

"Healthy sort of man. Very contemporary." Fletch tied the string around the package. "Inventive. Diplomatic. Always liked the ladies. A businessman, too. He was a good businessman, wasn't he?"

"How burned do you like your chops?"

"If you're asking, stop cooking." He tossed the package on the floor near the front door.

Sitting at the table, Barbara said, "I'm calling your mother."

"What did I do now?"

"You're getting married Saturday. Don't you think Jessica ought to hear from me, her daughter-in-law-to-be?"

"Oh, sure."

"Give her the opportunity to come to the wedding, you know? Make her feel really welcome."

"I wrote her. Don't know if she can afford to come. She's a poor writer, you know. I should say, she's a writer and she's poor. And if we pay her way from Seattle, we won't be able to afford a honeymoon."

"Still, her son's getting married."

"Naked?" Fletch asked. "Do you still mean for us to get married naked?"

"No." Barbara scooped mashed potato into her mouth. "I haven't been able to get rid of that eight pounds."

"Ah," smiled Fletch. "So you do have something to hide."

"I'll ask you once more about your father."

"What about him?"

She asked, "What about him?"

"He died in childbirth." Fletch shrugged. "That's what mother always said."

"Modern American marriage." Barbara sighed and looked at their reflection in the window.

"Yeah," Fletch said, "what's it for?"

"What do you mean, 'What's it for?' "

"Alston asked me at lunch if I was sure I want to get married. That was just after I asked him to be my best man."

"Alston works for Habeck's law firm, doesn't he?"

"Yeah."

"Is he happy there?"

"Not very."

"What did you answer?"

"I don't remember."

"Lawyers are always asking difficult questions. That's their job. Makes 'em feel superior, I think. Helps them create the illusion they're worth their fees."

"Frank Jaffe said something or other about the only point in getting married is if you intend to have children."

"He's right. Almost."

"Do we intend to have children?"

"Sure." Barbara's eyes glanced over the rough wooden floor of the beach house. "We have to have money, first. You're not earning much. In fact, you're not in a very high-paid profession. I'm not in a profession at all. Kids cost a lot."

"Someone mentioned that today, too."

"What did you do, go around today developing a brief against marriage?"

"I went around today announcing the joyful news you and I are getting married Saturday, and everybody asked, *Why?*" Barbara stared at Fletch. "In fact, I'd say for the most part, people's reaction was, *Bleh!*"

"That's not very nice of people."

"No, it isn't."

"Just because other people make bum marriages . . ."

"What criterion do we have, but other people's marriages?"

"I think our getting married makes sense."

"So do I."

"We can support each other."

"Right. Today I tried to help you get out of Cecilia's jodhpurs."

"Build toward a family, a way of life."

"As long as I keep accepting one miserable assignment at the newspaper after another."

"Companionship. Grow old together, seeing things from somewhat the same perspective, having the same memories, protecting each other."

"Correct," said Fletch. "You know anybody who's doing it?"

"Doesn't mean we can't."

"No. It doesn't."

"I definitely think we should get married," Barbara said.

"I do, too," Fletch agreed. "Definitely."

"Just think of marriage the way you think of everything else," Barbara said. "Playing through to truth. Only in marriage, you're playing through to a truth of you, and me, and us."

The telephone rang.

Startled, Barbara looked at it. "Who could that be?"

"I asked Alston to call. He may have some things to tell me about Donald Habeck."

"Habeck." Barbara carried her plate to the sink. "You're crazy."

"Yeah." Fletch stood up to answer the phone. "Factor that in, too."

FIFTEEN

"Hate to admit it, ol' buddy," Alston said. "But you just might be right."

"Of course I am." Fletch settled into a Morris chair by the phone. "About what?"

"As best I could, without my fingers getting caught in the files, I've been able to dig up a few things for you: Habeck's latest big case; his current big case; and — this is where you may be right — what old client of his just got out of the pen with, maybe, an irrepressible urge to send a bullet through Habeck's skull."

"There is one?"

"First, his last and current big cases. Doubtlessly you have comprehensive newspaper files on both."

"Yes. I got them this afternoon."

"So you know the current big case concerns the chairman of the State House Ways and Means Committee being charged with a kickback scheme. Bribery."

"Yeah."

"He's charged specifically with having accepted fifty-three thousand, five hundred dollars from an architectural firm contracted to design a new wing on the State Penitentiary at Wilton."

"Hope the state senator had them design a nice cell with a southern view for himself."

"Doubt he'll ever see it, if he did. The maneuvers here are too sophisticated for me to understand. I don't mean legal maneuvers, I mean political maneuvers. Habeck has filed all kinds of motions and petitions I don't understand. He's doing the most amazing fox-trot through the courts with this case. I don't understand why the courts put up with this kind of wriggling."

"Habeck was just trying to let the case get to be old news as far as the public is concerned, wasn't he? After a while the public, and the courts, too, I suppose, lose their anger over a case like this. We become tired of reading about it. Indifferent to what happens. Right?"

"Right. It would help if you journalistic types blew the whistle on this kind of maneuvering once in a while. Reported in depth the history of such a case. Demand that the courts make final disposition of it."

"Yes, sir."

"So you'd be interested in Habeck's personal notations on the records of this case?"

"You bet."

"The first notation says, *Get this before Judge Carroll Swank.*"

"Ah. The idea being that Judge Swank owes something from the deep, dark, shadowy past to Senator Schoenbaum."

"One assumes so. Some indebtedness safely hidden. You boys would never be able to find it."

"Or, Senator Schoenbaum holds something in the blackmail line over the aforesaid Judge Swank."

"Judges may deliberate like self-righteous prigs, but they must live as pragmatists."

"I'll write that down."

"A second note on the file in Habeck's own writing might also interest you. It reads, *Actual kickbacks Schoenbaum admits to over eight hundred thousand dollars. Tax-free, note. Plan fee in five-hundred-thousand-dollar range.* Both these notes are near the beginning of the file. The rest of the file is just a record of Habeck's jerking the courts around."

"Until he gets the case in front of Judge Swank."

"And that's when he really jerks the court around."

"Meanwhile, Senator Schoenbaum is vacationing in Hawaii."

"Yes. Poor jerk thinks he's going to come out of this a rich and free man."

"Well, he's half-right."

"I don't see Schoenbaum as anybody who wants to ventilate Habeck's head."

"No."

"The other cases Habeck is pleading, and there are more than twenty, are all being worked up by underlings, poor beavers like me. Several cases of embezzlement, two vehicular homicides, a half-dozen cases of insurance fraud, as many as ten cases of parental kidnappings — you know, when a member of a divorced couple loses the custody battle and arranges to have his own kid kidnapped?"

"That many?"

"It's a big business. If I ever decide to leave Habeck, Harrison and Haller, I might decide to go into it. I'd feel more useful."

"Gives one pause to think."

"Plus one rather funny case about a milkman."

"I met a witty milkman once."

"This one is real witty. Listen. First, he rented a sable coat for his wife, for a month, on credit."

"Loving husband."

"Then he walked his sable-adorned wife into a Rolls-Royce showroom, and leased a Rolls-Royce for a month, on credit."

"Liked good cars, too."

"With his wife in the sable coat, both of them in the Rolls-Royce, he was able to rent a small mansion in Palm Springs."

"Why shouldn't a milkman live well?"

"With the coat, the Rolls, and the house, he then went to a local bank, and wangled a five-hundred-thousand-dollar cash loan."

"Wow."

"And gave up his job as a milkman."

"Yeah. Why should he need to work with all he's got?"

"He returned the car, and canceled the lease on the house. And skipped to Nebraska."

"You can buy a lot of cows in Nebraska for five hundred thousand dollars."

"Even the bank didn't care, for three years, because the guy kept paying them interest out of the principal he had borrowed."

"Don't tell me. He was charged with Understanding America Too Well."

"Eventually, the well ran dry, of course, and the bank went after the retired milkman."

"Why would Habeck take on a case like that? I don't see how the milkman can pay him much."

"Okay. Habeck took on the milkman's case. As soon as the bank heard that, they began to shake in their collective boots. Habeck, Harrison and Haller bought a few shares in the bank, and then threatened the bank with full exposure. Charged loan-forcing, incompetent administration, and a loan policy so inept that clearly the bank's charter should be revoked. After all, Fletch, they made a half-a-million-dollar loan to a milkman!"

"Oh, boy. So the bank is going to swallow the five-hundred-thousand-dollar loss, or whatever part of it the milkman didn't pay back out of principal?"

"Not only that, two of the partners in the bank, who also happen to be bank officers, are buying back the few shares of stock Habeck, Harrison and Haller own at what you may describe as well above market value."

"Phew. What I'm learning about the law. Tell me, Alston, is that called 'settling out of court'?"

"I think it's called having a bank by the short hairs, and tugging."

"I think it's called blackmail. Of course, I never went to law school."

"At law school, it's called blackmail."

"So far today, I've learned Habeck, Harrison and Haller, as a law firm, is actively in the burglary business, the blackmail business, judge fixing . . . what else do you guys do for a living?"

"Don't ask."

"You sure all law firms aren't this way?"

"Absolutely not."

"What happened to the milkman?"

"He moved to New York State, where he's employed as —"

"A milkman!"

"No. As some kind of a psychotherapist. During his three years in Nebraska, he qualified for some kind of degree, got a professional certification which permits him to earn a living being understanding."

"I'll bet he's good at it."
"I'll bet he is."
"Upward mobility, Alston."
"The American dream"
"Through judicious use of credit."
"The name of the game."
"The creation of another debt-free professional."
"Warms my heart."
"The legal system works, Alston."
"Don't you ever forget it."
"And a bank had to sharpen its loan policy, from which we all benefit."
"Habeck's last case that reached the newspapers was about a year ago."
"The case of the Fallen Doctor."
"Yeah, the doctor who organized a certain number of his patients into drug pushers. The doctor was a wreck himself."
"And Habeck got him off by charging the Narcotics Bureau with entrapment."
"Ultimately, yes. First he went through a lot of dazzling footwork regarding the sanctity of the patient-slash-doctor relationship. To wit, doctors are not to be entrapped by the confidences of patients who turn out to be narcs."
"And, tell me, Alston, how did Habeck, Harrison and Haller get paid for that job?"
"There was a million dollars of cocaine never found by the authorities."
"Good God. Burglary, blackmail, drug pushing . . . why doesn't someone bring charges against Habeck, Harrison and Haller?"
"Who'd dare? In fact, talking to you right now, I feel my pants slipping down around my ankles."
"I appreciate that, Alston."
"Where you may be right is that a Habeck client got out of jail last Tuesday. And he's not a very nice person. He served eleven years the hard way. And I don't understand why Habeck took on the case in the first place."
"No personal notes?"
"All the files, except for a microfilm record of the case, are in the warehouse in Nevada and I can't get to them."
"He must have had a reason."
"A child molester. A real sweetheart. He had two trained German

shepherds. Apparently he'd enter a housing project, first attract little kids with his dogs. Then the trained dogs would herd and hold the little kids in a corner of the building, or the play yard, and this son of a bitch would then make free with them."

"Jesus."

"Say one for me. Takes all types, uh?"

"Jesus!"

"Lots of little kids gave evidence. There were lots of witnesses to the event with which he was finally charged. I guess he had been getting away with it for a long time. He counted on the dogs to help him make his escape. What he didn't count on were a couple of black brothers who weren't intimidated by German shepherds and kicked their heads in."

"And he got only eleven years?"

"Habeck must have done something for him."

"Eleven years!"

"I'm sure they were eleven hard years, Fletch. Child molesters are not popular in prison. They get very few invitations to the cellblock cocktail parties."

"What's his name?"

"Felix Gabais. Employed at various jobs, bus driver, school-bus driver, taxi driver. Lived with a crippled sister in the Saint Ignatius area. Would be about forty-one, forty-two years old now."

"If Habeck got him out of prison in eleven years on that kind of charge, I can't see why he'd go gunning for Habeck."

"He's crazy, Fletch. I mean, a guy who works all that out with trained dogs has to be crazy. Talk about premeditation."

"I guess so."

"In this case, he's had eleven years to premeditate."

"Alston, I have another thought. Supposing someone killed or maimed one of your loved ones. And Habeck got him off scot-free, or something meaningless, a suspended sentence or something. Wouldn't that incline you to go after Habeck?"

"Come again?"

"I heard of a case today in which Habeck was involved. Drunken teenager stole a car and killed someone with it. Habeck got him off with just a sentence of probation. What about the victim's family? Wouldn't they have reason to be pretty mad at Habeck?"

"I can see them wanting to harm the drunken kid."

"But not Habeck?"

"That would take too much thinking. First, in anger, I think people want to see people get the punishment they deserve. When the courts don't give perpetrators the punishment they clearly deserve, yeah, I think even the most decent people feel the temptation to go out and beat the perpetrator over the head themselves."

"But, if they think twice . . ."

"If they think twice, they're angry at something vague, you know, like *the legal system*, or *justice*, or *the courts*."

"You don't think anyone ever focuses on the defense attorney who twists the legal system to get genuine bad guys off free?"

"It's possible. Someone bright, maybe."

"Someone bright who sees a pattern in what Habeck is doing."

"And, maybe, has a personal grudge."

"And knows there is no way of ever bringing Habeck to justice."

"Yeah. Such a person might be able to justify shooting Habeck in the head. But, Fletch, think of the numbers. Over Habeck's thirty-five-year career, the numbers of victims' loved ones and families who have watched Habeck send the perpetrator to the beach instead of to jail must number in the hundreds, the thousands."

"I suppose so." Fletch took *The Knife, The Blood* from the table beside the telephone. "Anyway, I already know who killed Habeck."

"Bright boy." Alston sighed. "Why didn't you tell me that in the first place? Instead of spending all this long time talking to you, I could have gone jogging."

"You can still go jogging," Fletch said, turning the pages.

"I don't want to get mugged by a milkman."

"Listen to this." Fletch read:

Slim, belted hips
Sprayed across by automatic fire,
each bullet
ripping through,
lifting,
throwing back,
kicking
the body at its
center.
Thus
The Warrior In Perfection
bows to his death,
twists,
pivots and falls.

Waisted, he is wasted
but not wasted.
This death is his life
and he is perfect
in it.

"Jeez!" Alston breathed. "What's that?"

"A poem called *The Warrior in Perfection.*"

"You and I know a little better than that, don't we, buddy."

"Do we?"

"That dancing beauty just isn't there."

"It isn't."

"That's the sickest thing I've ever heard. It makes me angry."

"If I'm right, and I'm not sure that I am, it was written by Donald Edwin Habeck's son-in-law."

"Oh. Anybody who'd write that would do anything for kicks."

"I read one to Barbara called *Knife, Blood* and suddenly she decided she had to come off the beach to get dinner."

"I think you're right. You needn't look any further for the murderer of Habeck than the snake who wrote that poem."

"I think he's worth talking to."

"So, the newspaper wants you on this story?"

"No, Alston, they don't."

"Trying to prove yourself, boy?"

"If I come up with something good, do you think the newspaper will turn it down?"

"I have no idea."

"I'm getting married. I've got to get going in life. So far, I'm playing dumb jokes on the newspaper. And the newspaper is playing dumb jokes on me."

"You're taking a risk."

"What risk? If I don't come up with anything, no one will ever know it."

SIXTEEN

Barbara stood wrapped in a towel over Fletch in the Morris chair.

"You want to know why we're getting married?"

"The world keeps asking," Fletch answered.

She dropped the towel on the floor.

She stood before him in the dimly lit beach house like a sculpture just finished.

"This body and your body moving in concert through life, in copulation and out of copulation, coupled, always relating to each other, each movement to each, however near or separated we may be, will measure our minuet in this existence, tonight, tomorrow, and all tomorrows."

Fletch cleared his throat. "I've heard worse poetry. Recently."

"Are you coming to bed?"

"I guess I'd better." Fletch stood up, thinking of the immediate tomorrow. "It's now, or maybe never again."

SEVENTEEN

Barbara entered the bedroom, head down, reading the front page of the newspaper.

"Dammit," Fletch said from the bed. "Next time you house-sit, please check to make sure there are curtains on the bedroom windows first, will you?"

"Biff Wilson made the front page."

"Of course."

"Or Habeck did."

"The sun isn't even up yet."

"You want to hear this?" Folding one leg under her, Barbara sat on the bed.

"Yeah."

" 'Nationally famous criminal attorney, partner in the law firm of Habeck, Harrison and Haller, Donald Edwin Habeck, sixty-one, was found shot to death in his late-model blue Cadillac Seville this morning in the parking lot of the *News-Tribune.*' "

"This bedroom faces west, but still this room is as full of light before dawn as a church at high noon Sundays."

" 'Police describe the murder as, quote, in the style of a gangland slaying, unquote.' "

" 'Gangland'!"

"That's what it says. 'Mr. Habeck's law partners, Charles Harrison and Claude Haller, issued a joint statement before noon this morning.' "

"I'll bet they did. Dropped all other work and put themselves right down to it."

" ' "The legal profession has lost one of its most brilliant minds and deft practitioners with the passing of Donald Habeck. His incisive understanding and innovative use of the law as a defense attorney, especially in criminal cases, made Donald Habeck an example to attorneys nationally, and somewhat of a popular hero. We mourn the passage of our partner and dearest friend, especially under such despicable and inexplicable circumstances. Our heartfelt sympathy goes out to Donald's widow, Jasmine, his son Robert, daughter Nancy in parenthesis Farliegh, and his grandchildren." ' "

" 'Innovative,' " Fletch said. "First time I've heard that word to mean crooked."

"Was he crooked?" Barbara asked.

"There was a moment yesterday when I referred to Habeck as a *criminal lawyer* I was afraid someone would think I was making a joke."

"Some wordsmiths, these guys. 'Despicable and inexplicable circumstances.' "

"Lawyers are the only people in the world who get to say, 'Words don't mean what they mean. They mean what we say they mean.' A deft practitioner of the law. Ha! A perverter of the legal system."

"You seem to have formed a personal opinion, Fletch."

"I hear what I hear."

"Don't let personal opinion get in your way. There are other perfectly good ways you can destroy us over this story."

"You're right."

" 'Habeck's wife, Jasmine, was placed in seclusion by her doctors and therefore was not available for comment.' "

"There must have been a first Mrs. Habeck. Any reference to her?"

"Not that I see. 'Neither Harrison nor Haller would comment on the nature of Habeck's death pending police investigation.' "

"It was no gangland slaying."

" 'According to John Winters, publisher of the *News-Tribune*, Donald Habeck had requested a meeting with Mr. Winters for ten o'clock this morning to seek advice regarding the announcement of a charitable contribution Mr. Habeck intended to make in the city. "I did not personally know Donald," John Winters said. "Naturally, all of us here in the *News-Tribune* family express our regrets to his family and friends." ' "

"Wise old John Winters. Hold the sleazy lawyer at arm's length even in his death. Amelia Shurcliffe said no one would dare declare Donald Habeck either a friend or an enemy. I guess she was right."

" 'Mr. Habeck's body was discovered by *News-Tribune* employee Pilar O'Brien while she was reporting to work. Police Lieutenant Francisco Gomez stated Mr. Habeck had been shot once in the head at apparently close range by a handgun of as yet undetermined caliber. The gun was not discovered at the scene of the crime.' "

"It was not a gangland slaying."

" 'A graduate of the state system of education, and for years a visiting lecturer at the law school, Habeck . . .' Blah, blah, blah. The report goes on to recount his most famous cases." Barbara turned to an inside page. "At great length. Want me to read all that?"

"I went through all that yesterday. Even I know how to write obituaries."

"I think son-in-law Tom Farliegh should be arrested, charged, convicted, and imprisoned immediately." Barbara refolded the newspaper.

"You think Tom Farliegh murdered Habeck?"

"Tom Farliegh wrote that poem you read me last night. Isn't that enough to imprison him? A man who writes a so-called poem like that shouldn't be left loose to walk around in the streets."

"It was not a gangland slaying."

"Am I supposed to ask you why you keep saying that?"

"Are you asking?"

"I suppose so."

"In order to drive into the parking lot of the *News-Tribune* you have to stop and identify yourself and state your purpose to the guard at the gate. But anyone can walk in and out. Habeck's car was parked more toward the back of the lot than the front. I just can't see professional gangsters stopping and saying anything to the guard at the gate, driving in, doing their dirty deed, then driving out again. I also can't see a professional gangster parking his car outside the gate, walking in, popping Habeck in the head, and then walking out. Can you? A professional gangster would have hit Habeck somewhere else."

"Strange no one heard the shot."

"A small-caliber handgun makes a pop so slight, especially in a big, open-air parking lot, you could mistake the sound for a belch after eating Greek salad."

Barbara stretched out beside him on the bed.

"Guess I should start the long drive back to the city," Fletch said.

"You don't have to go yet."

"How do you know? There are many, many things I want to do today. And some I don't."

"Don't forget you're having dinner with Mother and me tonight. To discuss the wedding."

Fletch glanced at his watch. "We really did wake up awfully early. I guess we have time."

"I know." Barbara cupped her hands behind his neck. "That's because I took down all the window curtains in here last night, before you arrived."

EIGHTEEN

"Good morning," Fletch said cheerily to the middle-aged woman in an apron who opened the door to him at 12339 Palmiera Drive, The Heights. Her eyes narrowed as she recognized him as the man who had run through her kitchen the day before wearing nothing but a denim shirt hanging from his waist. He gave her a big smile. "I'm really not all the trouble I'm worth."

"Yes?" she asked.

"I just want to deliver this package." He handed the grocery bag filled with Donald Habeck's clothes through the doorway to her. "I'd also like to see Mrs. Habeck, if possible."

The woman kept the door braced with her feet when she took the package with both hands. The string had loosened. "In seclusion," she said. "Under sedation."

One of Donald Habeck's black shoes dropped out of the bag.

"Oh, my," Fletch said. He picked up the shoe and put it on top of the bundle in her arms.

The woman drew her head back from the shoe.

"One other question," Fletch went on. "There was an older woman here yesterday, sitting by the pool. Bluish hair, red purse, green sneakers. Do you know who she was?"

The woman looked at Fletch through narrow slits over Donald Habeck's shoe.

"She said she was Mrs. Habeck. She acted strangely."

"I do not speak English," the woman said. "Not a single goddamned word."

"I see."

She closed the door.

"I'll be back to see Mrs. Habeck when she's feeling better!" Fletch shouted through the door.

Getting into his car in the driveway, Fletch looked up at the house.

A window curtain in the second story fell back into place.

NINETEEN

"Thank you for seeing me," Fletch said slowly, "so promptly."

He was surprised the curator of contemporary art at the museum was seeing him at all, let alone at nine-thirty in the morning without an appointment. He expected museum curators to keep relaxed hours. He also expected any museum curator to be standoffish with someone presenting himself in blue jeans and T-shirt, however fresh and clean, sneakers however new and glistening white, who said he was from a newspaper.

He also did not expect any museum curator, however contemporary, to be sitting behind a desk in a Detroit Tigers baseball cap. On the desk, beside one huge book with MARGILETH written in script on the glossy cover and a few folders, was an outfielder's mitt and a baseball.

"You're from the *News-Tribune,*" curator William Kennedy confirmed.

"Yes. I was assigned to report on the five-million-dollar gift to the museum that was to be announced by Donald and Jasmine Habeck." Fletch smiled slightly at his accurate use of the past tense. "A lady in your Trustees' Office said she thought the gift was to be made to this department."

"I'm glad to talk to someone, anyone, about it," Kennedy said.

Fletch asked, "Are you from Detroit?"

"No." Kennedy took off his baseball cap and looked at its logo. "I just admire excellence, in any form."

"I see."

"I also collect video-cassettes of Nureyev, Muhammad Ali, and Michael Jackson. Recordings of Caruso, McCormack, Erroll Garner, and Eric Clapton. Do you think I'm odd?"

"Eclectic."

"I'm a perfectly happy man." Kennedy reached for his baseball mitt. "I don't know why everyone isn't like me."

"Neither do I," Fletch said.

"Do you collect things?"

"Yes." Fletch said. "People."

"What an interesting thought."

"I don't use people, just collect them. It gives me some interesting memories on the long drive."

"Is that why you're a journalist?"

"I suppose so. That, and a few other reasons."

"You have less of a storage problem than I have."

"First, I need to confirm with you that Mr. and Mrs. Donald Habeck were giving this department of the museum five million dollars."

"I'm not sure." Kennedy tossed the ball up into the air and caught it in his mitt. "And if they were going to actually make such an offer, in writing, I'm not sure we would accept it."

Fletch raised his eyebrows. "Wouldn't a museum accept money from any source?"

"The source doesn't bother us. In my fifteen-year museum career to date, I've never seen money turned down because of its source, even if it were tainted money. Remember that old wheeze about Mark Twain? A minister came to him saying that a gangster had offered him money to fix the church's roof. Twain asked, 'Why are you hesitating?' The minister said, 'Because it's tainted money.' 'That's right,' Twain said. 'T'ain't yours, and t'ain't mine.' "

"You collect good stories, too?"

"As they come along."

"I think I'm hearing you saying that you considered Habeck's money tainted."

Kennedy shrugged. "We know he was a tricky lawyer."

"By 'tricky' do you mean crooked? I think I'm collecting polite ways of saying crooked."

"How often do you hear of lawyers going to jail?"

"Not often."

"Doctors get sick, but lawyers seldom go to jail."

"Why would a museum turn down money?"

"Because of the stipulations that come with the money. Let me explain." Kennedy put his mitted hand on top of the baseball cap on his head. His other hand spun the baseball on the desk. "Late last week, Donald Habeck made an appointment to see me. I was dismayed when my secretary told me she had made the appointment. We had never pursued Donald Habeck. I have never heard that he cared anything about art, or the museum. Therefore, I suspected he wanted to talk me into being an expert witness for a case of his — something of that sort."

"And you wouldn't have agreed?"

"I don't think so. I have been an expert witness in court, of course. But only when I have felt I was on solid ground, could trust whichever side of a case requested me. I don't make a career of it. Only when I feel need for me is justified."

"And you didn't feel you could trust Donald Habeck?"

"I didn't know anything about him, other than an impression of him that has come through the newspapers and television press. Vaguely, my impression was that, through a lot of tricks, he kept people who ought to be in jail out of it. I had never met the man."

Fletch noted how quick people were to say they had never met, or had scarcely met, Donald Habeck.

"So Habeck was given an appointment, but not invited to lunch," Kennedy continued. "He came in last Wednesday afternoon, sat in the chair you're sitting in, and surprised the hell out of me by saying he was thinking of giving the museum five million dollars."

"What was your first question?"

Kennedy thought a moment. "My first question was, 'Of your own money?' Immediately, I was suspicious, of I don't know what."

"And he confirmed it was his own money he wanted to give away?"

"Yes. I then said, as politely as I could, that I had never heard he was interested either in art or the museum. He answered that he was very interested in art and, furthermore, that he had identified what he referred to as 'a vast hole' in our present contemporary collection."

"That got your attention."

"It certainly did. I could hardly wait to hear what 'hole' he felt was in our collection. Ours is not the strongest collection of contemporary art in the whole world, but it is very strong and really quite well balanced, thanks to my predecessor and myself." Kennedy was again playing catch with himself. "He said he wanted the five million dollars spent exclusively on acquiring contemporary religious art."

After a moment, Fletch said, "That's a puzzle."

"Isn't it?" Looking at Fletch apologetically, Kennedy said, "As you know, or don't know, there is almost no contemporary religious art. I mean, all art is religious, isn't it? In its own way, even the profane. Art depicts man in his relation to nature, himself, his fellow persons, and his deity. Not all of it may be worshipful, but each piece of true art, to me, is a powerful acknowledgment of the nature of our existence."

"How did you answer him?"

"Politely, I asked him whom he thought we should be collecting. In true legalistic fashion, he answered that we are supposed to be the experts in that, and that if we felt we couldn't find viable contemporary religious art to acquire, he'd take his money elsewhere."

"A tough guy even in his giving."

"Wait. You haven't heard everything. Gently, I tried to explain to Mr. Habeck that if there were much viable contemporary religious art, I'd be the first to seek it out and acquire it. Of course, prayer-card art, like the poor, is ever with us. Some churches have developed very contemporary-looking designs for their crosses, and stations thereof. But unless you consider a Jesus with female breasts on a cross a viable statement, there isn't much new in the field. As critics and curators, we find ourselves nowadays, perhaps mistakenly, considering the various religious genres, from Creation to Joan-at-the-stake, closed history." Kennedy tossed the ball high and caught it. "Then I realized I was lecturing the poor man, and that was not why he came here. I could see he was getting angry. I was on the wrong track altogether. So, more personally, I asked him why he wanted to contribute so much money."

"A question we all have."

"I expect the answer will astound you. After a few moments of writhing in that chair, I'm sure looking as uncomfortable as any witness under his own cross-examination, Habeck blurted out that his life was over, that he was packing it in; no one cared a tin whistle for him; he was dispossessing himself of all of his property, and" — Kennedy threw the ball high in the air; he had to lean forward to catch it — "he intended to spend the rest of his life in a Roman Catholic monastery."

After a moment of silence, Kennedy threw the ball across the desk at Fletch.

Catching the ball, Fletch said, "Glunk."

"Thought that would surprise you," Kennedy said. "You see why I'm happy to talk to you this morning. A very strange circumstance indeed."

"My, my. Who'd have thought it?"

"Aren't people amazing? Well worth your collecting."

"He wanted to become a monk?"

"Yes. So he said. A Roman Catholic monk. Spend the rest of his life reading Thomas Merton, or something. Matins and evensong. The whole bit."

"He always wore black shoes."

"What?"

"Never mind."

"Needless to say, we've had some staff meetings around here to discuss this whole Habeck business. No one has known what to think. Then, yesterday, when I was driving out to lunch, I heard on the car radio Habeck had been murdered. When he said last Wednesday that his life was over, he was more right than he knew."

"If he wanted to give away five million dollars and go into the monastery, why didn't he give the money to the monastery, or to the Church?"

"I asked him that. He said he was too old ever to fulfill a ministry. Furthermore, that he would have too much to learn. And, he wanted the peace and quiet of a monastery. He said he was tired of talking and arguing and pleading. Would you believe that?"

"So establishing a collection of religious art at the museum would do his public pleading for him?"

"I guess. He hoped such a collection would inspire religious feelings among contemporary people more than any sermons he could ever give, or ever want to give. If I understood him correctly."

Fletch tossed the ball back to Kennedy in a high arc. "I don't get it."

"He said he'd have something more than a million dollars left over, and that money he would give to the monastery."

"What about his wife? His kids? His grandchildren?"

"He didn't mention them. Except to say no one cared a tin whistle for him. His words exactly."

Kennedy tossed the baseball back to Fletch.

"The museum as church, uh?"

"A museum is partly a church. Maybe entirely a church."

"So how did you leave it with him?"

"I was so startled, I suggested he think it over. I think I even dared suggest he talk it over with his wife, his children, his law partners."

Fletch tossed the ball back in as high an arc as the room could take. "Curator as minister, eh?"

"Or shrink. And I told him we'd talk it over here. I indicated very strongly to him that I didn't feel we could take his five million dollars with the restriction that it be spent solely on acquiring contemporary religious art. It wouldn't be fair to him to accept money on conditions we couldn't observe." He tossed the ball back to Fletch. "If he could find some wording which would make the money available to us to use, with the understanding that we would acquire valid contemporary religious art when and if it became available, then maybe we could accept his money."

Fletch arced the ball back at the curator. "And he, being a lawyer, was perfectly sure that he could develop such wording."

"Probably. The story of his murder I read on the front page of your newspaper this morning said he intended to see your publisher regarding the announcement that he was giving five million dollars to something in the city."

"The museum was what was mentioned to me."

"Did you write that piece in this morning's paper?"

"No. Biff Wilson."

Kennedy tossed the ball into his glove. "It was a good piece."

"It was okay," Fletch said. "For an obituary."

TWENTY

In the very small reception room of the Ben Franklyn Friend Service, the young-middle-aged, distinguished-looking woman gave Fletch the once-over from behind her small wooden desk.

"If you take your left here at the corner," she said, pointing a manicured hand, "and left again in the middle of the block, you'll find yourself in the alley."

"Ecstatic!"

"Our delivery door is about halfway down, on the left." Over her pink sweatsuit she wore a long rope of pearls. "The door is clearly marked."

"Pure ecstasy!"

The woman frowned. "You are making a delivery, aren't you?" She looked more the type to be sitting at a checkout desk in a public library.

"What am I delivering?" Fletch asked.

"Linens. Towels."

"Me."

"You?"

"Me. In all my parts. Head, shoulders, hips, and knee joints, right down to the ankles. And everything in between." Fletch swallowed hard.

"Do you have an appointment?" She opened a desk calendar. "You're just not the sort . . ."

"Sort of what?"

Her eyes confirmed that he was wearing a T-shirt, faded jeans, and very white, new sneakers. ". . . the sort we usually see."

"I was welcomed by the museum dressed this way."

"Your name?"

"Jaffe."

"Ah, yes: Fletcher Jaffe." She made a pencil check in the IN box beside his name.

"You've heard the name before?"

"We don't pay that much attention to names."

"Jaffe is a name to which you should pay attention."

"That will be one hundred and fifty dollars."

"Good! I'll pay it!" He dropped seven twenties and a ten on the desk. "Make sure I get a receipt."

She looked quizzically at him. "Our clients don't usually ask for receipts."

"I do."

"I'll make out a receipt for you before you leave."

"Why not now?"

"Well, you might want to add on some extras."

"Extra whats?"

The woman seemed embarrassed. "Tips. Whatever."

"I see."

"You're not married, are you?"

Fletch shook his head. "No, ma'am. No one goes through my pockets."

"Diseases?" Her eyes enlarged as she looked at him. "Are you willing to swear you have no diseases?"

"This place is harder to get into than a New England prep school."

"I asked you about diseases."

"Chicken pox."

"Chicken pox!"

"When I was nine." Fletch pointed out a pockmark on his left elbow. "I'm better now, thank you."

The woman sighed. She pressed a button on the desk intercom. "Cindy? Someone's here to see you."

"Ah, Cindy!" exclaimed Fletch. "I was hoping for a Cindy. Nobody wants a Zza-zza, Queenie, or Bobo this hour of the day."

"I've seen you somewhere before," the woman said, almost to herself. "Recently."

"I'm around town," Fletch said breezily. "A bit of a *boulevardier*."

"Oh, Cindy," said the woman. "This is Fletcher Jaffe."

In the door stood a woman in her early twenties. She was dressed only in well-cut nylon gym shorts, sneakers, and footies. Her shoulders were lightly muscled. Her perky breasts were tanned in the round identically with the rest of her body. Muscles were visible in her stomach. Her black hair and wide-set eyes matched perfectly and had the same sparkle.

Looking at Fletch, she wrinkled her nose.

"Good morning, Cindy." Fletch again swallowed hard. "Glad you came to work early today."

Through the street door came another young woman. She was wearing white jeans and a loose red shirt. She had fly-away blond hair.

Approaching the desk, she openly studied the scene: Fletch standing in the middle of the small reception room; Cindy presenting herself in the doorway.

"Marta!" she whimpered to the woman at the desk.

"I can't help it, Carla," Marta answered.

"You told me I should sleep in, this morning!"

"I also told you," Marta said forcefully, "never to wear that color red. It doesn't go with your hair coloring."

"I know." Carla giggled. "It makes men in the street look away."

In the interior doorway, Cindy tossed her head. Fletch followed her.

He followed her down a paneled, carpeted corridor.

"You a cop?" she asked.

"No."

"I hope you are," Cindy muttered. "Time this place got busted." She slowed her walk. "Do me a favor, though, will you?"

"Anything."

"Bust this place if you want. See where it will get you. But don't bust me personally, okay?"

"What makes you think I'm a cop?"

"I'm splitting the end of this week. I swear to you. I don't want the hassle."

"If I'm a cop, you're ugly."

Even in the dark corridor, her skin had a lovely sheen.

She smiled at the compliment.

She opened a heavy drawer built into the wall, and pulled out another pair of well-cut nylon shorts. "These about right? Waist thirty?"

She tossed them to him.

"Sure."

She led him into a brightly lit room to the left off the corridor.

In the room was a single-frame exercise rig.

The walls were covered with mirrors. Mirrors hung from the ceiling. At one place there was even a mirror on the floor, inset into the carpet.

Fletch stood on the floor mirror and looked up and around. Through the angled ceiling mirrors he saw himself from directions he had never seen himself before. In the mirrors on the four walls he saw his body replicated to infinity.

Cindy closed the door to the corridor. "Where did you get your tan?"

"On my face."

"Anywhere else?" She crossed the room, went through a door to a bathroom, came back immediately, and tossed him a towel.

Standing on the mirror, looking around at himself everywhere, Fletch said, "Me, me, me."

"You got it, honey."

He held the towel and the shorts in his hand.

"Take a shower," she said. "Use the soap. Change into just the shorts, and come back."

Fletch held the shorts up. "These shorts ain't got nothin' in them."

"They will have," she said. "I expect."

The shower soap stung.

When he reentered the room, Cindy was at a small, recessed bar mixing a drink.

She glanced at him. "I thought so."

"You thought what?"

She was bringing him the drink. "What vitamins do you take?"

"P."

"Never heard of it."

"All the best beers have it."

She handed him the drink. Her other hand dropped five stuffed olives into his hand.

He sniffed the drink "What's in it?"

"Orange juice."
"Okay." He munched the olives.
"Some protein powder."
"That sounds healthy."
"A little yeast."
"Sounds explosive."
"And some ground elk's horn."
"I was hoping you'd say that."
"An aphrodisiac, you know?"
"Anything else?"
"No."
"Specialty of the house?"
"Drink it, honey. Perfectly safe."
He sipped it. "Yummy."
"Chug-a-lug," she said.
"Really," he said, choking a little. "You thought of marketing this stuff?" Even while drinking it, his throat felt dusty. "Elixir of Ben Franklyn."
"Come on." She took the empty glass from him and put it on the recessed bar.
Then she took his hand and led him to the exercise machine.
"You know how to use these things? Of course you do. Lie down on your back. You're going to do bench presses. I have it set for one hundred and twenty pounds. That about right?"
"We'll see."
He lay down on his back on the bench. His knees were bent, his feet on the floor.
Looking up, he saw himself and the top of Cindy's head, and her shoulders, in the mirror.
"Lift," she said.
He lifted.
"That's about right," she said. "Feel good?"
"Like ice cream on a hot summer's day."
"Do eight in a row, slowly."
She sat on him, straddling his thighs. She spread her hands on his lower stomach, thumbs touching.
As he lifted, she pressed her hands into his stomach muscles.
He felt a sensation such as he had never felt before.
He groaned.
"Don't drop it," she said. "Makes a loud noise."
He let the weights down quietly and looked into her eyes.

"Come on," she said. "You're going to do eight of them in a row. I'm giving you every motive. Breathe."

He breathed and lifted.

On the third lift, he found his legs straightening, his heels sliding along the rug.

She did not fall off his thighs. Through the mirror he saw that she had hooked the calves of her legs around the legs of the bench. At each lift she pressed the palms of her hands into his stomach muscles.

"Breathe," she said.

"That, too?"

After he did eight lifts, she flicked the front of his shorts with her fingernails. "You're healthy enough. I thought so."

He raised his knees.

"I'll take your sweat," she said.

She leaned forward and put her breasts, her stomach on his. She raised her legs and put her thighs on his. She rolled on him, just a little.

As soon as he gave in to irresistible impulse and put his arms around her back, she was up and away.

She stood under the chin-up grips. "Come on."

"Who said exercise has to be boring?"

As they moved in the brightly lit room, their infinite reflections in mirrors on all sides made it seem as if each were a legion moving with martial precision.

"Put your hands on the back of the grips."

Standing on his toes, he stretched totally and put his hands around the grips.

"No," she said. "Put your hands further back on the grips." He did so. "Now do a chin-up." He did so while she watched. "Again," she said.

While he was lifting himself a second time Cindy jumped up and grabbed the grips just in front of his hands. Her body knocked against his.

She lifted herself with him, their bodies just brushing. She stared into his eyes as they lifted themselves slowly, together, lowered themselves to full stretch, up again.

"Now, stay up," Cindy said.

"As if I had a choice."

She wrapped her legs around his hips.

Slowly she relaxed her hands on the grips.

His body took her weight.

She wrapped her arms around his neck.

"Now let us down slowly."

She opened her mouth and put her teeth hard against his taut neck muscles.

As he lowered them, every muscle, ligament, tissue, and piece of skin in his body above his waist was stretched to its maximum.

There was a delirious crackling up his spine, a small explosion in the back of his head.

As his feet settled on the floor, his knees buckled.

Tangled, they both fell on the mat.

Cindy laughed. "Not everybody can do that."

Their legs were tangled. He put his arms around her. His shoulder muscles felt inflamed, inflated.

She kissed his neck, where she had bitten him.

"I'm lapping up blood," she giggled.

"Gym class was never like this."

"You went to the wrong school."

"I always suspected that."

"We've got lots to do yet," she said.

"Will I be up for it?"

"I'll see to that."

Cindy had not yet untangled herself from him when the door to the corridor opened.

She jumped. She looked up at the doorway in genuine surprise.

TWENTY-ONE

"What's your game?" Marta asked Fletch from across her desk in the executive office of the Ben Franklyn Friend Service.

"Game?" Sitting in a small wooden captain's chair in front of the desk, Fletch looked down. He was still breathing somewhat heavily, still sweating, and the front of his flimsy yellow shorts indicated to any observer that his attention was still elsewhere. "Warden, I'm suffering."

Marta picked up the phone on her desk and pushed three buttons. Into the phone, she said, "Cindy? Get dressed. Then come in here."

"Take pity on me!" Fletch said.

Reluctantly, he had followed Marta down the dark, carpeted corridor to the office behind the reception room. Walking, Marta had more of an athletic spring in her step than sexy wriggle in her hips.

"You'll calm down in a minute, boy."

"I don't think so. You may have created a permanent condition here."

"Don't you wish."

The ferns in this office were alive. *Venus de Milo* stood on a pedestal in one corner. On a wall was *September Morn*. Another wall had a large panel of color photographs of women weightlifters, flexed.

On Marta's desk was a stack of bills which looked suspiciously like seven twenties and a ten.

"Am I being expelled from the Ben Franklyn Friend Service?" Fletch asked. "Won't you be my friend?"

"I asked you what you're playing at."

"I'm just a red-blooded boy out for a morning of sport."

"Like hell you are." Marta fingered the pearls draping her stomach. "I remembered where I saw you before."

"I know!" Fletch said. "I just remembered, too. Sunday, at the Newcomers' Coffee, at St. Anselm's Church."

"You're right about Sunday," Marta said. "You want something. And I think I know what."

"You'd be right." Leaning forward, elbows on knees, Fletch put his face in his hands. "Nothing so wicked has happened to me since Sue Ann Murchison's parents came home early from the first *Star Trek* movie and caught us on the couch."

"I saw you on Sunday. You ran in the Sardinal Race."

"I didn't get any understanding then, either. They threw me out. It was a real cold night. There's a danger in brittleness, you know. If I hadn't kept my hips absolutely straight as I went down their front walk . . ."

"You hound-dogged the girls all through the race."

". . . why, I wouldn't be here today."

"Why?"

"If you excuse me, I think I'll go for a run now."

"Sit down."

"I've got to do something!"

"You've got to answer me, is what you've got to do. I asked you: Why did you follow us all through the Sardinal Race Sunday?"

Fletch sat back down in his hard chair. "Because I'm a dirty old man."

"I asked you: Why?"

"Because I used to be a dirty young man."

"You are a young man," Marta insisted. "A transparently healthy young man."

"Bursting."

"You are good-looking. In fact, I expect some women would consider you exciting to look at."

"Some women consider cabbage exciting to look at."

"A hundred and fifty dollars." Marta riffled the stack of bills on her desk with her fingers. "You can get anything you want, probably more than you want, without walking a full city block."

"Mind if I go try it right now?"

"Sit down, please. I was suspicious the minute I saw you. A hundred and fifty dollars is a lot of money. And that's just for starters."

"You know how to cool the client, huh?"

"The minute you walked in here, I knew no one like you was laying down two hundred dollars or more just to get a sexual thrill."

"I was enjoying it. I was headin' for ecstasy, when you opened that door."

"Then I remembered where I saw you before. I'll ask you one more time: Why did you stay right behind us through the entire Sardinal Race Sunday?"

"All right," Fletch said. "I confess. I'm a student of advertising. Publicity, actually. I was studying your technique." He held his hands out to indicate wriggling hips. "Your technique really worked. I mean, you really got mileage out of your publicity."

"Marta's smile was droll. "Really . . ."

"Didn't I see a big spread on the Ben Franklyn Friend Service on the sports pages of the newspapers, yesterday? Two pictures, at least. Was it the *Chronicle-Gazette*?"

The woman's smile became genuine. "The *News-Tribune.*"

"Yeah. That's right. All for the price of a dozen T-shirts. That's real mileage."

Marta said, "You're a spy."

Fletch widened his eyes at her. "I'm a spy?" He dropped his voice to a near whisper. "You mean, from Red China?"

"You're studying us all right." Marta nodded. "Is that it? That's why you followed us Sunday. That's why you came here this morning. You're studying our operation."

"Oh, you mean an industrial spy," Fletch said more loudly. "From Japan."

"After you learn what we do here, you intend to open one of your own exercise-to-sexual-ecstasy pavilions."

"You phrase things so well," Fletch said. "Truly, you have a natural talent for advertising and publicity."

"Isn't that true?"

"*Moi*?" Fletch asked. "Look at me. At my age, where could I get the money to open one of these gymnasiums-of-delight?"

"I don't know, but you're here."

"I don't even know how much one of these exercise machines costs, but, I'm sure, plenty. All these mirrors. Lights. Bathrooms. Ground elk's horn."

"Someone could be backing you."

"Heck, lady, at my age I couldn't get financial backing from a milkman."

Marta shuddered. "Don't call me 'lady.' "

"Right. Sorry."

"So, then: Why are you here, Fletcher Jaffe?"

Fletch looked at his toes. "I thought by now you would have figured that out," he said, not knowing what his next line of defense was, but hoping for one.

"You want a job." Marta looked pleased with herself.

"You got it," Fletch said quickly.

"I had to be circumspect." Marta straightened her back.

"I understand."

"In this business," Marta said, "one has to be careful."

"Of course." Fletch gulped. "Naturally. Me, too."

"Talking around, testing each other out, before we lay our cards on the table."

"You're good at it," Fletch said.

"That's why you've been making this strange approach to us. *Solicitation* is such a dirty word. You wanted to see if we'd make the offer to you."

"Right," Fletch said through his Adam's apple.

"You thoroughly expected your one hundred and fifty dollars back this morning." She picked it off the desk and handed it to him. "Here it is."

He took it.

She sat back in her swivel chair, and turned sideways to the desk. "At the moment we only have two suites operating for women, three days a week, Tuesday, Wednesday, and Thursday, when our male traffic is apt to be down. Don't worry. You'll make more money those three days than you could at any other profession, except of course, maybe neurosurgery. The women have a separate entrance, of course, but we're talking the same thing. The principle here is that sex is far more ecstatic after hard exercise. You know, exercise as foreplay." Listening to her, trying to swallow his Adam's apple, staring at her, Fletch thought Marta remarkably like Frank Jaffe sitting in his swivel chair behind his desk, trying to get across a few principles of journalism. "When it comes right down to it, of course you know, we don't expect you to use your own personal, shall I say, intimate equipment." She chuckled. "Except your fingers, of course. Unlike women, men can't bear that much traffic. Men can't phony it. Our clients understand that. We have machines, vibrators, mechanical dildos which I find quite satisfactory. We even have a vibrating dildo machine on a wide, leather belt you can strap on yourself, if you're not absolutely repulsed by the woman. Of course, we expect you to solicit an extra charge, for that service." There was a rap on the door. Marta called, "Come in, darling!"

Cindy opened the door and stood just inside it. She was dressed in loafers, white knee socks, a short kilt, and a light blue, buttoned down, preppy dress shirt with the sleeves rolled up. Without expression, she watched Marta's face.

"Say hello, again, to your new colleague, darling." Marta stood up. "Fletcher Jaffe will be joining the staff of the Ben Franklyn Friend Service. I want you to take him to lunch, Cindy, and give him the benefits of your wisdom and experience."

Now Cindy was watching Fletch without expression.

Fletch's throat was dry.

"He made a real smart approach to us," Marta said. "He knew he couldn't come here and just ask for a job, without making himself awfully vulnerable. He gave me a hard time," she chuckled. "Is he a cop? I asked myself. A spy? The cops wouldn't send anyone that young. And no one his age could run a place like this. Sexual dysfunction? Not from what I saw watching you two through the mirror."

"You're some detective," Fletch croaked.

He stood on wobbling knees.

Marta came around the desk and put her hand on the back of his neck. "He's exactly what we need, to build up the female side of this business. Isn't he, Cindy?"

"Sure." Cindy was still watching him. "I guess."

"He's just perfect. I've been looking for you, boy." She squeezed the back of his neck. "Exactly what we need. Welcome aboard. You can start work anytime."

"Thanks."

"Tell him everything, Cindy. Show him the ropes."

Fletch said to Cindy, "Mind if I take a shower before I get dressed?"

"*I'd* appreciate it."

"Have a nice lunch, kids. Today you're lunching on the Ben Franklyn Friend Service. But, remember, high protein, both of you, and watch the starch and fats." Back behind her desk, Marta beamed at Fletch. "And remember, Fletch. My door is always open."

TWENTY-TWO

"That never happened before," Cindy said. "Marta just opening the door and bursting in that way. I couldn't imagine what was happening." They were walking from her car to Manolo's sidewalk café. "Of course, I knew there was something weird about you. Something different. Remember my asking you if you were a cop?"

"You asked me to bust the Friend Service, but not you personally."

"Just in case you were a cop. You need the sense of privacy that that closed door gives you, you know? Set the right mood, control the client."

"Satisfy him, too."

Fletch carried his jeans and his T-shirt rolled up in his hand.

When he was about to get dressed, Cindy had walked into the bathroom and tossed him a T-shirt and a pair of light shorts. "Marta said you were to wear these. She said you understand about public relations." Across the front of the T-shirt and across the front waist of the shorts was written, in small letters, YOU WANT A FRIEND? and across the back of the T-shirt and the back of the shorts, BEN FRANKLYN.

Cindy had suggested lunching at Manolo's Café. Fletch suggested someplace else, but Cindy said Manolo's was the in place at the moment.

So they went along the sidewalk, Fletch a walking billboard, hoping no one knew precisely what the commercial message he was flashing meant.

Marta had been pleased to see him wearing the shorts and shirt. His job was secure.

"Of course, Marta can watch us through the mirrors anytime she wants."

"The mirrors are windows from their reverse side?"

"Not all of them. Just some."

"What does that do to your sense of privacy?"

"It's good. Makes you feel safe, you know, in case something goes wrong. In case you get some kook in there, who turns violent or something."

"You get kooks often?"

"No. But when you sense something might be wrong, there's a little button you can push in the bar that signals someone to come watch through the mirror."

"I see."

"And, of course, Marta sells the seats, and there are the cameras."

"What?"

"Behind the big wall mirrors, there are seats, in one or two of the gyms, you know, for voyeurs. Old, fat, repulsive, I don't know what they are. People who would rather watch it than do it."

"Men and women?"

"Sure. Marta nicks them one hundred bucks a seat."

"You perform for them?"

"We like to. I mean, supposing we get a reasonable young, healthy guy in there. Like yourself. Marta would have invited you back for a freebie, say, Friday night. You would have come back, and I would have put you through the routine, the only difference being that people would have been watching."

"And I wouldn't have known it."

"All you would have known was that you were getting the routine free."

"And what would it have meant to you?"

"More money. Also, having people watching somehow enhances the experience, you know? Especially when you're doing it all the time."

"Beats the sense of privacy?"

"Sure it does. Haven't you ever done it in public?"

"Not intentionally."

"Sometimes Marta rents us out for parties. We do it on the floor, after dinner. A guy and a gal, two gals, two guys. Really turns the old dears on. It's fun. You'll see. And the tips are marvelous."

"You said something about cameras."

"Yeah, that's necessary. To avoid difficulties. They're behind one of the smaller mirrors, in every gym. A videotape camera and a still camera. We get shots of every client."

"Why?"

"Well, sometimes they're drunk, or angry, or get frustrated. You know, clients are the same in any business, I suppose. They complain, threaten. If they seem truly dangerous to us, Marta shows them the pictures. That quiets them, you bet. It's not just that they're doing this, you know, it's that the pictures make them look so ugly and clumsy, big, gray guts hanging out, hairy asses sticking up being beaten by the exercise machines."

"And the pictures are used for blackmail sometimes, right?"

"Sure. Especially if the client stops being a client, and we know who he really is. Once you walk in the door of the Ben Franklyn Friend Service, a piece of you stays there forever."

"You've made a friend for life."

"It's a good business."

"Yeah," said Fletch. "It's up there with a solid law practice."

"Oh, look. There's a free table."

"So," said Fletch, stretching his legs under the shade of the café table. "Are you the prostitute with the heart of gold?"

With his arms folded across his chest, all his commercial messages were out of view.

"I don't think a heart of gold would pump very well," Cindy answered. "I have a better place to put my gold."

"Have you made much gold at Ben Franklyn?"

"Enough to leave the stupid place. Marta doesn't know yet. Please don't tell her. We want it to be a surprise, end of the week. Friday's my last workday. Got something else to do Saturday. Sunday, we're off to Colorado. For good."

"You're escaping."

"You bet."

"But, if you're making so much gold . . ."

"It's not very nice of me to say this. I mean, you're just joining the service, and I'm leaving. I should say only good things, I guess. You may not believe this, but, frankly, Fletch, the Ben Franklyn Friend Service is sort of a sleazy place."

Fletch tried to look surprised.

"I'm just fed up with it," Cindy said. "You remember when you were in the reception area that frowsy blond who came in and started kicking up a fuss?"

"Yeah."

"That was Carla. She was jealous because I got you as a client. She wasn't even expected in this morning, for cryin' out loud."

"She gets first pick of the clients?"

"She gets the first pick of everything. Hours, clients, gyms."

"Seniority has its benefits, in any business."

"Seniority! She's been there three months, I've been there two and a half years, since it opened, for cryin' out loud!"

"There's jealousy in every business, I guess. What's she got you haven't got?"

"Didn't you hear Marta say something about her wanting Carla to sleep late this morning? Guess who crept out of a double bed, and tiptoed out of a bedroom this morning, so Carla could sleep late?"

"I see."

"Marta."

The waiter Fletch had had the day before recognized Fletch. He looked around hopelessly, probably for another waiter. Reluctantly he approached.

Cindy leaned forward and said to Fletch with great vehemence: "I don't care what business you're in. No one should get special perks or advancement because of sex!"

Fletch cleared his throat. He looked up at the waiter.

The waiter said, "So interested to see you're alive and well today."

"Thank you, I think."

"And what will your 'usual' be today? I can't wait to hear. In fact, I'm sure our chef, who didn't sleep a wink last night, reliving your order of yesterday, cringes in his kitchen this noon upon the possibility of your return."

"You ate here yesterday?" Cindy asked.

"A memorable experience, Ms.," said the waiter. "In fact, we've asked the dining-out critic of the *News-Tribune* to pass us by until this particular customer either moves out of state or passes on to his eternal damnation of hiccups."

Fletch said to Cindy, "I just ordered a —"

The waiter held up his hand. "Please, sir. It does not bear repeating. Having heard your order yesterday, I barely got through the rest of the day and the night myself. If we can't believe each day can be better than the last where would we be?"

Fletch said to Cindy. "Do you think he's insulting me?"

"Oh, no," said Cindy. "I think he's trying to instruct you in the finer points of fast food."

"Fast food takes refinement?"

"You bet." She said to the waiter, "Anyway, I'm ordering for him today."

"Oh, thank God! Sir, someone has finally taken you in hand!"

"He'll have five scrambled eggs."

The waiter looked at her, astounded. "That's it."

"And a chocolate egg-cream," Fletch muttered.

"Yes," Cindy said. "You see, from now on, a certain kind of demand is going to be made upon his body, in his new job."

"He doesn't want to hear," Fletch muttered.

"And you, Ms.?"

"I'll have a banana split, three kinds of ice cream, fudge sauce, marshmallow, and chopped nuts."

"What will that do for you?" Fletch asked.

"Make my tummy happy."

Fletch said to the waiter, "I'll have you know this young woman this morning has already fed me a dose of ground elk's horn."

The waiter said, "I could have guessed that."

"It was not," Cindy said. "That's a fake. I think it's really pulverized cow's horn."

"Oh, sigh," said the waiter. "What happened to those nice people who used to say, 'Just a Coke and a hamburger rare'?"

"Young people can't get any respect from waiters," Fletch muttered, "no matter what they do for a living. No matter what they talk about."

"What's my job description?" Fletch asked between sucks of his chocolate egg-cream through a straw. "Call boy?"

"You're a whore, sir, like the rest of us, and don't you forget it." Cindy picked up her spoon. "If you think anything else, you lose control, of yourself, of your client. It's a profession, you know. You must not lose control. Losing control can be dangerous."

The waiter had brought their lunches announcing, "Five aborted chickens and a bowl of frozen udder drippings."

Fletch asked of Cindy, "How did we end up here?"

"We were brought up the same, I expect. All Americans are, to some extent." With her spoon she was spreading the whipped cream and the marshmallow evenly over her ice cream. "We were brought up primarily as sexual objects, weren't we? I mean, what were all the vitamins, pediatrics, orthodontistry really for? Why did parents and schools make us play sports? To learn a philosophy, to learn how to win, how to lose? Nonsense. Parents and coaches protested, complained, argued with referees and each other more than we did. For health reasons? Nonsense. How many of your friends survived school sports without permanent knee, back, or neck injuries?" Cindy put a heaping spoonful of ice cream, fudge sauce, marshmallow, and whipped cream in her mouth. "Must be outdoors, doing things, but not without sun blockage, to preserve the skin. Lotions morning and night. The sole purpose was to create beautifully shaped legs, arms, shoulders, flat tummies, in gleaming, fresh skin."

"I'm a sex object?" Fletch asked.

"That's all you are, brother. Growing up, what was the intellectual discipline you were given? The theology? philosophy? culture? Me, a thirteen-year-old girl, comes running home from school, bursting into the house, and says, 'Mama, Mama, I got an A in mathematics!' And Mama says, 'Yes, dear, but I've been noticing your hair is losing its sheen. Which shampoo are you using?' "

Quietly, Fletch was eating his plate of eggs.

"Who were held up to us as heroes?" Cindy asked. "Teachers? Mathematicians? Poets? No. Only those with beautiful bodies, athletes and film stars. They are the ones interviewed on television continuously. And are they ever allowed to talk about how they really become as fast on their feet, or how they get themselves into the character of a role they're playing? No. All they're ever asked about is their sex lives, how many times they've been married, and to whom, and what each affair was like. Prestige, Fletch, is in how many people you can attract to your bed."

"Therefore, you became a whore."

"Isn't that what it's all about?"

"Very clear-sighted of you."

"I think so."

"You enjoying your banana split?" It was half gone.

"Very much."

"I can see that."

"Very much."

"But, Cindy, I, uh, have some qualms, about, uh, actually doing it, uh, you know, for money."

"I hardly ever *actually do it*. At the spa, the machines beat the clients. They get all stressed and strained, and I see that they get excited, and I jerk 'em off before they know what happened. Then they get apologetic that they couldn't contain themselves and I 'missed a really good time,' in quotes. When I'm out at night as an escort, mostly I sit in the restaurants and the clubs watching some old boy drink himself blue in the face. I just listen to him, sort of. Usually, that's all he really wants. It's very boring. When he's totally drunk, I hustle him back to his hotel room, strip him, and put him in his bed. Next morning, he thinks he's had a wonderful time, done wonderful things with a wonderful girl. He hasn't. You'll learn. I've probably made love to fewer men, or, fewer times with a man, than that secretary over there."

She nodded to a young woman at a nearby table with an older man. On their table, besides their lunches, were notepads, pens, a folder of paper, and a calculator.

Cindy said in her throat, " 'Cept I get paid more."

Fletch said, "Maybe I mean emotionally. How am I supposed to handle, you know, being paid for being intimate emotionally? I worry a little about that."

"That's so much bullshit handed out by the psychiatrists. And let me ask you: Who's more intimate with a client, a whore or a psychiatrist?"

"Uh . . ."

"I know their text by heart. The guilt trip. Whores have an enormous need for love, but we don't know what love is. Our only way of valuing ourselves is by setting a price on our affections, our attentions. Isn't that true of psychiatrists, too? Man, they're just projecting. I don't care. They have to make a living, too. I just wish they wouldn't lay their own sickness off on us."

"But you, Cindy, after two and a half years of this, how can you ever really, truly relate to a man again, have a genuine experience?"

"I don't want to. I never did before. I never will." She was scraping her ice-cream bowl clean with her spoon. "See, that's where everybody's wrong, at least about me. About many of us. I mentioned a friend to you, a real friend. She works at Ben Franklyn, too. We've made our money. Next week, we're splitting. We're going to Colorado, going to buy a dog-breeding ranch, and live happily ever after."

"You're lovers?"

"You bet. See, making love to a man means nothing to me. Emotionally. Morally. Whatever those words mean. I don't care about men. Going to bed with a man doesn't bother me any more than it would bother you to go to bed with a boy, or a dog."

Fletch said, "What kind of a dog?"

Cindy sat back from her empty bowl. "The way I was brought up, eating that ice cream was more of a sin for me than going to bed with a man. Or men. Or a whole track team." She looked at her empty bowl. "I enjoyed it."

"Things are different, for me," Fletch said.

"I suppose so. That's your problem."

At the corner of the block, walking toward them, was a yellow skirt familiar to Fletch. So was the dark blue, short-sleeved blouse above the skirt.

"Oh, my God."

Cindy stretched her arms a little. "But, for you and me basically it's the same thing, I expect. I was developed into a supposedly brainless, cultureless beautiful body, a sexual object, and told men are materialistic oppressors and making babies is a no-no. I'm not really an athlete. I'm not an actor."

Fletch had sat up straight. Under the table he had moved his feet into a sprint position. His eye measured the distance between his table and the door of Manolo's. "Oh, wow."

"It comes time to make a living," Cindy continued. "What am I supposed to do? Pretend I'm a big intellect? Or, worse, pretend I'm a worker-ant?"

The woman approaching them spotted Fletch.

Then she spotted Cindy.

Fletch said, "Oh, no."

With certainty, Cindy said, "I am doing exactly what I am supposed to be doing. I am exactly who I am supposed to be."

"Fletch!" the woman said.

"Uh . . ."

Cindy turned around. Delight came on her face.

"Barbara!" she squealed.

Cindy jumped up and hugged Barbara around the neck.

Barbara hugged Cindy.

Fletch stood up. "Ah, Barbara . . ."

When the hugging and squealing abated, Barbara looked at Fletch. She was still holding Cindy's hand.

Barbara said, "I didn't know you two know each other!"

TWENTY-THREE

"You have a hickey on your neck," Barbara said to Fletch.

The waiter had brought a third chair to the table, heard with relief they wanted nothing more than the bill, and gone away.

"A passion mark," Barbara added, looking closely at him from under the shade of the umbrella. "It wasn't there when you left me this morning."

Fletch fingered the mark on his neck. "I, uh . . ."

Cindy's eyebrows wrinkled in confusion.

"And that's not the way you were dressed when you left this morning."

Barbara put her hand on his rolled T-shirt and jeans on the table. "How come you're in shorts?"

Fletch folded his arms across his chest.

"What does your T-shirt say?" Barbara leaned forward and moved his arms. " 'You want a friend?' What does that mean?" She reached into his lap. "Your shorts say the same thing."

"They do," Fletch admitted with dignity.

"Did you get a bargain?" Barbara asked.

Fletch croaked, "How do you two know each other?"

"We're old friends from school," Barbara said easily.

"You are? Old friends?"

"Yeah."

"Good friends?"

"I've mentioned Cindy to you. She's been advising me on the wedding."

Fletch said: "Ah!"

"Fletch!" Cindy yelled. She hit her forehead with the heel of her hand. "You're that Fletch!"

Accusingly, Fletch asked Barbara, "And why aren't you wearing jodhpurs?"

"Ho, ho, ho," Cindy laughed.

"I change for lunch," Barbara answered. "I hate the beastly things."

"This is the Fletch you're marrying on Saturday?"

"In the flesh." Barbara put her hand on his thigh. "Fletch, you're awfully hot. You're sweating. Your face is red. You all right?"

"Ho, ho, ho," said Cindy.

"Oh, my God," said Fletch.

"But how do you two know each other?" Barbara asked.

"Ho, ho, ho," said Cindy.

"I, uh, we . . ." said Fletch.

"Is there something funny?" Barbara asked.

"Not really," said Fletch.

"Ho, ho, ho," said Cindy.

"After we're married," Barbara said, "I have the small hope Fletch comes home at night dressed something like the way he goes out in the morning."

"Ho, ho, ho." Cindy was choking with laughter.

"Barbara," Fletch said slowly and seriously, "Cindy and I met in the course of business."

"Ho, ho, ho!" laughed Cindy.

The secretary and the older man at the nearby table were frowning at this disturbance.

"The course of business?" Barbara asked.

"The course of business!" Cindy laughed.

"In the course of business," Fletch affirmed. "Now, Barbara darling, if you'd just —"

"Barbara darling!" yelled Cindy.

Not understanding Cindy's raucous good humor, Barbara said to Fletch, "Oh, by the way, I just heard on the car radio that someone has confessed to murdering Donald Habeck."

Fletch snapped forward in his chair. "What?"

"A man named Childers, I think. Went to the police this morning and confessed to killing Donald Habeck. A client of Habeck's —"

"I remember," said Fletch. "The trial ended two or three months ago. He was accused of murdering his brother."

"Well, this morning he admitted murdering Habeck."

"But he was acquitted. I mean, of murdering his brother."

"So you needn't trouble your little head about the murder of Donald Habeck anymore. You can go back to doing the job you're assigned to do."

"Yeah," Fletch said grimly. "Thanks."

"We can get married Saturday, we can have a honeymoon, and maybe you'll even have a job when we get back."

"That's right." Cindy had stopped laughing. She was looking at Fletch with new eyes. "You're a reporter!"

Fletch sighed. "Right."

"For the *Chronicle-Gazette*," said Cindy.

"For the *News-Tribune.*" Fletch looked a dagger at Barbara.
"What's going on?" Barbara asked.
"Cool," said Cindy. "That explains everything!"
Fletch said, "I'm afraid it does."
"Have you written anything for the newspaper I might have read?" Cindy asked.
"Sunday," Fletch said. "Did you read 'Sports Freaks at End of Line'?"
"Yeah," Cindy said. "Sure I did. The lead piece in the sports section. Real good. Did you write that?"
Fletch said, "Just the headline."
"Oh."
"What were you doing?" Barbara grinned gamely, as if asking to be let in on a joke she might have already ruined. "Being undercover?"
"Thanks for asking," Fletch said.
Cindy began laughing again. She clapped her hands. "Super!"
" 'Super,' " Fletch quoted grimly.
The waiter gave the bill to Fletch. "Serving you, sir," said the waiter, "is an affliction I'd hate to have become an addiction."
Fletch stared at him.
Cindy took the bill. "No. This is on the company, remember?" She laughed out loud again. "You might say, it's on the house!"
"Anyway, Cindy," Barbara said. "We're going to be married on a bluff, overlooking the ocean. Did I tell you that? The weather's supposed to be nice Saturday."
Cindy was paying the bill in cash.
"Remember, we're having dinner with my mother tonight," Barbara said uncertainly to Fletch.
"Tonight for dinner," Fletch said somberly, "I'm having my head on a plate."
"Cindy," Barbara said. "Around the corner there's a sports shop. There's this great-looking skiing suit in the window. You know, for our honeymoon. Want to walk over with me and see how I look in it?"
"Sure," Cindy said. She left the waiter a generous tip.
The two women stood up from the table.
Fletch remained, elbow on the table, chin on his hand.
"See you, Fletch," Barbara said.
Fletch didn't answer.
Cindy said happily, "See you, Fletch! At the wedding! Saturday!"
After Cindy had gone a few paces, she turned around, again doubled over in laughter. "Fletch!" she called. "You're being married on a bluff!"

TWENTY-FOUR

"Hello? Hello?" Fletch knocked loudly on the frame of the screen door. Inside the bungalow a television was playing loudly but nevertheless was drowned out by a child crying, other children yelling, and the noise of some mechanical toy. "Hello!" he shouted.

The front porch was a junkyard of broken toys, a scooter with its neck twisted, a crunched tricycle, a flattened plastic doll, a play stove that looked like it had been assaulted with an ax.

On the television, a woman's voice said, "If you tell Ed what you know about me, Mary, I'll see you rot in hell."

Inside the house, a woman's voice shouted, "Keep up that bawlin', Ronnie, and I'll slay you silly!"

A man's voice said, "Now, now. Let's get this eating process completed. The kiddies must eat, Nancy. Keep up their strength!"

Associate Professor Thomas Farliegh's bungalow was eight blocks from the edge of the university campus. Other humble houses surrounding it had vestiges of paint on them and at least undisturbed stands of weeds in their front gardens. Farliegh's house was yellow and gray with rot, a front window was smashed in its center, and the front yard was packed dirt, holding, among other things, a wheelless, collapsed, rusted yellow Volkswagen.

Driving to Farliegh's house, Fletch had heard a repeat of the radio news report Barbara had mentioned. Stuart Childers had confessed to murdering Donald Habeck. He had confessed — and been released.

Fletch stood as close to the screen door as he could and shouted as loud as he could, "Hey! Hello!"

Noise within the house dimmed fractionally.

A shadow the other side of the screen door grew into a woman who said, "Who are you?"

"Fletcher."

"Who? I don't know you. Better come in."

Inside it was discovered it was not the screen door which had made him less audible.

"Are you a student?" the woman asked.

"I'm from the *News-Tribune!* The paper!"

"Tom's back here," she said. "I don't know if he's corrected your paper yet." She led him into the kitchen at the back of the house. "You said your name is Terhune?"

The house smelled of diapers, burned food, spilled milk, and ordinary household dirt.

"I'm from the newspaper," Fletch said.

In the kitchen, beside the blaring television set, a battery-operated toy tank treading noisily along the floor, up and down piles of laundry, garbage, and books, were five children, all of whom seemed to be under the age of seven. Two were in diapers, three in underpants. Each seemed to have been freshly bathed that morning in used dishwater.

A short, bald, chubby man was at the chipped kitchen table spooning mushed prunes into an infant in a high chair. The man's eyes, visible as he glanced up at Fletch for a brief instant, were a startlingly pale blue. Four of the children also had blue eyes, but none as light as his.

The woman said nothing.

"What?" Fletch asked.

The television said, ". . . transporting a cargo of dum-dum bullets . . ."

The woman turned it down, which left just the noises of the tank overcoming all obstacles on the floor, two children shouting and kicking each other, and one small child sitting on a torn cushion against the wall bawling lustily.

"Ronnie," the woman said to the bawling child, "stop crying, or I'll kick you in the mouth." Her threat went unheeded. Her feet were bare.

"Do you have a car?" the woman asked Fletch.

"Yes. Are you Nancy Farliegh?"

"He wants to see you," the man at the table said.

"I'm sure he wants to see you, Tom. Something about a paper."

"I want to see you, Nancy. I'm from a newspaper."

"Oh," she said. "About my father's death." She was wearing a loose, bleach-stained skirt and a green, food-stained blouse. Her arms and legs were thin and white, her stomach distended. Her hair hung in greasy strands. "I don't care to say anything about that, but I do need a ride."

"I'll give you a ride."

"Our car is broken," the man at the table said. "Smashed. *Kaput*. Ruined."

"I should have gone yesterday," Nancy said.

"Yes, yes," the man said. "Bobby likum prunes."

"Sit down." Nancy picked up a pile of newspapers and a telephone book from another chair at the table, and dropped them on the floor. "I'll just change." She looked down at her clothes. "Tom, should I change?"

The child on the cushion stopped bawling. Determination entered his face.

"Never change, darlin'."

The determined-looking child got up from his cushion. He crossed the floor. He caught the tank and picked it up. He hurled it through the window.

Now three children were in the middle of the floor shouting and flailing each other. Hair-pulling seemed their best strategic device. It caused the best shrieks.

"I'll just change," Nancy said.

Fletch looked through the kitchen window. In the yard, the toy tank was assaulting a collapsed baby carriage.

He sat down.

"Choo, choo, choo, choo!" said Tom Farliegh. "Now the choo-choo comes to the open tunnel. Open the tunnel!" The baby opened her mouth. Tom stuck the mushed prunes into it. "Now," he said, scraping the bottle of the jar clean, "chew, chew, chew, chew."

"*Social Security*," Fletch quoted. "*The sidewalks of the city/Offer up without pity/Little old ladies to be mugged.*"

"Ah!" Tom wiped the baby's mouth gently with a crusted rag. "You're familiar with my work."

"Do you call it the Poetry of Violence?"

"That's what it's called." Tom lifted the baby from the high chair and placed her carefully on the floor.

He crossed the kitchen to where an even smaller baby was lying in a plastic basket-chair on the edge of the stove, looking like something to be roasted. The man was shaped like a rutabaga. He brought the baby in the basket-chair to the kitchen table.

"Your poetry is different," Fletch said.

"Different, yes." Tom was trying to unscrew the cap off a bottle of baby formula. "Why don't you call it beautiful?"

He handed the bottle to Fletch, who unscrewed the cap and handed it back.

"Would *beautiful* be the right word?" Fletch asked.

"Why not?" Tom screwed a nipple onto the bottle. "Choo, choo, choo." The baby opened his mouth. Tom inserted the bottle. "There must be a beauty in violence. People are so attracted to it."

Holding the bottle tipped to the infant's mouth, he looked down at where four children now fought and cried on the floor. One was bleeding from a scratch on an arm. Another had a new welt over an eye.

"That's why I have so many children," Tom Farliegh said. "Look at their fury. Isn't it wonderful? Unbridled violence. I can hardly wait until this crop get to be teenagers."

"May your dreams come true," Fletch prayed. "How many do you think will make it?"

"You are attracted to violence," Tom said.

"Not really."

"Do you watch football?"

"Yes."

"They aren't violent?" Tom's hands were the softest, pudgiest Fletch had ever seen on a man. "The vast preponderance of human entertainment is violent." He nodded at the television. "That instrument of popular human communication dispenses more violence in a day than most humans, without television, normally would see in a lifetime. What attracts us to such violence?"

"Fascination," said Fletch. "It is the second greatest puzzle, in life, that people are willing to do unto others violence which, apparently, they want done unto themselves."

"Beauty," Tom said. "The fascinating beauty of violence. The ultimate irony. Why has there never been a poet before to admit it?"

"Slim, belted hips/Sprayed across by automatic fire/each bullet/ripping through,/lifting,/throwing back,/kicking/the body at its/center. Thus/The Warrior In Perfection/bows to his death,/twists,/pivots and falls," quoted Fletch.

"Beautiful," said Tom.

"I have seen such things," said Fletch.

"And it is beautiful. Admit it." Tom Farliegh tipped the baby bottle higher. *"Waisted, he is wasted/but not wasted. This death is his life/And he is perfect/In it."*

"What courses do you teach at the university?"

"The works of Geoffrey Chaucer. Another course comparing the works of John Dryden and Edmond Spenser. Also, my share of freshman English courses."

"You teach *The Faerie Queene?*"

"Oh, yes." Tom took the bottle out of the baby's mouth. There was a small quantity of formula left in it. He put it to his own mouth, and drank it.

The baby cried.

Tom took the bottle to the sink and rinsed it.

Fletch asked, "Did you do violence to your father-in-law?"

"Yes," Tom said. "I married his daughter. He never forgave either of us."

"He never came to see his grandchildren?"

"No. I doubt he knew how many he had, or their names. Too bad. He would have appreciated them."

Fletch watched one Farliegh child throw a carrot at the head of another. "I think so."

"There was no honesty in Donald Habeck."

"You're living in squalor here," said Fletch. "Your father-in-law was a multimillionaire."

"Did I murder my father-in-law?" The short, pudgy man turned around from the kitchen sink and dried his hands on a piece of newspaper. "There would have been no irony in it."

"No?"

"No. It's the innocence of victims which makes a poetry of what happens to them. And I'm a poet."

"Did you know he intended to give almost his entire fortune to a museum?"

"No."

"If he had died without a will, as I understand lawyers are apt to do, your wife might have inherited enough for you to take up poetry full-time. That is, if his fortune were still intact. Are you saying poets aren't practical people?"

"Some are." Tom Farliegh smiled. "Those who get published in *The Atlantic* and win the Pulitzer Prize. They might be practical enough to do murder. But, surely, you're not accusing the most unpopular published poet in the country, of practicality?"

Nancy Farliegh reentered the room. She was wearing ballet slippers, a hotter-looking full skirt, and a once-white blouse gray from repeated washing. An effort had been made to brush her hair.

"Are we ready to go?" she asked.

Not knowing where he was going, Fletch stood up.

"Morton Rickmers, the book editor of the *News-Tribune,* might like to do an interview with you, Mr. Farliegh. Would you be available to him?"

"See?" Tom Farliegh grinned at his wife. "I'm reaping the benefits of my father-in-law's sensational murder already." To Fletch, he said: "Sure, I'm available to him. I do anything to deepen my unpopularity."

TWENTY-FIVE

"Is it all right to leave him with the children?" Fletch buckled himself into the driver's seat.

"Why do you ask?" Nancy Farliegh found her seat belt.

"Your husband sees beauty in violence. Those kids are beatin' up on each other in front of him."

"He's better with the kids than I am. He has much more patience."

"Much more tolerance." He turned the ignition key. "Where are we going?"

"The Monastery of St. Thomas, in Tomasito."

"Tomasito!" Fletch looked at her. "That's a hundred kilometers from here!"

"Yes," she said. "It is."

"I thought I was just dropping you off downtown."

"My brother is in the monastery." Nancy stared at the unmoving landscape through the windshield. "It is a cloistered monastery. I don't think he yet knows Father is dead. I feel I must go talk to him. I have no other way to get there."

"Your brother is a monk?"

"A monk, a monk," she said. "I suppose Tom could make a vicious nursery rhyme from that. *A monk, a monk/hiding in a trunk/to have nothing to do/with his father, the punk.* Not very good."

"Not very."

"Guess I'll leave poetry to my husband. I'll just keep birthing his little monsters."

Fletch put the car in gear. "Sorry," he said. "There's a hole in the muffler."

"I don't hear it."

"Are you a Christian?"

"Me? God, no. Bob's going into the monastery was his own thing. It had nothing to do with the family, I mean, our upbringing, at all. I suspect he's trying to atone for the sins of his father. Aren't they supposed to be visited on the son? He's got his job cut out for him."

Across from the university, Fletch drove up the ramp to the freeway and accelerated.

He said, "Someone who talked with your father just last week told me your father said he intended to enter a monastery."

Nancy gasped. "My father?" She laughed. "I knew newspapers print nothing but fiction."

"It's true," Fletch said. "At least it's true that somebody said it."

"Maybe my father would enter a monastery if he heard the Judgment Day Horn. It would be just like him. A clever legal defense."

"He was getting older."

"Not that old. About sixty."

"Perhaps he wasn't well?"

"Hope so. If anyone deserved leprosy of the gizzard, he did."

"Were you never close?"

"Emotionally? I don't know. I never saw him that much, growing up. Black suit and black shoes coming and going in the driveway. Intellectually? After I grew up, I realized how he'd been screwing the system all his life. A real destroyer of values. For profit. He never believed in good, or evil, or justice; any of the things we have to believe in, to center our lives, to focus. He believed in having his own way, despite the social consequences; in lining his own pockets. He was the most completely asocial and amoral man I ever knew. If he weren't educated as a lawyer, he probably would have been a psychopathic killer himself." After a moment, she laughed wryly. "My father, a monk!"

"Your husband," Fletch said, "extolls violence."

"You don't see a difference?" Nancy asked. "My husband is a teacher. A poet. At sacrifice to himself, he's pointing out the beauty in violence. We are attracted to it. He's making us confront the violence in ourselves. He's teaching us about ourselves. His poetry wouldn't be so damned effective, if it weren't true."

"What sacrifice to himself?"

"Come on. People cross the street when they see him coming. They won't even talk to me. We haven't been invited to a faculty cocktail party in three years. Most of the faculty want to get rid of him. He could never get another job teaching. We're going to end up in Starvation Lane. Just so Tom can make this statement, not about the nature of violence, but about the nature of you and me. Don't you understand?"

"Anyway." Fletch stretched in his car seat. "This man, who should know, told me your father intended to give five million dollars to the museum. The money was to be spent on contemporary religious art. He was going to give the rest of his worldly goods to a monastery, which he was going to enter."

Nancy shrugged. "He had an angle somewhere. I'd guess someone had the goods on him. The Justice Department. The Internal Revenue Service. The American Bar Association. I expect that after the dust settled, you would have found my father living luxuriously somewhere with his sexy, pea-brained young wife behind the facade, the protection of some religious or cultural foundation, all brilliantly, legally established, and funded, by himself."

"Maybe. But did you know your father had stated the intention of disposing of his worldly goods?"

"I read something of the sort in the newspaper. This morning's newspaper. After he was murdered."

"No one had told you before?"

"No."

Fletch said, "It's always hard to prove that you don't know something."

They rode without speaking for a while. They listened to The Grateful Dead on the radio.

Finally, Fletch said, "At your father's house yesterday, I met a woman who was about sixty years old, white-haired, or blue-haired, whatever you want to call it, wearing a colorful dress and green sneakers. I asked her if she was Mrs. Habeck, and she said she was. All she'd say about your father was that he wore black shoes and wandered away. She referred to Habeck, Harrison and Haller as *Hay, Ha, Haw.*"

"Ummm," Nancy said.

"That your mother?"

"Um." Nancy shifted in her seat. "What it says on your shorts is correct. You can be a friend, I guess."

"That's not quite what the legend means." Fletch had changed T-shirts. He had hoped his own, pure T-shirt, left outside his shorts, had covered the advertisements.

"You put your finger on it," Nancy said. "Growing up, my father and I ignored each other. He wasn't interesting. When I got older, I learned contempt for him. 'Brilliant legal practitioner.' Bullshit. He was a crook. When he put Mother away, had her legally committed to a home for the mentally unwell, I absolutely despised him. I never spoke to him again, or voluntarily saw him again. Sorry. I didn't tell the exact truth, before. I hate the son of a bitch."

"Oh."

"Mother didn't need to be thrown out of her home. Confined to an institution, however swank and gentle. She's just pixilated."

Fletch remembered Mrs. Habeck looking down at her green sneakers and saying, *I don't have any privacy.*

"Pixilated," Nancy repeated. "Year after year, Dad left her alone in that house. No one wanted to know her. At first, she tried to get out, go do things, you know, join the Flower Club. The other ladies didn't want her. Some sensational case of my father's would be in the newspaper, a small editorial outcry about Donald Habeck getting a not-guilty verdict for some rapist. And Mother's flower arrangements wouldn't get into the show. Her phone wouldn't ring. Once, when I was a teenager and getting independent, Mother marched downtown and got herself a job behind the counter in a florist's shop. My father put a stop to that, quick enough. Poor, damned soul. She moldered alone in that house. Talked to herself. She began setting the dining-room table for luncheon and dinner parties, for six people, eight people, a dozen. There were no people." Tears streamed down Nancy's face. Her voice sounded dry. "What could I do? I went home as much as possible. She used to go to six different hairdressers in one day, just to have people to talk to. Her hair was getting burned out. Then she took to spending all day in the shopping malls, buying everything in the world, lawn mowers, washing machines, towels. There were about twenty washing machines delivered to the house one week. When she was being packed up to go to the Agnes Whitaker Home, it was discovered she had over two thousand pairs of shoes! She liked to talk to the salespeople, you see."

Fletch took the exit for Tomasito. "Does she escape from the home often?"

"Almost every day. At first the institution staff would be alarmed and call me, I suppose call my father. Scold her when she came back. But she's harmless. She has no money, no credit cards. I have no idea how she gets around. Have never been able to figure that out. On nice days, I guess she goes and sits in the park, walks around the stores pretending she's buying things, goes back to her old home and sits by the pool."

"Yeah. That's where she was yesterday."

"She must appear to Jasmine as sort of the Ghost of the First Wife," Nancy laughed. "So what. She turns up at my house two or three times a week. Sits and watches the television. Sits and watches the children. Tells them absolutely crazy things, like about the time she made friends with a great black bear in the woods, and the bear taught her how to fish. The children adore her."

"And she loves the children?"

"How do I know? She keeps showing up."

"And you don't think this woman should have been confined?"

Nancy's jaw tightened. "I don't think she should have been left in isolation for years. I don't think she should have been socially ostracized. No. I don't think she should have been thrown out of her home. When strange symptoms began appearing, I don't think my father needed to continue what he was doing. They could have retired, started another life somewhere. Or, if it was too late, some sort of a paid housekeeper-nurse could have been hired to stay with her, give her some company." Nancy was silent for a long moment, the muscles in her jaw working. Then she said, "My father got rid of her through some legal trickery, divorce and confinement, because he wanted to marry pea-brained Jasmine."

"You don't like Jasmine, of course."

"Like her?" Nancy looked across the car at Fletch. "I feel sorry for her. The same thing is happening to her as happened to my mother."

They went down a ramp from the freeway onto a two-lane road through fairly decent farmland.

Nancy said, "I heard on the television this morning that someone confessed to my father's murder."

"Yes," Fletch said. "Stuart Childers. A client of your father's. Accused of murdering his brother. Acquitted two or three months ago."

"So?" Nancy said.

"He was released by the police immediately. I don't know why."

Nancy said, "What are you getting at, friend?"

"I don't think it was a gangland slaying," Fletch said, "despite the suggestion in this morning's *News-Tribune*."

"You think I did it?"

"Someone in the family heard your father intended, or said he intended, to dispose of all his worldly goods, for reasons sacred or profane. Incidentally, my source reported that your father said, last week, that no one gave 'a tin whistle' for him. His words."

Nancy snorted. "I suppose that's true."

"Someone decided to do him in before he decided to do the family out. You, your husband. Your mother, for your sake or the sake of your kids. Your father's second wife."

"You don't understand Tom."

"He may be the important poet, the intellectual you say he is. But where was he Monday morning?"

"At the university."

"What time is his first class on Mondays?"

Nancy hesitated. "Two in the afternoon."

"Okay."

"Poverty is important to Tom. The fact that he, his work is being scorned. It makes the sacrifice more real, the poetry," she stuttered, "most significant, monumental."

"You weren't brought up in squalor," Fletch said. "Your daddy may not have bounced you on his knee, but you had a stocked refrigerator in a clean home, with a swimming pool in the garden. Plus a lot of washing machines."

"Frankly, friend, I don't want a penny from my father. People are still getting mugged, raped, and murdered because my father took their money."

"Ah, the beauty of violence!" Fletch said. "You've got five kids crawling around the floor. You said you are headed for Starvation Lane. Not many mothers let their kids starve, if there's an alternative."

After a moment, Nancy said, "Monday morning I was home alone with the kids."

"Great witnesses. Got any other?"

"No."

Fletch slowed as they passed a sign saying THE MONASTERY OF ST. THOMAS. He turned right through the gates.

"There's a guard at the gates to the *News-Tribune* parking lot," he said. "Checking cars. I see someone, knowing your father was going to the newspaper that morning to arrange for the announcement of his giving away his fortune, walking into the parking lot, shooting him as he was getting out of his car at the back of the lot, and walking out again, unquestioned."

The car was rising on the road through a well-kept forest.

"Who, Mother?"

"She does have her own way of coming and going," Fletch said. "And her own point of view. And what does she have to lose? She's already been committed as insane."

"You haven't mentioned Jasmine."

"I haven't met Jasmine. By the way, your father has a cook now."

"Good. Jasmine has someone to talk to. I doubt she can fry eggs."

"A young wife, possibly about to be left high and dry through her husband's spiritual conversion or his legal trickery . . ."

Atop a gardened knoll ahead of them was a large, stuccoed, Spanish-style building.

"Tom's self-image would be destroyed by our having money," Nancy said. "My mother couldn't focus on anything long enough to do murder. I don't care enough about my father or his money to have murdered him."

"And then there's Robert." Fletch put the car in the gravel car park and turned off the engine.

"Now you're really crazy."

"I'll wait here for you."

Her hand on the car door handle, Nancy didn't move. Again she stared through the windshield at unmoving scenery.

"I'm sorry for you," Fletch said. "This will be tough on both of you. I'll be here."

"No," Nancy said. "Come with me, will you, friend? This place gives me the creeps."

TWENTY-SIX

"Have you been in a monastery before?" Robert Habeck took Fletch by the elbow and steered him toward a backless bench across the small courtyard.

"No," Fletch answered. "The silence is ear-splitting."

"I heard the noise of your car." Robert smiled. It seemed an admonition.

Fletch and Nancy Habeck Farliegh had been shown silently into a small, cool waiting room immediately inside the main door. They sat on a carved wooden bench.

In a few minutes, the abbot entered. He did not greet them, or sit down. Nancy explained she had come to the monastery to tell her brother their father was dead. The abbot nodded and left without uttering a single word.

Waiting, Nancy explained to Fletch that this room and the small, adjacent, high-walled courtyard were the only places females were allowed in the monastery. She had last visited Robert after her first baby was born, almost seven years ago. Since then she had written him once a year, at Christmas. She had never had an answer from him.

They waited a little more than forty-five minutes.

When Robert entered the room, he smiled and held out his hands to his sister. He did not embrace her or kiss her. He did not say anything.

Nancy introduced Fletch as "a friend."

Looking down at Fletch's shorts, Robert asked, "Are you a Quaker?"

"What? No."

Robert's ankle-length white robe was belted by a length of black rope. He wore sandals. He was scrawny and balding. His beard looked like it had been struck by a plague of locusts.

His eyes went from the dull, inward-directed to a more lively substitute for verbal communication.

Following them across the courtyard, Nancy said, "I have five children now, Robert. Tom still teaches at the university, but he's becoming quite well known as a poet. Mother is still at the Agnes Whitaker Home. Physically, she's quite well. We see her often."

Robert sat on the bench, and looked up at them with happy eyes.

Nancy sat beside him.

Fletch sat cross-legged on the ground-stone path in front of them.

"Robert, I have something difficult to tell you." Contrary to everything she had said, Nancy then began to weep. "Father is dead." She sobbed. "He was murdered, shot to death, yesterday, in a parking lot."

Robert said nothing. His eyes became inward-directed. He did not look at, reach out a hand to, touch his sister in any way. He offered her neither sympathy nor empathy.

Desperate to collect herself, Nancy wiped her eyes with the hem of her heavy skirt.

Finally Robert sighed. "So."

"I don't know what's happening about the funeral," Nancy said. "Jasmine . . . the partners . . . Robert, will you come to the funeral?"

"No." He put his hand on the bench and looked around the small courtyard as if he wanted to get up and go away. "Here we are used to death . . . the flowers . . . the farm animals . . . It comes to us here. We need not go out to it."

Fletch asked, "Do you ever get to leave here?"

"Who would want to?"

"Do you ever leave here?"

"Sometimes I go in the truck, to the markets. In the station wagon, to the dentist."

"Do you ever go alone?"

"I am never alone. I carry the Savior with me in my heart."

Nancy put her hand on Robert's hand. "No matter what we thought of him, Robert, it's a shock, it's hard to take, that he was murdered. That someone actually took a gun, and ended his life with it. Stood before him. Shot him."

"Ah, The Great Presumption," Robert said, clearly speaking in capitals. "Why do people keep making The Great Presumption, that we each have the right, moral and legal, to die a natural death? When so many, many of us die by accident, violence, wars, pestilence, famine. . . ."

Nancy glanced at Robert, then looked at Fletch. She moved her hand.

"Well . . ." Fletch said, "your father died of violence."

"Murder makes it seem that someone has corrected God." Robert smiled. "We must believe someone has. But, no. One cannot really correct that which is perfect."

Nancy straightened the hem of her skirt over her knees with shaking hands.

"Robert," Fletch said, "the story is that yesterday morning, your father went to the *News-Tribune* to consult with the publisher, John Winters, about the announcement of your father's intention to donate five million dollars to the art museum. He had had a meeting at the art museum, to discuss this gift. The museum was not sure that it wanted such a gift, as long as your father stipulated that the money be spent exclusively on contemporary religious art."

Robert looked interested.

"Furthermore," Fletch continued, "your father told the curator at the museum that he intended to give the rest of his wealth to a monastery, which he intended to enter, to join."

At first, Robert raised his eyebrows and stared at Fletch.

Then his jaws tightened. He squeezed his eyes shut. Elbows on his knees, hands clutching each other, Robert lowered his head.

Nancy and Fletch glanced at each other.

Finally, Fletch asked, "Are you angry?"

"That man," Robert said through clenched teeth.

Fletch asked, "Was he possibly trying to come to you? His son?"

Looking at Fletch, Nancy's eyes popped.

Robert said, "That man."

Fletch asked, "Do you believe any of what I've just told you?"

For a long moment, Robert sat on the bench silently, apparently holding himself together with effort. He breathed deeply through his nose. "Impossible," he said. His breathing became easier. "Nancy wrote me that my father, after disposing of my mother, institutionalizing her, took a second wife. . . ."

"Jasmine," Nancy said.

Robert's eyes opened. Much of the strain left his face. "I don't suppose she's dead?"

"No," Nancy answered.

"One may not divorce a wife," Robert said, as if elucidating a fine point of law, "for the sake of entering a monastery."

Fletch said, "Oh."

"So all this is not true," Robert said. "Like the rest of my father's life. It is some complicated lie. Even if he were free, months, if not years, of prayerful instruction and reflection would be required."

Fletch looked down at the ground stone between his folded legs. "He had perhaps more than another million dollars to donate to a monastery."

Looking at Fletch, Robert said nothing.

Fletch turned the question. "Robert, you must believe in redemption. Is it totally inconceivable to you that your father could make such a change in his life at the age of sixty, sixty-one?"

"My father," Robert said with difficulty. "My father spent his life shortcutting the law. In fact, short-circuiting it. There is no shortcut to eternal paradise. One cannot short-circuit the laws of God."

Nancy uttered a short laugh. "Robert. You sound so unforgiving."

Finally, Robert turned to his sister. "And are you forgiving?"

"No," she said. "Not of what he did to Mother."

"One never knows," Robert said. "Perhaps the man died within the grace of God. I sincerely doubt it."

Fletch had the impression Robert did not want his father's company either in the monastery, or in paradise.

"What he did to Mother," Robert said. "What he did to all of us."

"What did he do to you?" Fletch asked.

Robert's eyes became as inflamed as the subject's of an El Greco portrait. "He taught us the one thing that must not be taught children, that must not be taught society: that one can commit evil with impunity, if one lies about it successfully." Robert's voice rose. "And do you expect that a person with such a philosophy, such a practice, can ever come to God?" His voice lowered, but his hands, even his shoulders shook. "I am spending all my adult life trying to separate myself from such a wicked belief. It is the one belief which can destroy society. It is the one belief which can corrupt irretrievably a person's soul." Trying to smile at Fletch, Robert asked, "And do you believe a person with such a mind-set could confess, with honesty, and come to God?"

Fletch felt he ought not answer.

Robert modulated his voice. "What he did to us that is unforgivable is that he corrupted us beyond belief."

Fletch stood up from the ground-stone path.

Robert spoke, looking at his callused fingers. "It doesn't matter who killed him. We are all murdered by life, by our own way of life, by how we live. Of course he died a violent death. His life condoned, encouraged violence. We are all victims of ourselves." Nancy was standing up, too. "All that matters is that he died in God's grace. Although I can't believe he did, and is condemned to suffer in hell through all eternity, we will not know. Such was his life; such was his death: all between his Divine Creator and himself."

"Despite the circumstances," Nancy said, straightening her skirt, "it's good seeing you, Robert."

Robert did not rise from the bench. Robert did not answer.

"Right," Fletch said. "Try to get some peace."

Between the waiting room and the monastery's main door, Fletch said to Nancy, "Wait one moment for me, will you?"

He crossed the foyer and entered a small outer office lined with filing cabinets.

He then went through an open door into a larger, well-furnished office, where the abbot sat behind a large, wooden desk. The abbot looked up from some eye-saving pale green papers on his desk.

"Pardon the intrusion," Fletch said.

The abbot didn't say he did, or didn't, pardon the intrusion.

"Robert's father, Donald Habeck, not only died yesterday, he was murdered." There was no response apparent from the abbot. "It is important for us to know if Donald Habeck came and talked with you, recently."

The abbot pondered as if this might be a trick question from the body of scholastic philosophy.

"Yes," the abbot finally said slowly. "Donald Habeck came to see me recently. Yes, we talked."

"More than once?"

The abbot looked at the open door behind Fletch.

"When he came to see you," Fletch asked, "did he also see Robert?"

"To my best knowledge, Robert did not know he was here," the abbot answered.

"Was Robert here yesterday morning?"

"Monday morning? I expect so."

"May I ask the nature of your conversation with Donald Habeck?"

"No."

"You can be subpoenaed," Fletch said.

"You have my address," the abbot answered. "I am always here."

Nancy awaited Fletch in the car.

Before Fletch had the key in the ignition, she said, "I need a beer break. The odor of sanctity makes me want to puke."

TWENTY-SEVEN

"Cecilia's Boutique. Cecilia speaking. Have you considered jodhpurs?"

"Good afternoon," Fletch said. "I ordered a pair of jodhpurs for my wife, this morning. A color you don't have in stock?"

"There's a color we don't have in stock?"

"Special order. Green, white, and black stripes, vertical at the thighs and calves, horizontal at the knees."

"We certainly don't have that in stock."

"It's all right. I understand. You're a small shop. Can't have all the jodhpurs in the world in stock."

"I thought we did," Cecilia said beguilingly.

"I told the salesgirl, who said her name was Barbara, that I'd call her this afternoon with my wife's exact size."

"That would be Barbara Ralton."

"May I speak with her, please?"

"Of course."

After a pause, Barbara said, "Hello?"

"Hiya, sweetie."

"Fletch? How did you get through to me?"

"I lied. But it's all right. I can forgive myself. When people are corrupt enough to oblige lies, I oblige them."

"Where are you?"

"In the only bar in Tomasito."

"Tomasito? What are you doing there?"

"Having a lukewarm beer."

"You went a long way for a beer."

"Listen, Barbara, I won't be able to have dinner with you and your mother tonight. There are things I still have to do."

"You promised."

"I promise for tomorrow night."

"That will leave only two days till the wedding."

"Absolute promise."

"Fletch, did you hear on the radio that the police released the man who confessed to Habeck's murder?"

"Yes."

"Oh, no. That's why you're in Tomasito! That's why you're going to be late tonight! The week we get married, you are determined to get yourself fired over that Habeck story!"

"Barbara? I had another assignment from the *News-Tribune*. But, you know, somehow or other the rug got pulled out from under my feet on it."

"The travel story. What has Cindy got to do with a travel story?"

"You can go a long way with Cindy. How did she like the ski outfit?"

"She liked it. I bought it. Cindy has excellent taste in sportswear."

"I'll say. Er, Barbara, do you have any idea what Cindy does for a living?"

"Yeah. She works for one of those diet-health spas. Which is why I was so surprised to see she had a banana split for lunch. I guess she can take such a thing, but she sets people like me a real bad example."

"She works it off, I guess. One way or another."

"I forget which spa she works for. One of the fancy ones, downtown, I think."

"Do you think she might be gay?"

"Cindy? Lesbian? No way. I've seen her out with lots of men."

"I'm sure you have."

"Cindy's real nice."

"Yes, she is. See you tonight."

"You are coming to the beach house?"

"Absolutely. I'll just be late. You might put some curtains up in the bedroom."

"Don't you like getting it up early?"

"Not that early."

TWENTY-EIGHT

"Hey! Damn it all! Open up!" Again Fletch pounded on the door. Again he looked to the street corner. Again he tried the doorknob. Again he read the sign: EMERGENCY EGRESS ONLY. MAIN ENTRANCE AROUND CORNER. AGNES WHITAKER HOME. He was about to sprint again. He banged the door one more time with his fist. "Hey!"

It opened.

Inside, on the cement floor, were green sneakers.

"I saw you through the window," Mrs. Habeck said. "You'd better come in."

Fletch entered quickly and closed the door behind him.

"Why was that policeman chasing you?" Mrs. Habeck asked.

"Damned if I know." Fletch breathed deeply. "Just after I parked, about five blocks from here, this cop jumped out of his car, yelled at me, and started chasing me. His partner got stuck in traffic. Thanks for letting me in."

"You certainly had a good lead on him," Mrs. Habeck said admiringly. "Of course, you're dressed for running. If it's the police's job to catch people, why don't they wear shorts and sneakers too?"

In the utility hall where they stood, her flowered dress seemed particularly bright.

Fletch said, "I don't know your first name."

"Why should you?" Mrs. Habeck turned and led him through a door and along a corridor. "I've been awaiting you, you'll see. But now you're late. They'll be setting supper for us soon. A ridiculously early hour, I know, but, as you know, institutions set out their three meals within the same eight-hour workday. As a result, some institutionalized people are too fat; some are too thin: none can outrun a policeman, I'm sure."

They went into a large room at the front of the building.

A television at the back of the room played a quiz-game show for three depressed-looking people. A man in a full suit sat at a bridge table, mulling over a hand of cards. The three empty positions at the table had cards neatly stacked in front of them. At the side of the room, a young woman in jeans and a T-shirt that said PROPERTY I. C. U. ATHLETIC DEPT. worked a computer terminal.

Fletch and Mrs. Habeck sat in chairs in a front corner of the room. She had an excellent view of the street from her window.

"My name is Louise," she said.

"Is that what you friends call you?"

"Don't have any friends," Louise Habeck said. "Never have, since I was married. My husband's friends genuinely didn't like us, you see. None of our friends did. Your shorts ask if I want a friend. Well, I did want a friend, at one time. It's like wanting a cup of tea in a desert. I'm sure you know what that's like. After a while of not having a cup of tea, it becomes all right. You stop wanting it." She lifted a large, brown, paper shopping bag from the floor beside her chair and put it in Fletch's lap. "I've been nothing less nor more than Mrs. Habeck for a good long time now."

In the bag, neatly folded, were his jeans, T-shirt, undershorts, and socks. They smelled clean. At the bottom of the bag, he could feel his sneakers.

"You did wash my clothes for me!"

"I said I would."

"My favorite sneakers!"

"My, they made an amusing noise going 'round in the dryer. The noise a camel might make, after having been trained for an Olympic track event."

He changed from his new, white sneakers to his old, dirty, holey sneakers.

She watched him wriggle his toes in them.

"You might have been able to run away from the policeman even faster, if you'd been wearing those." Outside the window, the policeman stood, arms akimbo, on the curb. "My husband, of course, always wore black shoes. Somehow or other, he always managed to wander away in black shoes."

They watched the police car come down the street, make a U-turn, and pick up the policeman.

"I honestly don't know what the policeman's chasing me was all about," Fletch said. "Maybe I should have stopped and asked, but there's a lot I want to do yet today."

"I love the way you arrive places," she said. "Yesterday, reeking of bourbon. Today, chased by a cop. Reminds me of no one whatsoever."

"You depart places pretty well." He remembered her disappearing yesterday with his clothes.

"Oh, yes," she agreed. "Once you're put out of your own home because you're too much trouble, after that, you know, departing anywhere becomes easy. Like not wanting a cup of tea."

"Tea," he said. "Yes."

"Sorry I can't offer you any," she said. "All these people around here dressed in white are not paid to fetch and carry." A large man dressed in white was now standing just inside the recreation-room door. "They make that quite clear when you first arrive. They're paid to stand around like dolts and grimace." She grimaced at the large dolt. He didn't see her. His eyes were totally bloodshot. "Scat!" she said to him. "Go set supper!"

The well-dressed bridge player put down his hand, took the seat to his left, and picked up that hand.

"I'll be a cup of tea," Fletch said.

She smiled and nodded with understanding.

"Tell me," Fletch said gently. "Do you know by now your ex-husband is dead?"

She laughed. She slapped her knee. "That would make him ex enough! Ex-pired!"

Again, in her presence, Fletch did not know if he ought to laugh.

He cleared his throat. "I've spent today visiting your family."

"You're trying to discover who done Donald in!" she said gleefully.

"Well, I'm trying to get the story. Trying to understand . . ."

"There's no understanding Donald. Never was. If he himself told me he was dead, I'd wait for the obituary, before believing it."

"Obituaries," Fletch said solemnly, "are not always to be believed either."

"I hope they had some source for the news of his death other than himself. Or his office."

"They did. He was shot to death. In the parking lot of one of the newspapers."

"He must have a jury deliberating somewhere."

"What do you mean?"

"Donald always calls attention to himself when he knows a jury is going to bring in a positive verdict. He says it's good for business."

"He didn't shoot himself," Fletch said. "The gun wasn't found."

"It wandered away," she said. "Wandered away on black shoes."

"Yes. Okay. Tell me, do you often go back to your old house and sit in the garden? The gardener didn't know you."

"Not often. Usually I don't sit there unless I know no one's there. I'm used to that house being empty, you know. Sometimes Jasmine surprises me. She comes out of the house and sits with me and we talk. She's discovered living with Donald is lonelier than living alone. He wanders away, you know."

"On black shoes. What was special about yesterday?"

"Yesterday? Let me think. Oh, yes, Donald got shot."

"I mean you stayed at the house even though the gardener was there."

"Such a nice day."

"When I met you yesterday, did you know Donald had been killed?"

"I knew it some time. I don't know whether I knew it before or after meeting you. Meeting you didn't seem that significant, originally. You weren't drunk, were you?"

"No."

"You smelled it."

"Did you know before I told you that Donald intended to announce he was giving five million dollars to the museum?"

"I washed your clothes for you. *Bumpity-bumpity-bump!* went the sneakers in the dryer. Exactly like a camel running the four-forty."

The bridge player was now in the fourth position at the table.

"How do you get around, anyway?"

"Vaguely."

"I mean, how do you get around the city? To your daughter's house, to — "

"I sit in an open, empty car. When the driver comes back, from shopping or whatever, I tell him or her where I want to go. They take me."

"Always?"

"Always. I'm a little, old, blue-haired lady in a bright dress and green sneakers. Why wouldn't they? Sometimes they have to go someplace else first. I go, too. The secret is that I'm never in a hurry. And," she noted, "sometimes I get to see places I wouldn't otherwise see."

Fletch frowned. "Your daughter did somewhat the same thing this afternoon."

"Did she? I never explained to her how to do it. She never asked. But, poor dear, she hasn't any money, either."

"I went with your daughter to the Monastery of St. Thomas this afternoon and spoke with Robert."

"That sinner!"

"Why do you say that?"

"Have you ever heard of the sin of omission?"

"No."

"Robert's omitting life in that monastery. I suspect he'd rather be in jail, but he knew his father would prevent his going to jail, no matter what he did. I think some people want to be in jail, don't you?"

"Shooting his father would accomplish two goals, wouldn't it?"

"Splendidly!"

"I think I heard your son, the monk, actually saying something like he doesn't much care if his father goes to hell."

"Oh, we all felt that way about Donald. Didn't you?"

"Didn't know him."

"Not a pity."

"When Nancy was telling Robert their father was dead, she wept."

"Nancy! I brought her up to be such a pretty girl and, for a while there, she was such a whore."

"Was she?"

"She married her college professor, you know. What's his name?"

"Tom Farliegh."

"Yesterday you didn't know his name. Today, you do. You see? You've learned something."

"Not much."

"I try to get his name around, in my own small way."

"Rather a strange man, don't you think?"

"Oh, he's a darling. Very good to me. He publishes my poetry."

"What?"

"Well, he gets it published. Under his own name, of course."

Fletch sat forward. "What?"

"Well, you just indicated you wanted to learn something."

"What are you saying?"

"That little book, *The Knife, The Blood*. Those are my poems."

Fletch stared at the blue-haired lady in the corner of the Agnes Whitaker Home's recreation room. "You do like playing with words."

"Very much," she said firmly. "Very much."

"Ex-pired husband. With sounds. *Hay Ha Haw*."

"They're good poems, aren't they?"

"I think I believe you. The Poetry of Violence written by . . ."

"The few critics who reviewed the poems referred to them as that. 'Poetry of Violence'? I suppose so. Poetry of Truth and Beauty. I don't like labels."

"Your writing those poems changes the meaning of them altogether."

"Does it? It shouldn't."

"It changes the perspective. *The sidewalks of the city/Offer up without pity/Old ladies to be mugged*. If you think a young man wrote that, it seems cruel. But if you know a sixty-year-old woman wrote it —"

"I don't know about criticism. I know Tom needed to publish something, to keep himself employed at that university. His own poems wander around on black shoes like Donald. Never can get ahold of them. So verbose they should be verboten. Well, they are forbidden, essentially. Couldn't get them published. So I gave him mine. He has my five grandchildren to support."

"My God. Life is crazy."

"Interesting thought."

"Tom talks as if he wrote those poems!"

"He's supposed to. It's a secret, you see. Even Nancy doesn't know. You mentioned perspective. Who'd publish the poems of a little old lady in a private mental home? Tom is a university professor. If he presents something to a publisher, at least it will be read. Right? I can't help it if the world's perspective is crazy."

"When people are corrupt enough to oblige lies, you oblige them."

"Tom's working on the second volume now. I'm helping him. It's very difficult for him, you see. When a person has to lecture almost every day in fifty-minute lumps, it must be nearly impossible for him to think in terms of a simple, concise line, each word pulling more than its own weight, a cadence that works in the briefest moment. Don't you think?"

"I have no idea."

"But you see, I, on the other hand, have lived more or less in silence. A silence so profound that when a sound, a word emerges into it, I realize it in the most complete sense, hear it, feel it, touch it, taste it, turn it over and over, in its isolation, in my isolation. Sound, to Tom, in his busy life, with five children, must be resisted, somewhat. Sound to me is cherished, and I coax it into fullness, into meaning."

"Explored, exploited, explained, exploded," Fletch said. "Expired."

"I do think I've identified for Tom a previously unadmitted, shall we say? source of beauty. He's getting the hang of it. Pretty soon some of these poems will be entirely his." Louise Habeck looked around the recreation room. "And pretty soon it will be time for supper."

"There's a story I've heard," Fletch said slowly, "that Donald Habeck was taking a turn for the religious."

"Donald was always religious," Louise Habeck said.

"No one else seems to think so."

Louise Habeck shrugged.

"He was a liar," Fletch said. "A paid liar, a professional liar. You yourself said you wouldn't believe him if he told you he was dead."

"A liar has a regard for the truth such as the rest of us do not have," Louise Habeck said. "A liar believes that truth is somehow difficult, mysterious, mystical, mythical, unobtainable, to be pursued. I'll bet you that while Demosthenes was wandering the earth, searching for an honest man, he was selling gold bricks on the side and cheating his landlords. To the rest of us, truth is as obvious, as common, as plain, as a simple poem."

"Would you believe Donald would retire into a monastery?"

"Oh, yes. It would be just like him. Just what he would do. He was forever poring over religious tracts, books of sermons, proofs of this and that."

"How could his children not know that?"

"They know nothing about him, other than what they read in the newspapers. Nobody did. After you read about Donald in the newspapers, you don't want to know him."

"Did he ever take instruction in any religious faith?"

"All of them. That's how he spent most of his evenings. That's why I never saw him. The children never saw him. Never knew him."

"Listen," Fletch said softly, "Donald Habeck had a mighty unusual lady we both know committed to a mental institution."

"Yes," Louise Habeck said. "Me. It was very kind of Donald, very correct. Living here is much nicer than living with him. I get to watch other people eat. All of the people here" — she waved her arm around the room — "are better company than Donald was. I come and go as I please. People give me rides. They talk to me, usually. I tell them stories about Peru. And Donald was right: I was buying rather too many washing machines and lawn mowers."

"Have you ever been to Peru?"

"No, but neither have they."

"Mrs. Habeck, your son is a monk who can't find peace. Your daughter and grandchildren live in squalor. Your son-in-law is a pudgy impostor."

"What does that have to do with Donald?"

"Donald could have helped them, gotten help for them, at least have been accessible to them, tried to know them, see them."

Louise Habeck stared at the floor between them for a long moment. "Donald wandered away," she said, "after God. I hated him for it." Somewhere in the building a soft gong sounded. Her eyes rose to meet his. "The poetic irony would be," she said, "if Donald were shot before he could escape his life of lies."

"Did you shoot him?"

She smiled. "At least now I know where he is."

People were hurrying out of the room.

"Come on," she said. "I'll show you out the side door. It's much simpler than going through all that rigamarole at the front door. Your not signing in would confuse your signing out."

"Thanks for doing my laundry," he said, following her. "Although your delivery system leaves something to be desired."

Walking down the corridor ahead of him, she said, "Washing your clothes, I came to love you."

At the EMERGENCY EGRESS ONLY, Fletch said, "Okay if I come by someday and take you for a cup of tea?"

Louise Habeck shook her head. "I doubt I'll be thirsty."

TWENTY-NINE

Fletch rang several times and waited several minutes but no one answered the door at 12339 Palmiera Drive. The sun was lowering. It was getting cooler. There were no cars in the driveway, no wreath on the front door. Louise Habeck was in a home for the mentally unwell. Robert Habeck was fretting in a monastery. Nancy Habeck was living in squalor with a husband who was a fraud. And Donald Habeck was dead, murdered.

And Jasmine?

Fletch backed up from the front door and looked up at the curtain that had moved as he was leaving that morning.

It moved again.

He smiled, waved at the curtain, turned, and walked to his car at the curb.

As he was getting into his car, the front door at 12339 Palmiera Drive opened. The silhouette in the door was as the gardener had drawn it in the dirt.

Fletch closed his car door and started back up the flagstone path.

She came down the steps to the walk. Behind her, the door closed.

"Oh, damn," she said. "I just locked myself out."

"Are you Jasmine?"

She nodded. She was older than she looked at a distance. Older, heavier, face more scarred by cosmetics, eyebrows more plucked, hair more dyed.

"My name is Fletcher. I work for the *News-Tribune.*"

"How am I going to get back into the house?"

"Cook's not here?"

"I couldn't pay her. She went."

"Why did you come out?"

"I was curious." Jasmine was wearing an unmournful, low-cut, yellow sweater blouse, lime-green slacks, spike-heeled shoes. "That bundle of clothes you dropped off this morning. They were Donald's clothes."

"Sorry I couldn't have them cleaned before I dropped them off."

"Are they part of the investigation?"

"No."

"I mean, I know they weren't the clothes he was, uh, dead in."

"No. They were just his clothes. I was returning them."

"Oh." That seemed to satisfy her. She looked worriedly at the house.

"Jasmine, I'm puzzled."

"Aren't we all. I mean, really!"

"Did Donald discuss giving five million dollars to the museum with you?"

"No."

"Not at all? He never mentioned it to you?"

"Not a peep. To the museum? I read in the paper he was planning to give money away to somebody."

"Did he ever mention religious art to you? Show you any?"

"I don't even know what it is. Religious art? I thought only people could be religious."

"Did he ever talk about religion to you?"

"No. Lately he's been reading big books instead of sleeping. Big novels."

"Did he ever mention to you his visiting the monastery in Tomasito?"

"Where his son is? No. I've never been there."

"Did he ever suggest to you that he might like to enter a monastery?"

Her eyes widened. "No!"

Fletch too looked at the house. "So. We're all puzzled."

"He lived like a monk," she said. "Up all night, reading. *War and Peace. The Brothers Karaminski.*"

Fletch's eyes narrowed. "Harm no more?" he said. "Something like that. Go away and do no more harm?"

"Yeah," she said. "He said something like that. Two or three times." She shrugged. "I never knew what he was talking about. When he talked."

"He never mentioned going away with you?"

"No. Why should he?"

Fletch shook his head. "I get less puzzled for a second, and then more puzzled. You are Jasmine Habeck, aren't you?"

"No. The newspaper was wrong about that."

"Your name is Jasmine?"

"Only sort of. We never married. Donald never divorced his first wife. Louise. Have you met her?"

Fletch heard himself saying, "Yuss."

"Sort of weird lady. Sort of nice, really. She'd sit and say nothing for the longest while, and then she'd ask. 'Jasmine, what do you think of the word *blue*?' and I'd say, 'I don't think about the word *blue* all that much,' and then she'd say something really weird like, 'Blue Donald blew away in a blue suit.' Really! Very strange."

"I'm becoming less puzzled."

"That's good."

"You were just living here as his friend?"

"Well, sort of I had to, you see." She shifted on her heels. "Maybe you can tell me what to do."

"Try me."

She took a step closer to him. "I'm in the Federal Witness Program, you see."

"Oh."

"I testified in a trial in Miami against some bad guys, for the government. They really weren't bad guys, I didn't think so, they had lots of money, and didn't care whether it was day or night. But they were in trouble, and the government said I should help them out, testify against them, or I could go to prison, too, and I hadn't done anything bad, taken a few jewels from Pete" — she pointed to a turquoise ring on her finger — "my favorite fur, so I said, 'Sure,' hung around a long, long time, went to court and answered all sorts of dumb questions about seeing the naked women working in the coke-cutting factory, things like that, you know? So I was to be protected by the federal government. You think I should call someone in Washington?"

"What did all that have to do with Donald Habeck?"

"Nothing. I was in this lawyer's office in Miami, and Donald came in to see a friend. At that time they were going to send me to St. Louis when I was done, and my girl friend, this Hispanic *chanteuse*, said that's where the Bibles are printed and it's awfully muggy there, and that didn't sound like me. Donald invited me for a drink. Two days later I came back here with him. We was never married." She concluded with, "My real name isn't Jasmine, of course."

"Of course."

"No one's is, I think."

"I suspect not."

"I mean, have you ever actually met anyone named Jasmine?"

"Never before. Not even now, I guess."

"That's why I chose it. If I had to go be anoniminous, at least I wanted an outstanding name. Wouldn't you?"

"I suppose so."

"So what should I do now Donald's dead? Call someone in Washington, or what?"

"What federal officer did you deal with in Miami?"

"That's the trouble. I can't think of his name. It was either John or Tom."

"What about Habeck's partners? Do they know you are in the Federal Witness Program?"

"I don't think so. I think they thought I was Mrs. Habeck Part Two. The few times we were together they never spoke to me. I mean, except for, 'Get me a drink, will you, Jasmine?' Pete and those guys were much nicer. At least they knew I was a woman, you know what I mean? They didn't treat me as no equal, for God's sake. I'm glad I came out here with Donald before I finished testifyin' against them."

"I see." Fletch looked at a few of his toes through the tops of his sneakers. "So you're sitting here without any money, any friends. . . ."

"Yeah. I want a friend."

"You're not Donald Habeck's widow, you're not even Jasmine. . . ."

"I'd be little Miss Nobody, 'cept I was married twice once."

"Do you have any idea of Donald's plans for you, if he went away, if he went into a monastery?"

"I had no idea he was going into a monastery. It must have come over him sudden like. I had a girl friend like that. Suddenly it overcame her to be a WAC."

"I guess we'd better get you in touch with some federal officer here in town."

"I thought of talking to the mailman about it. Well, I mean . . . really."

"Someone will call you."

"Plus, I'm locked out of the house." She turned around and looked at the quiet brick house floating on rhododendrons. "My fur is in there."

He started toward the house with her. "Is there a burglar alarm? I didn't notice."

"No. Isn't that stupid? Think of a big criminal lawyer like that, and his house don't even have a burglar alarm. He should have known some of the guys I knew!"

"I think he did, Jasmine. I think he knew all of them."

THIRTY

"I see someone's arse sticking up from the bushes!" Definitely, that was Frank Jaffe's voice. No other voice was that gravelly. "And on that arse is written 'Ben Franklyn Friend Service'!"

In the dark, in the bushes in front of the *News-Tribune*, momentarily Fletch wondered if he went all the way in his imitation of an ostrich and stuck his head into the ground he would disappear entirely from view.

Instead, he stood up and turned around. He had not realized he had moved so far into the building's security lights.

" 'Evening, Frank. Time you'd gone home."

"Oh, it's you!" Frank Jaffe exclaimed in mock surprise. "Don't you think we've given that particular institution of physical excess enough free advertising this week?"

"Yes. I do."

"Then why are you in front of the *News-Tribune* building waving a flag at passing traffic advertising their services?"

The manila envelope and the pencil Fletch had taken from his car were on the ground behind the bushes.

"That's not really what I'm doing, Frank."

"What else are you doing?"

"I'm looking for a gun, Frank."

"You're looking for your gum?"

"Okay."

"How could you drop your gum way over there in the bushes?"

Fletch held up his index finger. "Don't you feel that wind?"

"You were trying to throw up in the bushes," Frank accused.

"No, I wasn't."

"You were trying to catch a buggerer?"

"Frank . . ."

"Besides advertising their services across your arse, have you penetrated any deeper into the whorehouse story?"

"I wanted to talk to you about that, Frank."

"Clearly you've exposed yourself. Are we going to expose them?"
"Frank, I think the story is going to take a little longer than we originally thought."
"Ah," said Frank. "Really getting involved, are you, boy?"
"Something unpredictable has happened . . . a setback . . ."
"Discovered you really dig this assignment, that it? Getting your bones ground at office expense, who wouldn't? Ah, Fletch, I wish all the employees at the *News-Tribune* threw themselves into their work as enthusiastically as you do! I knew you'd like this assignment, once you got into it!"
"I threw myself into it, all right, Frank —"
"That's my boy!"
"Trouble is, you see, this girl, Cindy —"
"Now, I'll bet, even *you're* asking yourself why you're getting married Saturday!"
"Well, you see, Barbara —"
"Carry on, Fletcher, whatever you're doing. But, please! The publisher and I would both appreciate it if, in keeping your chin up, you keep your arse down!"
"All right, Frank."
"Good night, Fletch."
"Good night, Frank."

THIRTY-ONE

"Is Lieutenant Gomez in?"
The counter in the lobby of the police station was so high it made even a helpful citizen feel like a humble miscreant.
"Why do you want to know?" the desk sergeant asked.
"I want to talk to him," Fletch said. "I want to give him something."
"Leave it with me. I'll see that he gets it."
The sign on the desk said SERGEANT WILHELM ROHM.
"I'd like to talk to him: Is he in?"
"What's in the big envelope?" Sergeant Rohm read the advertisement on Fletch's clothes.
"What I want to give him."
"Delivery service from a whorehouse; that's pretty good. What's in

the envelope, handsome? A case of clap for the lieutenant? It won't be his first."

"A gun."

"Used?"

"I think so."

"I'll give it to him."

"He's not in?" The sergeant took the envelope and felt the contents. "Don't mess up the prints," Fletch said.

"Ah, a junior G-man," the sergeant said. "I can see you're used to working under covers."

"At least let me write the lieutenant a note."

"Sure." The sergeant slid a turned-over booking sheet and a ballpoint pen across the desk. "Write anything you want, stud. We just love full confessions. Sometimes even the lawyers find them an obstacle to getting their clients acquitted."

"Why was Stuart Childers released?"

"What's that got to do with you?"

"Curious."

"Stuart Childers is always released. He comes in here once a day. Sometimes twice. He confesses to any murder he hears about on the radio. Also robbery, arson, and aggravated littering. He must have really gotten a kick out of his day in court. Wants to play defendant again."

Fletch wrote:

Lieutenant Gomez:

Your search for the Habeck murder weapon couldn't have been extensive. Guard checking cars at News-Tribune *parking lot gate indicates murderer walked into and out of parking lot. I followed logical walking path from back of parking lot, where Habeck was murdered, to street, and found this gun in the bushes in front of* News-Tribune *building tonight. I lifted it with pencil through trigger ring, so prints should be complete. Also look forward to ballistics report. Tell your pal, Biff Wilson, I'm always glad to be of assistance. Clearly he needs help writing obituaries.*

I. M. Fletcher

"You writing your life's story?" The desk sergeant was trying to ignore a weeping black lady at the other end of the counter. "I'd love to know what it is you male whores do that's worth paying for. Nobody's ever offered to pay me."

Fletch handed him the folded note. "Put this in the envelope with the gun, will you?"

"Sure, stud. I'll take care of it." He put the note on top of the envelope.

"Please," Fletch said. "It's important."

"Sure, stud, sure. Now why don't you get out of here before I throw you in a cell where you'll get to do whatever you do for free?"

THIRTY-TWO

"What are you two doing, playing *Uncle Wiggily in Connecticut?*"

"Yeah." Cindy quoted: " 'I was a nice girl, wasn't I?' "

Barbara and Cindy were in lounge chairs on the deck of the beach house. The small, round table between them held their glasses, a half-empty bottle of Scotch, and an ice bucket.

"A banana split for lunch and Scotch at night," Fletch said. "Better be careful you don't go to hell, Cindy."

She stretched her arms. "That's okay. I'm retiring real soon."

"Yeah," Fletch said. "You're going to the dogs."

There was a quarter moon over the ocean. Far out to sea a good-sized freighter was moving south.

"Have a drink," Barbara said. "Join us."

"Yeah," Cindy said, "you've had a long day, I think, getting a job this morning, when you already had one, then a business lunch . . ."

"You don't know the half of it."

"A discouraging day, too, I think," Barbara said.

"Yeah, yeah," Cindy said. "Discouraging, presenting yourself so well at the job interview, then being discovered a liar, an impostor, so quickly at lunch."

The women laughed.

In the kitchen Fletch half-filled a glass with tap water.

"Poor Fletch," Barbara said. On the deck he added Scotch and ice to the water in his glass. "He was so discouraged he drove himself all the way to Tomasito, just for a drink."

"A warm beer," he muttered. "What's to eat?"

"Nothing," Barbara said. "Remember, you canceled dinner with my mother."

"We haven't eaten," said Cindy.
"It's ten o'clock," Fletch said.
"We've been talking," said Cindy. "Story of my life."
"Maybe you'll go for pizza," said Barbara.
Fletch sat in the chair near the railing. "So Cindy . . . Did you ruin my prospects for employment? Did you tell Marta I'm an impostor? That I'm not really a male whore but rather an honest journalist out to screw the Ben Franklyn Friend Service?"
"I thought about it," Cindy said. "I thought a lot about what to do. This afternoon my clients didn't get my undivided attention. Seeing I wasn't controlling the situation as well as I should have been, one guy came on real strong. I had to make an accident to cool him off. One of the lift bars swung against his nose accidentally-on-purpose." She was dressed as she had been at lunch, in a short kilt and loafers. "It's okay. No blood got on the rug."
"You were ready with a towel," Fletch guessed.
"I'm always ready with a towel. Men are always spilling one fluid or another."
Barbara took a gulp of her drink.
"Did you tell Marta, or not?" Fletch asked.
"I decided either I had to tell Marta who you are and screw you," Cindy said, "or tell Barbara who I am, and screw Marta."
"A tough decision." Fletch watched Barbara. "So you've told Barbara, your old friend, who you are, what you do for a living . . . et cetera?"
"Yeah."
Fletch asked Barbara, "How do you feel about that?"
Barbara didn't answer immediately. "I guess I understand. I'm more surprised at myself, than anything."
"What do you mean?"
"That I could have a friend and really know so little about her. It makes me doubt myself, my own sensitivity, my own perceptions." For a moment Barbara looked into the glass she held in her lap. "This is difficult to explain. I mean, now I'm wondering who the hell you are, Fletch, the guy I'm going to marry in three days. What don't I know about you? How good are my perceptions?"
"Jitters," Cindy said.
"Today," Fletch said, "I discovered things about a few people I would never have guessed. I added some real interesting people to my collection."
"I mean, here we go along in life assuming everybody is more or less as he or she appears to be, as he or she say they are. Forgive my bad grammar. Enough of that he-or-she shit. And, wham-mo, in one

minute over a drink or something you discover they've been living this whole life, having thoughts, doing things, being someone you never knew about, never even dreamed possible."

Cindy said, "I think with orthodontics and psychiatry, health care, clothing fashions, too, with the great American idealization of normalcy, which doesn't exist, people think they want to love people similar to themselves."

"All that's the mother of prejudice," said Barbara. "Economics is the father."

"It's the differences between people that we ought to love," said Cindy.

"If we were just exactly what people think we are," Fletch said, "we wouldn't have much of ourselves to ourselves, would we?"

"Yeah," Cindy giggled. "Hypocrisy is our last bastion of privacy."

"My." Barbara waved her glass in front of her mouth. "Pour a little booze into this trio and we pick up a philosophical text fast enough, don't we?"

"It wasn't much of a decision," Cindy said. "I'm leaving Ben Franklyn Friday. I don't mind letting the Ben Franklyn Friend Service know I have a sting in my tail."

Fletch said, "And there's Marta's fondness for Carla. . . ."

Cindy smiled at him. There was light coming through the window from the living room. "The human element is in everything we do. Isn't that what we're talking about?" She plopped two ice cubes into her glass. "Anyway, that's no way to run a business. People should not be allowed to win career advancement in bed."

Barbara giggled into her glass. "You're talking about a whorehouse here, Cindy! I'm sorry, old pal, but that's funny."

"My business has less to do with sex than you think," Cindy said.

"I'm sure."

"So what have you really decided?" Fletch asked.

"I've decided to help you get your story," Cindy said. "Let's expose Ben Franklyn."

"Great!"

"It will be my wedding present to you and Barbara. I was going to give you a collie when you came back from your honeymoon. . . ."

"A collie!" Barbara exclaimed. "If Fletch doesn't keep his job, we won't be able to feed ourselves!"

"Tell me what you need," Cindy said to Fletch.

"I need to know who owns the Ben Franklyn Friend Service."

"Something called Wood Nymph, Incorporated."

"That's beautiful."

"Nymphs would," Barbara giggled.

"Who owns Wood Nymphs?" Fletch asked.

"I have no idea."

"Nymphomaniacs always would," Barbara said. "Isn't that the point?"

"I need to know that. I need to know specifically and graphically what services you provide, and the specific fees for those services."

"I can tell you that right now."

"Please don't," Barbara said. "Not while I'm drinking."

"I'll need some sort of a deposition from you regarding the performances you put on for voyeurs. And that the man frequently doesn't know he's being watched, that his ass is being sold."

"Oh, charming!" said Barbara.

"Also, a description of the whole escort service, that you're really operating as call girls, call people. The parties at which you have performed, how that works, how much it costs. The whole blackmail thing, the cameras —"

"Cameras!" clucked Barbara. "Hypocrisy is the last bastion of privacy."

"Listen," Fletch said to Barbara, "a week ago you suggested you and I get married naked in front of everybody."

"I was kidding."

"Were you?"

"I thought I could lose eight pounds."

"Can you get all that by tomorrow?" Fletch asked Cindy.

"I'll try."

"Pizza," Barbara said. "I am feeling a distinct need for pizza."

Cindy looked fully at Fletch and asked, "What about a list of our clients?" She watched him closely as she waited for his answer.

"Sure," he said evenly. "Prostitution can't exist without the johns."

"Will you publish their names?" Cindy asked.

"I don't know," Fletch said. "I honestly don't know. I will present their names for publication."

"Uh!" Cindy said. "It's still a man's world, Master!"

"Will you please go get some pizza, Fletch?" Barbara asked. "Better make mine pepperoni. Right now I don't think I could look an anchovy in the eye."

THIRTY-THREE

"We called ahead," Fletch said to the counterman. "Three pizzas in the name of Ralton."

The sweating counterman did not smile at him. "It will be a few minutes."

The counterman then picked up a phone between two ovens. He dialed a number, and turned his back.

There were six other people waiting for pizzas. Four men, two in shorts, one in work clothes, one in a business suit. A teenaged boy in a tuxedo. A young teenaged girl in shorts, a halter, and purple high-heeled shoes. She also wore lipstick and eye shadow.

"Aren't you afraid of spilling pizza on your dinner jacket?" the man in running shorts asked the teenaged boy.

The boy answered him, apparently courteously, in rapid French.

"Oh," the man said.

Fletch opened the door to the vertical refrigerator and took out a six-pack of 7-Up. He put it on the counter.

"Schwartz?" the counterman called.

The boy in the tuxedo paid for his pizza and left.

The man in working clothes got his pizza next. Then one of the men in shorts. A woman in tennis whites entered and gave the name Ramirez. The young girl clicked out of the store on her high heels carrying her pizza like a tray of hors d'oeuvres.

"We must have called a half-hour ago," Fletch said to the counterman. "Name of Ralton?"

Again the counterman did not smile at him. "It will be a few minutes."

The man in the business suit picked up his pizza.

Two policemen strolled in. Their car was parked just outside the front door. They didn't give a name.

They looked at the counterman.

The counterman nodded at Fletch.

The cops jumped at Fletch, spun him around, pushed him.

Fletch found himself leaning against the counter, his hands spread, his feet spread. One cop had his hand on the back of Fletch's neck, forcing his head down. The other's fingers felt through Fletch's T-shirt, his shorts, checked the tops of his athletic socks.

"What did he do?" the man in running shorts asked.

The eyes of the woman in tennis whites widened. She stepped back.

"He was robbing the store," a cop answered.

"He was not!" the man said. "He's been standing here fifteen minutes!"

"He was about to rob the store."

"He gave a name! He was waiting for pizza!"

They pulled Fletch's arms behind his back.

He felt the cool metal of the handcuffs around his wrists, heard the click as they locked.

"He's robbed lots of stores," the cop said. "Liquor stores, convenience stores. Once he got his pizza, he'd rob this store."

"Oh," the man said.

The other cop said, "Even a robber's got to eat, you know."

"He doesn't look like a bad guy," the man in running shorts said. "Fast. You'd never catch him, once he started runnin'."

"Well," a cop said. "We caught him."

The man said to Fletch, "Your name Ralton?"

"No."

"That does it for me," the man said. "He gave the name Ralton. Phony name."

"His name's Liddicoat," said a cop. "Alexander Liddicoat."

"That's probably phony, too," said the man.

"Ramirez?" the counterman called.

The woman in tennis whites paid for her pizza.

"Let's go," the cop said.

Both hanging on to Fletch, they waited for the woman to go through the door with her pizza.

"Can we take my pizza with me?" Fletch asked. "I'll let you have some."

"Thanks anyway," a cop answered. "We just had Chinese take-out."

Outside they put him in the back of the police car carefully and slammed the door.

As they settled in the front seat, the cop in the passenger seat looked at his watch. "Eleven-forty. We take him all the way downtown, we'll never get back in time to go off duty at twelve."

"What's so special about him?"

"Dispatch said take him straight downtown to headquarters."

"Yeah." The driver started the car. "We run a taxi service."

"I could save you the trip," Fletch said. He was trying to fit his handcuffed hands into the small of his back against the car seat. "My name's not Liddi-whatever. I've got identification in my wallet."

"Sure. I bet you have. Might as well get goin', Alf."

"You've got the wrong guy," Fletch said.

The cop in the passenger seat said, "Twelve years on the force and I've never yet arrested the right guy."

The car started forward. "We didn't read him his rights."

The other cop looked through the grille at Fletch.

"You know your rights?"

"Sure."

"That's good. He knows his rights, Alf."

"Cruel and unusual punishment already," Fletch said. "Lettin' a guy smell pizza for fifteen minutes, then not lettin' him have any."

"Tell your lawyer."

The police car bumped over the curb from the pizza store's parking lot onto the road.

Fletch said, "Next stop, the guillotine."

THIRTY-FOUR

"Fletcher?"

On the cell bunk that reeked of disinfectant, Fletch sighed with relief. The guard opening the cell door had called him Fletcher. Confusion regarding who he was was now over. Now he could go to his apartment and get some sleep.

He stood up. He figured it must be about four in the morning.

For about three hours he had lain on his bunk listening to two men, not synchronized, vomiting, one old man whimpering, another singing, for more than an hour, over and over again, the refrain *I'll be blowed, Lucy, if you will. . . .* In the cell next to him, two male streetwalkers argued endlessly and passionately about barbers. One had asked Fletch how to get a job with the Ben Franklyn Friend Service. Fletch answered he didn't know, he was just a bouncer there. Fletch's cellmate was a portly, middle-aged man in white trousers and sandals who said he was a schoolteacher. The afternoon before, he said, he had stabbed one of his students. There was blood on his trousers. After telling Fletch this, he curled on his bunk and fell asleep.

"Come on," the guard said. "Move it."

"Am I free to go?"

He followed the guard between the cells to the steel door.

While he was being booked as Alexander Liddicoat, for more than twenty incidents of armed robbery, Fletch's wallet and watch had been taken from him. Photographs of Alexander Liddicoat were with the warrants. Looking at them upside down, Fletch saw a remote resemblance. While handing it over, Fletch showed the booking officer identification in his wallet, his driver's license and press card, proving who he was. Without really looking at the identification photographs, the booking officer charged him with stealing the wallet of Irwin Maurice Fletcher, as well.

The other side of the steel door, Fletch turned right, toward the stairs to the booking desk and the lobby.

The guard grabbed him by the elbow. "This way, please."

They went to the left, past offices. Most of the doors were open. Lights were on, people working in the offices.

At the end of the corridor, they came to a closed door. The guard opened it with a key. He snapped on the inside light.

Six chairs were around a long conference table. Nothing else was in the room. High up on the far wall was a barred window.

"Wait here," the guard said.

"Why are you holding me?"

The guard closed the door behind him.

Fletch snapped off the light, crawled onto the table in the dark, and fell asleep.

The light snapped on. The door was open.

Lieutenant Gomez was standing over Fletch.

"You make yourself at home wherever you are, don't you?"

Fletch sat up. "What time is it?"

He was cold.

"Five-thirty A.M. The jailhouse swimming pool doesn't open for another half-hour. The mayor and his top aides are down there cleaning it for you now. They know you like to go skinny-dipping every morning."

"Glad to see you." Fletch remained sitting on the table. "You get to work early."

"Working on an important case," Gomez said. "The murder of Donald Edwin Habeck. You know anything about it?"

"Yeah. Read something about it in the newspapers." Fletch yawned and rubbed his eyes. "Did you get the gun?"

"What gun?"

"The gun I left for you last night. I left it upstairs at the desk for you, with a note."

Gomez repeated: "What gun?"

"I think it's the gun used to kill Habeck. I found —"

Gomez looked at the door.

Biff Wilson stood in the door, shaved and suited as well as ever, wrinkled and rumpled.

"Oh, hi, Biff," Fletch said. "Did you bring the coffee?"

Biff snorted. "I guess I was a wise guy once. Was I ever this much of a wise guy, Gomez?"

"You were never a wise guy," Gomez said. "Always the altar boy."

"I thought so." Biff closed the door. "I'm not even sure I remember precisely what it is one does to a wise guy."

"On the police, we break his balls," Gomez offered. "Do all the guys in journalism have balls?"

Biff stood closer to Fletch. "Hi, kid. I heard you were incarcerated."

"Case of mistaken identity," Fletch said. "Robber named Liddicoat. Apparently his picture had been circulated to all the liquor stores, pizza parlors —"

Biff said to Gomez, "Can we make the charge stick awhile?"

"Awhile," said Gomez.

"You can't," Fletch said. "Booking desk has already checked the identity in my wallet. That's how you know I'm here, right?"

"Wallet?" Biff asked Gomez.

"He didn't have a wallet," Gomez said. "Just a stolen wristwatch."

Biff nodded at Fletch.

"We were talking about a gun," Fletch said.

Biff looked at Gomez. "What gun?"

"A gun I found," Fletch said. "Outside the *News-Tribune*. I turned it in to Sergeant Wilhelm Rohm last night, with instructions to give it to Gomez."

"I don't know about a gun," Gomez said.

"You're a good boy." Biff stroked Fletch's leg with the palm of his hand. "A real good boy."

Fletch moved his leg.

"Muscle." Biff dug his fingers into Fletch's thigh. "Look at that muscle, Gomez."

Fletch got off the table and moved away.

"And what do those shorts say?" Biff squinted. "I can't quite read it, can you, Gomez? Some high-school track team?"

"Ben Franklyn Friend Service," said Gomez.

"Football," said Biff. "I think that means a football team."

"That's another story," Fletch said.

"I sure would like to know what you've found out," Biff said.

"Lots," Fletch said. "You write lousy obituaries, Biff."

"Why do you say that, Liddicoat?"

"For one thing, Jasmine and Donald Habeck never married. He never divorced Louise."

"Yeah? What else?"

Fletch looked from Gomez to Wilson and shook his head.

"What else?" Biff asked.

"Have you talked with Gabais yet?"

"Who?"

"Felix Gabais. Child molester. An ex-client of Habeck. Served eleven hard years. Released from prison last week."

"Have you talked with him yet?"

"Not yet."

"You've been bird-doggin' me all week, kid. Talked with everybody in the Habeck family, as far as I know, even the brother in the monastery. You're stealin' our thunder. What for, Liddicoat?"

Again, Fletch shook his head. "This was no gangland slaying, Biff. You're on the wrong track."

"You know better than we do, uh? The newspaper assign you to this story?"

"The museum angle."

"Oh. The museum angle. That make sense to you, Gomez?"

"No sense whatever, Biff."

"I think this kid ought to get lost."

Gomez said, "We can lose him."

"Some sort of bureaucratic tangle," Biff said. "You know, kid, once you get entangled with the cops, any damned fool thing's liable to happen."

"Sure," said Gomez. "We'll put him in the van for the funny farm this morning. It will be a good ten days before anyone straightens out that bureaucratic tangle."

"What will that get you?" Fletch asked. "A few days. You think I'd shut up about it?"

"Can't blame us for a bureaucratic tangle," Biff said. "I'm not even in this building this morning. You're not here either, are you, Gomez?"

"Naw. I'm never in this early."

"This is a real wise guy. Our offer of a few days' vacation at the funny farm doesn't frighten him. We should stick a real charge on him, Gomez. Get him off my back forever. Is that what you do with wise guys? I forget."

"Generally, Biff, if you're going to hit somebody, you should hit him so hard he can't get up swinging."

"Yeah." Although speaking softly, the veins in Biff's neck and temples were pulsing visibly. His eyes glinted like black pebbles at the bottom of a sunlit stream. "I've heard that somewhere before. Let's hit him with a real charge, so he can't get up again swinging. Let's see. He was picked up as Alexander Liddicoat. While he was being booked, it was discovered he had a seller's quantity of angel dust in his pocket. You got any spare PCP, Gomez?"

"Sure," said Gomez. "For just such an occasion."

Fletch was hot. "All because I'm bird-dogging your story, Biff?"

"Because you're a wise guy," Biff said. "There's no room for wise guys in journalism. Is there, Gomez?"

"You were always an altar boy," Gomez said to Biff.

"We play by the rules, kid. You get convicted for possession of a seller's quantity of PCP, Fletcher, and somehow I doubt John Winters and Frank Jaffe are going to want to see you around the *News-Tribune* emptying wastebaskets anymore. Or any other newspaper."

"What am I supposed to say?" Fletch asked. "That I'll back off and be a good boy?"

"Too late for that," Biff said. "I've decided you're a real wise guy. We want you gone."

"I'm supposed to say I'll go away?"

"You'll go away," Gomez said. "At taxpayers' expense. We'll see to it."

Fletch laughed. "Don't you think I'll ever come back, Biff?"

Biff glanced at Gomez. "Maybe. Maybe not. Who cares?"

"You'll care."

"I doubt it. You spend a few years inside now, and, what with one thing and another, you won't even be able to walk straight when you get out. Not much of a threat." Biff said to Gomez: "Find out about this gun he's talking about. Where's the PCP?"

"Got some in the locker."

"Get it. We'll go to your office and rewrite this kid's booking sheet."

"Got some real coffee in the office. We'll have some real coffee."

"I could use some."

Fletch said, "Jesus, Biff! You're serious!"

"Have I ever made a joke?"

"Ann McGarrahan said you're a shit."

"She should know. Biggest mistake of her life was marryin' me. Everybody says so."

Gomez laughed. "You the reason she never had any kids, Biff?"

"Had something to do with it. The lady didn't like to be screwed by anybody with whiskey on his breath."

Fletch said, "Jesus!"

"Guess I won't be seeing you around anymore, kid," Biff said. "Can't say I'll miss ya."

"Biff —"

"Someone will come get you in a while," Gomez said. "Enjoy waiting. It will be a lot of years before you ever get to spend any time alone again."

"We're going to go cook your papers, kid." Biff held the door open for Gomez. "And, believe me, Gomez and I are the greatest chefs in the world."

Fletch stood alone in the fluorescent-lit room. The door had thwunked closed. Wilson's and Gomez's footsteps faded down the corridor. Muffled shouts came from the cellblock.

Louise Habeck crossed his mind.

Fletch looked up at the dirty, barred window. Even with the bars on the outside, an electric wire ran from the closed window into the wall.

There was no air-conditioning/heating vent.

The walls were painted cement.

Green sneakers, blued hair, and a flowered dress . . .

It was crazy. Fletch went to the door and turned the knob. He pushed.

The door opened.

He looked out. The corridor was empty.

His heart going faster than his feet, he ambled along the corridor and up the stairs.

There was no one at the counter of the booking office.

In the lobby the same black woman who had been weeping there the night before was now sitting quietly on a bench. The sergeant at the reception desk was reading the sports pages of the *News-Tribune.*

It took Fletch a moment to get the sergeant's attention. Finally, he looked up.

"Lieutenant Gomez and Biff Wilson are having coffee in the lieutenant's office," Fletch said. "They'd like you to send out for some doughnuts. Jelly doughnuts."

"Okay." The sergeant picked up the phone and dialed three numbers. "The lieutenant wants some doughnuts," he said into the phone. "No. He has his coffee. You know Gomez. If it ain't mud, it ain't coffee."

"Jelly doughnuts," Fletch said.

The sergeant said, "Jelly doughnuts."

THIRTY-FIVE

"*News-Tribune* resource desk. Code and name, please."

"Hiya, Pilar. How're you doin'?"

"Good morning. This is Mary."

"Oh. Good morning, Mary."

"Code and name, please."

Still ravenously hungry, Fletch was glad at least to be back in his own car, headed for his own apartment. "Seventeen ninety dash nine. Fletcher."

Jogging to the bus stop, his eyes scanning the storefronts for a place open for breakfast, Fletch then realized he had no money. The police had stolen his wallet and keys. The thought amused him that if he robbed a convenience store, Alexander Liddicoat would be blamed.

His car was in the parking lot of a pizza store way out at the beach. He hitchhiked. The first driver who picked him up was a middle-aged man who sold musical instruments. He tried to interest Fletch in the roxophone. He was then picked up by a van filled with kids headed for the beach. At that hour of the morning they were passing around a joint of marijuana and already had finished one quart of white wine. A group of youngsters headed for the beach on a fine morning, each was near tears. It was past nine o'clock by the time Fletch arrived at his car, removed the parking-violation notice from it, hot-wired it, and started the drive back to his apartment.

"Messages for you," said the resource desk's Mary over the car phone. "Someone named Barbara called. Sounds like a personal message."

"Yes?"

"We're not supposed to take too many personal messages, you know."

"Ah, come on, Mary. Be a sport." Fletch's hunger, the morning's heat, the bright sunlight, made his eyes and head ache.

"Message is, 'Did you eat all the pizza yourself? All is forgiven. Please phone.' "

The reference to pizza made his tum-tum beat a tom-tom.

"Well?" Mary asked.

"Well what?"

"Did you eat all the pizza yourself?"

"Mary, that's a personal question. No personal questions, please."

"You did. I think you ate the pizza yourself. There's nothing worse than expecting someone to bring you a pizza and that someone eats it all himself."

"Mary, have you had breakfast this morning?"

"Yes."

"I haven't."

"You don't need breakfast, with all the pizza you ate."

"Is there another message?"

"I wouldn't forgive you. Yes. Ann McGarrahan wants to hear from you. Message is, 'Fletch, know you have your hands full with present assignment but please phone in. Beware B.W. and other social diseases."

"Okay."

"What's B.W.?"

"Mary, that's another personal question."

"I never heard of B.W."

"You're lucky."

"I thought I knew all the social diseases. I mean, I thought I knew of them."

"Fine. Now I need the address of Felix Gabais." He spelled the name for her. "In the St. Ignatius district."

"Aren't you going to warn me about B.W.?"

"Mary? Stay away from B.W."

"I mean, how do you catch it?"

"Sticking your nose in places it doesn't belong."

"Oh, we never do things like that. There's only one Gabais in the St. Ignatius district. First name, Therese."

"That's it. He lives with his sister."

"That's 45447 Twig Street. Mapping shows the address to be a half-block west of a car dealership on the corner."

"Thank you. One more: I need the address of Stuart Childers." Again he spelled the name.

"That's disgusting," she said. "Anyone who does that deserves B.W."

"Mary . . ."

"That's 120 Keating Road. Mapping shows that to be Harndon Apartments. Swank."

"Okay. Thanks."

"I shouldn't tell you this, I suppose, but Mr. Wilson called in a while ago. He wanted that address, too."

"Which address?"

"The one in St. Ignatius. Therese Gabais."

"Mary, you've already got B.W."

"Oh, don't say that."

"Be careful, Mary. B.W. can lay you up a long time."

"This is an answering machine," Fletch said into his apartment phone on the third ring. "I am not able to come to the phone just now —"

"Fletch!" Barbara shouted through the phone. "You don't have an answering machine!"

"Oh," Fletch said. "I forgot."

Fletch didn't have much. Across from the rickety, secondhand couch where he sat, posters were on the wall of the harbor of Cagna, on the Italian Riviera, of Cozumel, in eastern Mexico, of Belize, of Nairobi, Kenya, of Copacabana, in Rio de Janiero, Brazil. He hoped someday to have some really decent photographs on his wall, a proper collection. Someday, maybe, he'd have walls big enough to hold some decent copies of the paintings of Edgar Arthur Tharpe, Jr., the western artist.

"Are you all right?"

"Of course." On the chipped plate on the chipped coffee table in front of him there was very little left of his breakfast of scrambled eggs, waffles, and bacon. "Why do you ask?"

"You went out for pizza last night at eleven o'clock! And you never came back!"

"Oh, God! I didn't! Are you sure?"

"You never even phoned!"

"I did not eat all the pizza myself. I didn't get any of it."

"Were you in an accident, or something?"

"Or something. How come you're free to phone me? Cecilia finally get a customer for her jodhpurs?"

"I'm doing an errand for her, at the drugstore. We damned near starved to death."

"Did you lose those eight pounds you don't like?"

"I think I did."

"What did you and Cindy do?"

"Went to bed, finally. What else could we do? We waited for you until past one o'clock."

"Did Cindy stay the night?"

"Of course. What else? We'd had drinks, remember? She knew she shouldn't drive."

"Yeah."

"Damned inconsiderate of you. You could have at least phoned."

"I could've?"

Hung from the ceiling across the room was his surfboard, a thing of beauty, a joy forever.

"We were worried. I phoned the pizza store. The man said no one named Fletcher had been there."

"You ordered in the name of Ralton."

"Oh, yeah. I forgot. Where did you spend the night?"

"Long story. Mind if I tell you later?"

"Does it have to do with Habeck?"

"I guess so." Fletch looked at his plate. His headache was gone.

"Did you read Biff Wilson's piece this morning?"

"Yeah." The *News-Tribune* was on the couch beside Fletch. It was not reported that a gun, the possible murder weapon, had been turned in to police the night before.

"His piece strongly indicates, Fletch, that Habeck was bumped off by the mob because he knew too much."

Fletch sighed. "Maybe he's right."

"I mean, really, Fletch, how long has he been covering crime for the *News-Tribune?*"

"A long time."

"He must have contacts everywhere."

"He must have."

"I mean, sure, people must talk to him: the police, mobsters, informants. He probably has it all figured out."

"Probably."

"There's little point in your being up all night, losing sleep over it. There's no point at all in your losing your job over it."

"Listen, Barbara, I've got to shave and shower and get to work."

"Ate all the pizza, and slept late. And I'm marrying you?"

With a flick of his fingers, Fletch knocked the *News-Tribune* onto the floor.

"I'd have second thoughts, if I were you," Fletch said.

"Too late. I'm on my umpteenth thought. Remember you're having dinner with my mother tonight."

"Absolutely."

"Six o'clock at the beach house. If you disappoint her again, all her doubts about you will turn into certainties, for sure."

"For sure."

"You'll be there?"

"Absolutely."

"Okay. By the way, Cindy said to call her at twelve-thirty sharp at 555-2900. She'll answer the phone herself."

"Say again? That's not the number of Ben Franklyn."

"No. She said she'll just be there at that time, waiting for you to call. That's 555-2900. She'll have things to tell you then."

"Okay."

"Fletch, this is Wednesday."

"Already?"

"We're getting married Saturday. You absolutely must be at dinner tonight."

"Okay."

"There are things to discuss."

"Okay, okay."

"I've got to get back to work," Barbara said.

Fletch said, "Yeah. Me, too."

THIRTY-SIX

"I'm from the *News-Tribune,*" Fletch said. The woman who opened the door of the ground-floor apartment at 45447 Twig Street was in a wheelchair. "Are you Therese Gabais?"

Her eyes were black, her face gray, her hair unwashed, uncombed. "We can't afford a daily newspaper, I don't like them, anyway."

"Has anyone else from the *News-Tribune* been here?"

She shook her head no.

The car dealership at the corner of Twig Street seemed to be offering special sale prices on rusty, six-passenger sedans. Fletch had parked near the dealership and walked the half-block, scuffing through the wastepaper and empty tins on the sidewalk. He almost stumbled over the legs of a woman asleep in a doorway.

He was watching for a police car, or Biff's car. While he breakfasted, talked with Barbara, shaved and showered, his doorbell had not rung.

If it had rung, he planned to go through a back window and down the fire escape. Being falsely arrested as Alexander Liddicoat for more than twenty robberies was slightly amusing. Having Wilson and Gomez contrive real charges against I. M. Fletcher for drug dealing was totally alarming. The police had not appeared at Fletch's apartment. They were not now visible in the street.

But Wilson and Gomez had every reason to believe Fletch would show up at the Gabais apartment.

"Has anyone been here?" Fletch asked. "The police?"

Again the woman shook her head no. Her eyes were dull.

She wheeled her chair aside. Perhaps she next would close the door in his face.

Holding the door open, Fletch stepped into the foul odor of the apartment. "I'm looking for Felix Gabais."

Expression briefly came into her eyes as she looked up at him. She was surprised he was still there. "He doesn't want a newspaper, either."

Fletch pushed the door closed. "Need to talk to him."

There was a bed, a mattress and some blankets on a box, in the room.

Moving no further, the woman's attention went to a television turned to a quiz-prize show on a dark, heavy bureau.

Fletch stepped through the only door into another room, a kitchen, of sorts. There was a small refrigerator, a stove top, a sink. Everything was filthy. Empty food cans overflowed the sink. The smell of garbage and excrement was stinging. Against the wall on the floor was a double-sized mattress without pillows or blankets.

There was a massive, brown upholstered chair between the mattress and refrigerator.

And in the massive chair was a massive man. His gaze remained on the corner of the walls behind the stove top. A half-finished quart bottle of beer was in one hand on the chair arm. Slobbered food and drink were on his shirt and prison-issue black suit.

Fletch sat on the edge of the mattress. "What have you done since you've been out of prison?"

"Bought this chair." Felix Gabais's free hand raised and lowered on the chair arm. "Bought that mattress." Felix looked at the mattress. "Bought beer." The counter in the corner beyond the refrigerator had more than twenty empty quart beer bottles. "Beer's the only thing that fills me up now." The fat creases on Felix's neck rearranged themselves as Felix turned his head and looked down at Fletch. "I'm doin' okay, first week out."

"Looks like you got enough to eat in prison anyway."

"Yeah. But she suffered." Felix tipped the bottle toward the other room. "No one took care of my sister in eleven, twelve years. Scrounging food stamps. Sends kids out for cat food. Eating cat food off scrounged food stamps, you got it?" Fletch nodded. "Look at this place. Landlord took the living room and the other bedroom away from her. Only 'cause he couldn't throw her out. See that wall he put up?" From the layers of filth on it, Fletch supposed the wall had been there for most of the eleven years. "You call that legal?" Fletch didn't opine. "What are you going to do about it? She didn't do anything wrong. Why should she suffer?"

"Did you do something wrong?"

Instantly, there were tears in Felix's eyes. "I shouldn't have been put in prison. I was sick. What would you call someone who bothers small children?"

"Sick."

"Sure. They had to put me away. Couldn't let me be loose. Had to keep me in prison until I was no good anymore. Had to wreck me. I don't know about prison, though. That's an awful insult to a sick person."

"At your trial, you didn't plead insanity."

"At my trial, I didn't say nothin'!" Felix made no effort to control his tears. "You know what a defendant feels like at a trial?" Fletch shook his head. "He's in a daze. He's shocked this could be happenin' to him. He's shocked by what he's hearin' about himself, about the things he did. All these people are talkin', talkin', talkin' about you and about the things you did. What they're sayin' has nothin' to do with what you've always thought about yourself. All the time they're talkin', you're sick. You're struck dumb, you know what I mean?"

"Your lawyer was Donald Habeck, right?"

"Mr. Habeck. Yeah. I could have said a lot, if he didn't talk so much. See, I had my reasons. I had my own idea of things. I could've explained."

"You could explain molesting children?"

"I had things to say. I was just tryin' to make it up to them."

"How did you pay Habeck? How could you afford him?"

"I never paid Mr. Habeck. Not a dime."

"I don't get it. Why did he take your case?"

"I don't know. One day he walks into the jail and says, 'I'm your lawyer.' He never asked me nothin'. He never let me explain. I could have explained, from my perspective, why I was such a bad guy. He never let the judge ask me nothin'. Day after day after day I sat there in the courtroom while all these people came out, one after another, and said they saw me do this, they saw me do that, the two dogs, this, that, this, that." Felix put the bottle of beer to his mouth, but didn't swallow much. "Every day the television and newspapers made a big thing of it. They hounded my sister. They hounded my sister crazy. Showed where we lived. Drew maps. Showed the playgrounds, the schoolyards where I used to walk the dogs and meet the children." Felix was crying copiously. "The newspapers were lousy! Drove her stupid!"

"I'm beginning to understand."

"You ever hear of trial by newspaper?"

"You were the case Habeck lost. Lost big. Why not? A child molester . . ."

"Why did he do it? Why did he let it drag on so long? Why did he tell 'em everything? Why didn't he let me tell 'em anything?"

"He used you for publicity. Through you, he proved that Habeck could lose a case, big. And get his name in the newspaper every day while he was doing so. What I don't understand is, how come you served only eleven years?"

"That's the point! After all this punishment of my sister in the newspaper, after wreckin' her, one day this Mr. Habeck stands up in court and says, 'Your Honor, my client changes his plea to guilty on all counts.' "

"Wow. And he never told you he was going to do that?"

"Never! He never said a word to me. And I had things to say. I didn't mean to bother the children! I was just lovin' 'em up!"

"You were 'lovin' 'em up' with two dogs on them."

"Sure! They loved the dogs. The children always came to the dogs!"

"You'd corner the children with the dogs."

"Listen! Have you ever seen a schoolyard? The little kids are always in the corners! The dogs didn't put 'em there! The dogs would go see 'em. They'd call the dogs!"

Fletch made a gesture of impatience at himself. "I don't mean to harass you."

"I understand all about it! I had things to say. See, there was this psychiatrist who spent a lot of time with me when I first went to prison. I felt guilty about my sister. When we were little kids I pushed her behind my father's car when he was backing out of the driveway. She got crippled from that. My father got mad. He went away. Never heard from him. See? I was tryin' to make it up to little kids. I was just lovin' 'em up. Tryin' to love 'em up."

"A psychiatrist told you all that?"

"Helped me to realize it, he said. I was sick. I had things to say at that trial. Habeck just fucked me over, and threw me to the pits."

Fletch shook his head. "How did you get so fat in prison?"

"None of the crews wanted me on 'em. None of the work crews. I was sent to the prison farm. I'd go in a corner. They all knew all these terrible things about me, from the newspapers." Felix Gabais was sobbing. "If Mr. Habeck was going to tell the court I was guilty of everything, why did he let the newspapers wreck my sister so long?"

"So you killed Habeck."

"I didn't kill nobody!" Felix's angry, reddened eyes blazed at Fletch. "I needed to be gotten off the streets. The dogs were dead! I had to be wrecked!"

"But not your sister."

Felix pointed at himself with both hands. "I'm going to go out in the streets and kill somebody? I'm a wreck!"

"You're pretty angry at Habeck."

"I don't want to go in the streets for nothin'! The mattress, this chair, I had to have. What day is this?"

"Wednesday."

"Thursday. Tomorrow. I have to go to the parole office. You'll come with me?"

"What? No."

"My sister can't come. It's way downtown."

Fletch stood up. "I think you'd better check in with your parole officer."

"You won't come with me?"

"No."

"What are you going to do about my sister?"

"Have I heard that question somewhere before?"

"Now that you finally show up, you just wanted to sit and hear the story of my life?"

"I wanted to hear you say you murdered Donald Habeck."

"Who are you?"

"I. M. Fletcher."

"You're not from the public agency?"

"I said I'm from a newspaper." Fletch was standing at the door of the room. "Didn't you hear me?"

Felix Gabais's eyes grew huge. He tried to get up from the big chair.

Fletch said, "The *News-Tribune.*"

Felix fell back into the chair. He switched the beer bottle to his right hand.

Fletch ducked through the door. In the dark outer room he bumped into Therese Gabais's wheelchair.

The beer bottle smashed against the doorframe.

Therese Gabais said, "My brother doesn't like the newspapers."

"I understand."

"Blames 'em for everything," Therese Gabais said.

Down Twig Street, Fletch ducked into his car quickly.

Opening the door of his car, Fletch had seen the car Biff Wilson used, lights, antennae, and NEWS-TRIBUNE all over it, stop in front of number 45447.

THIRTY-SEVEN

"555-2900."

It was exactly twelve-thirty.

There were many places Fletch felt he ought not be. His apartment was one. The *News-Tribune* was another. Driving around the streets without his driver's license or car registration, both of which had been taken by the police with his wallet and keys, and, with the police prone to recognize him as Alexander Liddicoat, the robber, and probably looking for him as Irwin Maurice Fletcher, angel-dust merchant, also struck him as imprudent.

So, after he watched Biff Wilson lift himself out of his car, button his suit jacket, and lumber into number 45447 Twig Street, Fletch drove into the used-car lot. He parked his Datsun 300 ZX in the front row of used cars, facing the street. All the other cars in the row, bigger than his, nevertheless were newer and cleaner.

No car salesmen were around. Undoubtedly they were off reenergizing their smiles and chatter with soup and sandwiches.

Fletch took a cardboard sign off the windshield of another car and put it on his own. The sign read: SALE! $5,000 AND THIS CAR IS YOURS!

Seated behind the FOR SALE sign in his car, Fletch could make his phone calls. He also could watch number 45447 Twig Street.

Cindy answered immediately. "Fletch?"

"You feel okay?"

"Sure. Why not?"

"Sorry about the pizza last night."

"Isn't that what men do? Negotiate with women and then walk out on them, ignoring their agreements? I mean, even about bringing back pizza? It was no surprise to me. Of course, Barbara mentioned being both hungry and disappointed in you."

"Hey, Cindy. Don't be angry. If you only knew what happened —"

"I don't want to be told. From what I know of men, they're as incapable of telling the truth to women as snakes are of singing four-part harmony."

"You've met a lot of snakes."

"I'm not doing this for you, Fletcher. I'm doing this for Barbara."

"Wedding presents are for brides and grooms, aren't they? Isn't that why, so often, there are rods and reels among the packages?"

"We all have to give men everything their little hearts desire so that a few of the good things of this world will dribble down to their dependent wives. Isn't that the way the world works?"

"You're doing it to screw Marta."

"That, too."

"Where are you?"

"None of your business."

"Cindy, I just want to make sure you're on a safe phone. That no one is listening in."

"No one is listening."

"Good. Who owns the Ben Franklyn Friend Service?"

"Okay. Wood Nymph, Incorporated, as I said. I got into the filing cabinet in Marta's office this morning. She spent most of the morning at the reception desk. Found references to two other corporations. One is called Cungwell Screw —"

"That's funny."

"A riot. The other is called Lingman Toys, Incorporated."

"Someone has a sense of humor. What's the relationship among these three companies?"

"I don't know. I wouldn't expect terribly accurate or complete evidence of ownership to be lying about Marta's office, would you?"

"No. But it's more of a lead than we had, I guess."

"I think Cungwell Screw and Lingman Toys are investors, owners of Wood Nymph."

"Any reference to any of the officers of any of the companies?"

Down Twig Street, Biff Wilson dashed out of number 45447. He slammed the door behind him. Looking back, he stumbled down the steps.

"Marta. President of Wood Nymph, vice-president of both Cungwell Screw and Lingman Toys. President of Cungwell Screw is a Marietta Ramsin."

The door of 45447 Twig Street opened again. Felix Gabais, empty beer bottle in hand like a football, stood on the front stoop. Really, he was a massive person.

Felix threw the empty bottle at the fleeing Biff Wilson.

The bottle hit Biff on the ear. It fell into the gutter and smashed.

"Jokes everywhere," Fletch said.

"And president of Lingman Toys is an Yvonne Heller. Treasurer of all these companies is a man named Jay Demarest. I know him."

"You do?"

The ground-floor window of 45447 Twig Street opened. Therese Gabais leaned as far out the window as she could from her wheelchair. She was shaking her arm and shouting at Biff in the street.

"Yeah. Comes in all the time. Uses the place, you know, as if it were all for him. Never gets a bill. Exercises, gets what he wants when he wants it."

"What's he like?"

Now Felix was bending over as well as he could in the gutter and scooping up broken glass from his beer bottle.

"Actually, over the two years I've known him, he's gotten himself into pretty good shape, one way and another. He's in his thirties, not married."

"Why would he marry, with the friends he's got?"

"What?"

Head tilted, hands pressed against his wounded ear, Biff turned back to attack Felix.

Felix threw the bits of glass in Biff's face.

"Nothing."

"I've even been out with him on dates, you know, as escort. When he takes friends out for dinner, that sort of thing."

"What are his friends like?"

Brother and sister Gabais screaming at him from the street and the window, Biff hustled into his car.

"Losers. You know what I mean? People who think that if they ever get their lives properly organized they'll make it big and be as good as other people."

"Do you think Jay Demarest is a real owner?"

Biff seemed to be having trouble getting his car started.

All the lights on the *News-Tribune* car began to whir and flash.

"I think he keeps the books, and orders the ground elk's horn. The fall guy."

"Being given a few good years and meant to take the fall for the real owners."

Now Felix was beating up the car. He kicked the rear left fender hard enough to rock the car and leave a good-sized dent. Arms joined at the fists, he landed his considerable weight on the car's trunk. That made an impression.

"Yeah. He and Marta better look out below. I think they're both just employees."

Biff's car engine roared.

"When can you have the rest of the stuff for me?"

Twice dented, lights whirring and flashing, rear end skittering, Biff's *News-Tribune* car fled down the street.

A stone Felix had ready in hand caught up to it and broke its rear window.

Skittering around the far corner, Biff almost hit a bus.

"Ah," Fletcher said. "The reportorial life does have its ups and downs, its ins and outs."

"What?"

Retreating slowly, unwillingly, back into their depression, Felix and Therese Gabais intermittently shouted and shook their fists at the corner around which Biff had disappeared.

"When can you have the other stuff?"

"Anytime you want to meet me, I'll be ready. I'm preparing a list of the services and charges. I've got the names and addresses of some of the clients. I've even pinched some of the still photographs and videotapes for you."

"Great! Any of Marta?"

"Sure. She's not beyond takin' a trick now and again. She has her vanity."

"Jay Demarest?"

"You bet. Marta probably took those, to keep Jay in line, should the need ever arise. Nice lady, uh? All in the same cesspool together."

"I don't want you to risk yourself, Cindy."

"Not to worry. You can't make pie without crust."

"What? Right! Sure. I suppose so. Will you be at this number later?"

The window and the door to 45447 Twig Street were now closed.

Therese and Felix Gabais were now back inside their own morosity.

"If not, I'll be back. Don't call me at Ben Franklyn."

"Course not. Marta would ask me when I'm coming to work."

In the street in front of Fletch, a police car cruised by slowly.

Alston Chambers said, "Glad you called. I've been trying to get you. Your apartment doesn't answer, the beach house doesn't answer, your car phone hasn't answered. No one at the newspaper seems to know where you are. I've got some news for you. By the way, where are you?"

"At the moment, I'm hiding out in a used-car lot disguised as a satisfied mannequin in a Datsun 300 ZX."

"Why didn't I guess that?"

"I need a couple of favors, old buddy."

"Why should I do you favors? Aren't I already marrying you off, Saturday, or something?"

"Cause I'm trying to find out who murdered your boss, ol' buddy."

"Not even a topic of discussion around here. Bunch of cold-blooded bastards. It won't interest anyone at Habeck, Harrison and Haller who murdered Donald Habeck unless and until they get to defend the accused, always presuming he or she is rich, or, good for publicity. By the way, who did murder Donald Habeck?"

"You're always good for the obvious question."

"That's my legal training."

"I don't know who killed Donald Habeck. So far, I have spent time with each member of the Habeck family, and I believe any one of them could have and would have done it, if, and that's a big if, any of them knew Habeck was disinheriting them in behalf of a museum and a monastery."

"Monastery! What in hell are you talking about?"

"I forgot. You and I haven't talked lately. Believe it or not, ol' chum, I believe a liar for once told the truth."

"And no one believed him?"

"Of course not. I believe Donald Habeck really wanted to give five million dollars to the museum and, knowing how to use the press, by making the announcement through the press, embarrass the museum into accepting the gift and promising to use it to develop a collection of contemporary religious art. Of that Habeck crafty scheme, I and the *News-Tribune* were to be the unwitting tools."

"Telling the truth once in your life doesn't make you a monk. Does it?"

"I believe Donald Habeck wanted to enter a monastery. If you can believe any of my insane and otherwise unreliable sources, you can believe it. Over the years, he had taken religious instruction. He had not divorced the only wife he ever had. She had been permanently endowed in an institution years before. Maybe Donald was trying to relate thusly to his son, a monk. Maybe they each had the same instinct. Maybe, as sometimes happens, the son, thinking he was rebelling from his father, instinctively and inadvertently perceived and fulfilled his father's innermost ambitions. Also, of course, Habeck was not lying when he said no one cared 'a tin whistle' for him. No one did. Plus, lately Habeck had been reading Russian novels, in which icons abound and the theme of personal withdrawal is very strong, especially as written by Dostoevski."

There was a long pause before Alston next spoke. "Er, Fletch?"

"Yes, Alston?"

"Do you also believe you are following approved, police methods of investigation here?"

"Of course I am. Why not?"

Alston's voice sounded distant from the phone. "I've never known the police to consider the victim's recent reading list as evidence of anything."

"Why not? What better way is there of knowing what a person is thinking?"

"Back to hard facts." Alston's voice became stronger. "You know Habeck and Jasmine never married?"

"Donald and Louise never divorced. I know Jasmine is not Mrs. Habeck. I know she isn't even Jasmine. Which brings up one of the favors I ask, ol' buddy."

"Jasmine isn't what?"

"She thinks she's in the Federal Witness Protection Program. In fact, while she was giving evidence in a trial in Miami, Donald Habeck absconded with her."

"In the middle of her giving testimony?"

"I believe so. Donald apparently gave her the impression she was through testifying, free to go, and that he was some sort of an official. Jasmine has a one-cell brain. She believed him because he was a lawyer, was kind to her, in his fashion, and, I suppose, wore a nice suit."

"He did have nice suits," Alston mused.

"Not from the internal view. Would you please ask a federal officer to call upon her at Palmiera Drive and attempt to straighten out her life for her? She might still have evidence which would interest courts in Miami, as well as points north and west."

"That's a favor? Sure. Always glad to get in good with the feds. My news is that Donald Habeck did indeed have a will, drawn up five years ago, and not altered since."

"And this will stands?"

"Yes. Under its terms, everything goes straight to the children of Nancy Habeck and Thomas Farliegh, as they come of age."

"Wow! This shoemaker's children have shoes. Or will have."

"Nothing remarkable about leaving everything directly to the grandchildren."

"You haven't seen these grandchildren fight over a noisy toy tank."

"Brats, uh?"

"Given an inheritance, the violence those kids will be able to raise might astound the Western World, as we know it."

"Great. Sounds like they'll each need lawyers."

"Of one sort or another."

"And you don't think their papa, the poet of violence, bumped off their grandpapa?"

"What Tom Farliegh is best at is engineering mud into his babas' maws."

"Come again?"

"Violence is not natural to Tom Farliegh. He gets it from his in-laws."

"I was hoping you'd pin the punk. So none of the family bumped off Habeck?"

"Any one of them could have, including Louise, including Nancy, even including the son, Robert, who is a monk. Each in her or his own way expressed the sentiment, *to hell with Donald Habeck.* Two elements, one big, one small, bother me. The big one is that I can't establish that any of them knew before Donald was murdered that he planned to disinherit them all in behalf of a museum and a monastery. Of course, it's hard to prove what people know and when they know it. But with the wife in an institution, the daughter in squalor, and the son in a monastery, when each says she or he didn't know the change in Donald's life and death plans, how can one not believe them?"

"A lawyer never believes anyone, and that's the truth."

"The weird thing that bothers me is how these people get around. Would you believe, in this day and age, none has a car? The Farlieghs' car is just one more broken toy in their front weed-patch. Robert's use of vehicles is limited. Louise sits in cars until their owner comes back and takes her where she wants to go, ultimately. None would seem to be able to time things, such as murder, too well. I don't think the murderer drove into the parking lot of the *News-Tribune,* but how did he or she get there without a car?"

"Pardon me for saying so, Fletch, but there are other lines of investigation to be followed. I hope you're leaving something for the police to do. Wash out my mouth, but Habeck's partners, for example."

"You're right. But the family came first. Donald Habeck was about to announce he was disinheriting them. That's a clear motive for murder, isn't it?"

". . . The list of his present and past clients . . ."

"Yeah. I saw Gabais. Habeck used him for publicity; in Gabais's words, wrecked not only him, but his crippled sister. Hates Habeck. But I don't think Gabais could organize himself enough to do murder. I think he pretty well gave up on his life when he saw his dogs' heads bashed in."

". . . Stuart Childers."

"Yeah. Tell me about him. How strong was the evidence that he killed his brother?"

"Very strong, but, unfortunately, all self-admitted. I've got the file somewhere here on my desk. Thought you'd want it. Here it is. Richard was the elder brother, by about two years. A complete playboy. Never worked, never married, sponged off his parents, hung out with the yachty set, wrecked about one sports car a year. In his last car wreck, the girl who was with him was killed. Variously over the years Richard had also been charged with possession of small amounts of controlled substances, paternity twice, vandalism, one case of arson. He tried to burn down a boat shed. His parents always got him off."

"Using Habeck, Harrison and Haller?"

"Yes. That's how I know."

"Parents are rich?"

"You've heard of Childers Insurance. Biggest, oldest, richest insurance brokerage firm in the city."

"On City Boulevard, right?"

"That's where their main office is, yes. Stuart, on the other hand, was the good son, dutiful, diligent, all that, never any trouble, graduated college with honors, worked for Childers Insurance every summer since he was sixteen, entered the firm as a qualified broker the November after he graduated."

"Good son, bad son, bleh," Fletch said.

In the street in front of him, another police car cruised by slowly.

"After the last car wreck, in which the girl was killed, Mama and Papa Childers turned Richard off. No more family money for him. He had to prove himself, go get a job, stay out of trouble, etcetera, etcetera."

"There's always an *instead* right about here in this story."

"Instead, Richard proved himself by blackmailing his brother. Or attempting to."

"What had Stuart done wrong?"

"Gotten his honors degree by cheating. Paid some instructor to write his honors thesis for him. Richard, of course, never graduated from college, but had contacts at the old place, knew the instructor, etcetera."

"And the thought of being exposed, especially to his parents, proven to be no better than his brother, drove Stuart crazy."

"So he said."

"Who said?"

"Stuart said. Richard was found dead on the sidewalk fourteen stories below the terrace of his apartment. There was lots of evidence of a fight having happened in the apartment, turned-over chairs, tables, smashed glass, etcetera. Stuart's fingerprints were found in the apartment. So were others'. Because of Richard's wild acquaintances, the inquest's finding was Death by Person or Persons Unknown."

"I know Stuart confessed."

"Loud and clear. He walked into a police station late one afternoon, said he wanted to confess, was read his rights, taken in to a room where he confessed into a tape-recorder, waited until the confession was typed up, then signed it."

"Enter Donald Habeck."

"Donald Habeck entered immediately, as soon as the Childerses knew their son was at the cop house confessing to killing his brother. Habeck ordered an immediate blood-alcohol test. Apparently, Stuart had braced himself with almost a quart of gin that day, before going to confess."

"So the confession was no good?"

"Not only did the cops know he was drunk while making the confession, they even gave him maintenance drinks, of whiskey, to keep him going during the confession, and before he signed."

"How could they be so stupid?"

"Listen. Cops try to get what they can get before the lawyer shows up. And that's usually when they make their mistakes."

"*In vino veritas* is not a tenet of the law, huh?"

"In Habeck's own handwriting, I read you from the file: *'In court, keep Stuart sedated.'* "

"They drugged him."

"Right."

Fletch remembered Felix Gabais saying, *"You know what a defendant feels like at a trial? He's in a daze. . . . What they're sayin' has nothin' to do with what you've always thought about yourself. . . . You're struck dumb. . . ."* "Maybe they needn't have bothered."

"The confession was found inadmissible by the court. And, even though Richard and Stuart were known not to be friends, Habeck pointed out that a person's fingerprints found in his brother's apartment is insufficient evidence for the charge of murder, especially when there were many unidentifiable fingerprints there."

"You said everyone has a right to the best defense."

"Of course."

"Even involuntarily?"

"I don't know. All Habeck had to do here was raise a question of reasonable doubt, and that's what he did."

"Stuart Childers confessed!"

"Now, Fletch."

"What?"

"Now, Fletch . . . Have you always meant absolutely everything you've said after too much to drink?"

"Absolutely!"

"If I believed that, I wouldn't be talking to you. Or you to me."

"In *vino* a germ of truth?"

"Inadmissible. Especially when the *vino* came out of the cops' locker."

"I give up." At the edge of the used-car lot a man wearing a ready smile and a lavender necktie dropped a lunch bag from a fast-food store into a waste receptacle. "In behalf of leaving no stone unturned, I guess I better go see Stuart Childers. The cops won't listen to him again."

"Maybe he keeps confessing to every crime in town just hoping for another free drink at the police station."

"I've listened to every other nut in town. Might as well listen to him."

"Got a story to tell you."

"No more stories."

"You like stories about lawyers."

"No more, I don't."

"I remembered that in the old days, when my grandfather was a lawyer in northern California, lawyers used to charge by the case, rather than by the hour. So in their offices they would saw a few inches off the legs of the front of the chairs their clients would sit in. You know, to make them lean forward, state their case, and get out."

"What's funny about that? The chairs in modern fast-food restaurants are designed that way."

"What's funny is that when lawyers began charging by the hour instead of the case, they all bought new chairs for their clients, and sawed a few inches off the back legs. You know? So the clients would relax and talk about their last vacations?"

On the sidewalk, the car salesman stood, arms akimbo, smile ready, looking for a customer.

Fletch cleared his throat while Alston laughed. "My second favor, ol' buddy . . ."

"Yes?"

"Would be a real favor. Three corporations called Wood Nymph, Cungwell Screw, and Lingman Toys. . . ."

"I don't think they're on the exchange."

"Even the telephone exchange. I need to know their relationship to each other. And, of most importance, who owns them."

"I'll trace them right now."

"No need. Anytime within the next half-hour will do."

"No. Seriously. I'll do it right now."

The salesman spotted Fletch sitting in the Datsun. "Doesn't Habeck, Harrison and Haller give you any other work to do?"

"Not anymore. I resigned from Habeck, Harrison and Haller an hour ago."

"What?"

Alston Chambers had hung up.

"So. How do you like it?" the used-car salesman asked Fletch through the car window.

"Like what?" Fletch asked.

"The car. Want to buy it?"

"I hate it." Fletch turned the key in the ignition. "Listen to that! Muffler's no damned good!"

To the amazement of the used-car dealer, Fletch put the Datsun in gear, roared off the lot into the street, and away. The FOR SALE sign blew off the windshield and landed on the sidewalk, not far from the salesman's feet.

THIRTY-EIGHT

"You're from the *News-Tribune*?" Stuart Childers looked young and neat in his business suit and necktie behind his wooden desk. He looked basically healthy, as well, except for bags of sleeplessness beneath his eyes. His teeth kept tearing at his lips.

"Yes. Name of Fletcher."

"I take it you're not here to see me about insurance?"

"No. I'm not. The doorman at your apartment house said you were here at your office."

"You may be the answer to a prayer." Stuart Childers took a .22 caliber revolver from the top drawer of his desk. He placed it in the center of the desk blotter in front of him. "If I'm not arrested for murder by five o'clock today, I intend to blow my brains out."

"That's some threat." Fletcher sat in a chair facing the desk. He quoted, " 'When the gods wish to punish us, they answer our prayers.' "

The office was small but paneled with real wood. There was a Turkish rug on the floor.

"You want to find out who murdered Donald Habeck, is that right?" Childers asked.

"That's the job of the police and the courts," Fletch answered.

"The police!" Childers scoffed. "The courts! Oh, my God!"

"I want the story," Fletch said. "I'm a journalist. My own purpose is to understand Donald Habeck, as much as possible, and why he was murdered."

"Have you gotten far?"

"Yes. I've gotten some good background."

Childers contemplated the handgun on his desk. "I murdered Donald Habeck."

"The hell you say."

"The police won't listen to me."

"You've confessed to everything that's gone down in this area in the last two months."

"I know," Childers said. "That was a mistake."

Fletch shrugged. "We all make mistakes."

"Don't you think we have a need for punishment?" Teeth tearing at his lips, Childers looked to Fletch for an answer, waited. "If we are being punished for what wrong we did, at least we can live with ourselves, die with ourselves." He waved his fingers at the handgun. "Just going bang is not the better way."

Still Fletch said nothing.

"What do you know of my brother's death?"

"I know you were drunk when you confessed to the police. I know Habeck kept you drugged during the trial."

"Yes. Tranquilizers. Habeck said he always gave them to his clients during a trial. I had no idea how strong they were. The trial went by in a blur, like a fast-moving railroad train." Childers's teeth worried his lips. "I murdered my brother."

Fletch said, "I expect you did."

"How is that forgivable?" Again, he seemed to be asking Fletch a real question. "Richard said he was going to blackmail me, for money to keep up his whacky, careless life. Even if I was paying him, he couldn't be trusted to keep his mouth shut. His need to hurt me, and my parents, was too great. My mistake was that I was horrified at the threat of the college, the world, my parents learning that I had cheated, hired an instructor to write my honors thesis. I went to Richard's apartment. I didn't intend to kill him. We fought like a couple of shouting, screaming, crying, angry kids. Suddenly we were on his little balcony. Suddenly the expression on his face changed. He fell backwards. Fell."

"You confess very convincingly."

"I woke up on the other side of the trial. I was back living in my apartment, coming to work here every day. Everybody was telling me the incident was over, closed, that I had to get on with my life. How could I get on with my life? The so-called incident wasn't over. My parents knew I had cheated on my honors thesis. One son was dead. The other son had murdered him. And my parents knew it. I had destroyed my parents' every dream, every reality. I might as well have killed them, too." From the way he was looking at him, Fletch knew another unanswerable question was coming. "My parents did what they thought was best in hiring Habeck, in getting me off. But wouldn't they feel better in their hearts if their sole remaining son took responsibility for what he had done?"

Fletch said nothing.

"You asked for a story," Childers said.

"So you took to confessing."

"Yeah. I'd read enough about a crime to be able to go in to the police and say I committed it. They had to listen, at first. I'd make up evidence against myself. That was my mistake. The evidence wouldn't check out. So they wouldn't believe me at all."

"You're sure you just didn't want to play a starring role in court again?" Childers gave him the look of a starlet accused of being attractive. "Some people get a kick out of that."

Childers sighed and looked at the gun.

"Stuart, you can't be tried again for murdering your brother."

"I know that. So I murdered Habeck."

"Now the story gets a little hard to swallow."

"Why?"

"Murdering your brother was a crime of passion. Two brothers, very angry with each other, probably never having been able to talk well with each other, finding each other tussling, hitting each other, all kinds of angers at each other since you were in diapers welling up out of your eyes. And one of you got killed. That's very different from the fairly intellectualized crime of killing the person who had prevented your receiving punishment for the first crime."

"Is it? I suppose it is." He looked sharply at Fletch. "Frustration is frustration though, isn't it? Once you've taken a life, it becomes easier to take another life."

"That's a cliché. People who commit crimes of passion seldom do so again. The object of your rage was dead."

"Couldn't I have transferred my rage from my brother to Habeck?"

"Keep trying, Stuart. You'll work it out."

"Who says a person who commits a crime of passion, as you call it, isn't capable of commiting an entirely different, rational murder?"

"What's rational about your murdering Habeck? The son of a bitch got you off!"

"Yes, he got me off!" Leaning forward on his desk, Childers spoke forcefully. "And the son of a bitch knew I was guilty! He obstructed justice!"

"In your behalf! You're the one who is walking around free!"

Childers sat back. "I don't know that much about the law, but I'd call Donald Habeck an accessory to murder, after the fact. Wouldn't that be about right? Think about it."

Fletch thought about it.

"How many times was Donald Habeck an accessory to a crime, after the fact?"

Fletch said, "Before the fact, too, I suspect."

"What?"

Fletch remembered saying to Louise Habeck, about her son, Robert,

"Shooting his father would accomplish two goals, wouldn't it?" And her answering, *"Splendidly!"*

"Okay, Stuart. If you shot Habeck because you wanted to be punished so much, how come you didn't stay there? How come you weren't found standing over him with the gun?"

Childers smiled. "Would you believe I had to pee?"

"No."

"Go shoot someone, and see what happens to your bladder." Sitting behind his desk, Stuart Childers was then speaking as evenly as someone might discussing a homeowner's fire-and-theft policy. "I did wait there. I had thought someone would hear the gun. I shot Habeck sort of far back in the lot, where he parked. I shot him as he was getting out of the car. No one was around. The guard at the gate was talking to someone entering the parking lot. I could see him. I waited. I had to pee in the worst way. I mean, really bad. I didn't want to have to go through the whole arrest process, you know, having shit my pants. So I went into the lobby of the *News-Tribune* and asked the guard there if I could use the men's room."

"Why didn't you come out again? There were police, reporters, photographers who would have been interested to actually see you at a scene of one of your crimes."

"I felt sick. Jittery."

"That would have been understood."

Stuart Childers said something Fletch didn't hear.

"What?"

"I wanted a drink. A few drinks before I gave myself up."

"You wanted to get drunk before you confessed again, is that it? What did you supposedly want, Stuart?"

"I wanted to get control of myself. I went home, had a few drinks, a bath, a night's sleep. In the morning, I had breakfast. Then I went to the police station to confess." Childers shrugged. "A gentlemanly routine, I suppose. I was brought up that way."

Fletch shook his head. Then he asked, "How did you know Habeck was going to be in the parking lot at the *News-Tribune* a few minutes before ten on Monday morning?"

"I didn't. Murdering Habeck was something I decided over the weekend. So Monday morning, I drove to his house. Got there about seven-thirty. Waited for him. He drove out of his garage in a blue Cadillac Seville. I followed him. He drove to the *News-Tribune*. While he talked to the guard at the gate, I parked outside and walked in. It was the first stop he made. When he opened his car door, I shot him."

"Then you had the irresistible need to pee."

"I had been sitting in my car since before seven o'clock! Then, after I peed, I felt really sick in the stomach. My legs were shaking. I had a terrible neck ache." Childers rubbed the back of his neck. "I wanted time! Isn't that understandable?"

"I don't know. You say you wanted to get caught, but you ran away. There is no evidence at all that you were at the scene of the crime. Everything you've told me so far, that Habeck drove a blue Cadillac Seville, that he was shot at the back of the lot getting out of his car, all that was reported in the press."

"Sorry if my story conforms to the truth."

"You didn't confess until after you'd been able to read the details of the crime in the newspaper."

Childers stared at the gun on his desk.

"Okay, Stuart. What did you do with the murder weapon?"

"You know what?"

"What?"

"I don't know."

"You don't know what you did with the gun?"

"I don't know. When I got home, I didn't have the gun. I've tried to remember. I was upset. . . ."

"You had to pee."

". . . Tried to reconstruct."

"I bet."

"I couldn't have had the gun in my hand when I walked into the lobby of the *News-Tribune*. I must have thrown it into the bushes."

Fletch watched him carefully. "You threw it into the bushes in front of the building?"

"I must have."

"What kind of gun was it?"

"A twenty-two-caliber target pistol."

"Stuart, your twenty-two-caliber target pistol is on your desk in front of you."

"I bought that last night. The one I used on Habeck I've had for years. My father gave it to me on my sixteenth birthday." Childers grinned. "He never gave Richard a gun."

"Oh, my God!"

"What?"

Fletch stood up.

Childers said. "Why didn't the police find the gun?"

Fletch said, "Why didn't you find the gun?"

"I tried to. I went back to look for it. It wasn't there."

Fletch nodded to the gun on the desk. "May I take that?"

Childers put his hand over it. "Not unless you want to get shot trying."

"Oh, no," said Fletch. "That would just put you to the bother of confessing again!"

THIRTY-NINE

"Hello, hello?" Fletch heard his car phone buzzing while he was unlocking the door.

"This is the *News-Tribune* resource desk. Name and code, please."

"Oh, hi, Mary."

"This is Pilar. Code, please."

"Seventeen ninety dash nine."

"Mr. Fletcher, you're wanted at a meeting in Frank Jaffe's office with Biff Wilson at three o'clock."

"Oh. That's what's happening."

"That's what's happening."

The dashboard clock said two-twenty. "Doubt I can make it."

Pilar said, "The rest of the message from Mr. Jaffe is, 'Either be in my office at three o'clock for this meeting, or don't bother coming back to the *News-Tribune,* period.' "

"Life does offer its choices."

"So does the *News-Tribune.* Any last words?"

"Yeah," Fletch said. " 'And that was all he wrote.' "

Glancing time and again at the clock on his dashboard, Fletch sat in the parked car and thought, for as much time as he had.

When it became too late to make the *News-Tribune* reasonably by three o'clock, he started the car.

Slowly, he pulled into traffic and headed toward his apartment.

"Alston? I know you haven't had the time . . ."

"Sure, I've had the time, ol' buddy." Fletch's car was slouching down the boulevard's slow lane toward home. "As soon as I announced my resignation from Habeck, Harrison and Haller this morning, a woman came by and took all the folders from my desk. Even the case I was working on! What do you think of that?"

"Oh, yeah. You resigned. Tell me about that."

"I didn't become a lawyer to become a crook. I don't think they'd mind right now if I went home and only came in Friday to pick up my final paycheck. Maybe I will. Want to meet at Manolo's for a beer?"

"Alston, I don't think there's going to be anyone at my wedding on Saturday who is employed."

"Don't tell the caterer. By the way, ol' buddy, wedding present from your best man will be forthcoming, never fear, but, obviously, a bit late."

"Aren't I supposed to give you a present, for being best man, or something?"

"Are you?"

"That will be late, too."

"As long as the wedding comes off on time, and it's a rollicking affair."

"Yeah." Fletch stopped the car to let a pigeon investigate a cigar butt in the road. "Rollicking."

"So, for the last hour or so, using the considerable resources of Habeck, Harrison and Haller, I've been working for you. Don't worry: you can't afford it."

"That's the truth."

"About those companies you asked me to look into . . . Are you ready?"

"Yeah."

"Lingman Toys and Cungwell Screw seem to exist for the sole purpose of each owning half of Wood Nymph, Incorporated. In turn, Lingman Toys and Cungwell Screw are owned by one corporate body called Paraska Steamship Company. All this is a typical structuring of corporations designed to discourage curiosity and conceal interests. The purpose of all these corporations seems to be none other than owning a single business called the Ben Franklyn Friend Service, essentially a whorehouse, situated at . . ." A woman in chartreuse shorts, halter, and high-heeled shoes was walking a poodle on a leash along the sidewalk. The gray of the woman's hair matched the poodle's. The woman's shorts were cut halfway up her ass cheeks. Alston was reciting the names of the officers of the various corporations. Names kept being repeated, Jay Demarest, Yvonne Heller, Marta Holsome, Marietta Ramsin. The woman and the dog turned into a passport-photo shop.

"Alston, okay, stop. Who the hell owns Paraska Steamship, or whatever it is?"

"Four women." Alston then began to repeat, recite a mishmash of names.

Fletch stopped at an orange traffic light. The car behind him honked. "Say what? Say again?" A police car drew alongside Fletch. The cop studied Fletch's features carefully.

Alston repeated the names.

" 'Bye, Alston!" He dropped the phone in his lap.

Fletch stomped on the accelerator.

He went through the red light, made a U-turn in the middle of the intersection, and went through the red light again.

The police car pursuing him did the same thing.

"Lieutenant Francisco Gomez, please. Emergency!"

It certainly was an emergency. There were now two police cars pursuing him through city streets. His trying to outdrive them while talking on the car telephone clearly was a traffic hazard.

"Who's calling?"

Fletch hesitated not at all: "Biff Wilson."

He put on his left directional signal and turned right from the left lane. Not a good enough trick to throw off his pursuers, but it did cause noisy confusion at that intersection.

"Yeah?" Gomez sounded as if he were in the middle of a conversation instead of beginning one.

"Gomez, Biff Wilson's in trouble."

"Who is this?"

"Fletcher, a.k.a. Alexander Liddicoat. Remember us?"

"Shit! Where are you?"

"Hell, don't you know?" Fletch spun his wheel mid-block and scurried down an alley. "I thought the police were the eyes and the ears of the city."

"What are you talking about? What's all that noise I hear? Sireens? Screeching tires?"

"Yeah, thanks for the police escort. I am in a hurry. Have you got the forensics report on that gun yet?"

"What gun?"

"The gun I gave you. The gun I told you about."

"Who cares about that? Kid tryin' to make a name for himself . . ."

"You haven't even looked into it?"

"You're as bad as Charles, what's his name, Childers, Stuart Childers. Want to play cops and robbers. You want to be the cop, he wants to be the robber."

"The ballistics report ought to be ready by now, too." Fletch had a moment of comparative peace as he went wrong-way up a one-way street.

"I've got a warrant out for you, Fletcher. Possession of a seller's quantity of angel dust. I've got the evidence right here on my desk."

"I look forward to seeing it." Three police cars spotted Fletch at the corner. They accelerated after him. "Aren't you hearing me, Gomez? Your pal Biff is in trouble."

"Yeah?"

"At the newspaper. He's in Frank Jaffe's office. On the carpet, you might say. In danger of losing his job."

"No way."

"You know it's possible."

Gomez said nothing.

Fletch turned on his lights and pulled into the middle of a funeral cortege. Demonstrating little respect, the three police cars screamed by the cortege.

"He needs your help," Fletch said. "He needs the ballistics and forensics reports on that gun. Immediately."

"Yeah?"

"Would I lie to you?"

"What is this?"

Fletch turned off his lights and ducked down a side street. "As soon as you've got the reports, call the *News-Tribune*. Ask for Frank Jaffe's office. Biff's in Frank's office."

Two blocks up from the next corner, a police car hesitated in the middle of the intersection. As soon as the police saw Fletch's car, they turned and came after him, lights flashing, sirens screaming.

"Gomez, you want to see Biff out on his rear?"

The line went dead.

Fletch dropped the phone in his lap again. He could see the roof of the *News-Tribune* building. The three police cars were back in V formation pursuing him.

There were only two more corners to skitter around. . . .

FORTY

"Hey! You can't leave your car there!"

The guard in the lobby of the *News-Tribune* was known to get red-faced easily. Fletch had left his car half on the sidewalk at the front door of the *News-Tribune*.

Fletch was on the rising escalator to the city room.

"What?" he asked.

At the bottom of the escalator, the guard looked toward the front door. "What are all those sireens?"

"I can't hear you," Fletch said. "Too many sireens."

He passed Morton Rickmers, the book editor, in the city room.

"Did you see Tom Farliegh?" Morton asked. "Is he worth an interview?"

"Naw," Fletch answered. "He's a little, blue-haired old lady in green tennis shoes."

Morton wrinkled his eyebrows. "Okay."

Through the glass door of Frank's office, Fletch saw Frank, behind the desk, and Biff Wilson, in a side chair. The color of their faces was compatible with the color of the face of the guard downstairs, now doubtlessly talking to six policemen.

Frank's secretary said, "You're late."

"It's all relative." He breezed by her.

Fletch closed Frank's office door behind him. "Good afternoon, Frank. Good of you to ask me to stop by." Frank's watery eyes took in Fletch's T-shirt, jeans, and holey sneakers. "Good afternoon, Biff." Biff's jaw tightened. He looked away. His right ear was swollen and red. Fletch commiserated. "That looks like a real ouch." Biff's face was splotched with little cuts from having glass thrown in it. "Lucky for you none of the glass from that beer bottle got in your eyes." Biff looked at Fletch wondrously. Fletch said to Frank, "That's nothing. You should see the *News-Tribune* car Biff drives. Big dents. Rear window smashed. Doubt you'll be able to get much for it on the used-car market."

"How the hell do you know about it?" Biff demanded.

"I'm a reporter." Fletch sat in a chair. "Well, Frank. I'm glad to report that Mrs. Donald Habeck does not slip vodka into her tea. In fact, the poor thing doesn't get to have any tea at all. I've learned my lesson in humility. Never go out on a story with preconceptions. Right, Biff?"

Frank said to him, "I'm surprised you showed up."

"Frank," Fletch said. "In a moment your phone is going to ring. It will be police lieutenant Francisco Gomez calling Biff. He knows Biff is in your office. I would like you to take the message for Biff, please."

"Jeez!" In his chair, Biff threw one leg over the knee of his other leg. "Now the wise ass is telling you what to do!"

Through the windows of Frank's office, Fletch saw six uniformed policemen milling around the city room.

"What's going on between you two guys?" Although high in color, Frank was trying to sound reasonable. "Fletch, Biff tells me you're screwing up in ways even I can't believe. Everywhere he goes on this Habeck story, you've already been there, screwing up, swimming bare-assed in the Habecks' pool, so upsetting Habeck's son, a monk, he refuses to see Biff, angering another suspect so much that when Biff shows up this thug throws a beer bottle in his face. Twice." Fletch was grinning. "It isn't funny. You know you weren't assigned to the Habeck story. Ann McGarrahan and I made that perfectly clear to you. There are easier ways to get fired."

"No rookie should ever come anywhere near me," Biff said. "Especially no wise-guy punk screw-up."

Frank smiled to himself. "I thought you'd burn off your excess energy over the whorehouse story. Instead, last night I heard you say you can't do that story."

"I can do it."

"You said you needed more time on it. Maybe if you spent your time on the story assigned to you instead of bird-dogging Biff . . ."

Through the window, Fletch saw Morton Rickmers talking to one of the policemen. Morton pointed toward Frank's office.

"Screw it." Biff made a move to get up. "This is a waste of time. Just can the son of a bitch and let me go back to work."

"Do you like bullies, Frank?" Fletch asked. "I don't like bullies."

Frank forced a laugh. "Biff's been with the *News-Tribune* all his adult life. You've been with us what? Three months? He's the best crime reporter around. He's got a right to do his work without being bird-dogged by a screw-up kid."

"He's a bully," Fletch said. "I don't like bullies."

"You went after Biff because he's a bully?" Frank asked. "Like hell. You went after Biff because you thought you could beat him at his own story. Little you know."

"I have beaten him."

"Sure," said Biff. "You're ready to wrap up the story of the Habeck murder? Like hell!"

"Right," said Fletch. "I am."

Frank was watching Fletch closely. "I told you two days ago, Fletch, Monday, that we've had about enough of your crap around here. I thought if I gave you a real assignment, the Ben Franklyn whorehouse story —"

"I've got that about wrapped up, too." Fletch looked at the silent phone on Frank's desk.

"Sure," Biff said. "Tell us who killed Donald Habeck, wise ass. We can hardly wait to hear it from your lips. A member of the family, I bet. Crazy Louise? No-brain Jasmine? Daughter Nancy left her five kids in wet diapers and ran out and shot her pa? How about her husband, the two-bit poet? Or better yet, the monk, Robert? Tell us the monk murdered his old man. That will sell newspapers."

The telephone on Frank's desk wasn't ringing. At that moment, Fletch would have appreciated some factual evidence. He took a deep breath. "Stuart Childers murdered Donald Habeck."

Biff laughed. "Jeez! I'll bet you know that 'cause he confessed to you!"

"Yeah," Fletch said. "He did." Biff laughed louder. "Gotta listen," Fletch said. "Sometimes liars tell the truth."

Frank looked through his office windows at the city room. "What are those cops doing out there?"

Six of them stood around Frank's secretary.

"A criminal is a victim of his own crime," Fletch said to Biff, "as you'll come to understand, I think."

The phone rang. Outside, the secretary was too busy with the police to answer it.

Frank picked up the phone in annoyance. "Hello! . . . Who is this? . . ." He glanced at Biff. "Lieutenant Gomez . . . Yeah, Biff is here. . . . No." Then Frank glanced at Fletch. "You tell me the message, Lieutenant. . . . The gun? Okay . . . Twenty-two-caliber pistol. Registered to Stuart Childers . . ." Biff looked up. "Stuart Childer's fingerprints . . ." Frank glared at Biff. ". . . Ballistics . . . It is the gun used to murder Donald Habeck. . . . Right. I'll tell him. . . ." Slowly, Frank hung up.

Frank sat back in his chair, hands folded in his lap. He looked from Biff to Fletch and back to Biff.

Biff sat erect, looking as alert as a rabbit.

Outside the office, the hubbub made by the six policemen was rising noticeably. Clearly, two were arguing with each other. Each was pointing through the window at Fletch.

The secretary, too, had raised her voice.

Irritated, Frank asked, "What's going on out there?"

"Okay." Biff straightened the crease in one trouser leg. "Gomez has been working closely with me on the Habeck murder." He cleared his throat. "That call was for me."

"You didn't even know he was calling," Frank said.

Outside, Hamm Starbuck had arrived. He stood between the police and the door to Frank's office.

Fletch leaned forward in his chair. "Now, Frank, about the Ben Franklyn story . . ."

"Fuck off!" Biff shouted.

Frank raised his eyebrows. He said to Fletch, "Tell me."

"The Ben Franklyn Friend Service is owned by Wood Nymph, Incorporated," Fletch said. "Which is owned by two companies, Cungwell Screw and Lingman Toys." Frank, looking from Biff to the ruckus outside his office door to Fletch, nevertheless appeared to be listening. "Cungwell Screw and Lingman Toys are entirely owned by Paraska Steamship Company, which is owned entirely by four women, Yvonne Heller, Anita Gomez, Marietta Ramsin, and Aurora Wilson."

The blood splotches disappeared against the color of Biff's face.

Outside now, even Hamm Starbuck was shouting.

Frank looked at his telephone. He said, "Anita Gomez." Then he looked at Biff. "Aurora Wilson." Frank moved his chair closer to the desk. "Gomez and Wilson. I guess you two did work closely together." He reached for his phone. "And that's how the pictures of those whores got on my sports pages Monday morning."

Biff exploded. "Son of a bitch!"

"Matt?" Frank said into the phone. "Frank Jaffe. Draw up a severance check for Biff Wilson. I want him out of here by five o'clock. Fired? yes, fired. Not another minute's protection does he, or his enterprises, get from the *News-Tribune*."

Biff jumped to his feet. His hands were fists. "You son of a bitch!"

He took the few steps toward Fletch and swung.

Fletch rolled off his chair, tipping it over onto the floor.

The door opened.

Hamm Starbuck said, "I'm sorry, Frank, the cops, something about Fletch." He looked at Fletch on the floor. "What are you, a rug fetishist?"

Biff swung a kick at Fletch, but Fletch rolled away from it.

The cops poured into Frank's office. Fat, slim, old, young, they were arguing with each other loudly. They were pointing fingers at each other and, occasionally, pointing fingers at Fletch on the floor.

Biff, feet planted either side of Fletch, bent over. He picked Fletch up by the neck.

"Alexander Liddicoat!" shouted one cop. "I recognized him at the stoplight!"

"You didn't check his license plates!" shouted another cop. "We did! He's Irwin Fletcher, wanted for selling PCP!"

Fletch gurgled. "Help! Police!"

"Armed robbery . . ."

"Were you asleep at roll call this morning?"

"Angel dust . . ."

"Listen, Fletch." Frank had come around his desk. Hands on knees, he bent over Fletch being strangled on the floor by Biff Wilson. Clearly, Frank was concentrating hard. "I want the complete story of Habeck's murder, Childers's confession and arrest in the morning edition. Gomez said they're arresting him this afternoon. The other press will have the story of the arrest, but we'll have complete background. Also the news that he confessed to a *News-Tribune* reporter. You'll do a follow-up for the Saturday newspaper."

"Grrr-uggg!" Fletch was trying to force Biff's arms apart.

"Cut that out!" Frank hit Biff's forearm.

"Every traffic violation in the book!" shouted a cop. "Whoever he is, we got him on all that! Even a broken muffler!"

Frank continued. "We want a complete wrap-up, all the background, on the Habeck story, for the Sunday newspaper. We'll need that by six o'clock Saturday."

Hamm Starbuck, after wondering awhile what he was witnessing, took action. Fletch's face, having gone from red to white, was turning blue. Putting his arms around Biff's shoulders, he locked his hands under Biff's chest. He lifted.

Not letting go of Fletch's neck, Biff lifted Fletch higher off the floor.

Six policemen argued vehemently.

The phone was ringing.

Frank stood up as Fletch rose. "Now, what about the Ben Franklyn story? I think that ought to be treated as an exposé in Sunday's newspaper. We'll publish teaser-promos on it tomorrow, Friday, and Saturday. That means we'll need that story, complete, by midday Saturday, for pictures."

Hamm finally wrestled Biff off Fletch.

Biff's grip on Fletch's neck broke.

Fletch fell flat on the floor. His head bounced on the carpet.

"Can you do that?" Frank asked.

Grabbing breath, Fletch said, "I'm getting married Saturday!"

"Ah, the hell with that!" Frank turned away in disgust. "There's no sense of sport in this business anymore!"

He looked around his office.

In one corner, Hamm Starbuck was struggling, restraining Biff Wilson.

Five cops were arguing with each other about Irwin Fletcher, angel dust, Alexander Liddicoat, armed robberies, and traffic violations. Two had their night sticks drawn.

The sixth policeman was bending over, trying to put handcuffs on Fletch.

Fletch's hands were rubbing his throat.

Almost the entire city-room staff was looking through the door and windows into Frank's office.

"What's going on!" Frank yelled. He grabbed the arm of the policeman about to handcuff Fletch. "Cut that out! I need him!" The cop did stop. "Jeez," Frank said. "Whatever happened to the sanctity of the newspaper office!"

" 'Just a breath of fresh air,' " Fletch quoted from the floor, " 'a young maverick who would shake things up a bit . . .' "

Frank Jaffe's secretary leaned over him. "Fletcher, there's a woman on the phone who says she must talk with you. She says it's urgent."

" '. . . See things differently, maybe,' " Fletch quoted as he got to his feet. " '. . . jerk people out of their ruts.' " On his feet, he swayed. "That was my assignment, wasn't it, Frank? Isn't that why I was hired?" Frank had six policemen talking to him, mostly at once. Fletch muttered, "Some ruts are deeper than others."

Among the people marveling through the office door was Ann McGarrahan. A smile played at the corners of her lips.

Hamm Starbuck was talking into Biff's ear. Biff nodded affirmatively twice. Hamm released him.

Straightening his jacket, then making fists of his hands again, Biff skirted all the arguing policemen. He marched out of the office.

"Biff!" Fletch held his throat as he shouted after him. "I know a good lawyer! He's available!"

The secretary said, "She said her name is Barbara something-or-other."

Frank was saying, loudly, to the assembled police, "Look, guys, he can't go to the police station now. He's needed here." Frank watched Fletch pick the phone up off his desk. "I'll go with you to headquarters. Straighten things out myself."

"Hello, Barbara!" Fletch croaked into the phone. "I won't be able to make it to dinner with your mother tonight. Not tonight. Not tomorrow night. Not Friday night. Absolutely. I've got work to do. Got a job. I'll try to see you Saturday. Wait a minute. Hang on . . ." Fletch put his hand over the receiver. "Frank?"

At the side of the room, Hamm Starbuck was breathing deeply.

Frank, surrounded by policemen, looked at Fletch.

"When I do the story on Ben Franklyn," Fletch asked, rubbing his throat, "You want me to report the full particulars of the involvement of Biff Wilson, late of the *News-Tribune?*"

"Damned right." Frank grinned. "Screw the bully."

FLETCH, TOO

Dedicated to

the WANANCHI.

Also dedicated to Joyce and Arthur Greene.

With special thanks to Kathy Eldon and Alexey Braguine.

ONE

What astounded Fletch was that the letter written to him was signed *Fletch.*

TWO

"Do you, Irwin Maurice Fletcher, promise to love, honor, serve, and support in all the ways a man can support a woman . . ." the Preacher shouted. Down the bluff the wind was whipping up whitecaps on the Pacific Ocean. A curtain of hard rain was visible a couple of miles offshore. ". . . cherish, respect, encourage, relinquish all interests and endeavors which do not serve the marriage, until death do you part?"

"Who wrote this?" Fletch asked.

At his side, wind whipping her skirt, Barbara said, "I did. You never gave me a chance to discuss it with you."

"Let's discuss it now."

Behind them on the bluff overlooking the sea stood their wedding guests, coat collars up, holding on to their hats.

"Be a good sport," Barbara said. "Say you do. We'll have plenty of time to discuss it."

"That's what I'm afraid of."

Barbara said to the Preacher, "He says, 'I do.' "

The Preacher looked at Fletch. "Do you do?"

"I guess I do."

"And do you, Barbara Ralton, promise to be a wife to this man to the best of your abilities?"

"I do."

The Preacher then began to read interminably from some word-processor printout. Some rabbits built their hutch in a dell. Spring rains came, and the hutch got flooded out. They built a new hutch in a high place. The winds knocked it over . . .

Watching the storm approaching from the sea, Fletch suspected the wedding party was going to get flooded out and blown over, too.

The wedding had been planned for two o'clock Saturday afternoon. Fletch had gotten all his copy in by two o'clock, shaved in the men's room at the newspaper, and had reached his wedding at two-forty.

"Surprised to see you here," Fletch said to Frank Jaffe, the editor of the *News-Tribune*. "Thought you pretend employees don't exist Saturdays."

"I've been standing in for you at various police stations and courts the last three days," Frank said. "Thought I might have to stand in for you today at your wedding, too."

"You almost did." Two pickup trucks with their tailgates down were parked across the field. In the bed of one truck, delicatessen food was laid out; in the bed of the other, plastic glasses, liquor, and ice. "Are all the various charges against me dropped? Can I get through an airport without being arrested?"

Frank tasted his drink. "Good follow-up on that lawyer's murder in this morning's edition. Got the big Sunday wrap-up in for tomorrow?"

"Yes, Frank."

"How about the big exposé of Ben Franklyn for tomorrow?"

"Ben Franklyn will be exposed in Sunday's newspaper, Frank. Pages and pages of it. With pictures."

"You've been working day and night since Monday."

"Very nearly."

"You look half asleep."

"Frank . . ."

"Have a nice honeymoon." Frank smiled. "You need the rest."

Alston Chambers said, "Fletch, thanks for coming. Being best man at a wedding without a groom was becoming a real strain."

"If you come across any hot stories on your honeymoon," Frank said, "be sure and phone them in. We may have found your talent in investigative reporting."

Alston looked down at Fletch's jeans and sneakers. "Didn't have time to change, uh?"

"Alston, I'm here, I shaved, I'm employed, I get to go on a honeymoon."

"I mean avalanches. Mud slides." Frank finished his drink. "Major earthquakes. Airplane crashes. Train wrecks."

Alston said, "I left some clothes for you at the City Desk. Didn't they tell you?"

"No."

Frank continued, "Mass murders. Acts of terrorism, like, you know, airport bombings."

Alston took Fletch by the elbow. "Your bride, having noticed you're here, would like you to go over and stand next to her in front of the Preacher. That's integral to the wedding."

"Be sure and phone in," Frank said. "If you get any good stuff."

Fletch said to his mother, "I'm surprised to see you here."

A long-stemmed flower bobbing from her hat hit Fletch in the eye as Josephine Fletcher leaned forward to kiss her son. "I wouldn't miss your first wedding for anything."

"This is the only wedding I have planned," Fletch said.

She waved airily. "After this, you're on your own."

" 'After this' ?"

Josie scanned his clothes. "I guess you're dressed appropriately for a picnic next to the sea."

She was dressed in watered silk.

"I've been working."

"Barbara's mother was quite certain you wouldn't show up at all. She says you never do."

"Where is she? I've never met the lady."

"So she says. She's the one over there, in jodhpurs."

"Of course."

Josie scanned the bush. "I don't see where she parked her elephant."

"Elephant?"

Cindy took Fletch's other elbow. "The Preacher says, if you don't get over there, all hell will break loose."

Fletch turned and shook her hand. "Can't thank you enough, Cindy, for everything. You've helped Barbara get ready for our skiing honeymoon. You've helped me keep my job."

Cindy took the hand of a young woman standing next to her. "I feel this is as much our wedding as yours."

"It is." Fletch shook the hand of the other woman. "Have a nice life."

"Fletch," Alston said, looking harried, "this person says she has to meet you right now. Her name is Linda."

"I don't suppose this is a very good time to tell you this." Linda pulled his shirt out of his jeans. She cupped the palms of her hands against the skin of his waist. "I'm in love with you."

"You've never seen me before."

"I see you now. This is it, for me. Wildly, passionately in love." Her eyes said she was serious.

"Alston, how much are you paying this person?"

Alston sighed.

Fletch said to Linda, "I'm just about to get married."

"Really?" Sticking her chin out, she slid her hands up his sides.

"That's why we're all here," Fletch said. The wind was beginning to come up. "Standing around in this horrible place."

Alston said, "I think weddings make some people romantic."

Linda asked, "When are you returning from your honeymoon?"

"Two weeks. We're going skiing in Colorado."

"Don't break anything," she said.

"I'll try not to."

"Because I'm going to be your next wife."

"You are?"

"I've decided that." Linda looked like what she was saying was entirely reasonable. "In fact, you might as well skip this wedding with Barbara altogether."

"Boy," Alston said. "Getting you married is something I'll never try again."

"Was she serious?"

"Call me when you get back," Linda said. "I work with Barbara."

"Oh, nice." Fletch was being guided strongly by the elbow across the field. "Actually, she is beautiful."

"Barbara?" Alston asked.

Fletch said, "Linda."

"Oh, boy."

The wind had come up enough so Fletch had to speak loudly to the woman in jodhpurs. "Hello, Barbara's mother! How are you?"

The woman looked at him as if accosted. "Who are you?"

Fletch tucked in his shirt. "Don't worry. You're not gaining a son."

"Oh, my God."

"Nice to meet you, too."

In front of the Preacher, Fletch pinched Barbara's bottom.

She wriggled. "Nice you could make the time."

"Hey, I filed two terrific stories this week." He shook hands with the Preacher.

To one side stood a man Fletch did not recognize. Standing alone, he was watching, not socializing. Middle-aged, he wore khaki trousers, khaki shirt, blue necktie, and a zippered leather jacket. His eyes were light blue. He held a sealed manila envelope.

Fletch said, "I just got a marriage proposal."

"Are you seriously considering it?" Barbara asked.

The bride wore walking shoes, leg warmers collapsed around her calves, skirt and sweater. She carried a bouquet of flowers.

Fletch said, "Nice posies."

"They're forget-me-nots. Alston remembered them."

Fletch looked across the field at the pickup trucks. "Someone arranged for caterers, too."

"Alston."

Fletch looked at Alston. "Guess I picked the right best man."

Alston shrugged. "Didn't have anything else to do. I'm an unemployed lawyer."

"And," Barbara said, "Alston has packed all your skiing things. And brought them to the airport. And checked them in."

Fletch looked at Cindy. "I'm getting chewed out here."

"Without Alston and Cindy . . ." Barbara's voice trailed off in the wind.

Alston touched the Preacher's arm as if searching for a starter button. "Sir?"

The Preacher smiled. "I've learned to wait until the bride and groom stop arguing. It makes for a nicer ceremony."

Alston said, "The weather . . ."

The Preacher looked out to sea. "Ominous."

The end of the allegory regarding rabbits was entirely blown away in the wind, despite the Preacher's shouting. Fletch wondered if he would ever know where the rabbits finally set up hutch.

The wind abated enough so that the Preacher could be heard to yell, "With the powers invested in me by the State of California, I now declare you man and wife. What God has put together, let no man put asunder."

A heavy raindrop fell on Fletch's nose.

Immediately Linda broke between the bride and groom and kissed the groom on the mouth.

"What about woman?" Fletch tried to say.

Cindy was kissing Barbara.

Hand on the back of his neck, Linda said, "Next time, baby. You and me."

The Preacher was kissing Barbara.

Alston shook Fletch's hand. "I do divorces."

"My vows seemed longer than her vows."

"I'm sure it always seems that way."

Barbara's mother was kissing Barbara.

The middle-aged man dressed in khaki came through the crowd. He handed Fletch the envelope.

"Thanks," Fletch said.

Immediately there were splotches of rain on the envelope.

Alston was kissing Barbara.

In the envelope were two passports, two thick airline ticket folders, a wad of bills, and a letter.

Fletch said, "Barbara?"

Frank Jaffe was kissing Barbara.

The man in khaki already was up on the road getting into a sports car. He had said nothing.

"Barbara . . ."

Dear Irwin:

What a moniker your mother hung on you. As soon as I heard that was who you were to be, Irwin Maurice, I said to myself, There's nothing I can do for him. With a name like that, either he'll be a champ or a dolt.

Which is it?

I'm mildly curious.

After having missed out on your whole life, I didn't want to break a perfect record by attending your wedding.

How curious are you?

Enclosed is a wedding present, which you may take anyway you want. You may take the money, cash in the tickets, and buy your bride a nice set of china or something. That's probably what I would do. Or, if you're mildly curious about me, you and your bride can come visit me in my natural habitat. Squandering money is always fun, too.

Seeing you've now put yourself in the way of being a father yourself (at least you've gotten married), I thought we could meet agreeably.

If you do come to Nairobi, I've made a reservation for you and Barbara at the Norfolk Hotel.

Maybe I'll see you there.

Fletch

* * *

The rain was making the ink run on the page.

"Barbara!"

It was raining hard. Across the field, people were dashing for their cars. As Josephine walked, the flower blossom from her hat bobbed in front of her face. Men were throwing tarpaulins over the beds of the pickup trucks.

"What's that?" Alston asked.

Hundred-dollar bills were fluttering out of Fletch's hand and blowing in the wind. Alston scurried around picking them up.

On the road, Barbara was getting into a car with her mother.

"Where's Nairobi?" Fletch handed Alston the dripping letter.

"Nairobi? East Africa? Kenya?" Reading the letter, Alston tried to protect it from the wind and the rain with his body. "Fletch! Your father!"

On the road, cars were going off in each direction. Josephine Fletcher was nowhere in sight. Even the pickup trucks went in different directions.

"Fletch, this has to be from your father. You always said he was dead."

"He always was dead."

Together they looked at the faint lines under the running ink of the writing paper.

"What the hell," Alston said. "Your plane for Denver leaves at six o'clock."

Peering inside the envelope, Fletch said, "These tickets are for a plane to London, leaving at seven-thirty."

Only a few cars were left on the road.

"Alston, where is my mother staying?"

"At the Hanley Motor Court. On Caldwell, just off the freeway north."

"Do you suppose that's where she's gone?"

"Of course." Alston shivered. "We're soaking wet."

"Oh, yeah."

Fletch took the illegible letter from Alston and stuffed it back in the envelope. "If you see Barbara, tell her I'll meet her at the airport."

"Where are you going?"

Rain ran down the faces of the two young men as they looked at each other.

Jogging up the slope to his car, Fletch slipped and fell. He landed on the envelope in the mud.

THREE

"Your father died in childbirth."

"Whose?"

"Yours."

They stood inside the door of Josephine Fletcher's room at the Hanley Motor Court. She had changed into slacks, blouse, and open sweater. He was dripping wet.

He clutched the muddy envelope to his side.

"That's what you've always said."

"You need a hot shower."

"You've always said that, too."

"Mostly, for you, I've recommended cold showers." Josie turned on the light in the bathroom. "You're muddy, soaked, disheveled, and, my son, you look more exhausted than Hilary at the top of Mount Everest. What have you been doing to yourself?"

"Working. Getting married. Normal things."

"They don't seem to agree with you. But I will correct myself: for that particular wedding, you were indeed dressed appropriately. If I had known what was to happen, I would have worn a swimsuit."

"Your silk dress got watered."

Josie crossed the room to him. She put her hand out for the envelope under his arm. "Do you think you had some communication from your father? On your wedding day?"

"Yes. I think so." He put the muddy envelope on the bureau.

"That would be interesting," Josie said. "Exciting. To both of us. First, let me ask you: is your wedding over?"

"Not the marriage."

"That was it? So much milling about and shouting on a stormy bluff over the ocean?"

"We didn't have a backup plan."

"Only an hour ago you married a nice girl named Barbara," Josie said patiently. "You have, or you think you have, some communication from beyond the grave. However interesting and exciting it might be possibly to hear from your father, don't you think this is one of those particularly special times you really ought to be with your wife, no matter what?"

"She'll understand."

"Don't be too sure, sonny." Josie's face saddened. She turned toward the rain-streaked window. "Love and understanding have nothing to do with each other. I loved your father. I did not understand him. Why not? Was he too masculine, and I too feminine? Maybe the modern expectation that men and women really can understand each other is so false that it destroys marriages. As a woman, however, I will report to you that having a man present in a marriage means rather a lot to a woman." She turned to Fletcher again. "Like on your wedding day. And other notable occasions."

Fletch put his finger on the envelope. "This appears to be from my father. You've always given me this stupid line, 'Your father died in childbirth.' Never anything more, no matter how I've asked. I've always let you have the literary conceit of this stupid line. But the humor of it has worn as thin as my skin at the moment."

"You're curious?"

Fletch took a deep breath. "Mildly."

"What I'm saying, sonny, is that I see your possibly hearing from your father causes you to do exactly as he would have done."

"What's that?"

"Leave your bride alone on your wedding day."

"Did he do that to you?"

"He spent the entire wedding reception at the other end of the hangar removing, repairing and replacing the engine in the airplane we were about to use for our honeymoon."

"You were married in an airplane hangar?"

"By now you know how wind and rain on a bluff exposed to the sea can drown out the sweetest words a woman should ever hear. Consider how much of the wedding ceremony is heard in an airport aluminum hangar, with thirty seconds between scheduled takeoffs and landings."

Fletch smiled. "Are you sure you were married?"

"Are you sure you were married?"

"He wanted to be sure of the engine before he took his bride up in the plane."

"That was my kind thought, too, back when I expected to understand because I loved."

"What do you think now?"

"I think he was avoiding the reception, the congratulations, the handshakes, the slaps on the back, the jokes, and the reasonable questions obliging him to speak of our future with responsibility." Her eyes narrowed. "What are you doing?"

"My editor, Frank Jaffe, says I may have a talent for investigative reporting."

"This is your wedding day."

Fletch shrugged. "I've spent most of it working."

"Why is it considered the height of masculinity for a man to avoid the biggest emotional moments of his life by burying his head, and his body, in work?"

"Trickcyclists say a man's urge to work is as great as his sexual urge."

She smiled. "I haven't heard that slang for the mental health brigade in decades."

"I read that lately."

"Wouldn't you say work can also be man's way of avoiding emotional responsibility?"

"Okay. Super. You should know. But you're not going to evade my question now."

Josephine Fletcher colored. She said, "Your 'mild curiosity,' the mystery about your father, is not worth your taking two minutes from your wedding day."

Fletch shivered. "I don't know that for a fact."

"Get into the shower," his mother said. "Barbara won't want you sneezing all over her during your honeymoon. This traveler's court, or whatever it is, must have a washer-dryer for those Americans who choose to live all their lives entirely behind windshields. There are towels in the bathroom."

When he handed his clothes to her through the bathroom door, she said, "You know, I'm 'mildly curious,' too. Would you show me what you think you got from your father?"

Wrapped in a towel he crossed the room to the envelope. "Some tickets to Nairobi, Kenya, and some cash and a letter."

"Yes," she said. "If he's alive, he probably would be in Africa. I've thought that. May I see the letter?"

Between index finger and thumb, Fletch pulled the drenched, blued piece of paper out of the envelope and handed it to her.

Josie held it in two hands. As she looked at the washed-out, blank page, her face crinkled. "Oh, Irwin. Don't you see? There's nothing there."

FOUR

"Ironic, and rather sad, that you are spending your wedding day with your mother."

Josie had ordered lunch for them from Room Service. They sat at odd angles obliged by the smallness of the motel room at the round table, taking the toothpicks out of their club sandwiches. Wind slashed rain against the window. "I say, more in worry than in bitterness, *See what your father has wrought?* First time you ever hear from him and you respond with behavior unnatural but typical of him."

"That much I've heard."

When Fletch bit into his sandwich a dollop of mayonnaise landed on the towel below his waist.

"Can't you at least telephone Barbara?"

"Not sure where she is."

"You just told me you're an investigative reporter. Surely you could find her."

"I've told Alston, my best man, to tell her I'd meet her at the airport."

"What does that mean?" Josie's bite of her sandwich was so small, mayonnaise had no chance to escape her.

"I want to do some thinking."

Her eyes widened. "You're not honestly thinking of going to Nairobi?"

He shrugged. "When will we ever get another chance?"

"Oh, Irwin! This man ignores you all your life; we presume him d ad; and suddenly he snaps his fingers and you cancel your honeymoon and fly halfway around the world to meet him!"

"It could be a honeymoon. Barbara might like it."

Fletch remembered. Growing up, he had not been exactly the center of Josie Fletcher's universe either. There were her detective novels, always. He called them her *defective* novels. Because none had sold particularly well, there had had to be a lot of them. Other people made jokes about his mother's books. She had not written many novels, people said, she had written one novel many times. People joked that her publisher kept her writing one novel until she got it right. True, her producing murder and mayhem for quiet libraries throughout the land had kept them reasonably sheltered and reasonably fed. For that he was grateful to her.

Josie Fletcher lived in a world in which fictional characters had reality and real people were forgotten, blinked at, treated vaguely. The characters in her novels seldom had breakfast, lunch, and dinner all in the same day, never had cuts on their elbows, black eyes, broken fingers, itchy pubic hairs, or teachers deeply mistaken in their student's mathematical potential. They never went shopping to replace trousers that had risen up the shank of the leg or split in the back when the wearer stooped for a drink from the school water bubbler.

Independence was not something for which Fletch had ever had to strive. There had been moments when he had deeply resented it.

Yet here he was, on his wedding day, in a moldy motel room, having a sandwich with his mother, listening to her surprise at his expressing "mild curiosity" regarding his father. She had never, never told him about their marriage.

In fact, he was curious about both of them. Always had been.

"Why haven't you?" he asked.

"Why haven't I what?"

"Ever told me about my father, your marriage?"

"Fear and fairness."

"Fear?"

"Your masculinity, too, my son, is something I've never been able to come to grips with. Don't think a mother doesn't know. You've been ripping your jeans on garden fences since you were nine years old."

In front of his mother, Fletch blushed. "Men aren't born virgins, you know."

"You weren't, at any rate."

"A man has nothing to give up but his energy." Fletch laughed.

"Oh, God."

"I can't help it if I'm energetic."

"Is that what you call it?"

"May I have some of your french fries?"

"Of course. Do keep up your energy."

"I had pizza about three this morning. Supper or breakfast. I don't know which."

"Despite all my last chapters, not all mysteries have solutions. How does a mother explain to a son that she doesn't understand a husband, a father? That she was in a marital situation she doesn't understand?"

"By beginning with Chapter One?"

"And there's the element of fairness. I could have spewed forth what I thought about your father, my confusion, my hurt, my puzzlement, the *mystery*, but he wasn't around, you see, to defend himself, to give you his side of whatever story. I loved him, you see."

"You could have told me he left you, not that he *died*, for Christ's sake."

"I never knew that, you see." Her face turned whiter. "You show up today with, frankly, a blank piece of paper . . ."

Fletch watched his mother try to gather together in one hand another quarter of her three-decker sandwich.

"You know that we had to have your father declared assumed dead, after seven years. Otherwise, I couldn't have married Charles."

"I remember him."

"He wasn't with us long, was he? Or Thad."

"You've kept the name Fletcher."

"Well, I had published books under that name, you see, and it was your name. And Charles, and Thad, and . . . weren't your father." She wiped under her eyes with her paper napkin. "It was the *impossibleness* of your father that I loved. If that blank piece of paper you showed me means anything, if he did go somewhere, I would have loved to have gone with him."

"But you say you didn't understand him."

"Oh, who the hell understands anybody? Damn fools keep asking me why I write mystery stories. Maybe because there's a big mystery in my life I've never been able to solve. So, neurotically, I keep setting up simulated mysteries and arriving at simulated solutions. Frustrated practicing."

"Writers have an uncontrollable compulsion," Fletch said. "I read that somewhere, too. Remembered it, in my effort to understand you."

"Lots of luck," she said.

"Chapter One." Fletch snuck a look at her wristwatch. "I'm trying to make a decision here. Am I flying to Denver, Colorado, or Nairobi, Kenya?"

"I don't know what to tell you."

"Chapter One," he repeated.

"Chapter One," she said. "High School. Montana. I was the pretty little thing. Cheerleader. Honor student."

"I've read this book," Fletch said. "Several times. And he was the big man on campus, president of the class, captain of the football team."

"Far from it. He was way out."

"Sorry. Wrong novel."

"Way out, skidding his overpowered motorcycle around his parents' dirt-poor ranch. Bright enough. He once wrote this paper for English class, this long, somber, brilliant analysis of a Shakespearean sonnet. The teacher gave him an A-plus-plus, and complimented Walter in class. Walter roared with laughter. He told everybody he had written the 'Shakespearean' sonnet himself and then analyzed it. Nearly destroyed the teacher."

"Ah," said Fletch. "So it was Daddy who wrote Shakespeare."

"When they expelled him for that —"

"They expelled him for that?"

"Suspended him. At the time, the object of education was obedience, not intellectual freedom. Has anything changed? Anyway, Walter took an airplane without permission from a neighboring ranch —"

"He could fly a plane in high school?"

"No one knew he could. First he buzzed the high school a few times, while it was in session. Then he bombed it. With a volume called *The Collected Plays of Shakespeare*. Made a perfect hit, too. Smashed the skylight over the stairwell. The book and all this glass came crashing down three floors."

"And you've never wanted to tell me about this man?"

"Wild. You mentioned football. One Saturday at a home game, suddenly he appeared on the field, standing up in the saddle of his motorcycle. He caught a pass, sat down, roared down the field and through the goalposts, ball cradled under one arm."

"Did he ever spend any time in jail?"

"Some. He was so handsome, so . . ." Josie shrugged. ". . . energetic, everyone should have loved him. Everyone hated him. Everything he did jeered at everything we held sacred. He jeered at the school by fooling the teacher with *his* Shakespearean sonnet. He jeered at football by saying, 'If the object is to get the football down the field, through the goalposts, use a motorcycle.' He'd show up at school dances drunk, and dance energetically, *satirically*, I now realize. Everybody else would go home."

"Dance with you?"

"To my embarrassment, yes."

"What was a nice girl like you doing with a rogue like him?"

"Maybe I had a little understanding of him. At least between someone very feminine and someone very masculine, if not much ability to understand, there is a very strong chemistry? Electricity?"

"Sex?"

"He wasn't an outlaw. As soon as everybody in the town thought he was, and the real baddies began to talk as if he were one of their own, Walter dressed in as close an approximation of a suit and tie as he and his family possessed, and went down to the local baddy hangout, a really horrible roadhouse about eight miles out of town, and started a riot I expect they're still talking about. He jeered at *everybody*."

"How old was he then?"

"Would you believe fifteen?"

"How could you not tell me about him?"

"Energetic," his mother said. "Bright, handsome, and energetic. Saw things his own way, and never asked for agreement. I mean, it's not everybody who is expelled from school *and* the local roadhouse. I thought him simply marvelous."

"Is that why you've never sought agreement from me?"

Josie looked at her son from under lowered lids. "Anyway, we were married literally over my father's dead body. I've told you your grandfather died of a heart attack during my senior year of high school."

"Yes. Must put that fact in my medical folder, if I live long enough."

"Walter had a flying job. Flying ranchers around, mining executives, emergency medical equipment, out-of-state crop-dusting, in season. Sometimes, frankly, I wasn't absolutely sure where he was. Weather's always a problem in a job like that." Josie poured coffee for them both. "I got pregnant immediately. I thought that was the right thing to do, that was the way life was, that we both wanted it. It never occurred to me you were supposed to *think* about such things. We were buying a house trailer. I thought we were perfectly happy."

"What do you guess he thought?"

Josie sighed. "Everyone was telling this *boy*, Walter, that he was married and about to be a father and ought to give up flying and riding motorcycles. That he ought to give up being *Walter*. At the time, I thought such talk was natural, too. I've wondered since how he heard it."

"Come on, get to the good part: me."

"You were born ten days ahead of expectations. Walter had promised he would be with me when you were born. In fact, he was across the state. My mother telephoned him the good news. He said he would take off and fly home right away. There being a major storm in his path, he was advised against flying. He took off. He never arrived."

"He crashed?"

"Seven years later we were able to assume him dead. After the snows melted in the spring, a search was made for his plane. It was never found."

"He died in childbirth."

"An enigmatic statement, for which I apologize. I always thought it rather graceful. What I mean by it is, What was in his mind when he climbed into that airplane, when he took off, while he flew alone across the state of Montana in the dark, presumptively to his wife and son, me and you? Do you understand? What was in his mind at that point has always been more important to me, in a way, than whether he lived or died."

"Maybe I understand. A little."

"Who *was* Walter? Who *is* he?"

"I need my clothes."

Josie looked at him as if awaking suddenly. "Where are you going?"

"I don't know."

"When will you know?"

Fletch said, "It's a long drive to the airport."

FIVE

"May I kiss the bride, too?"

Fletch decided where he wanted to go only as he walked down the airport corridor with the muddy envelope under his arm and saw Barbara and Alston waiting outside the gate.

"Where have you been?" Barbara asked.

"Where did you go?" Fletch asked.

"Where did you go?"

"I didn't know where you went."

Alston rolled up his eyes.

"Have Cindy and her friend gone?" Fletch asked.

Barbara said, "They've gone."

"Where's our luggage?" Fletch asked.

Barbara said, "It's gone."

"I checked it in this morning," Alston said. "So you wouldn't have to be bothered with it at this point."

"It's gone?"

"It's gone."

"We need to get it back."

"Oh, no," Alston said. "It's gone."

"The plane's about to go," Barbara said.

"It hasn't gone," Fletch said.
Alston looked at his watch.
"We're not going?" Barbara asked.
"We're going." Fletch said to Alston, "You didn't tell her?"
"I'm not going to."
"We're not going to Colorado."
"Our luggage is," Barbara said.
"Must get it back," Fletch said.
Alston hit his forehead with the palm of his hand. "Skis."
"Come on," Fletch said. "Let's go."
They were rushing up the corridor.
"We're not going?" Barbara asked.
"I've got the tickets," Alston said. "Turn them in. I've got the baggage tickets. Get the luggage."
Barbara said, "We're not going."
"We are going," said Fletch. "Alston, we need to get the luggage to British Air at the International Terminal."
"The plane's changed?" Barbara asked.
"We're changing planes."
"For Colorado?"
"London."
"London, Colorado?"
"Kenya."
"London, Kenya?"
"Nairobi, Kenya."
"Nairobi, Kenya!"
"Africa."
"Africa!"
"East Africa."
Barbara mouthed the words: "East Africa . . ."
"Didn't you say you'd follow me to the ends of the earth?"
"Never! You can't even find a pizza parlor in Malibu!"
In the terminal's main concourse, Barbara jumped ahead of Fletch, turned around, and stopped. Facing Fletch, she put her fists on her hips.
"Fletch! What's going on?"
"London," Fletch said. "Then we're going on to Kenya."
Alston had kept walking.
"Tell me what's happening!"
"We've got a wedding present," Fletch said. "A trip to Nairobi, Kenya."
"Who from? Tell me another." Barbara's face flushed. "Fletch! You

accepted an assignment from the newspaper on our honeymoon!"

"No, no. Nothing like that."

Flapping boarding passes, airline tickets, baggage stubs, Alston was at the airline's courtesy information booth clearly straining the attendant's courtesy.

"You did too!"

"Would I do that to you?"

"I'll be damned if I'm going to sit in some hotel room, or some, some grass shack while you run miles in circles trying to fill up one damned inch of that newspaper! Not on my honeymoon!"

"I told you: the trip is a present. A wedding present. It will be fun."

"I'll bet. A present from the newspaper!"

"No. Not from the newspaper."

"Who else would give you a trip to Africa?"

The courteous man at the information counter now had a phone to each ear while also, apparently, listening to Alston.

"My father."

Barbara's eyes popped. "Your father?"

"I guess."

"You didn't say, *I do* at the wedding, you said, *I guess I do*. Now you're saying you *guess* you got a wedding present of a trip to Africa from your father?"

"It's turned into a highly conjectural day."

At the counter, Alston's lips were moving rapidly.

"You've never had a father. Or you've had four of them, or something."

"What's the difference?"

"What father?"

"The one who died."

"You've inherited something?"

"No. We really don't have time to discuss this now, Barbara."

"You didn't have time to discuss the wedding, either."

"And it happened, see? It came off without a hitch. All right. Things work out."

Barbara wagged her head. "This can't work out."

"Sure it can."

"I can't go to Kenya."

"We haven't had any shots, have we?"

"I don't have a passport!"

"Oh, that." Fletch reached into the muddy envelope. "You have a passport." He handed it to her.

Alston was striding toward them, smiling.

"Alston," Fletch said. "we haven't had any shots."

"You only need them for medical reasons," Alston said. "Not legal reasons."

"I'm glad you became a lawyer."

"Yeah." Alston glanced at Barbara. "Don't forget: I do divorces."

"Where did this picture of me come from?" Barbara said into her passport.

Fletch glanced at it over her shoulder. "It's a nice one."

"Okay." Alston was sorting various tickets and stubs in his hands. "Your tickets to Colorado are canceled. Not sure I'll be able to get your money back."

"Can we get the luggage back?"

"That's my green sweater," Barbara said at her passport picture.

"What they're going to try to do is get your luggage off that plane, then they'll send it over to the International Terminal, British Air, and get it aboard your flight to London, checked straight through to Nairobi."

Fletch put Barbara's passport back in the muddy envelope. "We won't know if our luggage is with us until we get to Nairobi."

"The skis," Barbara said.

"Can't separate the luggage now." Alston shook his head. "No way. Things are too confusing as it is."

"Are you confused?" Barbara asked. "I'm not confused."

Alston glanced at his watch. "We've got to get over to the International Terminal quick-quick. Got to tell them what your connecting flight to Nairobi is."

"Quick-quick." Fletch grabbed Barbara's elbow.

"We're not going skiing," Barbara said. "We packed ski clothes! Nothing but ski clothes!"

"Barbara, we have to hurry."

"Where?"

"International Terminal," Fletch said.

"British Air," Alston said.

They were dashing across the concourse.

"London, England," Fletch said.

"Passport Control," Alston said.

"Nairobi, Kenya," Fletch said.

"Fletch! I told my mother I'd call her from Colorado!"

"Can't stop," Fletch said.

"Tonight!"

Fletch steered her into the revolving door.

"Ain't married life fun?" After he went through the revolving door himself, he said, "So far?"

SIX

"All my mother wanted to do was meet you." Barbara fastened her seat belt.

"I met her. At the wedding."

"Would you believe she really wanted to meet you *before* the wedding?"

"I met her before the wedding. She was wearing jodhpurs. Right? She seemed real surprised to see me."

"Dismayed, more likely. She arranged dinner for us every night last week. You never made it. Not once."

"I was working. Did I tell you I have a job?"

"And you're dragging me halfway around the world to meet your father?"

"Maybe."

"What do you mean, 'maybe' ?"

"He's known to evade important occasions." Buckled up, Fletch put the side of his face against the back of his seat.

"You're going to sleep, aren't you?"

"Barbara, I have to. I haven't slept in days and nights, and days, and . . ."

Barbara sighed. "How long before we get to Nairobi, Kenya?"

"Two days."

"Two days!"

"Two nights? Maybe three days."

"Fletch. Wake up. Get your head off my shoulder. Listen to what the steward's saying about what to do when the airplane crashes."

"That's okay," Fletch mumbled. "You're coming with me."

"Oh, my God! Seven-twenty on our wedding night, and he's asleep!"

"The thing is," Fletch said, "I never knew there was a possibility my father is alive."

Many, many hours later on the flight from London to Nairobi, they were terribly scrunched up. The airplane was full. The seats were narrow and close to each other. There was hand luggage spilling out from under every seat.

"Did your mother know? Did she know there was a possibility he was alive?"

"I think she convinced herself he was dead. To keep her pride. To keep her sanity. In order to marry again, she had to legally assume him dead after seven years."

"I guess in order to go to court to declare your husband dead, you have to believe he's dead."

"But she never really knew. When I'd ask questions about him, you know, growing up, her answers would always be so glib, so casual, you know? I'd get the idea the topic wasn't worth discussing."

"Maybe it wasn't."

"She says she loved him, though."

"What sort of things would she tell you?"

"She'd say, 'Hey, I was only married to your father ten months, and I never understood him.' "

"Then what would she say?"

" 'How do you spell "license"?' "

"Why would she say that?"

"Well, you know, she writes these detective novels. And she never could spell. She'd ask me to look words up in the dictionary for her. It was her way of getting rid of me."

"What did you know about your father?"

"I knew he was a pilot. I knew, or thought I knew, he died about when I was born. Therefore, I always assumed he died in a plane crash shortly after I was born. Or before. I knew my mother was alone when she gave birth to me. I didn't realize she was awaiting a husband who never showed up. A child accepts what he's told."

"Did you ever see a picture of your father?"

Fletch scanned his memory. "Never. That's odd, isn't it? Naturally, there would be pictures of your father around, if he were dead."

"But not if there was a possibility he was alive, and had abandoned you both."

"So that possibility must have been very much in my mother's mind."

"Very much, I'd say."

The areas under the seats in front of them were filled, too.

Instead of waiting at Heathrow eight hours for their connecting flight to Nairobi or finding a place to sleep, Barbara and Fletch had bussed into London. Fletch had no clothes but the jeans and shirt he was wearing. Barbara insisted upon buying sweaters. They had lunch in a not-very-good place. They bought books. They got lost. They had to taxi back to the airport.

"This little guy just came up to me after the wedding, while everyone but the groom was kissing the bride, and just handed me this envelope."

"I didn't see him."

"He was there, I swear it. He didn't say a word. Just handed me the envelope and left."

Barbara asked, "Are you sure he wasn't your father?"

"I would think if he were, my mother would have recognized him."

"It's been a long time."

"Still . . . they knew each other all through school."

"Maybe your mother didn't even see him. We were outdoors, somewhat of a crowd, bad weather . . ."

"And you never know whether my mother is seeing real people or socializing with figments of her imagination."

"Right," Barbara said. "She must have been deeply hurt by all this."

"And deeply puzzled."

Barbara smiled. "The mystery Josie Fletcher couldn't solve. Better not let her fans in the libraries know."

"Her only fans are in the libraries, and are silent."

"What else was in the envelope?"

"The tickets, the passports, ten one-hundred-dollar bills, and the letter."

"You haven't shown me the letter."

"There's nothing to see." Fletch reached under the seat in front of him and picked up the envelope. "It all washed away in the rain."

He handed her the wrinkled piece of paper.

"That's sad." She stared at it in her hand. "Maybe your mother could have recognized the handwriting. How do you know it was from your father?"

"It was signed 'Fletch.' "

"What's his real name?"

"Walter."

"Walter. I wonder how I would have thought of you as a Walter junior."

"A fletcher by any other name is still an arrow maker."

"So what did the letter say?" She handed it back to him.

"In fact, it said something about my name." He leaned forward as much as he could to put the envelope back. "Something about not liking my names, Irwin Maurice, something about my mother's giving me these names, not him, or not with his agreement, as if he'd had nothing to do with it."

"What are you talking about?"

He sat back again. "The letter read almost as if my mother gave the baby, me, the names which he didn't like, didn't relate to, on her own, and this made the baby, me, more her baby than his: that he couldn't relate to anyone named Irwin Maurice."

"Neither can you."

"But I've stuck around. I haven't disappeared."

"You disappear all the time."

"He said he was 'mildly curious' in meeting me and asked if I was 'mildly curious' in meeting him."

"That's the word he used? 'Mildly'?"

"Yes. 'Mildly.' But the airline tickets to Nairobi and back are expensive."

"Maybe he's rich."

"Maybe he was giving us each an out. He wrote I certainly didn't have to come if I didn't want. He said I could cash the tickets in and buy you a set of china or something."

"A set of china," Barbara said. "I might have liked that."

"You'll never see your china, but you will see Kenya."

"Maybe this isn't from your father at all." Barbara wriggled uncomfortably in her seat. "Maybe somebody was trying to get you out of the country for a while. One of these stories you've been investigating."

"I suppose that's possible."

"Keep you out of court, keep you from raising more trouble, or something."

"Maybe everyone on the newspaper took up a collection to get rid of me. Maybe the return tickets are no good." Fletch smiled.

"Maybe a wild-goose chase."

Fletch asked, "Aren't you 'mildly curious'?"

"Only mildly."

Fletch continued looking at Barbara.

"I'm trying to say something here," she said.

"I know. What?"

"I don't think it's good for you to be more than 'mildly curious.' You know what I mean?"

"So I won't be more than mildly disappointed?"

"Yeah," Barbara said. "Something like that."

SEVEN

"*Jambo,*" the customs official in Nairobi airport said. He eyed the two pairs of covered skis Fletch held upright.

Very carefully, Fletch said, "*Jambo.*"

"*Habari?*" He was a short, pudgy, balding man in well-pressed shirt and trousers.

"Fletch said, "*Habari.*"

"So you have been to Kenya before."

"Never," Fletch said. "Never been in Africa before."

"That's the way it is." The man chuckled softly. "Everyone in the world speaks Swahili."

Barbara said, "I've got to take off this sweater."

The two pairs of skis in their soft plastic covers had drawn the particular attention of the customs official to Barbara and Fletch. In fact, the two pairs of wrapped skis were drawing the attention of many people in Nairobi airport. These people stood in a loose circle around Fletch, Barbara, and the skis. Two of these people were in uniforms. Nightsticks and handguns dangled from their belts. One carried a machine gun.

The customs official took his eyes off the wrapped skis long enough to look at the passports Fletch handed him. "Are you visiting Kenya for business or pleasure?"

"Pleasure," Barbara answered. "We were just married. Days ago. A million years ago."

Fletch then heard, for the first time, the sound he was to hear many times in Kenya, the little song exhaled on three notes: "Oh, I see."

The customs official made a note on his clipboard. "And what sort of shooting equipment is that, in the rifle covers, you are bringing into Kenya? Very long rifles, I think." He pointed the back of his pen at them as if they really needed pointing out.

"Oh, these." Fletch looked up and down the skis he held beside him. "These are for shooting down mountains."

The official looked alarmed. "Shooting down mountains? Is that possible?"

"Skis."

"Skis . . . Mombasa?"

Very carefully, Fletch said: "Mombasa."

"I have skied off Mombasa. Behind a speedboat." The official took the position of one skiing behind a speedboat, knees bent, hands forward to hold a towline. "The skis I used were short. Perhaps in proportion to the feet?" He looked down at Barbara's and Fletch's feet. "I don't think so."

"Snow skis."

"Oh, I see. I have seen those in films. This large, are they? You are in Kenya en route to someplace else."

Fletch was hoping that soon he could get to a men's room. "Not really."

"Where do you go after Kenya?"

"Home. Back to the States."

"You return to the United States? With the skis?"

Fletch craned his neck to look through the door of the controlled area to see if possibly anyone was waiting, looking for them. "Yes."

The official thought a long moment. "You always travel with snow skis, even to the equator?"

"No."

"There was some confusion," Barbara said.

"Oh, I see."

"At the airport. We ended up bringing the skis with us."

"At the airport, did you not know you were coming to Africa? Did you get on the wrong plane?"

"We knew," Fletch said. "We got on the right plane."

"So you knew what you were doing when you brought your snow skis to Kenya, just to bring them home again?"

"Well, that's the fact." Barbara looked at Fletch. "We did bring our skis to Africa."

"There is snow on Mount Kenya," the official conceded, "but it's at the top, you see. There are no skiing safaris. Perhaps you brought these snow skis to Africa to sell them. They are a curiosity."

"We can't sell them," Barbara said. "They're borrowed."

"Oh, I see. You borrowed skis to bring to Africa and home again."

"Fletch," Barbara said, "quite reasonably, this gentleman wants to know why we brought snow skis to equatorial Africa."

"Wait till I take off my sweater." Fletch leaned the skis against Barbara and wriggled out of his London-bought sweater. "Hot."

"Perhaps someone here could use snow skis for a wall decoration," mused the official. "Someone who has a very large wall."

"Originally we were going to Colorado," Fletch said. "Skiing."

"And you failed to get off the plane when it stopped in Colorado?"

"It didn't stop in Colorado," Barbara said. "If it had, I would have called my mother."

The official smiled at her.

Fletch said, "It's a little difficult explaining just why we have landed in Kenya carrying snow skis. I admit that."

The official wagged his head. "I love my job."

"We'll definitely take the skis with us when we leave," Fletch said.

"We have to return them," Barbara said. "They're borrowed."

"I would love to see them," the official said, "while they're here."

"Of course." Fletch opened the zipper on one of the ski covers. The man carrying the machine gun stepped back a pace. "There," Fletch said. "Skis."

The official seemed surprised. "And those . . ." He bent his knees again and now used his hands as paddles. ". . . those are ski walking sticks?"

"Ski poles."

The official concerned himself with his clipboard. "Snow skis are very large items to carry with you when you can't use them."

"Cumbersome, too," Barbara said.

Fletch said, "I'm very fond of them." He zippered the cover closed again.

"May I see what is in your luggage, please?" the official asked.

"Of course." Fletch handed the skis to Barbara and unzipped his large knapsack. As he folded back the cover he saw on top of the clothes a book entitled *How to Screw Around*. "Oh, my," he said. He remembered Alston had packed for him. Quickly, he picked up the book and held it by his side.

The official stroked the palm of his hand over the nylon surface of Fletch's ski pants. "That feels beautiful," he said. "Like the skin of a woman. Do you wear these?"

Fletch swallowed. "When I go skiing."

"Oh, I see. These are skiing trousers."

"Yes."

The official's hand went layer through layer down the bag. "They're like moon clothes."

"We're not from the moon," Barbara said.

"They're ski clothes," Fletch said.

The official said, "This bag is full of ski clothes."

Fletch said, "I suppose it is."

"Usually when people come to Kenya for pleasure," the official said, "they bring shorts. Safari jackets. Sun hats. Swimsuits. Hiking boots."

Fletch said, "Oh, I see."

The official waved his hand at the bag, indicating it could now be closed. "I'm afraid you won't have a very good time in Kenya, if you insist on going snow-skiing."

Fletch dropped *How to Screw Around* back into the knapsack. "We'll try our best."

EIGHT

Fletch handed Barbara a one-hundred-dollar bill. "Would you please go to the exchange booth and get some local currency?"

Immediately when they came out of the controlled area five small boys had grabbed the skis and carried them on their shoulders out to the sidewalk. A man had grabbed the rest of the luggage. Others had just shouted *Taxi!* at them.

"Where are you going?"

"Men's room. We need taxi fare."

"What's the exchange rate?"

"Tit for tat. Roughly."

"Thanks."

There was only one other man in the men's room. Slim, he wore a full-length safari suit. Thinning hair was stretched across his pate. He had a pencil-thin moustache. He was washing at a basin.

Sitting in the cabinet, Fletch watched the man's brown boots make the little movements on the floor a person makes while thinking he is standing still. The water was splashing into the basin.

The main door to the men's room opened. Heavy black shoes beneath dark trousers came into view beneath the cabinet door. The brown boots turned. The two men spoke a language Fletch didn't understand. He could barely hear it over the sound of the running water. Then one man shouted. The other man shouted. They both were shouting. The feet began moving, agitated. Forward, back, sideways, some sort of crazy dance. The brown boots came nearer the men's room door. One of the black shoes landed on the floor on its side, on the man's ankle. The black shoes pulled backward to the right. The brown boots turned and sprinted for the door. The water was still running.

Fletch came out of the cabinet, pulling up his jeans. He pressed the flat of his hand against his stomach. His other hand covered his mouth.

Blood was on the mirror, the white washbasins, the floor.

A man's body was in the corner, his neck twisted against the wall. His white shirt was soaked with blood, from just below the chest down. Some blood was on his dark trousers, as far down as his knees. His jaw was slack. His eyes, glassy as a stuffed animal's, stared toward the men's room door. On the side of the sink above his head was his bloody, streaked hand print.

Water was still running in the basin. A knife had been dropped into it. Water swirling around the knife was still bloody.

Fletch's two hands could not stop what was about to happen. He went to a basin nearer the door. He vomited. He rinsed out the basin. He vomited again.

After rinsing the sink a second time he stood against the basin a moment to steady himself. Then he rubbed cold water on his face, the back of his neck.

Using the bottom of his shirt around his hand, he opened the men's room door.

Eyes stinging, temples throbbing, knees shaking, Fletch tried to walk straight across the airport terminal while he tucked in his shirt.

NINE

The sunlight on the sidewalk outside the Nairobi airport was brilliant. Barbara was showing the taxi driver how to weight down one end of the skis with a knapsack so they could stick out of the trunk without falling. Many people stood around very interested in this problem of transporting skis by taxi.

Trembling, Fletch crossed the sidewalk directly to the taxi. He sat on the backseat. He rolled down the window. He sucked warm, dry air into his lungs.

Bending, Barbara looked through the back door of the taxi at him. "Fare to the Norfolk Hotel should be about one hundred and seventy shillings. I exchanged a hundred-dollar bill for local currency, inside, at the bank window." Adjusting to the light inside the taxi, her eyes narrowed. "What's the matter with you? What happened?"

"Get in, please."

She sat on the backseat. "Can't take a little jet lag?"

"Close the door, please."

"Do I look as badly as you do? Fletch, what's the matter?"

Speaking softly, he said, "I just saw someone get murdered. Stabbed to death. Blood." He tried to rub the brilliant sunlight out of his eyes. "Blood everywhere."

"My God! You're serious!" She sat closer to him on the seat. "Everywhere where?"

"Men's room."

She, too, spoke softly. "What do you mean, you *saw* a murder? My God, this is terrible."

At the back of the car, the driver was trying to arrange the trunk lid so it would not fly up and bounce as they went along the road.

Eyes closed, facedown, Fletch pressed his fingers against his forehead and cheekbones. "When I went into the men's room, a guy was standing at the basin washing his hands. I went into a cabinet. While I was sitting there, another guy came in. They began shouting at each other. Below the cabinet door I saw their feet get excited, do this crazy dance. There was a loud shout from one of them, agony, distress." Barbara put her arm over Fletch's shoulder. "I came out as quickly as I could. The second man, the man I hadn't seen before, was slumped in a corner, dead. There was blood everywhere, coming from just below his ribs. There was a bloody hand streak on the wall. His eyes were open, staring at the door. The water was still running in the basin. In the basin was a knife. The water in the basin was red."

"You're sure he was dead?"

"He wasn't blinking."

"My God, Fletch. What are we going to do?" She looked through her closed window to the airport terminal.

"I don't know. What can we do?"

"What have you done so far?"

"I've thrown up."

"You look it."

"Into one of the other basins. I cleaned up after myself."

"Nice boy." She took one of his hands in hers. "Do you think anyone else knows about this yet?"

Fletch looked through the window at the people standing on the sidewalk. "No one seems very excited."

"We must tell someone." Her hand went for the door handle.

"Wait a minute." He took her hand. "Let's think a minute."

"What good is thinking going to do? Something terrible has happened. Somebody got murdered. You saw it. We have to tell someone."

"Barbara, just wait a minute."

"Can you identify the murderer? The first man in the men's room?"

"Yes."

"What did he look like?"

"Middle-aged. Slim. Thinning, sandy hair. Pencil moustache. Khaki clothes. Safari jacket."

"What were they arguing about?"

"I couldn't tell. Foreign language. Portuguese, I think."

"Fletch, we have to tell someone."

"Barbara, you're not thinking."

"What's to think about? You saw a murder."

"We've just arrived in Kenya. We don't know how things are here. Because of the skis, the ski clothes, we made clowns of ourselves coming through customs."

"Come on. That was funny."

"Yeah. And the press will report we were not acting normally going through customs. We seemed confused."

"I am confused."

"I know. I've written reports like that. Barbara, we attracted the attention of the two gun-carrying soldiers."

"True."

"What are we doing in Kenya?"

"What are we doing in Kenya with skis?"

"We're here to meet my father. *Prove it.* There's this washed-out letter inviting us. *It's illegible!* We're not on very solid ground here."

"You're just reporting a murder."

"I don't want to have anything to do with a murder. This isn't California. We've just arrived in a foreign country. We don't know what it's like here. I go into a men's room. There's someone in there alive. I come out and report there is someone else in the men's room who is dead? And you expect people to believe I had nothing to do with it? Come on, Barbara. What would you think? I didn't come halfway around the world to be taken off immediately in handcuffs and leg irons to the local police warehouse."

"Did anyone notice you go into the men's room?"

"How do I know?"

"Or come out?"

"Barbara . . ."

"You're right. Until a better suspect comes along, you're the best the police would have."

"Just an airport incident."

"You have no evidence that there was another guy, a third guy, in the men's room?"

"Nothing but my word. And that's the word of a guy who has just arrived on the equator carrying skis and ski clothes, waving an illegible invitation from a man whom the courts in California declared dead years ago."

"Shaky ground."

"Without a leg to stand on."

"Fletch, we have been moving pretty fast here."

"Yeah. Lots of fun. Until something goes wrong."

Annoyed, Barbara looked through the window at the terminal again. "Why didn't your father meet us at the airport? He's a pilot. He has to know where the airport is!"

Fletch didn't say anything. He exhaled slowly.

"Your breath smells like an old cat's," Barbara said. "Do you still feel sick?"

"Good thing British Air didn't give us much breakfast."

The driver passed by Fletch's window.

"Barbara, don't say anything about this the driver can hear."

Barbara sighed. "Your decision."

Before starting the engine, the driver turned around in the front seat and looked at Fletch. *"Jambo."*

"Habari," Fletch breathed.

The driver's forehead wrinkled. *"Mzuri sana."*

"My husband's sick," Barbara said. "Must be something he ate."

For the first time, Fletch heard the two-note song, B flat, F: "Sorry."

In a land where people, even a broad-shouldered taxi driver, sang so sweetly, so gently, their simple courtesies, *"Oh, I see. Sorry,"* how could Fletch possibly have seen what he just saw? A clean, public lavatory turned into a blood-splattered, blood-streaked, blood-puddled room of horror in less time than it took for him to relieve himself. Like seeing a snake come out of a hen's egg. Again, Fletch rubbed his eyes with his fists. The man sat in a pool of blood, spraddle-legged on the floor in the corner of the room, his neck twisted, his eyes staring unblinking at the door, blood everywhere below his rib cage.

"Damn!" Barbara expostulated. "Your father didn't come to meet us at the airport."

Softly, Fletch said, "I guess he didn't."

As the taxi pulled away from the curb it passed a group of people packing into a van. From behind the van walked quickly the first man

Fletch had seen in the men's room, thinning combed hair, pencil moustache: the murderer. He carried his safari jacket rolled up in his hand. Small sections of his khaki trousers were dark brown, wet.

Fletch said, "Hey, wait a minute."

The taxi slowed. The driver looked at Fletch through the rearview mirror.

Barbara asked, "Are you going to be sick?"

The man, the murderer, had his hand on the door handle of a parked car. He was looking around.

Fletch did feel sick again.

"Go ahead," Barbara said to the driver. "He'll be all right."

The taxi proceeded through the gate. The moment had passed.

Barbara took Fletch's hand onto her lap. "You going to be all right?"

"I'll be all right. Just a shock. The last thing I expected to see."

"It was the last thing someone did see." She squeezed his hand. "Welcome to Africa."

"What in hell are we doing here?"

"When you arrive at a ski lodge in Colorado you're handed a cup of hot chocolate."

"Somehow," Fletch said, "I don't think this welcoming was arranged by the Kenyan Tourist Bureau."

"No," Barbara said. "But I would have expected your father to be here. He arranged the tickets. He knew when we were arriving. Altogether, it would have been a help having him here."

Again, Fletch exhaled, heavily.

Slowly, on the drive into Nairobi from the airport, Fletch became more alert to his surroundings.

The taxi went at a sedate pace. Worriedly, the driver kept glancing in the rearview mirror. As they went along, the trunk lid bounced higher and higher.

The snow skis sticking out of the trunk of a taxi driving into Nairobi, Kenya, attracted a lot of attention. Other drivers smiled at them, blew their horns, waved at what appeared to be a joke or, at least, something funny. People on the sidewalks pointed. A few people seemed to know, or were able to figure out, what they were. Others just found two blue fangs sticking out the back of a flapping Mercedes funny enough.

As they began to go around a rotary, Fletch saw, on his left, a children's playground. Everywhere in the playground were oversize traffic signs, STOP, RAILROAD CROSSING, WAIT, WALK, CAUTION.

Fletch said, "People here like their kids."

Barbara frowned at him. "People everywhere like their kids."

"I've never seen an urban park dedicated to teaching kids traffic signs before."

The car slowed before making a U-turn to pull up at the front door of the Norfolk Hotel.

"Oh, no," Barbara said.

"Oh, no, what? It's beautiful."

The hotel looked like a Tudor hunting lodge in tropical sunlight. In front, a deep, covered veranda, a bar/restaurant, ran half the length of the building.

"Look at all those people."

"So what?"

"Oh, nothing," Barbara said. "I don't mind pulling up in front of all those people, getting out of the car with a ghostly young man who clearly has been sick all over himself, putting my snow skis on my shoulder, and walking into a tropical hotel. Why should I mind?"

"Okay." Fletch started to get out of the taxi. "Stay here. I'll send you out a poached egg."

"Either we're going to end up in a Kenyan jail," Barbara said, following him, "or an asylum for the insane."

"Pay the driver, Barbara. You've got the money."

"I'll tip him," Barbara said, "asking him to forgive us and forget
us."

In fact, the big doorman took the skis out of the trunk, brought them into the lobby, and stood them up against the wall as if this were something he did hourly.

A few people on the veranda looked up and nodded at Fletch and Barbara.

In the people's eyes was little more than mild curiosity.

TEN

"Hello?"

There was a hesitation. "Is this Mr. Fletcher?"

"Is this Mr. Fletcher, too?" Fletch answered.

There was another pause. "My name's Carr. I'm a friend of your father's. Are you all up there?"

"All who?" Fletch asked. "Up where?"

"Is your father with you? With you and your wife, in your room?"

"I haven't seen him," Fletch said. "Ever."

"Oh. He told me we'd all meet here, on Lord Delamere's Terrace. For a drink. Rather think the old boy wanted me along for moral support, don't you know. I understand the situation. Father and son meeting for the first time."

Barbara was in the shower.

"More than I do, I expect."

Fletch had opened the knapsacks, gotten his shaving kit out.

"Well, I've got a table on the terrace. He'll turn up."

Slanted along the wall, propped against the windows, were the two pairs of snow skis. Outside the window, brilliant flowers were everywhere.

"I'll come down," Fletch said. "How will I know you?"

"Well, we'll be two proper-looking gentlemen, I trust, with drinks in front of our faces, all eyes on the front door of the hotel."

Fletch chuckled. "Okay. But I'll be a few minutes. We've spent the last several months on airplanes and you won't want to recognize me if I don't shave and shower."

"Right," Carr said. "We'll look for someone clean."

"Did I hear the phone?" Barbara came out of the bathroom. Her head and torso were wrapped in towels.

"Yes." Shirt off, Fletch was going into the bathroom with his shaving kit.

"Was it your father?"

"No."

"Was it the police?"

"Why would it be? A friend of my father's, someone I guess my father wants present at the meeting for moral support. They'll be waiting for us downstairs on the veranda."

"Why didn't your father make the call?"

"He's not here yet. Barbara!"

"Yes, darling?"

"If we're to be married —"

"We were married. We are married."

"—either I'll have to grow a beard or be able to see in the mirror so I can shave."

"You told me I had first dibs on the shower."

"Why steam up the room? Why shower with the door closed?" There was a phone extension in the bathroom. "What century do you belong to, anyway? Why ever shower with the door closed?"

"The air's very dry here. See?" She reached her hand into the bathroom, closed her fingers, and threw the steam out. "All gone."

"I look lousy," he said, shaving.

"Yes," she said solemnly. "I was trying to spare you that view of yourself."

"Yeah, yeah."

"How do you feel?"

"I'm no more jet-lagged than you are. We'll live through the day."

"I can go down and say you're sick. You can meet these . . . your father, tomorrow."

"Why do that?"

"One shock to your system at a time. Isn't that what Aristotle said?"

"Aristotle said, 'The roast lamb is very good today.' "

"You're so contemporary."

When he came out of the shower, Barbara was still in her towels but there were clothes all over the room. Ski clothes. Sweaters. Ski boots. Ski goggles. Gloves. A kit of ski wax.

Barbara looked perplexed.

"Where are my clothes?" Fletch asked.

"In the laundry."

"What laundry?"

"A man came to the door and said he wanted clothes for the laundry so I gave him yours."

"Very generous of you."

"Mine, too. Everything we were wearing on the plane."

"Do I have any other clothes? I mean, to wear?"

"No," she said. "Neither do I. Apparently not." She waved her hand around the room. "Ski clothes."

"Not even jeans?"

"I told Alston I wasn't going to see you in jeans on our honeymoon. Or sneakers. Just ski clothes."

"Great."

He sat on the edge of the bed. Feet still on the floor, he lowered his back onto the bed. He was completely surrounded by ski clothes.

"You are still wet," she said.

"I won't catch cold."

She took off her torso towel. She wiped him down lightly, just once, from his shoulders to his ankles.

"You missed the soles of my feet."

"Raise your legs," she said. "Seeing everything else is up."

She knelt. He put his knees over her shoulders.

"Maypole," she said. "Flagpole. Tower of London." She was waving it back and forth. "There's nothing quite like it. Rigid, yet flexible."

"Millions of things just like it, so I hear."

"This is the one I've got ahold of."

"Right. That's the one."

"What will I do with it?" she asked.

"As you will. I can always grow another."

"Mmmmmm."

"My father . . ."

"My sneakers?" he asked.

"I gave them to the laundry man. I doubt you'll get them back."

Fletch stood in the middle of the room, dripping from a second shower.

"They'll be crocked by now." She was lying on some ski clothes on the floor, still looking at the ceiling.

"Who?"

"Your father and his friend. They'll be relaxed. You're relaxed."

"I figured he could wait."

Barbara rolled on her side and put her head on the palm of her hand. She bent one knee. "You look much better now. Your color has come back."

"Barbara, I have to meet my father, for the first time, dressed in ski clothes, in equatorial Africa. Powder blue or rich yellow?"

"Wear your blue. It's sort of a formal occasion."

"Ski boots!"

"Am I coming downstairs with you?"

"What do you think?"

"I think I could try to call my mother. She must be worried silly. I was supposed to call her—how many days ago?—from Colorado!"

"Maybe I should meet him first myself. No distractions."

"No moral support?"

"My morals don't need support." He was pulling on nylon, form-fitting, powder-blue ski pants.

"She's probably been bothering the airlines, the police, hospitals, the ski lodge. She must be frantic."

"I'm sorry. I should have asked Alston to call her."

"What sense would he have made? 'Hello, Mrs. Ralton. Fletch took your daughter to Africa. Said something about the white slave trade.' "

She rolled onto her back. "Oh, God. What am I going to say? 'Hi, Mom. The snow here is not all that great for skiing. We're in Africa.' "

"Is one of these sweaters at least lightweight?"

"Wear the red one."

"It looks hot."

"Roll up the sleeves. 'We missed doing what we said we were going to do by two whole continents and one huge ocean!' "

"Just tell her you're all right."

Keeping her legs straight, she raised them off the floor and held them, tightening her stomach muscles. "You're not going to talk to the police?"

He was stomping into his ski boots. "One thing at a time. As you just said."

" 'Hey, Mom! You know those aquamarine shorts of mine? Could you send them to Nairobi?' How's that for starters?"

"Sounds good." He clicked his boots shut and knelt on the floor. He leaned over and kissed Barbara.

She ran her hand along the inside of his leg. "Ummm. You feel good, even with pants on."

"The customs official thought they felt good, too."

"Strange customs."

At the door, he said, "You'll come down in a while?"

She rolled onto her stomach. "Sure. What did I say?"

" 'Don't be disappointed'?"

She winked at him. "You got it, babe."

ELEVEN

There was only one proper-looking gentleman with a drink in front of his face, eyes on the front door of the hotel, when Fletch appeared on Lord Delamere's Terrace in ski boots, powder-blue ski pants, red sweater (sleeves rolled up), and sunglasses. At least there was only one proper-looking gentleman with drink in front of his face, eyes on the front door of the hotel, who gulped at the sight.

Others glanced and continued chatting.

That man began to rise, so Fletch went over to him.

The man held out his hand. "I'm Carr. The four-door model."

Shaking hands, Fletch said, "My father not here yet?"

"Can't think what happened to him." The man sat down again. His beer glass was half empty. It was a round table, with four chairs. Fletch sat across from him. Carr said, "You're a dazzler. Absolutely a dazzler. Is that what they wear in America these days?"

"When they're skiing."

At a table near them sat two paunchy men in short safari suits, balding, florid-faced, wearing competitive handlebar moustaches. At another table sat a woman in black, with a black picture hat. The man with her was in a double-breasted blue blazer, white shirt, and red tie. His hair was brilliantined. Jammed around another table were six students, male and female, black and white, jabbering excitedly, dressed in cutoffs and T-shirts. Two businessmen, briefcases on the floor beside them, talked earnestly at another table. Their white shirt cuffs and collars were between the perfectly matching blackness of their skins and suits. Many tables away three women sat together in brilliantly colored saris. Almost everyone else on the terrace was dressed in long or short khakis.

Carr asked, "Do you play guitar?"

"No," Fletch answered. "No talents."

Carr himself was dressed in khaki shorts, long khaki stockings, a short-sleeved khaki shirt. He was a solidly built middle-aged man with big knees, big forearms, big chest, and not too much gut. His hair was thinning, sandy. Even though his skin was deeply tanned, there was a light sunburn on top of it, and a few freckles on top of the burn. His hands were large, strong, heavily callused. His eyes were perhaps the clearest Fletch had ever seen.

"How do you like the Norfolk?" Carr asked.

"It seems authentic," Fletch said. "Perhaps the most authentic place I've ever been."

Carr chuckled. "I expect it is. In the old days, you know, the cowboys would come in so dusty and thirsty they'd ride their horses straight into the bar. The bar used to be through there in those days." He pointed to a blocked-off door. "Now that's a posh dining room. They'd be so dehydrated half a drink would make them looped, and they'd start shootin' the place up." He chuckled again. "I've been thrown out of here more times than I can recall."

"I bet." Fletch doubted it.

"Red, white, and blue."

Fletch looked down at his powder-blue pants and red sweater. "What's white?"

"You are."

"Oh, yeah. I forgot."

A young waiter said to Fletch, *"Jambo."*

"Jambo. Habari?"

"Habari, bwana?"

"Mzuri sana."

Good God!" Carr said. "You speak Swahili?"

"Why not?" Fletch checked his watch. "I've been here two and a half hours."

Carr gave Fletch a long look. Then he said to the waiter, *"Beeri mbili, tafahadhali."* He felt his glass. *"Baridi."*

Very carefully, Fletch said, *"Baridi."*

Laughing, Carr said, "You're a dazzler!" The waiter went away. "Americans never used to make an effort at languages."

Fletch looked across Harry Thuku Road to Nairobi University. "Does my father speak Swahili?"

"Oh, yes. Plus God knows what else. Has to, you see, flying small planes around the world. Here, ninety percent of the people speak English, ninety percent Swahili, and ninety percent speak at least one other, tribal language."

"What are you?" Fletch asked.

"What do you mean?"

"You could be English, American, South African, I suppose, Australian, from the way you sound."

"Not Austrylian," Carr said. "Not Austrylian. That takes too much bloomin' work. I'm Kenyan. Turned in a British passport for a Kenyan passport, and never regretted it. Live here awhile, and you're apt to sound like anything, I suppose. A cosmopolitan wee place."

"You're a pilot?"

"Still flying, as they say."

"The man who appeared at my wedding, last Saturday, said nothing, but handed me the package with the tickets in it to come here was probably a pilot, yes?" Fletch was hot. The red sweater was prickling his skin. "He was a little guy, dressed in khaki, a blue tie."

"The international brotherhood of bush pilots."

"Where else have you flown?"

"Latin America, India. Some in the States. Other places in Africa."

"Smuggle?"

"That's not my business."

"Does my father?"

"That's not his business, either."

The waiter brought the beer.

Fletch said, "Thanks, *bwana*."

Carr smiled. He put his half-empty glass of beer onto the waiter's tray.

"How is my father?" Fletch asked.

Carr looked across the road. "We've all seen better days."

"He must be rich."

"Why do you say that?"

"Tickets here, for two, plus a thousand bucks, this hotel. That's a lot."

"Not over a lifetime. Have you ever had anything else from him?"

"No."

"Did you come here only because you thought he might be rich?"

"No. I was 'mildly curious.' "

"He's not rich."

"How do you suppose he knew I was getting married? Exact time, odd place . . . I barely made it myself."

Carr seemed to be studying his rough hands. "I suspect your father's been hearing from you all your life."

"Not from me."

"Hearing of you. I've seen pictures of you."

"Of me?"

"In a school yard. Walking along a street. In a football jersey. On a beach."

"All those dirty old men taking pictures of me."

"Pilot friends, I expect."

Fletch grinned. "And all these years I thought it was because I was so pretty."

"I take it you've never seen a picture of him?"

"No."

"What were you told?"

"I was allowed to think he was dead. He was declared dead, legally, when I was in the second year of school. I didn't know until last Saturday that my mother has always allowed for the possibility that he is alive. I guess she didn't want me to go off on some half-baked father search, you know, only to be disappointed."

Carr's eyes opened wider. He shook his head. "Absolutely," he said, "this has to be Mrs. Fletcher."

Fletch looked around.

Outside the door of the hotel stood Barbara, in ski boots, powder-blue ski pants, and a red sweater, sleeves rolled up.

TWELVE

"Three rabbits," Carr said to the waiter, "and I guess a beer for the lady."

"Rabbit," Barbara said softly. "Americans don't eat rabbits."

Carr had said they might as well have lunch.

After he ordered, Carr was interrupted by a man who came by the table. There was a brief introduction. The man and Carr talked about flying some glass specimen boxes to Kitale.

"This isn't your father?" Barbara whispered.

"A friend of his. Another pilot. Name of Carr. First name unknown."

"Where's your father?"

"He doesn't know. I think he's rather embarrassed. He's here as moral support, and the old man isn't here at all. He's trying to be very nice."

The conversation about glass specimen boxes was ending.

"Peter Rabbit," Barbara said. "Peter Cottontail. The Easter Bunny. 'What's up, Doc?' "

Carr said to Fletch, "My first name is Peter. People call me Carr."

"Peter."

"I can't eat Peter Cottontail," Barbara said.

Carr said, "What?" as does a man who suffers some permanent hearing disability.

"Where's Fletch's father?" Barbara said.

Carr looked at the entrance in obvious pain. "I wish I knew."

"Isn't there someplace you can call him?"

"This isn't Europe," Carr said. "The States. When a person goes missing here, it's not likely he's standing next to a phone."

"I called my mother," Barbara said to Fletch.

"What did you tell her?"

"I said, 'I'm in Nairobi, Kenya, East Africa, on my honeymoon with Fletch darling, I am very well, and sorry if you were worried when I didn't call you from Colorado.' "

"That's the thing," Carr said. "You can make a transworld call from here easier than you can call across the street."

"What did she say?"

"She thought I was joking. Then she said, 'Is that *boy* you married ever where he'd supposed to be when he's supposed to be?' Then she said, 'There's some trick to everything he does. You can't live your life that way, Barbara.' "

Carr was trying to watch Fletch's eyes through Fletch's sunglasses.

Fletch put his sunglasses on the table.

"She said I should come home instantly and divorce you."

"Are you going to?"

"I was going to have lunch first. But rabbit?"

"Don't make a point in looking," Carr said, "but there's a man entering you mustn't miss."

The man went by the table like an aircraft carrier. He was six feet eight or nine inches tall and weighed nearly three hundred pounds. His head was a great, bald nose cone. He and Carr exchanged nods.

He sat at a table near the railing, back to the daylight, facing the entrance. He took a newspaper out and flattened it on the table.

Instantly, a waiter brought him a bottle of beer and a glass.

"He usually doesn't show here until about four o'clock in the afternoon," Carr said.

"Who is he?" Fletch asked.

Carr hesitated. The waiter was putting their plates in front of them. "His name is Dawes. Dan Dawes."

"What does he do?"

Barbara examined her plate. "They don't look like rabbits."

"He teaches high school."

"I'll bet his students call him *'Bwana.'* "

"I daresay," Carr said.

Barbara put her knife into what was on her plate. "Cheese."

"Rarebit," Fletch said.

"They're cheese rabbits." Barbara began to eat happily.

The waiter was gone.

"He shoots people," Carr said. "At night. Almost always at night."

Barbara choked.

"Bad people, of course. Villains. Some say he does it for the police. He kills people the police can't get sufficient evidence against to bring to trial; people the police feel aren't worth the expense of a trial, and jail, or hanging."

"He just goes out and shoots people?"

"A blast from a .45 through the back of the head. Always very neat."

Barbara's eyes were bulging out of her head. "And he teaches school?"

"High school math."

Barbara looked at Fletch. "Is he the man — "

"Shut up, he said kindly," Fletch said.

As they ate, Fletch kept glancing at the huge man studying his newspaper. His bald head was as big as a boulder one would have to drive around.

Carr said, "You work for a newspaper?"

"Yes."

"That's nice. What particular abilities do you need for that?"

"Strong legs."

"And what do you get out of it?"

"A hell of an obituary."

Eating with delicate manners, the man with the rough hands asked Barbara, "And you?"

"I've been working in a boutique. Selling jodhpurs."

"Jodhpurs? My word, you Americans dress funny."

As they were finishing eating, Carr said, "How do you two feel?"

"Hot," Barbara said.

Fletch pulled at his sweater. "Hot."

"It's not hot, you know," Carr said. "You're at five thousand feet altitude."

Fletch said, "The slopes are dry, though. Definitely you need snow."

"I mean, how do you feel, jet lag and all?"

Barbara said, "Numb."

"We're determined to live through the day," Fletch answered. "Otherwise, we'll never adjust."

Carr thought a moment. "Seeing your dad doesn't appear to be appearing . . . How ought I say that? You write for a newspaper."

"He's not here," Fletch said. "And it's not news."

"I have some private business this afternoon, out in Thika." Suddenly there was even more red in Carr's face. "You both seem open enough. I mean, you're open to the fact that there is a language called Swahili, and you might pick up a few words." Barbara was watching Carr closely, wondering what he was talking about. "Private business. An odd sort of appointment. Well," he sighed. "Your dad seems to have missed this appointment, and I don't mean to miss mine." He scratched his ear. "With a witch doctor."

"A witch doctor," Fletch repeated.

"A witch doctor," Barbara repeated.

"I have a problem." Carr wasn't looking at them. "I'm not having much luck with something. There's a question I might as well ask."

Barbara said to Fletch, "A witch doctor."

"Sounds interesting," Fletch said.

Carr looked at his watch. "No point your hanging around here for

Fletch to show up. I mean, the other Fletch. You might as well come with me. Take a ride through the suburbs of Nairobi."

"Are you sure we won't be in the way?" Fletch asked.

Carr laughed, "No, I'm not. But what's life without risk?"

Barbara said to Fletch, "I think if that other Fletch shows up, we don't particularly want to be here. Right now."

Carr skidded back in his chair. "I'll get the Land-Rover. It will only take a minute. It's over by the National Theater."

THIRTEEN

"Hurry up," Barbara said. "I want to do something."

They ran up the stairs at the back of the lobby.

"What?"

On the second floor they walked along a sun-dotted courtyard in which there was a Japanese garden.

"Get these clothes off me."

"Barbara, there isn't time. We kept this nice man waiting long enough this morning. He sat there sipping only half a beer while we screwed around."

"Will you tell Carr about what you saw this morning at the airport?"

"I was thinking of it." Fletch fitted their key to the lock. "*Witch doctor*!?"

In their room, all their clothes had been put away.

On the bureau was a pair of new sneakers. Next to them was a note.

Dear Mr. Fletcher:

Instantly your sneakers were damaged beyond repair in the wash so we have replaced them.

With apologies,
The Management
Norfolk Hotel

"My holey sneakers! How embarrassing!"

Barbara read the note over his shoulder. "How sweet!" She had a pair of scissors in her hand. "You're right. How embarrassing."

"What are you doing?"

"Take 'em off."

"Take what off?"

"I can't stand being in these clothes. I can't stand seeing you in those clothes. We can't go around on the equator dressed like this."

"My wife is attacking me with a scissors! We haven't been married a week!"

"Take your pants off or I'll cut them where you stand!"

"Help! Dan Dawes! Save me! There's a villain in my room!"

FOURTEEN

In the bright, midday sunlight, the shamba was country quiet.

Fletch and Barbara stood aside, along the stick fence inside the enclosure.

Carr, his big, rough hands looking useless hanging at his sides, stood in front of the witch doctor.

She sat on the ground in the doorway of her dung and thatch house. Her legs, wrapped in a black, thigh-length skirt, were straight and flat on the ground before her. Her feet were bare. There was a red Turkish cap on her head.

Her husband, in threadbare shorts, threadbare suit coat, no shirt, barefooted, sat on a low stool to her side, facing her, utterly attentive to her.

Together, the ancient couple did not weigh as much as one hundred pounds.

Across the enclosure there were three young men, late teenagers, dressed only in tawdry shorts, distantly present. Two were swaying drunk. The eyes of the third shone across the courtyard, attentive, alert.

The old lady witch doctor had drawn in white chalk a rectangle around her in the dirt, even over the dark little rug at her side. She had put white chalk dabs on each of her temples.

Then she had sung a nonmelodic song, prayer, incantation.

Her husband handed her a narrow-necked vase. Again and again, she would shake a few beads out of the vase into her hand, study them, flip them onto the dark rug, scatter them and regroup them with her fingers, watching how they came together. She would murmur a bit, sing a bit, gather the beads up, put them back in her vase, shake it, start over again.

The husband watched everything she was doing with reverent attention.

A clucking chicken crossed the enclosure.

Carr hadn't said much on the ride to Thika.

He had been waiting for them outside the hotel in his Land-Rover. He smiled when he saw Barbara and Fletch now in shiny powder-blue shorts, Fletch in thick ski socks and white new sneakers, his sweater cut from armpits to waist, sleeves cut off. Barbara was in one of Fletch's T-shirts and her rubber sandals. "That looks better," Carr said.

They stopped at an inn outside Nairobi called the Blue Post and had a cup of soup in a garden overlooking a short waterfall. "This soup cures all," Carr said. "Upset stomach. Broken heart. Although not traditional, probably even jet lag. Very special here. Made of bones." He waved at the hills behind him. "Various animals. Boiled bones. Herbs. God knows what." It was a soup that puckered the throat. Fletch did feel better after drinking it.

Bouncing along the hard-top road, Carr missed the turning. He had to back up, half off the road, half on. Everywhere, along every road they had been on, besides the cars and trucks, there was a heavy traffic of people walking, both sides, going both ways, mostly people dressed in dark, cheap pants and shirts, dresses, many barefooted; always a few schoolchildren in uniform shorts and shoes, socks, shirts, and incongruous sweaters. Many times, Fletch noticed, there would be a man walking with a child or children. Carr turned onto a dirt track that wound through a field of standing corn.

Completely invisible from the road, thirty meters inside this cornfield was a little village, a half-dozen wellspaced dung and conically thatch-roofed houses, each separated by its own thick stick fencing.

The witch doctor appeared and took her position sitting in the doorway as they arrived. This was a genuine appointment. Carr gave Barbara and Fletch a look indicating they should stand aside in silence. He stood in front of the old lady.

Suddenly, the third young man, the one with the lively eyes, strode across the enclosure in a full-blown gait that could carry him across the world. He stood between Barbara and Fletch. They made room for him. He faced Carr and the witch doctor. Then he sat down on his heels.

In a moment, he tugged Fletch's ski sock.

Fletch looked down.

"I'm James," the young man said. "Get down."

Fletch bent his knees but could not sit on his heels. Not for long. He sat cross-legged on the ground.

Barbara sat cross-legged, too.

Seeing this, James changed his position so that he, too, was sitting cross-legged. One of his knees was on Barbara's leg, the other on Fletch's.

Fletch jerked his thumb at his wife. "Barbara." He pointed his thumb at himself. "Fletch."

James's eyes widened. He stared into Fletch's eyes and then looked away. He gave Fletch the whole song, all five notes: "Oh, I see. Sorry."

"Say what?"

"I know of your father." James rushed on. "The reason I told you to sit down, you see," James said softly, "is because these things take a long time." He said to Barbara, "You must be careful not to get sunbite."

Barbara looked confused. She was against the fence. There was no place for her to move.

Whispering, James said, "Do you know what the man asked her?"

Carr had said something to the witch doctor after she had put the chalk around her and on her temples.

Fletch said, "I heard, but I didn't understand."

"He said he is trying to find something. He wants her to tell him where it is."

"Why did she put the white marks on her temples?" Barbara asked.

James looked at her as if she had asked if the sun rises in the east everywhere. "So she can communicate through the gods on Mount Kenya with your ancestors."

Fletch said, "Oh, I see."

"The white is the snow."

"*That's* the snow," Barbara said.

Sitting against the stick fence in the dirt under an equatorial sun, Fletch asked, "Has she ever seen real snow?"

"I doubt it. She's reading the beads. Five beads is for man, three for woman, two for house. Something like that. I don't know. Each bead means something different. It's all very complicated."

"It must take a long time to learn," Barbara said.

"Learn," James said. "Yes. But, you see, she is a witch doctor."

"You mean, she doesn't have to learn?"

"Yes, much," James said. "But you can't learn, if you haven't the ability."

James pulled a sun-bleached hair out of Fletch's leg. He looked at it closely between his fingers in the sunlight. Still holding it, he looked at Barbara's legs. Examining the hair again, he said, "It must be funny to be not black."

Fletch heard Barbara saying, "You are a blackness I've never seen before. You're so very black the way some people are so very white."

"I have no white blood," James said. "Probably in England or America or wherever you come from all the black people you see aren't black at all. They have white blood. Do you like being white?"

"Well enough," Fletch said.

James blew the hair off his fingers. "I haven't decided whether it's better being black or white."

"Is James your real name?" Fletch asked.

"Why isn't it?"

"It's not an African name, is it?"

"Would you rather call me . . ." James seemed to be making up a name. ". . . Juma?"

"Sure. I don't care."

"That's fine," James said. "You've probably known another James somewhere before, and you shouldn't confuse me with him."

Barbara said, "Not likely, Jim-Bob."

Juma giggled. "The witch doctor just said to the man, 'You are looking for something you haven't lost.' "

There was a conversation going on so quietly over by the doorway Fletch was scarcely aware of it. "Did Carr agree?"

"Carr said it's a place he's looking for. It's been lost a long time."

Now Carr was leaning over the witch doctor.

The old woman put her cupped hands up to him.

Carr spit in her hands.

Fletch looked at the ground. "Maybe I should ask her where my father is."

"Your father's not lost," Juma said. "He's here in Kenya. Fletch. I know him."

"What do you know about him?"

"He flies planes. I've seen him. I've seen Carr before, too. I get everywhere."

Barbara said, "Shhh."

Juma whispered, "She said he'll find the place, but it will be difficult. The dead people there want him to find it, so they will be remembered." He listened a moment. "She said he must go far, far south where there are hills and look for a river."

Carr looked around at Fletch. His face beamed with vindication.

"Oh, wow," Barbara said. "Mumbo jumbo."
Fletch asked, "How old are you?"
Again Juma seemed to take the time to invent something. "Thirty-seven."
Fletch said, "Okay."
Juma was listening intently. He put his hand on Fletch's knee. "She's talking about you." The witch doctor was looking at her beads on the little rug, rolling them back and forth. She appeared to be talking to them. "She's asking why don't you come forward."
Forehead creased, Carr was looking at Fletch. Juma pushed him. "Get up. Go forward. She's saying something to you."
Fletch got up. He dusted off the seat of his pants.
He stood in front of the tiny witch doctor.
Carr said, "She wants to know why you haven't talked to her."
"No disrespect," Fletch said. "Right. Where's my father?"
Carr started to speak to the old woman. Instantly she began to speak, not to Fletch but to the beads she was rolling around the rug.
When she paused, Carr said, "She says you have no question, but something you must say, or it will be worse for you."
"What will get worse?"
The witch doctor was continuing to make her little noises.
"She says you must speak to her. You are carrying a box of rocks which will get heavier and heavier until your legs break."
"I have strong legs."
"Do you know what she's talking about?"
"Maybe."
"She says you must drop this box of rocks or go away, as she does not want to see your legs shatter."
Fletch looked across the enclosure at the two teenagers swaying, dizzy-eyed drunk in the sunlight. He looked at Barbara and Juma sitting together against the fence like schoolchildren born and bred together. He looked down at the little old lady sitting in the dirt in the doorway of her dung house.
He looked into Carr's face.
Fletch said, "They're my rocks."

Fletch was the first one out of the enclosure, to spare the witch doctor the sight of his legs shattering.
Fletch hit his head against a thick branch forming an arch over the gate.
Juma said the two-note song: "Sorry."

Rubbing his head, Fletch said, "Why are you apologizing? I walked into it."

Juma said, "I'm sorry you bonked your noggin."

Barbara came through the gate, sunburned.

Carr exited, looking bemused, if not bewitched.

They went up the track to the Land-Rover.

Swaying, the two young men were fumbling with the gate.

Fletch said to Juma, "Your two friends are pretty drunk."

" 'Friends'?" Juma did not look at them. He did not look at Fletch. He looked deep into the standing corn.

Juma frowned, but said nothing.

FIFTEEN

"No, I don't know him." Carr smiled. "I thought he was a friend of yours."

On the dance floor at the Shade Hotel, Juma was breakdancing with some paid-for performers. It was early in the evening and only a few of the tables in the yard had people at them. The performers seemed to be showing Juma a few things, and Juma seemed to be showing them a few things. A tape machine at the edge of the stage/dance floor was playing "Get Out of Town" loudly.

"He just got into the car with us," Barbara said. They were at a little wooden table under an umbrella. "First he said his name is James. Then he said we could call him Juma."

Carr said, "He probably just wants a ride back to Nairobi."

Carr had gone across the yard to the barbecue pit and ordered their dinners. A waitress brought three beers.

Fletch said, "I asked him how old he is and he said thirty-seven."

"He is thirty-seven," Carr said.

They watched Juma on the stage/dance floor spinning like a top on the muscles of his left shoulder.

"There are two rainy seasons a year here," Carr said. "The short rains and the long rains. Ask someone how old he is, and he'll tell you how many rainy seasons he has behind him. In Juma's case, it would be thirty-seven. That means he's eighteen and a half years old."

Fletch said, "Oh, I see." He was getting the three little notes nearly right.

On their way from the witch doctor's shamba to the Shade Hotel, Carr had driven them on a detour through Karen. They had stopped at Karen Blixen's, that is, Isak Dinesen's farm, or what's left of it. Not a tarted-up tourist attraction yet, the low stone house and a few acres adjoin a business school. They had gotten out of the Land-Rover and walked around, under the trellis, through the roots and trunks of the great trees in back.

Barbara and Fletch had sat for a moment on the stone arrangements near the back door where Karen Blixen had held court with *her people* and maybe did some of her writing about them.

"Dinesen, Hemingway, Roark," Carr said. "That was all light-years ago, in African time."

"Time, space." Juma started back to the Land-Rover. "They were always light-years away from Africa, anyway."

In the deepening dusk at the table in the yard of the Shade Hotel, Carr said, "You must be aware of what time it is, too. You're on the equator. The sun rises at roughly seven each morning and sets at roughly seven each night, year-round. Sunrise is the beginning of the day, naturally, and sunset the beginning of the night. So if someone says he'll see you at three tomorrow, he might mean ten o'clock in the morning. Ten might be five o'clock in the afternoon. Five tomorrow night is midnight."

Fletch said, "Oh, I see."

"It is through such simple misunderstandings," Carr said, "that cultures clash."

The waitress brought them a large plate of cooked meat and a bowl of rice. She placed three paper plates on the table.

Carr took a piece of the meat in his fingers. With it he lifted rice from the bowl into his mouth.

"Shouldn't we ask Juma if he wants something to eat?" Barbara asked.

Carr said, "He doesn't want to eat now."

Barbara raised her eyebrows. "Say what, *bwana?*"

"Traditionally, people here eat only one meal a day, at nine or ten o'clock at night, after it cools down. A very high-protein meal, if they can get it. They believe eating during the heat of the day makes you sick, fat, and lazy." Carr looked around him at the few other people at that early hour. "Some come to the city, of course, put on polyester clothes, take to eating three meals a day, and in no time they took just as chubby and pasty as your average New Yorker."

Watching him dancing, Barbara said, "Juma is not chubby and pasty."

"So," Carr said. "He doesn't want to eat now."

Eating the meat and rice with his fingers, Fletch asked Carr, "What are you looking for?"

"Beg pardon?"

"For what are you looking? Or shouldn't I ask? At Thika, Juma was translating for us. He said you told the witch doctor you are looking for a place. You asked her where it is."

"Oh, that," Carr said.

"Private business," warned Barbara.

Fletch shrugged. "No one ever has to answer a question."

"No one ever has to ask a question, either," Barbara said.

"I'm a reporter."

"You're not working now."

"May the searchlight of the free press never darken," said Fletch.

In the glow of the kerosene lamp on the table, Carr's face looked more red than usual.

"The witch doctor was fascinating," Barbara said. "Thank you for taking us. You said people working in holistic medicine now are taking an interest in the witch doctor generally . . ."

Suddenly, Carr said, "I'm looking for a Roman city."

"Huh?" Fletch asked.

"Good!" exclaimed Barbara. "Finally an answer to one of your impertinent questions made you almost swallow your teeth!"

"Here?"

Carr nodded. "In East Africa."

Barbara sighed.

"Hell of a long walk from home," Fletch said. "Through Egypt, the Sudan, Ethiopia . . . ? How could they supply themselves through thousands of miles of desert?"

"The Arabians did," Barbara said. "It can't be all desert."

"Down the Red Sea," Carr said. "Into the Somali Basin."

"By boat."

"The reason people have always doubted it," Carr said, "is because once you get into the Somali Basin the southwest winds and currents are strongely against one."

"So?"

"So," Carr said. "They rowed."

"Hell of a long row."

"Difficult, I admit. But the Romans did difficult things."

"What would they want here?" Barbara asked.

"Spices. Minerals. Gems."

"The Romans conquered the known world," Fletch said. "This world was unknown."

"Right," said Carr. "Kenya would be farther than anyone has ever believed the Romans traveled."

"A Roman city in Kenya," Barbara said.

"Kenya is as far from Rome as is New York," Fletch said.

"The Romans came to America," Barbara said.

"They didn't build cities."

"No," said Barbara. "They ate lobsters and either died or went home. Typical tourists."

"I don't think the Romans ever went to America on purpose," Carr said. "They got blown there by mistake. No one from Europe ever got blown to East Africa by mistake. I think the Romans came here, settled here, and were here for a very long time."

"If Barbara will forgive another impertinent question," Fletch said, "what makes you think so?"

"To be honest," Carr said, "there is currently a small rumor circulating that some documentary evidence of there having been a Roman city on the East African coast south of the equator has turned up in London. That's all I known about it: there's a rumor. But long before I heard this rumor, I have believed it. Always."

"Why?"

"The Masai." Carr sat back in his chair. "How can you observe the Masai and possibly believe the Romans weren't here?"

Fletch shook his head as if to clear it.

"Right," Carr said. "There is a tribe called the Masai. Bantu origins, cousins of the Samburu. The Masai roam the south, the Kenyan-Tanzanian border; the Samburu the north. The Masai are a warrior tribe. They carry spears. Traditionally, they carry shields. They wear togas. Historically, Masai young men go through intensive training in the arts of war, to attain the rank of *moran*, warrior, including elaborate tests of courage. From what is known, the Masai were perfectly disciplined to use complicated, sophisticated military formations and tactics. So perfect were they as a military force that they succeeded in keeping the Western world, the white people, with their bows, arrows, crossbows, and gunpowder, out of inland East Africa until very nearly the beginning of the twentieth century. What finally made them retreat was the automatic rifle and the English railroad. The coast had been opened, Lamu, Malindi, Mombasa, fought over by the Arabians, Portuguese, whoever. But no one ever went inland, so terrified were they of the Masai."

Barbara picked gristle off her meat. "Why couldn't they have developed these military tactics on their own?"

"They could have," said Carr. "But some of their military tactics were appropriate only for urban areas. There weren't any urban areas for them to develop such tactics. And why, if they did develop these disciplines and tactics themselves, are these techniques, even their mode of dress, so similiar to the Romans'?"

"Come on," Fletch said. "Why would an African tribe maintain a military discipline imposed on them by a foreign culture for over two thousand years?"

"Because," Carr answered, "the Masai are a very fragile people. Extremely tall. Extremely thin. Traditionally, they eat only meat, milk, and blood."

"Good God," said Barbara.

Carr smiled at her. "They produce the best-smelling sweat in the world."

"What?"

"Their perspiration smells beautiful. It's a heavy, dense, clean odor you could bottle and sell in your boutique."

"Masai Perspiration *parfum*." Barbara shook her head. "I don't think it would be a hit."

"The Masai are so brittle," Carr said, "they can never win in hand-to-hand combat. As soon as their ancient enemies, the Kikuyu, would penetrate the Masai's disciplined formations and go at them with their hands and feet, the Masai would lose. Maintaining this Roman militarism was their only way of surviving as a people for two thousand years."

Electronic music was blaring from the stage.

"In fact," added Carr, "the Masai are so brittle they have trouble bearing children. Over the centuries they have needed the women of other tribes. The Masai were not just militarily defensive, but these enormously tall, skinny people had to be militarily aggressive to survive."

"Whew." Fletch shook his head. "Witch doctors. A lost Roman city. Carr, you are a surprising fellow."

Carr shrugged. "It's just a hobbyhorse of mine. If anything works out, I might make a bit of a name for myself. It's so crazy anyway, I didn't mind going to a witch doctor about it. You never know what little thing might come out of traditional wisdom."

"Are you actually spending time and money looking for this place?" Barbara asked.

"Time and money. I have a camp set up. Sheila's there now."

"Is Sheila your wife?"

"Might as well be. Dear old thing's been with me years now."

Barbara looked shyly at him. "Has either of you a degree in anthropology, archaeology, anything?"

"Good heavens, no. Barely finished school. But to paraphrase the ignoramous regarding art, I'll know when I see something out of the ordinary."

Fletch smiled. "And is your camp in the south, in the hills, near a river?"

Carr nodded. "Exactly. Figured the Romans needed a certain altitude, a supply of fresh water, and a river big enough to give them access to, yet protection from, the sea."

Fletch pushed his chair back. "We won't tell anyone."

He couldn't imagine Frank Jaffe's reaction to such a story anyway. *Avalanches, mud slides, major earthquakes, airplane crashes, train wrecks, mass murders, acts of terrorism, airport bombings . . . Be sure and phone in, if you get any good stuff . . .*

Hello, Frank? I'm onto a search for a lost Roman city on the East African coast. One of my sources is the witch doctor of Thika . . .

Uh, Frank . . . ?

"Tell anybody you like," Carr said. "*Harambee.* All in good clean fun. Better than poaching elephant tusks."

"Go for it."

Carr smiled at Barbara. "I thought you'd prefer the goat to the beef."

Barbara said, "What goat?"

"Anytime you have a choice around here between goat and beef," Carr said, standing up, "choose the goat."

Barbara was looking at the empty plates. "I've been eating goat?"

"It's much more tender," Carr said, "than beef. Tastier, too."

"I've been eating goat? I ate Billy the Goat?"

Suddenly, Barbara looked ill.

On the dark sidewalk outside the Norfolk Hotel, Juma crossed his arms over his chest. His feet were planted far apart.

Carr had just driven away in the Land-Rover.

Juma said to Fletch: "At the shamba in Thika you said my friends were drunk."

"Sorry," Fletch said. "Didn't mean to insult your friends. They looked pretty drunk to me."

"How do you decide friends?"

Fletch said, "I don't care about drunkenness."

"How do you decide who is your friend? Is that something you decide about?"

"What?" Barbara asked.

"How can you decide someone is your friend without deciding everyone else is not your friend?"

"I'm not sure I understand," Fletch said.

"Do you decide who is your enemy? That's not the way things happen," Juma said.

"Oh, I see."

"Things just happen," Juma said. "When you first saw me, I was with those boys. They were drunk. I don't decide if they are my friends or not my friends. Maybe they are my enemies. How could you decide?"

Barbara shook her head. "I am very, very tired. I don't have to decide that."

Juma grabbed her arm. "That's right!"

"Barbara said something right?"

Juma looked all around. "Deciding everything like that, all the time, north, east, south, west, is very hard."

Barbara asked, "Do you mean difficult . . . ?"

". . . or harsh?" Fletch finished.

Juma turned and began walking away from them down the street. He waved. "Nice time!"

Watching him, Barbara asked, "Does he mean, *Have* a nice time . . . ?"

". . . or We *had* a nice time?" Fletch finished.

"I don't know." Barbara took Fletch's arm as they started into the hotel. "But he understands Fletch is your father . . ."

". . . and he's sorry."

SIXTEEN

Fletch had a funny line ready but, although he had used it before, he couldn't remember it. Instead, he said, "Hello?"

"Did you both sleep well?"

"So far." Fletch remembered the line. "Is this Fletch, too?"

" 'Fraid not. Carr here again."

"Oh." Fletch finally got his head off the pillow and rolled over. "There was a message waiting for us at the hotel when we got back last night. My father had been here during the afternoon."

"I'm sure he was, old chap."

"And that he'd call us in the morning."

"I'm sure he meant to."

"This is morning?" The window was filled with gray daylight. In the bed beside him, Barbara had not noticed.

"Shortly before eight of the clock, Nairobi time. To my surprise, I'm downstairs about to have breakfast. I only have an hour or so this morning."

"That's very nice . . ."

"Hate to awaken you this way, your first real day here, and all that. Your father called me a couple of hours ago. Something's come up, you see. If you could pull yourself together and join me for a cup of coffee, I could fly away with a sense of duty done."

"Something's happened to my father?"

"Yes."

"I'll be right down."

"The Kenyan coffee is quite pleasant but you might want to cut it with milk or hot water."

The waiter was pouring black coffee into Fletch's cup. Carr was finishing a large bowl of fruit.

He said, "The pineapple here is probably better than anywhere."

"Barbara will be right down."

"Yes."

There was a huge, round, beautiful breakfast buffet inn the middle of the Lord Delamere dining room.

"What's up?" Fletch asked.

"The senior Fletcher called me about five-thirty this morning. It seems there's been a spot of trouble."

Carr was right. The coffee did need cutting. "What kind of trouble?"

"It seems that yesterday, the senior Fletch, doubtlessly nervous about your imminent arrival, began quaffing the local brew a bit early on."

"He got drunk."

"With the resultant loss of sense of time and place."

"Which is why he didn't show up."

"Sometime during the day, he's not sure just when, he found himself in an altercation at the Thorn Tree Café. Someone, he says, insulted the Queen."

"What Queen?"

"The Queen of England. Elizabeth Regina Twice."

"What does he care about the Queen of England? He's born and bred Montana."

"We all care about the Queen of England out here, old chap. She's very fond of Kenya. Been here twice."

Carr drew his knife across the surfaces of the two fried eggs the waiter had brought him. "What came up was his fist. He's aware of having done damage to two or three people, seems to remember the sounds of glass smashing, seeing one of those little tables in matchsticks on the ground, and of being very angry at a placating *askari*, although whether he actually hit him is something the senior Fletcher is trying to reason through this morning. Why don't you go get your fruit?"

"What's an *askari*?"

"A guard. Possibly a cop. It will make a difference when this matter comes to trial."

"He got into a bar fight."

"So he testifies."

"He was doing that sort of thing at age fifteen, or so my mother testifies."

"I'd give you a rhyming couple about the boy in every man, but I never was that strong on Wordsworth."

"So where is he now, in jail?"

"Not yet. He's gone to ground to reconstruct his head and think things through. I had the discretion not to ask from where he was calling. He'll have to face the tune sooner or later, of course. Nairobi isn't like London or New York, you know. Everyone here knows who Fletcher is. On the other hand, people here didn't used to take this sort of bash-up all that seriously."

"Mother warned me he was apt to evade emotional moments."

"Did she? Is that what she said? How very kind of her. Understanding, I'd say."

"So why did he invite me here if it was going to be so upsetting for him?"

"Sometimes you don't know your *kanga* has a loose thread."

"Is that from Wordsworth?"

"Maybe. It makes a great deal of difference whether the *askari* he hit was a private watchman or a real policeman."

"You indicated yesterday the law is very strict here."

"Very. It has lost its sense of humor."

"Listen, Carr . . ."

"Why don't you get some breakfast? Fried eggs you have to order from the waiter."

"You probably know where my father is."

"Probably."

"Why don't I go to him now, get this confrontation over? Maybe I can even be of help to him."

"I've got a better idea. Why don't you fly up to Lake Turkana with me today? I've got to deliver a scientist up there. I'll be coming right back. You can have a swim. We can have lunch. Nile perch. Nice time."

"My father . . . "

"Put yourself in his shoes, Fletch. He's got a hell of a hangover. Probably a bloody nose. He's liable for arrest. Last thing anyone would want under such circumstances is for a dazzling kid who looks like he's never farted to come walking in offering aid and assistance, calling him *Daddy*."

"I've farted."

"Glad you heard it."

Fletch looked at the buffet. "Guess I'll get some breakfast."

"Breakfast," said Carr, "is the only fortification left to modern man."

While Fletch circumnavigated the breakfast buffet, he saw Barbara enter the room, kiss Carr on the cheek, and sit down.

On his plate Fletch placed pineapple, scrambled eggs, sausage, bacon, and toast. He also took a glass of orange juice.

"Just explaining to your wife," Carr said, "that the senior Fletcher is held up today by a sticky legal problem. Suggesting you both fly up to Turkana with me . . ."

"Nice of you . . ." Barbara's eyes were filled with questions.

"About a two-and-a-half-hour flight each way. Lake Turkana is very interesting. Used to be called the Jade Sea. Plenty of room in the plane. Carries eight passengers and there's only this one small scientist going. A Dr. McCoy. He won't mind at all."

Barbara said, "I'm a little sick of airplanes . . ."

Carr looked at his watch. "Trouble is, I have to be going. I told Dr. McCoy I'd be ready to take off at ten."

"You go, Fletch," Barbara said. "I really need a down day. There's a swimming pool somewhere here. I've never even looked in the aviaries in the courtyard yet."

"Sure you'll be all right?" Fletch was eating rapidly.

"If I get bored I can go walk around that mosque near here. I've never seen a real mosque."

"I'll get the car. You'll be out front in five minutes, Fletch?"

"Sure."

After Carr left the breakfast room, Barbara said, "Fletch, darling. There is something about your father that doesn't make sense."

Fletch drained his cup of the strong coffee. "We knew that before we arrived."

SEVENTEEN

Barbara shoved Fletch away from the bathroom mirror. "Is this what life with you is going to be like?"

Fletch was brushing his teeth. "What do you mean?"

She put toothpaste on her own brush. "Always running away? Always being somewhere else?"

She already had changed into her swimsuit.

"Carr invited both of us," Fletch said. "You said you didn't want to come. You said you were sick of airplanes, want to spend the day resting by the pool."

"Lovely," Barbara said. "You fly me to East Africa, worry my mother frantic, then fly off into the bush, leaving me in some tropical hotel . . ."

"I agreed to go. I thought you would want to go, too."

"I said I wanted to stay here. I thought you'd say you wanted to stay here, too."

"Will you let me rinse my mouth? Please?"

Barbara stepped aside, but not much. "We got married. Big event in life. We flew halfway around the world, totally unprepared. Big event. To meet your father, for the first time, which should be a big event, except he decides he's got something better to do than meet us. Yesterday, you saw someone get stabbed to death in a bathroom. Big bloody event! And today you want to go flying off into the African bush to someplace we've never heard of, with someone we don't even know!"

"You losing your sense of humor?"

"When is enough enough for you? Can't you sit still a damned minute?"

"Okay," Fletch said. "I'll go downstairs and tell Carr I'm not going. We'll sit by the pool."

She had put the cap back on the toothpaste and placed the tube neatly on the counter.

Barbara turned and faced Fletch. "No. You go." Suddenly her tight fist, much smaller and harder than Fletch had realized, smashed into Fletch's stomach, low, just inside his right hipbone. "Take that with you."

Fletch lowered his head. He looked up at her. "No one's ever hit me there before."

"First time for everything."

Fletch walked into the hallway outside the bathroom. "I can't stay now."

"That's a nice excuse."

"Take it as you like it. See you at dinner."

EIGHTEEN

"How's married life so far?" Carr drove the Land-Rover along the left-hand side of Harry Thuku Road.

Half a block from the Hotel Norfolk, on the left, just before the rotary, Fletch noticed a police station/jail.

After a moment, Fletch answered, "There's a difference between men and women."

"Yes," Carr said. "There is. Shall I sing you a few million songs about that? Never mind. You may have only one life to live." He shifted down.

"Okay. You know Barbara and I had a disagreement."

Of the men who walked along the road, many were with children.

A few raindrops appeared on the windshield.

"Hope Barbara's having a nice day by the pool," Fletch said.

"Never begrudge Africa its rain," Carr said. "We'll go a bit out of our way to have lunch at the fishing lodge on Lake Turkana, which is nothing to write home about. But, before that, you can swim in their pool, which is."

"Which is what?"

"Something to write home about."

"How can a swimming pool be something to write home about?"

"You'll want a swim by the time we get there." Carr was smiling to himself.

Fletch noticed a dog-eared paperback on Carr's dashboard. *Murder by Rote.* By Josie Fletcher. Fletch picked it up. "You read my mother?"

"Her biggest fan. Have you read that one?"

Fletch was thumbing through the book. "How can I tell?"

"She must be a very sensible woman, your mother."

"Sensible?" Adjectives sometimes used to describe his mother always amazed Fletch. Sensible. Observant. Clever about clocks set wrong and dogs that don't bark. Practical. Wise. Logical. Adjectives used by her few fans. "Yes, she might notice if her house were on fire. But she'd probably finish writing her chapter before doing anything about it."

Carr shifted in his seat. "Have you seen her lately?"

"Last Saturday. The day I was married."

"Still, I gather, a woman, without much education, she's supported herself, and you, at a hard profession . . ."

"I appreciate it.'" Fletch tossed the book back onto the dashboard. "We had a good conversation. I really pinned her down about my father. My hearing from him forced the issue."

"Oh?" Carr cleared his throat. "What did she say about him?"

"She said she loved him. His disappearance left her in a state of permanent shock. She's been trying to solve mysteries ever since."

"Maybe the quality of a writer is determined by the universality of the mystery he's trying to solve."

Leaning against his door, right arm over the chair back, Fletch stared at Carr.

"A pilot has lots of time to think," Carr said, as if excusing himself. "Literally, his head is in the clouds. Why does human life take the forms it does? Families, friends . . . What are these institutions humans keep creating, destroying, and re-creating for ourselves? Religions, nations, families, businesses, clubs . . . What are they for? Given the uniqueness of life, how can one person purposely take the life of another, for any reason?"

"My mother supports herself by writing detective stories," Fletch said. "There's nothing mysterious about it."

They were stuck in traffic.

"What are we?" Carr mused.

Fletch said, "We are all mysteries waiting to be solved."

"Now you've got the beat." Carr beat out a little rhythm with his fingers on the steering wheel. "One has to think *something*." The traffic began to move. "Odd, though, that your mother never told you much about your father. She must be articulate."

"She really hasn't known all these years whether he's dead or alive."

"She had him declared dead?"

"She had to, to get on with her own life."

"Therefore you thought he was dead."

"Kids believe what they're told. When the courts say, 'Your daddy is dead,' the kid says, 'Okay. My daddy is dead. What's for lunch?' "

"What was for lunch?"

"Usually the question, 'How do you spell *hors d'oeuvres*?' My mother never could spell *hors d'oeuvres*. It's a wonder she kept serving 'em up in her books."

"All this is more of a surprise to you than I thought."

"You don't get used to not having a father. Then again, you do."

"Then someone comes along and says, 'Here's Papa!' "

"Where is Papa?"

Carr swung out to pass. "Walter Fletcher has screwed up."

"She also told me she never told me much about Walter because Walter wasn't there to defend himself."

Carr breathed a whistle through his teeth. "Nice lady."

"Sometimes, any news is better than no news."

"I'm not so sure." Carr turned left onto the airport road. "Barbara's not missing much of a trip. Too murky really to see the green hills of Africa. Still, she's getting her rest by the sunless pool. And your company is pleasant. I guess you're the one person in the world I don't have to worry about stealing *Murder by Rote* before I finish it."

NINETEEN

"Carr?" Fletch banged his fist on the pilot's shoulder. Carr shoved the radiophone forward off his right ear. "There's a body down there. A man on the ground."

Carr leaned over Fletch and looked through the starboard window of the airplane. He dipped the right wing so he could see better. "So there is."

The naked man was lying on his side, far from any bush.

Carr said, "I was wondering what the vultures had found for themselves."

The circling birds had drawn Fletch's attention to the man on the ground.

They had flown about two hours northwest from Nairobi, over the White Hills and the eastern edge of Lake Naivasha. Looking down, Fletch had seen the enormous, white Djinn Palace at the edge of the lake.

Carr had pointed out the great gash in the land called the Rift Valley. "Someday, we're told," Carr shouted over the sound of the engine, "the Red Sea will come flooding down that rift. Hope I've got my waders on that day!"

Now, Fletch knew by the chart in his lap, they were somewhere east of the Loichangamata Hills. There were no shambas below them.

The scientist they were transporting to Lake Turkana, Dr. McCoy, had taken a backseat in the airplane. A little, very white man in a seersucker suit, wide-brimmed safari hat, and canvas bush boots, he coughed continuously and spat into his handkerchief frequently. He had not asked why Fletch was accompanying them to Lake Turkana on the doctor's chartered plane. He had not asked anything or said much.

Carr turned the plane and swooped lower over the figure on the ground.

As Carr did so, Fletch pointed out the body to McCoy in the seat behind him.

"Is he dead?" Fletch asked Carr.

"Look at the hyenas." Carr could not point while he was turning the plane again. "They're just waiting. And the vultures are waiting for the hyenas."

Carr was bringing the plane around to land near the man.

Leaning forward, McCoy said, "Leave him!"

Carr looked over his shoulder at him.

"He was left there to die," McCoy said.

"Ah, culture clash," Carr said, facing forward. "He's an anthropologist or something. I suppose he's right."

Carr was still making for a landing.

"I said, leave him!" McCoy shouted. "You're not to interfere with their nature!"

McCoy began coughing.

Carr turned his head so McCoy could hear him. "I haven't your education, McCoy. It's my nature I must sleep with!"

McCoy spat into his handkerchief.

Just after the wheels of the plane touched the ground, Fletch threw up the door next to his seat and held it open. Carr had taught him to do that, taking off from Wilson Airport, to rid the cockpit of the terrible, immediate heat on the ground.

"Poor bastard. He's been *panga*ed."

The man's skull was split open. Brain matter was visible.

There was the great patience of the nearly dead in the man's eyes as he watched Carr and Fletch approach.

"How can he be alive?" Fletch asked.

"Tough nut."

Carr haunched next to the man and spoke with him. The man answered slowly, from a parched throat, through a swollen tongue. He never closed his mouth completely.

McCoy stood coughing under the wing of the plane. He had only gotten out of the cockpit to get out of the heat.

Carr said, "He says he stole six goats."

"Honest of him to say so."

"They caught up to him, cut his head open with a machete, and left him to die." Carr looked at the birds circling above them. "To be eaten." He looked over to where some hyenas sat next to a bush. "Rude justice."

"Why did he tell you the truth? Why doesn't he say *he* was robbed or something?"

Carr stood up. "Under prevailing circumstances, vultures about to pluck out one's eyes, hyenas about to begin their feed on one by first cracking off one's hands and one's feet, one is probably well advised, happier, if you catch my drift, if one is honest with oneself as to how one fell victim to such circumstances."

"For six goats?"

"Nothing is more important than goats. They rank right up there with wives in the local economy." Carr stooped to look into the skull wound. He had brought a medical kit from the airplane. "In every way, goats are the scourge of the third world."

A little fresh blood continued to trickle onto the dried, crusted blood. Flies were everywhere over the wound and over the naked man. The flies walked on the man's eyeballs. They probed his nostrils. They walked along his lips and entered and exited his mouth.

"Why didn't they kill him?" Fletch asked. "Why leave him like this?"

"Having six goats stolen can ruin a family, for at least a generation."

Carr wrapped gauze around the man's head. "Just trying to hold his brains in. Although I guess I cleaned up worse things off the cockpit floor. There. Let's get him up."

As they lifted the man upright and began to walk/carry him between them to the airplane, the hyenas began to yell angrily. They paced up and down in protest, coming nearer.

"We're certainly upsetting nature," Carr said. "May God forgive me."

McCoy did nothing to help them lift the man onto the rearmost seat of the airplane. Carr buckled him in.

At no point did the man cry out, groan, show pain. Nor did he seem to notice being rescued. He showed nothing but patience.

Buckling himself into his seat, Fletch said, "He seems to accept all this."

The hyenas surrounded the airplane.

Carr said, "He knows he done wrong."

TWENTY

"Strip and dip," Carr said.

Fletch already had his sneakers and wool socks off. Carr had said he did not want to guess the temperature in either degrees centigrade or Fahrenheit. He said figuring such an astronomical number would thin his hair.

It was hot.

The other side of the none-too-serious fence, behind the fishing lodge's cabins, were a few of the Turkana tribe. Not all wore clothes.

Fletch dropped his cutoff ski pants. He plunged into the swimming pool.

"YOW!"

Standing on the pool edge, Carr laughed. "Something to write home about?"

"This is impossible! It's freezing! Is it just the contrast, because I'm so hot?"

"No. The water temperature really is near freezing."

Fletch's teeth were chattering. "How do they do it?"

The fishing lodge at Lake Turkana was a terrace, an open wooden lodge, and a half-dozen wooden cabins on a sand bluff overlooking the lake.

"They don't do it. The rate of evaporation in this heat is so rapid the water in a pool like this gets very cold indeed. Would you believe it?"

Hugging his own shoulders, Fletch said, "I believe it. You coming in?"

"Not on your life. You think I'm crazy?"

Fletch did a fast crawl to the ladder and pulled himself out of the pool.

"Swimming pools are for tourists," Carr said.

"This one sure is."

Fletch stood shivering on the pool ledge. Carr looked down Fletch's body and frowned. "Is that a birthmark?"

Fletch looked down at himself. The lowest right side of his stomach was blue. The mark was bigger than a fist. It was as big as an outstretched hand.

Fletch said, "I must have been born again."

Carr leaned over and prodded Fletch's flesh with his fingers. "First birthmark I ever saw that's swollen."

"I didn't even feel it," Fletch said. "I must have bumped into something in the hotel room. A strange hotel room. In the dark . . ."

"Sorry," Carr said. "None of my business."

Fletch prodded with his own fingers the great blue welt where Barbara had hit him. It didn't hurt.

Carr said, "I'll be on the terrace, when you're ready. I'll buy us shandies before lunch."

For a moment, Fletch sat on the pool edge, his feet in the cold water.

Then he dropped forward into the water. He thought of drowning.

Shortly he climbed out of the pool. He pulled on his cutoff ski pants, his socks, laced his sneakers, and went to join Carr on the terrace.

TWENTY-ONE

Fletch sat with Carr at the little table on the terrace on the sand bluff overlooking Lake Turkana. "A lake in the middle of a desert," Fletch said.

Carr said, "The lake is down about a mile from its edges since I've known it."

In the airplane coming in, Fletch had watched the Kerio River wandering over sand toward Lake Turkana. The river dried up miles before it reached the lake. A sad, empty landscape surrounded the lake, miles and miles in every direction. The only marks upon the landscape, besides the few, widely separated shambas, were water catchments, which were empty.

"The lake of many names." Carr gazed over it. "Aman, Galana, Basso Narok, Jade Sea, Lake Rudolf, Lake Turkana. There are Nile River perch in it. Explain that to me. They used to grow to as much as two hundred pounds. Nowadays, they run thirty, forty pounds."

Naked men on logs were fishing the lake.

A waiter brought two glasses, two bottles of premium beer, two bottles of lemon carbonated drink. "Thank you, Fred," Carr said. He poured some of the beer and some of the lemon drink in each glass to make the shandies.

"Over there is Koobi Fora." Carr tipped his head to the east side of the lake as he poured. "Where they found the remains of extinct elephants, both African and Indian. Explain to me how the skeletons of Indian elephants come to be here. Also seven human footprints, dated a million and a half years old. And, although some debate it, the remains of our first human ancestor, *Homo erectus*. First man. The papa of us all."

To the eye, the other side of the lake was just rolling sand. Fletch said, "Lots to be explained."

"I'll say."

A small, naked boy with a tall stack of aluminum pots on his head was trudging straight-backed through the sand from the village behind the lodge toward the lake.

"One can't imagine what the landscape might have been like here when it first cradled human life," Carr said. "Sure makes one curious."

Fletch tried his shandy. "Is the research why McCoy flew here?" Then he took a thirst-quenching drink.

"I don't know." Carr blinked. "I didn't ask him. Science wallah named Richard Leakey is in charge of all."

"I can see why you're digging around, looking for a lost Roman city."

"What I'm doing is nothing. I'm just trying to go back a few thousand years." From the terrace, Carr was scanning the horizon. "The landscape sort of calls for it. Here, in East Africa, you have sort of a time capsule, or time map. All of animate life before our very eyes, much of it still walking around, the rest being ghosts calling to us to be discovered. Here we all want to read the bones."

Using only their hands as paddles, the fishermen straddling logs were coming in toward shore.

Fletch took another long swallow. "Carr, I was sort of surprised when you left our wounded man at the police station."

Flying in, Carr had buzzed the lodge in the plane, signaling the manager, Hassan, to send a car for them. He had not been able to get the lodge on the radio.

While they were waiting at the airstrip, a man looking more ancient than Fletch had ever seen, longevity walking briskly in a loincloth, carrying a spear, marched out from under a bush. Carr said this man would be in charge of the airplane while they were at the fishing lodge.

"I've never seen anyone so old," Fletch said. "How old is he?"

"Right," Carr said. "About my age." Fletch figured Carr to be in his late forties.

The Land-Rover which brought them to the village was driven so fast over the packed sand road Fletch was sure it would fall apart. He was sure the man's split skull would fall apart.

"Did you see a hospital?" Carr upended his glass. "The colonists were better at building police stations than hospitals."

They had left the wounded man propped on a wooden bench inside the police station. Carr had explained everything to the only officer there. When they left, the police officer was still working on papers at his school-sized desk. He had only glanced at the wounded man when Carr had said he was a thief.

And the wounded man had watched them leave with eyes of weary patience.

"What will they do with him?" Fletch asked.

"I don't know. Maybe put him back in the bush. Or into the lake." Crossing Ferguson Gulf to the lodge in an aluminum outboard boat, they went through a herd of crocodiles. Flamingos stood in the shallower water. "McCoy is right, you know. One shouldn't meddle too much. I was indulging my own conscience."

"You were being kind."

"Kind to myself. That's the hell of original sin, you see. One can never be quite sure what is kindness to another."

Near the water's edge, the little boy with the pots on his head was doing a crazy dance in the sand. None of the pots fell off his head.

Watching Fletch watching the boy, Carr said, "Once in a small village way out in the bush, I saw a woman buy a postage stamp. She put the postage stamp on her head face-down, and then placed a rock on the stamp, to walk home that way. Made great sense. That way the glue on the stamp wouldn't get sweated away, and the stamp wouldn't blow away."

"I doubt I could walk two meters with a rock on my head," Fletch said. "Or a postage stamp."

Carr said, "My witch friend in Thika says you're carrying a whole box of rocks."

Fletch said nothing.

One of the fishermen who had emerged from the lake, shoving his log ashore, grabbed up the small boy. Holding the boy to his chest, the man danced in circles. The pots flew off the boy's head and scattered everywhere in the sand.

"Instead of wondering what the land tells us," Carr said, "right now, I'm wondering what the sky is trying to tell us. I think we'd better eat."

"Okay."' Finishing his drink, moving slowly in the heat, Fletch watched the naked man and boy give the pots a quick rinse in the lake.

Entering the lodge's dining porch, Fletch saw the man and boy, hand in hand, begin their trudge through the sand back toward the village. Again, all the pots were stacked tall on the kid's head.

TWENTY-TWO

"What's that? What's happening?"

Facing the inside wall of the dining porch, Fletch looked to his left. The screens were bending toward him. Paper plates were three meters in the air. An empty beer bottle smashed on the stone floor.

Suddenly the air had darkened, yellowed.

"Eat fast!" Carr shouted over the roar. He cupped one hand over his plate. His other hand shoveled food into his mouth rapidly.

"What is it?" Fletch's eyes were stinging. He could barely see the great lumps of white fish yellowing on his plate.

"Sandstorm! My timing was off. The faster you eat now, the less of a peck of dirt you'll eat all at once."

Fletch put fish into his mouth. He coughed. Already his mouth was full of sand. Already a million particles of sand had adhered to the insides of his nostrils.

His filled plate wobbled on the table.

He and Carr both shoved back as the table was pulled up by the wind. It flipped over and skittered to the wall of the porch.

Carr and Fletch sat facing each other, hands in their laps, no table between them.

Fletch shouted, "Shall we go someplace else for dessert?"

Carr stood up. "I'll ask Hassan to get a cabin ready for us. The only thing for us to do in a sandstorm is get between walls and underneath a sheet."

As soon as Fletch stood up, his chair fell over. All the porch furniture was sliding by them. "How long does a sandstorm last?"

"A few hours. A day. A week."

"Can I call Barbara? Tell her we'll be late?"

"Sure," Carr said, "There's a telephone box at the corner. Right next to the pizza parlor!"

"Carr? I saw a murder."

They were in narrow beds in a small cabin. It had grown dark.

The wind howled. Sand blew through the walls. Lying under the sheet, Fletch had kept his mouth closed. Still, his tongue, teeth were gritty with sand. Occasionally, he had spat into a glass. Carr suggested he stop that, saying his body needed the fluid. Fletch kept his eyes closed until his lids became too heavy with sand. Then he'd roll over and wipe his face against the lower sheet. The sheets became coated with sand centimeters thick. Less than every hour, he would get up and flip the sand off his sheets. Sand was in his eyes, nose, mouth, sinuses, in his skin. He wished he could keep his nostrils closed.

There was a primitive shower in the cabin. It dripped in loud splats. When Fletch could hear the shower splattering he knew the wind was down somewhat. Mostly he couldn't hear the shower.

At the moment, he could hear the shower splattering.

Carr asked, "Is that the box of rocks you're carrying?"

"I guess so."

Carr said, "I've got strong legs, too."

The cabin was hit with another sustained blast of hot, sand-filled wind.

"At the airport yesterday," Fletch said when he was hearing the shower splattering again. "Just after we arrived." Talking, he realized just how much sand was in his throat, mouth, on his lips.

"I went into the men's room while Barbara changed some money.

There was a man in there, acting perfectly normal, just washing up. I went into a cabinet. Another man came in. I saw his feet. The two men argued. They were shouting in a language I didn't understand. Maybe Portuguese. When I came out, there was only one man there, and he was dead. Stabbed. Blood all over the place."

"The same man who was there when you entered?"

"No. The other man."

"So you saw the murderer."

"Yes."

"What did you do?"

"Carr, I threw up. I was careful to wipe my fingerprints off the door as I left."

"Could you identify the murderer?"

"Yes. I saw him again, in the parking lot, as we were driving away."

"A white man?"

"Yes. They were both white."

"I saw about it in *The Nation*."

"I forgot to look in the newspapers."

"Murders still make headlines here. Unless it's just Dan Dawes doing his nocturnal duty."

"It wasn't Dan Dawes."

"No. That's not how Dan executes people. Whom have you told?"

"Only Barbara. Now you."

"I see. You made your decision to shut up about this pretty fast."

"What do you mean?"

"You wiped your fingerprints off the door handle."

"Carr, I had just arrived in a foreign country. I knew very little about Kenya."

"There is justice here."

"A murder investigation is apt to take a long time."

"Right."

"Soon, I've got to go home, back to work, start my married life. You know?"

"Of course."

An extraordinary wall of wind slammed against the cabin. Fletch said, "Committed, but not involved."

After that thick wall of wind passed, Fletch said, "Did the newspapers say who the murdered man was?"

"I didn't really read it. Did you recognize either man from your airplane?"

Fletch thought a moment. "I don't know. The airplane was so crowded."
"Well," Carr said, "it seems to me you made your decision. You were a witness to a murder, and you chose not to come forward."
"Yeah, but, Carr? Suppose they convict the wrong guy?"
"There's always that possibility. They'll hang him. You'll never know. You'll be in the United States downing hot dogs and beer."
"I don't want to live with that possibility."
After a while, Carr said, "That's a box of rocks, all right. You can't wait around Kenya for a year or more serving as police witness. And you have a natural disinclination against letting the powers-that-be hang the wrong chap."
Carr didn't say any more.

"Carr?" It was hours later, but Fletch knew Carr wasn't asleep. Shortly before there had been another loud burst of wind. Now the splattering shower could be heard again. "Tell me about my father."
"What? Sorry. My ears aren't that perfect, you know."
"My father. Tell me about him."
"We're talking about the man Fletcher."
"Please."
"Well. He's a pilot. Like the rest of us, he's flown light planes here and there in the world. Somewhere in South America for a while, and then I know he flew in India. He was well off, for a while. He owned three airplanes, his own little airlines, in Ethiopia. Then that new administration took over, and took over his airlines."
"Just took them over?"
"Yes."
"Didn't pay him for them, or anything?"
"Because they wanted his airplanes, they also took over his house and his car, to get rid of him. Everything. That government enterprises freely only on its own behalf."
"Oh."
"So he arrived in Kenya broke. Flew for me for a while. Now he has his own airplane again."
"You have more than one airplane?"
"I have two."
The wind made conversation impossible for a few moments.
"Carr?" Fletch finally asked. "Is he a happy man? Does he give the impression life satisfies him?"
"Pretty much. Flying around is a great life. Aren't you having fun?"

* * *

"Carr?" It was the time of night any dawn would seem a wearisome blessing. The wind was down for the moment, but Fletch knew it would rise again. He felt like a stocking stuffed with sand. "We didn't anchor down the airplane. What's to keep it from flipping over?"

"Remember that little guy at the airstrip you thought was so old?"

"Yeah."

"He's out there in the wind, hanging on to a wing holding the airplane down."

"You serious?"

"Of course I'm serious."

"That skinny little old guy will get blown away, too."

"We'll see."

TWENTY-THREE

"So you two finally decided to show up?"

Barbara was in a long chair by the swimming pool at the Norfolk Hotel.

"What?" Carr said.

"What?" Fletch said.

Even the sky over Nairobi still wasn't that clear.

"Safe and sound." Carr rubbed his hands together. "But not home on the same day. Anyone else want a beer?"

Fletch stooped to kiss Barbara.

"You look all puffy," Barbara said.

"What?"

"Puffy!"

"We're full of sand."

"Don't shout."

Fletch sneezed.

"I want a beer." Carr signaled the pool *bwana* on the upper terrace.

"Were you guys up all night?" Barbara asked. "Your eyes are runny."

"She wants to know if we spent the night drinking and dancing."

"Yes," Carr said. "We spent the night drinking and dancing."

On the other side of the pool were an English couple in string bikinis and straw hats under an umbrella having a proper tea.

"We were in a sandstorm," Fletch said.

"Sure."

"We were in a sandstorm."

"I hear you."

"Not that bad a time." Carr sat in a poolside chair. "I don't mind sand." He was speaking as does a person who can't hear himself. "Your husband saw the cradle of humanity." He sneezed. "Perhaps where man first walked."

"Sure."

Fletch sat on the edge of Barbara's long chair. "This little old guy, he couldn't weigh sixty pounds, held the wing of the plane down all night, so it wouldn't flip in the wind."

"Why are you two talking so loudly?"

"What?" Carr asked. He now had beer in hand.

"My, you're gritty." Barbara's hand was on Fletch's forearm. "Don't they have water in whatever lake you were at?"

"Crocodiles, too."

"Sure."

Fletch's tongue continuously ran over the sand on his teeth.

Carr said, "Life's not all roasted goat."

Barbara said, "I hope not."

"What?" Fletch asked.

"I'll admit it wasn't a very good flight home." Carr shook his head. "Couldn't see."

"You were supposed to be back in time for dinner last night."

"There was a sandstorm, you see," Fletch said.

"I had some fruit in my room."

"Oh?" Carr said. "Did he leave politely?"

"Why didn't you call?"

"Wives always want to know why you don't call home," Carr said. "That's the way it is with wives."

"There were no phones, Barbara."

"A fishing lodge without phones?"

"The madame wouldn't let us,'" Carr said. "She said the brothel's phones were for paying customers only."

"Did it ever cross your mind I might be worried?"

"We were almost sanded down a full size." Fletch sneezed.

"Did you catch cold?"

"Air-conditioned brothel," Carr said.

"Sand." Fletch sneezed. "Sinuses." He sneezed again. "Oh, hell."

"Hope that's all you caught."

"Didn't go fishing." Fletch sneezed. The English couple looked over at him with concern. "Nile perch there. Crocodiles in the lake and the fishermen go out on it straddling logs, their legs and feet in the water."

"What was I supposed to do if you didn't show up?"

"We did show up." Carr sneezed.

"Any word from my father?"

"No."

Fletch stood up. "I've got to take a shower. Start getting this sand off. Thanks for a lovely trip." Fletch sneezed. "Carr."

Barbara came into the bathroom as Fletch was getting out of the shower. He had rinsed his mouth and nose and eyes, washed his hair, and scrubbed his body over and over again. He still felt like the inside of a cement mixer.

"I was worried," Barbara said. "Worried sick."

"There were no phones, Barbara. No radio that could work."

"All day yesterday I sat here feeling sorry for the way I acted yesterday morning. For the things I said. Then you didn't show up. Didn't call. All night."

"We were in a sandstorm near the Ethiopian border. There were no camels coming this way."

"Then I began to get angry all over again. Angry and scared."

Fletch banged the side of his head with the heel of his hand. "If my ears don't pop soon, I'm going to go nuts. I feel like I've got a balloon in my head."

"Then you two come prancing in this afternoon looking like a couple of kids who had been playing in the sandbox."

"We flew home at twelve thousand five hundred feet," Fletch said, "with the window open. Otherwise, Carr couldn't see. The sandstorm reached that high. Even the cockpit was full of sand. Can you understand all that? We're deaf. Our ears hurt. Carr kept having to open the window."

"Did you stay away all night because of the way I acted yesterday morning? Were you trying to teach me a lesson or something?"

"Oh Jesus, Barbara. If I ever play that sort of game on you, I'll let you know. Where are my swimming trunks?"

Fletch went into the bedroom.

"In the top drawer of the bureau."

"Good thing we knew there was a swimming pool at the ski lodge. At least we have swimsuits."

The two pairs of skis stood in a corner of the room. The other side of the window next to them, hibiscus flowered.

"What was I supposed to think when you didn't show up?"

"That we were caught in a sandstorm near the Ethiopian border. Maybe a swim will help blow the sand out of my sinuses."

"What's that?" Wide-eyed, Barbara was staring at Fletch's lower stomach.

"What do you think?"

"I don't know. What is it?"

"A wound, Barbara. A trauma. Vulgarly described as a blow below the belt."

"Where did you get it?"

"Are you serious?"

"Of course I'm serious. Where did that come from?"

"You belted me."

"I did not."

"No one else did. Ever."

"Not like that."

"Like that."

"I never did."

"Oh, stow it. You coming back to the pool for a swim?"

"I'll take a shower."

"Okay. I'll go for a swim. Then play in the sandbox for a while." Fletch sneezed. "When I come back, we can think about what we do next."

"If you don't make it," Barbara said, "telephone."

TWENTY-FOUR

"So," Barbara said.

"So," Fletch said.

They had ordered breakfast on the Lord Delamere Terrace.

"Here we are in Nairobi."

"So we are."

"Having a honeymoon at last."

"And a night's sleep." Across Harry Thuku Road, Nairobi University was awake with students coming and going in the bright sunlight.

"A nice, long night. Ten hours to sleep, and five hours to eat and play."

"That much?"

"By my clock."

"I feel like a new man." Fletch began to look through *The Standard*. "Except my ears are still clogged and my nose is still runny."

"This morning I'm glad I married you." Under the table, Barbara's leg went against his.

"Likewise."

"I was afraid that thing on your stomach would hurt."

"It doesn't. It never did. Just looks ugly."

"I don't know. I think it looks sort of erotic."

"One is apt to think well of one's own work."

"I didn't do that to you."

"Oh."

"I know I didn't. You must have bumped into something."

"Okay."

"It looks sort of like a codpiece pulled aside. A jockstrap or something, you know?"

"Maybe you ought to go into the business of Designer Bruises."

"Is that why hitting boxers below the belt is considered a no-no?"

"Their trainers haven't your sense of what's sexy, I guess."

"I didn't know men are so sensitive there."

"If you cut us, do we not bleed?"

Their fruit was served.

"There's nothing in this morning's newspaper about the murder at the airport," Fletch said after the waiter left.

"Did you tell Carr about it?"

"Yes." The mashed rhubarb was sweetened exactly right.

"What did he say about it?"

"He agrees I have a problem. A 'box of rocks.' "

"Did he understand why you didn't come forward?"

"Oh, yes. I can't spend my life in Kenya reviewing their suspects, one by one."

"Are you just going to forget about the murder?"

"I can't. Suppose they decide to hang the wrong sack?"

"Can't you just leave a description with the police?"

"Oh, yeah, sure. Middle-aged white man with brown hair and a moustache. Kenya probably has more men fitting that description than they have zebras. They'd have me flying halfway around the world and back again every week. Which I can't afford. Which Kenya probably can't afford. So I suspect they'd ask me to stay here, in voices sweet or stern. Which I also can't afford. Carr had no suggestions."

"Speaking of *afford* . . ." Barbara cleared her throat.

"I've already thought of it."

"Your father doesn't seem to be Nairobi's greeter, official or unofficial. This is the third day we've been here, and no Fletcher senior has showed up pulling a welcome wagon."

"I've noticed. There was a message from him, however. While we were out at Thika."

"Yes. Saying he'd be back."

"He must have had a flat tire."

"I think you'd better check with the hotel desk, to make sure our bills are being paid."

"I thought we'd have breakfast first."

"I doubt we'll get much of our money back from the ski lodge in Colorado. We don't deserve much back."

"They must be used to canceled honeymoons."

All sorts of interesting traffic was going by on Harry Thuku Road. Besides the cars, taxis, trucks usual to any city, there were *safari guarris* painted in zebra stripes, Land-Rovers with spare wheels plastered all over their bodies, Jeeps which looked like they had been rolled down mountains sideways and a few vehicles which looked distinctly homemade.

"So what will we do today?" Barbara asked. "Presuming we don't have to find a cheaper hotel."

Their eggs, bacon, and toast were served.

"I suppose I could go looking for my father. He must be here, somewhere. I am 'mildly curious.' "

"A lady at the pool yesterday told me about seeing some wonderful dancers, what did she call them? Bomas. The Bomas Harambee Dancers. Something like that. About ten kilometers from here. She said they tell this wonderful story in dance about an evil spirit who takes over a young girl while she and her husband are traveling, asleep in the bush. So the young husband goes and hires a witch doctor to rid his wife of the evil spirit. The doctor comes and scares the evil spirit away from the girl. But every time he gets close to the spirit, the spirit scares the followers of the witch doctor and runs away. The whole story is told in dance. I might like to see that this afternoon."

Fletch was watching Juma striding down the street toward them.

"And would you believe there's a game park just outside Nairobi that's something like forty-seven square miles? Lions, giraffes, everything. We could rent a car, if you don't mind driving on the left side of the road."

Striding along, shirtless, shoeless in dusty shorts, carrying a book in his left hand, Juma kept his happy eyes straight ahead. He did not survey the people on Lord Delamere's Terrace.

Fletch and Barbara were too far back in the terrace to call out to him.

"Someone else said there's a great restaurant called the Tamarind. Great lobster. And a Chinese restaurant near here, called the Hong Kong. Less expensive. Best soup in the world."

"You've been doing your homework."

Fletch was just getting up to go after Juma, to say hello to him, when he saw Juma turn into the entrance of the Norfolk Hotel.

Putting the book in his back pocket, Juma bounced through the tables and chairs at them.

He sat down at their table.

"Are you happy to see me?" he asked.

"Absolutely," Fletch answered.

"Does that mean yes?"

"Of course. Were you looking for us?"

Juma's eyebrows wrinkled.

"Have you spent all this time in Nairobi?" Barbara asked.

"Yes."

"Would you like something to eat?" Barbara asked.

"I will have some toast," Juma said, "to be polite." Barbara handed him her plate of toast. "Also because I like buttered toast."

"What have you been doing?" Fletch asked, attempting to make conversation.

"I've been thinking about your problem, Fletch."

"What problem?"

"You see, my father in in jail, too."

Barbara jumped.

"Very sad, very stupid." Juma munched his toast. "You see, he was a driver for the government. The department of education. At the end of an eleven-hour day, very tired and hungry, he went into this bar where his brother works, for some food. Someone reported seeing this government car parked outside this bar for forty-five minutes. For this, he was convicted and sentenced to jail for eighteen months."

"Good God," Barbara said.

Fletch felt the blood draining from his face. "Good God."

"It is not proper for a government car to be seen parked outside a bar."

"Eighteen months in jail?" Fletch asked.

Barbara was staring at Fletch.

"Also, he was fired. So my family has no money again. May I have more toast, please?" Juma took another slice.

Fletch cleared his throat. "Who said my father is in jail?"

"It is something you will have to accept, Fletch. I know you came all this way from America to see him. Have you seen him?"

Fletch felt a throbbing in his temples. "No."

"That's the problem," Juma said. "They won't let me see my father, either. Even now."

"How do you know my father is in jail?"

"This man at the jail, the one who keeps me out, no matter what I say, says not permitting my father to see his son all this long time is part of the punishment, you see. For parking the government car outside the bar."

Barbara said, "Poor Fletch."

"So I asked this man if he would make an exception for you, because you came all this way to see your father, and he said, maybe, but not until after the trial."

Fletch sat back in his chair. He exhaled deeply.

Barbara said, "Oh, dear."

Juma asked Barbara, "How do you like Kenya?"

"Just great," Fletch answered.

"We *wananchi* are very proud of Kenya. Everything is very scrupulous here. Do you see pictures of our president, Daniel arap Moi, just everywhere?"

"Just everywhere," Barbara answered. "In every shop."

"Although I admit it is difficult on a family when a father is sentenced to eighteen months in jail for parking a government car outside a bar."

"I daresay," Fletch said.

"So I have been thinking about your problem, Fletch." Juma shrugged. "I do not have a solution."

Barbara was still staring at Fletch. "Have you known about this?"

"Not really."

"What do you mean, *not really*?"

"Not now, Barbara. Please. Not here." Fletch felt he was being wrung out to dry.

"You did know about this. *Flat tire*, you said."

"I didn't."

"Why is he in jail?"

"It must have happened yesterday."

"There was some trouble at the Thorn Tree," Juma said. "Everyone knew about it."

"I didn't," Barbara said. "What's the Thorn Tree?"

So filled was Fletch's head and heart that he did not realize Carr was standing over them until Carr spoke.

"Irwin, I need a quiet word with you."

"Ah. Good morning, Carr."

"We've heard,'" Barbara said.

Carr looked at her. "You've heard what?"

"Fletch's father is in jail. Awaiting trial. No visitors."

"I see." Sitting down, Carr nodded hello at Juma. "He turned himself in yesterday. By far the wiser course."

"Has he got a lawyer?" Fletch asked.

"Yes."

Barbara asked, "What's all this about?"

"Two nights ago," Carr told her, "while we were eating at the Shade Hotel, there was some sort of a punch-up at the Thorn Tree Café. Such things didn't used to be unusual, in the bad old days. Walter Fletcher may, or may not, have started it. Damage to the glassware was done. Much worse, in the eyes of the authorities, a few tourists were discommoded. Walter Fletcher may, or may not, have knocked an *askari* silly."

"What's an *askari*?" Barbara asked.

"A guard. The official status of this particular guard is not yet established."

"You mean, there's still some doubt as to whether he was a cop or a private watchman?" Fletch asked.

"Yes," answered Carr. "Some private guards have police status. Some don't. May I have some coffee?" Carr asked the waiter. "It makes a difference. Kenya is very strict about respect for its things and people official."

"Eighteen months for parking a government car in front of a bar," Fletch mutterred. "It's a wonder they didn't send Dan Dawes to shoot Juma's father!"

"Why can't they find out?" Barbara asked.

"Because the *askari* is still moaning it up in the hospital, claiming this and that between bites of noodles. He says one of his wives has his employment papers, but he can't remember which one."

"Which *wife*?" Barbara asked.

"I guess a clip on the jaw causes one to forget which wife is which." Carr sipped his hot coffee. "In any case, no one can see Walter Fletcher, except his lawyer, until after the trial. And the trial date is not set."

Juma said, "It will be nice to get away from here."
Carr gave him a sharp look.
"What can we do for him?" Fletch asked.
"There's a mosque down the street." Carr sipped more of his coffee. "Be sure and take off your shoes. There's a sign on the main gate saying, DO NOT ENCOURAGE BEGGARS."
"Oh, dear," Barbara said. "Poor Fletch."
"We shouldn't have gone to Thika with you," Fletch said. "Because my father didn't show up when he was supposed to, I acted snotty. I wasn't here when he did show up."
"Water over the dam," Carr said.
"Well, there isn't that much water in Africa," Fletch said.
"Walter's over the dam," Barbara said.
"Which brings up the next point," Carr said.
"There's nothing I can do for him?" Fletch asked.
"No."
"I can't see him?"
"No."
"Shit!"
"Today I'm flying down to my digs," Carr said. "Get some work done on them. I thought I'd stop by first, bring you up to date on affairs Walter Fletcher, and ask if you'd like to come with me."
"To your digs?" Fletch asked.
"Oh," Barbara said. "Now we go looking for a lost Roman city."
"It's not a very grand camp. You'll be living under canvas. And it's hot there." Carr looked at the wall of the Norfolk Hotel. "But it would be cheaper for you than staying at this palace of eternal delights. And it might be interesting for you. See something of the real Kenya."
Fletch sighed. He looked at Barbara.
"Bomas Harambee," Barbara said.
"What?" Carr said. "That's right. Let's pull together for our own sakes. You might even help me root through the jungle. No telling what we might find."
Fletch, too, looked at the wall of the hotel. "Barbara? I want you to be precisely clear as to what you want to do."
Barbara sat up in her chair. She swallowed. Carr, Juma, and Fletch were watching her. She swallowed again. "How can I agree to something when I don't know what I'm agreeing to?"
"Rather nasty living," Carr said. "In tents, at the edge of the jungle. No telephones, electricity, or ice cream parlors. What we're doing is hacking our way through the jungle, either side of a river. Digging

holes, here and there, seeing if they turn up anything vaguely ancient Roman. Still, Sheila likes it."

Barbara was staring at Fletch.

"Barbara?" Fletch asked. "Would you like to go home?"

"It is our honeymoon," she said.

"One of the all-time great ones," Fletch said.

"Sheila could use a bit of company," Carr said.

"I don't see how we can go home," Barbara said. "We came all this way to meet your father."

"True," Fletch said. "But his absence here is just as real as his absence is in the States."

"But now you know he exists," Barbara said.

"True."

"And probably you'll never be able to come back."

"Probably not."

"And there is this other matter . . ." Barbara looked at Carr. ". . . no one knows what to do about."

Carr said nothing.

Barbara said, "Why are you leaving it to me?"

Fletch sighed.

"Is it something you want to do?" Barbara asked.

"I don't know any more than you do."

"Nice time," Juma said.

Everyone looked at Juma.

Carr then looked at his watch. "It's getting nigh onto checkout time. If you're checking out, that is."

Barbara said, "Okay."

Fletch said to Carr, "I'm afraid we're not being very gracious about your kind invitation."

Carr grinned. "Didn't I show you a nice time at Lake Turkana?"

TWENTY-FIVE

"I'm not sure just what arrangements have been made." Fletch, in speaking to the man in the hotel's cashier cage, hesitated. "The name is Fletcher." The sound of his own name made him slightly sick. The pin on the cashier's coat said his name was Lincoln.

"We wish to check out this morning. We don't know if we're coming back to the Norfolk. We hope to."

The cashier pulled a long card from a file box. "Yes, Mr. Fletcher." He looked at the card. "Your expenses are being paid. By Walter Fletcher. No problem."

"If we go and come back again will our expenses still be paid?"

"Unless Walter Fletcher directs otherwise, we'll leave the bill open. You just sign for your expenses so far, and we'll free the room." He turned the card around and slid it under the grille to Fletch with a pen. "Going on safari?"

"Yes." Fletch signed the bill, which was in *shillingi*. We're going on safari. We weren't invited until just now. Also, there'll be a breakfast charge coming in from the terrace."

"Are you going to Masai Mara?"

"I'm not sure where we're going. Someplace south. Near a river."

"You should go to Masai Mara," the cashier said. "It's nice there."

Fletch slid the billing card and pen back under the grille. "And I want to thank the hotel for the new sneakers."

The cashier smiled. "Nice time."

"Good grief." In their room, Barbara was stuffing ski suits, mittens, earmuffs, thermal underwear, and woolen socks into the big, framed knapsacks. "If you'd told me a week ago we'd be heading off today to search for a lost Roman city on the East African coast today, I wouldn't think you were crazy, I'd know it!"

"I wouldn't be so crazy as to predict such a thing."

"Do you think there's anything to it? Is there any chance of our finding such a place? I mean, my God, Carr's best source of information seems to be a witch doctor!"

Fletch shrugged. "It's Carr's thing. It's what he wants to do. He's inviting us into his life. I appreciate it."

"Daft," Barbara said. "How could the Romans have built a city here in East Africa without its being a known, established, historical fact by now?"

"I don't think very much of history is known," Fletch said. "Percentage wise, I mean. Look how hard it is to find out the facts of my own, personal history."

"Going into the African jungle to dig holes," Barbara said. "Are we sure we want to do this?"

"I just got a look at our hotel bill," Fletch said. "It's in *shillingi*, of course, but many thousands of *shillingi*. Carr says my father is not rich. I don't think we should stay here racking up such a bill, if we have a choice. Carr has given us a choice."

"Your blue jeans and T-shirt are back from the laundry. They're hanging in the closet."

"Great. I can dress like a bum again, instead of a streetwalker."

"Fletch, are you sure you and Carr aren't related?"

Hanger in hand, Fletch was looking at his jeans. "You mean, is Carr my father?"

"At the pool last night, when you came back from Lake Turkana, I don't know, watching you enter, the way you both walked, the way you sat, the way you both spoke . . ."

"We had both just been sandblasted, kept awake all night by a raging storm, deafened in the airplane . . . 'course we moved and sounded alike."

"He's being awfully nice to us."

"My jeans have been pressed. Look! My jeans have been pressed!"

"Oh, dear. That won't do." She took the jeans from him and started to rough them up in her hands.

"I've thought about this," he said. "Want the hard evidence?"

"About what?"

"While we were out at Thika and Karen with Carr, someone came to the hotel, identified himself as Walter Fletcher, and inquired for us."

"Couldn't do that by phone?"

"The man at the reception desk said that someone came to the hotel. He said it was Walter Fletcher." Barbara was kicking his jeans around the floor. "When we met Juma, he said he knows my father."

"He sounded regretful about Walter Fletcher, too."

"Juma identified Walter Fletcher as a pilot. Carr was with us. Juma knows Carr, and he knows a man here named Fletcher. When he came to the hotel this morning, before Carr, he knew Walter Fletcher is in jail."

"My father-in-law the jailbird."

"Please, Barbara."

"Well, it's true, isn't it?"

"Is hitting below the belt a characteristic of yours?"

"A man who starts a fight in a bar! And gets arrested for it! Mother will love that one. I married the son of a jailbird!"

"God damn it, Barbara!" Fletch snatched his jeans off the floor. "Is this what marriage to you is? You're nice to me in public and vicious in private. Downstairs, on the terrace, you were full of *Oh, dear! Poor Fletch!* and up here you call me the son of a jailbird!"

"Well, I've had time to think."

"I'm not in control of the facts, here, regarding my own life." Fletch was falling over trying to get into his jeans. "Sorry. We just have to go along discovering what we can discover."

"You said, 'Maybe he got a flat tire.' Really, Fletch. Yesterday, Carr said your father was delayed by some 'legal difficulty.' You call those *facts*?"

Fletch zipped his jeans. "I knew there'd been some unpleasantness in a café. I didn't know he was in jail. Clearly, I didn't know that."

Barbara said, "I don't want any of this to be true!"

"At least he turned himself in."

"Why wouldn't it have been natural for your father to meet us at the airport?"

"I don't know."

"He didn't do it."

"I guess he didn't."

Fletch was pulling on his T-shirt.

"You 'guess'? What is this with you and the word *guess*? When you married me, you didn't say *I do*, you said, *I guess I do*."

"I guess I did." Sitting on the edge of the bed, Fletch was pulling on his socks and sneakers.

"What do you mean, you *guess* your father wasn't at the airport to meet us? You know damn right well he wasn't."

"Do I?" Fletch headed for the door.

"Where are you going?"

"That's the point, Barbara. I don't."

"Are you going somewhere?"

"Yes." He opened the door to the corridor.

"Where?"

"Out."

"Carr's waiting for us."

"He said he'll pick us up at noon."

"You're disappearing again because you're mad at me."

"I'm going out . . ." Hand still on the door handle, Fletch hesitated. ". . . to answer your question; to find out something for myself: maybe to find out too much."

"Fletch . . ."

"If I'm not back by the time Carr gets here, you'll just have to wait for me."

TWENTY-SIX

"Hello." Fletch waited for the young policeman behind the high counter to look up, notice him, answer him.

"Hello," the policeman answered after only a glance.

Fletch sneezed. "How are you?"

"Well, thank you. And yourself?"

"I'm fine."

The policeman glanced at Fletch again. "What do you want at a police station?"

Fletch swallowed. "I want to see my father. My name is Fletcher. Is he here?"

"Oh, yes." The policeman checked the second sheet of paper on a clipboard. "Awaiting trial."

"May I see him?"

"That's not the way it's supposed to be," the policeman said. "He is being punished, you see."

"He is being punished before his trial?"

The policeman's forehead creased. "What is the point of keeping him here if we let everyone see him?"

"I have come from America," Fletch said. "Arrived two days ago. I don't know how long I will be able to stay here. I have come to see him."

"Oh, I see." Moving around behind the counter, the policeman fiddled with papers. His brow remained creased.

Fletch said nothing more.

After a few moments, the policeman went through a door behind the counter.

Trying to clear his eyes and his nose and his throat of sand, Fletch had walked the half block from the Norfolk Hotel to the police station. The sidewalk was busy with people his age carrying books to and from Nairobi University. He passed an older, Caucasian couple in plaid shorts and straw hats looking exhausted and confused.

No one else was in the lobby of the police station. The place was absolutely quiet.

Fletch sneezed again.

The policeman returned alone.

He said nothing. Behind the counter, he started to sort some papers.
Fletch said, "Well? Any chance of my seeing him?"
"Mr. Fletcher is not in."
"What?"
"He says to tell you he is not in."
"Did you tell him I'm his son? His son is here to see him?"
"Oh, yes. He asked me to say he is not in."
Going toward the door to the street, Fletch sneezed.
Quietly, the policeman said, "Bless you."
Fletch turned around. "Walter Fletcher? Is the man you are holding named Walter Fletcher, originally an American, Caucasian, somewhere in his forties?"
"Oh, yes," the policeman said. "We know him well."

TWENTY-SEVEN

"Distract her hands," Carr muttered.
Fletch tickled the back of the little girl's neck.
As her hands flew up, Carr's huge, strong hands slipped the little girl's leg bone back into alignment. First she giggled; then she yelped.
"It's over, sweet. You'll be a beautiful dancer when you get older."
Carr slipped a strongly elastic brace over the girl's foot and up her leg. The cut over the compound fracture was almost healed. The leg had been broken a week or more. He then splinted the leg.
"We do what we can," Carr said. "Patent medicines."
They had flown southeast from Nairobi.
At Wilson Airport, Juma had helped carry things from the Land-Rover to the airplane, had helped pack them in, then climbed into the backseat beside Barbara. Fletch had heard nothing said by anyone about Juma's accompanying them. The snow skis were in the airplane's aisle, almost the full length of the plane.
On the flight, Juma read a book, *Ake*, by Wole Soyinka.
Chin in hand, Barbara studied the landscape through the window.
From the air, Carr's camp was barely noticeable. It was on the west side of the river in a natural clearing north of thick jungle. About twenty-five kilometers east sparkled the blue of the Indian Ocean.
The airstrip was just a two-wheeled track. There was a long cook

tent, a small tent each side of it, and, at the front, a rectangular piece of canvas supported by four poles. A derelict Jeep was in the shade of a huge banyan tree.

Carr placed the airplane's wheels in the ground tracks precisely. Fletch pushed open the door beside him. The heat was immediate, intense, humid.

About fifty people moved slowly from under the trees to greet them.

Watching the people, Carr flipped off the switches on his instrument panel. "Clinic's open, I guess."

Monkeys were everywhere, on the ground, in the huge banyan tree, on top of the tents, on the table and chairs under the horizontal canvas. There were papa monkeys with baby monkeys on their backs; momma monkeys with infant monkeys at their breasts; children monkeys playing their own games up and down and around, everywhere.

"They bite," Carr said. "They steal. They are no respecter of persons."

Sheila, in tennis shorts and a preppy shirt opened at the collar, waited for them at the end of the runway track. On the tray she carried was a pitcher of lemonade and glasses. "All's right here," Sheila sang out to Carr the minute he stepped out onto the wing. "All's right with you? Then all's right with the world."

"Find anything interesting while I was gone?" Carr asked.

"Yes," Sheila said. "The spare keys to the Land-Rover you insisted you lost."

Carr shrugged.

After putting the tray on the ground and pouring out the lemonade, Sheila hugged and kissed Carr. "My sweaty beast," she said. She hugged and kissed Fletch when she understood who he was. "Good. We need some more brawn." Hugged and kissed Barbara. "Excellent! A woman to catch me up with the world!"

Juma stood away, looking at Sheila sourly.

When Carr introduced them, Sheila gave a little wave of her hand. "Hello, there, Juma. Glad you came to join us."

"I actually brought some half-decent steaks," Carr said.

"I'm sure they were very dear."

"Not as dear as the chicken." A monkey was peering into the lemonade pitcher on the ground. Sheila gently guided it away with her boot.

Juma spoke quietly to Fletch. "Listen. Is that Carr's woman?"

"I guess so. Sheila. Yes."

Juma said, "I didn't know that."

"Nothing Roman turn up?" Carr asked Sheila as they walked toward the tents.

"Just the usual. Spear tips. A tusk. A skeleton."

"Human?"

"Yes. A child. Fairly recent, I think."

For much of the afternoon, in the shade of the extended cook tent, Fletch watched Carr doctor the people. Many children had burns, and Carr dressed them. Many, many others had eye infections, which Carr bathed. He put ointment into each infected eye and sent each mother or father away with a small tube and exact instructions. Other people had boils and sores and cuts and broken bones, complained of aching stomachs, and, in each case, Carr questioned, examined, reached into his kit for something that would clean, cure, fix, do no harm anyway. The people knew enough not even to ask him about their many spots of skin cancer. For two old men Carr thought had internal tumors he could do nothing and said so. He told them where he expected the Flying Doctor to be in a week or ten days.

A man who carried himself proudly limped in on a crude crutch made of a tree branch. He said he had dropped a rock and crushed his toes. Carr clipped off two toes with garden shears. He stitched, trimmed, disinfected, dressed them. A third toe, only broken, Carr set.

Carr wrapped the two severed toes in a piece of gauze and solemnly handed them to the man.

"How did these people know when you were coming?" Fletch asked Carr.

Carr didn't answer.

"How did Juma know all about my father? How did he know Barbara and I were having breakfast on the Lord Delamere Terrace at that moment? He came straight to us, without inquiring or appearing to look around. How did he seem to know we were coming down here before we did?"

Carr said, "Never try to figure out how Africans know things. It's their magic. But I can give you a clue. Much of their magic is simple observation. They spend what is to us an inordinate amount of time thinking about people. I mean real people, the people around them. They think about people instead of things, possessions, cars, televisions, hair dryers. They think about the people they know instead of thinking about mythical people, politicians, sports heroes, and movie stars; instead of thinking about mythical events, distant wars, currency crises, and meetings of the United Nations." Carr dropped an empty tube of Neosporin ointment into an oil drum being used as a wastebasket. "Our magic, of course, comes from the pharmacy. Out here we have a beautiful relationship, as long as we respect each other's magic."

"But why were they waiting for you?" Fletch was taking off his sneakers and wool socks. "Sheila could have treated their burns and infections . . ."

Carr opened a fresh roll of gauze. "They don't trust Sheila. If you didn't notice, Sheila is an Indian lady. She's tried to help, but they won't let her. Magic, everywhere, has to do with the *persona*. They also wouldn't trust you to help them, even though you are a white man. The older people would not be able to bring themselves to complain to you, to tell you they have problems, because you are too young. So I get these dirty jobs."

A young man explained to Carr that he'd had a sore on the back of his hand. So he had stuck his hand in battery acid. Now the hand, wrist, forearm were horribly inflamed.

As Fletch helped Carr, held this, held that, fetched a new box of medical supplies from the airplane, he watched a tent being set up in the clearing under Sheila's direction. His and Barbara's knapsacks were carried up from the plane and put into that tent.

Because the snow skis were so long, and so unusual, two men carried them to the tent on their shoulders. Fletch heard the exclamations as Barbara took the skis out of their cases and showed everyone what they were. Standing in the dirt in the tropical sun, the jungle a green wall behind her, Barbara went through the skiing motions with the ski poles, knees bent, hips sashaying, slaloming down a snow-sided mountain, from the looks of her.

Juma, in pretending to ski, pretended to lose his balance. On one leg, arms pinwheeling for a long time, he pretended to be trying to regain his balance. Finally, he let himself fall. Dust rose around him.

A large monkey, scolding angrily, tried to take one of the ski poles from Barbara.

After Carr treated the people, they wandered back into the jungle or the bush on narrow footpaths.

"Terrible eye troubles," Carr said. "So close to the equator, without protection from the sun. And there are always the flies." He waved a dozen flies away from a child's face. "And burns. The children try to help out with the cooking. They play too close to the fires. Or they fall out of their mothers' breast-slings or back-slings into the fire. The mothers, you see: most of them are children themselves."

Most of the mothers were long-legged girls, skirted this way and that with *kangas*, wearing uncomfortably tight-looking metal bracelets and anklets, their breasts covered, if at all, with arrangements of necklaces. Whatever their troubles, all seemed in good spirits. They were attractively shy with Fletch, never looking directly at him, that he saw, but clearly talking about him, and Juma, and Barbara.

"Is this meddling?" Carr was getting tired. "I should ask the good Dr. McCoy if what we ordinary folks do here in the bush is meddling. What some of these bloody science chaps would like to do is put a glass case over Africa and view it all as history."

Looking across the compound, Fletch said, "Couldn't put Juma under a glass case. He'd break it."

"I believe he would," Carr said.

"By the way, Carr, I'm remembering that Barbara and I didn't take any medical shots before we left the States."

"You'll be all right," Carr said. "Be sure and take your whiskey." He glanced out to see where the sun was. "But, first, let's walk the riverbanks. I'll show you how far I haven't gotten with my crazy idea. Lost Roman city," Carr said. "Pah! I'm crazy!"

"Last night I read the previous two days' newspaper reports on the murder you saw at the airport," Carr said as he and Fletch ambled along the riverbank. "I also talked with Dan Dawes."

"You talk to Dan Dawes?"

"Why not? He's a schoolteacher."

"He's also a paralegal executioner."

"That, too. Here we refer to him as being 'very close to the police.' "

"He's a hit man for the cops."

"There is great diversity in this world, Irwin. One must not expect the same standards everywhere."

"Sorry. Go on." As he walked, Fletch slapped at the flies on his arms, his legs.

"The murder victim's name was Louis Ramon. He was carrying a French passport. In a money belt he was also carrying an extraordinary amount of German marks — about one hundred thousand United States dollars' worth."

"He wasn't robbed?"

"No. They found the money on him."

Fletch marveled softly, "He wasn't even robbed by the police."

"Interpol's return cable said that Louis Ramon was some sort of a low-life currency trader, opportunist, possibly smuggler. He first came to their attention five years ago when he was suspected of moving a large amount of Italian lire into Switzerland, and again, three years ago, of moving a large amount of French francs into Albania. He has been fined and admonished, but has never served time in prison, as far as they know. Here, come this way. I'll show you what we're doing."

They turned right into the jungle and followed a track wide enough for a Jeep about twenty-five meters from the river. Foliage was beginning to overgrow the track.

At the end of the track they came to a circular clearing.

In the center of the clearing was a hole in the ground so small Fletch wouldn't have noticed it if it weren't for the settling mound of dirt surrounding it.

"We dig holes with a giant corkscrew," Carr said seriously, "see what comes up. What we use is actually a sort of primitive machine they use to look for water, before digging a well. We can only go down about fifteen meters. Do you think fifteen meters, forty-five feet, is enough to reach back two or three thousand years? I doubt it." He kicked the earth with his boot. "Soft earth. Jungle growth."

Carr led the way back toward the river. "Every hundred meters or so along the river, we go about twenty-five meters into the jungle and dig our little hole. Do you think that's far enough from the river? Too far? I think it's more likely a settlement would have been on the west side of the river, the inland side from the sea, don't you? We're apt to dig more holes anywhere there's an elevation in the land."

"How long have you been doing this?" Fletch asked.

"About eighteen months. Lots of holes, up and down both sides of the river."

They headed south along the river again.

"Anyway," Carr continued, "Louis Ramon was on your plane from London. The suspicion is that he came to Kenya to pull off some sort of a currency scheme, and his partner, or accomplice, or whoever he met at the airport in Nairobi, simply did him in."

"Not his partner," Fletch said. "Not his accomplice."

"Oh? Why not?"

"Because a partner or an accomplice would have known Ramon was carrying a hundred thousand dollars in German marks, and taken them. He had plenty of time. He wasn't that conscious that I was there. I mean, if you're going to stab someone in a men's room, you might as well rob him, right?"

"I forgot you're an investigative reporter," Carr said. "Old Josie Fletcher must be proud of you. You have her brain."

"I deal in reality," Fletch muttered. They were passing another track into the jungle. "I think it was more of an accidental meeting. There was no prologue to the argument I heard. The voices were surprised. Immediately enraged. It was all very fast. It was as if two men met accidentally, two men who had known each other, hated each other before, had some ancient, powerful grudge between them, or maybe even saw each other as an immediate danger to each other, or one to the other. It was too fast," Fletch said. "I wish I understood Portuguese."

Carr was leading him up another jungle track.

In the clearing was what appeared certainly to be a giant corkscrew. An aluminum frame sat on the ground, four meters square at its base, one meter square at its top, about three meters tall. Sticking through it and twelve meters above it was a slim screw shaft. On each of the four sides of the frame was a wheel one meter in diameter with a perpendicular handle of the sort found on coffee grinders.

"I guess Sheila decided to backtrack," Carr said.

He stooped over the fresh mound of dirt and combed through it with his fingers. "Nothing. Do you think we're crazy?"

"What does it matter? Everyone's thought crazy until proven right."

Carr stood up and dusted off his hands. "Usually people are proven wrong, aren't they?"

"Yeah," Fletch said. "I guess most people are crazy."

"To choose your own way of being crazy," Carr said, stepping out again. "That's the thing."

When they were back walking the riverbank south, Fletch asked Carr, "How would such a currency scheme as Louis Ramon seemed to be attempting work?"

"I don't know," Carr said. "I'm not sure I want to know. But I do know that having that much foreign currency in Kenya is illegal."

"Why?"

"As far as its currency is concerned, Kenya's economy is closed. You may not take more than ten *shillingi* in Kenyan currency out of Kenya. The truth is, the Kenyan *shillingi* doesn't exist outside Kenya. It's like casino money. It only has reality within its own closed environment. Kenyan money is pegged to the English pound, but there is no international trading or market in the currency itself."

"How do they manage that?"

"By strict enforcement of the law. A while ago, an Indian lawyer was discovered by the police to have thirteen United States dollars in his pocket. He was sentenced to seven years in prison for currency violations."

"I'd call that strict enforcement of the law."

"Let's cross the river here. Walk back on the other side."

They stripped. Carrying their clothes head high, they waded across the sluggish river. The water was armpit high on them both.

Carr said, "You can see all sorts of signs this river used to be deeper. Can't you?"

While they were waiting on the eastern riverbank to dry off, Carr glanced at the black and blue mark on Fletch's lower belly, but said nothing.

Carr pointed back across the river, further south. "See that baobab tree there? Tomorrow I think we'll make a trail into the jungle past that. But we mustn't disturb the tree. Baobab trees are sacred here. Rather than disturb them, people here build major highways around them."

After dressing, they walked faster northward along the riverbank. They ignored the many trails into the jungle.

"Kenyans take anything having to do with the government very seriously indeed," Carr said.

"Juma says his father is in prison for a year and a half for parking a government car outside a bar. He used to be a government driver."

"Not long ago," Carr said, "one of your fellow Americans had dinner in a Nairobi restaurant. Two men waited on him. At the end of dinner, the man wanted to tip them both, but he only had a one-hundred-*shillingi* note. I guess he thought he was making a joke. He tore the one-hundred-*shillingi* note in half and tried to give half to each waiter. The newspaper report I read said, 'Shocked and embarrassed at this desecration of Kenyan money, the waiters called the police.' The man was arrested. He spent the night in jail. He was tried the next morning, fined one thousand dollars, and escorted by the police to the airport and put aboard the next airplane leaving Kenya."

"Some joke."

"It's illegal, of course," Carr said, "but here, in the bush, girls are still circumcised. But you tear a piece of paper money in half and you get yourself written up in *The Standard*."

Fletch asked, "So how would you work a currency scheme?"

Carr walked a long way before answering. "Generally it's true," he said slowly, "that the stricter such currency laws are, the greater are the rewards for violating them successfully."

The camp came into sight just at full dark. The live fire at the back of the cook tent was bright.

As they were wading back across the river, Carr said, "I guess we're crazy. Looking for a lost Roman city. But the past fascinates. Doesn't the past fascinate you? The past, where we came from, who we were, tells us so much about who we are. Don't you think so?"

Fletch ducked below the surface of the water to get some of the sweat out of his hair.

While they were drying on the western riverbank, Carr said, "I guess I'm just messing up the jungle."

"Not much."

"I've promise myself one thing, though." He was looking downriver. "The instant I find anything, the slightest evidence I'm right, if I ever do, I'll turn the whole thing over to proper scientists. If I'm right, I swear I won't muck the site up."

"Right," Fletch said. "What this place needs is Dr. McCoy. You won't catch him clipping off anybody's toes."

"As soon as you and Barbara are ready," Carr said, "join us for a whiskey. Bring your own ice."

TWENTY-EIGHT

Conversationally, Sheila said to Barbara, "You're enjoying your honeymoon?"

"He drives me nuts."

"Yes. There's always that."

They were sitting in a semicircle in camp chairs just outside the long stretch of canvas on four poles. Carr had provided each with a Scotch and soda. Bug-repellent candles were here and there around them. Over them hung a moon such as Fletch had never seen before. It was a black orb within a perfect silver circumference. The noises from the jungle were absolutely raucous. As he listened to the conversation, Fletch watched the monkeys playing about here and there in the candlelight. Under the canvas behind them, a man named Winston had set the dining table for four.

"He complains I speak nicely to him in public and nastily to him in private," Barbara said.

"There's a lot of that goes on in marriage," Sheila said.

Carr said, "We're not exactly married."

"So I've decided to speak nastily to him in public, too." Barbara giggled.

"Will you speak nicely to me in private?" Fletch asked.

"If there is ever anything to speak nicely to you about, I will say it both in public and in private."

Juma came out of the dark carrying a camp chair. He sat down with them.

Carr asked, "Would you like a whiskey, Juma?"

"No. Thank you. I don't like whiskey. It makes me drunk."

"Oh. I see."

Fletch said to Sheila, "Our honeymoon has not worked out as planned."

"Barbara mentioned something about your planning a skiing honeymoon. In Colorado."

"She did?" Fletch mocked surprise.

"Yes. She did mention it."

"Our wedding was not as planned, either," Barbara said. "It was on a bluff overlooking the Pacific Ocean. Fletch was late. The wedding got rained out. He spent the day with his mother."

Carr shot Fletch a quick glance.

"Weddings aren't all they're cracked up to be," Fletch advised Carr. "You haven't missed much."

"He showed up at his wedding in blue jeans, a well-used T-shirt, and torn sneakers."

"I'd shaved. You must understand, I'd been working day and night. I have a job."

Juma leaned close to Fletch and asked quietly, "Is Barbara your first wife?"

Fletch blinked. "Yes."

"Oh, I see."

"Clothes don't make the couple," Sheila said. "At least, not until later in life."

Carr said, "You both look hot."

Because of the flies, Barbara and Fletch had decided to wear long ski pants, sweaters with sleeves, and ski boots to dinner.

"I'm boiling," Barbara said. "Are you sure you're not having me for dinner?"

They had been surprised to find Sheila and Carr dressed only in pajamas and mosquito boots.

"Dining in pajamas is an old Kenyan custom," Carr said. "A natural result of *safarini*. After spending a day in the bush, the thing you most want, after a drink, is a bath. After a bath, what's more natural than slipping into cool, cotton pajamas? They even look more formal than our usual short-pants rig. In the bad old days, people used to go dine at each other's houses in pajamas. They'd even go out to dine at a hotel or restaurant in pajamas."

Close by, a lion roared.

"Good God!" Barbara said. "I'm being boiled for a lion!"

"Think of it as a tape recording, if you wish," Carr said.

"I shall be eaten alive."

"Whatever shall I tell your mother?" Fletch asked.

"No, no," Carr said. "Hungry lions are quiet lions. That roar sounds like he's had his kill, his fill, his sleep, and now he's calling around to see where his pride is, where his friends are." Either the lion roared more loudly, or the lion was closer. "Your average wild beast has seen man and doesn't think much of us."

"Even as dessert?" Barbara asked.

"Even as a snack."

A man named Raffles came by to freshen their drinks.

"We came out to Africa to meet my father," Fletch said to Sheila. "At our wedding a man showed up with a letter from him."

"A letter written in disappearing ink," Barbara added.

"Yes," Sheila said. "Peter told me there'd been some trouble at the Thorn Tree Café. It doesn't sound too serious."

Fletch looked at Juma. "It sounds to me that any trouble with the law in Kenya is very serious."

"A wonderfully attractive man, your father," Sheila said.

"He is?" Carr asked.

"Don't you think so?"

"No."

"A little immature, perhaps. But some societies prize immaturity in a man."

"Irresponsible," said Carr. "When he was flying for me, I never knew where the hell he was."

"Well," Sheila admitted, "he is a bit of a will-o'-the-wisp."

Barbara said, "I'll say."

"Enormously popular," Sheila said.

"Maybe with the ladies," Carr said.

"Oh, come on, Peter. You men like him, too."

Carr shook his head. "Too much the iconoclast."

Sheila said, "He does have his own way of doing things. But, after all, most of the people who have settled in Africa have done so because they're a bit too individualistic for other places. Take you, for example, Peter."

"Right," said Carr. "I have my own way of doing things. But usually

I stay out of the beds of other chaps' wives, and keep my fists out of other chaps' faces."

Fletch winced. "How come you're friends?"

There was a moment before Carr answered. "What are friends? The international fraternity of fliers. Roughly the same age. We find ourselves in the same place at the same time."

Sheila said, "Walter Fletcher is a man of great personal energy."

"Mostly misspent," Carr muttered.

"Why do you say that?" Sheila asked. "He has his own plane, plenty of work — "

"There's a reverse spin to everything he does," Carr said. "He flies in our faces, is what he does. Last year, as a group, we decided to stop flying in and out of Uganda. Too much paperwork. Too dangerous for our equipment and passengers. Your Walter Fletcher takes to flying in and out of Uganda like a hawk. Makes three years' pay in one year, at least." Looking at the moon, Carr asked, "And where is he now?"

"But you came with him to the hotel," Fletch said, "to meet us."

"Exactly," Carr said. "I was there, and he wasn't."

"You said you were there to be his moral support."

"Right." Carr put down his glass. "Walter's morals need propping up. Care to eat with us, Juma?"

Juma glanced at Sheila. "No, thank you. I've eaten."

In the candlelight, Carr was looking into Fletch's eyes. "All this has nothing to do with you, you know."

Fletch said, "Oh. I see."

"Will you be able to spend a few days with us, Peter?" Sheila asked.

"A few days. Then I have to fly some French *hôteliers* up to the Masai Mara. Pick them up in Nairobi. They're traveling around, studying the Block Hotels. I'll be gone two nights."

"The Masai Mara," Fletch said. "I hear it's nice there."

"Welcome to join me," Carr said. "There'll be room in the plane."

"If we don't hear from Walter first," Sheila said.

"Yeah. I told his lawyer where we'd all be."

"Who flies your other plane?" Fletch asked.

"A young Kenyan. He's flying hard for us these days, while I'm down here wasting time and money. The perks of age and ownership. He can't make the Masai Mara trip, though. He's chartered to fly to Madagascar."

"I'm afraid we're imposing," said Fletch.

"Why? Good company is worth anything in the bush. Tomorrow we'll all get some hard work in."

"Would you rather be sitting in a hotel room in Nairobi?" Sheila asked.

For the fifth time, Barbara waved flies away from her rice.

"Went to see the witch doctor of Thika, old dear," Carr said to Sheila. "Barbara and young Irwin here came with me. Actually, that's where Juma attached himself to us, too."

"Was she encouraging?" Sheila's gold bracelets jangled as she ate.

"Right on. Straightaway, she said I was looking for something I hadn't lost. When I said it was a place, she said I must go south where there are hills and a river."

"That's where we are," Sheila said.

"She said the people who used to live here want us to find their place, so they'll be remembered."

"Did she say we will find it?"

"Definitely yes."

Sheila said, "At this point, encouragement from any source is welcome."

In the cook tent, a tape of a contemporary Italian love song was playing. Juma and Winston and Raffles and the five or six other young men behind the tent were lustily and perfectly singing the lyrics, in Italian.

Fletch couldn't be sure if some of the bird noises he was hearing were from the tape or from the jungle around them. They, too, matched or followed the music perfectly.

"Barbara? Stand up, please?"

After dinner they had returned to their camp chairs in front of the dining awning. Carr had poured them each a Three Barrels brandy.

Juma appeared dressed now with just a cloth wrapped high around his waist. He was carrying an unfolded cotton cloth about four feet by five and a half feet.

Even in the candlelight, the reds, greens, yellows of both cloths were bright.

"Ah, Juma, the perfect solution!" Sheila said. "A *kanga*!"

Juma ignored her.

"When Barbara stood up, Juma wrapped the cloth around her, under her armpits, over her breasts, and tied it to itself, simply.

It was a full, free-hanging dress.

Barbara looked down at herself. "Far out!"

"Beats jodhpurs," Fletch said.

Juma slipped it off her and folded it lengthwise. He put it around her hips like a sling. Holding the two ends together with one hand, he ran his finger against both sides of the cloth up against her waist. He used that point as the fold. He tucked the top end of the cloth into the cloth itself against her other hip.

It was a skirt.

"That's all you need wear around here."

"Nothing on top?" Barbara asked.

"I can get you some necklaces, too, if you like."

Again he slipped the cloth off her. This time he folded it lengthwise in quarters and tucked it around her waist again, finding the fold with his fingers.

It was a short skirt.

"Very cool," Juma said.

Looking below the skirt to her thighs, knees in ski pants, Barbara said, "I'll say."

"It goes well with your ski boots," Fletch said.

"Also," Juma said, "as you see, a man can wear a *kanga*. Stand up, please, Fletch."

Fletch put his glass of brandy on the ground beside his chair and stood up.

Juma draped the *kanga* over Fletch's shoulders. "Keeps off the sun-bite," Juma said.

Then he folded the *kanga* in quarters again and using the same method tucked it around Fletch's waist.

There was the sound of a burp.

Holding the glass to his face with both hands, a monkey was finishing Fletch's brandy.

"Hold on." Carr got up abruptly. "Better restrain that fellow until the brandy wears off." He began to approach the monkey slowly. "No telling what he might do."

Barbara said, "Just like your father, Fletch."

Juma tugged the *kanga* off Fletch's waist and handed it to Barbara.

"For me? A present?"

"Yes," Juma said. "I got it for you. So you will be dressed right, and be cool."

"How nice," Sheila said.

The monkey had put down the glass. He scratched the top of his head.

"Thank you, Juma."

When Carr was almost ready to pounce on the monkey, the monkey suddenly laughed and darted away. He scrambled up the banyan tree.

Hands on hips, Carr watched the monkey climb high into the tree. "Now what do we do?"

"Can you see him?" Barbara asked.

Using only one hand, chattering wildly, the monkey was swinging from a branch ten meters above the ground.

"Come down here, you silly bastard," Carr said. "Do you suppose we can coax him down with a little more brandy?"

The monkey scrambled even higher. He was now fifteen meters off the ground. Putting one foot in front of the other, holding his arms out for balance, he teetered out a long branch like a tightrope walker. Looking down at them, he chattered a fairly long speech.

"He'll hurt himself," Sheila said.

"More than likely," Carr agreed.

"The whiskey made the monkey drunk, you see," Juma said.

The monkey stepped off the tree branch backward. He caught himself with both hands.

Using both arms, the monkey began swinging from the tree branch, swinging higher and higher.

"Oh, dear," Carr said. "I'm afraid he means to give us a flying lesson."

At the highest point of his swing, with no destination discernible, the monkey let go of the branch. He went up into the air feet first in a perfect arc.

Carr sprinted forward. "Can we catch him?"

In a great puff of dust, the monkey landed on his back a meter in front of Carr.

In the inflection of the disappointed, the monkey said, "Ohhhhh."

"Bastard knocked himself out," Carr said. "That'll teach him to fly too far too high too fast."

They were all looking down at the monkey unconscious on the ground.

"He will have a headache," Juma prophesied.

Fletch said to Barbara, "*Just like my father*?!?"

TWENTY-NINE

After gazing, not really looking, into the jungle for several minutes while taking a water/rest break from his work, Fletch jumped.

A young man was looking back at him.

The young man stood perfectly still on one leg. His other foot was off the ground. His body was in profile but his head was turned to look full-faced at Fletch. Extremely tall, extremely thin, the young man's body was an upright black stick among the foliage. He wore a feathered headdress. His earlobes had been opened and extended. They hung nearly to his shoulders. Over one shoulder he wore a strip of cloth which joined the narrow strip somehow around his waist. Bracelets were around the muscles of his arms. His anklets were red. His fingers loosely held a spear upright against his body.

"Hey!" Fletch said in surprise. "Hello!"

The young man did not speak or move.

"*Jambo!*" Fletch said. "*Habari?*"

Nothing.

Fletch held up his gallon jug of water. "*Magi baridi?*"

No response.

The young man stared at him silently, unmoving.

Fletch waved at him and went back to work.

With a *panga* he was cutting a trail wide enough through the light brush for the Jeep, from the riverbank into the jungle. He had not disturbed the baobab tree. Barefooted, in his swimming trunks, he worked alone.

Carr had told him never to take a step without looking carefully for snakes. During the morning, Fletch avoided a half dozen.

That morning Carr and the others were extending the path along the riverbank. The trees along the river were bigger, older, heavier. The ground needed filling in. That job required more of a team effort.

Doing this mindless work alone in the jungle, sweating profusely, felt good to Fletch. Besides lovemaking, his body had been confined too long to chairs and airplane seats, strange beds, the newspaper office. Since receiving the letter from his father the day of his wedding Fletch's mind had been belted with the unexpected too regularly: the conversation with his mother; flying out to Kenya; seeing the bloody, murdered man at the airport; his father not showing up; some of the things Barbara had taken to saying and doing. He did not understand the jungle noises, but he found them soothing. He admired the birds as they came and went. He watched for snakes and cleared a path through the brush.

During the morning, whenever Fletch would stop to straighten his back, drink some water, which was frequently, he would look at the young man standing silently, watching. The young man was more still, more unmoving, than any animate object Fletch had ever seen. Standing still for a long period is the hardest exercise. Being so still, first on one leg, then on the other, took great discipline. Fletch never saw him change his weight from one leg to the other. Why was the young man posing this way?

During his first few breaks, Fletch would hold up his water bottle in offering to the young man, then wave at him before going back to work.

But as the morning wore on and Fletch found himnself thinking about this and that, "Running for Love" humming in his mind, he forgot the young man was there. Gazing around, Fletch's eyes would not pick out the still figure unless he remembered him and focused on him. The young man's silence, stillness, made him drop from consciousness, almost disappear from view.

Juma spotted him immediately.

Late morning, Fletch heard Juma coming down the trail Fletch had cut. He was whistling that Italian love song. From one hand dangled a full gallon of water.

"Fletch must drink plenty of water," Juma said. "Fletch is not used to this heat. Fletch is not used to this work. Fletch comes from America, where the hardest work is pushing buttons."

Juma's body was as soaked with sweat as Fletch's.

Juma put the fresh jug of water on the ground. Looking up, he saw the young man standing on the knoll.

"Ug!" Immediately, Juma grabbed up two handfuls of dirt. He flung one handful in the direction of the young man. "Idiot!" He started toward the young man. Closer, he threw the other handful of dirt. "Go away! What do you think you're doing? Stupid!"

Juma stooped to pick up a stick.

His eyes now on Juma, the young man stepped sideways into the jungle. Immediately the foliage covered him.

"Son of a bitch!" Juma yelled after him. "Why don't you come into this century!" Turning back to Fletch, Juma said, "At least this half of the century." He dropped the stick.

"I wanted to see how long he'd stay that way."

Juma waved his hand. "For the rest of his life. He'd die that way."

"Why was he doing it?"

"Who knows? Who cares? Some of these people live in another world. They know about radios, telephones. Tiresome. Someone that age . . ."

"Thanks for bringing me the water."

Juma picked up the empty jug. "Carr said he'll be along later, with your lunch." Juma began to walk down the trail. "Go ahead. Eat in the midday. It will make you more hot, more tired, sweat more. You Europeans insist on consuming and wasting, consuming and wasting, just to keep yourselves sick."

The young man with the spear did not return, that Fletch could see, or feel.

Fletch was hungry for lunch well before Carr arrived.

They sat cross-legged on the ground in the center of a wide bare spot. They ate fish sandwiches with a third jug of water.

For all the water Fletch was drinking, he was urinating little.

Carr said, "I thought you'd appreciate a morning working alone."

"I enjoyed it."

Fletch told Carr about the young man who had spent much of the morning at silent attention watching him. And that Juma had come along and chased him away.

"Sounds like a Masai *moran*. A warrior. A *mti*. An *mtii*. They're not allowed to carry shields anymore."

"Why did he carry a spear?"

"Because of the snakes."

"Sounds sensible. Maybe I should carry a spear."

"Pretty far south for a Masai these days. But you never can tell. They're nomads. Follow the grazing."

"What tribe is Juma's?"

"I'm pretty sure he's Kikuyu. There are over forty tribes in East Africa."

"And over all these centuries the tribes have remained segregated enough, distinct enough, so that you can tell one from the other?"

"Pretty much so. To this point in history, the political struggles in Africa have almost nothing to do with ideologies, East versus West, socialism versus free enterprise, communism versus capitalism. The struggles for power are among the tribes. Wish you'd tell your chaps in Washington that."

"I'll write them a letter."

"There's even a tribe near here which denies it exists. No one but its own members knows its true name. You meet a member of that tribe and he will always tell you he's a member of some other tribe. Prove to him he's not, and he'll say, 'Well . . . ' and insist he is a member of even another tribe. They're a secret tribe. They camouflage themselves among all the other tribes. The true name of the tribe may be the Wata."

"Sure." Fletch grinned. "Wata tribe. I got it."

"You don't believe me?"

"Was Juma working with you this morning?"

"Yes."

"Are you paying him?"

"Am I paying you?"

"No."

Carr smiled. "You're working off that mosquito net you and Barbara wrecked last night."

"Oh." Feltch scratched his elbow. "You know about that."

"Raffles mentioned to Sheila this morning that someone will have to spend a day sewing."

"Sorry about that."

"There is a technique to doing what you want to do under mosquito netting. You'll learn."

"So why is Juma working for you if he's not being paid?"

"I don't know. I didn't ask him to come with us. I didn't ask him to work. I guess he just wants to be with us."

"Are you paying the other men?"

"Of course."

"Why does Juma want to be with us?"

"Perhaps because he loves you?"

"Loves who?"

"Loves you. Loves Barbara. Do I mean love? He's very curious about you both. He watches you very closely, how you walk, how you talk, relate to each other, and others, what and when you eat, drink, how you dress, what your bodies are like and how you use them, your minds."

"I'm curious about Juma, too."

"It's a very dear relationship, if you find you can relate to it at all decently. He's interested, but uncritical. Can you understand that?"

"The other night, standing on the sidewalk outside the Norfolk, he said something which totally baffled Barbara and me. He said he doesn't decide who are his friends and who are not his friends. He said something like making such decisions is very *hard,* but he may have meant very *harsh.*"

"Generally very uncritical," Carr repeated.

"He certainly made a fast decision about the young man with the spear standing in the bush over there. Instantly, he picked up things and started throwing them at him. He swore at him."

"Yeah. Well. A modern young man like Juma is apt to have great impatience with other people, especially people his own age, who cling to tribal ways. They don't like that spear-shaking image of Africa."

More quietly, Fletch said, "He certainly seems to have made a rather harsh decision about Sheila."

"Yes," Carr said. "He inherited that. There is a distinct prejudice here against people of East Indian extraction."

"Why?"

"Throughout Africa, throughout much of the third world in fact, Indians own most of the *duccas,* the stores. They do most of the trading, the buying and selling. Therefore, the native populations think the Indians have a disproportionate share of the goods and the money."

"Do they feel the Indians exploit them?"

"Don't we all feel a little exploited by the shopkeeper? We give him more money for something than he paid for it, and we know it. Then, with his profits, the shopkeeper goes off and builds a house better than any we could afford. Trouble is, some of the poorest Africans I know are of East Indian extraction. Some of the richest, too. Sheila was born in Kenya. She was a workingwoman when I met her. She worked for a car rental agency."

"So Juma crosses her off completely, as a Kenyan, as a woman, as a person."

Carr shrugged. "Prejudice is like that. Are you surprised to find prejudice in Africa?"

Fletch had finished his lunch. "Carr, I went to the jail yesterday."

Carr's eyebrows shot up. "Oh?"

"To see my father."

"They let you in?"

"They would have. My father sent out the message that he wasn't in."

"Cute."

"I thought so."

"Can't fault old Fletcher for his humor."

"At least I proved one thing to myself."

"What's that?"

"There is a Walter Fletcher."

"Did you doubt that?"

Fletch removed a speck from his eye. "I think Barbara was beginning to hope you are my father."

Carr laughed. "I'm flattered."

"We came to meet my father, you see, and we met you instead."

Carr refolded the brown paper in which he had brought lunch. "If you keep cuttin' trail, I'll go get the corkscrew."

"So I know Walter Fletcher exists," Fletch said, "which I really didn't know before." He sighed. "And for once in my life, I know exactly where he is."

THIRTY

"H*apana kitu.*"

Barbara and Carr knelt on the ground watching the soil as it came up the screw to the surface. Sheila stood over them, arms akimbo, watching, saying nothing.

On the four sides of the earth screw's frame, Juma, Fletch, Winston, and Raffles turned the wheels sending the screw into the ground. For the most part, the earth was soft. Forcing the screw slowly into the ground wasn't very hard work.

Carr's fingers crumbled a piece of rotten wood that surfaced. "Nothing," he repeated.

An hour or so after Carr had left Fletch, the derelict-looking Jeep snorted up the trail Fletch had cleared. Looking huge and ridiculous, the aluminum corkscrew stuck far out of the back of the Jeep. Twelve meters behind the Jeep men carried the top of the shaft. Barbara, wearing her *kanga,* rode in the Jeep with Carr.

The rest, including Sheila, walked beside the Jeep.

It seemed an invasion of the solitude Fletch had enjoyed in the jungle.

It was fairly easy, tipping the corkscrew up and making it even on the ground.

The top of the screw shaft reached its lowest point. The wheels could turn no further.

"Right," Carr said. "Bring it up."

It was easier, unscrewing the earth.

They continued to watch what earth came up with the screw.

"Pity we're not in the well-drilling business," Carr said. "At least sometimes we find water."

"Ever find oil?" Fletch asked.

"Not even hair grease."

Wrestling the corkscrew around, they tried three other places in that clearing that afternoon. Fletch tried a few pleasantries until he realized they weren't appreciated. They didn't find a lost Roman city, but he had enjoyed the day.

"*Hapana kitu,*" Carr said. "Nothing. Let's go back to camp. There's always tomorrow."

THIRTY-ONE

"Hello," Juma said. "Stay where the crocodiles are used to us. They are very territorial, you see."

Naked, Barbara and Fletch were swimming in the river.

Naked, Juma sat on a rock in the river watching them.

"Crocodiles?" Barbara stood up in the river.

"Haven't you seen them?" Fletch asked.

"Crocodiles that eat people?"

"I don't think they're particular."

"Fletch," Barbara whispered. "Juma's naked."

"So are we."

"What does he mean? That there's nothing *sexual* between us? Among us?"

"I'll ask him."

"Screw crocodiles." Barbara started for the riverbank in haste. "Never even got to wash my hair."

Fletch climbed up onto the rock and sat beside Juma.

"Barbara wants to know if there's nothing *sexual* among us."

"What does she mean?"

"Among us three, I guess she means. You and her."

"Barbara wants a baby by me? That would be odd."

"No. She doesn't. We three were just naked together."

"People put on clothes to be sexual, don't they?"

"People do many things to be sexual."

"What else are clothes for?"

"Pockets."

Juma was rubbing the fingers of his right hand against his leg. "Africans don't have pockets. We have nothing to put in them." The red stain on his fingers was not coming off. "People can be sexual with each other whether they wear clothes or not."

"True."

Juma was looking at the mark on the lower right side of Fletch's stomach. Juma said, "So you are partly black."

"And blue."

"I have never seen such a thing before. Is that the way a baby would look, if Barbara and I had a baby? I don't think so."

"No."

"It looks odd."

"Black people do not turn white where they are hit."

"Who hit you? Did someone in Kenya hit you?"

"Why are your fingers red?"

"*Miraa*."

"What's *miraa*?"

"You don't know *miraa*? It's a drug we chew. A pleasure drug."

"Like marijuana?"

"What's marijuana?"

"A pleasure drug."

"It leaves the fingers red, and the gums and tongue." Juma showed Fletch how red his gums and tongue were. "Also, I suppose, our insides. It's not very good. One of the men gave me some." Juma nodded up the riverbank toward the cook tent. "You can buy some in any store which has banana leaves over the door."

"I read some of that book you lent me, *Weep Not Child*."

Juma snorted. "Ngugi blames white people for almost everything."

"Including inventing war."

"As if they were gods." Juma put his hand on the back of Fletch's neck and squeezed. "Are you a god, Fletch?"

"Tell me about my father."

"He's all right." Juma returned to trying to rub the red stain off his fingers. "A bit of a *mutata*."

"What's *mutata*?"

"Troublesome."

"He's a nuisance?"

Juma laughed. "Once he rode into Narok on his motorcycle, slowly, slowly, dragging behind him with a rope around its neck a hyena."

"He still rides a motorcycle."

"He insisted some people bet him the night before he could not lasso a hyena and bring it into Narok by the second hour of daylight the next day." Juma laughed again. "Trouble was, no one remembered having made such a bet with him. No one would admit to such a bet."

"He sounds crazy."

"It's all right. No one likes hyenas much."

There was a particularly loud chattering from the jungle across the river.

"Juma, when Carr took me to Lake Turkana he told me there's an elephant skeleton, very, very old, buried near there, at Koobi Fora."

"Of course it's very old, if it's a skeleton."

"The skeleton of an East Indian elephant."

"Buried in East Africa?"

"It didn't swim across the Indian Ocean."

Juma thought a moment. "You're talking about Carr's woman."

"Her name is Sheila."

"Well, her skeleton will belong in India."

"She was born in Kenya. In Lamu."

"All the borders are colonial. Have you thought that? The borders of all these nations were set by the English and the Germans and the French, not by the tribes."

"I like Sheila. I like Carr."

"Perhaps while you are here, I will take you to Shimoni."

"What's Shimoni?"

"It means hole-in-the-ground. It's a place on the coast. I have been there."

"Sheila worked for a car rental agency when Carr first met her."

"Perhaps you and I will go to a three-in-one hotel."

"What's a three-in-one hotel?"

"You have never been to one?"

"I don't think so."

"Three in one bed. They are very popular here. I think they are very good especially for a man who must treat one wife at a time."

"I see. Are you married, Juma?"

"No. I want to go to school. I want to work in television. Don't you think it would be very good to work in television?"

"Yes. I do."

"What is your work?" Juma asked.

"I work for a newspaper."

"Oh, I see. That would be interesting work. Somewhat the same work as television, I think, except no one can see your face. If you are going to tell people something, don't you think you should say it so people can see your face?"

"I believe it is easier to find out what to tell people if they do not see your face."

"Oh, I see. Yes, perhaps that is true." Juma stood up on the rock. "Well, it is time for you to go have your Scotch whiskey."

"Why?"

Juma shrugged. "You had a Scotch whiskey last night at this time."

THIRTY-TWO

"They adore him."

"Who?"

"Carr. The women just eat him up."

Carr was having an after-dinner beer at the lodge's bar with the two women *hôtelières* they had flown up from Nairobi. Carr was sitting sideways to the bar on a stool. The two French women stood with their drinks, facing him. They laughed at everything he said.

Barbara and Fletch were drinking beer at a small table at the side of the veranda.

At the entrance to the veranda, a guard with a flashlight and rifle waited to escort the tourists to their cabins.

"Don't you find Carr attractive?" Fletch asked.

Barbara looked around at the few remaining tourists who had not yet gone to bed.

"Every woman in the place," Barbara said, "is just eating him up."

After clearing trails and digging holes and finding nothing significant one more day, Barbara, Fletch, and Carr had flown to Nairobi, refueled, picked the two women up, and then flown west to the Masai Mara.

Sheila said she preferred to stay in camp and dig holes along the freshly cut trails. She promised she would find a Roman city before they returned.

There was no discussion about whether Juma would accompany them. While they were getting ready to go, he simply did not appear.

The two women hotel executives from France were *très chic, très jolie.* They were on a business trip, but they were also having a good time. They handed around a bottle of champagne on the airplane. Carr did not drink any.

They marveled happily flying over the Rift Valley, the Loita Hills and Plains, ecologically the Serengeti Plains. Carr flew as low as he decently, legally could, so they could all see the herds of zebras, elands, giraffes grazing. The older woman, who sat in the copilot seat, snapped photographs from the air with a little camera genuinely useless at the distance of more than three meters. She thought she was getting wonderful pictures. Their first sight of elephants from the air sent them into raptures. In fast, stuttering English they were full of questions for Carr.

The women were warmly greeted by management and immediately taken on a tour of Keekorok Lodge. Even Fletch wondered how a lodge so far in the bush could provide such impeccable food and drink, accommodations and service.

Carr organized a *safari guari* and driver. That night and the next day, sunrise and sunset, while the hotel executives studied the operation of the lodge, Carr, Barbara, and Fletch toured the reserve.

They were to be at the lodge only two nights, before returning to Nairobi, and then Carr's camp.

The *safari guari* was a well-spirited, well-sprung, fairly quiet Nissan van, roofless so they could stand in it, the clean, bush-scented African-air wind in their faces, so they could see all sides at once from an elevation of three meters as they rode along. Carr provided binoculars for them. They learned to brace themselves against the van's frame so they could use the binoculars reasonably well as they joggled along. They also learned from the driver, Omoke, a Kisi, a new way of looking at landscape, of surveying vast areas quickly, mathematically, with just their eyes, going over it in sideways Z's, spotting anything moving, anything even slightly outstanding in color. Anything remarkable spotted Omoke would drive to, through the bush, quietly, drawing up and stopping at a decent, noninterfering, nonmeddling distance.

Almost immediately Omoke found for them a lion and two lionesses sprawled in the fading sunlight. The tail and the hind legs of the lion were embraced by the forelegs of one lioness; his head and one shoulder were on the shoulder of the other lioness. Their heads were up. They were looking around lazily, the light from the low sun in their eyes. The bellies of all three were so stuffed they lay on the ground almost separately, like suitcases.

Before sunrise the next morning, Omoke, who saw a landscape differently from any painter, any engineer, found a small grassy depression in the ground in the shade of a bush. Lying in the hollow, clearly exhausted, was a cheetah who, just hours before, had given birth to four.

Later that afternoon they watched this same cheetah on uncertain legs hunt, bring down and kill an eland, to feed on and to feed her young. Immediately, hyenas came and took her kill from her. They dragged it a few meters away and devoured it.

The cheetah sat, blinking in the sunlight, watching them, clearly too tired to protest, to go on, just yet, or to go back, foodless, to her young.

From the ground, even more than the beasts, the dik-diks, the zebras, Thompson's and Grant's gazelles, topis, tree and rock hyraxes, impalas, leopards, lions, waterbucks, elephants, giraffes, or, down by the Mara River, the vervet monkeys, patas monkeys, olive baboons, were the birds, big and small, fascinating, the marabou storks and sacred ibises, secretary birds, Egyptian vultures, black kites, peregrines, francolins, spur fowl, bustards, plovers, turacos, the white-bellied go-away birds. Omoke had a bird book which he passed around. He knew his birds, but it was fun for Barbara and Fletch to look from this amazing bird in the bush to the book to confirm that such a creature existed and had a name and that one could believe one's eyes.

Besides these specific observations, the general observation of African arithmetic is impressive. The social unit of many, if not most, species of birds and beasts is dominated by a single male. He has two wives, five wives, ten wives, fifty wives, seventy wives. Besides bearing the children, the wives do the work of hunting and feeding. All these wives and children belong to the single male, at least as long as he can fight off whatever young male would like to take his place. The only way this stupefying arithmetic can work out is if a shocking number of young males die trying. Or so Barbara and Fletch worked out in the back of the *guari*.

Giraffes stretch their long necks to graze off the top of trees, their four slim legs, bodies, long, graceful necks making something architectural out of whatever tree they graze/grace.

On the way back to the lodge that second night, they stopped to watch elephants graze through a stand of long, coarse grass. An elephant uses its tusk like a spoon, its trunk like a fork. With its tusk, an elephant digs down into the earth, loosens and lifts whatever it is eating. His trunk grabs it and swings it into his mouth, grass, root, soil, all together, all the while making this wonderful, rhythmical swaying movement, as if inviting someone to dance, or to box.

"The women are giving up," Barbara said. At the bar, the two French hotel executives had put down their empty glasses. "They are going to bed. Seeing we need an *askari* to escort us, I might as well leave with them."

"Okay. I'll have a nightcap with Carr."

After she stood up, Barbara said, "You might not find your father on this trip. But it looks to me as if you may have found your father figure."

THIRTY-THREE

"Barbara says every woman around is eating you up with her eyes," Fletch said.

Carr had brought two fresh beers to the table. "Occupational hazard. Women can think bush pilots attractive, but, for the most part, they'd never think of marrying one." He touched his glass to Fletch's. "Home tomorrow to the camp, and Sheila."

They drank.

Fletch said, "Barbara and I are very grateful to you, Mr. Peter Carr. Seeing the Masai Mara has been a most memorable treat."

"Then perhaps you'll permit me a personal question?"

"Of course."

Carr took another swallow of his beer before speaking. "You've got me a bit confused, young Fletcher. I'm speaking of the murder you saw, or half saw, at the airport."

"Yes."

"I understand your not running out of the men's room yelling bloody murder, or I guess I do. Jet-lagged, deeply shocked, sick, newly arrived in a country foreign to you, knowing no one here, unsure of your father, his invitation, all that."

"Did he ever indicate to you he might meet us at the airport?"

"But in the days since then, why haven't you come forward? Granted, the authorities here would want you to testify, might hold you over, and sooner rather than later you want to get back to your own lives in the States . . . but something could be worked out, don't you think?"

Fletch cleared his throat. "My ace in the hole."

"You're playing poker?"

"There are those who say life is poker."

"What's in the pot?"

"My father."

"Oh, I see. I think I see."

"I'm talking about a trade-off, Carr."

Carr's eyes narrowed. "The senior Fletcher for a murderer."

"Carr, I've been listening to you all. That's what a reporter does: he listens. I'm in a country, however you love it, where a tourist is jailed, fined, and expelled for tearing a hundred-*shillingi* note in half; where a government driver is jailed for eighteen months for parking a government car outside a bar; where an Indian lawyer is sentenced to seven years in prison for having thirteen U.S. dollars in his pocket. My father got into a drunken bar brawl and may or may not have slugged a cop. What's that worth in Kenyan prison time?"

"I see. You're looking forward to doing a deal."

"If it comes to it, I know a deal is possible. No police in the world would fail to forgive what is essentially a misdemeanor for an eyewitness account of a murder."

"You're not just playing Hamlet."

"I see my father's ghost, and that's about all."

Quietly, Carr said, "You don't even know the chap."

"He's my father."

"And that means something to you?"

"I don't know what it means to me."

"He ran off on you and your mother. He seems to have ignored you all your life. A few days ago, in prison, he refused to see you."

"Am I crazy?"

"I don't know."

"He also arranged for Barbara and me to come out here to meet him, spend some time with him, get to know him. There must be some feeling there. At least 'mild curiosity.' "

"There's a moral question here somewhere."

"Is there? How do I know what morals there are within a family, between a father and a son? No one ever taught me."

"I see."

"I know I don't want to see anyone who is my father spend months, years in an African prison for getting pissed and blindly swinging out at someone."

"Not quite what I mean. You can identify a murderer, someone who has murdered and is still at large."

"You mean you think he may murder again?"

"Exactly. Don't you have the responsibility to get the chap off the streets?"

Fletch shook his head. "No. That was a murder of impulse, of rage. I was there."

"The police aren't so sure," Carr said. "I made a phone call while we were in Nairobi."

"Dan Dawes?"

"The same."

Fletch chuckled. "The police informant."

"Right. The police inform him of everything. Bringing hard currency into Kenya isn't illegal; in fact, it's rather appreciated. Failing to declare the money upon arrival is illegal. In getting as far as the men's room without declaring this extraordinary number of *deutsche marks*, Louis Ramon, who, by the way, was on your airplane, had committed a crime."

"So?"

"So the Kenyan police are looking for a Kenyan financial acrobat who had desperate need for that much hard currency."

"Wrong. The man who killed, what's-his-name, Louis Ramon?"

"Right."

"Was not the man Louis Ramon came to meet. Whoever killed Louis Ramon did not know he was carrying one hundred thousand dollars in hard currency on him. You can't tell me someone's willing to do murder and not willing to stoop over and pick up one hundred thousand dollars if he knows it's there."

"Dan thought that point interesting."

"Was Dan interested in why you called?"

"Beg pardon?"

"Carr, in calling Dan Dawes, you're showing a lot of interest in a case which has nothing to do with you. Aren't you afraid of making him, and the police, suspicious of you?"

"Oh, I see. Well, in a small place like Nairobi, we all love the gossip."

"Yeah? How many other people have called Dan Dawes for inside information on this case?"

"I didn't ask him. And he didn't say."

"Sorry, but I'm afraid you're tipping our hand."

"Didn't realize we're playing poker."

"I'm waiting to hear the official charges against my father. Was the man he slugged a policeman or not? I'd appreciate knowing that as soon as possible."

"Is this all you're thinking, young Fletcher?" Even in the dim light shed by the hanging lanterns of the lodge's patio, Carr's face was without shadows.

"What do you mean?"

"I don't know. I don't know what I mean."

Surprising warmth flooded through Fletch's body. "Well. I don't know my father." He shook his head. "It would have been natural for him to meet us at the airport." He shook his head again. "I don't know. I may be mistaken."

Carr tipped his head back and finished his beer. "You're thinking something, at any rate. That's a relief."

THIRTY-FOUR

"My, my," said Carr. "What have we here? A crippled Sheila . . . ?"

". . . being held up by Juma!" Fletch yelled.

"What happened?" Barbara leaned forward and looked out Fletch's window.

Flying low over the camp, everything was visible. Sheila was hobbling down from the tents to meet them. A homemade crutch was under her right arm. His arm around her waist, Juma supported her from the left side. Sheila's right leg was in a long cast. They were both looking up at the airplane, laughing. Behind them hurried Raffles with a pitcher of lemonade and glasses on a tray. Sheila tripped on a tuft of grass. She and Juma nearly collapsed on the ground, laughing.

Carr landed the plane wheels perfectly on the slightly uphill track. "The old dear's splintered her drumstick."

Fletch banged the cockpit door open and held it up.

"Poor Sheila," said Barbara.

Fletch said quietly, "And no Walter Fletcher."

Raffles was first to the airplane.

Sheila and Juma were rollicking down the slope, holding on to each other, laughing like two roisterers in the wee hours.

Fletch got out of the plane, then Barbara. They jumped off the wing.

Carr emerged from the cockpit just as Sheila and Juma arrived.

"All's right here," Sheila called out. "All's right with you?"

Standing on the airplane's wing, arms akimbo, Carr said, "Clearly, all's not right here!"

"But it is!" Sheila waved her crutch. "Juma's a hero! At least, to me!"

"How did you crack your kicker?" Carr demanded.

"The bloody corkscrew tipped over on me! There I was, alone in the jungle, as they say, leg broken, full weight of the corkscrew on me, no more able to move than Buckingham Palace, while three snakes were exploring closer to me, thinking nasty thoughts, I'm sure, while also hearing hyenas laughing at a few ripe ones not far off, and out pops Juma from the flora like a Masai *moran*, spear in hand, to stigmatize the snakes, notify the hyenas the show was over, make me as comfortable as possible, run for the Jeep and men to get the bloody corkscrew off me with high alacrity — generally, to save my sanity and my life, in that order!"

" 'Spear in hand'?" Fletch muttered.

"Darling Juma!" Hand around his shoulder, Sheila grabbed him to her and planted a kiss on his ear.

Juma was laughing merrily.

From his elevation on the airplane wing, Carr was studying Sheila's cast. "Simple or compound?"

"Compound," Sheila said proudly.

"Juma set it for you?"

Holding up her encased leg, Sheila said, "Juma did a first-class job!"

"Good for Juma!" Carr said. "We all thank you, sir."

As they were drinking lemonade, Sheila chatted, "When Juma discovered me in the bush, he moved with such speed, brain, and brawn, I was put to right in no time at all!"

Carr shook his head. "Can't leave you alone for a minute."

"Oh, rot," said Sheila. "Next you'll tell me I spoiled your plans to go dancing tonight!"

"I don't know, though, Peter." Over coffee after lunch under the stretched canvas, Sheila looked around at the less than luxurious campsite, walls of jungle three sides, the derelict-looking Jeep, the sluggish river, the corkscrew lying on its side on the riverbank. "Perhaps it's time to pack it in."

Carr picked a cracker crumb out of his lap and put it on the table. "Been thinking the same thing, old dear. Enough gets to be enough."

Still looking around, Sheila said, "Enough is enough."

Carr, Barbara, and Fletch had flown from the Masai Mara early that morning. They had left the two *hôtelières* in Nairobi and refueled.

Awaiting them at the camp had been a mother with a baby whose back had been burned, whom Carr tended as well as he could, and an old man being blinded by cataracts Carr had to send away.

Lunch at the campsite was late, bigger than usual, slower. Sheila's broken leg had prevented her starting the day's digging, and thus it never did get started. They even had sherry before lunch while Sheila and Juma regaled them again, laughing, about Sheila's pain, terror, near death in the jungle; Juma's appearing from the jungle like a *moran*, slaying the snakes with his spear, dispatching the hyenas, reappearing driving the Jeep, engineering the corkscrew off Sheila quickly and painlessly, then setting her compound fracture and creating a beautiful, smooth cast for it.

"I'll be damned if I sell airplane number two over this project," Carr said. "I already sold one airplane to finance this."

"The one your father used to fly," Sheila said to Fletch. "The one your father now has."

"Did he finish paying for it?" Barbara asked.

"Oh, yes," Carr said. "He had that profitable year flying the Uganda border, while the rest of us were refusing to do so."

"And the house in Karen," Sheila said. "We sold the house in Karen."

Juma came and sat at the table with them.

"Hello, hero," Fletch said.

Juma grinned. "Now it's a bigger story than almost any other."

"It wasn't all that much of a house," said Carr.

"No. Not that much of a house. But it was ours."

Juma was looking quite fondly at Sheila. "Sorry you lost your house."

"With two airplanes flying," Carr said, "in a few years we should be able to afford another house. With only one plane flying, I'd expect to be an apartment dweller from now until my dotage."

A man Fletch recognized came out of the jungle toward them. He walked rapidly with a homemade crutch, heeling-and-toeing across the rough ground.

Sheila said, "You do like your peace and quiet."

"Yes." Carr looked around the camp and smiled. "I do."

"Still," Sheila said. "Enough, as you say . . ."

"Also the matter of the lost income. I'm not making money while I'm mucking about down here . . ."

The man on the crutch approached the table. The front of one foot was bandaged. One toe was in a splint. Two other toes Carr had removed with a garden shears a few days before.

In the man's hand were his two toes still wrapped in the gauze.

"A few more days," Carr said. "We'll give it to the end of the month. If we don't find anything encouraging by then, I guess it's back to Nairobi to find an apartment."

Carr looked up at the man on the crutch. *"Habari leo?"*

Leaning toward Carr, the man spoke softly in a tribal language. He held out the bloody gauze with the toes in it.

Juma grinned. He put his head down, near Fletch, and said, "The man wants to know where his toes are." Speaking in Swahili, Carr pointed to the gauze in the man's hand. "Carr says, 'There are your toes.' " Grin widening, Juma said, " 'No, no,' the man says, 'I mean where are the spirits of my toes?' Carr asks him what he means. The man says, 'My toes still pain me, but not the toes in my hand, the toes which are no longer on my feet.' "

"Oh, I see," said Fletch. "That happens. Nerves still signal pain to the brain from a severed appendage."

"Now the man wants Carr to cut off the spirit of his toes, so the pain will stop."

Fletch said, "That makes great sense."

Carr's face was looking as if he had just been told he had buried someone who wasn't dead. Clearly, he did not know how to answer the man.

There was a long silence while Carr looked at the man, the toes in the man's hand, the man's bandaged foot, to Sheila, and back to the man.

Juma said, "Witch doctor."

"Yes, yes," said Carr. "Witch doctor. Only a witch doctor can remove spirits . . ."

Carr launched into a long, gentle instruction to the man as to how he must now go to a witch doctor to have the spirits of his toes removed.

"Listen," Juma said to Fletch. "In three days someone is coming by in a truck. He is going to Shimoni. I would like to take you and Barbara with me to Shimoni in the truck. It is on the coast. We can camp there, and swim, catch fish . . ."

"Sounds like fun."

"Do you want to go?"

"Very much."

"And Barbara will want to come?"

"I think so. I'll ask her."

"It won't be such hot work as here."

"Of course, we'd like to help out Carr and Sheila, for as long as possible."

"We'll only go for a day or two."

"Sounds good."

Apparently satisfied, the man on the crutch was heeling-and-toeing it back along the jungle path.

Carr sighed. He looked at Sheila. "I don't know, old dear. Maybe we won't last the month, what with one thing and another . . ."

THIRTY-FIVE

"How do you know this truck is coming?" Fletch asked.

"It is coming."

"Can you hear it?"

"No."

Before dawn, Barbara, Juma, and Fletch went out to the jungle track west of Carr's camp and waited. They stood silently in the dew almost an hour, hearing the jungle noises turn from nocturnal to diurnal. They had one knapsack among them, which Fletch kept on his back. After a while, Barbara sat down on the dry track. Fletch lowered the knapsack onto the grass. Only after Fletch sat down did Juma.

After the sun was well up, they moved into the shade. Fletch left the knapsack in the middle of the track.

"Thirsty," Barbara said.

Juma disappeared into the jungle. He returned with two grapefruit, which they shared.

"It will come," Juma said.

"You sure you have the right day?"

No vehicle came along the track.

"Yes."

"It's almost noon," Fletch said. "We could have walked to the coast."

"Yes," Juma allowed. "We could walk to Shimoni."

Juma, Fletch, and Barbara had put in two more long days of clearing brush, digging holes, looking for Carr's lost Roman city. Muscle-weary, tired of being slick with sweat, tired of being thirsty, even Fletch had begun to believe, to wish that there was an ancient Roman city underfoot, that some evidence of a different time, a different people, a different civilization would surface. To himself, as he worked, he marveled more and more at Sheila and Carr selling their house, selling an airplane, a part of Carr's business, and devoting eighteen months rooting about in the bush on just hope.

They had started out that morning clean and cool and fed. Watching the birds and the monkeys sporting about near and across the jungle track, they were again glistening with sweat, even in the shade. They were developing a hunger and thirst grapefruit slices did not address.

Fletch said, "I feel guilty just sitting here. I feel we ought to be back helping Sheila and Carr. They said they're going to give up their search soon."

"The truck will come," Juma said.

Fletch said, "Juma. You seem to have become fond of Sheila."

"Yes." Juma's eyes danced in his head. "Nice lady. Good-spirited."

Barbara asked, "Did you actually talk to this friend of yours with the truck?"

"He's not a friend. Not an enemy, either, I don't think."

Fletch sighed. "Are we friends?"

Juma smiled. "We'll see."

"Did you talk to whoever this is who is supposed to be coming by in a truck?" Barbara asked.

"No."

"Then how do you know he's coming?"

"He is coming."

"Do you know the driver at all?" Fletch asked.

Juma said, "I don't know. Probably."

" 'Probably'?"

"Then what are we doing here?" Barbara asked.

"Waiting for the truck," Juma said. "There is nothing to decide about."

About one-thirty, a diesel truck carrying bags of cashews ground its gears slowly up the track. Juma asked the driver if they could ride to Shimoni with him.

Of course they were welcome.

Lying on the bags of cashews on the back of the truck, they jounced along to the coast. The truck generated a little breeze, and the cashews smelled good.

Fletch never did know if that was the truck for which they had waited all morning. It was a truck. Eventually, it had come along the track. It did pick them up. It did transport them to Shimoni.

Fletch wondered how to ask Juma if it was the *right* truck.

After wondering a long time, Fletch found himself asking himself the question, *What does it matter?*

THIRTY-SIX

"What do you think, Juma?" From their table at the roofed, wall-less restaurant on the crown of Wasini Island, Fletch looked across the ocean at mainland Africa. "Is it possible there is a lost Roman city in East Africa, or are our friends just wasting their time and money?"

Juma shrugged. "How can you decide, until you know?"

Barbara said, "Carr said some documentary evidence exists in London. The appearance and military traditions of the Masai are a kind of evidence, I suppose." She smiled. "And then there's what the witch of Thika said . . ."

"She was right about one thing," Fletch said. "I sure am carrying a box of rocks." Under the table, Fletch stretched out his legs.

Juma studied Fletch's face.

Barbara fingered crab meat into her mouth. "I sure would like to help out Sheila and Carr."

"I don't know." Fletch shook his head. "There are a lot of little things, impressions, things I've heard, rattling around inside my head. I haven't quite sorted them out, focused on them yet."

"Are they helpful?" Barbara asked. "What sort of things?"

"I don't know," Fletch answered. "I won't know until I sort them out."

In midday, Juma was eating steamed crab with them. This was a special picnic, in a special place, Juma had arranged for them.

The afternoon before, the cashew-bearing truck had stopped for them to climb down onto the road outside Kisite/Mpunguti National

Park. They walked the fifteen kilometers into the park, past the ruins of the district commissioner's house. Fletch carried the knapsack. They had to pay a few *shillingi* to enter the park.

Originally just a fishing camp, still there was little evidence of tourists there. Tents were sparse, well hidden, virtually invisible. The few visitors were so acclimated to the jungle, the beach, the sea, they did not jar the landscape, seascape. The few officials were casual, unobtrusive, helpful. And the commercial fishermen were still curious about, kind to, these visitors to their world.

Immediately upon arrival, Barbara, Juma, Fletch jumped into the Indian Ocean. It being almost as warm as they were, it welcomed them easily, held them a long time.

Later in the afternoon, they stood upon the lip of the cave, Shimoni, the hole-in-the-ground, and looked down. Fletch and Barbara did not know what they were seeing. To them, Shimoni was a hard-packed mud descent into darkness. Something, not a sound, not a smell, something palpable emanated from the cave.

"Do you wish to enter?" Juma asked.

Fletch glanced at Barbara. "Why not?"

"Going down is slippery." Juma looked at the knapsack on Fletch's back.

Fletch put the pack on the ground.

"There are bats." Juma looked at Barbara's hair.

"It's a cave," Fletch said.

"Is it a big cave?" Barbara asked.

"It goes along underground about twelve miles," Juma said.

"What am I feeling?" Fletch asked.

Juma nodded.

He led the way down the slippery slope.

They stood in an enormous underground room, partly lit by the light from the entrance. Barbara remarked on the stalactites, then giggled at the hollow sound of her voice.

Fletch noticed that all the rock, every square centimeter of floor, all along the walls two meters high, had been worn smooth. Even in imperfect light, much of the stone looked polished.

"What was this place used for?" Fletch said.

A bat flew overhead.

"A warehouse," Juma said simply. "For human beings. A human warehouse. People who had been sold as slaves were jammed in here, to await the ships that took them away."

Only the slow drip of water somewhere in the cave punctuated the long, stunned silence.

When Barbara's face turned back toward them, toward the light, her cheeks glistened with tears.

"How afraid they must have been," she said.

Juma said, "For hundreds of years."

"The terror," Barbara said. "The utter despair."

Juma said, "The smell, the sweat, the shit of hundreds, maybe thousands of bodies. The crying that must have come from this cave, day and night, year after year."

The entrance to the cave was wide, but not so wide it could not be sealed by a few men with swords and guns, clubs and whips. The rear of the cave was total darkness. That damp, reeking, weeping darkness extending twelve miles underground, no way out from under the heaviness of the earth, however frantic, however intelligent, however energetic the effort, to light, to air, to food, back to their own realities, existences, their own lives, loves, expectations . . .

There was only one way out of that cave: docile, enslaved.

Juma asked, "Did your ancestors buy slaves, do you think?"

"No," Fletch answered.

"I'm pretty sure not," said Barbara.

Juma ran his bare foot over the smoothness of the floor stone. "You see, that is how we must think of things."

"What do you mean?" Fletch asked.

"I'm pretty sure my ancestors sold slaves. Do you see? Which is worse — to buy people or to sell them?"

They bought a couple of handsome fish at the ice/trading house just after the fishing boats came in, and cooked them on the beach as the sun dropped into the jungle.

Just before full dark one of the casual officials found them. He brought them to a small tent among the palm trees just off the exposed beach, not far from the dock. There was scarcely room for the official, Fletch, Barbara, and Juma to crawl into the tent, but they all did.

Later, standing outside the tent, Fletch asked Juma, "Where will you be?"

The official had wandered off.

Juma said, "I'll be here."

Deciding everything like that, all the time . . . is very hard. Do you mean difficult? . . . or harsh? . . . Does he mean have *a nice time? . . . Or we* had *a nice time? . . . You said we'd be picked up by a truck which would take us to Shimoni, and, after six and a half hours, we were . . . but was it the truck you were expecting . . . ? . . . What is worse — to buy people or to sell them? . . . I'll be here . . .*

In fact, after being in the tent together awhile, Barbara and Fletch were too hot to stay there. Their skin was sticky from the salt water, abrasive with sand, wet with sweat.

They crawled out of their tent in the dark. Hand in hand, naked in what moonlight there was, they ambled down the beach. Without changing pace, they walked into the ocean, ducked, broke handclasp, and swam about, playing quietly, going away from each other, and coming back to each other, again and again.

It was a wonderfully important time in that Barbara and Fletch were having a honeymoon beyond any expectation.

Later, on their way back to their tent, they were widely circumnavigating a tall, broad boulder at the edge of the beach. They had been quiet for some time.

As they walked, the moon came to be behind the boulder, slightly above it.

Barbara gasped. She jerked Fletch's hand.

They stopped still.

"Is that a statue?" Barbara whispered.

Standing on the boulder in profile in the moonlight, absolutely still, stood a slim, male figure, feet together, arms at sides, head held high, perfectly erect, in every way.

"It wasn't there before."

"Fletch. I think it's Juma!"

"It is Juma."

Juma's erect penis was a straight rod extending at a perfect ninety-degree angle from the straight, slim rod of his figure. The stillness of Juma's silhouette on the boulder in the moonlight was stunning.

"What's he doing there?" Barbara whispered.

"Just standing."

"He's so beautiful!"

"Yes. He is."

They couldn't help staring at Juma's silhouette a short while.

Finally, silently, Barbara and Fletch returned to their tent.

Again, just before dawn, they crawled out of their tent, to go to the ocean, to swim, to awake fully, to play. The birds had awakened them. The heat, the heavy air under their low-slung mosquito net kept them awake.

In the morning, returning to the tent, hand in hand, they were walking around a bush when they nearly tripped over a tableau of human bodies.

Juma, naked, was asleep on the ground. Two girls, naked except for their necklaces, bracelets, anklets, hair beads, were asleep with him. Jum'a head was on the stomach of one girl. One of his legs was sprawled sideways, not heavily, across the hips of the other. Each of the three faces seemed concentrating on the contentment of sleep.

Juma's penis was rising before him.

"The arithmetic of Africa," Barbara whispered. "I'll never figure it out."

A fly was walking up the cheek of one of the girls, toward her eye. Her hand, across Juma's chest, did not rise to brush it off.

Fletch had the strong instinct to brush the fly off the girl's face.

Instead, he pulled Barbara away, silently, by the hand.

Barbara said, "Just like the lion we saw, his body sprawled comfortably over two lionesses."

Not much later, Juma found them at the *ducca* where Barbara and Fletch had bought bottles of Coca-Cola and a box of biscuits for breakfast.

Juma had organized the day for them.

Two Italian couples were all that were to sail on the dhow for that day's excursion. The dhow could take eight passengers comfortably.

The Italians and the dhow's crew had assured Juma that he and Barbara and Fletch were most welcome to join them.

Sailing away from the mainland in the dhow, Fletch asked Barbara, "Do you feel grungy?"

Barbara said, "I feel like Carr's Jeep."

Two husbands and one wife of the Italian couples were medical doctors; the second wife said she was the *madonna* of three children. The Italians spoke little or no English; Juma, Barbara, and Fletch had no Italian: they all came to be jolly together with gestures and *patois*.

At first, Barbara and Fletch were shy of the Italians. Sunburned, bug-bitten, their skin also scraped and cut from clearing jungle trails and digging holes, their hair washed only in salt water and conditioned with sand, dressed in cutoff and now ripped-to-shreds nylon ski pants, already they were seeing the healthy, wealthy Italian tourists as being from a different world altogether. They boarded the dhow in well-cut swimsuits, stripped to even better cut swimsuits. Their bodies were strong but pampered. The skin of each of them was unblemished from either sun or bugs. Each recently had had the attention of a good hairdresser. As the dhow approached the reef they all were to swim, the Italians pulled out of nylon sacks equipment which looked fabulous: masks and snorkels, tight-fitting rubber boots, rubber flippers, two underwater cameras. One man even strapped a sheathed knife to his ankle.

Barbara said, "Already I'm suffering culture clash."

"That's okay," Fletch consoled. "Back at Carr's camp, we have some wonderful skiing equipment."

"Shall I try to tell them?" Barbara asked.

"I think not."

Instantly, Juma was open to the Italians. He asked from them and learned the Italian for sails and ship and wheel and islands, water, fish. One doctor proudly showed Juma how the underwater cameras worked.

Fletch had the great temptation to ask Juma, *Where did the two girls go? Where did they come from?* but he didn't.

The dhow's crew of two were wonderful, full of good cheer and humor for everybody, in English, Italian, Swahili, and one other language they kept to themselves. As a joke, they kept offering to the well-equipped Italians the cheap, worn-out, torn goggles and snorkels they had for rent aboard the dhow. They pretended to be insulted when the Italians, laughing, insisted they preferred their own equipment.

The reefs along the Tanzania coast have been blasted and picked dead by entrepreneurs collecting fish and coral souvenirs for "tourist goats." The reefs just north and south of Mombasa are dying rapidly. So the reefs of Kisite are forcibly protected.

The dhow anchored just outside Mako Kokwe Reef.

The non-Kenyans swam for hours back and forth along the reef. Except for the two men with cameras they just goggled the sculptured coral magnified in the sunlight by the water. They were mesmerized by the lacy coral fans waving in the slight, shifting currents, their shadows moving from side to side on the coral or sand floor.

Swimming slowly in the warm water, not even disturbing the surface of the ocean much, Fletch toured the small schools of fish, many more brightly colored than any birds. Best he liked to look at and follow the bright yellow surgeons with the black lines drawn up from their mouths in an apparent, *Nice time* grin. Always, when he first saw these fish, Fletch inhaled too much, too quickly, to laugh, and would flood his mouth and nose with water. He would have to pull his head up above water to laugh happily at the appearance of the fish, at himself, to recover.

Barbara banged Fletch on the shoulder with her hand.

Treading water, she said, "Juma went back to the dhow."

Fletch looked at the dhow. He guessed he saw Juma's head amidship. The crewmen were in the stern.

"When?"

"Some time ago."

"Is he all right?"

"I was with him at first. He doesn't seem at all comfortable in the water. He kept thrashing about and coughing. At first, I thought he was kidding, then I thought he was drowning."

"He can swim?"

"He works too hard at it. He swims like he feels he's being pulled down more than we are."

"He's just catching his breath."

"He went back almost right away."

"He's all right."

"Maybe we ought to go back, too."

"Yeah. In a minute. In a while."

Sailing along then, in early afternoon, the dhow attracted dolphins which swam along with them for a long while, escorting them, appearing to race the dhow, torpedo it from the sides. Definitely they were relating to the dhow and the people on it, making noises back at them, and all the people on the dhow were relating to them, like friends unseen for too long.

After crossing intersecting currents among the islands, enjoying a short, rough ride in the dhow, the crewmen anchored off Wasini Island. The dinghy took the passengers into shallow water.

From shallow water, the passengers walked over ow-ow up to Ras Mondi.

"Hey." Barbara clutched Fletch's hand as they walked carefully over the ow-ow. "We're having a nice time."

"Things are beginning to come together," Fletch said.

Only the party from the dhow was at the restaurant.

Because of the language barrier, the Italians sat one one table; Juma, Barbara, and Fletch at another.

After the sail and the swim they were thirsty for fresh water and only a little beer. Their hunger made them compete playfully for the first food they saw, sesame-ball appetizers. They thought the enormous steamed crabs were a big enough lunch, all there was, and ate them slowly, savoring them. When plates piled high with *changa* and rice cooked in coconut sauce were set before them, they all rolled their eyes, and then cheered.

"Sheila and Carr will be right disappointed if they don't find anything," Barbara said. "Can't we think of something that might help out? At least to console them?"

"All over Africa, people are looking for their pasts," Juma said. "Digging up bones, and pots, and spear tips. You'd think Africa is nothing but a museum."

Fletch asked, "How come there are fish, perch, from the Nile River in Lake Turkana? The two bodies of water are hundreds of miles away from each other. Nothing, no river, flows from one to the other."

Barbara said, "They must have been joined at one time."

"Why are people so interested in their pasts now?" Juma asked. "Why do people come to Africa from all over the world to search for their ancestors, first man, first bone, first fossil?"

" 'Mild curiosity,' " Barbara said.

"What difference does it make?" Juma asked. "The way to the future is the present, not the past."

"It doesn't make a difference?" Fletch asked. "It doesn't make a difference to you that an East Indian elephant was found buried at Koobi Fora?"

"No," Juma said. "What difference does it make?"

Barbara said, "It suggests that at one time Africa and India might have been joined together. Doesn't that mean anything to you, Juma?"

"Sure," Juma answered. "You want me to say East Indians belong here, in Africa."

Fletch asked the air, "Why did I come to Africa to meet my father?"

" 'Mild curiosity,' " Barbara repeated.

"Why did you come, Fletch? You are who you are. What does your father have to do with you? You don't even know him."

"Cultural flow." Fletch spoke to his plate. "Moral flow."

Barbara said, "What are you talking about?"

"I don't know."

"When people look into the past," Juma said, "they only expect to find good, good things. Supposing they find bad, bad things?"

Fletch asked, "Am I going to find bad, bad things, Juma? You know my father. I don't."

"I think maybe people are better off going into their futures without worrying about, carrying bad, bad things that might be in their pasts."

"I think you're trying to warn me," Fletch said.

"There are people here," Juma said, "people my age, who insist on living the way their ancestors did thousands of years ago. Like that *moran* you saw near Carr's camp. That's too much of a burden, on all of us. You can't run a computer with a spear."

"Spears come in handy, too," Fletch said. "There are still snakes. You used a spear to rescue Sheila."

"And a Jeep," Juma said.

"Here's something about the future," Fletch said. "Carr told me that someday the Rift Valley is going to rip open at the top, and the Red Sea is going to come flooding down. There will be a sea where there is now a valley."

Barbara said, "They know the future, in this case, from studying the past."

"Things change," Fletch said.

"Yes," Juma said. "Things change. Nomads know that. Constantly we move away from our pasts, because things change."

Fletch said, "Things change . . ."

"You've stopped eating," Barbara said to him.

Juma asked Barbara, "You like leather fish?"

"Leather fish?" Barbara asked. "I'm eating leather fish?"

"*Changa,*" Juma said. "Leather fish."

"Oh, my God." Barbara looked at the little left on her plate. "I'm eating something called leather fish."

Fletch said, "I'm thinking about the Mississippi River."

"There are no leather fish in the Mississippi River," Barbara said. "Catfish. I don't like to eat catfish, either."

Fletch said, "It is also said the Mississippi River is going to change course."

"Right," said Barbara. "Then New Orleans will really be blowin' the blues."

"Rivers change course, sometimes," Juma said.

Fletch shook his head, as if to clear it. "I'm beginning to have an idea. All these things I've heard, rattling around in my head — "

Juma said, "Carr and Sheila are digging along a river that exists now." He laughed.

Fletch said, "Thousands of years ago . . ."

Barbara put down her fork. " . . . the river might have been somewhere else."

"So Carr's *theory* might be right . . ."

" . . . but the river might have moved," Juma chuckled.

"Oo, wow," said Barbara.

"Of course the river might have moved," Juma laughed. "Why didn't you ask me?"

"Nice time," Fletch said. "Let's go back to Carr's camp."

"Can't move," Juma said. "Ate too much."

THIRTY-SEVEN

"Absolutely!" Swooping the airplane through the sky in joy, Carr dipped the wings.

"No doubt about it!" Barbara was in the seat behind Carr. Juma was beside her, trying to look out all the airplane's windows at once. "Looks good!"

"Carr," Fletch said, "I need to be set gently on the ground."

"You mean, it's true?" Her encased leg stuck out into the airplane's aisle, Sheila had to shout from the rearmost seat. "There was another river?"

"Naam, Momma!" Juma shouted. *"Indio!"*

Everyone was shouting over the noise of the engine.

"Damn!" Carr swooped the plane lower for another horizontal look, this time from the west. "All the times I've flown over this area, and I never noticed. Damn me!"

"Soon," Fletch said.

"That line of trees, all the way to the ocean, is distinctly different," Barbara said.

"The whole line is indented," Juma said. "You see? A different growth. Deeper in the ground. Greener, too."

"Absolutely." Looking through his side window, Carr was flying just above treetop level. "From this level, you can see the gap."

"Carr . . . " Fletch moaned.

Juma, Barbara, and Fletch stayed at Kisite/Mpunguti one more night. It was late when they returned to the mainland. Juma said one did not start a long trek into the jungle an hour before sundown.

"Only superstition, of course" — Juma smiled — "but the ancient belief is that people might, just might, get lost in the jungle after dark, might just get hurt, might not be able to protect themselves so well from snakes, zebras, warthogs, cheetahs, and lions." He lowered his head as if ashamed. "Just an ancient African superstition."

"Then I guess I'm superstitious," Barbara said.

"Anyway," Juma said. "After eating so much we are too stupid and lazy-sick to do anything but trip around in circles until we fall down. We deserve to be snacked up by hyenas."

At dawn they stood by the main road. An iced fish truck going to Mombasa took them part of the way. After walking an hour, an old

Kenyan *née* English farm couple picked them up in a Land-Rover they said they had brought to Kenya thirty-six years before. It jounced along well. Juma knew when to start walking again through the bush.

They walked most of the way back to camp.

Early afternoon they found Carr and Sheila with a team of workmen setting up the corkscrew for another dig downriver. Sheila stumped around on her crutch, being as helpful as she could be. Clearly, though, from the expressions on their faces, the way they moved, Sheila's frustration had grown, Carr's patience had thinned.

That afternoon, in the steamy jungle, Sheila and Carr would have listened to any idea.

Sitting in the shade of a baobab, Barbara, Juma, and Fletch explained the possibility they had thought of, that sometime during the last two or three thousand years the river had changed course. They should look for signs of another river in the area, one that no longer existed, one that might have existed in times of the Roman Empire, upon the banks of which the Romans might have built their city . . .

Hearing the excited talk, the workmen worked themselves closer, then stopped, to listen.

After listening, Carr studied Sheila's face. "What do you think, old dear?"

Sheila shrugged. "It's possible, I suppose."

"Do you suppose we could spot such a thing from the air?" Carr asked.

"Yes," Barbara said firmly.

"Maybe," said Fletch.

Wearily, Carr stood up. "I suppose it's worth taking the plane up for a spin. I'm beginning to feel like an earthworm anyway."

Making a chair by clasping their hands and wrists together, Fletch and Juma speeded the laughing Sheila up the riverbank, through the camp, to the airplane.

Having the idea the dry riverbed might be there, they spotted it almost immediately. A wandering, snakelike trail departed from the river five kilometers north of the camp to the right, the west, and wandered discernibly through the jungle on a longer course to the sea.

Following it, Carr pointed through the windshield and shouted to everyone. "You see? At some time in history, the river fell to lower ground, took a shorter course to the sea."

"Water takes the course of least resistance," Sheila piped up from the back, "unlike some reasonably intelligent people I know."

Carr was taking them all for a spin in the airplane — literally. He followed the dry riverbed to the sea. He flew low, at treetop level along it, to the east of it. Swooping up and down, crossing back and forth, he was proving to himself and everyone that the dry riverbed was distinguishable from all heights, all angles.

Fletch was sick.

Quite suddenly, he found himself fighting not to vomit. Below them, the landscape was moving much too fast, tilting, coming and going. His vision blurred. His head pounded as if stuffed with rusty pistons in a rapidly accelerating engine. The back of his neck tightened to pain. As well as he could, he sucked huge amounts of air into his lungs.

A very different sort of sweat was on his face, the sort that made his skin feel distant to himself, and cold.

"Carr," he groaned. "I think you'd better put me on the ground soon."

"Look!" They were high in the air again. Barbara was pointing forward, so that Carr could see. "Look at that little hill."

"Look at that!" Carr banged the heel of his right hand against the control panel. "Right where I figured! A lovely big mound on a bend at the west side of the river, how far from the sea?"

"Maybe ten kilometers," Juma said.

"That much, you think?" Carr spun the plane around and down, down again to the large mound next to the dry riverbed. He flew over it and around it several times. "If there's not a city under that hillock," Carr said, "I'll eat a zebra raw!"

Barbara said, "You just might."

Carr was really showing what he could do with an airplane that afternoon.

When the airplane fell, Fletch's stomach remained in the air. When the airplane rolled, Fletch felt his stomach was going to be splattered out through his sides. When the plane climbed, his stomach met itself just coming down with a lurch.

His head wanted to burrow into the soft earth below.

Getting into the airplane and taking off, Fletch had felt well enough.

Shortly after takeoff, he felt a stab of pain in his eyes. Afternoon sunlight reflecting from the windshield of another airplane, far away, seemed to cut right through his brain.

Breathing hard through lips that felt like sausages, Fletch knew he could not contain vomit much longer.

He grabbed Carr's forearm. "Carr!" he shouted. "I'm sick! Really sick! Please put me down on the ground as soon as you can!"

"Tender tummy?" Carr examined Fletch's face. "You've never complained of it before." He rolled the plane into a left turn. "Hold on!"

Only to Fletch did the rest of the flight seem interminable.

He heard Carr say, "Hello. Look what the hyena dragged in."

Fletch opened his eyes. The airplane was approaching the landing track leading uphill to the camp.

At the top of the track was parked a yellow airplane with green swooshes. The cockpit hatch was open.

A man in khaki shorts and shirt stood beside the plane, watching them land.

Fletch not only had the cockpit door open, but his seat belt off before Carr's plane touched the ground.

While the plane was still taxiing, Fletch crawled out onto the wing. As soon as the plane slowed, he rolled off the wing onto the ground, which, thankfully, did not move.

Kneeling, Fletch vomited onto the ground.

The plane came to a complete stop fifteen meters up the track. Everyone was *hello*ing and offering to help Sheila disembark.

Trying to keep his back to everyone, while trying not to kneel in his own vomit, trying to find new places to vomit, Fletch walked sideways on his bare knees across the track.

Behind him, near the airplane, there was much excited talk. He heard the name Walter Fletcher. The names Barbara, Juma. Happy, happy talk about the new hope of their finding the lost Roman city. Comments about Sheila's broken leg and Juma's heroism. Something about the Thorn Tree Café.

The voices were approaching Fletch.

He scraped his knees a little further along the dirt.

"And this," he heard Carr say, standing over him, behind him, "is Irwin Maurice Fletcher. Bit under the weather at the moment, as you can see. 'Fraid I did one too many loop-de-loops for him."

Surveying the long trails of vomit and knee scrapes he had left across the track, Fletch wiped his nose and his lips and his chin with his hands.

Then, using his hands to push himself up from the ground, he stood up. His knees felt as if they had never worked, never bent, never clicked straight. They wobbled. His lower back felt like a rusty crane.

He took a deep breath.

He turned around.

Carr looking solid, arms akimbo, Sheila on her crutch, one foot off the ground, Juma smiling uncertainly, eyes dancing, Barbara dressed like a drugged Sunset Strip tart, hair dirty, sweat and dirt sworling on her skin, stood with a stranger among them, all looking at Fletch.

The stranger said, "He's a pretty poor-lookin' specimen, isn't he?"

Everything below Fletche's waist went numb.

He raised his face, for air. His eyes closed against a spinning sky.

When his knees hit the ground, the back of his neck snapped forward. His right shoulder was shot with pain as he landed badly on his arm, twisting it.

THIRTY-EIGHT

The hard rain did not begin until late the next afternoon.

Fletch had a raging fever.

Looking up, Fletch saw Carr's face looming above him, looking larger than normal. Above Carr's head was the peak of the tent. Fletch did not know how he came to be on the narrow cot in a tent. His legs ached. His head ached. He was cold. Sweating cold. His mouth tasted filthy. His right shoulder pained. He did not know the source of the pain in his shoulder.

"How do you feel?" Carr asked.

Fletch thought it all through again. "Wonderful."

"That's good."

"May I have a blanket?"

"Sure." Carr stuck a thermometer in Fletch's mouth.

Barbara's round-eyed face was over the end of the cot. Arms folded across his chest, Juma stood near the tent flap.

Raffles came in and covered Fletch's body with a brown blanket.

Carr removed the thermometer and studied it. "At least now we know it wasn't my superb flying that laid you low."

"I'm hot."

"I'll say you are."

Carr fed him a glass of cold soup and two pills.

"Pity," said Carr. "We're planning fettucini with a nice anchovy sauce for dinner."

Consciousness coming and going, Fletch marked time through the night. He heard pots and lids banging in the cooking tent and then talk and laughter from the eating tent. Carr came to see him again, shook him awake, said something Fletch couldn't remember long enough to answer, gave him two more pills, more cold soup. At some point, he saw Barbara's face in the low light of the kerosene lamp. Then silence, long, long silence. Carr came again during the night. He helped Fletch sit up, take more soup, more pills. For a while, Fletch remained awake under the mosquito netting, conscious now of the raucous jungle noises. Hot, he tossed the blanket off. Cold, he pulled it back up to his chin.

Carr was there again in the morning. He read the thermometer in the daylight near the tent flap. "May you live as old as this reads," he muttered. More soup. More pills.

"How do you feel?"

"Wonderful."

"That's good."

There were more happy noises from the cooking tent, eating tent. Someone kept whistling the first four bars of that popular Italian song. Over and over. Maybe it was a bird.

Juma stood beside Fletch. He said nothing.

After a long while, Carr was in the tent with Barbara and Sheila.

Carr said, "You awake?"

"Wonderful."

"We're going to trek through the jungle to that mound we saw yesterday. Do you remember?"

"Sure. Mound."

"See if we can dig up anything. Pick-and-shovel brigade. You'll be all right?"

"Sure."

"Sheila's staying here. Can't drag her through the jungle anyway. She'll keep putting fluids into you, and pills."

"Okay."

"We'll be back."

"Right. Good luck."

"You'll be better when we get back," Carr said.

"Absolutely."

Carr's big bulk moved away from the cot.

Barbara asked, "You want me to stay?"

Fletch wanted her not to have asked. "No."

"I can stay."

"No. It's an exciting day."

"You'll be all right?"

"Go find the lost Roman city. You don't want to miss that."

"I really believe it is there."

"Hope it is."

"If you rather I stay . . ."

"No. Go with them. Go."

" . . . okay."

Barbara left the tent sideways.

Sheila's voice seemed stronger. "You want anything now?"

"No. I'm fine."

Sheila left.

Distantly, Fletch heard the Jeep start. Voices called to each other. The Jeep's engine accelerated. There was a shout, a squeak of brakes. The Jeep started off again.

Raffles came in and washed down Fletch's body with cold, wet rags. It felt wonderful. Raffles even turned Fletch on each side, to wash his back thoroughly.

"Raphael?"

"Yes?"

"Will you bring every blanket in the camp, please, and pile them on top of me?"

"Well. Okay."

During the morning, Raffles and Winston entered the tent, not saying anything. They picked up the cot with Fletch in it and carried him outside. It was a surprisingly dark, gloomy day. They set him evenly on the ground under a tree.

Winston put a camp chair next to the cot.

"Rain?" Fletch asked.

"No," Winston said. "Many times it looks like rain here, but there is no rain."

Sometimes when Fletch awoke, Sheila was sitting in the chair, sometimes not. Sometimes she was leaning forward, working a wet rag over his face and chest. She gave him soup and a lighter, cold herb tea and the pills while either Raffles or Winston held his head up.

"Are they back yet?" Fletch asked.

Sheila said, "No."

"You should be with them."

"I'm glad to be with you."

"What time is it?"

"Never mind."

Going and coming. The day got darker rather than brighter. The air was heavy.

It was a long day.

Again, Fletch awoke in the tent. He didn't remember being carried back.

Carr was standing over him, smiling.

Fletch hadn't heard the Jeep.

"How do you feel?" Fletch asked.

"Wonderful!" Carr held his hand out. Fletch did not reach for it. Carr held something up for him to see.

"What is it?"

"Pottery shard. You can see a piece of what is distinctly a Roman soldier walking with a spear and a shield."

"Fabulous!"

Carr held up his other hand. Something glinted in the low kerosene light.

"And, in case you have any doubts about what we have found, look! A coin!"

"No!"

"Yes!" Carr laughed. "Showing the head of Caesar Augustus. Or so we think. Wasn't he the pretty one?"

"They were all pretty, as boys."

"Definitely Caesar Someone."

"My God!"

"And I think we may have found the top of an ancient wall. Pretty sure of it."

"Carr, that's wonderful!"

"I'll say. Sheila's outside doing the Masai jump, which ain't easy on a crutch."

"What's that?" Fletch heard something like clods of dirt being thrown against the tent.

"Rain."

"It's going to rain?"

"Probably not."

"Carr. Congratulations. Good news. Sorry I wasn't there."

Barbara came in behind Carr, to see how Fletch was.

"Fine."

Carr said, "I'll be back later, to take your temperature."

Later, the sound of the rain was wild. Fletch heard none of the cooking, dining noises. The tent sides were billowing from the gusts of rain.

Fletch watched the water seeping in from under the tent sides. A few rivulets first, turning into brave streams, as well as a general dampness growing in from the sides, all sides; soon there were good-sized puddles inside the tent.

Carr was soaking when he came in.

He turned up the kerosene light on the box to read the thermometer. Frowning, he said, "You're pretty sick, Irwin."

"Sick of Irwin."

"You should be better."

"I agree."

"You can only keep up these high temperatures so long, you know."

"How long?"

Hands on hips, Carr watched how the rain beat down on the tent. "Can't fly you out to the hospital in Nairobi in this weather. Can't take off." He looked sideways and down at Fletch. "You've got to get better."

"My legs, Carr."

"What about 'em?"

"They feel awful."

"Like what?"

"All broken up."

Carr pinched a toe on each foot. "Can you feel that?"

"Yes."

"Can you feel that?"

"Yes."

"It's just the fever."

"They feel all broken up."

More soup, more pills.

Fletch awoke while Raffles was washing him down again.

Fletch wanted all the blankets back on him.

The three blankets were soaked through. They weighed like lead.

Leaving, Raffles had to fight with the tent flap to secure it down against the wind and the rain.

Later, when Fletch awoke, Juma was standing over him silently. In the low light from the kerosene lamp, Juma's hair and skin glistened with rainwater.

Fletch said, "Not a nice time."

"You know what?"

"What?"

"You've got to put down that box of rocks."

The muscles in Fletch's lower stomach heaved.

Juma helped Fletch throw up, on the ground, on the side of the cot away from the tent flap.

Then Juma was there, wet again, with a broom, pushing the vomit and the mud around it out of the tent. He held the bottom of the tent up with one hand while he swept the vomit out under it.

Alone, Fletch listened to the rain. It was interesting watching the vomit seep back in, under the tent wall.

When his stomach felt better, he rolled onto his back.

"Oh!" Fletch jumped awake.

There was a terrible smell in his nostrils.

Huge, red-veined eyes were staring into his from only a few centimeters away. His ears were filled with a weird, high crooning. There was pressure, warmth, against his forehead, and against his heart, and his penis and scrotum were warm. It was not the warmth of the jungle heat or the warmth of the fever. It was a different, drier, more real, more human warmth.

Looking down as much as he could from the staring eyes, Fletch saw the nose, the cheeks of an old face. Orange streaks were painted on the face.

The breath of the crooning old man was horrible in Fletch's nose, mouth.

The old man's forehead was pressed against Fletch's. The old man's left hand was pressed against the skin of Fletch's heart. The old man's right hand was cupped in Fletch's crotch, over his penis and scrotum.

Breathing into Fletch's face, the old man was crooning up and down the scales.

Fletch said, "Jesus Christ."

When he awoke, the old man was gone. Had he dreamt it? The stink was still in his nostrils. The three wet-heavy blankets were smoothed over him again, from toe to chin.

He felt no better from the event, the reality, the dream. Except for the lingering smell, he felt no worse.

Box of rocks.

Then Carr, bare-chested, wet, was shaking more pills out of a bottle.

Fletch did not remember taking them.

The sound of the rain, pelting the ground outside, hammering against the tent, went on and went on and went on.

Suddenly, Fletch's eyes were wide open. The low light from the kerosene lamp had not changed. The box on which the lamp stood, as well as the wet towel on the box, was suddenly clearer in Fletch's eyes. The seams of the tent over his head were more distinct.

The air seemed cleaner in his nostrils. The ache in his head was gone, until he moved his head too quickly.

His arms were happy to move, lightly, as they were ordered.

He was free, free of the fever.

Through the sound of the rain he heard men talking. Two men. Their voices came and went under the sound of the rain.

No one was in the tent with him.

Realizing how heavy, wet the blankets were, he pushed them off him, to the bottom of the cot. Lying down again, he raised his legs, brought his knees to his chest, straightened them, let them down.

Free.

A decision had been made.

Bare feet in the mud, Fletch sat on the edge of the cot and tried to think about the decision. He listened to the rain. He felt cool, normal. There was nothing to think about.

The decision had been made.

This was right. This was normalcy. This was health. This was being alive. If he wanted to be open to life, health, normalcy, *rightness,* he also had to be open to the decision, commit himself to it, act on it, because the decision was based upon decisions made by everybody, everywhere, a long, long time ago, *in the beginning,* and those decisions, once made, determined how everything worked, life, health, defined normalcy, and if one, anyone, did not act basically within those deductions, or acted against them, or decided something else, then *legs,* which hold us up, support us, permit basic movement, progress, *shatter,* and shortly we are sitting in the dust, all of us, corrupt and cracked-headed, corrupting, awaiting the jackals.

Tired rising from the cot, dizzy at first, Fletch stood a moment sucking in the jungle air, heavy with rain. He could smell the jungle, the rotting roots and the slashed green leaves. He could hear the noises of the animals as they moved around in their world, acting within decisions, what was normal, what was health, what was life for them.

Making choices is the ultimate freedom in a world in which decisions have been made to permit such freedom. Failure to see that sometimes no choice can be made, that there is no personal decision, is the ultimate folly, the absolute destruction of self and all.

Fletch took the wet towel and tucked it around his waist.

Pushing aside the tent flap, he looked outside. There were signs of dawn in the sky. The rain was a nearly solid, straight-down torrent, hitting so hard it made the ground look almost jumping.

From which direction was the sound of two men talking coming? Two men, talking loudly over the sound of the rain, in English. Laughing. Listening through the opened tent flap, just inside his tent, Fletch could not make out what they were saying.

A tent across the way, newly put up, showed dim light around the edges of its flap.

Unsteadily, the rain beating on him, feeling good, feeling weary, feeling fresh, feeling slightly dizzy, Fletch splashed and slithered across the campsite mud barefooted.

Do I have to do this? Am I sure I have nothing to decide? The decision has been made. We exist within context. That is our first, our only, our last decision. Making choices is the ultimate freedom. There is no freedom without basic decisions having been made. Self-discipline is the greatest exercise of freedom.

He pulled aside the tent flap and looked in.

Inside, Peter Carr and Walter Fletcher sat in canvas, wood-framed camp chairs. Each had a glass in hand. On the box beside the kerosene lamp was a nearly empty bottle of whiskey.

They stopped talking. They stared at Fletch.

The lines in their faces moved up from around their mouths to around their eyes.

Fletch said to Walter Fletcher: "Thanks for coming to the airport to meet us."

THIRTY-NINE

The two men sitting in the tent staring up at Fletch through the dim light of the kerosene lamp said nothing.

"Do you speak Portuguese?" Fletch asked the man with the thinning, combed hair, pencil moustache.

"What do you mean?" asked Walter Feltcher.

Fletch stood just inside the open tent flap. Behind him, rain poured with a steady roar.

"I saw you," Fletch said. "At the airport. In the men's room."

"Oh, my God!" Carr sat forward in his camp chair. "Say it isn't so."

On the box beside Carr, next to the kerosene lamp, next to the whiskey bottle, were the pottery shard and the Roman coin.

Walter Fletcher stared full-eyed at Fletch. He put his whiskey glass on the box. He resettled himself in his chair.

Ankles crossed, boot heels in the mud, hands folded in his lap, for a long moment Wlater Fletcher studied Fletch's face.

Slack-jawed, Carr was staring at Walter Fletcher.

For only a second, Walter Fletcher glanced at Carr.

Then he looked at Fletch, for another long moment.

"Well." Abruptly, Walter Fletcher stood up. His boots were flat in the mud. He patted down the pockets of his safari jacket. Using both hands, he smoothed back his hair from his temples.

Chin up, not looking into Fletch's face, he brushed by Fletch. He walked out of the tent into the storm.

"Where is he going?" Fletch asked.

"Nowhere he can go." Carr remained hunched over in his camp chair. "What a box of rocks. All this time, you've been thinking the murderer at the airport could have been Walter Fletcher."

Fletch shrugged. "The murderer was a local who came to meet someone at the airport . . . whom he did not meet."

"Don't you think you'd better sit down?"

"Jesus, Carr!"

"What now?"

Fletch had heard an airplane engine ignite. Carr had not.

They both heard the roar of the engine as gasoline was pushed into it.

Carr jumped up.

Together, Fletch and Carr stood outside the tent looking through the heavy rain in the dawn across the campsite at the yellow airplane with green swooshes. The cockpit lights went off. The wing and tail lights were on.

The airplane was turning around over the rough, wet ground. Wings rocking, it skittered around Carr's plane and jounced onto the landing track.

"A plane that light can't take off in this heavy rain," Fletch shouted. "Can it?"

The glass in Carr's hand had a centimeter of rainwater in it already.

Carr said, "I wouldn't try it."

The airplane almost made it. It splashed and swayed down the track. Its engine roared through the sound of the rain. Throwing water behind it, it lifted off the track. It rose against the tree line. For a moment it looked as if it were above the treetops.

The left wing dipped. The plane fell.

The plane's left wing cracked against the top of a tree. The treetop shook. The tip of the wing fell into the woods. As if pivoting, engine roaring, the plane swung left around the top of the tree.

Then only the undercarriage of the tail of the airplane was visible against the sky.

From the woods was not a crash, but a thud.

Instantly, flame was visible through the undergrowth.

Carr thrust his glass into Fletch's hand.

"I'll go. You're in no condition — "

Carr ran splashing through the rain.

"The flames. Carr — "

Fletch threw the glass aside. He ran, tripping over the wet ground, slipping in the mud.

Fletch hadn't gotten far when he fell, facedown in the mud. He tried to get up, quickly. His head felt cement. Pain shot from his right shoulder. Weak from his days of fever, his arms and legs flailed the mud uselessly.

He lay stomach on the ground a moment, his right cheek, ear in the mud, just breathing.

He watched air bubbles in the mud break open.

FORTY

Rain-soaked, muddy from head to foot, a cut bleeding on his forearm, Carr entered Fletch's tent.

Carr shook his head, *No.*

Fletch was sitting on the edge of his cot. Mud ran down his face, the front of his body, his chest, his stomach, into the sodden towel around his waist; down his legs into the mud at his feet.

How many words did my father speak to me? He's a pretty poor-lookin' specimen, isn't he? *No. These were not words spoken to me, but about me. He said,* What do you mean? *He said,* Well. *Five words. My father spoke five words to me. In my life. In his life. In our lives.*

I had no decision to make.

The basic decision ordering how people behave, for survival, the social contract, was made a long, long time ago.

"Carr, he was trying to get away. Wasn't he?"

"Who knows?" Carr said. "Who cares?"

"My mother said he was apt to evade moments of emotional intensity . . ."

"How do you feel?"

" . . . like being hung from the neck."

In the dim kerosene light Carr watched Fletch from across the tent.

"He finally died in an air crash. In a storm. Not in Montana, but in Africa. *Presumed dead.* The courst made a presumption, which was almost right."

"All this noise apparently hasn't awakened anybody."

"The sound of the rain . . ."

"Yes. The sound of the rain."

"How did he get to be here? I never heard."

"You've been pretty sick."

"Were the charges against him dropped?"

"All that was a joke already. Another funny story. The *askari* had no official standing. He was just an unlicensed guard from a jewelry store across the street. So Walter was released from custody after paying a fine, damages to the Thorn Tree Café, the *askiri*'s hospital expenses, plus a few *shillingi* to make up for the weight the *askari* gained in hospital."

"I came halfway around the world to put my father out into a storm; to see him killed in an air crash. Poetry."

"Irwin . . ."

"Yes, Carr."

"I know you can't be feeling like a calisthenics director on a spring morning . . ."

"How I Spent My Honeymoon."

"This is Tuesday. A plane leaves for London tonight. I think you and Barbara should be on it."

"Yes?"

"As soon as the weather clears, I'll fly you up to Nairobi, book your seats."

"Okay." Fletch fingered mud from his eyes. "Anything you say. You've been a real friend, Carr. Thank you."

"Enough of that. I thank you. If it weren't for the intelligence of you and Barbara and Juma, we never would have found the world's latest ruin."

"Having found it will make a big name for you, Peter Carr."

"Yes. I want to go to Nairobi today and report the find. Show the evidence. Turn the whole dig over to the scientific wallahs.

After discovering the place, I don't want to be accused of messing it up."

"Right. Discover, but do not meddle. Be committed, but not involved."

"Also, of course, I have to report the death of Walter Fletcher to the authorities, get them down here."

"Yes."

"In the meantime, we still have the problem of the police accusing someone innocent of murder."

Fletch looked up at Carr's solidity. "We're not going to report Walter Fletcher was the murderer?"

"Not unless we have to. Why should we? Why totally wreck the name Walter Fletcher? It's a small world."

"You're thinking of me."

"If it looks like they're going to hang the wrong bag, you'll come forward?"

"Of course."

"Then there'd be a reason for coming forward."

"Maybe it will be an unsolved crime. But Dan Dawes — "

"This morning you might write out an eyewitness account, beginning in the men's room at the airport, including the events of this morning. Maybe I'll show it to Dan Dawes."

"Okay."

"If the authorities come even close to indicting someone else for the murder, I'll hand your account in officially. See if they want to bring you back to testify."

"Sounds like the best thing to do. I guess."

"I'll get you some paper and a pen. A spot of tea might go well about now, too."

"Carr? Why are Barbara and I leaving so soon? Why are we leaving tonight?" Across the tent, still standing, ignoring the cut on his arm, Carr looked at Fletch without expression. "I'm thinking about a funeral. My father . . . The excitement of the discovery . . . "

"The air crash will be investigated," Carr said. "The authorities will be here. University people will come to see the ruins. The press. They'll all be here by tonight."

"So what?"

Carr took a step closer to Fletch. Even in that dawn's light, Carr's eyes were clear, blue. Quietly, he said, "Don't you suspect your passports are phonies?"

At Los Angeles airport, looking into her passport, Barbara had said,

Where did this picture of me come from? Fletch had never seen his passport picture before either.

"Well. I know we didn't apply for them ourselves."

Carr nodded.

"I've heard all the news." Wet, bedraggled, Barbara stood inside Fletch's tent.

Propped up on the cot, the kerosene lamp pulled close to him, Fletch was writing out his account of the murder of Louis Ramon and the death of Walter Fletcher in an air crash during a storm.

Before starting, he had showered most of the mud off him in the rain.

My father did not die in childbirth.

Barbara said, "I don't know how I feel about it."

"How you feel?"

"No." She continued to stand a meter away from him.

Sweat, humidity: Fletch was having difficulty keeping the paper dry to write.

"We need to get packed," Fletch said. "We're starting home tonight."

"Once we came here to camp, we never really unpacked. Just underwear."

"I guess we don't need to pack the torn sweaters and cutoff ski pants."

"I'll hang them from the trees. Maybe the monkeys will wear 'em. Suits them."

"Still. We must repack."

"It's not as if I'm overburdened with souvenirs."

"You have some memories. For the long ride."

"I never even sent my mother a postcard."

"You can send her one from home. Where's Carr?"

"In his tent. He's writing something, too."

"His version of events."

"He says he thinks it will clear up enough for us to take off at noon."

Fletch looked out through the tent flap Barbara had left askew. "Can't take off in this rain."

Barbara said: "So I heard."

FORTY-ONE

"Your father was a murderer." Barbara was buckling herself into her airplane seat aboard the midnight flight to London from Nairobi. "Won't your mother love that? Think of all the books she's written looking for the murderer."

Fletch was already buckled into his seat. He sighed.

He said nothing.

He had a long way to go with the other passengers aboard.

He had a long way to go with Barbara.

After they were airborne and the No Smoking sign went off and the stewardesses demonstrated to the passengers what to do if the airplane ditched and the FASTEN SEAT BELT light went off, the voice over the public address system said, "Will passenger Fletcher please identify himself. Mr. I. M. Fletcher?"

Building a nest for herself in her seat, clearly Barbara did not hear the request.

Fletch took a deep breath and closed his eyes. *Don't you suspect your passports are phonies?* More trouble could wait.

The rain had not lightened enough for them to take off from the camp until afternoon. Packing the airplane, Carr made lame jokes about the skis. No one looked down the runway track to where an airplane had crashed that morning, burned itself up; where there was still a corpse.

There was a good-bye scene of mixed emotion. The workmen, including Winston and Raffles, said good-bye individually. Sheila had hugs and kisses for Fletch, Barbara, and Juma. They were all sad to be parting, sad to be standing near a terrible death, yet each quite glad that something sought at great expense had been found, that a historic discovery had been made, and that each had been part of it.

Nor did Fletch look down for the burn hole in the woods as they took off.

He did not put on his new white sneakers, courtesy of the Norfolk Hotel, until they landed at Wilson Airport.

Juma and Carr helped them with their luggage to the International Airport. Juma stood with them while Carr took their return ticket to the airline counter.

The few people who were in the airport at that hour looked curiously at the skis.

Fletch said to Juma: "Nice time."

Juma's head tilted. "Sorry."

"You have seats on tonight's flight." Their tickets and boarding passes were in Carr's hand when he returned. "You have to take your luggage through Customs yourself. Do you have any Kenyan money? You have to turn it in."

Both Barbara and Fletch dug out the few Kenyan shillings they had and handed them to Juma. Laughing, they both said: "No."

Money in hand, Juma bent over laughing.

Carr said, "I'm afraid you'll have to wait a long time. The plane doesn't leave until midnight."

"We'll be all right," Fletch said. "I need to sit down."

"You'll feel all right on the flight?"

"Sure. I need the rest."

"Well." Carr looked around the nearly empty terminal. "There are things I must go do."

Fletch said, "I understand."

"One happy, one sad."

"You'll arrange for a funeral?" Barbara said.

Carr hesitated. "Oh, yes."

Fletch said, "Carr . . . Peter Carr, we thank you — "

"No, no." Turning away, his face reddened, Carr waved down Fletch's speech. "Don't embarrass us."

Barbara said, "Thank you, Peter Carr."

Fletch hugged Juma. "I'll see you on television, kid."

"See you on the funnies pages."

While Barbara hugged Juma, Fletch hugged Carr. Then there was a general shaking of hands all 'round.

" 'Bye," Carr said. "Fletch."

Fletch said to Juma: "Friends?"

"Why not?" Juma asked. "Nice time."

Fletch tilted his head.

The wait at the terminal seemed interminable. Barbara read magazines. Fletch thought over the account of the murder of Louis Ramon and the death of Walter Fletcher he had written and handed Carr.

Slowly it dawned on him that he had another story to write. A story much better than the stories of avalanches, mud slides, major earthquakes, airplane crashes, train wrecks, mass murders, airport bombings Frank Jaffe had requested. He had the story to write of Sheila and

Peter Carr, the story of their historic discovery of the ruins of an ancient Roman city on the east coast of Africa.

After thinking about it, Fletch decided he would not mention to Barbara just yet that he would get a story for the newspaper out of their honeymoon.

Barbara nudged him. "That's you."

"What's me?"

"They just paged you. 'Would passenger I. M. Fletcher please identify himself?' she just said."

"Oh."

Fletch raised his hand. There were people milling about in the aisles.

"Maybe we get a free bottle of champagne," Barbara said. "That would be nice."

"You're always hoping."

"Mr. Fletcher?"

"Yes."

The stewardess handed him a letter.

"Mail delivery in midair?" he asked.

"Someone sent it aboard requesting it be delivered to you after takeoff. Would you like a drink?"

"No, thanks." Opening the envelope, Fletch said to Barbara, "It's from Carr."

"Oh. No champagne."

The letter read:

Dear Irwin:

The plan was that after meeting and greeting you and your bride, the man Walter Fletcher and I were going to take you aside and quietly explain ourselves.

Instead, the man Fletcher understood he was to meet you at International Airport and got himself into his own trouble, as you and I both know.

As you now must realize, the Kenyan government takes their official documents very seriously indeed. With the man Fletcher in jail, I suddenly saw him, and you and Barbara, as loose cannons careening around the deck. Forgive me, but I think you can understand I did not want my particular ship to sink, not at this point in my life.

The facts are these. I was in Kenya at the time English colonists had the choice of either going back to England or of turning their English passports in for Kenyan citizenship. I had flown planes in Chile, Australia, Colombia, then here. Even I had come to the point where I wanted to be a part of somewhere, of Kenya. While in Colombia, I had faked out heavy smuggler types, causing several to be shot, and they had proven slow to forgive. Occasionally, therefore, odd people would appear, looking for me, and I'd have to go hide in the bush until they went away. This was inconvenient. Always when they left they would leave the message that they would keep looking until they found me.

At the same time, Peter Carr had heavy debts he couldn't pay, both in England and France. I never inquired too deeply into the nature of his difficulties, but I believe they were severe.

Peter was English; I, American.

With only a little doctoring, during those days of official confusion, we switched passports, my American for his British, which I turned in for Kenyan. People who subsequently came looking for Walter Fletcher found Carr, and did not shoot him; people who came looking for Peter Carr found me, and left me similarly intact.

Thus we lived peacefully for years.

I realized I was taking a risk in inviting you and your bride here, but one, I thought, we could survive.

I was only half right.

I don't deserve to be reported well to your mother, I suppose. We are grown-up people now. For each other, we can never be children again.

We were children when we married.

There was a storm the night in Montana I took off to fly home, just having had the news of your birth, but I never saw the storm. I landed at a small, closed airport just before dark. See in your mind's eye, if you can, a boy, a teenager, sitting in the cockpit of his airplane at the end of a runway of a small, closed Montana airfield, a blizzard raging a few miles ahead of him, a very young husband who had just been told he was a very, very young father, shivering, feeling, thinking. More than my feet were cold. It was not Josie, my wife, I was rejecting. It was not you, Irwin Maurice, my son, I was rejecting (despite your moniker). I was rejecting myself that night, the idea of myself, as husband and father. That night I knew, as an absolute certainty, that I would be a terrible father, a terrible husband, a total disappointment, that I would cause more pain than we all could stand. There was no doubt in that boy's mind, sitting in the dark, shivering in the cockpit, that you would be better off without me. I could have flown into the side of a mountain that night. I didn't. For us all, I took the next option: disappear, get out of your lives, go have my own accidents without you as victims. Two days later, in British Columbia, I read of my probable demise. I left it at that.

Even so, I know I have caused you both much pain. Through the international brotherhood of flying buddies, I have had occasional reports, photographs of each of you. You've done okay without me; better I think, than you would have done with me. The history of my achieving my present maturity would gray the hair and crack the spine of even the most casual but consistent observer. I've barely survived it myself.

If you cannot report well of me to your mother, someday you might let her know I read her books as love letters I don't deserve.

To you, my son, I offer a simple, sustaining thought: one mellows.

I appreciate your having enough mild curiosity to come see me.

FORTY-TWO

What astounded Fletch was that the letter written to him was signed *Fletch*.

FLETCH AND THE WIDOW BRADLEY

ONE

"Hello," Fletch said. "My name is Armistad."

Behind his desk in his office, the manager of the Park Worth Hotel neither stood nor answered. His eyes telegraphed cold rejection of Fletch's sweater, with no shirt under it, jeans and sneakers. Clearly, in the manager's eyes, Fletch was not up to being a guest in the Park Worth Hotel, or a worthy candidate for a job. Dressed that way, he was not particularly welcome in the hotel lobby.

"Your name is Cavalier?" Fletch asked. A triangular piece of wood on the man's desk said the visage you'd see upon raising your eyes a mite would be that of Jacques Cavalier. Beside the olive wood desk in the managers' office was a large safe, opened, odd stacks of printouts, and a plaster cast of Donatello's *David* perched on a bookshelf full of *National Social Registers*.

The manager twitched his head as if recovering from a flick on the nose. "Yes?"

Fletch sat in one of the two semi-circular backed chairs. He held the wallet in his left hand. "As I said," Fletch said, "my name is Armistad." He pointed with the wallet to the manager's telephone pad. "You might take that down."

"You're not a guest here," the manager said.

"Geoffrey Armistad with a *G*," Fletch said. "One Three Four Nimble Drive, Santa Monica."

He watched carefully while the manager made the note.

"I'm awfully sorry," the manager said, while dotting the *i*'s. "You do come on like a storm, Geoffrey Armistad with a *G*, but we're not short of busboys or bellhops, and, if you want kitchen work, you should apply to Chef."

"James Saint E. Crandall," Fletch said.

"Beg pardon?"

"James Crandall. Found his wallet this morning beside my car. Not the usual wallet." Fletch opened it like a paperback book and indicated the plastic shield over the identification insert. "Name says James Saint E. Crandall. Only that. No address. No credit cards, pictures, etc."

Looking at it, Cavalier said, "It's a passport wallet."

"So it is," said Fletch.

"And you think this Mister — ah — Crandall is a guest of the Park Worth Hotel?"

"Yes and no. In this little pocket is a key." Fletch dug it out with his fingers and held it up. "The key reads Park Worth Hotel, Room 2019."

"Yes," drawled Jacques Cavalier. "You object is a reward."

"My object," said Fletch, "is to return the wallet to its owner."

"That seems simple enough," said the manager. "I'll check and make sure Mister Crandall is registered here. If he is, you may leave the wallet with me, and I'll see that he gets it."

"It does seem simple, doesn't it?" Fletch stared over the manager's head at the wall. "You haven't asked what's in the wallet."

Again Cavalier twitched his head. "A passport?"

Again Fletch opened the wallet. "Ten one thousand dollar bills this side . . . " He fanned the bills on his fingertips. " . . . Fifteen one thousand dollar bills this side."

"Oh, dear." The manager looked at Fletch with surprised respect. "I'm sure Mister Crandall will be very grateful to you."

"You'd think so, wouldn't you?"

"Indeed I would."

"He's not."

"You mean . . . " Cavalier cleared his throat. "He refused to negotiate a reward with you."

Fletch leaned forward and put his elbows on the desk.

"I came into your hotel about forty-five minutes ago," Fletch said. "Called Room 2019. A man answered. I asked him if he was James Saint E. Crandall, and he said he was. I told him I'd found his wallet. He seemed pleased. He asked me to wait in the coffee shop. He'd be down in five minutes. I told him I'm wearing a dark blue sweater. I waited in the coffee shop a half hour. Two cups of coffee. Not bad coffee, by the way."

"Thank you."

"He never showed up. After a half hour, I called his room again. No answer. I went up and knocked on his door. No answer."

"You must have missed him. When people say five minutes . . ."

"When a stranger is waiting to return twenty-five thousand dollars of your money in cash?"

"I don't know."

"Anyway, I checked at your desk. Between the time I first called Crandall and asked at the desk, he had checked out."

"Oh, dear," said the manager. "How very odd."

"Isn't it."

The manager put his hand on the telephone. "I'm calling Mister Smith," said the manager. "He's our hotel detective. We'll see what he can find out."

"Good." Fletch stood up. "While you're doing that, do you mind if I make a phone call? I need to call my boss."

"Of course." The manager indicated another small office. "There's a phone in there."

"Thank you."

"Mister Armistad."

"Yes?"

"Don't you find it amusing our hotel detective's name is Smith?"

Fletch grinned at him.

"People's names frequently amuse me," said Jacques Cavalier.

TWO

"Hello, Jane. Frank wants to talk to me?"

"Who is this?"

"Gone two days and you don't recognize my voice."

"Oh, hullo, Fletch. How are things up north?"

"Real excitin'. Would you believe I was in a place last night that featured a bald nude dancer?"

"Female or male?"

"What's exciting about a naked bald male?"

"I don't see what baldness has to do with it," Jane said.

"Where's Frank?"

"He didn't mention anything to me about wanting to talk to you."

"The message was waiting for me in the portable terminal this morning. *Call Managing Editor Frank Jaffe immediately. Most urgent.*"

"Oh, you know, everything becomes 'most urgent' with him after a few drinks."

"That's why he's a good managing editor."

"I'll see if he remembers why he wanted you," Jane giggled.

On hold, Fletch was obliged to listen to nine bars of *The Blue Danube Waltz*. A telephone innovation. The business side of the newspaper thought it real classy. The reporters thought it for the birds. Maybe it soothes someone calling up to order advertising space, but someone calls newsside with a hot story, like *The State House is burning down* or *The Governor just ran away with the Senator's wife* and he finds himself dancing a four-square in a telephone booth. It's hard to report temporary sensations and minor perfidies after having just heard violins work through *The Theme From Doctor Zhivago*.

"Hello, Fletch, where are you?" growled Frank Jaffe. Years of treating himself to whiskey had seared the managing editor's vocal chords.

"Good morning, esteemed leader. I'm in the accountant's office at the Park Worth Hotel."

"What're you doing there?"

"Filed from here last night. Incredible front-page story on the race track opening a new clubhouse. You mean it wasn't the first thing you read this morning?"

"Oh, yeah. It was on page 39."

"Can't make caviar from pig's feet."

"Jeez, you didn't stay at the Park Worth, did you?"

"No. Just stopped by to give away twenty-five thousand bucks."

"That's good. Only the publisher gets to stay at the Park Worth. Even he doesn't."

"Your message said I should call you. Urgent, you said."

"Oh, yeah."

Fletch waited. Frank Jaffe said nothing.

"Hello, Frank? You want me to pick up another story while I'm up here? What is it?"

Frank exhaled. "I guess the lead of this story is — you're fired."

Fletch said nothing. He inhaled. Then he said, "What else is new? How's the family?"

"Goofed. You goofed, Fletcher. You goofed big."

"How did I do that?"

"God knows. I don't."

"What did I do?"

"You quoted somebody who's been dead two years."

"I did not."

"Tom Bradley."

"Yeah. The Chairman of Wagnall-Phipps."

"Been dead two years."

"That's nuts. First of all, Frank, I didn't quote Bradley directly — I never spoke to him."

"That's a relief."

"I quoted memos from him."

"Recent memos?"

"Recent. Very recent. I dated them in my story."

"Dead men don't send memos, Fletch."

"Who says he's dead?"

"The executive officers of Wagnall-Phipps. The guy's wife. You make the *Tribune* look pretty foolish, Fletch. Unreliable, you know?"

Fletch realized he was sitting in the office chair. He didn't remember sitting down.

"Frank, there's got to be some explanation."

"There is. You took a short-cut. You took a big short-cut, Fletcher. Young guys in the newspaper business sometimes do that. This time you got caught."

"Frank, I quoted recent, dated memos initialed 'T.B.' I had them in my hands."

"Must have been some other 'T.B.' Anyway, you did this sloppy, casual story about Wagnall-Phipps, Incorporated, referring throughout to Tom Bradley as the corporation's top dog, quoting him throughout, and he's been dead two years. Frankly, Fletcher, I find this very embarrassing. How is the public supposed to believe our weather reports if we do a thing like that? I mean I know you're not a business reporter, Fletch. You never should have been assigned this story. But a good reporter should be able to cover anything."

Fletch put the wallet on the desk and rubbed his left hand on his thigh, removing the sweat.

"Let's talk about it as a suspension. Fletch. You've done some good work. You're young yet."

"How long a suspension?"

"Three months?" The managing editor sounded like he was trying the idea out on Fletch.

"Three months. Frank, I can't survive three months. I've got alimony to pay. Car payments. I haven't got a dime."

"Maybe you should go get another job. Maybe suspension isn't such a good idea. I haven't heard from the publisher yet. He probably won't like the idea of just suspending you."

"Jeez, Frank. This is terrible."

"Sure is. Everyone around here is laughing at you. It's going to be hard to live a story like this down."

"Frank. I feel innocent. You know what I mean?"

"Joan of Arc you're not."

"At least give me a chance to check my sources."

"Like who?" Frank Jaffe chuckled. "Saint Peter? You get him on the line, I want to know."

"Okay, Frank. Am I suspended, or fired, or what?"

"Let me try out suspension and see how it flies. The publisher's in Sante Fe with his wife. The financial editor wants your head on a plate. You're probably fired. Call me next week."

"Thanks, Frank."

"Hey, Fletch, want me to send you your paycheck? Janey can stick it in the mail to you."

"No, thanks."

"I just thought coming into the office would be sort of embarrassing for you."

"No, thanks. I'll come in."

"No one ever said you're short of guts, Fletch. Well, if you do come in to the office, wear your football helmet and your steel jock-strap."

THREE

"Wagnall-Phipps. Good morning."

"Mister Charles Blaine, please."

Fletch succeeded in keeping his voice steady. Still in the accounting office of The Park Worth Hotel he had dialed Long-distance Information and then called Wagnall-Phipps using his newspaper's telephone credit card. With his fingers he picked his sweater away from his sweaty skin.

"Mister Blaine's office."

"Is he there?"

"I'm sorry, Mister Blaine has left for the day."

Fletch glanced at his watch. "It's only eleven thirty in the morning."

"I know," the secretary said. "Mister Blaine has the flu."

"It's terribly important I talk with him. This is Jay Russell. I'm on a charity committee with Mister Blaine — the Committee to Preserve Antique Silver Clouds."

There was a long pause. "Silver clouds?" the secretary asked. "How do you preserve them?"

"They're a kind of car," Fletch said. "A kind of Rolls Royce."

"Oh," said the secretary. "For a minute there I thought you were really on to something."

"May I have Mister Blaine's home phone number?"

"No, I'm sorry. That's against company policy."

"This is terribly important."

"So's company policy. At least to me. You wouldn't want to get me fired."

"I wouldn't want to get anybody fired. Believe me. Mister Blaine will be very glad to hear from me. I can assure you there will be no recriminations if you give me his number."

"I know there won't be any recriminations — if I don't give it to you at all."

Fletch hung up.

His hand still on the receiver, Fletch said, "Damn, damn, damn!"

He checked his own billfold. He had two twenties, a ten, a five, and two one dollar bills, plus a blank check. He tried to remember whether he had a balance in his checking account of one hundred and twenty dollars, or if that had been the month before, or even the month before that. Sometime he had had a balance of one hundred and twenty dollars. At most he had less than two hundred dollars in cash, one paycheck due, and no job.

He picked up the phone and dialed a local number. He rang five times.

"Hello?" Moxie's voice said sleepily.

"Are you just waking up?"

"I don't know. What are you doing on the phone? Why aren't you in bed beside me?"

"Always a good question."

"Where are you?"

"Park Worth Hotel."

"Why?"

"I dunno. I went out to the car to check the computer terminal for messages. I found a wallet. That led me to the Park Worth Hotel. It's a long story."

"It's always a long story with you, Fletch."

"Some days you shouldn't get up in the morning."

"Most days you shouldn't get up in the morning. Is something wrong with you, Fletch?"

"Ha — ha," he said cheerily, "what could be wrong?"

"What's wrong?"

"Just one or two minor things. I'll explain later. Do you still want to drive down the coast with me today?"

"Yeah. What time do you have to be back in the office?"

"In about three months."

"What?"

"We've got plenty of time. Why don't you get up, pack, make us a picnic lunch, a picnic supper, a picnic breakfast — "

"Can't we stop along the way?"

"Not to eat."

"All I've got is a jar of peanut butter. I've been letting the supplies run down."

"Bring the whole jar. I'll pick up the bread and orange juice."

"Traveling with you sounds like a real treat."

"Fifth class all the way. I'll be by in about an hour."

"An hour and a half."

"It doesn't take that long to pack a jar of peanut butter."

"It does when I lost the top of the jar six weeks ago."

"How can you lose the top of a peanut butter jar?"

"I *think* I mistook it for an elephant, and you know those elephants —"

"Yeah," said Fletch. "Always getting lost. Don't be too long. Thought we'd stop on the way down, beach I know, for a swim."

"You have that much free time?"

"I have time," said Fletch. "And it's all free."

FOUR

"I'm sorry," Fletch said. "I didn't expect my phone call to take that much time."

Jacques Cavalier was sitting behind his olive wood desk, but in the chair where Fletch had been sitting was a short, middle-aged man with an angelic face. He was looking at Fletch with curiosity, and Cavalier was looking at Fletch with concern.

"Are you all right, Mister Armistad?" Cavalier asked.

"Sure, sure," Fletch said. "Just hot in that other room."

"Mister Armistad," Cavalier insisted. "You're pale. Have you had a shock?"

"Oh, that," Fletch said easily. "My boss just told me that a friend . . . of mine has been fired."

"How very distressing," said Cavalier. "Tell me, Mister Armistad: what do you do for a living?"

"I park cars."

"A humble enough job." Cavalier smiled. "Why was your friend fired?"

"He tried to park two cars in the same space. Almost succeeded. Chuck never did have a very good memory."

"This is Mister Smith, our house detective." Cavalier consulted his note pad. "Mister Geoffrey with a *G* Armistad — our honest friend who parks cars for a living."

"Hiya," said the middle-aged man with the angelic face.

Fletch sat in the free chair.

"I've repeated to Mister Smith your remarkable story, Mister Armistad. He is, you might say, incredulous."

"Lemme see the wallet," Smith said.

Fletch handed it to him. The detective counted the twenty five bills individually.

"Okay." Smith placed the wallet on the desk. "I've checked. A man giving his name as James Saint E. Crandall checked into the hotel at four P.M. three days ago. He checked out this morning just before Jacques called me. Paid cash." Smith read from the itemized bill in his hands. "He had room service for breakfast for one, for both mornings he was here. Yesterday he had a pair of trousers pressed. The night he arrived he had one beer brought to his room about ten-thirty, so we can guess he retired early. He had no other bar-bill or restaurant charges in the hotel. He made six local calls, all in all, and no long-distance calls. He gave as his address 47907 Courier Drive, Wramrud. He put down nothing on the line for Company Name, Business Affiliation."

Fletch had signaled Cavalier for a piece of paper and pen and was writing down the address.

"I've checked his room," Smith continued. "Nothing out of the ordinary. Usual wrinkled sheets and towels."

"He was known to your people at the Reception Desk?"

Smith said, "I asked the cashier, who checked Crandall out, for a description. He said the guy was either fifty and balding or seventy and stooped. I guess two people were checking out at the same time."

"But someone on your Reception Desk knew him."

"Why do you say that?" Smith asked.

"You said Crandall paid cash when he left. Reception desks like to run a credit card when a person checks in — don't they?"

Smith glanced at Cavalier.

"This is a first class hotel, Mister Armistad."

"You don't have first class crooks?"

"We try to bother our guests as little as possible. Of course, sometimes we get stuck . . . " Cavalier raised his hands and shrugged. " . . . but we consider it worth it not to distrust everybody. Our guests trust us; we should trust them."

Fletch asked, "How many people pay their hotel bills in cash?"

"A good many," said Cavalier. "At this hotel. We still have the little old ladies in tennis shoes, you know — and they're not all little old ladies — who do not put themselves in the way of being mugged by either someone in the street, or, a credit card company."

"We have other guests who pay cash, too." Smith chuckled at Crandall. "Every hotel has those — here on private business, we call it."

"Breakfast for one," Fletch said. "Two days running. Doesn't sound like Crandall was sharing his room with anyone."

"Doesn't necessarily mean anything," Smith said. "There are lots of other hours in a day."

"Yeah, but what percentage of your guests pay in cash?"

"About ten percent," said Cavalier.

"More like fifteen," said Smith.

"Mister Smith is obliged to think on the seamier side of things," Cavalier said.

"So there was nothing really unusual about this guest, James Saint E. Crandall."

"Yeah," laughed Smith. "He ducked out on somebody trying to return twenty-five thousand dollars cash to him. That's a new experience for us."

Cavalier had been studying Fletch. "Hope you don't mind my saying, Mister Armistad, but you're not my idea of a parking lot attendant."

"Have you known many parking lot attendants?"

Cavalier smirked. "Not intimately."

Taking the wallet off the desk, Fletch stood up. "Thank you both for your help," he said.

Cavalier asked, "You're taking the wallet?"
"What else?"
"Well, I don't know." Cavalier looked at Smith. "I'm sure I don't know what to do. This isn't a simple matter of Lost and Found. I suppose I had been thinking the next thing we would do would be to notify the police."
"Oh, I'm going to the police," said Fletch.
"Sure," Smith said.
"I came here, didn't I?"
"Yes, you did come here." Cavalier ran his middle finger over his creased brow. "And you did find the money. And not on hotel premises . . . you say."
"Not within twenty blocks of here."
"And the man did run out on you . . . are you sure you called the right room?"
"No," said Fletch. "Everybody gets a wrong number once in a while. But the hotel guest I spoke to didn't seem surprised when I told him he'd lost a wallet."
Fletch put the wallet in the back pocket of his jeans.
"I really don't know," Cavalier said. "I suppose we'll have to notify the police, in any case." He smiled at Fletch. "Just to protect ourselves, you understand."
"A kid walks in with twenty-five thousand dollars," muttered Smith, "and walks out with twenty-five thousand dollars."
"I expect you to call the police," Fletch said. "I gave you my name, didn't I?" He pointed at the pad on Cavalier's desk. "And my address?"
"Yes, you did, Mister Armistad," said Jacques Cavalier. "Indeed you did."

FIVE

"A jar of peanut butter, a loaf of bread, a jug of orange juice, and thou," Fletch said.
Bellies on the sand, head to head, at only a slight angle to each other, they were still wet from their swim. They were alone in the cove.
"Pretty romantic," said Moxie.
"Pretty romantic."

"Not very." The late afternoon sun sparkled in the dots of salt water on her arms, her back, her legs. "Peanut butter, bread and orange juice."

"And thou."

"And wow. Not chopped carrots and strained beans, but it still doesn't cut the mustard romantically, Fletch." Moxie rose up enough to brush sand off her bare breast, then settled her cheek against her forearm and sighed. "Not very romantic days, these."

"You don't think so?"

"Romance is gone from life. A thing of the past."

"Sob."

"Gone with crinolines and cramps."

"I thought I was pretty romantic."

"Sure. Pick me up at one thirty, ignore the reservation for two I made at the Café Mondrian, drive like a bobsled team captain to this abandoned beach down here, passing up several good places to stop for lunch — "

"You hungry?"

" — tumble me around in the surf like a — like a . . ."

"Like a what?"

"Like an equal." She wriggled forward on her elbows and kissed him on the cheek. "Do it in the sand without even a blanket, a towel, anything."

"Fair's fair. We did it on our sides."

"Not very romantic." Moxie blew in his face.

"Romance was an idea created by the manufacturers of wine and candlesticks."

"And smelling salts."

She licked his cheek.

"What could be more romantic than peanut butter and orange juice? That's protein and Vitamin C you're scoffing at, girl. Very energizing foodstuffs, you know."

"You getting energetic again, Fletcher?"

"Sure," he said. "It's been a whole five minutes."

They had examined the hillsides above them the first time. There was only one house overlooking the cove, and that was pretty far back. Its main plate-glass window looked blind.

They were sitting on the sand, washing peanut butter sandwiches down with orange juice.

"So?" Moxie said.

"So I took the twenty-five thousand dollars . . . " He took the orange juice carton from her and drank. "What do you want to know?"

"Last night, if I remember correctly, you were full of self-importance and duty and went on and on about getting back to the newspaper today in time to work the night shift and if I wanted a ride with you I had to be up and packed and ready to go before I woke up . . ."

"Self-importance?"

"Damned near pomposity."

"You're not famous for getting up early in the morning, Moxie."

"I'm not famous for anything. Yet. Sleeping late was the first thing I learned in Drama School."

"Really?"

"Yeah. All the classes were in the afternoon."

"You theater people have to be different."

"I don't know what time the night shift on a newspaper starts, Fletch, but that red frog crapping on the ocean over there is the setting sun. And I figure we're a good seven hours drive from your precious newspaper."

"I'm a changed man."

"What changed you?"

"I got fired."

Fletch watched the shallow crease in her stomach breathe in and out a few times. She said, "Oh." Then she said, "Hey." She resumed chewing. "You liked that job."

"It gave paychecks, too."

"You can get a job on another newspaper. Can't you?"

"I really doubt it."

"What happened?"

"Long story. Sort of complicated."

"Make it simple. If I don't understand first time 'round, I can ask questions. Right?"

"Well, I was assigned to do an unimportant story on an unimportant business company and I guess I got sold a big, fat lie." Fletch spoke rapidly. "My main source was a guy named Blaine. Charles Blaine. Vice-president and treasurer. He gave me a file of memos back and forth between him and the Chairman of the company, a guy named Tom Bradley, and said I could quote from them. So I did."

"So what went wrong?"

"Tom Bradley died two years ago."

"Died?"

"Died."

"Died dead?"

"Deader than romance."

"You quoted a dead man?"

"Very accurately."

Moxie giggled. "Jeez, that's pretty good, Fletch."

"I could have done worse," Fletch said. "I suppose I could have quoted somebody who'd never existed."

"I'm sorry." Moxie rubbed her nose.

"What for?"

"For laughing."

"It's funny. Wake me in the morning."

"Were these recent memos you quoted? They couldn't have been."

"They were recently dated memos. I put their dates in the story I wrote."

"I don't get it."

"That makes at least two of us."

Her eyes went back and forth over the sea. They were purple flecked with yellow in the setting sun. "Was it some kind of a mean joke?"

"Pretty mean. I guess someone meant to do mischief."

"Who? Why?"

"Blaine, I guess. He had to know what he was doing, giving me memos from a dead man. Maybe he's crazy."

"Have you gone back to him? Tried to get in touch with him?"

"Tried this morning. He'd left his office. Sick with the flu."

"No." Moxie shook her head. "That's too crazy. No one would do a thing like that. As a joke."

"Not a joke," Fletch said. "Maybe you've heard that some American businesses are waging a clever campaign to get back at the press. Make the newspapers and television look silly."

"How would I have heard that?"

"It's a growing thing. They say there are too many liberals in the press. Anti-business liberals."

"Are there?"

"Probably. More specifically, the *News-Trib* worked this particular corporation, Wagnall-Phipps, over pretty good two or three years ago."

"For what?"

"Influence buying. Wining and dining congressmen, mayors and others on the public payroll in a position to buy shovels and toothpicks from Wagnall-Phipps."

"Did you write those stories?"

"I wasn't even working for the *News-Trib* then. I was in Chicago."

"You're the fall guy."

"My own fault. I didn't care about this Wagnall-Phipps story. I was working on that football story, you know, at the same time. I cared a lot more about that story. I scanned the clips on Wagnall-Phipps, saw the key question was whether the corporation still owned that big ski house in Aspen they used to lend to congressmen and their families, and went off to interview Blaine. I remember I had a hard time staying awake listening to him. He finally put me in an office by myself and let me take notes from this sheaf of memos."

"So you don't have the memos, or copies of the memos yourself."

"No. I don't. Simple, stupid, unimportant story I didn't even think the newspaper would print, it was so boring. Who cares about Wagnall-Phipps?"

"I guess Wagnall-Phipps does."

"I was only assigned the story 'cause the reporter originally assigned to it, Tom Jeffries, broke his back hang-gliding."

"That's terrible."

"That is terrible. I'm no business writer. Shit. I don't even know how to read stock tables. I'd never heard of Wagnall-Phipps before."

"But why dump on you?"

"Nothing personal. They weren't dumping on me. They were making the newspaper look silly. They did a pretty good job."

"They took advantage of your ignorance."

"Sure. Along comes bushy-tailed Peter Rabbit with his mouth open and they feed him loaded carrots. They refer to the Chairman of their board, Thomas Bradley, show me memos from him, and I write down, *In a memo dated April 16, Chairman of the Board, Thomas Bradley, directed etc., etc.* I mean, wouldn't you believe the Vice-president and treasurer of a corporation regarding who was the Chairman of the company?"

Moxie shook her head. "Poor Peter Rabbit."

"Poor Peter Rabbit nothin'. He's a dope."

"So you're fired."

"Well, the managing editor is breaking it to me gently. He's talking about a three-months suspension, but that's only so he can insist later he tried to save my job."

"No chance?"

"I wouldn't hire me. Would you?"

"More orange juice? There's another quart."

"We'll need it in the morning."

"So what were you doing this morning at the Park Worth Hotel?"

"Oh, that's another story. We've got to stop by and see a guy about it in Wramrud tomorrow. Found his wallet."

"Fletch, I'm cold. If you glance westward, you'll notice even the sun has found a better place to go."

Fletch said, "I'll build a fire."

She stared at him. "You mean to spend the night here?"

"Sure. Romantic."

"On the beach?"

"How much money you got on you, Moxie?"

"I don't know. Maybe fifty dollars."

"I thought so. You begin rehearsing for the new play Monday. When do you get your first paycheck?"

"End of next week."

"So you've got fifty bucks to live off for a week and I've got about the same amount to live off for the rest of my life. Dig?"

"Credit cards, Fletch. You used one last night. At dinner. Even I've got a credit card."

"I've got a sleeping bag in the car."

"You're getting me to spend the night on the beach with you."

"I told you. I'm very romantic." Standing, Fletch brushed the sand off his skin.

"And I told you romance is dead."

"That's just wishful thinking," Fletch said. "I'll get the sleeping bag."

SIX

"Trying to find my uncle," Fletch said.

It had taken the creaky old policeman a long moment to stand up from his padded swivel chair and walk across the main room of the Wramrud Police Station to the counter. There was a hearing aid in his left ear.

"His name is James Crandall." Fletch spoke slowly and distinctly.

"Live here in town?"

"Supposed to."

"What do you mean 'supposed to'? Nobody's 'supposed to' live anywhere. Haven't you heard this is a free country?"

"My mother gave me this address." Fletch handed the policeman the piece of note paper he'd had from Jacques Cavalier's desk.

"I can't find Courier Drive," Fletch said.

"47907 Courier Drive, Wramrud," the old policeman read aloud.

"The man in the drugstore doesn't seem to know where it is."

The policeman looked at Fletch sharply. "Bob doesn't know where it is?"

"I guess not."

"This Crandall fellow. He your mother's brother?"

"Yes," said Fletch.

"You know you have sand on your face?"

Fletch brushed his face with his hand.

"Why do you have sand on your face?"

Fletch shrugged. "I was playing in a sandbox."

"You ought to shave before you see your uncle."

"Yeah. I guess I should."

The policeman looked again at the piece of paper in his hand. "Bob don't know where Courier Drive, Wramrud, is because there is no Courier Drive, Wramrud."

"There isn't?"

"You mother lie to you often, son?"

"First time ever."

"Far as you know. Nope. No Courier Drive. Fact is, we don't have anything called a Drive around here. Lots of roads and streets but nothing as fancy as a Drive."

"You have any street like Courier?"

"How do we know?"

"I mean, a street that sounds like Courier, or might look like Courier written out."

The man's rheumy eyes gazed through the plate glass window. "Century Street. Cold Water Road. We don't have any address numbers that run that high, either. Forty-seven thousand something. We only got nineteen hundred households this whole town."

"You know a man named Crandall?"

"You mean, your uncle?"

"Yes."

"Nope. Man named Cranshaw, not your uncle."

Fletch smiled. "How do you know?"

" 'Cause I'm Cranshaw and my sister don't lie."

"Okay," Fletch said. "I give up. You've never heard of a man named Crandall in this town."

"Nope. And we're the only town named Wramrud I ever heard of, too. You ever heard of another town named Wramrud?"

"No."

The policeman's eyes were inspecting Fletch's neck and sweater. "You got sand all over you, boy. You want a shower?"

"What?"

"You want to take a shower? Shave?"

"Where?"

"Back in the lock-ups. I can give you a fresh razor."

"Mighty nice of you."

"Well, seems to me you have a long way to go to find your uncle." The policeman lifted a section of the counter to let Fletch through. "Any boy whose mother tells whoppers like yours — ain't no tellin' where you might end up."

Fletch followed the policeman toward the door to the jail cells.

"Why do you suppose your mother would tell you a lie like that?" the old policeman asked. "Do you suppose you have an uncle at all? 'pect she told you he's rich . . ."

"Your hair is wet," Moxie said. She was waiting by the car. "And you shaved."

"I got cleaned up."

"Where?"

"In the jailhouse. Want a shower? Nice old policeman."

"How'd it smell?"

"Terrible."

"No, thanks. I'd rather shower at your apartment."

Fletch started the car and took the road back toward the highway. "There is no James Saint E. Crandall in Wramrud. Never has been."

Moxie rubbed her back against the back of the car seat and then scratched her elbow. "I am itchy. We are going straight to your apartment, aren't we?"

"No."

"Oh, lord. Fletch, I can understand your natural reluctance to get back to the city — we can hear the general laughter from here — but I do want a proper meal and a proper shower."

"Thought we'd stop at Frank Jaffe's house first."

"Who's he? Does he exist, or did he die?"

"He's my managing editor. My ex-managing editor."

"You think you can find his house?"

"I know where he lives. We go right by it."

"Boy, Fletch. Someone told me you're a great reporter. Can't even find a person in a little town like Wramrud, or wherever we just were."

"Who told you I'm a great reporter?"

"You did."

Coming onto the freeway, Fletch stepped on the accelerator, hard. "Guess I was wrong."

SEVEN

"My God." Moxie stood on the front walk looking at the lit facade of the house. It was an English Tudor-styled house with established shrubs. "This is where the managing editor of the *News-Tribune* lives?"

"Yeah."

"I'll bet those wooden beams are fake."

Fletch was ringing the doorbell.

"Moxie? Where are you going?"

Clara Snow opened the door. She had a half-empty martini glass in her hand.

"Fletch!"

"Evening, Clara. Didn't expect to find you here."

Clara did not smile. "Didn't know you were expected, Fletcher."

"You know, when Frank gives an at-home party for his employees —"

"This is not an at-home party."

"Well, Frank must be home, and you're at home with him, and you are an employee . . ."

"Come in, Fletch."

"Wait a minute. I have a friend."

Fletch looked along the side of the house, to the right, where Moxie was coming out of the established shrubbery.

"How do you do?" she said, shaking hands with Clara. "So nice to meet you, Mrs. Jaffe."

"This isn't Mrs. Jaffe," said Fletch.

Closing the door behind them, Clara said, "Fletch, you've got some balls."

"I've got Moxie," Fletch said.

Frank was in the livingroom, dressed in a ski sweater. He was putting another log on the fire. Fletch could feel the air-conditioning in the house was on.

"Evening, Frank," he said.

Frank looked over his glasses at Fletch. "You're fired, Fletcher. If you weren't before, you certainly are now."

"Why?"

"Because it's Friday night and this is my home and fired employees aren't supposed to come to their boss's home uninvited on Friday nights. Or ever. It just isn't polite."

"Even if I'm in pursuit of a story?"

"What story?"

"That's what you're going to tell me."

Frank was staring at Moxie. "You're a beautiful girl," he said.

"Thank you, sir," Moxie said prettily.

"Really beautiful."

Clara Snow moved around the coffee table and sat on the divan.

"This is Moxie Mooney," Fletch said. "She's an actress. Starting rehearsals Monday for a play at the Colloquial Theater."

"As long as you're here," Frank said "you might as well have a drink. Least I haven't lost my manners."

"Thanks, Frank. Where's Betty?"

Standing over the bar table, pouring two more martinis and freshening his own glass, Frank said, "My wife is in San Francisco. For a weekend of shopping and seeing her brother's family. Any other questions, Fletch?"

"Sure." Fletch looked at Clara Snow.

Frank said, "Clara is here for dinner with me and to talk over some editorial matters."

"Talking over editorial matters with a state house reporter. I see."

Clara had been cooking editor until letters of complaint had become overwhelming. Her recipes were making people sick. The Clara Snow Flu was a city room joke. Reporters with heavy hangovers would call up to say they were too sick to work because they had eaten something Clara Snow had recommended. Everyone had been perplexed as to how and why Clara had been transferred from that job to the highly prestigious job of state house reporter.

"Political matters," Frank said. "How do you want a drink, Fletcher, or do you want me to kick your ass through the front door without opening it?"

Fletch sat on the divan facing Clara. "Sure, Frank. I like martinis. Sorry to interrupt your meeting with Clara."

Frank handed Moxie a martini and put Fletch's on the coffee table. "Sit down, sit down," he said to Moxie. "Might as well make yourself at home. Fletch has."

Moxie sat beside Fletch, and Frank sat in a chair with his fresh drink.

"What's the name of the play you're in?" Frank asked Moxie.

"*In Love,* sort of a romantic comedy."

"Didn't know they produced romantic comedies anymore," Frank said. "I'd like to see one."

"You're the ingenue?" Clara asked. At thirty, Clara had blossomed into full womanhood.

"Yes," Moxie answered, "It's a comedy about rape."

"Hilarious," Clara said, "I'm sure."

"Not rape, really," said Moxie. "You see, it's about this young girl who was very strictly brought up and every time her young husband touches her, she thinks she's being raped. So every time he tries to make love to her, she has him arrested. You see?"

"Could be amusing, I suppose," Frank Jaffe said.

"But husbands can rape wives," Fletch said.

"The funny thing is," said Moxie, looking into her martinti glass, "the young couple really do love each other. They're just terribly confused, you know, regarding their rights to each other, and themselves."

"A lawyer in every bedroom," Frank said. "That's what we need."

"Wagnall-Phipps," Fletch said.

Frank looked at him. "What?"

"Can't say you're not talking business tonight, Frank. We interrupted a business meeting between you and Clara."

"I'm willing to talk newspaper business anytime," Frank said. "I'm just not sure how willing I am to talk over Wagnall-Phipps with you. A goof's a goof, Fletch. Hard to take, but there you are."

"A story's a story, Frank."

"Don't get you."

"The Vice-president and treasurer of Wagnall-Phipps refers to the chairman of his company as Thomas Bradley, shows me memos from him — recent memos — and someone else tells you that Thomas Bradley is dead. I need some facts."

"You needed some facts before you wrote the story," Clara said.

"Okay." Frank looked from one employee to the other. "I read the early edition here at my breakfast table per usual. I only scanned your story, wondering who in heck had assigned you to a business news story. You with your cut-off blue jeans and bare feet — "

"Barefoot boy with cheek," Clara said softly.

"You've never struck me as a business news writer," Frank said, smiling at Fletch.

"Tom Jeffries got hurt hang-gliding."

"I know. So I go into the office and there's a call waiting for me from an Enid Bradley. She says she's the chairperson of Wagnall-Phipps and has been since her husband died. While I'm listening to her mild voice on the phone, I open the newspaper to your story, scan it again and see that you've quoted her husband, Thomas Bradley, throughout. Recent quotes."

"From memos," Fletch said.

"You have copies of any of those memos?" Frank asked.

"No."

"So I called Jack Carradine, the business news editor, who had just returned from a trip to New York — "

"I know Jack's the business news editor," Fletch said.

" — and he doesn't seem sure whether Bradley's dead or alive. Apparently Wagnall-Phipps isn't that important a company. He calls the president of Wagnall-Phipps and is told the same thing — Bradley's dead. Didn't I tell you all this on the phone?"

"No. You didn't tell me Mrs. Bradley herself called you, or that she is now chairperson of Wagnall-Phipps, and you said you had confirmation from 'executive officers' of Wagnall-Phipps, not just one guy — the president."

Clara sighed and looked sideways at Frank.

Frank said, "Dead's dead."

Moxie said, 'It's none of my business, of course, but I think this Wagnall-Phipps company played a trick on Fletch. The *News-Tribune* did an exposé on Wagnall-Phipps a couple of years ago — "

"People play tricks on reporters all the time," Frank said. "No one ever tells the exact truth. People always say to a reporter what serves their own interest best. Good reporters know this and just don't get caught."

"Fletch got caught," said Clara. "And that's the end of the story."

"Frank, will you keep me on salary until I get this thing figured out?"

"What's to figure?" asked Frank. "Mrs. Phipps — I mean, Mrs. Bradley said she didn't want her children reading in the newspaper things her husband recently said. Can you blame her? She said they're just getting over the death now."

Fletch shook his head. "There's something wrong, Frank."

"Sure there is." Clara walked to the bar to pour herself a new drink. "Irwin Maurice Fletcher and his sloppy reporting. That's what's wrong."

Frank leaned forward, elbow on his knees. "Look, Fletch. Carradine called Mrs. Wagnall — I mean, Mrs. Bradley back and made all smooth. He even went to the house last night and spent an hour talking to the Bradley kids, saying newspapers sometimes make mistakes. Nobody's suing us. But the story that we quoted a dead man is all over the country now, and it hurts, Fletch. It hurts the paper. Our publisher picked it up out in Santa Fe and called me. I was going to wait until he got back."

"What'd he say?" asked Fletch.

Frank settled back in his chair. "I asked for a suspension. Honest, I did, Fletch."

"And he said no?"

"What do you think?"

"He said no." Fletch stood up.

"You didn't drink your drink," Frank said.

"I drank mine," Moxie said.

Frank smiled at her. "Anything as gorgeous as you are shouldn't drink."

Clara turned slowly from the bar and stared at him.

"Just one more question, Frank," Fletch said.

"What?"

"Is Clara cooking dinner for you?"

"Yes. Why?"

"I'll call the office," Fletch said, "and tell Janey you won't be in Monday."

EIGHT

"You supposed to be here?" The *News-Tribune*'s assistant librarian stood in the doorway glaring at Fletch.

It was a quarter to eight Saturday morning.

Looking up from the microfilm console, Fletch said, "I can be."

"I heard this newspaper no longer requires your services."

"I heard that, too."

"So you should no longer have access to this newspaper's excellent services. Such as our microfilm library."

Fletch turned the console off and gathered up his note papers. "Come on, Jack. Gimme a break."

"Wait a minute." The barrel-chested man stepped in front of Fletch and held out his hand. "Let me see what you're takin' out of here."

"Just some notes."

"On what? Come on, I want to see."

Fletch handed Jack his notes and waited while he scanned them.

"James Saint Edward Crandall. Address Newtowne. Who's he?"

"I don't know."

Jack's eyes flickered high-beam at Fletch.

"Charles Blaine. Address Bel Monte. You quoted him in that marvelous story of yours Wednesday. Everyone around here has given that story another real close read — as you might expect."

"I expect."

"Thomas Bradley. Chairman of the Board, Wagnall-Phipps. Married Enid Riordan. Two children. Address Southworth. You quoted him in that story too, didn't you?" He grinned at Fletch. "You don't give up easy, do you?"

"Should I?"

Jack handed Fletch back his notes. "I guess everyone has a right to try to save his own ass — even when his ass has already been whipped."

"May I use your phone, Jack?"

"Get out of here now and I won't have you arrested for trespassing."

"Okay, okay." At the door, Fletch turned and said, "Jack?"

"I'm still seeing you. Trespasser."

"Want to know something interesting?"

"Yeah. Who's going to win the third race at Hialeah this afternoon? Tell me so I can make points with Osborne. Knowing you you'll probably say Trigger."

"No obit."

"Trigger had a nice obit. Just before Roy Rogers had him stuffed."

"Yeah." Fletch pointed to the console. "But there is no obit for Tom Bradley in there."

"Lots of people die we don't print the obit. We're not properly notified. Bradley was no captain of American industry."

"I just find it interesting."

"Write a nice story about how they stuffed Tom Bradley. Only get the competition to print it this time, willya, Fletch?"

Standing over his own desk in the city room, Fletch dialed his own home number. The phone rang seven times.

Nearby, drinking coffee, sat four reporters and one photographer. They were gathered around Al's desk. Leaning back in his chair, Al had his feet on his desk. Al was a middle-aged reporter who complained of feet trouble and back problems and always managed to be the last one sent out on assignment. Mostly he held court, passed rumor and gossip in the city room.

They had grinned broadly at each other when Fletch had entered the city room from the library.

"Mornin', Irwin," Al sang to Fletch. "Don't remember ever seeing you here this early on a Saturday morning before. What happened? You get thrown out of bed, too?"

"Telephone," Moxie said. "I mean, hello?"

"Good morning, sunshine," Fletch turned his back on the reporters.

"Fletch? Why are you always waking me up in the morning?"

"Because that's the time of day people get up. Bounce out of bed. Do their breathing exercises."

"I didn't sleep well last night."

"You were asleep when I left."

Moxie yawned into the phone. "I lay awake a long time after you went to sleep. Thinking about the play. Watching you sleep. Thinking about how much trouble you're in. I mean, Fletch, you're ruined."

"Down but not out, old thing."

"Those people last night, your managing editor, Frank, and that dreadful woman, what's her name — "

"Clara Snow."

"They wouldn't have let you into the house if I hadn't been there. Frank would have thrown you through the door and that Clara person would have stomped on your head with a high-heeled shoe."

"If that's a question, the answer is: yes — I was using you. Do you object?"

" 'Course not."

"Frank has an eye for beauty. His left one, I think."

"By the way, I was right."

" 'Bout what?"

"You know those wooden beams on the outside of his house? They're plastic."

"No! And here he's supposed to be some kind of a tastemaker. Stylesetter. Trendspotter. Managing editor."

"Some kind of synthetic. A hollow synthetic at that. I knocked against them."

"You have the makings of a reporter, Moxie. Wish I had."

"Courage, Fletch."

"Listen, I have to do a lot of driving around today. Want to come?"

"Where?"

"No place interesting. The suburbs. Got to see people."

"Just spent two days in a car with you. Two days in a car and one night on a beach. Six peanut butter sandwiches, three quarts of orange juice, and home to your apartment for wet spaghetti made wetter by a can of tomato soup."

"Candlelit dinner."

"Yeah. Thanks for dragging out your hurricane lamp. Real romantic. Like being on a sinking ship. At least I got a shower Had a hell of a time not scratching myself at Frank's house."

"You did very well. Hardly twitched."

"Wasn't going to scratch in front of that Clara person."

"You don't want to come with me?"

"No. I'll go back to sleep for another few minutes. Should study the playscript."

"I might not be back until late."

"I'll take a walk, if I get bored."

"Right. Give the neighborhood a treat. See you."

"Hey. Is there any food in this house?"

"See you."

Fletch turned around and found the group of reporters watching him. Naturally, they had been trying to listen.

"Just trying to locate a *hara-kiri* sword," Fletch said, "With a booklet of instructions as to how to use it."

"Hey, Fletch?" Al drawled.

"Yes, Al?"

"Do me a favor, Fletch?"

"Sure, Al. Anything, for you. Want me to use my influence with Frank? Get you a raise?"

"I wish you'd interview someone for me." Al winked at the men sitting around his desk.

"Sure, Al. Who?"

"Dwight Eisenhower. I think ol' Ike still might have a few things to say."

"Sure, Al. I'll do it before lunch."

"Napoleon?" the photgrapher asked.

"Did him last month," Fletch said. "Thanks for reading the *News-Tribune*."

"Did you get any good hard quotes out of Napoleon?" Al asked.

"He really opened up on Josephine."

"Yeah? What did he say about Josephine?"

"Said she wore hair curlers in bed. That's why he spent so much time in the field."

"Really, Fletch," said a reporter named Terry. "You could get a job with one of those spooky magazines. You know? 'What Abraham Lincoln Said To Me.' That sort of thing."

"Or maybe a morticians' trade paper," the photographer said. "You could be their Consumer Affairs Columnist."

"Keep laughin', guys."

"Or you could quote Thomas Bradley again," said an old reporter, who was not smiling.

Fletch glanced at the big wall closk. "Guess I better hurry up, if I'm going to make that interview with *The New York Times*. Shouldn't keep 'em waiting too long. They want a new managing editor, you know."

"Gee, no, Fletch. We didn't hear that," said the photographer.

Terry said, "Ernie Pyle should get the job. Maybe H.L. Mencken."

Al called after Fletch, as Fletch was leaving the city room. "Aren't you cleaning out your desk?"

"Hell, no," Fletch said. "I'll be back."

"Yeah," the unsmiling reporter said. "Maybe in your next life."

NINE

"God, I hate this," Tom Jeffries said. On a high metal bed on wheels, on which he was lying on his stomach in the tiny patio behind his house, he was dressed only in shorts and, from his waist to his head, plaster casts and metal braces. His friend, Tina, was sitting on a stool spooning scrambled egg into his mouth. She was dressed in a light, loose dress. "Everything you eat sticks in your throat. Give me more orange juice, will you, Tina?"

She held a glass of orange juice up to his face and placed the flexible straw in his mouth.

"Hang-gliding sure looks pretty," Fletch said. He was sitting on the picnic table, his bare feet on the bench.

"It's a pretty thing to do," Tom said. "It feels pretty. It is pretty. Soar like a bird."

"Birds get broken backs very often?" Fletch asked.

"Sometimes you land pretty hard," Tina said. "This was to be Tom's last flight before we get married next Saturday."

"Yeah," Tom said. "I was going to give it up because Tina wanted me to. She said I might get hurt. Shows you what she knows." Tom grinned at her.

"Wedding put off?" Fletch asked.

"No," Tom said. "Instead of wearing a tuxedo Tina's going to put a big red bow ribbon on my ass."

"That'll be nice," Fletch said. "At least she'll know what she's marrying. How long you going to be wrapped up like that, in plaster and aluminum?"

"Weeks," Tom groaned. "Months."

"We'll be married a long time," Tina said quietly. "A few months won't matter."

She had offered Fletch breakfast, and he was hungry, but he had refused. He figured she had enough to do taking care of Tom.

"You heard what I did?" Fletch asked.

"Yeah," Tom said. "Jack Carradine called me. At first I thought he was telling me a funny story. Then I realized he doesn't think it's even slightly funny. Somebody ran your piece on Wagnall-Phipps on his pages while he was out of town. You quoted a dead man, Fletch."

"And got fired."

"And got fired. Makes me look all the better." Tom smiled at Fletch. "Which, under the circumstances, I don't mind at all. The only job security I've got. You screwed up royally on a story originally assigned to me."

"Tom, can you tell me any reason why Charles Blaine should show me, and let me quote from, recent memos he said were from Thomas Bradley?"

"Sure," Tom said. "He's a creep. They're all creeps at Wagnall-Phipps. Tom Bradley was a creep."

"In what way?"

"I don't know. Bradley lived way back, down deep inside himself — somewhere near his lower spine. He never seemed very real to me, if you know what I mean. Every word, gesture seemed calculated. Very self-protective. Always gave you the feeling he was hiding something — which is why we started that investigation into the financial dealings of Wagnall-Phipps a couple of years ago. Creepy. Made us suspicious. Sure enough, there he was, doing kick-backs, pay-offs, running the ski house in Aspen neither he nor any of the other executives, employees of Wagnall-Phipps ever used. He was his own worst enemy."

"Want some coffee, Tom?" Tina asked.

"Luke-warm decaffeinated coffee through a glass straw," Tom said. "No, thanks."

"You, Fletch?"

"No thank you kindly, Tina."

"Then I'll go wash up the breakfast dishes."

She carried the dirty plates and cups into the house.

Fletch asked, "Bradley never used the Aspen ski house himself?"

"Naw. Wasn't much of an athlete."

"How do you know?"

"We checked pretty thoroughly on who was using that ski house and who wasn't. Just politicians and purchasing agents. Bradley never went there. He never took his kids there. Sometimes his sales manager would go and play host for a drinking weekend. If you ski and have a ski house available, you use it, right?"

"I guess so."

"Bradley's thing was making mosaics, you know? Putting together mosaics with tiny bits of colored tile. Sort of pretty. He had some he had made in his office."

"How did he get to be chairman of something called Wagnall-Phipps? Family?"

"Naw. Wagnall-Phipps was a defunct supply company. Probably they'd played the game honestly and gone broke. Bradley bought it for its debts. Doubt he put very much cash into it. Then he sold off the stock from the warehouses. I'm sure he put the price of everything up, but he made sure whoever bought from him got a kick-back, something with which to line his own pocket. So he had much more cash than he had put into the company, bought more supplies, more warehouses — he was off and running."

"When was this?"

"Oh — twenty years ago I'd guess. Then, over the years, when one of the companies that supplied him got into financial difficulty, he'd buy all of it, or part of it. So now Wagnall-Phipps is a holding company owning lots of unrelated little companies manufacturing things like rubbish barrels and sidewalk brooms and nails — stuff like that. Nobody ever said he wasn't smart. And, of course, it's still a general supply company. You should know all this, Fletch. You did a story on the company last week. Remember?"

"Will I ever forget?"

"Blaine is sort of a turkey. I've talked with him. Always seems sort of confused, lost. Treasurer of the company. You know, one of those guys who wants to do his job nine-to-five and go home. Corcoran's all right. At least he looks you in the eye and talks straight at you."

"Alexander Corcoran, president."

"Good for you, Fletch. Did you talk to him?"

"No. Blaine said he was at a golf tournament somewhere."

"So Blaine was the only person you talked to?"

" 'Fraid so."

"Gee, Fletch. You never do any story with only one source."

"Tell me."

"Sorry, Fletch. You don't need me hitting you over the head, too. Some time I'll tell you about some of the mistakes I've made."

"As far as I knew I was doing a financial update on a little company the *News-Tribune* had already raked over the coals. Why should I talk to anyone other than the Vice-president and treasurer? I knew all the facts and figures he'd give me had to be on file somewhere — State Bureau of Corporations, or something. I felt safe. Why would he lie to me?"

"White people lie," Tom Jeffries said. "Black people do, too."

"Jeez, I don't understand this. Tom, had anyone ever told you Thomas Bradley was dead?"

"I don't know. I don't remember. I think if anyone had ever mentioned it to me I would have considered it with complete indifference. I mean, the company employs two, three thousand people at most. It's not a publicly held company. Wagnall-Phipps is so-what's-ville. The only reason we did that exposé on it a couple of years ago — whenever we did it — was to show that it's not just the giant corporations that spread the loot around illegally."

"So if Wagnall-Phipps isn't a public company, who owns it?"

"I think it's entirely owned by Bradley. Bradley and his wife. Corcoran might have held some of the stock, but I doubt it. Wagnall-Phipps wasn't that sort of a company, you know? I never had much of a sense of family, we're-all-in-this-together kind of feeling you get from some small companies. Bradley was too laid back for that. Too much his own man. And Corcoran — call him president if you like — he was really sales manager. He didn't run the company at all. Bradley did — as chairman. I think he gave Corcoran the title of president so he'd be more effective as sales manager."

"What about the rest of Bradley's life?"

"What do you mean?"

"I mean, how could he die and nobody notice?"

"Lots of people do."

"Wasn't he important to anybody?"

"His wife. His kids. His company. Why should anyone else care?"

"Charities. Clubs. I mean you go hang-gliding, Tom."

"Used to go."

"Used to. Didn't Bradley play golf? Tennis? You said he wasn't athletic."

"Well, I don't know, but he looked soft to me. Not like anyone who jogged, or anything. Maybe he wasn't well."

"Politics. Didn't he have any life other than the company?"

"I didn't know him that well. I'd see him in his office. Very quiet spoken. He made those mosaics I told you about. They were nice, but I don't suppose they excited too many people. I don't know what you want, Fletch."

"I'm trying to get a handle on this guy."

"Try the cemetery."

"Very funny. I want to know why Blaine referred to him as alive when he's dead."

"Ask Blaine."

"I'm going to."

"Listen, Fletch, screwing the press isn't exactly a new game. Purposely feeding us false information so they can deny it later and make us look bad? People do it all the time. You know that."

"Talking about a dead man as being alive?"

"It's a weird one," Tom said.

"There were kids involved. Bradley's kids. People say to them 'I saw your Daddy's name in the newspapers the other day. What a fine man he must be!' Shit, Tom, that's cruel."

"That's sick."

"Sick and cruel. So why would anyone do it?"

"Go ask the guy who did it."

"Yeah," Fletch jumped off the table. "Have a happy wedding."

"I will," Tom said. "I told Tina she'll always be able to say I took this marriage lying down."

"Anything you need before I go?"

"Yeah. Tell Tina I need her black hands out here spongin' me off. I'm gettin' sweaty."

TEN

James Saint E. Crandall was seventy and stooped.

He stood on the porch of his shabby house in Newtowne, hands in the pockets of his dark green, baggy work pants. His eyes had not left Fletch's face since Fletch had driven onto the dirt driveway.

"Morning." Fletch smiled as he approached the steps to the porch.

"Don't want any," Crandall said.

"Any what?"

"Any whatever you got."

"You don't know what I've got."

"Don't care to know."

"You sure?"

"Absolute sure. You might just as well back that tin can you're drivin' back out into traffic and be on your way."

"Are you James Saint E. Crandall?"

"None of your business."

"Are you James Saint E. Crandall or not?"

"Want me to call the cops?"

"Sure," Fletch said. "I'll wait."

The weathered skin around Crandall's eyes puckered. "What makes you think you have a right to know anything?"

"I have a right to know everthing."

"Who says?"

Fletch grinned. "Why do you ask?"

"You're a young punk."

"That may be."

"Don't even wear shoes. Standin' there in the dirt like white trash. Where'd you come from? You go to church? Where'd you get my name?"

"So you are James Saint E. Crandall."

"Maybe."

"If you are, then I found your wallet."

"Didn't lose my wallet."

"Your passport wallet."

"Never had a passport. Never had a passport wallet."

Have you stayed at The Park Worth Hotel lately?"

"Haven't stayed anywhere but at home."

Fletch ran his eyes over the bungalow. The paint was so thin the wood was dried out. On the porch was one rocking chair. A burst cushion was in its seat.

"I guess you never stayed at The Park Worth Hotel."

"Never heard of it."

"Do you have a son, a grandson named James Saint E. Crandall?"

"None of your business."

"Look, mister. I found this wallet, see? It has money in it. And the name James Saint E. Crandall. I'm trying to give the wallet back to its owner."

"It's not mine. I said that."

"Your son's?"

"Never had any children. My damned wife died thirty years ago, God rot her soul. Never had any nephews I ever heard of, and if I did, I hope they're perishin' in jail."

"You're a nice guy. You go to church?"

" 'Course I do."

"You ever heard of anyone else in the world named James Saint E. Crandall?"

"Wouldn't care if I had."

"Sorry to have bothered you," Fletch said. "Nice passin' the time of day with you."

"Let me see your license and registration."

Fletch was still within the limits of Newtowne when the police car came up behind him, growled its siren at him, and pulled him over.

He handed the officer his papers.

"Irwin Maurice Fletcher," the policeman read. "What kind of a name is that?"

"A stinky name. My parents were expecting a skunk."

"Did they get one?"

"No, they had a nice kid,"

"And what kind of a scam is their nice kid pullin' now?"

"I don't get you," Fletch said.

The policeman continued to hold Fletch's papers in his hand. "Well, you go up to a man's door and tell him you found his wallet and there's money in it. What's the swindle?"

"Jeez. Crandall did call the cops."

"Never mind who called."

"What a grouchy guy."

"You want to come down to the police station and explain yourself?"

"I'll explain myself here, officer."

"I'm listenin'."

"I found a wallet with the name James Saint E. Crandall in it. No address. I'm trying to find the James Saint E. Crandall it belongs to. I asked the one you've got here in your town and he damned near threw me off his place. And called you."

"Let me see the wallet."

"Why?"

"To save yourself from being arrested for trying a confidence game."

"You haven't enough proof for that."

"To save yourself from being arrested for driving with no shoes on."

"You can only give me a ticket for that."

Referring to Fletch's license, the policeman wrote out a ticket. "Twenty-five dollars fine," the policeman said.

"Don't retire until you get my check."

The policeman handed Fletch the ticket. "Let me see the wallet."

"No."

"Are you leaving town?"

"Trying to."

The policeman handed Fletch his license and registration. "Just keep on drivin', Irwin."

"Yes, sir."

"By the way," the policeman said, "your parents did have a skunk for a kid. What would you call someone tryin' to swindle senior citizens?"

"I wouldn't call him," Fletch said. "I'd wait for him to call me."

ELEVEN

The odor of cooked hamburger wafted through the screen door. All that morning Fletch had only had coffee.

"Hi, good lookin'," the woman said to him through the Blaines' screen door. Through the door she looked down at Fletch's bare feet and smiled and ran her eyes up his body again. "What can I do you for?"

She was a bosomy woman in her mid-sixties, wearing a yellow turtleneck sweater, tight slacks and sneakers.

"How's Mister Blaine today?" Fletch asked.

"How would I know?" The woman's brown eyes were lively.

"Isn't this Charles Blaine's house?"

"Yes."

"Doesn't he have the flu?"

"Hope not. It would ruin his vacation.."

"He's on vacation?"

"San Orlando. 'Way down on the Mexican coast. They've been in Mexico before, 'bout two years ago."

"Sorry," Fletch said. "I'm not explaining myself. I'm just surprised. I was told he had the flu. My name is Fletcher. *News-Tribune.* Mister Blaine helped me with a story last week on Wagnall-Phipps. There were some things wrong with the story. Thought I'd better come back and talk with Mister Blaine again."

"Fletcher, Fletcher, Fletcher," the woman said. "You the one wrote that story on what rip-off artists some funeral directors are?"

"No."

"Thought I knew your name. You hungry?"

"Of course."

"That's the right answer. All good men are hungry all the time." She held the screen door open for him. "I'll make you a hamburger."

"Wow."

"You're going to say that's right nice of me."

"Yeah."

"No need. It gives this woman a great deal of pleasure to feed a hungry man." The screen door swung closed behind Fletch. "My name's Happy Franscatti," she said.

"You are happy. I mean, you are a happy person."

"Yes, I am." She led the way through the livingroom and diningroom into the kitchen. "I've lost a husband and two children in three separate accidents."

"That's God-awful."

"Yes, it is. But I'm still a happy person. I was just born cheerful, I guess." She slapped three hamburger patties onto the grill. "I suspect it has something to do with the body chemistry. It's in the glands, or something. I know people who have no particular problems, but they act terrible sad all the time." She spoke loudly over the sizzle of the hamburgers. "They just have no capacity for happiness. I wake up every morning five-thirty, and the day's song is already goin' in my heart. I run to the window and peek out at the world to see what the day will bring. Why aren't you sitting down?"

Fletch sat at the small kitchen table.

"I'm Mary Blaine's aunt," Happy said. "You met Mary? Mrs. Blaine?"

"No. I've only met with him. In his office."

"I'm just house sitting." She turned over the hamburger, saying: "This is how you keep the juice in. Turn 'em over quick. They called me Thursday noon and said they had a chance to get away to Mexico and could I come right away? I was happy to. You should see my apartment. No, you shouldn't see my apartment. It's so small if I gain ten pounds I won't even be able to visit myself."

"They didn't know they were going ahead of time?"

"I guess not. Had supper with them Saturday night, and they didn't mention it. Not at all like Charley. He doesn't even go to the grocery store without preparing an hour and a half ahead of time, making a list, checking it twice, counting his money, changing his clothes twice. Until you're ready to yell at him. I came over Thursday noon, drove them to the airport. They were on the three-thirty flight."

"Okay," Fletch said. "His secretary told me Thursday he had the flu."

"Maybe he did. He looked pale and didn't have that much to say, although Charley never does."

"How long are they gone for?"

"Two weeks. Maybe three. Said they'd let me know. Something was wrong with the story you wrote for the newspaper?"

"My fault. I didn't check something I thought was obvious."

"You in trouble for it?"

"No," said Fletch. "I was fired."

Happy put the three hamburger patties on three buns, pressed their tops down on them, and piled them all in one plate. "If someone gave you a bum steer," she said, "it wasn't Charley. He's not capable of it. I've known him twenty years. He's too literal-minded to lie." She put the plate in front of Fletch. "He's a pest, the way he has to know the lieteral truth about everthing: how much did this cost, how much did that cost, what store did this come from, whom exactly did you see and what exactly did they say. Drives Mary and me nuts. Truth is, we can't remember all those little things. What store did we buy something in? Who cares except Charley?"

Looking at the hamburgers, Fletch said, "Are all these for me?"

"Can't you eat them?"

"Of course."

"I've eaten. Want milk?"

"Yes. Please."

Happy brought a glass to the refrigerator and filled it with milk. "Mary's more like me. More happy-go-lucky. Of course next to Charley the Statue of Liberty looks like a stand-up comedian."

"These are good," Fletch said munching. "Has Charley worked twenty years with Wagnall-Phipps?"

"No. Just the last four. Before that he was with IBM." Happy brought the glass of milk to the table and sat down across from Fletch. "You don't know Charley very well."

"I don't know him at all," Fletch said.

"He's one of those people, you know, you make a joke and instead of laughing he analyses it. And then he explains it back to you — the person who made the joke in the first place. I like Charley. He makes me wonder. I think he had the body chemistry of a mica schist."

"What's a mike-a-shits?"

"A kind of rock. I should have said basalt. Enough ketchup?"

"Thanks. Do you know the Bradleys, Happy?"

"Charley's boss? Yeah. Met them two or three times when Charley first went to work at Wagnall-Phipps. Haven't seen them in two or three years. I don't think they socialize much. I suspect that after Mary and Charley and Tom and Enid had dinners back and forth when Charley first went to work for Wagnall-Phipps — you know, did the necessary boss–new employee drinks and dinner things — everybody retreated into their own little holes. They're all a bunch of deadheads. Except Mary."

"Did you go to Tom Bradley's funeral?"

"How can you tell when a guy like that is dead?" Happy laughed. "I don't mean to be unkind. No, I buried my younger daughter only a year and a half ago. I knew Tom Bradley had been sick — in and out of hospital — had gone east to the specialists. He was so sick his wife, Enid Bradley, was running the company. Wouldn't think her capable of it, even with the help of Charley and Alex. That's Alex Corcoran, president of Wagnall-Phipps. Alex has got some life. You know — what's your name — Fletch? — when you go through three deaths of your own, as I did, people aren't apt to rush at you with news of every other death. Invite you to every funeral, you know?"

Fletch bit into his third hamburger. "Good."

Her eyes were smiling at him. "It's very nice watching a man eat."

"Wish you'd popularize that notion."

"Not married yet, Fletch?"

"Divorced."

"At your age? What happened? Couldn't your wife figure out how to work your diaper pin?"

"Something like that."

"She didn't feed you. Girls today. It's against their pride to feed a man. It's also against their pride a man should pick up a restaurant check. So everybody's starving."

"Tell me about Enid and Tom Bradley, Happy."

"What do you mean?"

"You said he was sick. Sick with what?"

"I forget. One of those long-range things. What would that be?"

"I don't know."

"Not a very big man. No bigger than his wife. He used to tell dirty jokes I liked. There was something especially dirty about them when he told them. I don't know. I suppose it was because he was the boss. And I always felt the dirty jokes sort of embarrassed Enid. She'd laugh, but only as if she had to."

"Maybe she'd heard them before."

"I suppose so. I really didn't know them very well." Happy looked at the wall clock. "I've got to get going."

"Oh. Okay." Fletch drained his glass of milk. "Anything I can do for you, Happy? Can I give you a lift anywhere?"

"No, thanks." She took Fletch's empty plate and glass to the sink. "I'll just get my guitar and be on my way."

"Guitar?"

"Yeah, I always bring it when I go to the Senior Citizens' Home. I play for them, and we sing. Some of them sing quite well. An old person's singing voice can be very fine. Too bad the world doesn't notice."

She went into a bedroom. Fletch waited in the front hall.

"Here we are," Happy said. She came through the bedroom carrying a guitar case and five or six copies of *The National Review*. Fletch opened the screeen door for her. "Just slam the door behind you."

"Happy, thank you very much for lunch."

"My pleasure."

"Have a nice time at the Senior Citizens' Home this afternoon."

"Sure," Happy said. "I've got to go burden the old folks with my cheer. I've got too much of it to keep all to myself."

TWELVE

Fletch drove by the Bradley house in Southworth, saw the Cadillac in the driveway, saw a man in the driveway two houses down painting a thirty foot sailboat on a trailer hitch, continued through the executive-homes neighborhood until he came back to the main road, turned left, stopped at a gas station, took slacks, a jacket, shirt, loafers and socks from the trunk of his MG, went into the rest room and changed.

Then he drove back to the street the Bradley house was on and parked three houses beyond it.

He walked back to the driveway where the man was painting the boat. He went up the driveway and stood next to the man, who was dressed in shorts and a paint-spotted sweat shirt. "Hi," Fletch said. "That's a wood boat."

The man smiled at him. "She sure is." The man was in his late thirties and still had freckles across his nose. "She's my wood boat and she'll never be your wood boat. Not for sale."

He had put green garbage bags on the driveway to catch the paint. Not much had spilled.

"I'm in real estate," Fletch said. "The question I have to ask you is one I really hate to ask."

"My house isn't for sale, either."

"Not yours," Fletch said. "The Bradleys'."

"Oh, them." The man glanced in the direction of the Bradleys' house.

"When we hear of a death of the head of a household, we have to ask if anybody thinks that house might go on the market. At least my boss says I have to."

"What firm you work with?"

"South Southworth Realty." Fletch said it in such a way the man might think he was stuttering.

"You work for Paul Krantz?"

"Yeah."

"I know Paul. He helped put together a real estate deal for my father a few years ago."

"Nice man, Paul is," Fletch said.

"So you'd rather ask a neighbor about a widow's intentions than ask the widow herself."

"Wouldn't you?"

"Yes. Except the neighbor might not know."

"Your guess would be better than mine."

The man was applying the creamy white paint thickly to the wood. "Is Tom Bradley dead?" the man asked.

"So we hear."

"I thought so, too. In fact I could say I knew so. Then I read an article in the newspaper the other day, the *News-Tribune,* that made him seem very much alive. Couldn't believe my eyes. I read the piece twice and then showed it to my wife. I had to ask her if I'd gone crazy."

"Yeah." Fletch stood on one foot and then the other.

"Did you read it?"

"I never read the financial pages." Fletch said. "Perhaps I should."

"Not that the financial pages of the *News-Tribune* are that good. Their sports pages are better."

Fletch looked up at the clean, curtained windows of the house. "Is Tom Bradley dead or not?"

"Enid Bradley said so."

"When?"

"At a Christmas party we gave. Every year we give one, just for people in the neighborhood. Every year we invite the Bradleys — just because they live here. They never came. This year, Enid came. At some point during the party, my wife came to me and said, 'Did you know Tom Bradley is dead? Enid just mentioned it.' I went and spoke to Enid. First we'd heard of it. This neighborhood isn't that close, but, gee, when a guy dies two houses away from you, you expect to hear about it."

"Enid Bradley told you Thomas Bradley is dead?"

The man squinted through the sunlight at Fletch. "Enid Bradley told me Thomas Bradley is dead," he said exactly. "She told me last Christmas. Then I see his name in the newspaper the other day. Do you understand it?"

"Ah," Fletch said. "I guess newspapers have been known to be wrong."

"Come on. Quoting a dead man?"

"I suppose it can happen," Fletch said.

"Will you tell me how?"

"I wish I could. If Mrs. Bradley says her husband is dead . . ."

". . . then he must be dead. Right?"

"They have a couple of kids, haven't they?"

"Yeah."

Fletch waited for more, but none came. He gathered the neighborhood did not have much positive enthusiasm for the Bradley young. The man spent longer than usual putting paint on his brush.

"Nice boat," Fletch finally said. "You take good care of it."

"I guess I can say to you." the man said, "seeing you work for Paul, Krantz — and I consider him a friend — that the Bradleys are not the most popular neighbors."

"I see."

"I'd be polite to say they're loud."

"Loud?"

"They've had their problems, I guess. Loud — you know what I mean — screams in the night, shouting, doors slamming, the kids burning rubber as they drive away from the house two, three o'clock in the morning. The occasional smashed window."

Fletch looked around. All the houses were set well back from the road, and from each other. "You hear things like that here?"

"You wouldn't think so. And talking to Enid Bradley, looking at her, you'd think she was the quietest, most demure little lady you ever met. But sometimes at night we'd hear her screaming like a stuck pig. Hysterical shouting and screaming. We never heard his voice at all." Again the man stirred the paint thoughtfully with his brush before lifting it. "Tom Bradley tried suicide two or three years ago."

"You know that?"

"The rescue squad came early Sunday morning. We saw them bring the stomach pump into the house, and then carry him off strapped to a stretcher. The whole neighborhood saw it. And he didn't take too many pills by accident. It was after one of those all-night shouts, you know?"

"Maybe he was sick," Fletch said. "Maybe he had been told he was fatally ill, or something, you know? I mean, he did die."

"I don't know, either. But I do know the screaming and shouting went on in that house for as long as we've lived here. Five or six years. Deep emotional problems. That family had deep emotional problems. I suspect there's a family like that in every neighborhood, from the slums to a neighborhood like this, for the lower-rich. Feel sorry for them, but what the hell can we do?"

"Has all that stopped? I mean, the noise and the smashed windows, since Tom Bradley died?"

"Yeah. It's become a very quiet house. The kids come and go, but there are no more slamming doors and burning rubber. Of course, she — I mean Enid — goes off to work nearly every day now. Or so my wife tells me. I think someone told me she's trying to run her husband's company — I forget the name of it, oh, yeah, Wagnall-Phipps is what the *News-Tribune* said — until she can get someone else to take over. Of course if the *News-Tribune* said Wagnall-Phipps, the company might be called anything including Smith, Smith and Smith."

"Yeah," Fletch said. "*News-Tribune*. Yuck. Punk paper."

"They have a good sports section."

"Mrs. Bradley didn't say anything to you about selling the house?"

"Haven't seen her since Christmas. Months ago. Live two houses away and I don't think anyone in the neighborhood actually converses with anyone in that house, year after year. We've heard enough of their noise. We're all embarrassed, I guess. You understand."

"Sure."

"I wish you would go ask Mrs. Bradley if she's moving. It might give her the idea that she should."

"Yeah."

"This is a nice neighborhood. It would be great to have a nice family in that house. You know, a family that didn't embarrass us all when we look at them?" The man moved his paint bucket nearer the stern of the boat. "Tell her her house is worth a lot of money, and you can find her a nice condominium down nearer the center of town — one with padded walls."

THIRTEEN

"Would you like a drink, Mister Fletcher?" Enid Bradley asked.

"No. Thank you."

"I think I will."

Fletch was sitting in the broad, deep divan of Enid Bradley's livingroom. Through sliding glass doors sparkled a good-sized swimming pool.

Enid Bradley moved across the livingroom to a bar disguised as a book case and poured herself a large glass of white wine. "Seeing I must go to the office every day during this period, relaxing with a drink Saturday afternoon is quite all right, isn't it? Isn't that the excuse you men aways use for drinking on the weekend?"

"No."

"You are younger than I was expecting, Mister Fletcher."

Enid Bradley did not seem relaxed to Fletch. She seemed someone eager to show she was relaxed. Her eyes had been too searching in his face when she opened the door to him; her sigh had been too deep when he identified himself. She was an overweight woman in her mid-forties in a slightly out-of-date dress and high-heeled shoes. Fletch could not guess what she might have been doing before the doorbell rang. The only image that came to his mind was that of her standing somewhere in the house, fearfully anticipating him, or some other threatening visitor.

She sat in a chair placed at a slight angle to the coffee table, and to him. The surface of the coffee table was bright inlaid tile.

Fletch put his fingertips on the mosaic. "Did your husband make this?"

"Yes."

"It's very nice."

"There are several around the house. In the den. In our bedroom. In a table by the pool." Her eyelids hooded as she turned her face toward the light from the glass doors. Then her free hand gestured over her shoulder. "And, of course, there's that one, on the wall."

There was a large mosaic of precisely shaded concentric circles, brightest at the center, on the wall next to the fireplace.

"I don't blame you for coming to see me, Mister Fletcher. If I'm offended, I'm also curious." She put her glass on the coffee table. "I read your article about our company in Wednesday's *News-Tribune*. I was obliged to call your managing editor. It was just too upsetting to my children and, of course, the employees."

"I regret that."

"Where did you ever get the idea of quoting my husband?"

Saying nothing, Fletch just looked at her.

"We're not suing the newspaper. What's the use? I didn't even ask your managing editor, that Mister Jaffe, to print a retraction. I can't imagine what it would say. 'The recent article on Wagnall-Phipps Incorporated by I.M. Fletcher erroneously had quotes by the late Thomas Bradley'? No, that would just stir up more confusion. More hurt."

"You might let the *News-Tribune* print an obituary on your husband. They never have."

"Rather late now, isn't it?"

"When exactly did your husband die, Mrs. Bradley?"

"A year ago this month."

Fletch sighed. "A year ago this month. I saw memos from him dated as recently as three weeks ago."

"You couldn't have. I mean, how could you have? Why do you say you did? The idea is absurd. You see, Mister Fletcher, I have the choice of thinking you're a very sick young man. You've done a very cruel thing to me and my family."

"Or — ?"

"What do you mean, 'Or — '?"

"You said you had a choice. Either I'm very sick, or, what?"

"Or someone else is. The reason I'm talking to you, didn't close the door in your face, is because I have a suspicion. At first I thought your article was just another effort on the part of your newspaper to smear Wagnall-Phipps — as you did a few years ago. But, no, what you did was too, too absurd. It doesn't leave your newspaper a leg to stand on. I was even going to ask your Mister Jaffe if I could see you, talk to you, but — well, he discouraged me."

"How did he do that?"

"He said you're very young, which you are, and that young people make mistakes, which they do."

"You settled on the conclusion that I'm very sick."

"Yes and no. I did and I didn't." She brought her glass of wine to her lips and replaced it on the coffee table. No wine seemed missing from the glass. "I've taken another step . . . " She hesitated. ". . . which is more to my purpose, if you know what I mean."

"No. I don't."

Enid Bradley shrugged. "It really can't be important to me, Mister Fletcher, if you are a sick, cruel man — as long as you don't hurt me or my family again." In her lap, her fingernails worried each other. "It's very hard for me. You must understand. Wagnall-Phipps was Thomas's company. He built it and he ran it. For the last twenty years I've been a housewife and mother. But at least for now I'm trying to run the company."

Sympathetic phrases plodded through Fletch's mind but he gave voice to none of them.

"But your editor, Mister Carraway, came out Thursday night."

"Carradine."

"Is his name Carradine? I was so upset. He sat with me and my children, Tom and Ta-ta. He was very kind. He was more explicit."

"About what?"

Her eyes flashed into his. "He said you're a fool, Mister Fletcher. That you're always doing wild and stupid things. He said you're an office joke. He said you're a compulsive liar." Her eyes fell. "He also said you were to be fired the next day, and that you'd never work in the newspaper business again."

"Say, he was kind."

Her eyes looked into his again, with less anger. "Were you fired?"

"Of course."

"Then, from your own point of view, why are you pursuing this matter further?"

"Because I'm a good journalist and I've got two statements, or impressions, which don't match."

"Are you sure you're not just being cruel?"

"Mrs. Bradley, I wrote a newspaper article quoting your husband. I never heard of your husband before, or you, or your family, and if I'd ever heard of Wagnall-Phipps it meant nothing to me. Then I'm told your husband is dead. I'm shocked. I'm hurt by this, too."

Her voice squeaked drily. "Do you think I'm lying to you?"

"The *News-Tribune* did not print an obituary on your husband. I haven't been able to check the Bureau of Vital Statistics yet, because it's Saturday and I just got back to town last night. But I will on Monday."

"It will do you no good," said Enid Bradley. "At least, I don't think so. My husband died in Switzerland."

"Oh."

"I thought everyone knew that. He was cremated there."

"I see."

Expressing exasperation, she rose from her chair, crossed the room, took a hand-sized, decorated box from the mantel and place it on the coffee table in front of Fletch. "These are his ashes, Mister Fletcher."

Fletch stared at the filigreed box lid.

"Open it," she said. "Go ahead. Open it."

"I don't need to."

She opened it. Inside were ashes, looking as if they had settled toward the center while still wet.

"Do you have any more questions, Mister Fletcher?"

"Yes," he said. He cleared his throat. "Yes."

She sat in the chair again. "I will tell you everything," she said, "if you will just go away and stop this insane harrassing of us."

"Yes," he said. "Of course."

"My husband had a form of blood cancer. Which means that, in order to stay alive, his blood had to be changed regularly. That is, his own blood had to be drawn out while fresh blood was being pumped into him. You can imagine what a horror that is."

"Yes. I'm sorry," he said. He closed the lid of the box.

"You're going to hear me out."

"Yes. Of course."

"You can imagine how debilitating all that is — having your own blood drained out while new blood is being pumped in. No, of course you can't."

"Yes," Fletch said. "No."

"Over time, of course, it weakened him more and more. Poor Thomas. Running the company he wanted no one to know how sick he was. Alex Corcoran, the president, is really only chief of sales — a big, hale-and-hearty fellow whose mind is permanently stuck on golf. In fact, he's playing in some tournament over at the Southworth Country Club this afternoon. Charley Blaine, the Vice-president and treasurer, is a superb backroom man, but one of the most dependent characters you ever saw in your life. If everything isn't just perfect, he overreacts and does crazy things. And Thomas was the kind of man who didn't want his children worrying about him. They're beautiful, happy, successful children. Ta-ta — our daughter, Roberta — is teaching at her old prep school, Southworth Preparatory, and half-way through her first teaching year they've made her Head of House. And Tom is finishing up his premedical studies at the College. They are both doing extremely well. My husband wanted to live. But these treatments, these blood exchanges, had to happen more and more frequently. It was a cumulative disease, Mister Fletcher. He was getting weaker and weaker.

"Then we heard about this new technique the doctors in Switzerland had developed. I can't pretend to understand it, or explain it. It has something to do with not letting the new blood mingle with the old blood, during the exchange. I take it you don't know anything about medicine, either?"

"No."

"Vacuums or something were to be created in the body. I'm not sure only Swiss doctors are doing it, but Thomas heard about this doctor in Switzerland who was the first, or the the best, or something. The most respected. So, while I stayed to run the company as well as I could, he went to Switzerland for these extensive treatments. All the news was good. He was doing fine. And then he died."

She was looking directly at Fletch as she spoke, rather in the manner of someone insulted. Then she put a hand to her brow and squeezed her eyes shut.

"Mister Fletcher, will you please leave us alone, and stop this insanity of yours?"

Fletch tried to make himself comfortable in the soft divan. He took a deep breath and exhaled slowly. "Mrs. Bradley," he said, "why did your Vice-president and treasurer, Charles Blaine, refer last week to your husband as alive? Why did he show me recently dated memos purportedly from your husband?"

Enid Bradley raised her head and blinked her eyes around the upper corners of the room. She spoke gently. "That's why I'm seeing you, Mister Fletcher. I'm now convinced of your innocence — that you meant to do nothing cruel. I'm afraid we're both victims of someone else's sickness."

"Whay would he do such a thing, Mrs. Bradley?"

"Charley is a worrisomely tight man, if you know what I mean. Anything out of the ordinary rattles him. He was terribly fond — worshipful — of my husband. Thomas would make the silliest little joke, and Charley would repeat it and laugh all night. I tried to break the news of Thomas's death gently. No, I did not offer the local newspapers obituaries. No, I did not run a memorial serviece for him locally. Maybe I should have. Maybe if I had done so all this painful confusion would have been avoided. You see, I took over the company only in Thomas's absence. Everybody believed he was coming back. Then Thomas died. I didn't know what to do. Thank God for Francine. She's been such a help." Enid Bradley looked into her lap. "She suggested I break the news slowly, gently, to each person individually — which I did. I even waited months — until last fall — to tell people, so the hurt of his death would be somewhat removed from them. I don't think Charley ever accepted Thomas's death. I think it drove Charley off the deep end. He didn't see Thomas die, so he doesn't believe Thomas died."

"Who is Francine?"

"Thomas's sister. She lives in New York. She and Thomas were always extremely close."

"Mrs. Bradley, how do you explain the memos I saw from your husband?"

"If you saw such memos, Mister Fletcher, then they were forgeries. Obviously. Charles Blaine forged them. What else am I to think? Once or twice, Charley has referred to Thomas as alive, in speaking to me. You know, referred to Thomas in the present tense. I thought his tongue was just slipping. Then, when I saw your article . . . Wednesday night . . . I figured it out. Charley must be having some sort of a nervous breakdown. Thursday morning I told Charley, as forcefully as I could, that Thomas is dead and has been dead for a year. Then I sent him and his wife away for a long vacation."

"Mexico."

"Is that where they went? Oh, yes, I think they've gone to Mexico before for their vacations. We'll just have to see how he is when he comes back. If he really went so far as forgery . . . I don't know. You don't have any copies of those memos, do you, Mister Fletcher?"

"No."

"Well. You see. I haven't known what to do. It's all been very difficult."

"Do you intend to continue running the company, Mrs. Bradley?"

"No! Thank God." She appeared horrified at the thought.

"Are you selling out?"

"No. That wouldn't be fair to the children. No, Francine is coming West to take over the company, as soon as she can settle up her own business in New York. She's much cleverer than I. As I said, she and Thomas were very much alike. It's almost as if they had the same mind. She's run businesses before." Enid Bradley looked absently across the room. "She should be able to come West in a couple of months."

Fletch said, "I guess I don't know what to say."

Enid said, "There is nothing to say. I'm sure you didn't mean any harm. It's just that the man you were talking to was temporarily deranged. How could you have known that? If you like, I'll call your managing editor. Tell him that you and I talked. Tell him about Charley, and how insanely fond he was of my husband . . ."

"Thank you, but it wouldn't do any good. I'm famous in the business now for having quoted someone who wasn't alive at the time. I'll never live that down."

"Mister Fletcher, is there anything I can do to help you? Reporters don't make much money, I know, and now you've lost your job. I guess it's partly our fault. I should have known Charley Blaine was going off the deep end."

"That's very nice of you, but no, thanks. It was nice of you to see me, under the circumstances."

"This is all very distressing."

Enid Bradley rose and showed Fletch to the door. Neither said another word.

FOURTEEN

"Cold beer," Fletch said. "If you've got any left."

The barman at the Nineteenth Hole, the bar of the Southworth Country Club, looked Fletch in the face, obviously considered challenging him, then drew a beer and put it in front of Fletch.

"Thanks," Fletch smiled. During a tournament weekend there were apt to be many strangers in and out of a golf club.

At the end of the bar near the windows overlooking the greens was a large and noisy group of men dressed casually. Two couples in the room, at tables, were dressed for dinner.

"Pebble Beach," said one of the noisy men. "Nobody believes what I did at Pebble Beach. Even I don't believe what I did at Pebble Beach!"

And they said this and they said that and they laughed at almost everything. Fletch sipped his beer.

His glass was nearly empty when one of the men turned to another, a heavily-built man wearing bifocals, and said, "Alex, I thought you'd never really get over your bug-a-boo about approaching the seventh green."

"Well," Alex smiled. "I did. Just in time."

Fletch picked up his beer, moved down the bar and, laughing with the men, looking interested at the next thing to be said, insinuated himself into the group. He nodded in appreciation at their slightly drunken inanities. He stood next to the man called Alex.

After many minutes, at a fairly quiet point in the conversation, Fletch said to the man, "You're Alex Corcoran, aren't you?"

"Sure," the man said.

"Second place winner of not the biggest but surely the friendliest golf tournament in the US of A," slurred one of the group.

"Congratulations," Fletch said.

"It's you young guys who beat me now," Corcoran said. "And you don't even go to bed at night to sleep." He pulled on his gin and tonic. "I said, to sleep."

"You and I met briefly before," Fletch said. "What's the name of that club over there . . .?" He pointed vaguely to the East.

"Euston."

"Yeah. Euston."

"Did I play you?"

"No, I wiped out in the first round. Watched you. We talked in the bar, later."

Alex Corcoran laughed. "Pardon me for not remembering."

"We talked about Wagnall-Phipps. You work for Wagnall-Phipps, right?"

"No!" said a golfer. "He doesn't work for Wagnall-Phipps. He's the president!"

"He doesn't work at all," said another.

Fletch nodded. "Yeah, I thought we talked about Wagnall-Phipps."

"Been with W-P seven years," Corcoran said. "Didn't become president, though, until the company suddenly decided to get out of the ski house business."

Everyone laughed.

"Jerry was really screwed by that." A golfer shook his head. "Jeez. Business entertaining. Suddenly it becomes illegal, or un-American or something."

"Depends on who you entertain."

"Depends on who you bribe."

Everything was funny to these golfers after the tournament.

"Alex, what happened to Jerry?"

"He's gone skiing," one of them joked.

"Yeah. Retired to Aspen."

"The ex-president of Wagnall-Phipps," said the current president, "is living in Mexico on a pension bigger than my salary."

"Really?" marveled one of the men. "The wages of sin."

"Pretty big pension, Alex said. "The scandal did him no harm. Wish I could work up a good scandal myself. Then I'd never have to go to the office."

"You hardly ever go now, Alex."

"You can't sell our crap from behind a desk," Alex said. "You gotta get out there and dazzle by foot-work!" The big man shuffled his feet in a boxer's step. None of his drink spilled.

"Thomas Bradley," Fletch said. "Your boss. Didn't he die?"

All the men guffawed.

"Depends on which paper you read," one of them said. "Another round of drinks, Mike," he said to the bartender. "What for you?" he asked, looking into Fletch's glass. "I don't know your name."

"Mike," Fletch said. "Mike Smith."

"And a beer for Mike, Mike."

"Mike Smith? You were on the U at Berkeley golf team, weren't you?"

"Is Thomas Bradley dead or not?" Fletch asked.

"Everywhere but in the *News-Tribune.*"

Fletch looked confused.

"Yes," Alex Corcoran said in a more serious tone. "He died. About a year ago. Did you know him?"

"I knew his sister," Fletch said. "In New York. Francine."

"Oh, yeah?" Corcoran's face expressed great interest.

"Well, met her once," Fletch said. "At a party, you know?"

"What's she like?" Alex asked.

"You mean you've never met her?"

"No. She's coming out to take over the company, and I've never met her. Tom used to say she was brilliant. Never came West, as far as I know."

"How did Tom die?" Fletch asked.

"Went to France for some medical treatments and didn't survive them, is what I understand."

"France?"

"Never knew he was as sick as he was. He used to be moody, and act down-in-the-dumps once in a while. Jeez, I didn't know the guy was fatally ill — dyin'!"

"But you did know he was sick?"

"No. Not really. The only comment I made about it to my wife was that he seemed to be getting smaller. Don't ask me what I mean, because I don't know. I guess his shoulders got thinner. He must have lost weight. He wasn't very big to begin with. Poor ol' Tom. Here's to you, Tom." Alex raised his glass and tipped it like a censer before drinking.

"Nice trophy," Fletch said, nodding to it on the bar.

"Say, so you know his sister, Francine Bradley, eh?" Alex Corcoran said.

"Well, as I said, I only met her once."

"Enid says she's a real clever business woman, that this Francine and Tom used to talk all the time. Some of Tom's best ideas came from Francine, Enid said."

"I guess she's pretty clever," Fletch said.

"Tom left it in his Will that Francine was to take over operation of the company — if she was willing and able. Tell you — what's your name?"

"Mike."

"I'll tell you, Mike, I'll welcome her with open arms."

"You will? Company not running so well?"

"Well, you know, a company needs a head — someone to make the people decisions, give it a direction. I'm president, by the grace of Tom Bradley, but I'm not good that way. What I'm very good at is selling things to people. That's all I can do; that's all I want to do. I mean, really, my wife says I could sell snowballs to Siberians. Long-range corporate planning, the day-to-day stuff — I'm not good that way. Enid tries, but, you know . . ."

"Enid is Tom's wife?"

"Yeah. Nice lady. Once in a while she has a good idea, but, you know . . . long-range planning. Listen, anything Tom Bradley decided to do with his company is all right with me. He could have left it to his horse, and I'd say, sure, fine, good idea."

"Tom rides?"

Alex looked at him. "A figure of speech. Don't you know your Roman history?"

"Oh."

"As a matter of fact, Tom did ride. Kept a horse out in the valley, somewhere. Rode on Sundays, some weekday mornings. Yeah, he liked riding. He'd go alone, I guess."

"Sounds like you were fond of him."

"Listen." Alex's eyes became a little wet. "Fond of him . . . I loved that guy. He was a real gentleman. Except for his stupid, raunchy jokes everybody had always heard before. That's what was so funny about them. He was one hell of a nice man. People like that shouldn't die so young. When you consider all the shits who live a lot older — like me!"

"Gotta split." Fletch put his beer glass on the bar, and held out his hand to Alex Corcoran, "Nice talking with you. Sorry about Tom Bradley."

"Yeah, yeah. I gotta go too. My wife will be lookin' for me." Two of the other golfers in the group had left. Alex Corcoran picked his trophy up off the bar. "Come here, you little darlin'." He kissed it. "Where the hell would a man be, it it weren't for golf?"

"Home with the wife," said one of the other golfers.

And they all laughed.

FIFTEEN

Fletch drove home in the dark, but the lights in his apartment were on and Moxie came to the door as soon as she heard his key in the lock. She was wearing an apron and nothing else.

"Gee," Fletch said. "Just like a wife."

"Not like wife." With her fingers Moxie held the edges of the apron's skirt away from her skin and curtsied, as a geisha might. "Like Moxie Mooney."

He kissed her. "Your ex-wife called," she said. He kissed her again. "Tom Jeffries called. Wants you to call him back." He kissed her again.

"What did good ol' Linda want?"

"Oh, we talked a long time. She told me what a male nymphomaniac you are, how unreliable you are, how funny you are. She told me about the time you called her from the office and said you were on your way home and then went to Hawaii."

"There was a story in Hawaii."

"She said the meatloaf got cold. How cruel you were to her cat. I believe she loves you."

"And what did you tell her?"

"I told her I believe you still love her."

"Thanks a heap. I love paying her alimony."

"Oh, she said you haven't. Paid her any alimony, that is. I told her I didn't understand that, as you have scads of money, have just ordered a sixty-foot motor cruiser, and anytime she needs money she's to come to you, alimony be damned."

"Terrific. What else did you do for me?"

"Told her you'd iust given me a diamond tiara and a mink coat."

"I'm sure she believed you."

"I don't think so, somehow. Go telephone what's-his-name. He's the guy with the broken back, isn't he?"

"Yeah."

"I'll run you a bath."

"Why don't we — ?"

She put her hand against his shoulder and pushed. "Yucky, dirty, smelly boy. If I'm going to give my all for you, least you might do is remove the outer layer of pollution."

"But, but — "

"Lots of evening left."

She turned her back on him and hopped into the bathroom.

"Tom? Fletch. How's life at ground level?"

"Never, never, Fletch, have I known there were so many ants in the world. All day I spend in the patio watching ants."

From the livingroom, Fletch could hear the bath water running. "You don't see many ants when you're hang-gliding I guess."

"Actually, ants are sort of interesting. Just like people, only more so."

"The Darwin of the patio."

"Listen, I called you not only because I'm bored out of my mind but also to tell you a funny story. Cheer you up. A story under the heading *Incompetent People Who Do Not Get Fired From The News-Tribune.*"

"There are some?"

"Jack Carradine called this morning, after you left. About Clara Snow."

"What's she done now?"

"You know she's been assigned to the State House, just as if she were a real reporter?"

"Yes."

"Well, while assigned to the State House she failed to report that the Governor's press secretary's brother owns a car dealership which, if you can believe it, has been selling cars to the state police."

"Clara didn't report that?"

"She put her nose up in the air, looked all haughty, you know, as only she can, and said she felt the matter was too personal."

"To whom?"

"A private matter, she said. Having to do with family life. Not in the public interest to report. Then she said the state police have to buy their cars from somewhere. Can you believe that?"

"It makes me angry."

"Good. I thought it would cheer you up. Of course you know Clara's been going to bed with the press secretary."

"I thought she was going to bed with Frank Jaffe."

"Him, too. Clara goes to bed with anyone who can help her career. You can't say Clara doesn't give her all. Which is why she's being allowed to get away with this little slip of hers."

"Are you telling me Frank still isn't going to run the story?"

"Jack says Frank called the governor and told him to put an end to this corruption within a month, or the *News-Tribune* would blow the whistle. How do you like those sweet peas?"

"Jeez. I hope the competition gets wise to it."

"You could always make sure they do, Fletch."

"No. I wouldn't do that."

"Just trying to get you a job, man."

"Not that way."

"How do you feel, Fletch?"

"Lousy. How do you feel?"

"Lousy. See ya."

"See ya."

Fletch called the *News-Tribune*. There was no chance of the bathtub overflowing. Water ran into it at about the speed of decisions reached by committee.

"Classifieds," the girl said. "May I help you?"

"Yes, please," Fletch said. "I'd like to run an item in your Lost and Found column."

"Yes, sir. What's the message?"

"Wallet found name James Saint E. Crandall write Box number — whatever box number you give me."

"236."

"236."

"James Saint E. like in James Saint Edward or something?"

"Yes."

"C-r-a-n-d-a-l-l?"

"Yes."

"And what name and number shall I bill this to?"

"I.M. Fletcher."

"You're kidding."

"Don't think so."

"That you, Fletch?"

"Yeah."

"Hey, real sorry you got booted. What did you do, set fire to Frank Jaffe's pants?"

"I thought everyone knew."

"Yeah, I know. You quoted a stiff."

"Who is this?"

"Mary Patouch."

"Well, Mary. Want my address?"

"Fletch, I've always wanted your address. You know that."

Fletch gave her his address and then called the *San Francisco Chronicle* long-distance and placed the same ad.

"How did I meet Fletcher?" Moxie said like a child talking to herself. She had dropped her apron on the bathroom floor and gotten into the tub of warm water with Fletch. "I was buying a hot dog and this nice man standing next to me at the counter paid for it and then said nothing to me. So I said, 'Thank you very much, sir,' and you said, 'Seeing we're having such a terrible lunch, why don't we have dinner together?' "

"Your story is true so far. And you said, 'Yes, all right.' Why did you say, 'Yes, all right'?"

"Because you're beautiful and smooth and have funny eyes and I wanted to touch you."

"Oh. Perfectly good reason."

"Your eyes look like they're laughing all the time. Almost all the time."

"I see."

"You can't see your eyes. And at dinner I told you I had to come down here this weekend to start rehearsals Monday and you said you were driving this way next day, you had to be back at the office, ho ho ho, and why shouldn't I save bus fare by coming with you. So, seeing we were friends already, we went back to my place and . . ."

". . . and what?"

"And touched each other."

She kissed his throat and he kissed her forehead.

"So tell me about this day," she said. "I've known you three days, but only been with you two."

"A very ordinary day," Fletch said. "Just like all the others. Met a grouchy guy who tried to throw me off his place while I was trying to do him a favor, I thought, called the cops and tried to have me arrested."

"And did the cops give you a shower and shave today?"

"Not today. A ticket for driving barefoot. Then I met a marvelous happy woman named Happy who invited me in and cooked me up three hamburgers."

"Nice of her. She wanted your bod?"

"For three hamburgers?"

"I got you for less. Jar of peanut butter."

"Charles Blaine's wife's aunt. Charles Blaine, by the way, the source of my suicidal story, has gone to Mexico."

"So you can't beat him up."

"I think I'd like to. Then I met a solid-looking man working on his boat in Southworth who looked less like a neighborhood gossip than Calvin Coolidge but who told me all the gossip about the Bradley family he could think of, and maybe then some."

"Did he know who he was talking to?"

"Of course not. Then I met the widow Bradley."

"Jeez, you're brave. Are these brass?"

"Can't take that. The gossipy neighbor said Mrs. Bradley is a midnight screamer who probably drove her husband to attempt suicide. Speaking of her, she is dignified, quiet, reasonable. She says this whole thing happened because Charles Blaine is suffering a nervous breakdown or something, which is why she sent him on vacation."

"So is Tom Bradley dead?"

"Then I went to the Southworth Country Club for a beer."

"I know."

"How do you know?"

"I can see it. Right there in your stomach." She pressed her finger against his appendix.

"Cannot."

She kissed his mouth. "I smelled it when you came in."

"Met Alex Corcoran, president of Wagnall-Phipps. Everyone says Tom Bradley's dead. The widow Bradley showed me his ashes."

"But, of course, you don't want to believe it."

"Of course I believe it. I believe everything. That's how I got into trouble in the first place."

She pushed his head below water.

"Glub."

"Face it, Fletch. You're sunk."

"Glub. Where you going?"

She was stepping out of the tub.

"Forgot the steak. Can't you smell it burning?"

"Steak! How'd you get steak?"

She had called to him, *Don't bother getting dressed — everything's ready.* She had the plates of steak and salad set out on the livingroom rug. She smiled at him when he came in.

"Opened a charge account," she said.

"Your name?"

"Of course." She poured wine into the glasses. "Can't starve forever."

"It's good. Great!"

"It's cheap and burnt," she said. "At least you'll never have to divorce me."

"Why's that? Not that I was thinking of it, already."

" 'Cause you'll never marry me."

"Oh. I was thinking of asking."

"I'll never marry anybody."

"Never ever?"

"Never ever. I'm an actor and actors should never get married."

"A lot do."

"You know about my father."

"Frederick Mooney."

" 'Nough said."

"You told me he's playing Falstaff in Toronto."

"When he's sober. Then he's playing *Salesman* in Chicago. When he's sober. Last Christmas he did a baggy-pants comic routine at a dinner theater in Florida. When he was sober."

"So he's an actor who likes to drink. Not the first. Not the last. Your dad was known as a damned fine actor. Still is, as far as I know."

"I haven't told you about my mother."

"No."

"She's in a very expensive home in Kansas for the mentally absent."

"Oh. You think that's your father's fault?"

"Packing, unpacking, packing. Putting him to bed. Getting him up. Sobering him up. Looking for him in the bars. Reminding him which Goddamn play he's performing. Years of it. Taking care of me, on the road. Putting up with his women. His disappearances. His tensions. His paranoias. She couldn't take the day anymore, let alone the night. Something just snapped."

"Okay," he said. "How much of that had to do with his acting?"

"All of it."

"You sure?"

"I'm sure."

"Then why do you want to be an actor?"

"I don't want to be an actor." Instinctively she moved her head so that the light fell on her nose beautifully. "I am an actor."

He drank his wine. "Come on. Eat up."

"Also I'd like to be able to pay my mother's bills when that day comes that Freddy no longer can do."

"Thanks for the steak," Fletch said. "Eat yours up, or I'll attack you instantly."

Moxie picked up her knife and fork. "So what are you going to do tomorrow?"

Fletch shrugged. "Guess spend another day going around apologizing to people."

"Who's left?"

"The Bradley kids."

Moxie nodded. "Your piece must have been a real shock to them."

"I wouldn't feel right not touching base with them."

"You'll come to the cocktail party tomorrow night at the Colloquial Theater?"

"Sure. I'll go with you."

"Do me a favor, though, uh?"

"Anything."

"Don't mention Freddy."

"Frederick Mooney. A famous name."

"Infamous," she said. "Infamous."

SIXTEEN

As Fletch walked by he noticed the boat still in the driveway, gleaming white under its fresh coat of paint under the three o'clock in the morning moonlight. Except for the street lights, there was only one light visible in the neighborhood, a coach lantern several houses down.

In bare feet he went up the Bradleys' driveway and into the opened garage. The door to the house was locked. He went around the house to the kitchen door, which was also locked.

The glass door between the livingroom and the pool area slid open with a rumble. Houses away, a dog barked.

The moonlight did not do much to lighten the livingroom. Fletch stood inside the door a moment, listening, letting his eyes become used to the deeper darkness.

Putting each foot forward slowly, he walked to the fireplace. The box of ashes was not on the mantel.

He went to the coffee table and stooped over it. With loose fingers he combed, slowly, the surface of the table. His hand identified Enid Bradley's wine glass; he did not knock it over. Then the box of ashes.

Taking an envelope out of his back pocket, he opened it and held it in one hand. With his other hand he opened the lid of the filigreed box.

He took a pinch of ashes out of the box and put it in the envelope. He closed the lid, sealed the envelope.

Turning, he walked into the chair in which Enid Bradley had sat that afternoon, talking to him. It move only a few centimeters on the carpet.

When he slid the sliding door shut, the dog did not bark.

SEVENTEEN

A gaggle of teenaged girls joggled across Southworth Prep's green quadrangle in the bright Sunday morning sun. Fletch was waiting on the sidewalk outside an empty dormitory house.

As he came closer he saw the resemblance between the oldest girl, the only one not a teenager, and Enid Bradley — except that she was not at all oveweight and her slit shorts and running shoes were not a bit out-of-date.

"Roberta?" he asked.

The girls were huffing along the sidewalk, pounding up the steps to the porch and into the house.

"Showers, everyone!" Roberta said. "Be ready for chapel in half an hour!"

She looked at Fletch.

"Roberta Bradley," Fletch said.

"Have we met?" she asked. She wasn't at all out of breath.

"We're just meeting now," Fletch said. "For probably the first and last time, no foolin'. I'm Fletcher."

"So?"

"I.M. Fletcher."

"You already said that."

"The jerk who wrote the piece in the newspaper Wednesday about Wagnall-Phipps."

"Oh, I see." Her look was not at all unfriendly. "You want to talk. It isn't necessary."

"I wanted to come by . . ."

She glanced at the clock in the church tower across the quadrangle. "I like to run another couple miles while the little darlings use up all the hot shower water. Mind running with me?"

"No. That's okay."

Her pace was faster than it had looked. She had long, skinny legs and a long stride. They got off the sidewalk and went behind the school buildings and along a dirt road.

"I run just to get a few minutes alone," she said.

"Sorry. Pretend I'm part of the landscape, if you want. Rock, tree, tumbleweed."

"The little darlings at Southworth Prep never give me time to go exercise Melanie. Dad's horse."

"You still keep your father's horse?"

Roberta ran silently for a minute or two. "Guess nobody's made a decision about it yet," she said. "Look, what do you want from me?"

" 'Pologize, I guess. I screwed up. Must have been a shock to you."

Her face looked more annoyed than poised. "Why is everybody making such a big deal of this? Weirder things have happened in the world. You wrote an article about Wagnall-Phipps and referred to my father as chairman. So what? You were just out of date, that's all."

"Still . . ."

"That three-piece suiter from the newpaper came over the other night, sat Tom and me down and gave us solemn apologies from the *News-Tribune*. Said mistakes happen. Don't you suppose we know mistakes happen? Jeepers!"

"It shouldn't have happened." Fletch's feet were raising bigger puffs of dirt than hers. "I hear Carradine had some nice things to say about me!"

Roberta smiled at him and waggled her head. "Boy, if you're half as bad as he says you are, you're awful! Incompetent, fool, compulsive liar, wow." She stretched her leg just slightly to avoid a rock embedded in the road. "Nice of you to come by, though, I suppose."

"I can't explain how it happened."

"No need to. You screwed up. So what? Last week I handed out a French test to a roomful of kids who were supposed to be taking a Spanish test. Would you believe two or three of the kids actually started to do the French test? No one should ever believe teachers or newspapers entirely."

"Your dad's dying in Switzerland and all. . . . Your mother taking over the company in his absence . . . then he died . . . your mother keeping the chair warm for your Aunt Francine. . . ."

Roberta appeared to be listening carefully.

"There was some confusion," she said.

"Yeah. I guess you could say that."

"You can't understand everything that happens," Roberta said. "I tell that to my students. You can even act like you understand, when you don't yet. But some things . . ."

"What are you saying?"

"I hear jogging's good for the soul. Turns you philosophical."

"Especially on Sunday mornings."

"Here, we go back this way."

They ran together in silence for awhile.

"Nice of you to come by," she said again, finally. "There was no need to. Do you intend to see Tom, too?"

"Yes."

"I wish you wouldn't. He's busy with his pre-med studies, you know. What a grind! How that kid works! Let's just consider this incident closed. Okay?"

"Trying to do the decent thing."

"Well, you've done it." They were approaching the dormitory house. She said, "I'll be sure and tell Tom you stopped by." Then she said again, "Okay?"

Fletch said, "Was that really two miles we just ran?"

"Two measured miles. You can go around again, if you want."

They stopped in front of the house.

"No, thanks."

She was looking him over. "Looks like there's an envelope about to slip out of your pocket." She pointed to the back pocket of his jeans.

"Oh, that. Thanks." He slipped the sealed envelope containing the ashes deeper into his pocket.

The house reverberated with giggles and shouts.

"Good thing you didn't lose it," she said. "You'd have to run around again to find it." She took the porch steps two at a time. "Thanks for coming by. I'll tell Tom."

"You want to see Tom?" The responsive, open face of Thomas Bradley, Jr.'s college roommate was almost as wide as the dormitory room door he held open to Fletch. "He's here but he's gone."

At Fletch's puzzled expression, the roommate said, "We keep him in the bathtub."

He led Fletch around scrungy doorways to a scrungy bathroom.

In the bathtub, back and head resting on pillows, was a twenty-year-old man. His hair stuck up in stalks; his thin whiskers stood out from his chin and cheeks in patches, his eyes were closed. He looked a sad young man seriously contemplating the state of the universe.

"Figure he can't hurt himself so much in there. It's hard for him to get out. Hard for him to climb the sides, you know?"

"What's he on?"

"Downers, man. Downers all the way."

The roommate leaned over and opened one of Tom Bradley's eyes with his thumb. "Hello," he said. "Anybody home? Anybody in there?"

Fletch had told the roommate he had wanted to see Tom Bradley on *family business* and the roommate had said, *Somebody's come at last, thank God.*

"Hey, man," Fletch now said. "He can't live this way."

"Well, he does. Mostly. Sometimes he's cleaner than others. Gets up a bit, goes home, gets money. This is a new down."

"When did it start?"

"Friday. Two days ago. Was that Friday?"

"Shit. I was told he was a hard-working pre-med."

"Never was, really. He's always goofed. Came back to school last fall without much decision left. Attended classes irregularly a few weeks. Kept it up until, I guess, November — long after there was any reason to, he was so far behind already."

"So how come he's still living at the college?"

"What are we gonna do with him? Tried mailing him home, but the post office said he was too bulky a package. No, seriously. We carried him — physically carried him to the infirmary one night. Next day he was gone."

"When was that?"

"Way back before Christmas. Showed up here two weeks after New Year's all beat up. Looked like he had walked the jungles of Borneo. So we let him drive the bathtub some more. I went out to his house in Southworth — his mother's house. I told her she has a problem. Tom has a problem. At first, she looked frightened out of her wits. Then she denied everything I said. She said Tom shows up at the house every week or two, and I guess he does. She said he's just tired from his studies. Bullshit. Said he's been under heavy strain lately."

"What strain?" Fletch asked. "Did she say what strain?"

"Said something about his father's death."

"Supposedly that was a year ago."

Kneeling by the bathtub like a child playing with toy boats, the roommate looked up at Fletch. "Why do you say 'supposedly'?"

"He's got a pretty nice sister," Fletch said. "Healthy."

"Ta-ta? Yeah, I've talked to her, too."

"What does she say?"

"She says this is a world in which everybody's got to go for himself. She's a wind-up toy, and she thinks everybody else is, too. She says there's no understanding some things. There's no understanding her." Leaning over the tub side, the roommate slapped Tom Bradley's face a few times, lightly, until Tom opened his eyes. "Hey, Tom. Person to see you. Says his name is Satan. Wants to interview you for a job as a stoker."

Tom Bradley's glazed eyes were aimed at the ceiling. They darted to his roommate's face.

"Come on, Tom. You awake?"

Tom's eyes passed over Fletch and settled about a half meter to Fletch's left.

The roommate stood up. "Get somebody to do something about this kid, willya? I feel like someone who inherited an aquarium, you know? I have to take care of it and keep looking at it, when I'm not a whole lot interested, you know?"

"I don't know what I can do," said Fletch. "Not much, right away."

"Besides," the roommate said at the bathroom door. "I like to take a bath, you know?"

After Fletch heard the outer door close, he sat on the edge of the tub, near the faucet.

"Tom, people call me Fletch," he said. "I've talked with your mother and your sister. Wanted to talk with you."

As Fletch had moved, Tom Bradley's eyes had remained looking a half meter to the left of Fletch's head.

"I wrote something about your father in the *News-Tribune* the other day. Some sort of a mistake. I don't know whether that's what's throwing you, or not. I suspect it didn't help any."

"My father?" Tom braced his neck against the back of the tub. His voice was louder than Fletch expected. "You going to tell me my father's dead again?"

"Hey, man."

"You talked to my father, lately?"

"Could I have?"

"Sure." Tom's smile came slowly, and his words were coming slowly. "Just go to the mantelpiece over the fireplace, open the little box, and say what you want to say. Or . . ." His unreal smile broadened. "You could use the telephone."

"Tom: is your father dead?"

"Sure." Again the response was overly loud. "Everybody says so. Even he says so."

"What's the joke, Tom? Come on, tell me."

After a long pause, Tom Bradley said, "My father's dead. He's worse than dead. You know?"

"No. I don't know. What's worse than dead?"

"He killed himself." Tom made the motion of sticking a knife into his stomach and rooting it around there.

"I see. He'd tried suicide before, hadn't he?"

Tom looked warily into the space beside Fletch's head.

"Tom, where did he die?"

"Southworth in the Spring. Vienna."

"France?"

"No. Not France."

"Switzerland?"

"Yeah. That's it. He died in Switzerland. Of blood cancer. Many, many operations."

"Okay, Tom. Why do you blame him for his death?"

Tom's eyes went around the small bathroom very, very slowly. "He didn't like."

Fletch waited until Tom's eyes settled back to the left of Fletch's head. "He didn't like what?"

Tom Bradley's eyes closed. "No. He didn't." Tom muttered, "That's the surprising thing, you see? Where does that leave me?"

"Where does that leave you?"

Tom's eyes opened, seemed to focus on the faucet between his legs, and closed again. He answered, "In the bathtub."

"Tom. One more question."

"I haven't heard any questions." With his eyes closed, Tom spoke more quickly.

"Where was your father born?"

"He wasn't. I guess he wasn't born. People only thought he was born."

"Where was he brought up?"

"In purgatory, he says. You know the word, purgatory?"

"Yeah."

"That's where he was brought up."

"In what town. What town is your father from, Tom?"

"Let me think."

Fletch waited until he believed Tom Bradley was gone into space again, and then stood up.

"Dallas, Texas," Tom Bradley then said.

For a moment, Fletch stood over him. Then he said, "Tom? Can you hear me?"

"No."

"Tom, I'm gonna try to help you. You don't need this thing — whatever it is. It might not look like I'm helping you. And it may even hurt. But I'm gonna try to help you."

After a while, Tom Bradley, Jr. said. "Good-bye."

"Later, Tom."

EIGHTEEN

"Drink? Beer? Joint?"

Alston Chambers, law clerk in the District Attorney's office, took the five steps necessary to cross the livingroom and turned off the television set.

"Sunday afternoon," Fletch said. "Caught you sitting in front of the TV watching baseball and guzzling beer. Who'd ever think he'd live to see the day? Why aren't you out working around the palace? Painting, scraping, mowing and hoeing?"

Alston gave him a sardonic sideways glance. "Crappy little house. Who cares about it?"

"It's your mortgage, bud."

In the hot, dark livingroom an imitation early American divan, imitation Morris chair, pine wood coffee table, single standing lamp and ancient Zenith television left almost no place to stand. There was a bedroom in the house, and a kitchen-dinette. Houses each side were only a meter or so away, and there was a back yard big enough for the rubbish barrels.

"That's what it's all about," Alston said. "You don't buy a house. You buy a mortgage. I hate this house. I need the tax deduction. I need to establish credit. Everybody our age does. You, too, buddy. Wait till you get started. We're all waiting till you get started. Join the human race."

Clearly, Alston Chambers had joined the human race and clearly he was paying his dues. On a spring Sunday afternoon he was dressed in long trousers and moccasins and in his mid-twenties a beer belly made his dress shirt protrude and he was indoors drinking beer and looking at baseball on television. And since getting his law degree, he had been working nine-to-five as a clerk in the District Attorney's office.

Fletch and he had gone through Marine Corps basic training, and a great deal more, together.

"I would join the human race, Alston, honest, but something keeps going wrong. Every time I apply, something happens. Some doggoned thing."

"You paying Linda her alimony like the judge told you to? Like a good boy?"

"No, sir."

Alston said, "I wouldn't expect anything else from you."

"Every month I sit down to write her a check, Alston, honest, but after the rent, the car payment, the utilities, the groceries . . ."

"There's nothing left. I know. I couldn't afford to pay alimony right now, either. You at least keeping up with your credit card payments?"

"I don't have any credit cards. I had one the office gave me for, you know, expenses, but I lost that Thursday."

"What do you mean you lost it?"

"Well, it's more accurate to say I lost the use of it."

Alston looked at him incredulously. "You mean lost your job?"

"Or you could say I regained my freedom"

Alston chuckled. He turned around in the doorway and called his wife. "Audrey! Fletch is here."

"I'm just putting on a dress," she said through the wall. She sounded like she was in the room with them.

"Don't need to put on a dress for me, Audrey," Fletch said. "Wish you wouldn't."

"I know that, Fletch," she said, coming into the room and putting her arms around his neck. "But Alston's home, and we don't want to embarrass him, right?" She kissed him on the mouth.

"Right."

"Right," Alston said. "Now would you like a drink?"

He had picked up his pewter beer stein from the top of the television. Alston had bought the Austrian-style beer stein in Tokyo, Japan, when he and Fletch had been there on Rest and Recuperation.

"No, thanks." Audrey had sat on the divan. Fletch flopped into the single chair. "Moxie's got me going to this cocktail party at her theater tonight."

"Moxie?" Alston smiled down at him. "Is Moxie back on the scene?"

"Yeah. I guess so. Come to think of it, she is. Bumped into her at a hot dog stand the other day. She's doing her thing — pretending that was the first time we ever met."

"That's Moxie," Alston said.

"That's Moxie."

"Did you say she's pretending you two just met for the first time, the other day?" Audrey laughed.

"Yeah. Come to think of it, she is."

"Moxie, Moxie," Alston said into his beer.

"Maybe it is the first time we ever met," Fletch said. "Moxie is a lot of different people, you know."

"All of them women," Alston said.

"Moxie's an actor," Fletch said, "whether she wants to be or not. She gets into an elevator and uses everybody else standing there as a captive audience. Once in a crowded elevator she turned to me and said, *Really, Jake, it hain't fair I got pregnant, when you said I wouldn't — you bein' my brother and all. What you go sayin' it wasn't possible for, when it was, all time? You heard what the doctor just said — don't make no difference you bein' my brother. You tol' me a tootin' lie, Hank.*"

Laughing, Audrey said, "What did you do, Fletch?"

"Well, the temperature in the elevator went up to about one-hundred-and-thirty degrees Fahrenheit. Everyone was glowering at me. I wasn't sure I was going to get out of there alive."

"What did you do?" Audrey asked.

"I said, *Can't be sure it was me, Stella. Might ha' been Paw.*"

Alston slopped a little beer onto his shirt laughing.

"Was that the last time you two split?" Audrey asked.

Fletch thought a moment. "Time before that, I think. Last time, her father called from Melbourne, Australia, sobbing, saying he needed her to come play Ophelia, or he had to cancel the tour. She was packed and gone within fifteen minutes."

"I never knew Moxie played Ophelia in Australia," Audrey said.

"She didn't. She got there and the role had been filled. Freddy didn't even remember telephoning her. He said, *How nice of my little girl to come all this way to see her old daddy!* Something like that. Old bastard didn't even pay her way out, or back. She worked six months on a sheep ranch. Loved every minute of it. Said it was the best time of her life."

"So now she's pretending . . . what?" Audrey asked. "That you two never met before?"

"Yeah. She pretends we just met and then refers to a knowledge of me going back years. Sort of eerie."

"You two," Alston said. "Birds of a feather cluck together."

"You're both nuts," Audrey amplified. "Why don't you get married? I mean, neither of you should marry anyone else."

"Moxie will never marry," Fletch said. "She has this strange, necessary thing with being in love with whoever she's playing at the moment. Anyhow, she blames ol' Freddy for putting her mother in the hospital."

"Is she afraid she'll put you in the hospital?" Alston asked. "Fat chance."

"Making love to her has always been interesting," Fletch said. "You're never sure with whom you're making love."

Alston cleared his throat. "I think the two of you alone in a bedroom would make for quite a crowded room."

Fletch took the envelope out of his back pocket. "I came because I need a couple of favors."

"You name it," Alston said.

"There are some ashes in this envelope. I need them analysed chop-chop."

"Sure." Alston stepped over and took the envelope and put it in his own pocket.

"Second," Fletch said, "are you of sufficiently august rank in the District Attorney's office, Alston, to make a call to the United States Embassy in Geneva?"

"Never have done such a thing before," Alston answered. "Guess that's one of those things you do first and ask permission for second — Marine style."

"Good. I need the particulars on the death of an American citizen named Thomas Bradley. About a year ago. He may have died in hospital, or some kind of a special sanitorium. He may have committed suicide."

"From California?"

"Yes."

"You say about a year ago?"

"His widow says a year ago this month. His death was not announced here, though — or so it seems — until about six months later. The operation of a family business, Wagnall-Phipps; Bradley's wife running the company while she's waiting for someone else to take over — it's all mixed up somehow."

"How?"

Fletch said, "I don't know. I guess you could say: confusion has been caused, I suspect, deliberately."

"Suicide," Alston said. "You said the possibility of suicide. Isn't that enough of an explanation?"

"Not really."

"You'd be amazed," Alston said, "to know what my office still puts up with to permit people to conceal the fact of suicide. I don't disagree," he said. "I'm sympathetic. I go along with it."

Audrey said, "Alston, I think Fletch is considering the possibility of murder."

Alston looked at Fletch and Fletch continued looking at Audrey.

Alston said, "Are you, Fletch?"

"Suspicious death," Fletch said. "The guy may have died a year ago. But I suspect his kids weren't told until six months later. His neighbors and the president of the company he owned weren't told until eight months later. And, I have good reason to believe, his own Vice-president and treasurer wasn't told — really told — until last Thursday."

"It would be nice to have a look at the probate record," Alston said.

"Would there have to be one?"

"Sure. Property within the state . . ."

"Then I'd appreciate that, too."

"My fast answer is," Alston said, "really off the top of the head, is that somebody is trying to postpone, or evade altogether, death taxes, inheritance taxes. Was this a young guy?"

"Less than fifty."

"Death caught him with his pants down. In what kind of financial shape is this company of his, what's it called?"

"Wagnall-Phipps. I don't know."

"I suspect that's the answer," Alston said. "People don't expect to die so young. He died in Switzerland. Sounds to me like the estate's trying to take advantage of that fact to get the estate in shape, fiddle the taxes."

"I never thought of all that," Fletch said.

"You never went to Law School."

"Gee," Fletch said. "Is that why I haven't got either a mortgage or a credit card?"

"That's why," Alston said.

"I do have all those people called Moxie waiting for me." Fletch stood up. "Will tomorrow be too soon to call you, Alston?"

"Nope. I'll put highest priority on the chemical analyses, D.A. Demands, and I'll put in the call to Switzerland before I leave the house. Might even have the answers before noon. I'll call probate when I get to the office."

Audrey looked at him. "Don't you have anything else to do? I mean, any work of your own?"

"I seem to remember once or twice in the past Fletch dropping everything to help me," Alston said. "In case I haven't mentioned this before, Audrey, I wasn't a very with-it Marine."

"Bye, Fletch." She kissed him on the cheek. "Thanks for saving my husband's ass."

"Hell with his ass," Fletch said. "It's his sense of humor I saved."

On the sidewalk in front of the house, Alston Chambers said, "Fletch, I've got a bank balance of over five hundred dollars. All or part of it are yours, any time you want it."

"Poo!" Fletch said. "What's money? Tissue paper! Who needs it?"

Sitting in the car, Fletch said through the window, "Thanks, Alston. Call you tomorrow."

NINETEEN

"Shit on a windy corner!" Moxie muttered as she got into the passenger seat of the car in the dark. "You even beat Freddy Mooney!"

"Don't bother giving me directions. I know where the Colloquial Theater is."

"I never in my life came across such a weird man as you are!"

"Across the bridge, right?"

She didn't even glance in the direction they were going.

"I mean, my God! In the three days I've known you all you've done is cry poor. Poor me! I've lost my job, wail, wail, wail! You haven't bought me any food in three days!"

"Orange juice. I bought the orange juice."

"I put my name on the dotted line for a steak, pal. And a bottle of wine. Had to pretend I was a bride new to the neighborhood with a husband working in a bank."

"You're good that way."

"You've got fifty dollars — I've got about the same, for the rest of my life." Even to Fletch her imitation of him sounded accurate. "You leave the house to run around the countryside in your sports car." She slapped the dashboard of the MG with her hand. "I spot a wallet hanging out of your dirty jeans, say, *What's this?*, pull it out, open it up, and there — right there before my eyes as surprising as Mount Everest in the Sahara

Desert — is twenty-five thousand dollars cash in one thousand dollar bills!"

"It's not my money, Moxie. I told you that, at the apartment."

"You wouldn't even buy us lunch with a credit card!"

"I told you. The money belongs to James Saint E. Crandall."

"Losers weepers!"

"Twenty-five thousand dollars worth of weepers?"

"Mister Fletcher, may I point out to you that anyone who can drop twenty-five thousand dollars cash on the sidewalk and not even look around is also someone who knows where his next poached egg is coming from?"

"I don't know that. Neither do you."

"I do know, on the other hand, that you do not know where your next poached egg is coming from."

"That has nothing to do with it."

"That's why you drove about one-hundred-and-fifty miles out of your way to stop at that dead-water town, Worrybeads, or whatever it was, right?"

"Wramrud."

"Whatever. Here's a guy trying to give away twenty-five thousand dollars in cash while he's starving. I ask you, is that sensible?"

"I'm not starving."

"You never even mentioned you were carrying so much money. And there we were, sleeping on a beach!"

"That was nice. And I did, too, mention it."

"Yeah. *So I took the twenty-five thousand dollars.* That's what you said. Is everything you say a joke? Are you a joke, Irwin Fletcher?"

Going onto the bridge Fletch's eye caught something fluttering in the breeze, a piece of cloth, to his right, half-way across.

"You sound like a wife," he said.

She grinned across at him, her face picking up the light from the dash-board. "Hoped you'd say that. I rehearsed."

He was slowing the car.

It was a skirt that was fluttering in the breeze. Fletch could see one leg below it, very white, and above it, hanging onto a bridge cable, an arm.

He pulled the car's hazard lights switch, and pulled over to the right as far as he could.

"Get out of the car, Moxie, and stand as much out of the way as you can. Don't stand in front of the car."

"You're stopping in the middle of the bridge?"

"That's why you're getting out and standing as much out of the way as you can. The car might get hit."

"What's the matter?"

"Be right back."

Fletch got out of the car and ran back along the bridge. He saw one of the cars approaching him was a taxi. He stood in front of the taxi, making it stop.

"Bastard! You crazy?" the taxi driver shouted through his window. "Son-of-a-bitch! You some kind of a nut?"

Fletch leaned through the window. "You got a radio-phone? CB?"

"Yeah. What are you?"

"Call the cops," Fletch said. "Jumper."

"Yeah. Oh, yeah." The taxi driver reached for the microphone hanging from his dashboard. "Where?"

"There." Fletch waved his arm toward the edge of the bridge and then pointed to his own car. "Pull your car behind mine, will you? You got bigger lights. A roof light."

"Yeah. Sure."

The car rolled forward. "You goin' out there?"

"Near enough to talk, I guess."

"Jeez. Crazy bastard."

Fletch watched the taxi, its roof light on, its hazard lights flashing, stop behind his car. Moxie's face looked white in the headlights of the taxi.

Then Fletch stepped onto the knee-high guard rail. Looking down he saw the lower ledge of the I-beam and stepped down onto it. From there he saw the river far, far below him, some lights, moonlight, city lights, bridge lights, reflecting off, wavering on the oily, sluggish water. He tried to decide the water was too far away for him to care about it.

There was an L-shaped strut extending away from the bridge to a cable running parallel with the bridge road. The cable was as thick as a sewer pipe. He put one foot on the strut. There was not much wind, but there was some. He looked at the woman who was standing farther along the cable, over the water to his right. There was enough wind to make her skirt flutter and stand out.

"Fletch?" Moxie's voice came from behind him. Her voice sounded sincerely inquiring, as if she were about to ask him a question.

Both of Fletch's feet were on the strut. He stood up straight, his hands free in the air. Then purposely fell forward, grabbing the cable with both arms, hugging it.

He held on a moment, his cheek against the cable's fabric.

"Fletch?" Moxie said. "I think I'll shut my face, now."

Fletch pulled himself more onto the cable, pulled his hips onto it. His empty stomach sent an inquiry to his brain regarding the dark water swirling far below him. He pulled his feet closer to the cable and putting weight on them, on the strut, flipped himself over. For a second, neither foot, neither hand was on anything.

Then he was sitting up, his feet on the strut, his hands on the cable each side of him, the breeze in his face. On the bridge, car horns were complaining about the two parked cars. Moxie and the taxi driver, facing him, were in silhouette.

To Fletch the woman standing to his left on the cable still appeared mostly as a fluttering skirt. She was wearing one green, plastic, ballet-style slipper. The other slipper was gone. Her legs were white and heavy and broken with varicose veins.

Easily, Fletch said, "Hi."

The woman's head turned. Two large, dark eyes stared down at him from deep, hollow sockets. Thick black hair waved around her face.

"What do you like?" Fletch asked.

She stared down at him.

"Do you like chocolate?"

She turned her head back into the wind, the dark, back into space, and said something.

"What?" Fletch asked. "I didn't hear you."

She turned her head back to him, annoyed.

"What do you like?" she asked. "Tell me that."

"I like chocolate," Fletch said. "I like to see birds hopping on the grass. Do you like to see little birds hopping on the green grass?"

She said something that was lost in the wind.

"What else do you like?" Fletch asked. "Who do you like on television?"

There was no answer.

"Mike Wallace? Merv Griffin? How about *As The World Turns*? Do you ever watch that?"

No answer.

Fletch's throat was dry.

"Hey," he said, "do you remember the smell of a brand new car? Really new?"

No answer.

"How about the smell of brownies baking? Isn't that the greatest?"

From above she was staring down at him.

"What kind of sounds do you like?" he asked. "Harmonica? Violin? Guitar?"

No answer.

"You know what I like?" he asked. "I love seeing a newspaper page blowing along a city street. I love to hear rain — really hard rain — when I'm in bed. The yap of a puppy. Do you like to hear the yap of a puppy sometimes?"

"Hey," the woman said. "Kid."

"Yeah?"

"Take my hand, willya? I'm scared shitless."

"So am I," Fletch said.

She began reaching for him, immediately tottering.

"Wait a minute," Fletch said. "There has to be a right way to do this."

To sidle toward her, Fletch would have to take his feet off the strut.

"Just sit down," Fletch said. "Right where you are. Slowly, carefully."

Slowly, carefully she sat down on the cable, facing the bridge. The green plastic slipper dangled from her foot.

"Hold onto me," she said.

Fletch took her hand.

"Wait for the cops," Fletch said. "We'll wait for the cops."

"What the fuck we doing out here?" the woman asked.

"I don't know," he answered. "Sometimes we find ourselves places like this."

She was shivering then. "It's not my fault, you know. It really isn't."

"I'm sure it isn't," Fletch said. "Tell me what you like. What's the nicest book you ever read?"

"That's a funny question."

"Well, what is the nicest book you ever read?"

"*Black Beauty*," the woman said.

"Tell me about it."

The woman thought a moment. "I don't remember nothin' about it," she said, " 'cept that I liked it."

"Hey, great," Fletch said. "You get to read it again."

"This really isn't my fault," the woman said. "Believe me."

"I believe you," Fletch said. "Believe me I believe you."

And there came onto the bridge the swirling lights of two police cars, then a fire truck, then the Rescue Squad truck. A policeman and then a fireman had spoken to Moxie and the taxi driver.

The man in the fire hat called to Fletch and the woman. "All right to come over?"

"Sure," Fletch answered.

"All right," the woman said.

A canvas-backed ladder was run across to them, landing on the cable between them, and a fireman walked across on it and took the woman by the arms and helped her to stand up. He guided her feet on the ladder, putting himself behind her, holding her arms, bearing most of her weight himself, urging her to move her feet along. From behind he looked a giant child walking a rag doll.

Halfway across, the fireman turned his head back to Fletch. "Want me to come back for you?"

"Just give me a minute," Fletch said. "I'll be right there. Put the coffee pot on."

Once the woman and the fireman were off the ladder, Fletch crawled along it back to the bridge on all fours.

TWENTY

"Really, Moxie," said the theater director in the light-weight, double-breasted blazer, "this does not bode well. If you're so late showing up for a cocktail party, how can I expect you to show up on time for rehearsals and performances?"

"We got held up on the bridge," Fletch said.

"Everyone gets held up by a bridge," the director said. "That's what bridges do."

"We were delayed on the bridge," Moxie said.

The Colloquial, like most theaters not putting on an illusion at that moment, looked a cross between a dirty warehouse and an impoverished church. On one side of the stage, lumber was stacked. On the other side, a long, flimsy table held half-eaten wheels of cheese and many empty wine bottles. Out front were rows of dispirited, sagging chairs, existentially weary of tears and laughter, tragedy and comedy.

When Moxie and Fletch had entered the stage from the wings other members of the cast and crew summed up Moxie coolly, professionally watching the way she walked and stood. None evinced a more human interest in her. Only the director had come forward to greet her.

"At least you're alive," the director said. "And you're here. We must be grateful for small favors."

"And I've studied the *In Love* script," Moxie said in a small voice. "Paul, I think it's wonderful."

"You'll meet the author tomorrow, I trust," the director said. "He flew in from New York this afternoon and was just too exhausted to stand up, he said. I suspect the truth is he intends to use his time out here trying to get a paying job in television." The director elevated his eyebrows at Fletch. "Is this the boy you wanted me to meet?"

"This is Fletch," Moxie said. "You said on the phone you're not all that keen on Sam . . ."

The director stood back, eyebrows still half-way up his forehead, and looked Fletch up and down and up again, as if to gauge his suit size.

"Nice looking," the director said. "Natural. I suppose your bodies would work well together."

"They do," commented Fletch.

"How do you feel about being naked?" the director asked.

Fletch answered, "I was born that way."

"But you weren't born on a stage," the director said. "Although, of course, Moxie was. How is dear Freddy Mooney, Moxie, your inveterate Pa?"

"Inveterate, thank you."

"But, my God, doesn't he bathe?" the director said of Fletch. "I mean, I know dirt turns some people on, but not enough of them to fill a theater at these prices."

"Am I dirty?" Fletch asked Moxie.

"Grimy," Moxie said. "Streaked."

"I'll swear I took a shower in the fall."

"He's really as clean as a whistle, usually," Moxie said. "It's just that, on the way over, he . . ."

"He what?" asked the director. "Did the backstroke through the city dump?"

"He saved a woman's life," Moxie said. "Sweaty work, that."

"But can he act?" the director asked.

"No." Fletch said. "Not at all."

"How refreshing of you to say that. Finally, in California, I've heard a new line: No, I can't act. If you're seriously applying for the male lead in *In Love*, Mister Fletch, or whatever your name is, you must know you have to appear nude on stage not once, but twice. I'll see to it that you take a shower before each performance. Afterward, you're on your own."

Fletch turned to Moxie and asked, in a reasonable tone, "Moxie, darling, what are you doing?"

"Tell him what a great actor you are, Fletch."

"I can't act at all."

"Nonsense," said Moxie, "you've been acting all your life."

"Never."

"You need the job, Fletch."

"Not a job acting."

"It would be fun," Moxie said. "You and me."

"It would be horrible."

"You don't have anything else to do."

"In fact, I do have something else to do."

"What? Interview more dead people?"

"Moxie?"

"Anyway," the director said, "you should meet Sam, Moxie. Your present male lead. Tell me what you think of him. Oh, Sam!" the director called.

Across the stage a dark-haired, heavy-browed young man stood up from a pile of lumber and started to walk over.

"Ape," the director said quietly. "He walks like an orangutan with gonorrhea. Heavy thighs. Today's audiences do not like heavy thighs. Oh, Sam, meet Moxie Mooney."

"Hullo," Sam said.

"Hullo," said Moxie.

"Why don't you two children greet each other with a kiss? You'll be working together."

Both Moxie and Sam put their faces forward to be kissed, neither to kiss. After indecisive, awkward maneuvers, the kiss was perfunctory.

"Theater history is made," said the director sardonically.

"It will be nice working with you, I'm sure," Moxie said.

"Yeah," Sam said. "I saw your dad play *King Lear*. Is it true he once ran a carnival knife-throwing act?"

Moxie's eyes became slits.

"Instant electricity," the director said. "Serendipity. I must rush home and get it all down in my journal, for posterity."

"See you," Sam said.

"Ten A.M.," said the director.

Sam ambled off-stage through the scenery.

The director sighed. "What do you think?" he asked Moxie.

"I don't think," Moxie said. "I act."

"At least you have the sense to realize it, dear. I wish other actors wouldn't think they could think. Listen," the director said to Fletch. "Hang loose a few days. I don't think Sam is going to work out. I hate to fire someone for thick thighs — "

"What?" Fletch said. "No."

"Okay," Moxie said. "He will."

"I can see you two as much more of a team. I mean, you'd be beautiful together, if one of you would take a shower. Really exciting to watch."

"I'm sorry to come to your party with a dirty face," Fletch said.

"Dirt can have its charms," the director said. "Especially when used to grow tulips."

"May we go now, Moxie?"

"We just got here. I haven't met the crew."

"I need a shower."

"He does need a shower, Moxie. You can meet the rest of the cast in the morning. Do try to be here at ten A.M. Excuses will not be tolerated." The director pointed at Fletch. "Take this boy home and wash him!"

TWENTY-ONE

"I've done you a favor," Moxie said a few times during the evening.

In bed, after they'd showered, after they'd eaten peanut butter sandwiches, after Fletch had explained to Moxie again he had no intention of trying to be an actor and she had explained to him, again, patiently, that, yes, he would so try, that doubtlessly he would be far better than Sam in the role, Fletch's legs were straighter, and after they, again, physically penetrated who each other was at that moment, lying back in the dark room, Moxie asked, "Fletcher?"

"Yes, Ma'm?"

"Where were you this morning?"

"When this morning?"

"I woke up at three o'clock. You weren't in bed. You weren't in the bathroom. You weren't in the apartment at all."

"I went out to do a spot of housebreaking."

"Jeez," Moxie said. "The way you say things I'd almost believe it. Not an actor, uh?"

"Not to worry. I got away with it."

"Well." She contracted and expanded, put her arm and her leg on his, so she'd be more comfortable. "I've done you a favor. A thousand-dollar favor. Or, a twenty-four thousand dollar favor, depending on your point of view."

"How's that again?"

"I've stolen a thousand dollars from you. From the wallet."
"What? What do you mean?"
"Well, it makes sense, Fletch. You're not spending the money when you really need to because you want to be able to return the whole twenty-five thousand dollars to the man. Right?"
"Right."
"Well, now you can't return the whole twenty-five thousand dollars to the man. Because I've got a thousand dollars of it. So you might as well do the sensible thing and spend the rest of the money yourself. Right?"
"Are you serious?"
"As serious as a flash flood in Abu Zabi."
"Perverted."
"What?"
"Perverted reasoning."
"Hardly."
"Moxie, you've stolen a thousand dollars that doesn't belong to me."
"Right. Thus giving you use of twenty-four thousand dollars."
"That's corrupt. You're a crook."
"I'm a sensible, clever lady."
"What have you done with the money?"
"Hidden it."
"Where?"
"Some place you'll never find it."
"Where would that be?"
"That's for me to know and for you not to find out."
"You're serious about this."
"Entirely."
"Do you intend to spend the money?"
"I will if I want. If there's something I want that costs a thousand dollars, I'll spend it."
"Is there something you want that costs a thousand dollars?"
"Not that I know of. Probably I'll think of something. I didn't really steal the money to spend it."
"Oh, no. Of course I believe that."
"You make me sound like a suspicious person."
"You're not suspicious. You're a crook."
"Fletcher, if you'd lost twenty-five thousand dollars in cash, do you think anyone else would drive all around the country trying to get it back to you?"

"I certainly hope so."

"Than you're an idealist slightly more demented than Icarus."

"Which Icarus is that?"

"The guy who flew toward the sun with wings attached by wax. The melting kind of wax."

"Oh, that Icarus. That kind of wax."

"Demented."

"Moxie, there's such a thing as a social contract. It makes the world go 'round."

"I don't notice Frank Jaffe, or your newspaper, observing any social contract with you."

"Of course they have. It appears I goofed, and they fired me. That's perfectly agreeable."

"You were lied to by someone at Wagnall-Phipps."

"Charles Blaine. And Enid Bradley did try to observe the social contract with me. She offered me money to make up for the damage I've suffered at the hands of Wagnall-Phipps."

"Did you accept?"

"No."

"More likely she offered you money to make you go away."

"I think so, too."

"It's also written into the social contract, Losers weeper, Finders keepers."

"Where is that written?"

"Page 38. Clause 74."

"That's the social contract for young readers. Ages four to seven."

"Really, Fletch."

"Moxie, what am I going to do if I find the man, this James Saint E. Crandall, and I haven't got the full twenty-five thousand dollars?"

"I have just given you reason — necessity you might call it — to stop looking for James Saint E. Crandall. Don't you get the point? You're such a slow boy."

"You're a crook. You've stolen a thousand dollars."

"I've done you a favor."

"Stop doing me favors. At seven o'clock you're doing me the favor of trying to get me a job as a male stripper. At eleven o'clock you tell me you've done me the favor of stealing a thousand dollars from me. What's the next favor you're going to do me? Give me whooping cough?"

"I'll think about it."

"Jeez!"

"You think about it, too."

"Think about what?"

"All the nice favors I've been doing you. You'll feel much better in the morning. You'll wake up and realize you have twenty-four thousand dollars to spend. You're so rich you can even afford to work in the theater."

"Good night, darling."

" 'Night, lover. Sweet dreams."

TWENTY-TWO

Fletch opened his apartment door to the corridor and found himself looking down at himself, his face streaked with grime and sweat, on the front page of the *News-Tribune*.

"Oh, no."

MOTORIST PREVENTS BRIDGE SUICIDE ATTEMPT was the headline over the photograph.

Towel wrapped around his waist, he picked up the newspaper, closed the door, and sat down on the divan in his livingroom.

An observant passerby with a willingness to risk his life to save the life of another climbed out onto the superstructure of the Guilden Street Bridge after dark last night and talked a middle-aged female potential suicide victim back to safety.

"In this life we're all in the same car together," said Irwin Maurice Fletcher, 24.

Until Friday of last week, Fletcher was a member of the News-Tribune *editorial staff.*

Fletcher said his eye happened to be caught by the potential victim's skirt fluttering in the breeze as he drove onto the bridge . . .

The telephone rang. Absently, still reading, Fletch picked up the receiver.

"Hello?"

"Fletch? Janey. Frank wants to talk to you."

"Frank who?"

"Hey, Fletch!" Frank Jaffe's voice sounded too cheery for a Monday morning. "You made the front page."

"Not the first time, Esteemed Managing Editor."

"The *News-Tribune* gave you quite a spread."

"I have it in my lap. Nice of you guys to report in the third paragraph you fired me last week. Really helps in the care and feeding of Irwin Maurice Fletcher."

"Makes us look like shits, don't it?"

"It do."

"Had to report it. Journalistic honesty, you know?"

"You had to report it in the lead?"

"Yeah, well, I agree — that stinks. Some of the people around here are pretty burned off at you, in case I didn't tell you before. One old desk man wondered aloud this morning why you didn't let the woman jump so you could then interview her. After she drowned, that is."

"I got the point, Frank."

"Some of these guys have a truly vicious sense of humor."

"Tell them if they don't restrain themselves I won't interview them after they're dead."

"I don't suppose you want to hear the headline they really wanted to run."

"I don't suppose I do."

"You might."

"I doubt it."

"I mean, with your irrepressible sense of humor?"

"Okay, Frank. Give it to me. I haven't had breakfast yet."

"The headline they wanted to run was GUILDEN STREET BRIDGE HERO FIRED BY THE NEWSPAPER YOU TRUST."

"Too long for a headline. Why did you call, Frank. To congratulate me?"

"Hell, no. I've always known you could talk the bark off a tree. No big feat, talking a woman off a bridge. Not for you."

"So why did you call?"

"It's Monday morning. I'm in the office."

"So?"

"You said I wouldn't be. You cast aspersions at Clara Snow's cooking."

"You must have a goat's stomach, Frank. I know you've got his horns."

"Actually, I was thinking, Fletch."

"I can smell the smoke."

"You write pretty well."

"When I have a chance."

"You have the chance. I'm giving it to you. What I'm thinking is, this is a perfect opportunity for a first-hand account, you know? Big feature."

"You mean, like, HOW I TALKED THE SUICIDE OFF THE BRIDGE BY I.M. FLETCHER?"

"You got it."

"No, thanks, Frank."

"Why not? You got something else to do today?"

"Yes. I have."

"We'll pay you. Guest writer's rates."

Guest writer's rates were on the lower side of adequate.

"Gee, thanks, Frank. But I don't work for you anymore, remember?"

"Might clean up your reputation a little."

"Might sell you a few newspapers."

"That, too."

"Know what, Frank? You're not a bad managing editor — even if you are burying that story about the Governor's press secretary's brother selling cars to the state police."

"Know what, Fletch? You're not a bad kid — even if you do interview dead people."

"See you, Frank."

"See you, Fletch."

When Moxie came into the livingroom, she looked at the newspaper and said, "You're not twenty-four."

Still sitting on the divan, Fletch shook his head sadly. "Goes to show you. You should never believe everything you read in a newspaper." He looked up at her, dressed only in his old, torn denim shirt. "Come on. Get dressed. I'll drive you to the theater."

"Where's breakfast?" she asked.

"Same place that thousand dollar bill is, you stole from the wallet yesterday."

She looked at him sharply. "Where's that?"

He shrugged. "I wish I knew."

TWENTY-THREE

"Are you the manager of this bank?" Fletch asked the skinny man in a worn-out suit who sat at a big desk the other side of a railing.

"Indeed I am." The man smiled at him warmly. "You look like someone who could use a car loan. We can do very well for you on a car loan."

"No, thanks. I have a car loan." Fletch waved a thousand dollar bill. "I want to know if this is real."

The manager saw the bill and gestured Fletch around the railing to his desk. The manager took the bill in the fingers of both hands and felt it as would a clothing merchant feeling material. He examined it closely through his eye-glasses. Expecially did he examine closely the engraving of Grover Cleveland.

"Do you have any reason to doubt its authenticity?" the manager asked.

"Sure. I've never seen one before."

"You don't see too many pictures of Grover Cleveland."

"Is that who it is? I thought it might be Karl Marx."

The manager looked at him in shock. "Karl Marx?"

Fletch shrugged. "Don't see too many pictures of him, either."

"The manager chuckled. "It looks okay to me."

"Will you cash it for me?"

"Sure."

Fletch took another thousand dollar bill out of the pocket of his jeans. "This one, too?"

The manager examined the second thousand dollar bill even more closely. "Where did you get these?"

"My employer is a little eccentric. Hates to write checks."

"You must be well paid." The manager looked closely at Fletch. "I've seen you somewhere before."

"Have you?"

"Your picture. I've seen your picture — very recently."

"Oh, that," said Fletch. "I'm on the five-thousand dollar bill."

"Maybe on a Wanted Poster?" The skinny man laughed. "How do you want these bills broken up?"

"Hundreds, fifties, twenties, tens, fives."

The manager stood up. "You just want it spendable, right?"

"Right."

"I'll be right back."

The fistfuls of money the manager brought back to Fletch were bigger than Fletch expected. The manager counted it out again, on the desk in front of Fletch.

"Thank you." Fletch was having difficulty stuffing the bills into the pockets of his jeans.

"I'm just slightly uneasy." The manager looked closely again at Fletch's face. "I've seen a picture of you somewhere — I think, this morning."

"Did you read the funnies?"

"Yes," the manager answered. "I read the funnies on the bus."
Fletch said, "That must be it, then."

"When will the suit be ready?"
"Ten days."
"Not soon enough."
"When do you need it?"
"Wednesday."
"This is Monday."
"Thursday morning then."
"We'll see what we can do."
Besides the well-cut, serious blue business suit, Fletch had bought, in the very expensive men's shop, shirts, shoes, neckties, tennis sneakers, shorts, sport shirts, and, a suitcase.
"Going on a vacation?" the salesman asked.
"Yes," answered Fletch. "I'd like to take everything with me, except the suit."
"Certainly, Mister Fletcher. How do you choose to pay? We'll accept your check."
"Cash." Fletch took a mess of bills from the pocket of his jeans.
"Very good, sir. I'll have everything wrapped for you."
"No need. I'll just put everything in the suitcase."
"If that's what you wish."
While the salesman added up the bill and made change, Fletch packed the suitcase.
"Mister Fletcher," the salesman said slowly. "I wonder if you'd accept a gift from the store."
"A gift?"
"That was qute a wonderful thing you did last night — taking that woman off the bridge."
"You know about that?"
"Everyone knows about that." The salesman's eyes studied the deep carpeting. "Our cashier, last year, found herself in similar straits. You see, no one knew, understood . . ."
"So people do read newspapers."
"We're proud to have you a customer of our store."
Other salespersons, Fletch now noticed, were standing around watching him.
The salesman handed Fletch a boxed silver-backed brush and comb.
"Wow," said Fletch.
"They're made in England," the salesman said.

"Real nice." Fletch shook the salesman's hand. "Real nice of you."

"People make efforts so seldom for other people . . ." The salesman seemed embarrassed.

"Thank you," said Fletch.

With suitcase in one hand and the boxed brush and comb in the other, Fletch proceeded to leave the store.

All the salespersons smiled at him as he went by, and applauded him.

"You don't want to go to San Orlando," the heavily made-up woman in the tight-fitting jacket said. On the wall of the travel agency posters recommended Acapulco, Athens, Nice, Naples, Edinburgh, Amsterdam, and Rio de Janiero. Fletch wanted to go to all of them.

"I must," Fletch said.

"No one *must* go to San Orlando." She had the phone to her ear, waiting for information from the airline. "You know where Puerto de San Orlando is? Way down the Mexican coast. Takes forever to get there. They haven't finished building it yet. Barely started. One hotel. The place is insuperably hot, dusty — hello?" She noted information from the airline. "That's terrible," she said, hanging up. "Terrible connections all the way through. It's a far more expensive trip than it's worth, at this point. If you waited a few years, until after they've developed the place a little . . ."

Leaning on the counter she told Fletch about the bad connections to San Orlando, and the expense.

"Fine," said Fletch. "Reservations for one, please."

"For one?" The woman looked truly shocked.

"One," Fletch said.

"Boy," the woman said. "Is being a hero *that* bad?" She sat down at the small desk behind the counter. "Return when?"

"Wednesday."

"Wednesday? This is Monday."

"Got to pick up a new suit," Fletch said. "Thursday morning."

She put the airline's ticket form into the typewriter. "Some people's idea of fun. It's all right, I suppose, as long as they have the travel agent to blame."

TWENTY-FOUR

"Hey, Fletch!" Alston Chambers said, answering the phone to him. "You're an unemployed hero again!"

In his apartment, sitting on the divan, Fletch put his coffee mug precisely over his own mug on the front page of the *News-Tribune*. Moxie had left the newspaper on the coffee table.

"I'm beginning to think that's your natural condition," Alston said. "Heroically unemployed."

"Aw, shucks. 'Twarn't nothin'."

"I wouldn't have gone out on that bridge cable for a million dollars. A million plus loose change. Especially in the dark."

"Actually, I never did decide to do it, Alston. I just did it."

"It's a good thing you're thoughtless, Fletch."

"Am I calling too early?" Fletch's watch read two thirty.

"Nope. I called the U.S. Embassy in Geneva before I left home, and they answered here at the office before noon. Was the name you gave me Thomas Bradley spalled B-r-a-d-l-e-y?"

"Yeah."

"No American citizen named Thomas Bradley has died in Switzerland."

"Ever?"

"Ever."

"No Thomas Bradley has ever died in Switzerland?" Fletch admired his new suitcase standing on the floor just inside the apartment's front door. "Do they know about deaths in private sanitoriums?"

"They say they do. They assure me their records regarding in-country deaths are one hundred percent accurate. I should think they would be."

"Even if the guy was cremated?"

"I asked them to check deaths and burials, removals, what have you, under all circumstances. Swiss paperwork, you know, leaves the rest of the world blushing. Wherever your man died, it wasn't Switzerland. Did you hear the announcement on the noon news the mayor is giving you The Good Citizen of The Month Citation?"

"The month isn't over yet. What about the ashes I gave you, Alston?"

"Oh, yeah. I dropped them at the police lab on my way to work. Why did you give them to me, anyway?"

"What was the result?"

"The result was that the good gentlemen in white coats called when I got back from lunch and asked if the D.A. had really wanted those ashes analysed. I assured the gentleman solemnly that the D.A. did. I didn't tell him that by 'D.A.' I meant a damned ass named Fletch."

"Alston — "

"Carpet."

"What?"

"Carpet. You know, rug? They were the ashes of a tightly woven, high quality carpet. Probably Persian."

"A carpet?"

"A quantity of petroleum, it says here, probably kerosene, a few wood ashes, probably pine, and a small measure of earth and sand."

"Are those guys always right?"

"Listen, Fletch, these guys do the lab work for every suspected arson in the state. They know a burned rug when they see one. They were very curious as to which case of arson we're working on. By the way, Fletch, which case of arson are we working on?"

"None I know of."

"Is Moxie burning up the family heirlooms so she can get a job playing in *Die Walkure*?"

"Something like that."

"Fletch, was Audrey right?"

"Probably. About what?"

"Are you on to a murder?"

"I don't know that at this point."

"What do you know at this point?"

"At this point . . ." Fletch thought a moment. ". . . I know Thomas Bradley was a carpet."

Dear Moxie,

Gone to Mexico to see a man about a carpet. Try to manage dinner by yourself. If you take anything from the refrigerator, please leave a $1,000 bill in the ice tray. Probably I'll be back Wednesday night.

—F.

TWENTY-FIVE

In late morning the sun on the Pacific Ocean and on the white sand of the beach at San Orlando was dazzling, dizzying to anyone who had spent most of the previous night jackrabbiting in airplanes. Fletch had arrived at the hotel at two forty-five A.M.; discovered there was nothing for him to eat, slept for three hours, awoke too hungry to sleep more, swam in the hotel pool until the breakfast room opened at seven, ate steak, eggs, bacon, homefries and fried tomatoes, then went out to the beach and fell asleep again.

The travel agent had been right. The airline's connections had been terrible: three different flights, each with a wait longer than the flight. She had been right that Puerto de San Orlando was just beginning to be built: whole walls were missing from the hotel; the landscaping was typified by weeds growing through cement blocks; beaten paths led from decorated bar to diningroom to pool. The sounds of bulldozers grinding, hammers bamming, saws buzzing filled the dusty air. She also had been right about Puerto de San Orlando's insuperable heat.

Late morning, Fletch took a table for two in the palm-roofed, open-sided bar on the beach and ordered a beer. Hot though he was, the beer was not cold. His eyes stung from the three jet airplane hops during the night, the brilliant sunlight reflected from the ocean and the beach, from swimming in the salt water. He drank his beer slowly and then ordered a Coca-Cola. The Coke wasn't cold, either.

Just before noon he saw Charles Blaine, in long plaid shorts and a yellow sports shirt, heavy horn-rimmed glasses and sandals, come through the hotel's arched doorway and plod across the sand to the beach bar.

When Blaine came into the shade of the palm-leaf roof he stopped, looked around. His eyes passed over Fletch, sitting at the table in just swimming trunks, blinked, and looked back. Blaine frowned like an accountant spotting red ink on books he had felt were not perfectly sound. He turned to go, apparently thought better of it, looked again at Fletch, hesitated, and then walked over to Fletch's table.

"You'd make a good accountant," Charles Blaine said to Fletch. "You don't give up."

Fletch turned his head toward the sea. "I'd make a good reporter, too. Pity I can't get a job as either."

Blaine put his hand on the other chair. "Shall I sit down?"

"I didn't come to Puerto de San Orlando," Fletch said slowly, "to drink the water."

Blaine sat down.

"Drink?" Fletch asked. "Warm beer or warm Coke?"

"Gin and tonic."

"Sounds good," Fletch said. "Me, too."

"Mexico has excellent limes," Blaine advised.

"I should think so."

They ordered from the young waitress whose hips were stacked on her like lava flow on a volcanic mountain.

"Nice vacation?" Fletch asked Blaine.

"Yes, thank you."

"Sort of an out-of-the-way place you chose for a vacation."

"It' s not too expensive — once you get here." Charles Blaine then listed the exact price of everything purchaseable in Puerto de San Orlando, Mexico, in both pesos and dollars — every article of food, drink, clothing, every souvenir.

Fletch asked, "How's your nervous breakdown doing?"

"Am I having one?"

"Enid Bradley says so."

"Does she? One of us may be having a nervous breakdown — either Enid or myself."

"She says you are. She says you were so fond of her husband you can't let him rest in peace. You can't believe he's dead. You keep referring to him in the present tense."

"Me, fond of Thomas Bradley?"

"Weren't you?"

"Thomas Bradley was my boss. I was as fond of him as I am of my desk, chair, filing cabinet, and desk calculator. He was a necessary piece of office equipment. As replaceable in my life as any other boss."

"There's some evidence," Fletch said, "that you're so eager to perpetuate the myth that Thomas Bradley is still alive that you even go so far as to forge memos from him."

A small, quirky smile flashed on Blaine's face.

"Why did you come here, Fletcher? What's your question?"

Fletcher looked innocently at Charles Blaine. "Was Thomas Bradley really a carpet?"

Blaine's eyebrows wrinkled. "I don't get you."

"I don't wonder. I don't get you, either."

Blaine finished his drink and signaled the waitress for another. "Vacationing in Mexico," Blaine said, "is enough to make a rummy of anyone. It's hot and it's dry and the injunction not to drink the water is well advertised. I calculate that because Mexico's water is famous for causing diarrhea, Mexico's liquor sales are approximately three hundred percent higher than they otherwise would be."

"No one's more cynical than a good accountant," Fletch said.

"That's true," Blaine said. "Or a good reporter, I guess."

"If we're both so good," Fletch said, "how come we're both sitting here on the edge of the world, about as popular with our employers as a toothache and an earache?"

Blaine sipped his new drink. "Do I understand, from what you said before, that you've lost your job?"

"I've lost my job. I've lost my career. I couldn't get a job now even working for the *Leavenworth Levity*."

"Is there such a newspaper?"

"Your wife's aunt said you're relentlessly literal-minded."

"Happy? You talked with Happy?"

"Of course. That's how I found you."

"My wife's aunt is sort of . . ."

". . . happy?"

"Yeah."

"She's a nice lady. Which, by Fletch definition, means she fed me."

"I'm surprised you had the resources to come find me," Blaine said. "I mean, the financial resources. The money."

"I don't," Fletch said. "Is Wagnall-Phipps paying for your so-called vacation?"

"Yes," Blaine admitted.

"I'm glad Enid Bradley didn't order you to go have your nervous breakdown on McDonald Island."

"Where's that?"

"Why don't you stop being so literal about the trivial, Mister Blaine, and become literal regarding the material."

Charles Blaine nodded his head, as if agreeing to difficult terms after a long negotiation. "All right." He sat back in his chair. "I guess I owe you an apology."

"Finally we're getting somewhere."

"I admit I was using you. Intentionally. Not you, personally. For that, I'm sorry. I was using the press. I guess I was thinking it's okay to use the press. I didn't realize, I forgot, that the media is made up of people, flesh and blood, who can be hurt, damaged."

"Damn," said Fletch. "I forgot to bring my violin."

"That was an apology," Blaine said.

"Consider it accepted, until you hear otherwise. Now please move to the facts."

"That's what I don't know," Blaine said. "That's what I want to find out. You can hardly blame me."

"That, too, will be decided later."

"Okay, I worked — work — for Wagnall-Phipps, Inc. Not one of the world's top forty companies, but a nice, solid little concern turning over a healthy profit. Thomas Bradley, founder, creator, Chairman of the Board. A sensible man, a quiet man, a good businessman. A quiet man except for the long, dirty stories he liked to tell."

"You didn't like his dirty jokes?"

"Didn't understand most of them. My wife and I lead a fairly — what should I say — conventional life. Always have." Blaine sneezed.

"I bet."

"An able businessman. He'd been married to Enid for twenty years or more. Two kids."

"I've got all that."

"Rode horseback for exercise, or pleasure, or for . . . whatever reason one rides horseback."

"Good for the digestion."

"Then I began hearing he was ill."

"From whom? When?"

"Well, from Alex Corcoran, who, if you don't know by now, is president of Wagnall-Phipps."

"I do know."

"Of course, next to Alex almost everyone looks ill. He's a big, florid man, plays golf almost every day of the week. That's all right. He makes more money for Wagnall-Phipps on the golf course than all the other sales personnel combined."

"When did Alex mention to you he thought Bradley was ill?"

"About two years ago. I don't know, really. I like to think I had noticed it myself, first."

"What did you notice?"

"About Tom? A weight loss. He seemed to be . . . becoming quieter. More reserved. He seemed distracted. I really don't know."

"So you understood something was wrong with him."

"Right. Then came the announcement that he was going to Europe for medical treatments. Prolonged medical treatments. Nothing was specified. When nothing is specified in a case like that, I guess, well, I guess we all thought the worst. Cancer."

"So no one, as far as you know, pressed for a full explanation."

"Of course not. It was announced that in his absence Enid Bradley would step in as Acting Chairperson."

"How come men are Chairmen and women are Chairpersons?"

"I don't know. Enid did just fine. Sometimes I'd ask her a question and she didn't have the answer, or hadn't thought it out, but by next morning she would have the answer, and it would always prove to be the correct one."

"How did you explain that to yourself? Did you think she had talked with Thomas Bradley overnight?"

"Yes, I did. At first. That made perfect sense to me, because many mornings, once or twice a week, I would get rather detailed memos from Bradley — I mean, Thomas Bradley. Nothing personal in them. Just memos regarding the backroom bookkeeping of Wagnall-Phipps."

"What do you mean, you *got them*? In the mail? From where?"

"No. They'd just be on my desk. I assumed Enid Bradley was bringing them into the office and leaving them for me."

"Okay. So the guy was in the hospital somewhere, maybe in Europe, keeping in touch with his wife by telephone, and, keeping his hand in the business by communicating with his treasurer by detailed memoranda."

"Yes. Then, last November, a Friday afternoon, the rumor went through the office that Thomas Bradley was dead. You know how rumors go through an office?"

"Ask the man who is one. A rumor, I mean."

"No one really says anything. The sound level, the tone, of an office changes. People walk differently. The expressions on their faces are different. Sometimes you just figure something is wrong, and then try to figure what is wrong. Do you know what I mean?"

"Sure. But I can't see a literal-minded man like you leaving matters like that. If there's a fact out there, somewhere, I suspect you pursue it."

"I did. I was worried, anxious. At about eight o'clock that night, I telephoned Alex Corcoran. Well, how do I say this? He had been drinking. He sounded terribly upset. He confirmed my suspicion."

"He said Thomas Bradley was dead?"

"He did. His speaking was uneven, his breathing was uneven. He said Enid was going through a terribly hard time. He asked me not to talk to Enid about it. She was being strong. She wanted no condolences, no flowers. She wasn't planning a memorial service."

"And that struck you as odd."

"Not really. The Bradleys were very quiet, sort of withdrawn people.

They had few friends, if any, that I know of. The socializing they did with people in the office was perfunctory, if you know what I mean. Anyway, Alex, in a sort of drunken manner, asked me not to confront Enid with the fact of her husband's death."

"And you didn't."

"No. I was surprised to see her in the office on Monday. She didn't leave for Switzerland until Tuesday."

"Do you know she went to Switzerland?"

"Let me think. I know Alex Corcoran said she went to Switzerland."

"Because that's where Thomas Bradley died?"

"Yes. So I understood."

"How long was she gone?"

"Oh, she returned the end of the next week. Thursday or Friday."

"Ten days, roughly."

"Ten days. And all that's all right. But, like an intelligent man, like any employee, intelligent or otherwise, I wondered what effect the death would have upon the company."

"What effect did it have?"

"Zero. Except for Alex Corcoran's statement to me, it was never stated that Thomas Bradley was dead."

"You accept that."

"Only more or less. I mean, Enid's not a warm woman, but you'd think she'd plant a flower somewhere for her dead husband. She continued to be listed as Acting Chairperson, instead of Chairperson."

"I understand that. Francine . . ."

"The routine remained as it was before. I mean, of course, I was expecting financial shifts in the company, little tell-tale signs, a cutting back of expenses, divestiture of certain assets, shifts of stock ownership. There was none of that. Of course the stock is held by an instrument called The Bradley Family Company."

"You're talking about the need to pay death taxes, estate taxes, whatever they're called."

"I presumed that the family had enough personal wealth to pay taxes without touching the assets of the firm."

"Is that likely?"

"It's possible. The Bradleys have never been big spenders. As far as I know, as a family they own one house, four cars, and a horse. How much does it cost to feed a horse? The only other family expense I know of is tuition for the son."

"Might as well be poured down the drain."

"Why do you say that?"

"So everything, so far, Mister Blaine, is understandable."

"Not at all. I said the routine remained identical. In conference with Enid Bradley, clearly she would not know the answers, what to do, how to decide. The next day, she would indeed have the answer for me, and, again, it would prove to be the correct answer."

"And she wasn't talking to her husband by telephone."

"Not unless the telephone company has made a technological advance they haven't publicized." Charles Blaine's paunch trembled with his own humor.

"Do you know about Thomas Bradley's sister, Francine?"

"Yes. I understand she and Tom were very close. That she is very clever in business. That Tom frequently consulted her."

"So Enid could have been getting advice from Francine on how to run the company."

"Yes. I suppose so."

"Do you kow that Enid may be only filling in for Francine? That Francine might come out to take over Wagnall-Phipps?"

Charles Blaine smiled. "It seems to me you know more about this company than you did last week when we talked, Fletcher."

"I'm doing this week what I guess I should have done two weeks ago. But, frankly, I still don't think a twelve graf story about a piddly little company like Wagnall-Phipps is worth the effort."

"So why are you doing it?"

"I'm worth the effort. I'm a good reporter."

Blaine shoved his glasses back up his sweat-slippery nose. "Yes, I know about Francine. And, yes, I think your conjecture that Enid was consulting with her is legitimate. Reasonable. Sensible."

"Thank you."

"But that doesn't explain the memos."

"Now we come to the memos."

"The memos kept coming. At first, I simply assumed they were in the pipe line — late in coming to me."

"Another reasonable assumption."

"Until they began referring to matters in the company which took place after Thomas Bradley's death."

"After."

"I said, *after,* dammit, *after.*"

"Spooky."

"Sufficient to make one wonder."

"I should think so."

"Initialed, of course. Not signed. Anyone can imitate initials. You saw the memos. You saw the initials."

"Yes. I did. That's rather the point. You showed them to me."

"Can you blame me being curious? Not only were they initialed, as always, the style of writing never varied. Not that I'm any expert on that. Purposely I showed you memos from before I heard about Bradley's death and after. Did you notice any difference?"

"I was not warned to look for any difference, thank you."

"I was curious."

"As well you might be. Did you ask anyone about these memos?"

"Yes, I mentioned the matter to Alex Corcoran. He didn't seem to understand a word I was saying. He's never understood me. I think I don't speak loudly enough for him, or something."

"He must have had some reaction. You showed him the memos, didn't you?"

"He scarcely glanced at them. He didn't understand what I was saying. He didn't listen. I went to him twice, trying to get him to see what I meant. Finally, he said, *For cryin' out loud, leave Enid alone, will you?*"

"And did you?"

"I'm an employee, Mister Fletcher."

"Okay, Mister Blaine. What was your best guess, at that point? Unless, of course, you believe that certain people have memo privileges from the beyond."

"I don't like to guess. I like to know."

"You lived with this spooky situation for some months."

"A few months."

"What were you thinking?"

"Obviously, I thought that either Enid Bradley had been writing the memos all along, and signing her husband's initials, you know, to give them added weight, authority, or . . ." Blaine shrugged.

"I'm filled with breathless anticipation."

". . . or the memos had been being written all along by his sister, Francine, who was forging his initials, or . . ."

"Two oars row a boat."

". . . . or Thomas Bradley was not dead."

"Three oars row us in a circle."

"What do you mean?"

"You could have been forging the initials yourself."

"Why would I do that?"

"Because you're crazy."

"I suppose from your point of view there's that possibility."

"What was your best guess?"

"You're missing another possibility, Mister Fletcher. One that worried me very much. I don't know if you can understand this. I consider myself a responsible businessman. I'm a Certified Public Accountant. This other possibility kept me awake nights."

"Which was?"

"That a complete unknown was running the company, through Enid Bradley. Some completely irresponsible person, who had no true authority. Enid wouldn't be the first widow to fall into the clutches of an unscrupulous parvenu, soothsayer, gigolo with ambitions, what have you."

"Did the memos sound that way? Were they ignorant, irresponsible?"

"No. But some confidence men are awfully bright, or, so I understand. A soothsayer, or whatever you call 'em, can be right nine times out of ten. It's the tenth order you obey that puts everything into a cocked hat."

"Well, Mister Blaine, that's a possibility that I never considered."

"Well, I did. And it worried me. You've referred to me several times in this conversation as literal minded. What I am, is honest. Something funny is going on here, clearly, and I had to find out what."

"So along comes the reporter from the *News-Tribune* — "

"And, in honesty, I showed you the true instruments that are running the company of Wagnall-Phipps."

"Memos from a dead man."

"Yes."

"However, you weren't honest enough to identify them to me as such. You didn't tell me Bradley is dead."

"I've apologized for that."

" 'Oops,' said the hangman, after he dropped the hatch."

"I never realized you'd get fired. I admit to using you. I was trying to bring this matter out into the open. Clear this matter up. I have my responsibilities. Who the hell is running Wagnall-Phipps?"

"Mister Blaine, who benefits from the death of Thomas Bradley?"

"I don't know. I don't see that anyone would. The stock in Wagnall-Phipps is held in a family fund sort-of-thing, the exact nature of which I don't know. And I don't know about any personal insurance Bradley had. And I don't know who might benefit emotionally from his death."

"Interesting point that: emotionally."

"Are you suggesting he may have been murdered?"

"Mister Blaine, I have a surprise for you. Are you ready for a surprise?"

"I'd love some answers."

"This isn't an answer. It's just a surprise."

"What is it?"

"Thomas Bradley did not die in Switzerland. I checked."

Charles Blaine stared at Fletch a long moment. "That's more of a question than an answer, isn't it?"

"Precisely."

Blaine leaned forward, his elbows on the table. "To answer your question more specifically: financially, I suspect the chief beneficiary of Thomas Bradley's death would be the Internal Revenue Service."

"And you said you can see no signs of estate taxes being paid."

"Exactly. Which is another worry. I do not intend to be party to a tax fraud. I do not even want to look like I might have been party to a tax fraud."

"Right," said Fletch. "Better my career be ruined than yours."

Sweating, his face colored, Blaine sat back. "I'm sorry it looks that way to you. It must. I did a very wrong thing."

"Tut tut, think nothing of it. Petroleum on a duck's feathers."

Blaine looked at his empty glass. "I don't get that expression. What happens when you put petroleum on a duck's feathers?"

"The duck drowns."

"Oh." Blaine cast his eyes slowly over the beach, which was empty at noon time. "We don't seem to know any more than we did when we started, do we?"

"Has Enid Bradley ever explicitly stated to you that her husband is dead?"

"Yes. Last Thursday. After your newspaper report came out. Just before she said I must be crazy and insisted Mary and I take a nice long vacation to this Mexican paradise." Blaine sneezed and then laughed.

"Was it Enid Bradley who specified Puerto de San Orlando?"

"Yes. She's paying."

"But you've been to Mexico before."

Blaine sneezed again. "Acapulco."

"I see."

"Dusty place, this. When are you going back?"

"Can't get a plane until tomorrow noon."

"What are you going to do until then?"

"Snooze on the beach, I guess."

"Will you permit Mary and me to entertain you at dinner tonight?"

"Certainly," Fletch said. "Nice of you."

"Not really," said Blaine. "Seems to me, without really meaning to, I did you a lot of harm." He stood up. "Will nine o'clock be all right?"

"See you then," Fletch said.

"The hotel's terrace diningroom." Blaine put out his hand to shake. "Why don't we stop this 'Mister Blaine, Mister Fletcher' nonsense? I suspect we're both victims of the same accident — or, I got you into my accident, or something."

Fletch stood and shook hands. "Okay, Charley."

"Do I call you Irwin?"

"Not if you want to live till dinner. I answer to the name Fletch."

Blaine leaned toward Fletch, his eyes magnified through his glasses. "Fletch, am I crazy, or is the world crazy?"

"That," said Fletch, "seems an eminiently sane question."

TWENTY-SIX

Three people, Mary Blaine, Charles Blaine, and Fletch, at dinner under the stars on the hotel terrace in Puerto de San Orlando, Mexico.

CHARLES: Gin and tonics, please, with lime.

FLETCH (to MARY BLAINE:): I've met your Aunt. She's a real nice lady. She fed me.

MARY: Isn't she marvelous? She says she was born happy, and I believe it. That woman has had such suffering, such tragedy. Yet she is relentlessly happy.

FLETCH: I know her nickname is Happy. What's her real name?

MARY: Mabel.

MARY: Look at the moon.

CHARLES: Even in Puerto de San Orlando I suspect prices are a little higher per item than they need be. It know it's a new resort, or a resort-to-be, and the Mexican government is trying to attract people here. But I daresay, if you drive a few miles inland, into some of the real villages, you'll find everything from limes to curios at half the prices . . .

CHARLES: Gin and tonics, please. With lime.

MARY: There's something unreal about Enid Bradley. I mean, she's the only contemporary woman I know who seems to have been born in a corset.

FLETCH: Originally, Tom Bradley was from Dallas, Texas?

MARY: You mean from where men are men?

CHARLES: I don't know.

MARY: Enid always looks terrified of what the next moment will bring — you know, as if she's afraid someone is going to say something dirty.

CHARLES: Her husband usually does. I mean, did.

CHARLES: Gin and tonics. Lime.

MARY: Look at the moons.

CHARLES: Didn't I say something this morning, Fletch, about people vacationing in Mexico drinking three times more alcohol than usual? They make a lot of money off our fear of drinking the local water.

MARY: I mean, I just don't see anyone ever having a rollicking time in bed with Enid Bradley, ever. I mean, I just can't picture Enid Bradley without her sensible shoes on.

MARY: Isn't this romantic, Charley? Look at the moons in the ocean. I have an idea. Why don't we take this nice boy to bed?

CHARLIE: Mary, I think we should order dinner, don't you?

FLETCH: Is Thomas Bradley dead?

MARY: Why wouldn't he be?

CHARLES: Frankly, I don't think so. I think he committed some gross irregularity and decided to disappear. Trouble is, I can't find what gross irregularity he committed. As Treasurer of Wagnall-Phipps, it's my damned responsibility to find it. I'm a Certified Public Accountant, and I can't find anything wrong. Please forgive me, Fletch. Please understand. This is very worrisome to me.

MARY: He's dead. It's just that nobody cares much.

TWENTY-SEVEN

Upon his return to his apartment late Wednesday night, Fletch found on the coffee table, beside the bills and junk mail, a note and three letters of interest.

F —

Your X, Linda, called. I told her you're cruising off Mexico on your yacht.

— M.

Dear Mister Fletcher:

The Mayor has informed his office that he has decided to honor you with the Good Citizen of The Month Award in recognition of the heroic risking of your own life to save the life of another citizen on the Guilden Street Bridge Sunday night.

The ceremony is to take place in the Mayor's office Friday at ten o'clock sharp.

You are to report to Mrs. Goldovsky at The Mayor's Office, City Hall, at eight-thirty sharp Friday morning. Mrs. Goldovsky will instruct you in what you are to do and to say during and after the ceremony. Any tardiness in meeting with Mrs. Goldovsky will not be tolerated.

The ceremony will be by nature of a press conference, which is to say, members of the press — reporters, photographers, and cameramen will be in attendance. Your being dressed in normal business attire will be suitable.

Sincerely,

The Office of The Mayor

Dear Mister Fletcher —

I read about how you rescued that lady off the bridge? I need rescuing. My parents treat me awful bad. They're never taken me to FANTAZYLAND — not even oncet, in all my life. Please come quick and rescue me up.

Tommy address above

Dear Mister Fletcher:

Although I'm sure I join millions in praising your act of heroism Sunday night, in saving that expectant woman from suicide, perhaps only my associate, Mister Smith, of this hotel, and I know you to be not an entirely honest man. There was a report of your deed in this morning's Chronicle. *We were able to recognize from your picture the man who was in my office last Thursday, identifying himself as Geoffrey Armistad. You showed us a wallet you said you found somewhere off the hotel's property containing twenty-five thousand dollars cash, apparently belonging to a recent guest of this hotel, a Mister James Saint E. Crandall. Such were the names we gave to the police, in reporting this incident. You gave us every assurance you, too, would report to the police. Apparently, you did no such thing. In fact, the newspaper reports you resigned your job with the* News-Tribune *last Friday. (You stated to us you were employed as a parking-lot attendant.) All this indicates to us you have no intention of returning the money to its rightful owner. Mister Smith and I think it only fair to warn you that we have set matters right this end, and provided the police with your correct name, and, having spent two minutes with the telephone directory, your correct address. Doubtlessly they will be in touch with you, requiring you to turn the money over to them until proper disposition can be made.*

Yours, Sincerely,

Jacques Cavalier,
Manager
Park Worth Hotel

TWENTY-EIGHT

"Where's the thousand dollars?"

"Hell of a way to greet me." At nearly midnight Moxie stood in the doorway of the apartment and dropped her airline's bag onto the floor. The zipper of the bag was broken and sticking out of it were the playscript, a sneaker, and a towel.

"Hello," Fletch said from the divan.

"Hello."

"You look bushed."

"I am bushed. Been rehearsing since noon. You look bushed with a sunburn. Oh, no! You have a sunburn!"

Through the dim light of the livingroom she was looking at him like a cosmetician.

"I have a sunburn. I fell asleep on the beach."

"Do you have it all over?"

"All over what?"

"All over your bod."

"No. Thank you for asking."

"That's all right. I guess it will fade before opening night. You'll just look funny tomorrow, that's all. At rehearsal."

"I'm not going to rehearsal tomorrow."

"Fletch, you have to."

"I do?"

"Sam is just impossible in the role. His manners are just so heavy. He's so self-conscious."

"And don't forget he's cursed with thick thighs or something."

"You'd think he was playing *Streetcar Named Desire.* His timing is all off for comedy. I told Paul you'd absolutely be at the rehearsal tomorrow."

"Paul the director?"

"Paul the director. He's good to give you the chance, seeing you've never really acted before. I mean, in the theater."

"I will not be at the theater tomorrow absolutely. Or tomorrow or tomorrow or tomorrow. Isn't that a line from somewhere?"

"Almost. I told you you can act."

"I've already done the strip-tease once today. And that was without music."

Moxie was taking things out of her airline's bag and spreading them around the floor. "Tell me: you were kidnapped and raped by a gang of Mexican Girl Scouts — right?"

"Almost. Customs. Coming back. The United States Customs. They hustled me into a little room, made me strip, and proceeded to prod and poke in my every crevasse and orifice."

"Serious?"

"I thought it was serious. I didn't like it much. They X-rayed my boots, my suitcase, my teeth."

"That's terrible."

"They spent over two hours on me. Or in me."

"What for?"

"They were unwilling to believe anyone my age flew on three airplanes to Puerto de San Orlando, Mexico, and back on three airplanes for thirty hours on the beach. I told them I had some time off."

"They thought you were smuggling drugs or something."

"Something." Fletch flicked a finger at the letter from the Mayor's Office on the coffee table. "Hardly the way to treat the Good Citizen of the Month."

Moxie knelt on the divan next to him and took Fletch's head in her arms. "Aw, my poor Fletch. Were you able to fart on cue?"

"Of course it didn't help convince them of my innocence that I was carrying over one thousand dollars in cash in my pocket."

"Did they finally apologize to the Good Citizen?"

"They said they'd catch me next time. Now may I ask where the thousand dollars is?"

"What thousand dollars?"

"The thousand dollars you took from the wallet."

"Oh, that thousand dollars."

"The very same."

"I bought a sweater."

"A thousand dollar sweater?"

"A skirt. Some records. And some baloney. Want a baloney sandwich?"

"We're living higher on the hog."

"And a car."

"A car!"

"A little car. Even smaller than yours."

"What kind of a car?"

"Yellow."

"A *yellow* car. I see."

"And it does beep-beep nicely."

"A small yellow car with a horn. Have I got it right so far?"

"I suppose it has an engine. It has an ignition key, which works."

"What a relief. No one should look at the engine until the ignition key doesn't work. Might be bad luck."

"I needed a car. You know, to get around."

"So the thousand dollars is gone."

"No such thing! I have a skirt, a sweater, some records — some nice records — a car, and some baloney. That's not *gone*, like, you know, if I threw it out the window. Want a baloney sandwich?"

"Sure."

At the kitchen counter Moxie spread the mustard so thin the baloney didn't even look slippery.

"Are you trying to make it last until all men are free?" he asked.

"What?"

"The mustard." He took the jar and knife from her and slathered it on properly.

Sitting at the kitchen table, she asked, "What were you doing in

Mexico? I mean, other than smuggling diamonds and drugs and cruising in your yacht?"

"I went to see Charles Blaine, Vice-president and treasurer of Wagnall-Phipps."

"Oh."

"And he tells me," Fletch said, placing the top pieces of bread on the sandwiches carefully so they would not slip, "that he's been receiving memos from a dead man."

"Seems I read that in the newspaper. Sort of."

"Indirectly, I suppose you did."

"So what's new?"

"Obviously, he has not been receiving memos from a dead man."

"It's nice to hear you say that. For a while, you had me worried."

"So from whom has he been receiving memos?"

"Must be Madame Palonka."

"Must be." He handed her a sandwich. "Who's Madame Palonka?"

"A medium in San Francisco. She transmits messages from the dead. Wow. Too much mustard."

"Who has been continuing to write memos signed Thomas Bradley after Thomas Bradley died?"

"A secretary stuck on routine?"

"Who is running Wagnall-Phipps?"

"Who cares?"

"I think they thought no one would care — much."

"They're right. Who are 'they'?"

"The great 'they'. I dunno."

"You care."

"I either have to care, or consider myself a non-entity, you see."

"Phew! What a choice! To be a something or not to be a nothing . . . how does that work out? To be a something, or a something . . . ? God! I can't keep up with you."

"Something's rotten in Denmark. Is that the same play?"

"Nothing's rotten in Denmark," Moxie said. "I've been there. Surely no one in Denmark would give me a mustard sandwich which even the baloney is trying to slip away from."

"Charles Blaine cares who's running Wagnall-Phipps."

"Fletch, do you think — just possibly — you're slightly obsessed with this matter?"

"It's not often one sees memos from a dead man."

"I admit that."

"And it's not often, I hope, that one's career is ruined by the selfsame mysterious memos."

"So you insist that your compulsion to find out who wrote those memos and why is legitimate?"

"I insist."

"Why don't you forget this whole silly thing, come to rehearsals tomorrow, try out for the lead in *In Love,* work hard with me, and enjoy a smashing success? You might find a whole new career for yourself in the theater."

"Sure. And ever after I'd still be known as the journalist who got fired because I quoted a dead man."

"At least come to rehearsal tomorrow."

"Can't."

"Why not?"

"Going to New York."

"Going to New York? You can't!"

"Can too. Made my reservation on an early flight while I was waiting for you."

"Why are you going to New York?"

"Because there's still one person concerned with this whole matter I haven't yet seen — Tom Bradley's sister, Francine."

"What can she know about it? She's all the way across the country!"

"Yeah. I know. But she's the only one I see benefitting from Bradley's death. Unless, of course, you subscribe to the theory Mrs. Bradley benefits emotionally by having gotten rid of the old boy."

"I don't subscribe to any theory. Except that there comes a time to give up! And you're long past that time!"

"Francine Bradley," Fletch said patiently, "is going to come West at some point and take over, run Wagnall-Phipps. Tom Bradley has been consulting her for years. Enid Bradley consults her. Don't you think I ought to at least go look in her eyes and try to figure out what all this means to her?"

"I suspect she'll look you back in the eyes and say you're a nut. All this can be explained by a secretarial mistake, Fletch."

"I don't think so. Charles Blaine doesn't think so."

"Anyhow, it was announced in this morning's *News-Trib* you're being honored Friday in the Mayor's Office for being Good Guy of The Week."

"Good Citizen of the Month, if you please."

"You can't go to New York. You have an appointment with the Mayor."

"The Mayor has an appointment with the press. I don't expect to be there."

"For goodness' sake, why not? If we could announce by Friday you're a member of the cast of *In Love* opening soon at The Colloquial Theater — "

"Everybody's got an angle."

"You bet."

"I'll be in New York Friday. You're not eating your sandwich."

Moxie pushed her plate away from her. "Your culinary skills aren't up to baloney sandwiches, Fletch. Better stick to peanut butter sandwiches for a while yet."

TWENTY-NINE

The doorman of the expensive, tall East Side New York apartment house put his hand over the mouthpiece of his telephone and said, with mild surprise and perfect respect, "Ms. Bradley says she doesn't know you, Mister Fletcher."

Fletch held out his hand for the phone. "May I speak to her myself, please?"

"Of course, sir."

He handed the phone to Fletch and stepped back half a pace. He was young and lean and had steady eyes and the gold braid on his uniform looked as ridiculous as a spinnaker on an aircraft carrier.

"Ms. Bradley?" Fletch said into the phone.

The woman's voice was throaty. "Yes?"

"Ms. Bradley, my name is Fletcher. I need to speak to you regarding the management of your late brother's company, Wagnall-Phipps. I have come all the way from California just to do so."

After a pause, Francine Bradley asked, "Who are you, Mister Fletcher?"

"I'm a reporter — an ex-reporter — who did a story for the financial pages of the *News-Tribune* on Wagnall-Phipps. I guess I made some sort of a mistake in writing the story. Yet I still don't know what the truth is."

"How could I help you?"

"I don't know. But I've talked with your sister-in-law, Enid Bradley, your niece, Roberta, your nephew, Tom — "

"The person you should speak to is Alex Corcoran. He's the president."

"I have spoken with him. I've also spoken again — a few days ago — with Charles Blaine."

There was a long pause. "You've spoken within the last few days with Charles Blaine?"

"I went to Mexico to do so."

"Well, you certainly have gone far out of your way. Weren't Corcoran and Blaine able to help you?"

"Not much."

"I don't see how I can help you. But come up. Anyone who's gone to as much expense and trouble as you have shouldn't be turned away at the door."

"Okay," Fletch said. "I'll give you back to the doorman."

"Really, Mister Fletcher — do I have the name right?"

"Yes."

"You could have saved yourself an awful lot of expense and bother if you'd simply called me from California. I probably could have told you on the phone whether I could help you . . ."

Francine Bradley had opened the door of Apartment 21M, flickered her eyes at him in some surprise, and immediately began talking as if she were continuing the conversation they had had on the apartment house's telephone.

Her hair was blonde and well set. Her face looked as if she had had expensive skin care. Her necklace was of heavy gold braid; her earrings matched. Her dress was a well-made, comfortably formal green satin, cut low in front. She was noticeably slim for a lady in her mid-forties.

". . . I doubt I know as much about Tom's company as you think." She led the way into a livingroom furnished well but sparsely. Glare filled the room from the large window overlooking the city. "I know none of the personnel out there, personally. I am acquainted with the figures, of course. Since Tom's death, well, Enid has had to lean on me more than somewhat. Enid, as you probably know, had no experience in business."

Her back to the window, Francine faced Fletch, hesitated as if wondering if she had already answered all his questions. Only at his silence did she gesture toward the divan. "Well, sit down. I'm expected out for dinner, shortly, but let me help you however I can in whatever time I have."

Sitting, Fletch unbuttoned his jacket, hitched up his trouser legs to avoid wrinkling his new suit.

On the coffee table in front of him were her handbag and gloves.

"I appreciate your seeing me," Fletch said. She sat on a brightly flowered chair, her back to the light from the window. "You may think me odd before I'm done, but I hope at least you will understand my confusion."

"I'm sure I won't think you a bit odd, Mister Fletcher." She smiled as if she already thought him odd. "Although, I must admit, when you said you're a reporter, an ex-reporter, I guess I was expecting to open the door to someone . . . more mature, older, I mean . . . someone who might look like he's been through more wars than you do."

"I keep an innocent look." Fletch smiled. "It comes from mixing orange juice with my cereal."

Francine Bradley laughed happily.

Now that his eyes had adjusted to the glare in the room, Fletch saw the photographs on a bookshelf of Roberta Bradley, Thomas Bradley, Jr., school photographs of them at various ages, two photographs of Enid Bradley, a younger and an older, and a large group photograph of the family. Fletch assumed the dark-haired man with his arm around Enid's waist was Thomas Bradley. On the wall facing him, Fletch saw a brown and black tile mosaic. On a low table near the window was an unfinished mosaic.

"Did your brother do the mosaic on the wall?" Fletch asked.

"Yes." Francine looked sadly at it. Then she sighed and gestured at the unfinished mosaic on the low table. "And that's one he was working on. Tom used to stay with me, you know, when he was in New York to see the doctors. He was working on that just before he went off to Switzerland. I've left it there. Silly of me, I suppose. It just makes him seem — well — sometimes when I come in at night I almost feel I can see him sitting there, in his robe and slippers, working on it."

"I guess my questions will seem strange to you."

"That's all right." She glanced at her watch. "I am being picked up . . ."

"Yes. I guess the point of my questions is that when I went to do a report on Wagnall-Phipps I was shown recent memos from your brother, and quoted from them. As a result, of course, I was fired."

At first she looked at him as if he were speaking a language she didn't understand. "What do you mean, 'recent'?"

"Dated as recently as a few weeks ago."

"Tom died a year ago."

"That's why I'm here."

Francine looked at her red-polished fingernails in her lap. "What an odd thing."

"Yes. It is odd."

"What's the explanation?"

"I wish I knew."

"Who showed you these memos?"

"Charles Blaine. Vice-president and treasurer of Wagnall-Phipps. Generally, one would think, a reliable source."

"Oh, Blaine. They've had trouble with him before. Enid has mentioned it. I think he might be very good at what he does, but . . . Enid says he takes everything so seriously. Sort of an ogre to his own department." Francine nodded her head. "Yes, I can see that, from what I've heard of Blaine. If every *T* isn't crossed, every *I* dotted apparently he has conniptions."

"This isn't a case of *T*'s not crossed and *I*'s not dotted, Ms. Bradley. This is a case of memos which were initialed — by someone who wasn't alive to initial them."

Francine shrugged. "Then someone's playing a bad joke. Someone in the secretarial pool. One of the people working with Blaine. I can see where someone working under a tight man like Blaine might want to play a game on him, shake him up, confront him with something inexplicable."

"It could be."

"What did Enid say, when you asked her?"

"She thinks Blaine is having a nervous breakdown. She sent him to Mexico for a vacation."

"Then that is probably so."

"I went to Mexico. He doesn't seem to be having a nervous breakdown. He seems to be having a hot, dusty time."

"Are you qualified to judge, Mister Fletcher? Have you a degree in psychiatry?"

"I left it in my other suit."

"I don't mean to sound like a prosecuting attorney. It's just that . . . most people can put on a good face. There's always more going on under people's surfaces than we'd suspect."

"Charles Blaine assures me he did not forge those memos."

Again Francine shrugged. "Then someone's playing a nasty trick on him." She smiled at Fletch pleasantly. "The Halloween spirit still walks the earth. People in offices love to play games on each other."

"Ms. Bradley, when precisely did your brother die?"

"I've already said — a year ago."

"Enid says the same thing. Yet Corcoran and Blaine both say he died six months later — last November."

"Oh, that. I don't blame you for being confused by that. Tom did die a year ago. We weren't prepared for it. Enid had been put in as Acting Chairperson of Wagnall-Phipps in Tom's absence, and she had hardly gotten her feet wet. I think people tolerated her in the job because they knew Tom was coming back. She was backed by Tom's authority, you see. She talked to me about it. We decided to, let's say, delay the news of Tom's death until she was more firmly established as Chairperson. Can you understand that?"

"Yes. I suppose."

"There was another consideration. A more human reason. Enid was terribly in love with my brother. From all I know, people working for Wagnall-Phipps — people like Corcoran and Blaine, others — were terrifically fond of him. Enid wanted to mourn alone a while. Trying to run the company — well, she just couldn't take the long faces, the commiseration, of the people upon whom she had to depend. Do you see?"

Fletch wrinkled his brow.

"There were lots of reasons for delaying the news of the death. The younger staff would have deserted the company, at least until they had more confidence in Enid . . . lots of reasons."

"Your brother died a year ago. The news wasn't given the people at Wagnall-Phipps until six months later, on a Friday afternoon in November. And it wasn't until the following Tuesday that Enid left for Switzerland. Is that right?"

Francine's eyes ran over the mosaic on the wall as if she were trying to remember. "Yes. That's about right." Her eyes then met his. "You're asking why we didn't go to Switzerland immediately, six months earlier, at the news of Tom's death?"

"That's the question."

"It was our decision of the moment. Tom was dead. We'd had no warning of it. The news didn't reach Enid until twenty-four hours after the death. A cremation was recommended. Enid cabled permission. It wasn't until six months later that we went to Switzerland, had a memorial service, for just the two of us, brought home Tom's ashes."

"You went to Switzerland with Enid?"

"Didn't I just say so?"

"Where in Switzerland?"

"Tom died in a small clinic outside Geneva."

Fletch took a deep breath and shook his head. "Ms. Bradley, your brother didn't die in Switzerland."

Looking at him, her eyebrows shot up. "Now what are you saying?"

Tiredly, Fletch said, "I've checked with the American Embassy in Switzerland. No American citizen named Thomas Bradley has died in Switzerland last year, or at any time in recent history."

Her lips a perfect little O, Francine sucked in breath. "They said that?"

"So said the American Embassy in Geneva."

"That's not possible, Mister Fletcher."

"And I'm sure they're not playing a prank."

"Well." And Francine opened and closed her mouth silently. "I don't know what to say."

"Neither do I."

"I guess we'll just have to chalk it up to a bureaucratic mistake. I'll have someone look into it."

"This information came with the assurance from the Embassy that regarding in-country deaths, their records are one hundred percent accurate."

"Oh, Mister Fletcher. If you can ever show me any bureaucracy of any country being one hundred percent accurate about anything I'll jump over the moon in a single leap."

Fletch sat forward in the divan. "You see, Ms. Bradley, I have many questions, about many things."

There was a buzzing from the foyer.

"Excuse me," she said. She went into the foyer and there was the sound of a phone being picked up and Francine Bradley said, "Hello? . . . yes. Please tell Mister Savenor I'll be down in five minutes."

When Francine Bradley returned to the livingroom, Fletch was standing near the window. He said, referring to the unfinished mosaic on the low table, "You've even left the loose tiles out."

"Yes," she said. "They're pretty in themselves."

"May we meet again?" he asked.

"Yes. I'm sure you mean to be helpful."

"I suspect I've surprised you enough for the moment, anyway."

"I'm sure there's a reasonable explanation for everything," Francine Bradley said. "A nasty office prank . . . a death certificate misfiled at the Embassy."

"Probably."

"Are you free for dinner tomorrow night?"

"That would be nice. Where, when?"

"Do you like French cuisine?"

"I like food."

"Why don't you meet me at eight o'clock at Chez Claire? It's only two blocks from here." She pointed more or less south.

"Eight o'clock," he said.

She followed him into the foyer. "I'm sorry I have to go now," she said. "I'm curious about what more you have to say." She held the door open for him. "I'm sure we can figure all this out," she said. "Together."

Beside the doorman, there was only one man waiting in the lobby. He was a silver-haired man in his fifties in a pearl gray suit seeming to look comfortable in an impossibly stiff-looking, narrow-seated, high-backed chair.

THIRTY

Friday morning at quarter to eight, Fletch stood in the drizzle across the street from Francine Bradley's East Side apartment house. He had bought a raincoat and a rainhat and, the night before, in Times Square, a pair of clear eyeglasses, and he was wearing all this, and under one arm he carried a copy of *The New York Post*. He supposed he looked like someone not wanting to be noticed.

He was waiting for Francine Bradley to come out of the apartment building, but to his surprise, at ten minutes past eight a taxi stopped in front of the building and Francine Bradley got out of the cab and dashed into the building. She was wearing a short rain coat and high boots.

At nine .twenty she came out of the building dressed in a longer raincoat and apparently a suit or skirt and began hailing cabs. The doorman was blowing his whistle for her.

On his side of the street, Fletch got a cab more quickly.

Getting into the taxi, Fletch said, "U-turn and stop, please."

The driver did so.

Fletch said, "See that woman trying to get a taxi?"

"Yeah."

"I want to see where she's going."

The driver looked at him through the rearview mirror. "You some kind of a pervert?"

Fletch said, "Internal Revenue Service."

The driver said, "Bastard. Better you should be a pervert."

They followed Francine's cab downtown where it stopped in front of the Bennett Bank Building.

"See?" Fletch said. "The lady's leading me to her money."

"I wish I could charge you more." The driver leaned over to read his meter. "I got to pay taxes, too, you know. Do you guys from Internal Revenue Service tip?"

"Yeah," said Fletch. "And we report the person to whom we give the tip — name, date, and place — just to see if you report it."

The driver turned around in his seat. "I don't want your damned tip! Get out of my cab!"

"Okay," Fletch said.

"Jeez!" the driver slapped the change into Fletch's hand. "Government in front of me in blue uniforms . . . government in my back seat!"

"Sure you don't have change of a dime?"

"Get outta my cab!"

Fletch waited a few minutes before entering the Bennett Bank Building.

On the sign board in the lobby was listed BRADLEY & CO. — INVESTMENTS.

He returned to the bank building at noon and followed Francine Bradley to Wayne's Steak House. She was accompanied by a man not much more than twenty carrying a brief case. His suit was not particularly good, his shoes were dull, he was without a raincoat, but his brief case was new-looking. They were in the restaurant fifty minutes. Fletch followed them back to the building and loitered in the lobby an hour. During that time the young man did not leave the building.

Fletch returned to the Bennett Bank Building again just before five o'clock. At five ten Francine Bradley came out and took a taxi. At five twenty-five, the young man came out and began walking down the street.

Fletch followed him into the subway, onto the platform and, while ostensibly waiting for a train, drew attention to himself by staring at the young man. Eventually the young man gave Fletch a look of distaste, and it was then that Fletch approached him.

"Sorry," Fletch said. "Trying to figure it out. Didn't I see you at lunch today at Wayne's Steak House with Francine?"

The young man's facial expression cleared. "You know Ms. Bradley?"

"Sure," Fletch said. "I've consulted her about some of my investments. Brilliant lady."

"She is." The young man nodded emphatically. "I think I'm damned lucky to be working for her. An education."

"She handles her brother's money, doesn't she? It was Tom who sent me to her."

"Well, we handle the Bradley Family Company. Mostly Wagnall-Phipps, you know. Other stuff. Not much I mean, not millions. But she's damned clever with what there is."

"Why doesn't Tom handle it himself?"

"The young man looked surprised at Fletch, hesitated, then said, "Didn't you know? Her brother died. A year ago."

"Gee, I didn't know. Too bad. Guess it's been a while since I've seen good ol' Tom. How long you been working with Francine?"

"Seven months." A train was coming in. "Real education."

The young man waited for Fletch to board the train first.

"Not my train," Fletch said.

"This is the only train you can get from here," the young man said.

"I'll wait for a less crowded train," Fletch said before noticing the train wasn't crowded at all.

As the train pulled off, the young man stared at Fletch through the window. On his face, expressionlessness battled curiosity, and lost.

At eight o'clock, Fletch entered Chez Claire and found Francine Bradley waiting for him, already seated at a table for two against the back wall.

There was a candle on the table.

THIRTY-ONE

"I think your nephew, Tom, is in serious trouble," Fletch said. They had ordered vodka gimlets on the rocks. "I saw him last Sunday."

Over the candle, he checked Francine's facial expression and saw that it conveyed the proper concern. More than proper — genuine. Francine Bradley did not strike Fletch as simply the distant maiden aunt going through kind, formal motions toward her late brother's family. Still, he realized, there had to be limits to her knowledge and her involvement with the family.

"What do you mean?" she asked, her tone near fear. "I understand Tom is in pre-med and doing very well."

"Not quite. He's using whatever education he has in chemistry to swallow oblivion."

"Drugs? Tom's on drugs?"

Fletch said, "Seems a mess. Hasn't attended classes since last fall. His roommate has him ensconced in a cushioned bathtub where he dreams away his days and nights. Doesn't know what else to do with him."

"Oh, no! Not Tom."

"I promised I would try to do what I could for him — which is another reason I'm seeing you. Of course, he makes no sense at all about his father's death."

"What does he say about Tom's death?"

"He sort of says your brother killed himself. He sort of blames your brother for dying. Sort of common, I believe, for a young person to be angry at a parent for dying, for leaving him. Sometimes young people blame themselves for a parent's death."

"You're playing psychiatrist again, Mister Fletcher."

"I'm called Fletch," Fletch said. "And I'm not playing psychiatrist. I'm in a crazy situation — and so are you — and I'm trying to understand it."

"I'm not in any situation at all."

"You are, too," Fletch said. "The preponderance of funds you're investing through your little company in the Bennett Bank Building came from your brother." Instantly, her eyes narrowed. "I'm checking to find out what probate action has been taken on your brother's estate — I suspect, none has. There's a pretty good suspicion that you and Enid are simply avoiding taxes. It's been stated to me by none other than Enid Bradley that you intend to go to California and take over the running of Wagnall-Phipps yourself. Anyone who didn't guess you've been forging your brother's initials to those accounting memos the last year would have to be myopic."

The waiter laid their gimlets before them. As in most dimly lit restaurants Fletch had experienced, the waiter's hands were dirty.

"You seem to be upset, Fletch." Francine sipped her drink. "Will you call me Francine?"

"With pleasure."

"Per usual with you," Francine said, "I don't really know what to say. You come in from California with all this information, all these questions . . . I am most upset by what you just said about Tom."

"He needs help. Heavy help. Quicker than soonest."

"I just had no idea . . ."

"Apparently he can fool his mother. He gets cleaned up, goes home, says he's doing well in school, gets money, then settles back in his bathtub with a six pack of downers."

In the candlelight, tears glistened in Francine's eyes. "I assure you," she said, "something will be done about it — immediately. Quicker than soonest. I appreciate your telling me."

"In a way," Fletch said, "Ta-ta, your niece, worries me just as much. Tom's roommate refers to her as a wind-up toy. She seems to be straight-arming existence, protecting herself in a girls' school, protecting Tom. I know their father died — a year ago — but they both seem inordinately troubled."

"When I get out there . . ." Francine said. "There's only so much Enid can handle."

"When are you going?"

"I'm afraid it will be another few months. I still have things to wind up here."

"You are going to run Wagnall-Phipps?"

"Tom wanted me to. Enid wants me to. I sold my business — a small business — a few years ago."

Fletch considered his gimlet, sipped it, looked across the flame at her. "Do you have any answers to the questions I just asked?"

"You mean, are Enid and I perpetrating a tax fraud?"

"Yeah, for starters."

"Not as far as I know. Of course, it's entirely possible Enid hasn't done things exactly right. In fact I'd say it's highly likely. She's not a Charles Blaine. She hasn't any training, any experience, except for having lived with Tom. I would expect she's screwed up mightily, but I'm sure with no intention to defraud."

"Have you been forging those memos?" Fletch asked easily.

"I've been consulting with my sister-in-law by telephone. Almost daily. Seeing you're so good at doing your homework — knowing about my office in the Bennett Bank Building and what I do there — you might check our telephone bills. Enid's and mine. They're monumental."

"Then we're still without explanations."

"Why don't we fortify ourselves with another drink, a good dinner, then go back to my apartment? We can talk more there. I suppose no one's ever told you that you're attractive?"

"Only a United States Customs Officer."

She put her hand on his. "Don't worry. I'm not one of these middle-aged women eager to get into the trousers of young men. Your orange juice-and-cereal innocence will remain intact with me." She took her hand away and picked up the menu. "They serve a very good orange duck here."

"Let's go over this one more time," Fletch said.

It was eleven fifteen when they entered Francine's apartment. They had had three cocktails, four courses, shared two bottles of wine and finished up with brandy for him, crême de menthe for her. During most of the entree Francine had told a long, wandering story which had ended with a punchline more barnyard than funny.

At the apartment, Fletch dropped his coat on the divan and then himself. He loosened his shirt collar, and, slumped, put his head on the back rest.

Quietly, she said, "Anything you say."

The lights were subdued. Francine Bradley was moving noiselessly around the room. The sounds of violins began coming from the walls.

"I'll just put on the coffee."

He concentrated on the violins. Their breathing was reminiscent of a full-bosomed girl whose passion had been awakened. He heard the rustle of Francine's dress as she entered the room.

Softly, her voice asked, "Now what are your questions?" She was sitting, relaxed, in the flowered chair.

"Who told you your brother was dead?"

"Enid. She called me at the office. She was terribly upset. Crying. Incoherent. I called her back an hour later. In fact, we talked most of the night."

"And you both decided not to go to Switzerland immediately?"

"Actually, we decided that the next morning. When the news first came, we weren't of any mind to decide anything. By the next morning, when we had both had some rest, Tom had already been dead two days. It would take us another two days to get to Switzerland, what with Enid being in California, and I being in New York, and each of us working. Instead, Enid cabled permission for the cremation."

"Okay. And then business went on as usual, you counseling Enid daily by phone."

"Yes."

"Then, in November, you both went to Switzerland?"

"Yes."

"Together?"

"Yes. Enid stopped over here, a night and a day. We flew over together."

"What did you do when you got there?"

"Rented a car. Checked into a hotel. Rested. Next day, Enid collected the ashes from the mortuary. It took time for us to arrange a little prayer service, in a chapel. We knew no one. In fact, we did not apply to the Embassy for help — we didn't think of it. We did have a service, late in the afternoon, Tuesday, I think, in a little chapel not far from the clinic. Just Enid, myself, and the minister. He spoke English. Enid brought the ashes to the service, and the minister had them on a little table, on an altar, throughout."

"Then you and Enid returned together to New York with the ashes."

The water pot in the kitchen was whistling.

"Yes," Francine said. "Enid flew on to California."

"How come the kids didn't go to Switzerland with you?"

"Tom and Ta-ta?"

"Yes."

"At that point, Enid thought they were just beginning to get over the death. She didn't want to stir up their grief all over again. Remember, this was six months later." Francine stood up. "Let me get the coffee."

When she returned to the livingroom, Fletch was sitting up, his elbows on his knees. In her absence he had paced up and down the livingroom. On the low table near the window the mosaic was more nearly finished than he remembered. He looked out the window at the roofs and lights of other buildings before returning to the divan. She placed a cup of coffee in front of him and took her own cup to her chair.

"Francine," Fletch said, stirring his coffee. "I think your sister-in-law murdered your brother."

Her cup jumped in her saucer. "God!" she said. "Now what are you saying?"

"I think your dear, incompetent sister-in-law cleverly has walked you through a complete illusion — which you have believed."

Francine's breathing was suddenly shallow, her jaw muscles tight. She swallowed twice, rapidly. "Really, Fletch! You are putting me through an awful lot!"

"Sorry," he said. "I'm afraid I have some evidence."

"Of murder?" Her voice was almost a shriek.

"Of murder," he said softly. "I haven't been confronting you with this evidence until I knew you, a little bit, and, well, until I was sure . . ."

"Sure of the evidence, or sure I can take it?"

"Oh, I'm sure of the evidence."

"All right, Fletcher." Francine Bradley was sitting straight and stiff in her chair, staring white-faced through the dim light at Fletch. "What's your evidence?"

"Ashes, represented to be your brother's, are not."

"Ashes . . ." She seemed to be trying to repeat what he had just said. "Not my brother's ashes?"

"No. They are not your brother's ashes."

"How can anyone tell a thing like that?"

"Last Saturday night — early Sunday morning — I went to Enid's house in Southworth and took a small sample of the ashes from the urn. The previous afternoon, Enid had showed them to me and said they were your brother's ashes."

"You broke into my brother's house?"

"The door was unlocked. I had the ashes analysed."

"You stole my brother's ashes?" Her throat muscles were so constricted her voice was barely audible.

"That's the point, isn't it?" Fletch asked. "They weren't your brother's ashes. They weren't anybody's ashes. They were just ashes."

"What? How can anybody tell the difference between one person's ashes and another person's ashes? You just tell me that! So a mortuary mixed up ashes. Do you have to tell us that?"

"These aren't human ashes at all, Francine. It isn't a case of a mortuary mixing up ashes. It's a case of your sister-in-law saying, *These are human ashes, These are Tom's ashes* — when they aren't."

"Then what are they the ashes of?"

"Carpet," said Fletch. "A tightly-woven carpet. Some pine wood. Some sand. A petroleum product, probably kerosene."

Francine put her coffee cup and saucer on the coffee table so forcefully the saucer shattered and the cup fell over.

"I can't stand any more of this."

"Francine, you just told me that when you and Enid arrived in Switzerland last November, Enid collected the ashes from the mortuary. You did not go with her. She arrived back at your hotel carrying ashes she said were Tom's."

"Did I say that?"

"Is it the truth?"

"You have me so confused."

"Enid brought the ashes of her Persian carpet to Switzerland with her."

In the dim light of the livingroom, Francine's eye sockets seemed hollow. The violin music from the wall-speakers was grating on Fletch's ears.

"Listen, Francine." Fletch sat forward and spoke reasonably, quietly into Francine's white, slack face. "Enid told you your brother was dead. Her saying so is the only evidence you have that he's dead. At her suggestion that news of Tom's death would make the running of Wagnall-Phipps impossible for her, you did not rush off to Switzerland. You waited six months. You did not see your brother's body. From what you just said about your trip to Switzerland with Enid, you did not talk with Tom's doctors, or with the undertaker. The United States Embassy in Switzerland says that no American citizen named Thomas Bradley has died in Switzerland in recent years. The ashes on the mantelpiece in your brother's home in Southworth are not your brother's ashes."

Fletch waited a long moment. Francine's chin looked pinched. Then he took her hand.

"Listen, Francine. It wasn't a happy marriage. I spoke with a neighbor of theirs, in Southworth. He didn't seem your typical neighborhood gossip. But he said he and his wife used to hear Enid screaming all night, doors slamming, things breaking. Not just once in a while, but all the time. While this would be going on, the kids used to roar off in their cars in the middle of the night."

"This is impossible."

"I don't know whether your brother was genuinely sick. Maybe you do?"

"He was."

"Enid might consider herself well off without Tom, especially if she can get you to come run the business."

"You think Enid killed Tom." Francine's statement landed between them like a thrown rock. She withdrew her hand.

Fletch said, "Tell me what else to think."

"I think all this is unnecessary." Francine got up from her chair and strode firmly across the room. She opened the door of a wall cabinet and threw a switch and the music went off. Then she turned a three-way lamp to its brightest. "I think you've assaulted me enough, Irwin Fletcher."

"Assaulted?"

Across the room, standing next to the bright lamp, her dinner dress wrinkled, her hair needing a combing, for the first time in Fletch's eyes, Francine Bradley looked small, vulnerable.

"You've assaulted me and Enid. Over nothing at all."

"I wouldn't call the evidence I've presented 'nothing at all.' I'd call it pretty indicative."

"There's no evidence at all, Fletcher. You're trying to save your job. That's it — pure and simple. I really don't know whether you've made all this up, but you certainly have a motivation to see facts as they aren't. If you don't know it by now, you will by the time you're my age: if you look at any event closely enough, you'll find supposed facts which conflict, contradict what you know to be the truth — memos that are unfiled, or mistakenly initialed, records lost in a bureaucracy — "

"Carpet ashes in a funeral urn?"

"God! It was six months later when we went to Switzerland! How do we know what some obscure Swiss undertaker did? He'd never expect the ashes he gave Enid to be analysed."

"I suspect he could have supplied human ashes — if a Swiss undertaker was the source of the ashes, that is. We all have our pride."

She turned her side to him. "Fletcher, I just can't stand any more of this. Not tonight. I understand that something happened in my brother's company which caused you to lose your job, and that that Charles Blaine has filled you up with all sorts of nonsense. I've tried to be nice, and open with you, and answer your questions." Even with her back to the light, Fletch could see Francine was crying. "And I do appreciate your concern for young Tom, and Ta-ta, and telling me about them. I believe that part. But when you say Enid murdered Tom! I've never heard anything so insane in my life! It's just too much, too . . . too insane!"

He stood up and put on his jacket. "Will you at least think about it?"

She looked at him through wet, blinking eyes. "Do you think I'll be able to think about anything else?"

"I'm just asking you to think about it. You've underestimated another woman, Francine. You're being had."

She opened the apartment door. "Good night, Fletch." Her red-rimmed eyes pleaded with him. "Would asking you to go away and leave us alone do any good?"

Fletch kissed Francine Bradley on the cheek. "Good night, Francine. Thanks for dinner."

THIRTY-TWO

"Good morning, Moxie. Did I wake you up?"

"Of course you woke me up. Who is this?"

"Your landlord. Your banker."

"Jeez, Fletcher, it's Saturday. I don't have to be at rehearsal until two o'clock."

"California time or New York time?"

"Are you still in New York?"

"Yeah, but I'm leaving for Texas in a few minutes."

"Why are you going to Texas?"

"I'm looking for a body, old dear. I keep not finding one."

"Thomas Bradley is not alive and hiding out in New York?"

"Apparently not. Despite my best efforts to shake up his sister, she does not produce him."

"What does she say?"

"She seems genuinely upset by everything I tell her. She's a smart, cool, efficient lady. She has to know that sooner or later I'm going to blow a whistle, bring what evidence I have to the authorities. I really believe she would produce her brother by now — if it were possible."

"Gee, whiz, Fletch, I have an idea — maybe Thomas Bradley died, despite that article in the *News-Tribune*. Did you ever think of that?"

"I'm beginning to believe in my own theories."

"Oh, no."

"Oh, yes."

"So far, Fletch, darling, your theories have been worth about as much as a grin in a wrestling match."

"Trial and error, trial and error."

"What's in Texas?"

"Everything, if you ask a Texan. It's the original home of the Bradley family."

"So what, she said, eager to roll over and go back to sleep."

"So when you're looking for someone, dead or alive, don't you look in his home?"

"Not nowadays. We don't have homes anymore. Just places where we live. The truth is, Fletch, you have no idea what you're doing."

"You are correct."

"You are spinning your wheels and going nowhere."
"Correct again."
"You're dashing from Mexico to New York to Texas and to God-knows-where because way down in your conceited little heart you just can't believe you did the utterly stupid thing of publicly quoting a dead man as if he were still among the quick."
"Your exactitude, Moxie, is doing nothing to encourage me."
"I hope. It's also correct you wouldn't be zipping around the landscape like a bitch in heat if you hadn't received a legacy from one unknowing James Saint E. Crandall, and, I might add, my permission to use it."
"Too, true."
"Foolish me."
"I hope you're contrite."
"I'm not contrite. I'm cold in bed alone. A different emotion altogether."
"You should be with me, in an overheated New York hotel room. Steam heat and mirrors everywhere."
"Well, I hope you're having a nice vacation with yourself. If you care, you've lost another job."
"Didn't have another job."
"You did, too. I told you so. The male lead in *In Love.*"
"I've lost that job? Oh, woe is me! Woe! I say, woe!"
"Sam is gone. Replaced by Rick Caswell. He's absolutely marvelous."
"I'm so glad."
"He's physically beautiful, with big lashes, you know?"
"No."
"His timing is perfect."
"No trouble with thick thighs, eh?"
"What? Oh, no. Ran cross-country for Nebraska. He's beautiful."
"I think you said that."
"Did I? Sorry. He's beautiful."
"Oh."
"Really."
"I've got the point. Say, Moxie — ?"
"May I go back to sleep now? I mean, I only answered the phone hoping it was your ex-wife again, so I could tell her more lies."
"How'd you like to do some spade work for me?"
"On this Bradley thing?"
"I know you don't believe in it; you're willing to chalk the whole thing up to my own incompetence and stupidity . . ."
"I really don't have much time, Fletch. The play is opening — "

"Just a little spade work, Moxie."

"Anything, darling. Oh, landlord and banker."

"Would you get a gang together — maybe your pals from the theater — and go dig up Enid Bradley's backyard? She's gone pretty regularly from nine-to-five."

"What?"

"You can tell them it's a treasure hunt, or something."

"Is that what you mean by spade work?"

"You'll want to bring more than one spade, to get the whole yard dug up in eight hours."

"Now you want to help Enid Bradley do her gardening?"

"No, no. You don't get the point. I'm looking for something."

"What?"

"What I'm always looking for: Thomas Bradley."

"What? Fletch, you're not serious!"

"I think Enid planted her husband in the backyard."

"Fletch."

"Yes."

"Fletch, you're not thinking."

"I'm not?"

"If you find Thomas Bradley under his wife's rhododendrons, you'd be proving that he is dead."

"It would strongly so indicate."

"And if Thomas Bradley is dead, you're ruined."

"That certainly has occurred to me."

"So why do you, of all people, want to find his body?"

"Two reasons. It would satisfy my curiosity."

"You have an expensive curiosity. What's your second brilliant reason?"

"It would be a helluva story, of course."

"Fletcher — "

"Will you do it?"

"No."

"You all need the exercise by now. Especially that Rick fellow. Think of spending a nice day digging in the garden."

"Rick does not need the exercise. He's — "

"I know."

" — beautiful."

"Moxie, you make up the damndest, most unacceptable reasons for not doing as you're asked."

"You just don't know how to take being fired gracefully! Roll over, Fletch! Play dead!"

"I'm on to something here, Moxie. I really am. Go dig up the garden. Please!"

"Bye, Fletcher. I just fell back to sleep."

"Moxie? . . . Moxie? . . . Moxie?"

THIRTY-THREE

Finally a taxi rolled up to the curb in front of the Dallas Registry. The driver rolled down his window.

"Three forty-nine Grantchester Street," Fletch said.

"Why would you want to go there?" The expression on the taxi driver's face was the one taxi drivers all over the world use while talking to *damned furriners who don't know what they're talkin' about.*

"Why wouldn't I want to go there?"

"You lookin' for somebody?"

"You might just say so," Fletch drawled.

"Well, you won't find him."

"I'm beginning to get that idea."

"I'm pretty sure all that way's a big owell."

"A big what?"

" 'Course not sure of that number in particular. What'd you say the number is?"

"Three forty-nine."

"Might's well get in. You look more like you can stand to lose the fare'n I can."

Inside his clothes Fletch's body was running with sweat from the dry heat. After he closed the door of the back seat he heard the air conditioner whirring high. The interior of the car was degrees colder. The driver started the car and, not interfering with anyone in Dallas who wanted to get ahead of him, followed the traffic sedately. As he drove he rolled up his window, making the interior of the car even colder.

"All that way's up there a big owell."

At nine o'clock Monday morning Fletch had been at the Registry of Births and Deaths in downtown Dallas, Texas. A slim, gray-haired woman had taken his simple enquiry not only as a great interest and cause of her own but also as an opportunity to be hospitable to someone clearly not native Texan. She poured Fletch coffee from the office pot, offered him a doughnut, which she insisted had been ordered by mistake, disappeared into the stacks and returned with a volume really too big for her to carry and dusty enough to make her white blouse look like it had been run over by a bus. Besides the date of birth, she established that Thomas Bradley indeed had been born in Dallas, Texas, at the Dallas Hospital, of Lucy Jane (McNamara) and John Joseph Bradley, of three forty-nine Grantchester Street.

"I'm just tellin' you it's a big owell, sonny, so when we get that way you won't turn on me mad for bringin' you that way."

"I won't turn mad," Fletch promised.

" 'Less you're in 'struction."

"In what?"

"You looked like you're in 'struction I never would say nothin'. But you don't."

"Oh, yes," Fletch said.

The sunlight reflected from a million mirrors as they drove along, from the windows of buildings, the windshields and chromium of cars. The driver was wearing sunglasses.

The sweat on Fletch's body froze. He held his arms close to his body.

The lady at the Registry of Births and Deaths had been very kind and very helpful, dragging out volume after volume for him. He doubted her blouse would ever be pure white again.

The taxi driver took a right turn, then another. The sign saying GRANTCHESTER was tipped.

Ahead of them, both sides of the street, was an enormous construction site. Chain-link fence ran along both sidewalks. An idle bulldozer dozed among the rubble. There were no workers in sight. Whatever buildings, houses, trees that had been there had been knocked down. On neither side of the road had new building commenced.

"Urban removal," the driver said. He slowed the car and brought it nearer the dusty curb. "A big owell."

"Oh," Fletch said. He had never gone so far to see a hole. "A neighborhood gone."

"No one here," the driver said simply. "Whoever you're lookin' for."

"Guess not."

"No one even to ask after him."

"No."

"Lotsa 'struction goin' on in Dallas," the driver said.

"Makes you proud, don't it?" Fletch said.

He gave the driver the name of the hotel where he had spent Sunday night and would not spend Monday night.

* * *

"Francine?"

Fletch had not been sure she would pick up the phone to him. He had identified himself properly to her secretary.

Returning to the hotel he had showered, changed to trunks, played around the hotel's rooftop pool awhile, until he felt his Puerto de San Orlando sunburn beginning to sting again. Now he was sitting on the edge of his bed, wondering which way to dress before checking out.

"Yes, Mister Fletcher. I mean, Fletch." Francine's voice was low, sounded cautious and tired.

"Any new thoughts?" Fletch asked. He had direct-dialled station-to-station. There was no way either the secretary or Francine could know he was calling New York from Dallas.

"About what?"

"About what we talked about Friday night."

"Well, I see that you've been damaged, Fletch. I understand that. Some mix-up at Wagnall-Phipps caused you to lose your job. Your profession. I'd like to talk to Enid about making it up to you."

"How do you mean?"

"Financially. Whether it was Charles Blaine's mistake, or some office mischief — or because of Enid's and my decision to delay news of Tom's death six months — the fact remains you got caught in the middle and suffered damage. It's partly our fault — I see that — or the fault of Wagnall-Phipps. You've suffered damage at our hands. So much so that you're imagining things. Wild things."

Her throaty voice was so soft Fletch realized he was pressing the phone receiver hard against his ear.

"I'd like to recommend to Enid we make it up to you somehow — like give you half a year's pay. Enough to let you go to Europe, or whatever, take a vacation, think out what you're going to do next with your life."

"That's kind of you," he said.

"Well, I really believe we owe it to you. I figure all this confusion happened just to protect Enid's authority in the company, get her through a bad time. There's no reason you should be wiped out by it."

"Francine, where were you born?"

There was a silence before she said, "My father, you know, was an engineer. I was born on station."

"Where was that?"

"Juneau, Alaska."

"I see."

"Fletch, why don't you let me talk to Enid about all this?"

"You don't seem to have thought much of the evidence I presented you, Francine."

"Oh, I've thought about it. And I find simple explanations, for everything, incredibly obvious. The one thing I will never tell Enid about, though, is that that Swiss undertaker gave her the ashes of a burned rug, or whatever you said. That's horrid. I trust you'll never let Enid know, either."

Looking at his toes, Fletch smiled.

"May I see you again?" Fletch asked.

"I wish you would. Toward the end of the week?"

"Thursday night?" Fletch asked.

"Yes. Come to the apartment Thursday evening. By then I'll have talked with Enid at length about all this. I will know what she thinks. I'm sure she'll agree with me. A trip abroad might be nice for you, at this point in your life. Help you sort things out."

Fletch said, "I'll see you Thursday night."

After putting the telephone receiver back in its cradle, Fletch walked across his Dallas hotel room to his suitcase and pulled out his sweater.

THIRTY-FOUR

"Moxie?"

"Fletch?"

"Hello."

"Hey, we're running through the last scene. Someone said I had a call from Juneau, Alaska, for Pete's sake. I don't know anyone in Juneau, Alaska."

"You know me."

"You're in Juneau, Alaska?"

"Yup."

"Boy, you can't do anything right. You aim for Dallas, Texas and hit Juneau, Alaska. Fletch style. Linda warned me about you coming home from the office by way of Hawaii. At least she had a meatloaf to keep her company."

"Stop a minute."

"Are there dead people in Juneau, or what?"

"I was in Dallas yesterday."

"Hey, Fletch. You're not supposed to interrupt rehearsals, you know? I mean, suppose everybody got called to the phone. Opening night would never happen."

"So why did you come to the phone?"

"Thought it might be dear old Freddy calling, demanding the presence of Ophelia again, or something. A lady with nerves of steel for his hard-times knife-throwing act."

"I want to ask you something."

"What? I've got to go back to rehearsal."

"Have you ever been confronted with something you absolutely cannot understand?"

"Sure. My father."

"I mean something which you just can't put your mind around?"

"Sure. My father."

"Where all the facts add up to something which simply isn't possible?"

"Sure. My father."

"I'm serious."

"So am I."

"I'm real serious, Moxie. When you prove out something which absolutely cannot be true?"

"No. I guess not."

"If you were in such a situation, what would you do?"

"Be very suspicious of my conclusion."

"Yeah. I've tried that."

"Doesn't work?"

"No."

"Well, I've got to go back to work."

"I have another question."

"What? When will you be home?"

"Maybe Friday night."

"What's your question?"

"How's Rick?"

"Oh, he's — "

"I know. Bye, Moxie."

THIRTY-FIVE

Before dawn Thursday morning, Fletch was waiting across the street from Francine Bradley's New York apartment house. It was a warm spring morning but he wore his raincoat, his hat. He also wore his clear glasses. He stood in the doorway of a dry cleaning store which had not yet opened. He was surprised to hear the sound of birds in New York City. As dawn broke, he could hear but still not see them. And, of course, he could hear the sirens. Standing anywhere in New York City, anytime, day or night, one can hear a siren from somewhere.

At a quarter to six a taxi cab pulled up in front of Francine's apartment house. Briskly, dressed in a short raincoat and high boots, she left the building and got into the cab.

The taxi was several blocks away, on its way uptown, before Fletch was able to get his own cab. Traffic was light and it was easy to catch up. Fletch told the driver that in the other cab was his wife, who had forgotten her wallet.

They crossed Central Park at fairly high speed and again turned north.

Francine was let out at the corner of West 89th Street.

Fletch let his cab go and walked slowly to the corner. As he arrived at the corner, he saw Francine enter an alley halfway down the block.

Strolling with his head down, he walked past the mouth of the alley, glancing in. What he saw was an oddity in New York — a cobblestoned stableyard, complete with box stalls, a horse's head above each half-door but one, bales of hay stacked in the corners of the yard. Three grooms were moving around, doing their morning chores. One groom was helping Francine mount a dappled gray.

Fletch continued walking. By the time he reached the end of that block he heard the clatter of hooves on a hard surface, and looked back.

Francine rode out of the alley and turned toward the park. She had removed her short raincoat.

THIRTY-SIX

"Hi," she said, opening the door of apartment 21M to him.

Fletch looked at Francine's breasts.

It was just after six in the evening and the doorman had said Fletch was expected. The doorman would call Ms. Bradley to say Fletch was on his way up.

"Hi."

Francine Bradley's face had been freshly made up. She wore a pearl necklace. Her cocktail dress was a soft gray, cut low in front. Francine Bradley's breasts were not large but appeared firm for a woman of her age, and, from the cut of her dress, Fletch surmised Francine Bradley was proud of her breasts.

"You look a little tired," she said, closing the door behind him. "New York City life too much for my orange-juice-and-cereal innocent?"

"I've been visiting the suburbs," he said.

She led the way into the livingroom but stopped near the liquor cabinet. He continued on to the far side of the room, to the big window, and looked down. Then he looked out the window.

"Would you like a drink?" she asked.

"Not just yet."

"I guess I'll wait, too."

Francine sat on the divan. "You do seem tired." She resettled a throw-pillow. "A little stiff, too."

"No," Fletch said from the window. "I'm not stiff."

"I daresay you're eager to hear our decision."

"What decision?"

"I've had two or three long talks with Enid. Of course, I never told her all your crazy notions. I told her you'd turned up here and seemed distraught. I took you to dinner and heard you out. It was my understanding you lost your job, really, only because she and I deliberately had delayed news of Tom's death, until Enid had become more established at Wagnall-Phipps. You got caught up in the middle somehow, what with Charles Blaine's craziness and all. In fact, I told Enid you are more or less ruined in your profession — for life. Is that more or less correct?"

"More or less."

"She said you'd been round to the Southworth Prep School, annoying Roberta. She didn't seem to know you'd seen Tom. I told her you'd gone to see both of them, just to apologize. That's true, isn't it?"

"More or less."

"Enid finally came to understand that we're at least partly to blame for what happened to you. She came to my way of thinking, and agreed we should help you out. I mean, financially."

On a roof across the street Fletch could see an older man and woman sitting in garden chairs under a parasol. A martini shaker and a plate of crackers and cheese were on a small metal table between them. A newspaper lay at the man's feet. As he watched, the woman said something that made the man laugh.

"Of course, we don't know precisely what a reporter earns," Francine continued. "But we figure it will take a good half-year for you to straighten out your life again, find a new interest, a new profession. To calm down and get over this obsession about us. Maybe travelling for a while would help. You could even use what we give you to go back to school."

Fletch heard Francine take a deep breath.

"Of course, for my part, I'm grateful to you for telling me about Tom. We had no idea. Enid has gone to his rooms at college and discovered the sad truth about him. He was dozing in the bathtub — just as you said. Quite given up on life. Enid lost no time in putting him in the hands of experts. Of course it will take a while," she said softly, "but he'll be all right. If nothing else you've done or said makes any sense, Fletch, your making us realize the state Tom was in leaves us entirely in your debt. But that's a human thing . . ."

Her voice trailed off.

On the roof across the street the man was pouring the woman another martini.

"So." Francine's voice brightened. "Enid and I have decided to try to make things up to you by giving you half a year's pay. We'll arrange it through Wagnall-Phipps somehow, so it won't cost us so much. To do with as you like, go where you like. Give you a chance to straighten out your own life."

"No."

"What?"

Fletch continued to look through the window. "No."

"Really, " Francine said after a moment. "Isn't that really why you went to see Enid, and came to see me, Fletch? You felt we owed you something? Be honest with yourself. Weren't you really hoping we'd have some understanding of what you're going through, and, shall we say, help you out?"

"No."

"What's wrong? Aren't we offering you enough? You do want our financial help, don't you?"

"No."

There was a long silence in the darkening room.

Fletch watched the older couple across the street fold up their garden chairs, gather up their newspaper, martini pitcher, glasses, plate of crackers and cheese, and disappear through the roof hatch.

THIRTY-SEVEN

Fletch said, "I'm sure Melanie is looking forward to your reincarnation."

He turned from the window in time to see Francine's hands flutter, her effort to keep surprise, alarm from her face. Her final expression was patronizing. "Now what are you talking about?"

"Melanie. Your horse. Your horse in California. No one ever sold your horse."

"What do you mean, *my horse?*"

"I don't get this even slightly." Standing in front of the window, Fletch shrugged. "You're Tom Bradley."

"My God!" Francine said. "Now the man has totally flipped!"

His face screwed in perplexity, again he looked at her breasts. "Maybe."

"First you told me Enid murdered Tom, and now you're telling me I am Tom!" Her laugh came entirely from her throat. "Maybe you do need more than half-a-year off!"

Fletch, with the light of the window behind him, peered at her on the divan. "I must say," he said, "you're marvelous."

"Enid hasn't sold Tom's horse — Melanie, or whatever her name is — *ergo* I'm my brother? Enid's been busy, you know — very busy. She's been running a family, and a good-sized company. Selling a horse is the last thing she has to worry about."

"You ride horseback," Fletch said. "I watched you this morning, on West 89th Street."

"Yes, I enjoy riding. My brother enjoyed riding. Does that make me my brother?"

"The night we had dinner," Fletch said, "last Friday night, you spent the entire time telling me a long, convoluted, not-very-funny barnyard story."

"So what? I'm sorry if you didn't like my story. I'd had a drink. I thought it was funny."

"Long, not-very-funny dirty jokes are characteristic of Thomas Bradley. As reported to me by Mabel Franscatti, Alex Corcoran, Mary Blaine and Charles Blaine."

"Tom and I had certain characteristics in common. We're brother and sister. Fletch, are you insane?"

"Brother . . . sister. You are your brother."

"I'm also my own grandfather."

"Could be."

"What's the point of this joke?"

"The point is I have only one piece of paper, when I should have, by this time, three pieces of paper." He took from his inside jacket pocket Thomas Bradley's birth certificate and placed it on the coffee table in front of her. "Thomas Bradley was born in Dallas, Texas."

She nodded. "Thank you. I knew that."

"I went to Dallas, Sunday," he said. "By the way, your old neighborhood's torn down."

She shrugged. "There goes the neighborhood."

"You were not born in Dallas, Texas."

"I told you. I was born in Juneau, Alaska."

"Tuesday I was in Juneau, Alaska. You were not born in Juneau, Alaska."

"Francine stared at him.

"And Thomas Bradley did not die in Switzerland." Fletch had returned to stand by the window, but he was still watching her. "So, instead of having two birth certificates and one death certificate, I've got only one birth certificate. And that's yours. The Bradleys had only one child — a son named Thomas."

"I was born well outside Juneau, about a hundred miles — "

"You weren't born at all, Francine."

She sighed and looked away. "My God."

"And Tom Bradley didn't die."

"You do believe in pieces of paper, Fletcher. Bureaucracies, clerks, secretaries — "

"And Swiss undertakers. I believe in Swiss undertakers. You've been writing those memos to Accounting yourself, Francine, and initializing them 'T.B.,' probably without even realizing you were doing it. We all have low-level habits that are just second-nature to us. We all do certain things in certain ways, and we continue doing them, under all circumstances, unconsciously." Looking at her, he gave her a moment. "True?"

"No," she said.

"Francine, would you come here, please?"

She looked a scared, unwilling child.

"Please come here," he said.

She rose and came across the room to him unsteadily, leaving the low table between them.

"Look down," he said.

She looked at the tile mosaic on the low table.

"Almost finished, isn't it?" he asked.

"Yes."

"When I first entered your apartment, a week ago, it was less than half finished."

Looking down at the mosaic, her mouth opened slowly.

"I see."

"Come on, Tom," Fletch said. "I'm not trying to embarrass anybody. As you said, I'm just trying to save my own ass."

Francine cupped a hand to her face, bridging cheekbone and forehead, turned, and started across the livingroom toward the foyer. She bumped into a freestanding chair.

Fletch heard her high heels click across the foyer's hardwood floor. And then he heard her knock on a door.

"Enid?" she called. "Enid, would you please come help me, dear?"

THIRTY-EIGHT

"Fletch, do you believe in the soul?"

"The soul is immaterial," he said.

Francine asked, "Is that meant as a pun?"

"Of course."

Enid Bradley had entered the livingroom from the foyer, putting one sensible shoe unsteadily ahead of the other as if unsure of where she was going. "Hello, Mrs. Bradley," Fletch had said. She looked worried, confused, and said nothing.

Francine entered more briskly behind her, and took her by the arm. Together they sat on the divan.

Fletch loosened his tie and collar and sat on the freestanding chair. "Sorry," he said. Again he looked at Francine's breasts. "I just don't understand." Seeing the two of them together he realized Francine was the shorter. In the photograph behind him, Thomas Bradley was shorter than his wife. "And I need to understand. I have to save myself."

Each woman had her hands in her own lap. Francine sat the straighter. *Enid always looks terrified of what the next moment will bring — you know, as if she's afraid someone is going to say something dirty,* Mary Blaine had said that night in Puerto de San Orlando. *Her husband usually does,* Charles Blaine had answered. *I mean, did.*

"Fletch," Francine asked. "Do you know what a transsexual is?"

"I can't say I understand. I'd like to be able to say I do."

You can't understand everything that happens, Roberta, Ta-ta, had said jogging through the California woods . . . *You can try to understand, of course. You can even act like you understand, when you don't yet. But some things . . .*

"A male can be born in a female body," Francine said simply. "Or a female born in a male body."

"What defines us as male or female, except our bodies?" Fletch asked.

"Our souls," Francine said. "To use your word, there is an immaterial self independent of the material self — our bodies. I was a female born in a male's body. That's all there is to it. I've known it since I was two or three years old. As long as I can remember I had feminine desires. A great interest in feminine clothes. I had a feminine perspective on everything. I liked dolls and babies and pretend tea parties and having my hair done up. I remember the first time my father introduced me as *his son, Tom,* I stared at him in shock. I was a girl. That was all there was to it. I knew I was a girl."

Francine went to the bar and began to pour out three Scotch and waters.

"I went through high school, as a boy, in Dallas, Texas. I wore trousers and sweat shirts and played on the varsity baseball team. I wasn't a bad shortstop. Gee, you know, I almost just said I could throw like a boy." She smiled at Fletch. "I dated girls and was elected treasurer of my senior class. I became a superb actor. With every word, every expression on my face, I acted the complete male. I was the complete male. I had the equipment, and I could get it up on demand. Don't ask me what I was really thinking, in the back seat with Lucy, or Janey, or Alice. Girls loved me especially because I understood them so well. All through college — boys' dormitories, boys' fraternity houses, well, all that was sort of nice. But I felt a cheater — because I was a girl."

She brought Fletch's drink to him.

"Can you imagine a worse conflict than being a girl in a boy's body? Or a woman in a man's body? No life can be worse than the life which obliges you to be dishonest with every word, every expression, in every living moment."

She took the two remaining drinks from the bar to the divan, and, sitting down, handed one to Enid, who drained half of it immediately.

To Fletch, Francine said, "You repeated to me that some nosy neighbor of our's in Southworth told you he could hear Enid screaming and shrieking at night. That wasn't Enid. That was me — Tom Bradley — shrieking to get out of my body." Francine tasted her drink. "Then came the Sunday morning that I swallowed everything in the medicine cabinet. I would rather have died than continue this lie, this life, this act, the agony of this conflict within myself." Francine's free hand took Enid's free hand and held it. "Enid promised to help me make the change. Enid is my dearest friend and greatest love."

Fletch asked Enid, "You knew about this before?"

"Of course," Enid said.

"For years?"

"Yes."

"It's something a husband really can't conceal from a wife," Francine said, "for long. I married thinking I could carry it off, carry on the act forever. But I couldn't. You see, Fletch, a person like me has the suspicion that every male — even you — would rather be a female. I know it's not true. I just don't see why you'd want to be a male."

"Why did you get married?" Fletch asked.

"Because," Francine said, "I had a very strong maternal instinct. It was my only way of having babies. Can you understand that? Also I loved Enid, very much." She continued to hold Enid's hand. "I won't ask you to understand that."

"Are Roberta and Tom your own children?"

"Of course." Francine smiled. "I told you. I was fully equipped. There was no reason why I shouldn't have children — as a father."

Fletch said, "Wow."

Francine smiled. "Do you need a moment to catch up?"

"Enid," Fletch said, "I thought you'd murdered him."

"I murdered myself," Francine said, "in the only way I could stay alive. Sometimes, young Fletch, we must do radical things to keep on living."

Again Fletch found himself staring at Francine's breasts.

"Yes," Francine said, "for two years before the surgical transformation began, I took hormonal shots. They softened my body, changed the shape of it, enlarged my breasts." *The only comment I made about it to my wife was that he seemed to be getting smaller,* Alex Corcoran had said in the golf club bar. "I also underwent two years of intensive psychotherapy, to make sure this was the right thing for me."

The room was growing entirely dark. No one moved to turn on a light.

"Surgery?" Fletch asked.

"Yes," Francine said. "Surgery."

Fletch remembered the motion Tom, Jr. had made sitting in his bathtub, of sticking a knife into the lower part of his own stomach, and rooting it around there.

"I still have one more operation," Francine said happily. "Then I can go home again."

"As Francine Bradley."

"Yes. As Francine. I can carry it off. You see, after all these years of acting, I'm not acting anymore. I really am Francine Bradley. I never was Tom."

"You convinced me."

"Enid and I carefully built the myth, over time, that there was a Francine. Tom's sister. Smart, competent at business, knew everything there was to know about Wagnall-Phipps. Would take it over, if ever anything happened to Tom."

"Your children — Ta-ta and Tom — they know the truth, don't they?"

"Yes," Francine said. "We thought they were old enough. They had seen enough of my pain, my agony. I guess Tom wasn't quite old enough. Of course, this sort of thing is much harder on fathers and sons than on daughters. Ta-ta can understand my transforming myself into a woman, because she is one. We sincerely did not know, Fletch, until you told me, how much trouble Tom was in. He has to make his own life, you know. I have to make mine."

Fletch realized he had been drinking his Scotch absently. It was gone. "And you just kept writing those memos to Blaine, and initialing them 'T.B.' without even knowing you were doing it."

Through the dark, he heard Francine sigh. "In a way, that's the worst part of a transformation like this. The little things. Changing the name on bank accounts, credit cards, Social Security. There's always one more thing — something you forget. It would be easier if one did die and go through probate. A few months ago I got stopped for speeding on the Connecticut Throughway. There I was, a blonde, middle-aged female, in a cocktail dress and high heels, driving on the California license of Thomas Bradley. Half my identification said I was Francine, half Thomas. The policeman was deeply perplexed, poor man. He took me to the police station. I told them the truth. Do you know, they understood it. It took them a while, but they were really very understanding and respectful. Well, they have to be now. There are thousands of us in the United States now. Thank God, we haven't become a statistic yet. We're still too much under-the-rug. But we exist. By the way, I still got that ticket for speeding. In the name of Francine." She laughed. "I paid the fine, gladly. I love anything that tells me I'm Francine. I'm finally Francine! Of course," she said more seriously, "getting a speeding ticket in Connecticut isn't the same as having you expose me in the newspaper."

Quietly, Fletch said, "I think you'd better tell Charles Blaine about this."

"Oh, no," Francine said. "How would Charley ever understand? He's so straight, so literal."

"He and Mary are more understanding than you think," Fletch said. "They have a good influence on them — her aunt."

"Oh, yes. Happy," Francine said. "How I used to hate that woman. She is so much a woman, and so happy at being a woman, being alive. I guess I don't have to hate her anymore."

In the dark, Enid blurted, "What are you going to do?"

"Me?" Fletch asked.

"We didn't murder anyone," Enid said. "All we did is lie. Are you going to ruin us, ruin the company, because we lied? We have a right to privacy, you know. Francine has a right to live her life in the only way possible for her."

More calmly, Francine said, "Forgive us our elaborate lies, Fletch. But you know the world isn't ready for this. It would hurt the company. I'd be seen as a freak. Key people would quit the company. Alex Corcoran wouldn't be able to sell a fire extinguisher to someone on his way to hell."

"Are you going to write about us in the newspaper?" Enid's voice was ready to sob.

"I'd like to tell my managing editor about all this," Fletch said. "I'd like my job back."

"He'll print it, for sure!" said Enid.

"No, no," Fletch said. "A newspaper knows a lot of stories it doesn't print. There's one now Frank Jaffe is sitting on, about where the state police used to get their police cars. This story, especially, is not in the public interest. Tom's becoming Francine is nobody's business but Francine's."

Francine snapped on the light beside the divan. Her face was charming, smiling. She said, "We never expected you to have so much persistence, Fletch. Mexico, New York, Dallas, Juneau, back here — phew!"

"We never thought you could afford it," Enid said. She was almost smiling.

"I couldn't," Fletch said. "I — uh — sort of borrowed the money."

Francine got up and took her glass to the bar. "Can we make it up to you?"

"I think I'll be all right."

"Francine, dear." Enid held up her empty glass. "My glass has been empty a long time."

Laughing, Fletch came over and collected Enid's and Fletch's glasses, taking them to the bar.

"That was your mistake, in fact," Fletch said.

"What was?" Francine asked indifferently.

Fletch said to Enid, "When I went to your house, essentially you offered me money. Never offer a reporter money."

"Or what?" Francine asked from the bar.

"Or he'll sink his teeth into you," Fletch said. "And never let go."

THIRTY-NINE

"Thomas Bradley is not dead," Fletch said, walking into Frank Jaffe's office. "He is alive and living in New York city in a different *persona*. Essentially, he is running Wagnall-Phipps. He did write and initial those memos. I quoted him fairly and accurately. I want my job back."

There had been boos and catcalls as Fletch walked across the City Room of the *News-Tribune* Friday afternoon. Someone had shouted, 'Hey, there's Fletch! Back from the dead! Again!" Others had been silent and looked away.

"Janey," Fletch said in the managing editor's outer office, "Frank in?"
"Yes, he is," she said. "Why are you?"
"Please tell him I'm here with something important to tell him."
"What do you have to tell him?"
"It's unprintable."
Fletch was made to wait in Frank Jaffe's outer office more than an hour. People went by him, in and out of Frank's office. If they knew Fletch, they scowled at him and said nothing — all but one old reporter, whose look and nod were friendly. He said, "Hi, Fletch."
"Hi."
"You all right?"
"Happy as a baker at breakfast."
"That's good."
Frank Jaffe had looked up from his desk sideways at Fletch when he entered, "It's nice of me to see you."
"Yes, it is," Fletch said, closing the door behind him.
Fletch's face remained quizzical through Fletch's statement and demand. Then he snorted.
"It's time I had a little entertainment." Frank looked at his watch. "Late Friday afternoon. You got a story?"
Without being asked, Fletch sat in one of the two chairs facing Frank's desk. While Fletch talked, Frank's eyes wandered behind their permanent film, looking impatient at what appeared to be the prologue to a rather long story, curious when Fletch began mentioning all the airplanes he had been on, intrigued when the facts Fletch recited continued to be contradictory . . . Fletch told him about meeting the Bradleys, Enid, Roberts, and Tom, Jr., their neighbor, about his friend in the District Attorney's office establishing that Thomas Bradley did not die in Switzerland, that the ashes in his funeral urn were not human ashes, about going to Mexico to interview Mary and Charles Blaine, to New York to interview Francine Bradley, to Dallas, Texas, to Juneau, Alaska, and back to New York . . .
Frank Jaffe's face colored as Fletch reported his final conversation with Francine Bradley, the night before, in New York, and described Francine and Enid sitting next to each other on the divan, holding hands, being brave in their fear, finally being honest in their difficulty.
"My God," Frank said. "A murder story without a murder. You do come up with some beauts, Fletch. We can't print that."
"Glad to hear you say that. I assured the Bradleys we wouldn't run the story."
" 'We'? Who are 'we'? You still speaking for the *News-Tribune*?"

"Journalistic 'we,' Frank. I won't write the story, and you won't run it. Right?"

"Of course not." Frank ran a dry hand over the stubble on his cheeks and jowl. "Not without their permission."

"That you'll never get."

"I suppose not. The Bradleys would lose too much by our running the story. Wagnall-Phipps would dry up faster than a drizzle in Las Vegas. What Tom Bradley — I mean, Francine Bradley has done does not affect the public interest in any way. People have a right to their personal lives."

Frank Jaffe's watery eyes looked long at Fletch. It was clear to Fletch that the managing editor — despite what he said — was tempted by the story. It was also clear to Fletch that Frank Jaffe had every reason to protect people's right to privacy. He wanted his own personal privacy, and privacy for Clara Snow.

Fletch smiled at his managing editor. After a moment, Frank smiled back.

"Helluva story, though," Frank said.

He squared his swivel chair with his desk. "You broke into and entered the Bradley's house? Is that what you said?"

"I didn't break anything. The door to the swimming pool was not locked."

"You broke and entered," Frank said. "Are the Bradleys pressing charges against you?"

"I wasn't stealing human ashes — I was stealing the ashes of a rug."

"What made you so sure they weren't Tom Bradley's ashes?"

"I wasn't sure. I was hoping. What made me do it? All you knew is that I'd said I'd seen memos dated recently and signed 'T.B.' I knew I'd really seen them. Second, of course, Enid Bradley had been quick to offer me money to go away."

"That's the best way to stimulate the curiosity of a good reporter," Frank smiled. "Or corrupt a bad one."

"Honest, Frank, I wasn't sure of myself, even last night, standing in Francine's apartment — until she offered me half-a-year's pay to go away and get off their case. Only then did I decide to blunder ahead."

"You still didn't realize the truth?"

"How could I? Here was a middle-aged woman — I mean, a woman, Frank, a real woman, with breasts — and a missing middle-aged man, father of two children — "

"Ah, the naiveté of the young."

"Would you have known better?"

Frank smiled and nodded his head at the wall. "There's a guy in the City Room whose name used to be Elizabeth."

"You're kidding."

"I'm not kidding. You know him well. The wonders of contemporary science."

Fletch shook his head. "I'm going to give up on my orange juice-and-cereal innocence pretty soon."

"If it weren't for human differences, Fletch, you and I would have nothing to write about." Frank's forearms were on the desk, his hands folded. "By the way, how do I confirm this story of yours? Not that I think you made it up."

"Call Enid Bradley. She and I flew back on the plane together last night. We're friends. You can even call Francine Bradley, in New York."

"I will," Frank said. "I will."

"Frank, do I get my job back?"

"Sure. Report Monday morning."

"And my expenses. I had big expenses sorting this business out, Frank. Will you refund my expenses?"

"No way."

"Why not?"

"No story."

"Jeez, Frank."

"Why should we pay expenses on a story we can't print?"

"At least you're going to refund my last two weeks' pay."

"We are not."

"You're not?"

"The fact remains. Fletch: you goofed. You were called upon to defend an important element in a story you wrote for this newspaper, and you couldn't defend it right away."

"But I have defended it."

"Two weeks later. And we can't publicly defend your story. The newspaper remains embarrassed. You're lucky to have your job back."

Fletch was standing over the desk. "You mean to say, Frank Jaffe, that in order to write a lousy twelve-paragraph story on a lousy, no-'ccount, two-bit company, for the lousy, gray pages of the Financial Section of the *News-Tribune,* I was supposed to have found out the Chairman of the Board had gone off for sex-change operations?"

"Yep," Frank said. "That's what I mean."

"You know what you're full of, Frank?"

"Lemme see. Do you spell it with four letters?"

"Damnit, Frank!"

"Report Monday," Frank Jaffe said. "And don't ever write anything again you can't defend immediately."

"Blast you, Frank Jaffe."

"Cheers, Fletch."

Amid a widening pool of silence, Fletch sat down at his desk in the City Room. Someone had placed a sign on his desk which read R. I. P.

Fletch took the sign off the desk, and dropped it in the waste basket. Then he smiled at all the other reporters sitting at desks around him.

Al said, loudly enough for everyone around him to hear him, "Finally come to clean out your desk, Fletch?"

"No. I'm not doing that."

"Then what are you doing?"

"Just stopped by to make sure it's still here. I'll need it Monday."

The silence became brittle enough to crack with a hammer. Even the police radios became quiet.

Randall, the religion news reporter said, "You mean, Frank has taken you back? Given you your job back?"

"That's what I mean," Fletch said. "That's exactly what I mean."

Everyone around him exchanged looks — significant looks, angry looks.

"See you Monday," Fletch said, getting up from his desk. "Nice weekend, everybody."

He crossed the City Room. At the door to the foyer, he looked back. What was clearly a delegation of editors and reporters was barging into Frank's office. Clara Snow was in the middle of the pack.

Fletch knew the delegation thought they were going in to protest his rehiring to the managing editor. What they were really doing, being journalists, was going in to get a story — whatever story Fletch had told Frank.

And Fletch knew they would not get the story from Frank.

Laughing, Fletch left the building.

A meter maid was putting a parking ticket on his car.

He took it from her, thanked her, then made her blush by kissing her lightly on the cheek.

FORTY

In the shower, Fletch thought he heard the doorbell ringing, but didn't care much. Then definitely he heard a banging on the front door sufficient to wake the asleep in the a burning building.

Having grabbed a towel around him, he opened the front door. Two men stood in the corridor. One was small and well-dressed and had mean, glinty eyes. The second was large, not well-dressed, and had mean, glinty eyes.

"You have the wrong apartment," Fletch said. "I hope."

"Irwin Maurice Fletcher?"

"Well, as long as you asked." Dimly, Fletch remembered the large man had been in the lobby of the apartment house when Fletch had entered, watched him pick up his mail, and came up in the elevator with him. Vaguely, Fletch had thought he looked like a carnival wrestler with much experience, and wondered if he might not make an interesting interview.

Now he thought avoiding an interview with this man might be the more prudent course.

The small man said, "I'm James Saint Eustice Crandall."

"Eustice?"

"You have something that belongs to me."

"I have?" Like tanks the men entered the apartment. Like a wet, near-naked laborer, Fletch backed up before the tanks. "Oh, yes. So I have. Sort of."

"What do you mean, 'sort of'?" the small man asked.

The large man closed the front door.

Fletch hitched his towel firmly around his waist.

"May I see proof you're James Saint Eustice Crandall?"

"Sure," the small man said. "Sure. That's reasonable."

He took a driver's license from his wallet and handed it to Fletch.

Who held it in his hand and stared at it as long as he could.

"What's the matter?" the small man asked.

"I'm sure it's just a bureaucratic error, but your license says James Reilly."

The small man snatched it from him, stuffed it back into his wallet without glancing at it, took out another license and shoved it into Fletch's hand.

"Ah!" said Fletch, examining it. "You're James Saint E. Crandall, too! I can tell. The pictures match." He handed the license back. "It must be nice being a schizocarp. You can scratch your own back."

"Come on," the small man said. "I want my wallet."

"Sure," Fletch said. He stepped back into the livingroom. The large man stepped with him. The large man was keeping Fletch within striking range. "I was wondering how much of a reward you're considering?"

"For what?"

"For finding your wallet and returning it to you."

"You didn't return it to me. I had to come get it."

"I advertised," Fletch said. "Two newspapers."

"Bullshit you did. I didn't see no advertisement."

"Then how did you find me?"

"The San Francisco police. Some hotel manager turned you in. They said you were scarperin' with my dough. They even showed me a picture of you in the newspapers, caught pushin' an old lady off a bridge or somethin'. They said, 'That's the guy.' You, ya punk."

"Oh, boy."

Red appeared around the small man's eyes. "I been waitin' for you all week! Make with the wallet!"

"No reward?"

"Get outta here with that shit!"

"I'd like to." The front door wasn't even visible behind the large man. "I was just thinking a reward of about three thousand, nine hundred and eighty-two dollars might be nice."

"Nice, mice!' The small man put his index finger against Fletch's chest. "Tearin' your skin off in strips would be nice."

"That's the amount I don't have."

The small man's eyes popped. "You don't have?"

"I spent it."

"How could you spend my money? Son-of-a-bitch!"

"Something came up, you see. Had to take a jaunt."

The small man shook his head and made every apparent effort to sound reasonable. "Listen, kid, this is my gambling money, got that? Know what that means?"

"Oh, no. Not that syndrome."

"That's my poke. My take. That's exactly where my winnin's are, in a particular enterprise. I need the whole stake. Intact. Or it's no good for me."

Fletch sighed. "Oh, boy."

"I lost my poke!" the man complained. "In the street somewhere. I can't use no other money in this particular enterprise. Last two weeks, you've cost me a fortune!"

"Oh, yeah," Fletch said.

"Maybe two, three hundred thousand dollars."

"Yeah, yeah. Sure."

"I gotta have every dime of it back! The original money I won!"

Fletch turned more sideways to them, so he would have a back leg to balance a blow. "I haven't got three thousand, nine hundred and eighty-two dollars of it."

"What right you got spending from my poke?"

"None," Fletch admitted.

"The small man's little fist hit Fletch hard in the shoulder. The large man did not move. He just continued to pollute the environment with garlicky breath.

"You get my money back! Every damned dime of it! Or Lester here will use your head for a basketball!"

"Lester," Fletch said sincerely, "I believe what the man says."

To the small man, Fletch said, "I think I can make up the money, get it for you. But it will take a while."

The small man threw himself petulantly into a chair. "We'll give you an hour."

"Enid?" Even turned away from Lester, speaking into the phone, Fletch could smell the garlic. "Fletch."

"Hello, Fletch. How's the jet lag? You must feel like a tennis ball at Wimbleton."

"I'm as well as can be expected."

"Your managing editor, Mister Jaffe, called. I told him everything — confidentially, of course."

"Thank you. Listen, do you remember I mentioned to you and Francine that I sort of borrowed money to do all the travelling?"

"Yes."

"Well, the thugs I sort of borrowed it from — " There was suddenly a sharp pain just below Fletch's right rib cage. — I mean the philosophers I took it from are here, wanting it back, right away."

"Fletch, you went to the loan sharks. Oh, dear. You should have said something."

"I'm saying something now."

"How much?"

"Let's phrase it as three thousand, nine hundred and eighty-two dollars in crisp, new one thousand dollar bills. In a big hurry."

"I'll be there as soon as I can. What's your address?"

Fletch told her and then said, "Enid, this isn't blackmail."

"I know that, Fletch. We gave you every opportunity for that. I'll be right there."

After he hung up, rubbing his side, Fletch said, "May I go put some clothes on?"

"No sense in spoiling 'em," the large man said. "They'll just get all bloody, most likely."

"Yeah," said the small man in the armchair. "You might as well leave 'em clean, so someone else can use 'em. Salvation Army."

They waited just over an hour. During that time the large man remained standing over where Fletch sat on the couch.

Lester seemed to have a fascination for Fletch's ears. He kept staring at them. Every time Fletch looked at him, Lester nodded at Fletch's ears and grinned. Obviously Lester's own ears had been maliciously treated. There were teeth marks in them.

Fletch tried to turn his mind to other matters.

On the coffee table, among many bills, was a letter from the Office of The Mayor. It read,

Dear Mister Fletcher:

This letter expresses the extreme displeasure of this office, and of the Mayor himself, at your failure to appear to receive your good Citizenship of the Month Award last Friday morning. The Mayor and the press were looking forward to seeing you. Your indifferent attitude (you did not even contact this office ahead of time to notify us of your inability to appear) has gone a long way toward jeopardizing the Mayor's entire Good Citizenship of the Month Award program.

The Mayor has directed me to inform you that your award has been rescinded.

Sincerely,
The Office of The Mayor

Fletch looked toward his own front door, and said, in a small voice, "Help! Police!"

Not succeeding in turning his mind to other matters, Fletch asked the small man, "When I called you from the lobby of the Park Worth Hotel, and told you I had your wallet, why didn't you come right down and take it from me? I mean, seeing you want it so much?"

"That wasn't you."

"Of course it was me."

"Naw." The small man was definite. "There was this other guy, see? He knew I had the wallet with the twenty-five grand in it. At that particular time I owed this other guy considerably more than the twenty-five grand. He was just connin' me, to get me down into the lobby. I got another friend to check out for me. I went out the back way."

"But you knew you'd lost your wallet."

"I thought it was in the car. I'd left it under the car seat. It must have fell out. Or you, or the other guy stole it."

Fletch sighed. "Now do you know it was me — trying to give you your money back?"

The small man grinned. "I know it wasn't."

"Why?"

"You find twenty-five grand in cash and try to give it back to me? Come on. You think I'm crazy?"

Fletch reflected a moment, and then said, "You shouldn't ask personal questions."

When the doorbell rang, Lester moved quickly to open the door. He said nothing. Enid's voice said, "Fletch! Are you all right?" Lester slammed the door. When he turned he had four one-thousand dollar bills in his hand.

"Sure!" Fletch yelled. "Thank you!"

"Ugly old broad," Lester said.

The small man had rushed to Lester and grabbed the money. He counted the four bills five times.

"Where's the rest?" he asked Fletch.

Fletch got up and went into the bedroom closet and took the wallet from where he had hidden it in Moxie's purse and brought it back to the livingroom. He tossed it to the small man.

After catching it the small man gave Fletch a look of outrage. His gambling money shouldn't be so desecrated.

And the short man counted the twenty-one bills five times. Then he placed the four one-thousand dollar bills neatly and smoothly in his wallet, and put the wallet in his jacket pocket.

Before opening the front door, the small man said, "Work him over, Lester. Break his head. All the trouble he's caused me. And four of these bills — " He tapped his wallet through his suit jacket " — just aren't the originals! It will cost me, you bet! You bastard!"

"Lester?" Fletch asked. "Did you hear the one about the near-sighted veterinarian and the garden hose?"

Fletch's observation had been correct: Lester had a fascination for ears. He beat on other parts of Fletch's body as well, but most of those blows were merely intended to get Fletch's forearms down from protecting his head. Lester hit Fletch's left ear repeatedly, then his right ear repeatedly, then alternated between the left ear and the right ear.

The large man might have become bored with his task sooner, if Fletch had not landed a hard one on his nose, making it bleed.

The small man came back, stuck his head through the open front door, and said, "Lester, come on! I've got the elevator waiting."

Wiping his nose on his sleeve, Lester left, closing the front door behind him.

From the floor, which was the only place Fletch had found he could retreat from Lester's final enthusiasm for his job, Fletch heard the men, small and large, walk down the corridor. He heard the elevator door slide shut.

Fletch said, "Finders weepers."

FORTY-ONE

The loud ringing in his head took on a slightly different tone, a harmony, once again, so Fletch reasoned the telephone was ringing. Still on the floor, still not breathing evenly, he pulled the telephone cord. It clattered to the floor in two pieces, but Fletch did not hear the clatter. He pulled the two pieces of the telephone to him.

"Hello?" he said into it.

"Oh, Fletch, you are home."

"What about phone?"

"Why are you shouting?"

"Moxie?"

"Fletch, Rick has asked me to move into his pad with him."

"Had with him? Had with who?"

"Stop shouting. It's been damned difficult. I've been spending every damned day and night with him doing this play, and, you know, it's not *Major Barbara* we're rehearsing, I mean, Paul has been a complete nut about our getting the nude scenes right, and, frankly, Fletch, Rick is beautiful, and very nice, perfect timing, and how do you expect a girl to take the strain? You haven't been here much, you know."

"How's Rick?"

"Fletch, are you deaf? Why are you breathing hard? Been exercising?"

"When are you coming home?"

"Will you come get me?"

"How could I forget you?"

"I lost the little yellow car that went beep-beep nicely. Parked it in front of the theater and it wasn't there when I came out. I told the police about it, but they didn't seem to much care."

"I'll come pick you up."

"Well, listen, Fletch, are you going to be home from now on? I mean, no girl can take this kind of strain."

"Train? Why take a train? What train? I'll come get you. It will take me a few minutes. I'm in the middle of a shower."

"Oh. That's why you're shouting."

"Hey, Moxie? I got my job back."

"That's wonderful."

"What? Sure. Be right there. Just wait for me."

Fletch hung up the phone, rolled over and sat up. The floor heaved. The walls wobbled. His eyes said they wanted to close. His stomach complained of having nothing to vomit.

He decided he should lie still a moment, on the rug, before washing off the blood, getting dressed, attempting to drive. He rolled over again, slowly, onto his stomach. He put his sore right cheekbone down gently on his sore right forearm.

And fell asleep.